THE DOVER ANTHOLOGY OF AMERICAN LITERATURE

DOVER THRIFT EDITIONS

Volume I

From the Origins Through the Civil War

Edited by

Bob Blaisdell

DOVER PUBLICATIONS, INC.
MINEOLA, NEW YORK

DOVER THRIFT EDITIONS

GENERAL EDITOR: MARY CAROLYN WALDREP
EDITOR OF THIS VOLUME: SUSAN L. RATTINER

Copyright

Bibliographical Note

The Dover Anthology of American Literature, Volume I: From the Origins Through the Civil War, first published by Dover Publications, Inc., in 2014, is a new anthology reprinted from standard sources. For the sake of authenticity, inconsistencies in spelling and punctuation have been retained in the texts unless otherwise indicated.

Library of Congress Cataloging-in-Publication Data

The Dover Anthology of American Literature, Volume I : From the Origins Through the Civil War / edited by Bob Blaisdell.
pages cm. — (Dover Thrift Editions)
Summary: "Ranging from colonial times to the mid-nineteenth century, this compact and inexpensive anthology offers a fascinating overview of early American literature. The authoritative texts are supplemented with informative introductory notes and suggestions for further reading. Starting with Cherokee creation myths and Powhatan's moving speech, "Why Should You Destroy Us, Who Have Provided You with Food," the eighteenth-century selections include the writings of poets Anne Bradstreet and Phillis Wheatley; preacher Jonathan Edwards; statesmen Benjamin Franklin, Thomas Paine, and others. From the early and mid-nineteenth century come excerpts from the journals of Lewis and Clark; stories by Nathaniel Hawthorne, Edgar Allan Poe, and Louisa May Alcott; the poetry of Henry Wadsworth Longfellow and Walt Whitman; and essays, speeches, verse, and memoirs by other prominent Americans"— Provided by publisher.
Includes bibliographical references.
ISBN-13: 978-0-486-78076-4 (paperback) — ISBN-10: 0-486-78076-7
1. American literature. I. Blaisdell, Robert, editor of compilation.
PS507.D68 2014
810.8—dc23

2014010332

Manufactured in the United States by LSC Communications
78076708 2020
www.doverpublications.com

Contents

NOTE

. . . all this to explain, would be to dive deeper than Ishmael can go.
—HERMAN MELVILLE, *MOBY-DICK*

THIS ANTHOLOGY SERVES as a whirlwind tour of American literature. We don't make all the stops, but we bring you to numerous classics and several out-of-the-way marvels of American writing. We have taken "literature" to include not just poetry and fiction but essays, letters, journals, memoirs and autobiography, as well as historical documents and speeches. The American voice is particularly unbound by genre and is usually distinct wherever it is heard. If your experience of these pieces tempts you to make a return journey to particular authors or works or genres, we will have accomplished our primary goal.

Had America's most famous poet, Walt Whitman, guest-edited this anthology, he could have sung a celebration of the tremendous variety encountered on this literary tour: from the forceful statements of the seventeenth-century tribal leader Powhatan to the modest but muscular and careful sentences of our greatest president, Abraham Lincoln; he could have evoked simultaneously an appreciation of the practical and humorous writings of Benjamin Franklin and the poignant memories of Frederick Douglass. In this brief introductory note, Whitman could have described the rich clamor of such disparate voices as Edgar Allan Poe's and Harriet Beecher Stowe's, the one with his dramatic, twisted phrasings depicting psychological torture, and the other with her passionate and inspired narrative that helped America finally undermine its immoral "peculiar institution" of slavery. Whitman could have done justice to the preachers—the American literary tradition is a preaching tradition! Jonathan Edwards, Phillis Wheatley, Ralph

Waldo Emerson, Henry David Thoreau and Red Jacket had the ringing voices of prophets, though only Edwards did the majority of his preaching from a pulpit. The others spoke for themselves, representing not God but the Individual American Spirit. The variety of these literary voices is a chorus, and we can't help but wish that Whitman were here to draw out and show off the strengths of the All as well as of the Soloists.

On our own, unaccompanied by the electrifying soul of Whitman, we must settle for a short explanation of our method of presentation. We have relied on our sense of the works and authors whose fame has endured into or revived in the twenty-first century. The several excerpts from novels drive themselves and can but needn't stand alone; those that captivate in a sampling must be pursued in full (all of the novels and many of the nonfiction works are available in complete Dover editions). We have gone light on the notes, trusting and hoping that the materials in themselves will provide enough of their own context. Our custom in this volume, rather than a strict law, is that we chose the first selected publication by an author to determine the chronological order rather than, for instance, birth years, though publication date is overridden occasionally by the date of writing or, for speeches and political events, their performance or manifestation. We begin with Native American creation stories (though they were not written down until the 1800s), and conclude the volume with the person who has come to symbolize and embody the purpose and tragedy of the Civil War, Abraham Lincoln. The chronology of the materials is, admittedly, awkward, with Lincoln's first selection coming from 1838, for example; another awkwardness is that we know some of the writers, among them Whitman, Douglass, Alcott and Emerson, wrote right on past the 1865 finish line.

I am indebted to Susan L. Rattiner, my editor at Dover, for her patient and painstaking work; her guidance, corrections and suggestions have continually steadied and focused this volume.

CHEROKEE CREATION STORIES (JAMES MOONEY)

The Cherokee Nation spanned much of today's Southeast, from North Carolina to Georgia and into Tennessee, until the early nineteenth century, when a majority of the population was deprived of its land by the U.S. Government and forcibly relocated via "The Trail of Tears" to reservations in Oklahoma. The ethnographer James Mooney (1861–1921) collected the stories from 1887 to 1890 and published them in Myths of the Cherokee. *"It is almost certain that most of the myths . . . are but disjointed fragments of an original complete genesis and migration legend, which is now lost," writes Mooney. We have placed them first in this anthology on account of their original versions having existed previous to American English writings.*

How the World Was Made (1897–1898)

THE EARTH IS a great island floating in a sea of water, and suspended at each of the four cardinal points by a cord hanging down from the sky vault, which is of solid rock. When the world grows old and worn out, the people will die and the cords will break and let the earth sink down into the ocean, and all will be water again. The Indians are afraid of this.

When all was water, the animals were above in Gălûñ′lătĭ, beyond the arch; but it was very much crowded, and they were wanting more room. They wondered what was below the water, and at last Dâyuni′sĭ, "Beaver's Grandchild," the little Water-beetle, offered to go and see if it could learn. It darted in every direction over the surface of the water, but could find no firm place to rest. Then it dived to the bottom and came up with some soft mud, which began to grow and spread on every side until it became the island which we call the earth. It was afterward fastened to the sky with four cords, but no one remembers who did this.

At first the earth was flat and very soft and wet. The animals were anxious to get down, and sent out different birds to see if it was yet dry, but they found no place to alight and came back again to Gălûñ'lătĭ. At last it seemed to be time, and they sent out the Buzzard and told him to go and make ready for them. This was the Great Buzzard, the father of all the buzzards we see now. He flew all over the earth, low down near the ground, and it was still soft. When he reached the Cherokee country, he was very tired, and his wings began to flap and strike the ground, and wherever they struck the earth there was a valley, and where they turned up again there was a mountain. When the animals above saw this, they were afraid that the whole world would be mountains, so they called him back, but the Cherokee country remains full of mountains to this day.

When the earth was dry and the animals came down, it was still dark, so they got the sun and set it in a track to go every day across the island from east to west, just overhead. It was too hot this way, and Tsiska'gĭlĭ', the Red Crawfish, had his shell scorched a bright red, so that his meat was spoiled; and the Cherokee do not eat it. The conjurers put the sun another hand-breadth higher in the air, but it was still too hot. They raised it another time, and another, until it was seven hand-breadths high and just under the sky arch. Then it was right, and they left it so. This is why the conjurers call the highest place Gûlkwâ'gine Di'gălûñ'lătiyûñ', "the seventh height," because it is seven hand-breadths above the earth. Every day the sun goes along under this arch, and returns at night on the upper side to the starting place.

There is another world under this, and it is like ours in everything—animals, plants, and people—save that the seasons are different. The streams that come down from the mountains are the trails by which we reach this underworld, and the springs at their heads are the doorways by which we enter, it, but to do this one must fast and go to water and have one of the underground people for a guide. We know that the seasons in the underworld are different from ours, because the water in the springs is always warmer in winter and cooler in summer than the outer air.

When the animals and plants were first made—we do not know by whom—they were told to watch and keep awake for seven nights, just as young men now fast and keep awake when they pray to their medicine. They tried to do this, and nearly all were awake through the first night, but the next night several dropped off to sleep, and the third night others were asleep, and then others, until, on the seventh night, of all the animals only the owl, the panther, and one or two more were still awake. To these were given the power to see and to go about in the dark, and to make prey of the birds and animals which must sleep at night. Of the trees only the cedar, the pine, the spruce, the holly, and the laurel were awake to the end, and to them it was given to be always green and to be greatest for medicine, but to the others it was said: "Because you have not endured to the end you shall lose your hair every winter."

Men came after the animals and plants. At first there were only a brother and sister until he struck her with a fish and told her to multiply, and so it was. In seven days a child was born to her, and thereafter every seven days another, and they increased very fast until there was danger that the world could not keep them. Then it was made that a woman should have only one child in a year, and it has been so ever since.

The First Fire (1897–1898)

IN THE BEGINNING there was no fire, and the world was cold, until the Thunders (Ani´-Hyûñ´tĭkwălâ´skĭ), who lived up in Gălûñ´lătĭ, sent their lightning and put fire into the bottom of a hollow sycamore tree which grew on an island. The animals knew it was there, because they could see the smoke coming out at the top, but they could not get to it on account of the water, so they held a council to decide what to do. This was a long time ago.

Every animal that could fly or swim was anxious to go after the fire. The Raven offered, and because he was so large and strong they thought he could surely do the work, so he was sent first. He flew high and far across the water and alighted on the sycamore tree, but while he was wondering what to do next, the heat had scorched all his feathers black, and he was frightened and came back without the fire. The little Screech-owl (*Wa´huhu´*) volunteered to go, and reached the place safely, but while he was looking down into the hollow tree a blast of hot air came up and nearly burned out his eyes. He managed to fly home as best he could, but it was a long time before he could see well, and his eyes are red to this day. Then the Hooting Owl (*U´guku´*) and the Horned Owl (*Tskĭlĭ´*) went, but by the time they got to the hollow tree the fire was burning so fiercely that the smoke nearly blinded them, and the ashes carried up by the wind made white rings about their eyes. They had to come home again without the fire, but with all their rubbing they were never able to get rid of the white rings.

Now no more of the birds would venture, and so the little Uksu´hĭ snake, the black racer, said he would go through the water and bring back some fire. He swam across to the island and crawled through the grass to the tree, and went in by a small hole at the bottom. The heat and smoke were too much for him, too, and after dodging about blindly over the hot ashes until he was almost on fire himself he managed by good luck to get out again at the same hole, but his body had been scorched black, and he has ever since had the habit of darting and doubling on his track as if trying to escape from close quarters. He came back, and the great blacksnake, Gûle´gĭ, "The Climber," offered to go for fire. He swam over to the island and climbed up the tree on the outside, as the blacksnake always does, but when he put his head down into the hole the smoke choked him so that he fell into the burning stump, and before he could climb out again he was as black as the Uksu´hĭ.

Now they held another council, for still there was no fire, and the world was cold, but birds, snakes, and four-footed animals, all had some excuse for not going, because they were all afraid to venture near the burning sycamore, until at last Kănăne´skĭ Amai´yĕhĭ (the Water Spider) said she would go. This is not the water spider that looks like a mosquito, but the other one, with black downy hair and red stripes on her body. She can run on top of the water or dive to the bottom, so there would be no trouble to get over to the island, but the question was, How could she bring back the fire? "I'll manage that," said the Water Spider; so she spun a thread from her body and wove it into a *tusti* bowl, which she fastened on her back. Then she crossed over to the island and through the grass to where the fire was still burning. She put one little coal of fire into her bowl, and came back with it, and ever since we have had fire, and the Water Spider still keeps her tusti bowl.

SOURCE: James Mooney. *Myths of the Cherokee.* Extract from the *Nineteenth Annual Report of the Bureau of American Ethnology*, 1897–98, Part I. Washington, D.C.: Government Printing Office, 1900.

POWHATAN

Before the arrival of Europeans, the Native peoples of North America did not write; instead, they preserved their various histories and cultures through oral traditions. Their cultures were more diverse than those of the Europeans who began settling here in colonies in the beginning of the seventeenth century, and the immigrants became impressed by the rhetorical sophistication and beauty of Native spokesmen (there are few instances before the twentieth century of Native women making speeches).

Powhatan (c. 1547–1618), also known as Wahunsonacock, was the head of an Algonquian confederacy that spanned hundreds of miles and thirty-two tribes. (He is well-known today because of his favorite daughter, Pocahontas, who rescued the English captain John Smith from execution in 1608.) In 1607 Powhatan's confederacy allowed the English to establish their first colony at Jamestown, Virginia. In 1609, when the same Captain Smith, dissatisfied with trade negotiations, resorted to bluster and threats, Powhatan made the following reply.

Why Should You Destroy Us, Who Have Provided You with Food? (c. 1609)

I AM NOW grown old, and must soon die; and the succession must descend, in order, to my brothers, Opitchapan, Opekankanough, and Catataugh, and then to my two sisters, and their two daughters. I wish their experience was equal to mine; and that your love to us might not be less than ours to you. Why should you take by force that from us which you can have by love? Why should you destroy us, who have provided you with food? What can you get by war? We can hide our provisions, and fly into the woods; and then you must consequently famish by wronging your friends. What is the cause of your jealousy? You see us unarmed, and willing to supply your wants, if you will come in a friendly manner, and not with swords and guns, as to invade an enemy. I am not so simple, as not to know it is better to eat good meat, lie well, and sleep quietly with my women and children; to laugh and be merry with the English; and, being their friend, to have copper, hatchets, and whatever else I want, than to fly from all, to lie cold in the woods, feed upon acorns, roots, and such trash, and to be so hunted, that I cannot rest, eat, or sleep. In such circumstances, my men must watch, and if a twig should but break, all would cry out, "*Here comes Captain Smith*"; and so, in this miserable manner, to end my miserable life; and, Captain Smith, this *might* be soon your fate too, through your rashness and unadvisedness. I, therefore, exhort you to peaceable councils; and, above all, I insist that the guns and swords, the cause of all our jealousy and uneasiness, be removed and sent away.

SOURCE: Samuel G. Drake. *Biography and History of the Indians of North America, from Its First Discovery*. 11th edition. Boston: Benjamin B. Mussey and Company, 1851.

ANNE BRADSTREET

Anne Bradstreet (1612–1672) composed the first published book of verse written in America, The Tenth Muse, Lately Sprung Up in America *(1650). Born in England, educated by tutors, she married and moved with her husband and parents to the New World. Her father became the governor of the Massachusetts Bay Colony as, later, so did her husband. She addresses her book in the introductory poem as if it were one of her several children "snatcht" from her and "expos'd to public view." The plain-spokenness of her love for her family and husband diminishes her temporal distance from us, and her poems of mourning are as wise as the ages. We have maintained the fitful capitalization and punctuation as rendered in Robert Hutchinson's excellent edition of Bradstreet's work.*

The Author to her Book (1650)

Thou ill-form'd offspring of my feeble brain,
Who after birth did'st by my side remain,
Till snatcht from thence by friends, less wise than true,
Who thee abroad expos'd to publick view;
Made thee in raggs, halting to th' press to trudg,
Where errors were not lessened (all may judg).
At thy return my blushing was not small,
My rambling brat (in print) should mother call.
I cast thee by as one unfit for light,
Thy Visage was so irksome in my sight;
Yet being mine own, at length affection would
Thy blemishes amend, if so I could:
I wash'd thy face, but more defects I saw,
And rubbing off a spot, still made a flaw.
I stretcht thy joynts to make thee even feet,
Yet still thou run'st more hobling than is meet;

In better dress to trim thee was my mind,
But nought save home-spun Cloth, i'th' house I find.
In this array, 'mongst Vulgars mayst thou roam.
In Criticks hands, beware thou dost not come;
And take thy way where yet thou art not known.
If for thy Father askt, say, thou hadst none:
And for thy Mother, she alas is poor,
Which caus'd her thus to send thee out of door.

To my Dear and loving Husband (1650)

If ever two were one, then surely we.
If ever man were lov'd by wife, then thee;
If ever wife was happy in a man,
Compare with me ye women if you can.
I prize thy love more than whole Mines of gold,
Or all the riches that the East doth hold.
My love is such that Rivers cannot quench,
Nor ought but love from thee, give recompence.
Thy love is such I can no way repay,
The heavens reward thee manifold I pray.
Then while we live, in love lets so persever,
That when we live no more, we may live ever.

Before the Birth of one of her Children (1650)

All things within this fading world hath end,
Adversity doth still our joyes attend;
No tyes so strong, no friends so dear and sweet,
But with deaths parting blow is sure to meet.
The sentence past is most irrevocable,
A common thing, yet oh inevitable;
How soon, my Dear, death may my steps attend,
How soon't may be thy Lot to lose thy friend,
We both are ignorant, yet love bids me
These farewell lines to recommend to thee,
That when that knot's unty'd that made us one,
I may seem thine, who in effect am none.
And if I see not half my dayes that's due,

What nature would, God grant to yours and you;
The many faults that well you know I have,
Let be interr'd in my oblivious grave;
If any worth or virtue were in me,
Let that live freshly in thy memory
And when thou feel'st no grief, as I no harms,
Yet love thy dead, who long lay in thine arms:
And when thy loss shall be repaid with gains
Look to my little babes my dear remains.
And if thou love thy self, or loved'st me
These O protect from step Dames injury.
And if chance to thine eyes shall bring this verse,
With some sad sighs honour my absent Herse;
And kiss this paper for thy loves dear sake,
Who with salt tears this last Farewel did take.

Upon a Fit of Sickness, Anno. 1632. Aetatis suae, 19 (1650)

Twice ten years old, not fully told
   Since nature gave me breath,
My race is run, my thread is spun,
   lo here is fatal Death.
All men must dye, and so must I
   this cannot be revok'd
For Adams sake, this word God spake
   when he so high provok'd.
Yet live I shall, this life's but small,
   in place of highest bliss,
Where I shall have all I can crave,
   no life is like to this.
For what's this life, but care and strife?
   since first we came from womb,
Our strength doth waste, our time doth hast,
   and then we go to th' Tomb.
O Bubble blast, how long can'st last?
   that alwayes art a breaking,
No sooner blown, but dead and gone,
   ev'n as a word that's speaking.
O whil'st I live, this grace me give,

I doing good may be,
Then deaths arrest I shall count best,
because it's thy decree;
Bestow much cost there's nothing lost,
to make Salvation sure,
O great's the gain, though got with pain,
comes by profession pure.
The race is run, the field is won,
the victory's mine I see,
For ever known, thou envious foe,
the foyle belongs to thee.

To the Memory of my dear and ever honoured Father Thomas Dudley Esq; Who deceased, July 31. 1653. and of his Age, 77 (1650)

By duty bound, and not by custome led
To celebrate the praises of the dead,
My mournfull mind, sore prest, in trembling verse
Presents my Lamentations at his Herse,
Who was my Father, Guide, Instructer too,
To whom I ought whatever I could doe:
Nor is't Relation near my hand shall tye;
For who more cause to boast his worth than I?
Who heard or saw, observ'd or knew him better?
Or who alive than I, a greater debtor?
Let malice bite, and envy knaw its fill,
He was my Father, and Ile praise him still.
Nor was his name, or life lead so obscure
That pitty might some Trumpeters procure,
Who after death might make him falsly seem
Such as in life, no man could justly deem.
Well known and lov'd, where ere he liv'd, by most
Both in his native, and in foreign coast,
These to the world his merits could make known,
So needs no Testimonial from his own;
But now or never I must pay my Sum;
While others tell his worth, I'le not be dumb:
One of thy Founders, him *New-England* know,
Who staid thy feeble sides when thou wast low,

Who spent his state, his strength, and years with care
That After-comers in them might have share.
True Patriot of this little Commonweal,
Who is't can tax thee ought, but for thy zeal?
Truths friend thou wert, to errors still a foe,
Which caus'd Apostates to maligne so.
Thy love to true Religion e're shall shine,
My Fathers God, be God of me and mine.
Upon the earth he did not build his nest,
But as a Pilgrim, what he had, possest.
High thoughts he gave no harbour in his heart,
Nor honours pufft him up, when he had part:
Those titles loath'd, which some too much do love
For truly his ambition lay above.
His humble mind so lov'd humility,
He left it to his race for Legacy:
And oft and oft, with speeches mild and wise,
Gave his in charge, that Jewel rich to prize.
No ostentation seen in all his wayes,
As in the mean ones, of our foolish dayes,
Which all they have, and more still set to view,
Their greatness may be judg'd by what they shew.
His thoughts were more sublime, his actions wise,
Such vanityes he justly did despise.
Nor wonder 'twas, low things ne'r much did move
For he a Mansion had, prepar'd above,
For which he sigh'd and pray'd and long'd full sore
He might be cloath'd upon, for evermore.
Oft spake of death, and with a smiling chear,
He did exult his end was drawing near,
Now fully ripe, as shock of wheat that's grown,
Death as a Sickle hath him timely mown,
And in celestial Barn hath hous'd him high,
Where storms, nor showrs, nor ought can damnifie.
His Generation serv'd, his labours cease;
And to his Fathers gathered is in peace.
Ah happy Soul, 'mongst Saints and Angels blest,
Who after all his toyle, is now at rest:
His hoary head in righteousness was found:
As joy in heaven on earth let praise resound.
Forgotten never be his memory,

His blessing rest on his posterity:
His pious Footsteps followed by his race,
At last will bring us to that happy place
Where we with joy each others face shall see,
And parted more by death shall never be.

His Epitaph

Within this Tomb a Patriot lyes
That was both pious, just and wise,
To Truth a shield, to right a Wall,
To Sectaryes a whip and Maul,
A Magazine of History,
A Prizer of good Company
In manners pleasant and severe
The Good him lov'd, the bad did fear,
And when his time with years was spent
If some rejoyc'd, more did lament.

In memory of my dear grand-child Anne Bradstreet. Who deceased June 20. 1669. being three years and seven Moneths old (1650)

With troubled heart and trembling hand I write,
The Heavens have chang'd to sorrow my delight.
How oft with disappointment have I met,
When I on fading things my hopes have set?
Experience might 'fore this have made me wise,
To value things according to their price:
Was ever stable joy yet found below,
Or perfect bliss without mixture of woe?
I knew she was but as a withering flour,
That's here to day, perhaps gone in an hour;
Like as a bubble, or the brittle glass,
Or like a shadow turning as it was.
More fool then I to look on that was lent,
As if mine own, when thus impermanent.
Farewel dear child, thou ne're shall come to me,
But yet a while, and I shall go to thee;
Mean time my throbbing heart's chear'd up with this
Thou with thy Saviour art in endless bliss.

To my Dear Children (1650)

This book by Any yet unread,
I leave for you when I am dead,
That, being gone, here you may find
What was your liveing mother's mind.
Make use of what I leave in Love
And God shall blesse you from above.

In my Solitary houres in my dear husband his Absence (1650)

O Lord, thou hear'st my dayly moan,
  And see'st my dropping teares:
My Troubles All are Thee before,
  My Longings and my feares.

Thou hetherto hast been my God;
  Thy help my soul hath found:
Tho' losse and sicknes me assail'd,
  Thro' thee I've kept my Ground.

And thy Abode tho'st made with me;
  With Thee my Soul can talk
In secrett places, Thee I find,
  Where I doe kneel or walk.

Tho' husband dear bee from me gone,
  Whom I doe love so well;
I have a more beloved one
  Whose comforts far excell.

O stay my heart on thee, my God,
  Uphold my fainting Soul!
And, when I know not what to doe,
  I'll on thy mercyes roll.

My weaknes, thou do'st know full well,
  Of Body and of mind.
I, in this world, no comfort have,
  But what from Thee I find.

Tho' children thou hast given me,
And freinds I have also:
Yet, if I see Thee not thro' them,
They are no Joy, but woe.

O shine upon me, blessed Lord,
Ev'n for my Saviour's sake;
In Thee alone is more than All,
And there content I'll take.

O hear me, Lord, in this Request,
As thou before ha'st done:
Bring back my husband, I beseech,
As thou didst once my Sonne.

So shall I celebrate thy Praise,
Ev'n while my Dayes shall last;
And talk to my Beloved one
Of all thy Goodnes past.

So both of us thy Kindnes, Lord,
With Praises shall recount,
And serve Thee better than before,
Whose Blessings thus surmount.

But give me, Lord, a better heart,
Then better shall I bee,
To pay the vowes which I doe owe
For ever unto Thee.

Unlesse thou help, what can I doe
But still my frailty show?
If thou assist me, Lord, I shall
Return Thee what I owe.

"As weary pilgrim, now at rest" (1650)

As weary pilgrim, now at rest,
Hugs with delight his silent nest
His wasted limbes, now lye full soft

That myrie steps, have troden oft
Blesses himself, to think upon
his dangers past, and travailes done
The burning sun no more shall heat
Nor stormy raines, on him shall beat.
The bryars and thornes no more shall scratch
nor hungry wolves at him shall catch
He erring pathes no more shall tread
nor wild fruits eate, in stead of bread,
for waters cold he doth not long
for thirst no more shall parch his tongue
No rugged stones his feet shall gaule
nor stumps nor rocks cause him to fall
All cares and feares, he bids farwell
and meanes in safity now to dwell.
A pilgrim I, on earth, perplext
with sinns with cares and sorrows vext
By age and paines brought to decay
and my Clay house mouldring away
Oh how I long to be at rest
and soare on high among the blest.
This body shall in silence sleep
Mine eyes no more shall ever weep
No fainting fits shall me assaile
nor grinding paines my body fraile
With cares and fears ne'r cumbred be
Nor losses know, nor sorrowes see
What tho my flesh shall there consume
it is the bed Christ did perfume
And when a few yeares shall be gone
this mortall shall be cloth'd upon
A Corrupt Carcasse downe it lyes
a glorious body it shall rise
In weaknes and dishonour sowne
in power 'tis rais'd by Christ alone
Then soule and body shall unite
and of their maker have the sight
Such lasting joyes shall there behold
as eare ne'r heard nor tongue e'er told
Lord make me ready for that day
then Come deare bridgrome Come away.

The Prologue [to *The Tenth Muse*] (1650)

1

To sing of Wars, of Captains, and of Kings,
Of Cities founded, Common-wealths begun,
For my mean pen are too superiour things:
Or how they all, or each their dates have run
Let Poets and Historians set these forth,
My obscure Lines shall not so dim their worth.

2

But when my wondring eyes and envious heart
Great *Bartas* sugar'd lines, do but read o're
Fool I do grudg the Muses did not part
'Twixt him and me that overfluent store;
A *Bartas* can, do what a *Bartas* will
But simple I according to my skill.

3

From school-boyes tongue no rhet'rick we expect
Nor yet a sweet Consort from broken strings,
Nor perfect beauty, where's a main defect:
My foolish, broken, blemish'd Muse so sings
And this to mend, alas, no Art is able,
'Cause nature, made it so irreparable.

4

Nor can I, like that fluent sweet-tongu'd Greek,
Who lisp'd at first, in future times speak plain
By Art he gladly found what he did seek
A full requital of his striving paine:
Art can do much, but this maxime's most sure
A weak or wounded brain admits no cure.

5

I am obnoxious to each carping tongue
Who says my hand a needle better fits,
A Poets pen all scorn I should thus wrong,
For such despite they cast on Female wits:
If what I do prove well, it won't advance,
They'll say it's stoln, or else it was by chance.

6

But sure the Antique Greeks were far more mild
Else of our Sexe, why feigned they those Nine
And poesy made, *Calliope's* own Child;
So 'mongst the rest they placed the Arts Divine,
But this weak knot, they will full soon untie,
The Greeks did nought, but play the fools and lye.

7

Let Greeks be Greeks, and women what they are
Men have precedency and still excell,
It is but vain unjustly to wage warre;
Men can do best, and women know it well
Preheminence in all and each is yours;
Yet grant some small acknowledgement of ours.

8

And oh ye high flown quills that soar the Skies,
And ever with your prey still catch your praise,
If e're you daigne these lowly lines your eyes
Give Thyme or Parsley wreath, I ask no bayes,
This mean and unrefined ure of mine
Will make your glistering gold but more to shine.

SOURCE: Anne Bradstreet. *To My Husband and Other Poems.* Edited by Robert Hutchinson. Mineola, New York: Dover Publications, 2000.

BENJAMIN FRANKLIN

The most interesting American who ever lived was born in 1706 and died in 1790. The Boston-born son of a tallow chandler had two years of schooling and a few years of apprenticeship under his older brother's stern watch before he fled New England at age seventeen and found himself almost penniless and yet ever resourceful in Philadelphia. He became a printer, writer, businessman, community activist, militiaman, scientist, diplomat and philosopher, as well as a family man, philanderer and social animal. Though extraordinary, our most famous and respected citizen was regarded in Europe as America's "representative man." As much as any American, he helped develop the idea of "American" as a national identity, and through his official and unofficial diplomacy in the 1750s and '60s tried to bring about colonial compromise with England before he became the budding Revolution's most eloquent and important spokesman.

An Apology for Printers (1731)

In this first selection, from a Philadelphia newspaper, we see Franklin's teasing and testy defense of freedom of speech.

BEING FREQUENTLY CENSUR'D and condemn'd by different Persons for printing Things which they say ought not to be printed, I have sometimes thought it might be necessary to make a standing Apology for my self, and publish it once a Year, to be read upon all Occasions of that Nature. Much Business has hitherto hindered the execution of this Design; but having very lately given extraordinary Offence by printing an Advertisement with a certain N.B. at the End of it, I find an Apology more particularly requisite at this Juncture, tho' it happens when I have not yet Leisure to write such a thing in the proper Form, and can only in a loose manner throw those Considerations together which should have been the Substance of it.

I request all who are angry with me on the Account of printing things they don't like, calmly to consider these following Particulars:

1. That the Opinions of Men are almost as various as their Faces; an Observation general enough to become a common Proverb, *So many Men so many Minds.*

2. That the Business of Printing has chiefly to do with Mens Opinions; most things that are printed tending to promote some, or oppose others.

3. That hence arises the peculiar Unhappiness of that Business, which other Callings are no way liable to; they who follow Printing being scarce able to do any thing in their way of getting a Living, which shall not probably give Offence to some, and perhaps to many; whereas the Smith, the Shoemaker, the Carpenter, or the Man of any other Trade, may work indifferently for People of all Persuasions, without offending any of them: and the Merchant may buy and sell with Jews, Turks, Hereticks, and Infidels of all sorts, and get Money by every one of them, without giving Offence to the most orthodox, of any sort; or suffering the least Censure or Ill-will on the Account from any Man whatever.

4. That it is as unreasonable in any one Man or Set of Men to expect to be pleas'd with every thing that is printed, as to think that nobody ought to be pleas'd but themselves.

5. Printers are educated in the Belief, that when Men differ in Opinion, both Sides ought equally to have the Advantage of being heard by the Publick; and that when Truth and Error have fair Play, the former is always an overmatch for the latter: Hence they chearfully serve all contending Writers that pay them well, without regarding on which side they are of the Question in Dispute.

6. Being thus continually employ'd in serving all Parties, Printers naturally acquire a vast Unconcernedness as to the right or wrong Opinions contain'd in what they print; regarding it only as the Matter of their daily labour: They print things full of Spleen and Animosity, with the utmost Calmness and Indifference, and without the least Ill-will to the Persons reflected on; who nevertheless unjustly think the Printer as much their Enemy as the Author, and join both together in their Resentment.

7. That it is unreasonable to imagine Printers approve of every thing they print, and to censure them on any particular thing accordingly; since in the way of their Business they print such great variety of things opposite and contradictory. It is likewise as unreasonable what some assert, That Printers ought not to print

any Thing but what they approve; since if all of that Business should make such a Resolution, and abide by it, an End would thereby be put to Free Writing, and the World would afterwards have nothing to read but what happen'd to be the Opinions of Printers.

8. That if all Printers were determin'd not to print any thing till they were sure it would offend no body, there would be very little printed.

9. That if they sometimes print vicious or silly things not worth reading, it may not be because they approve such things themselves, but because the People are so viciously and corruptly educated that good things are not encouraged. I have known a very numerous Impression of *Robin Hood's Songs* go off in this Province at 2s. per Book, in less than a Twelvemonth; when a small Quantity of *David's Psalms* (an excellent Version) have lain upon my Hands above twice the Time.

10. That notwithstanding what might be urg'd in behalf of a Man's being allow'd to do in the Way of his Business whatever he is paid for, yet Printers do continually discourage the Printing of great Numbers of bad things, and stifle them in the Birth. I my self have constantly refused to print any thing that might countenance Vice, or promote Immorality; tho' by complying in such Cases with the corrupt Taste of the Majority, I might have got much Money. I have also always refus'd to print such things as might do real Injury to any Person, how much soever I have been solicited, and tempted with Offers of great Pay; and how much soever I have by refusing got the Ill-will of those who would have employ'd me. I have heretofore fallen under the Resentment of large Bodies of Men, for refusing absolutely to print any of their Party or Personal Reflections. In this Manner I have made my self many Enemies, and the constant Fatigue of denying is almost insupportable. But the Publick being unacquainted with all this, whenever the poor Printer happens either through Ignorance or much Persuasion, to do any thing that is generally thought worthy of Blame, he meets with no more Friendship or Favour on the above Account, than if there were no Merit in't at all. Thus, as Waller says,

> Poets loose half the Praise they would have got
> Were it but known what they discreetly blot;

Yet are censur'd for every bad Line found in their Works with the utmost Severity.

I come now to the particular Case of the N.B. above-mention'd, about which there has been more Clamour against me, than ever before on any other Account.—In the Hurry of other Business an Advertisement was brought to me to be printed; it signified that such a Ship lying at such a Wharff, would sail for Barbadoes in such a Time, and that Freighters and Passengers might agree with the Captain at such a Place; so far is what's common: But at the Bottom this odd Thing was added, N.B. *No Sea Hens nor Black Gowns will be admitted on any Terms.* I printed it, and receiv'd my Money; and the Advertisement was stuck up round the Town as usual. I had not so much Curiosity at that time as to enquire the Meaning of it, nor did I in the least imagine it would give so much Offence. Several good Men are very angry with me on this Occasion; they are pleas'd to say I have too much Sense to do such things ignorantly; that if they were Printers they would not have done such a thing on any Consideration; that it could proceed from nothing but my abundant Malice against Religion and the Clergy: They therefore declare they will not take any more of my Papers, nor have any farther Dealings with me; but will hinder me of all the Custom they can. All this is very hard!

I believe it had been better if I had refused to print the said Advertisement. However, 'tis done and cannot be revok'd. I have only the following few Particulars to offer, some of them in my Behalf, by way of Mitigation, and some not much to the Purpose; but I desire none of them may be read when the Reader is not in a very good Humour.

1. That I really did it without the least Malice, and imagin'd the N.B. was plac'd there only to make the Advertisement star'd at, and more generally read.

2. That I never saw the Word Sea-Hens before in my Life; nor have I yet ask'd the meaning of it; and tho' I had certainly known that Black Gowns in that Place signified the Clergy of the Church of England, yet I have that confidence in the generous good Temper of such of them as I know, as to be well satisfied such a trifling mention of their Habit gives them no Disturbance.

3. That most of the Clergy in this and the neighbouring Provinces, are my Customers, and some of them my very good Friends; and I must be very malicious indeed, or very stupid, to

print this thing for a small Profit, if I had thought it would have given them just Cause of Offence.

4. That if I have much Malice against the Clergy, and withal much Sense; 'tis strange I never write or talk against the Clergy my self. Some have observed that 'tis a fruitful Topic, and the easiest to be witty upon of all others. I can print any thing I write at less Charge than others; yet I appeal to the Publick that I am never guilty this way, and to all my Acquaintance as to my Conversation.

5. That if a Man of Sense had Malice enough to desire to injure the Clergy, this is the foolishest Thing he could possibly contrive for that Purpose.

6. That I got Five Shillings by it.

7. That none who are angry with me would have given me so much to let it alone.

8. That if all the People of different Opinions in this Province would engage to give me as much for not printing things they don't like, as I can get by printing them, I should probably live a very easy Life; and if all Printers were every where so dealt by, there would be very little printed.

9. That I am oblig'd to all who take my Paper, and am willing to think they do it out of meer Friendship. I only desire they would think the same when I deal with them. I thank those who leave off, that they have taken it so long. But I beg they would not endeavour to dissuade others, for that will look like Malice.

10. That 'tis impossible any Man should know what he would do if he was a Printer.

11. That notwithstanding the Rashness and Inexperience of Youth, which is most likely to be prevail'd with to do things that ought not to be done; yet I have avoided printing such Things as usually give Offence either to Church or State, more than any Printer that has followed the Business in this Province before.

12. And lastly, That I have printed above a Thousand Advertisements which made not the least mention of *Sea-Hens* or *Black Gowns*; and this being the first Offence, I have the more Reason to expect Forgiveness.

I take leave to conclude with an old Fable, which some of my Readers have heard before, and some have not.

A certain well-meaning Man and his Son, were travelling towards a Market Town, with an Ass which they had to sell. The Road was bad; and the old Man therefore rid, but the Son went a-foot. The first Passenger they met, asked the Father if he was not ashamed to ride by himself, and suffer the poor Lad to wade along thro' the Mire; this induced him to take up his Son behind him: He had not travelled far, when he met others, who said, they were two unmerciful Lubbers to get both on the Back of that poor Ass, in such a deep Road. Upon this the old Man gets off, and let his Son ride alone. The next they met called the Lad a graceless, rascally young Jackanapes, to ride in that Manner thro' the Dirt, while his aged Father trudged along on Foot; and they said the old Man was a Fool, for suffering it. He then bid his Son come down, and walk with him, and they travell'd on leading the Ass by the Halter; 'till they met another Company, who called them a Couple of sensless Blockheads, for going both on Foot in such a dirty Way, when they had an empty Ass with them, which they might ride upon. The old Man could bear no longer; My Son, said he, it grieves me much that we cannot please all these People; Let us throw the Ass over the next Bridge, and be no farther troubled with him.

Had the old Man been seen acting this last Resolution, he would probably have been call'd a Fool for troubling himself about the different Opinions of all that were pleas'd to find Fault with him: Therefore, tho' I have a Temper almost as complying as his, I intend not to imitate him in this last Particular. I consider the Variety of Humours among Men, and despair of pleasing every Body; yet I shall not therefore leave off Printing. I shall continue my Business. I shall not burn my Press and melt my Letters.

—*The Pennsylvania Gazette* (June 10, 1731)

Poor Richard's Almanack

After a "preface" by Franklin, which we have excerpted from the posthumously published Part 3 of his Autobiography, *we share a selection of several dozen of Poor Richard's sayings. Franklin, writing in the character of "Poor Richard," derived and recomposed his sayings from many sources, among them religious texts, folk wisdom and proverbs. In his bestselling annual publication, "Poor Richard's Almanack," Franklin "filled all the little Spaces that occurr'd between the Remarkable Days in the Calendar, with Proverbial Sentences." They became a basis for what we think of as characteristic American practical philosophy.*

In 1732 I first published my Almanack, under the Name of *Richard Saunders;* it was continu'd by me about 25 Years, commonly call'd *Poor Richard's Almanack.* I endeavor'd to make it both entertaining and useful, and it accordingly came to be in such Demand that I reap'd considerable Profit from it, vending annually near ten Thousand. And observing that it was generally read, scarce any Neighborhood in the Province being without it, I consider'd it as a proper Vehicle for conveying Instruction among the common People, who bought scarce any other Books. I therefore filled all the little Spaces that occurr'd between the Remarkable Days in the Calendar, with Proverbial Sentences, chiefly such as inculcated Industry and Frugality, as the Means of procuring Wealth and thereby securing Virtue, it being more difficult for a Man in Want to act always honestly, as (to use here one of those Proverbs) *it is hard for an empty Sack to stand upright.* These Proverbs, which contained the Wisdom of many Ages and Nations, I assembled and form'd into a connected Discourse prefix'd to the Almanack of 1757, as the Harangue of a wise old Man to the People attending an Auction. The bringing all these scatter'd Counsels thus into a Focus, enabled them to make greater Impression. The Piece being universally approved was copied in all the Newspapers of the Continent, reprinted in Britain on a Broadside to be stuck up in Houses, two Translations were made of it in French, and great Numbers bought by the Clergy & Gentry to distribute gratis among their poor Parishioners and Tenants. In Pennsylvania, as it discouraged useless Expense in foreign Superfluities, some thought, it had its share of Influence in producing that growing Plenty of Money which was observable for several Years after its Publication.

1733

The poor have little, beggars none, the rich too much, *enough* not one.

God works wonders now & then;
Behold! a Lawyer, an honest Man!

Beware of the young Doctor & the old Barber.

Nothing more like a Fool, than a drunken Man.

Great Talkers, little Doers.

Hunger never saw bad bread.

A good Wife lost is God's gift lost.

1734

He does not possess Wealth, it possesses him.

Better slip with foot than tongue.

He that knows nothing of it, may by chance be a Prophet; while the wisest that is may happen to miss.

No man e'er was glorious, who was not laborious.

Laws like to Cobwebs catch small Flies,
Great ones break thro' before your eyes.

Where there's Marriage without Love, there will be Love without Marriage.

If you wou'd have Guests merry with your cheer,
Be so your self, or so at least appear.

There have been as great Souls unknown to fame as any of the most famous.

Take this remark from Richard poor and lame,
Whate'er's begun in anger ends in shame.

A learned blockhead is a greater blockhead than an ignorant one.

1735

A lie stands on one leg, truth on two.

To be humble to Superiors is Duty, to Equals Courtesy, to Inferiors Nobleness.

A man is never so ridiculous by those Qualities that are his own as by those that he affects to have.

Necessity never made a good bargain.

Approve not of him who commends all you say.

Sal laughs at every thing you say. Why? Because she has fine Teeth.

Early to bed and early to rise, makes a man healthy, wealthy, and wise.

1736

None preaches better than the ant, and she says nothing.

Do not do that which you would not have known.

Wealth is not his that has it, but his that enjoys it.

Fish & Visitors stink in 3 days.

The absent are never without fault, nor the present without excuse.

Creditors have better memories than debtors.

Lovers, Travellers, and Poets, will give money to be heard.

He that speaks much, is much mistaken.

'Tis easy to see, hard to foresee.

Diligence is the Mother of Good-Luck.

1737

The greatest monarch on the proudest throne, is oblig'd to sit upon his own arse.

Don't go to the doctor with every distemper, nor to the lawyer with every quarrel, nor to the pot for every thirst.

Well done is better than well said.

He that can compose himself, is wiser than he that composes books.

1738

There are three faithful friends, an old wife, an old dog, and ready money.

Eat to please thyself, but dress to please others.

Buy what thou hast no need of; and e'er long thou shalt sell thy necessaries.

As we must account for every idle word, so we must for every idle silence.

If you do what you would not, you must hear what you would not.

You may be more happy than Princes, if you will be more virtuous.

Keep your eyes wide open before marriage, half shut afterwards.

None but the well-bred man knows how to confess a fault, or acknowledge himself in an error.

Each year one vicious habit rooted out,
In time might make the worst Man good throughout.[1]

Since I cannot govern my own tongue, tho' within my own teeth, how can I hope to govern the tongues of others?

Search others for their virtues, thy self for thy vices.

Who has deceiv'd thee so oft as thy self?

Wink at small faults; remember thou hast great ones.

Write with the learned, pronounce with the vulgar.

If you wou'd not be forgotten
As soon as you are dead and rotten,
Either write things worth reading,
Or do things worth the writing.

---

1. See *The Autobiography*, Part 2, page 33, below.

Reading makes a full Man, Meditation a profound Man, discourse a clear Man.

1739

Sin is not hurtful because it is forbidden but it is forbidden because it's hurtful. Nor is a Duty beneficial because it is commanded, but it is commanded, because it's beneficial.

Blessed is he that expects nothing, for he shall never be disappointed.

Hear no ill of a Friend, nor speak any of an Enemy.

He that falls in love with himself, will have no Rivals.

1740

Observe all men; thy self most.

When you speak to a man, look on his eyes; when he speaks to thee, look on his mouth.

Fear not Death; for the sooner we die, the longer shall we be immortal.

To bear other People's Afflictions, every one has Courage enough, and to spare.

Lend Money to an Enemy, and thou'lt gain him, to a Friend and thou'lt lose him.

An open Foe may prove a curse;
But a pretended friend is worse.

There are lazy Minds as well as lazy Bodies.

A wolf eats sheep but now and then,
Ten Thousands are devour'd by Men.

Who says Jack is not generous? he is always fond of giving, and cares not for receiving.—What? Why; Advice.

Those who in quarrels interpose,
Must often wipe a bloody nose.

None are deceived but they that confide.

1741

Learn of the skilful: He that teaches himself, hath a fool for his master.

Quarrels never could last long,
If on one side only lay the wrong.

If you would keep your Secret from an enemy, tell it not to a friend.

1742

Have you somewhat to do to-morrow; do it to-day.

To err is human, to repent divine, to persist devilish.

1743

How many observe Christ's Birth-day! How few, his Precepts! O! 'tis easier to keep Holidays than Commandments.

Experience keeps a dear school, yet Fools will learn in no other.

Let all Men know thee, but no man know thee thoroughly: Men freely ford that see the shallows.

Speak with contempt of none, from slave to king,
The meanest Bee hath, and will use, a sting.

The World is full of fools and faint hearts; and yet every one has courage enough to bear the misfortunes, and wisdom enough to manage the Affairs of his neighbour.

1744

He that has not got a Wife, is not yet a compleat Man.

If you'd lose a troublesome Visitor, lend him Money.

What you would seem to be, be really.

Drive thy Business, or it will drive thee.

God heals, and the Doctor takes the Fees.

Fear God, and your Enemies will fear you.

Make haste slowly.

Those who are fear'd, are hated.

Tart Words make no Friends: a spoonful of honey will catch more flies than Gallon of Vinegar.

Sloth (like Rust) consumes faster than Labour wears: the used Key is always bright.

1745

Many complain of their Memory, few of their Judgment.

'Tis easier to prevent bad habits than to break them.

All blood is alike ancient.

You may talk too much on the best of subjects.

It's common for Men to give 6 pretended Reasons instead of one real one.

1746

It's the easiest Thing in the World for a Man to deceive himself.

The Tongue is ever turning to the aching Tooth.

Dost thou love Life? then do not squander Time; for that's the Stuff Life is made of.

1747

There is no Man so bad, but he secretly respects the Good.

A good Example is the best sermon.

A Mob's a Monster; Heads enough, but no Brains.

The Devil sweetens Poison with Honey.

A Slip of the Foot you may soon recover:
But a Slip of the Tongue you may never get over.

Write Injuries in Dust, Benefits in Marble.

A Father's a Treasure; a Brother's a Comfort; a Friend is both.

What is Serving God? 'Tis doing Good to Man.

1748

When you're good to others, you are best to yourself.

1749

Drink does not drown *Care*, but waters it, and makes it grow faster.

Many Foxes grow grey, but few grow good.

A Man in a Passion rides a mad Horse.

The wise Man draws more Advantage from his Enemies, than the Fool from his Friends.

Doing an Injury puts you below your Enemy; *Revenging* one makes you but *even* with him; *Forgiving* it sets you *above* him.

Having been poor is no shame, but being ashamed of it is.

All would live long, but none would be old.

1750

Genius without Education is like Silver in the Mine.

What signifies knowing the Names, if you know not the Nature of Things.

Glass, China, and Reputation, are easily crack'd, and never well mended.

There are three Things extreamly hard, Steel, a Diamond and to know one's self.

1751

To-day is Yesterday's Pupil.

Friendship increases by visiting Friends, but by visiting seldom.

Who judges best of a Man, his Enemies or himself?

Not to oversee Workmen, is to leave them your Purse open.

1752

If Man could have Half his Wishes, he would double his Troubles.

The busy Man has few idle Visitors; to the boiling Pot the Flies come not.

Success has ruin'd many a Man.

1753

Anger is never without a Reason, but seldom with a good One.

A Pair of good Ears will drain dry an hundred Tongues.

Serving God is Doing Good to Man, but Praying is thought an easier Service, and therefore more generally chosen.

He that is of Opinion Money will do every Thing, may well be suspected of doing every Thing for Money.

1754

The learned Fool writes his Nonsense in better Language than the unlearned; but still 'tis Nonsense.

1755

The Master's Eye will do more Work than both his Hands.

Diligence overcomes Difficulties, Sloth makes them.

A long Life may not be good enough, but a good Life is long enough.

Being ignorant is not so much a Shame, as being unwilling to learn.

The Doors of Wisdom are never shut.

> *Who is wise?* He that learns from every One.
> *Who is powerful?* He that governs his Passions.
> *Who is rich?* He that is content.
> *Who is that?* Nobody.

1756

Laziness travels so slowly, that *Poverty* soon overtakes him.

Love your Enemies, for they tell you your Faults.

1757

Work as if you were to live 100 Years, Pray as if you were to die To-morrow.

It is Ill-Manners to silence a Fool, and Cruelty to let him go on.

1758

Silence is not always a Sign of Wisdom, but Babbling is ever a Mark of Folly.

He that's content, hath enough; He that complains, has too much.

Great Modesty often hides great Merit.

Half the Truth is often a great Lie.

Autobiography ["Arriving at moral Perfection"] (1793)

In the most noted passage from his posthumously published Autobiography, *Franklin describes what has become the most famous of all systematic resolutions at self-improvement. He began "the bold and arduous Project of arriving at moral Perfection" in 1733, when he was 27.*

IT WAS ABOUT this time I conceived the bold and arduous Project of arriving at moral Perfection. I wish'd to live without committing any Fault at any time; I would conquer all that either Natural Inclination, Custom, or Company might lead me into. As I knew, or thought I knew, what was right and wrong, I did not see why I might not *always* do the one and avoid the other. But I soon found I had undertaken a Task of more Difficulty than I had imagined: While my Care was employ'd in guarding against one Fault, I was often surpriz'd by another. Habit took the advantage of Inattention. Inclination was sometimes too strong for Reason. I concluded, at length, that the mere speculative Conviction that it was our Interest to be compleatly virtuous, was not sufficient to prevent our Slipping; and that the contrary Habits must be broken, and good Ones acquired and established, before we can have any Dependence on a steady, uniform Rectitude of Conduct. For this purpose I therefore contrived the following Method.—

In the various Enumerations of the moral Virtues I had met with in my Reading, I found the Catalogue more or less numerous, as different Writers included more or fewer Ideas under the same name. Temperance, for example, was by some confined to Eating & Drinking, while by others it was extended to mean the moderating every other Pleasure, Appetite, Inclination, or Passion, bodily or mental, even to our Avarice & Ambition. I propos'd to myself, for the sake of Clearness, to use rather more Names, with fewer Ideas annexed to each, than a few Names with more ideas; and I included under Thirteen Names of Virtues all that at that time occurred to me as necessary or desirable, and annex'd to each a short Precept, which fully expressed the Extent I gave to its Meaning.

These names of Virtues, with their Precepts were:

1. TEMPERANCE.

Eat not to Dullness. Drink not to Elevation.

2. SILENCE.

Speak not but what may benefit others or your self. Avoid trifling conversation.

3. ORDER.

Let all your Things have their Places. Let each Part of your Business have its Time.

4. RESOLUTION.

Resolve to perform what you ought. Perform without fail what you resolve.

5. FRUGALITY.

Make no expense but to do good to others or yourself; *i.e.,* waste nothing.

6. INDUSTRY.

Lose no Time.—Be always employ'd in something useful.—Cut off all unnecessary Actions.

7. SINCERITY.

Use no hurtful Deceit. Think innocently and justly; and, if you speak, speak accordingly.

8. JUSTICE.

Wrong none, by doing Injuries, or omitting the Benefits that are your Duty.

9. MODERATION.

Avoid Extreams. Forbear resenting Injuries so much as you think they deserve.

10. CLEANLINESS.

Tolerate no Uncleanness in Body, Clothes or Habitation.

11. TRANQUILLITY.

Be not disturbed at Trifles, or at Accidents common or unavoidable.

12. CHASTITY.

Rarely use Venery but for Health or Offspring; Never to Dullness, Weakness, or the Injury of your own or another's Peace or Reputation.

13. HUMILITY.

Imitate Jesus and Socrates.

My intention being to acquire the *Habitude* of all these virtues, I judg'd it would be well not to distract my Attention by attempting the whole at once, but to fix it on one of them at a time; and, when I should be Master of that, then to proceed to another, and so on, till I should have gone through the thirteen. And as the previous Acquisition of some might facilitate the Acquisition of certain others, I arranged them with that view, as they stand above. *Temperance* first, as it tends to procure that Coolness & Clearness of

Head, which is so necessary where constant Vigilance was to be kept up, and Guard maintained against the unremitting Attraction of ancient Habits, and the force of perpetual temptations. This being acquired & established, *Silence* would be more easy; and my Desire being to gain Knowledge at the same time that I improved in Virtue, and considering that in conversation it was obtained rather by the use of the ears than of the tongue, & therefore wishing to break a Habit I was getting into of Prattling, Punning & Joking, which only made me acceptable to trifling Company, I gave *Silence* the second place. This and the next, *Order,* I expected would allow me more time for attending to my project and my studies. *Resolution,* once become habitual, would keep me firm in my Endeavors to obtain all the subsequent virtues; *Frugality* & *Industry* freeing me from my remaining Debt, & producing Affluence & Independence, would make more easy the Practice of *Sincerity* & *Justice,* &c., &c. Conceiving then, that, agreeably to the Advice of Pythagoras in his Golden Verses, daily Examination would be necessary, I contriv'd the following method for conducting that examination.

I made a little Book, in which I allotted a Page for each of the virtues. I rul'd each page with red Ink, so as to have seven Columns, one for each Day of the Week, marking each column with a letter for the day. I crossed these columns with thirteen red Lines, marking the beginning of each Line with the first Letter of one of the Virtues, on which line & in its proper Column, I might mark, by a little black Spot, every Fault I found upon Examination to have been committed respecting that Virtue upon that Day.

I determined to give a Week's strict Attention to each of the Virtues successively. Thus in the first Week my great Guard was to avoid every the least Offence against Temperance, leaving the other Virtues to their ordinary Chance, only marking every Evening the Faults of the Day. Thus if in the first Week I could keep my first line marked T clear of Spots, I suppos'd the Habit of that Virtue so much strengthen'd and its opposite weaken'd, that I might venture extending my Attention to include the next, and for the following Week keep both Lines clear of Spots. Proceeding thus to the last, I could go thro' a Course compleat in Thirteen Weeks, and four Courses in a Year.—And like him who having a Garden to weed, does not attempt to eradicate all the bad Herbs at once, which would exceed his Reach and his Strength, but works on each one of the Beds at a time, & having accomplish'd the first proceeds to a second, so I should have (I hoped) the encouraging Pleasure of seeing on my Pages the Progress I made in Virtue, by clearing successively my Lines of their Spots, till in the End by a Number of Courses, I should be happy in viewing a clean Book after a thirteen Weeks daily Examination. . . .

. . . I always carried my little Book with me. My Scheme of ORDER gave me the most Trouble, and I found, that tho' it might be practicable where a Man's Business was such as to leave the Disposition of his Time, that of a Journeyman Printer, for instance, it was not possible to be exactly observ'd by a Master, who must mix with the World, and often receive People of Busines at their own Hours.—*Order*, too with regard to Places for Things, Papers, &c., I found extreamly difficult to acquire. I had not been early accustomed to it, & having an exceeding good Memory, I was not so sensible of the Inconvenience attending Want of Method. This Article therefore cost me so much painful Attention & my Faults in it vex'd me so much, and I made so little Progress in Amendment, & had such frequent Relapses, that I was almost ready to give up the Attempt, and content my self with a faulty Character in that respect. Like the Man who in buying an Ax of a Smith my Neighbour, desired to have the whole of its Surface as bright as the Edge; the Smith consented to grind it bright for him if he would turn the Wheel. He turn'd while the Smith press'd the broad Face of the Ax hard & heavily on the Stone, which made the Turning of it very fatiguing. The Man came every now & then from the Wheel to see how the Work went on; and at length would take his Ax as it was without further Grinding. No, says the Smith, Turn on, turn on; we shall have it bright by and by; as yet 'tis only speckled. Yes, says the Man; but—*I think I like a speckled Ax best.*—And I believe this may have been the Case with many who having for want of some such Means as I employ'd found the Difficulty of obtaining good, & breaking bad Habits, in other Points of Vice & Virtue, have given up the Struggle, & concluded that *a speckled Ax was best.* For something that pretended to be Reason was every now and then suggesting to me, that such extream Nicety as I exacted of my self might be a kind of Foppery in Morals, which if it were known would make me ridiculous; that a perfect Character might be attended with the Inconvenience of being envied and hated; and that a benevolent Man should allow a few Faults in himself, to keep his Friends in Countenance. In

Truth I found myself incorrigible with respect to *Order*, and now I am grown old, and my Memory bad, I feel very sensibly the want of it. But on the whole, tho' I never arrived at the Perfection I had been so ambitious of obtaining, but fell far short of it, yet I was by the Endeavor made a better and a happier Man than I otherwise should have been, if I had not attempted it. As those who aim at perfect Writing by imitating the engraved Copies, tho' they never reach the wish'd for Excellence of those Copies, their Hand is mended by the Endeavor, and is tolerable while it continues fair & legible. . . .

My List of virtues contain'd at first but twelve; but a Quaker Friend having kindly inform'd me that I was generally thought proud; that my Pride showed itself frequently in Conversation; that I was not content with being in the right when discussing any Point, but was overbearing, & rather insolent, of which he convinced me by mentioning several instances; I determined endeavoring to cure myself, if I could, of this Vice or Folly among the rest, and I added *Humility* to my list, giving an extensive Meaning to the word.—I cannot boast of much Success in acquiring the reality of this Virtue, but I had a good deal with regard to the *Appearance* of it. I made it a Rule to forbear all direct Contradiction to the Sentiments of others, and all positive Assertion of my own. I even forbid myself, agreeably to the old Laws of our Junto, the Use of every Word or Expression in the language that imported a fix'd Opinion, such as *certainly, undoubtedly, &c.*, and I adopted, instead of them, *I conceive, I apprehend,* or *I imagine* a thing to be so or so; or it so appears to me at present. When another asserted something that I thought an Error, I denied myself the Pleasure of contradicting him abruptly, and of showing immediately some Absurdity in his Proposition; and in answering I began by observing that in certain Cases or Circumstances his Opinion would be right, but in the present case there *appear'd* or *seem'd* to me some difference, &c. I soon found the Advantage of this Change in my Manners; the Conversations I engaged in went on more pleasantly. The modest way in which I propos'd my Opinions procured them a readier Reception and less Contradiction; I had less Mortification when I was found to be in the wrong, and I more easily prevailed with others to give up their Mistakes & join with me when I happened to be in the right. And this Mode, which I at first put on with some Violence to natural Inclination, became at length so easy, and so habitual to me, that perhaps for these fifty years past no one has ever heard a dogmatical Expression escape me. And to this Habit (after my Character of Integrity) I think it principally owing that I had early so much Weight with my Fellow-Citizens when I proposed new Institutions, or Alterations in the old, and so much Influence in public Councils when I became a Member; for I was but a bad Speaker, never eloquent, subject to much hesitation in my choice of Words, hardly correct in Language, and yet I generally carried my Points.

In reality, there is, perhaps, no one of our natural Passions so hard to subdue as *Pride*. Disguise it, struggle with it, beat it down, stifle it, mortify it as much as one pleases, it is still alive, and will every now and then peep out and show itself. You will see it, perhaps, often in this History; for, even if I could conceive that I had compleatly overcome it, I should probably be proud of my Humility.

SOURCE: Benjamin Franklin. *Autobiography*, Part 2. Edited by John Bigelow. Philadelphia: J. P. Lippincott & Co., 1868.

JONATHAN EDWARDS

The Puritan minister Jonathan Edwards (1703–1758) was a genius of persuasion and rhetoric, and seemed to revel and glory in the fire and brimstone that he conjured up in clear and violent speech for his various congregations. His aim was to convert the unconverted to Christianity and to shock the complacent with God's "everlasting wrath." Why? Because for them it "would be dreadful to suffer this fierceness and wrath of Almighty God one moment; but you must suffer it to all eternity: there will be no end to this exquisite horrible misery: When you look forward, you shall see a long forever, a boundless duration before you, which will swallow up your thoughts, and amaze your soul; and you will absolutely despair of ever having any deliverance, any end, any mitigation, any rest at all; you will know certainly that you must wear out long ages, millions of millions of ages, in wrestling and conflicting with this almighty merciless vengeance; and then when you have so done, when so many ages have actually been spent by you in this manner, you will know that all is but a point to what remains. So that your punishment will indeed be infinite. Oh who can express what the state of a soul in such circumstances is! All that we can possibly say about it, gives but a very feeble, faint representation of it; 'tis inexpressible and inconceivable: For who knows the power of God's anger?" As David Dutkanicz writes in the Dover edition (see Source note below), "Delivered in a stunning and severe monotone, this sermon brought Edwards' congregation to tears and convulsions. It's since come to be known as one of the first and finest expressions of American Puritan thought."

Sinners in the Hands of an Angry God (1741)

A SERMON PREACHED at Enfield [Connecticut], July 8th 1741. At a time of great awakenings; and attended with remarkable impressions on many of the hearers.

Amos 9, 2, 3. *Though they dig into Hell, thence shall mine Hand take them; though they climb up to Heaven, thence will I bring them down. And though they hide themselves in the top of Carmel, I will search and take them out thence; and though they be hid from my sight in the bottom of the sea, thence I will command the serpent, and he shall bite them.*

Deut. 32, 35

—*Their foot shall slide in due time.*—

IN THIS VERSE is threat'ned the vengeance of God on the wicked unbelieving Israelites, were God's visible people, and lived under that means of grace; and that, notwithstanding all God's wonderful works towards that people, yet remained, as is expressed, ver. 28. void of counsel, having no understanding in them; and that, under all the cultivations of heaven, brought forth bitter and poisonous fruit; as in the two verses next preceding the text.

The expression that I have chosen for my text, *Their foot shall slide in due time;* seems to imply the following things, relating to the punishment and destruction that these wicked Israelites were exposed to.

1. That they were *always* exposed to destruction, as one that stands or walks in slippery places is always exposed to fall. This is implied in the manner of their destruction's coming upon them, being represented by their foot sliding. The same is express'd, Psal. 73. 18. *Surely thou didst set them in slippery places; thou castedst them down into destruction.*

2. It implies that they were always exposed to sudden unexpected destruction. As he that walks in slippery places is every moment liable to fall; he can't foresee one moment whether he shall stand or fall the next; and when he does fall, he falls at once, without warning. Which is also expressed in that, Psal. 73. 18, 19. *Surely thou didst set them in slippery places; thou castedst them down into destruction. How are they brought into desolation as in a moment?*

3. Another thing implied is that they are liable to fall of themselves, without being thrown down by the hand of another. As he that stands or walks on slippery ground, needs nothing but his own weight to throw him down.

4. That the reason why they are not fallen already, and don't fall now, is only that God's appointed time is not come. For it is said, that when that due time, or appointed time comes, their foot shall

slide. Then they shall be left to fall as they are inclined by their own weight. God won't hold them up in these slippery places any longer, but will let them go; and then, at that very instant, they shall fall into destruction; as he that stands on such slippery declining ground on the edge of a pit that he can't stand alone, when he is let go he immediately falls and is lost.

The observation from the words that I would now insist upon is this,

There is nothing that keeps wicked men, at any one moment, out of hell, but the meer pleasure of God.

By the meer pleasure of God, I mean his sovereign pleasure, his arbitrary will, restrained by no obligation, hinder'd by no manner of difficulty, any more than if nothing else but God's meer will had in the least degree, or in any respect whatsoever, any hand in the preservation of wicked men one moment.

The truth of this observation may appear by the following considerations.

1. There is no want of power in God to cast wicked men into hell at any moment. Mens hands can't be strong when God rises up. The strongest have no power to resist him, nor can any deliver out of his hands.

He is not only able to cast wicked men into hell, but he can most easily do it. Sometimes an earthly prince meets with a great deal of difficulty to subdue a rebel, that has found means to fortify himself, and has made himself strong by the numbers of his followers. But it is not so with God. There is no fortress that is any defence from the power of God. Tho' hand join in hand, and vast multitudes of God's enemies combine and associate themselves, they are easily broken in pieces. They are as great heaps of light chaff before the whirlwind; or large quantities of dry stubble before devouring flames. We find it easy to tread on and crush a worm that we see crawling on the earth; so 'tis easy for us to cut or singe a slender thread that any thing hangs by; thus easy is it for God when he pleases to cast his enemies down to hell. What are we, that we should think to stand before him, at whose rebuke the earth trembles, and before whom the rocks are thrown down?

2. They deserve to be cast into hell; so that divine justice never stands in the way, it makes no objection against God's using his power at any moment to destroy them. Yea, on the contrary,

justice calls aloud for an infinite punishment of their sins. Divine justice says of the tree that brings forth such grapes of Sodom, *Cut it down, why cumbreth it the ground?* Luke 13:7. The sword of divine justice is every moment brandished over their heads, and 'tis nothing but the hand of arbitrary mercy, and God's meer will, that holds it back.

3. They are already under a sentence of condemnation to hell. They don't only justly deserve to be cast down thither; but the sentence of the law of God, that eternal and immutable rule of righteousness that God has fixed between him and mankind, is gone out against them, and stands against them; so that they are bound over already to hell. Joh. 3:18. *He that believeth not is condemned already.* So that every unconverted man properly belongs to hell; that is his place; from thence he is. Joh. 8:23. *Ye are from beneath.* And thither he is bound; 'tis the place that justice, and God's word, and the sentence of his unchangeable law assigns to him.

4. They are now the objects of that very same anger & wrath of God that is expressed in the torments of hell: and the reason why they don't go down to hell at each moment, is not because God, in whose power they are, is not then very angry with them; as angry he is with many of those miserable creatures that he is now tormenting in hell, and do there feel and bear the fierceness of his wrath. Yea God is a great deal more angry with great numbers that are now on earth, yea doubtless, with many that are now in this congregation, that it may be are at ease and quiet, than he is with many of those that are now in the flames of hell.

So that it is not because God is unmindful of their wickedness, and don't resent it, that he don't let loose his hand and cut them off. God is not altogether such an one as themselves, tho' they may imagine him to be so. The wrath of God burns against them, their damnation don't slumber, the pit is prepared, the fire is made ready, the furnace is now hot, ready to receive them, the flames do now rage and glow. The glittering sword is whet, and held over them, and the pit hath opened its mouth under them.

5. The Devil stands ready to fall upon them, and seize them as his own, at what moment God shall permit him. They belong to him; he has their souls in his possession, and under his dominion. The Scripture represents them as his goods, Luk. 11. 21. The Devils watch them; they are ever by them, at their right hand; they stand waiting for them, like greedy hungry lions that see their prey, and expect to have it, but are for the present kept back;

if God should withdraw his hand, by which they are restrained, they would in one moment fly upon their poor souls. The old serpent is gaping for them; hell opens its mouth wide to receive them; and if God should permit it, they would be hastily swallowed up and lost.

6. There are in the souls of wicked men those hellish principles reigning, that would presently kindle and flame out into hell fire, if it were not for God's restraints. There is laid in the very nature of carnal men, a foundation for the torments of hell: There are those corrupt principles, in reigning power in them, and in full possession of them, that are seeds of hell fire. These principles are active and powerful, exceeding violent in their nature, and if it were not for the restraining hand of God upon them, they would soon break out, they would flame out after the same manner as the same corruptions, the same enmity does in the hearts of damned souls, and would beget the same torments in 'em as they do in them. The souls of the wicked are in Scripture compared to the troubled sea, Isia. 57. 20. For the present, God restrains their wickedness by his mighty power, as he does the raging waves of the troubled sea, saying, *Hitherto shalt thou come, and no further;* but if God should withdraw that restraining power, it would soon carry all afore it. Sin is the ruin and misery of the soul; it is destructive in its nature; and if God should leave it without restraint, there would need nothing else to make the soul perfectly miserable. The corruption of the heart of man is immoderate and boundless in its fury; and while wicked men live here, it is like fire pent up by God's restraints, whereas if it were let loose, it would set on fire the course of nature; and as the heart is now a sink of sin, so, if sin was not restrain'd, it would immediately turn the soul into a fiery oven, or a furnace of fire and brimstone.

7. It is no security to wicked men for one moment, that there are no visible means of death at hand. 'Tis no security to a natural man, that he is now in health, and that he don't see which way he should now immediately go out of the world by any accident, and that there is no visible danger in any respect in his circumstances. The manifold and continual experience of the world in all ages, shews that this is no evidence, that a man is not on the very brink of eternity, and that the next step won't be into another world. The unseen, unthought-of ways and means of persons going suddenly out of the world are innumerable and inconceivable. Unconverted men walk over the pit of hell on a rotten covering, and there are

innumerable places in this covering so weak that they won't bear their weight, and these places are not seen. The arrows of death fly unseen at noon-day; the sharpest sight can't discern them. God has so many different unsearchable ways of taking wicked men out of the world and sending 'em to hell, that there is nothing to make it appear that God had need to be at the expense of a miracle, or go out of the ordinary course of his providence, to destroy any wicked man, at any moment. All the means that there are of sinners going out of the world, are so in God's hands, and so universally and absolutely subject to his power and determination, that it don't depend at all less on the meer will of God, whether sinners shall at any moment go to hell, than if means were never made use of, or at all concerned in the case.

8. Natural men's prudence and care to preserve their own lives, or the care of others to preserve them, don't secure 'em a moment. This divine providence and universal experience does also bear testimony to. There is this clear evidence that men's own wisdom is no security to them from death; that if it were otherwise we should see some difference between the wise and politick men of the world, and others, with regard to their liableness to early and unexpected death: but how is it in fact? Eccles. 2. 16. *How dieth the wise man? as the fool.*

9. All wicked men's pains and contrivance which they use to escape hell, while they continue to reject Christ, and so remain wicked men, don't secure them from hell one moment. Almost every natural man that hears of hell, flatters himself that he shall escape it; he depends upon himself for his own security; he flatters himself in what he has done, in what he is now doing, or what he intends to do; every one lays out matters in his own mind how he shall avoid damnation, and flatters himself that he contrives well for himself, and that his schemes won't fail. They hear indeed that there are but few saved, and that the greater part of men that have died heretofore are gone to hell; but each one imagines that he lays out matters better for his own escape than others have done. He don't intend to come to that place of torment; he says within himself, that he intends to take care that shall be effectual, and to order matters so for himself as not to fail.

But the foolish children of men miserably delude themselves in their own schemes, and in confidence in their own strength and wisdom; they trust to nothing but a shadow. The bigger part of those that heretofore have lived under the same means of grace, and are now dead, are undoubtedly gone to hell: and it was not because they were not as wise as those who are now alive: it was not because they did not lay out matters as well for themselves to secure their own escape. If it were so, that we could come to speak with them, and could inquire of them, one by one, whether they expected when alive, and when they used to hear about hell, ever to be the subjects of that misery, we doubtless should hear one and another reply, "No, I never intended to come here; I had laid out matters otherwise in my mind; I thought I should contrive well for my self; I thought my scheme good; I intended to take effectual care; but it came upon me unexpected; I did not look for it at that time, and in that manner; it came as a thief; death outwitted me; God's wrath was too quick for me; Oh, my cursed foolishness! I was flattering my self, and pleasing my self with vain dreams of what I would do hereafter, and when I was saying peace and safety, then sudden destruction came upon me."

10. God has laid himself under no obligation, by any promise to keep any natural man out of hell one moment. God certainly has made no promises either of eternal life, or of any deliverance or preservation from eternal death, but what are contained in the covenant of grace, the promises that are given in Christ, in whom all the promises are Yea and Amen. But surely they have no interest in the promises of the covenant of grace that are not the children of the covenant, and that don't believe in any of the promises of the covenant, and have no interest in the Mediator of the covenant.

So that whatever some have imagined and pretended about promises made to natural men's earnest seeking and knocking, 'tis plain and manifest that whatever pains a natural man takes in religion, whatever prayers he makes, till he believes in Christ, God is under no manner of obligation to keep him a moment from eternal destruction.

So that, thus it is, that natural men are held in the hand of God over the pit of Hell; they have deserved the fiery pit, and are already sentenced to it; and God is dreadfully provoked, his anger is as great towards them as to those that are actually suffering the executions of the fierceness of his wrath in hell, and they have done nothing in the least to appease or abate that anger, neither is God in the least bound by any promise to hold them up one moment; the Devil is waiting for them, Hell is gaping for them, the flames gather and flash about them, and would fain lay hold on 'em, and swallow them up; the fire pent up in their own hearts is struggling to break out: and they have no interest in any Mediator, there are no means within reach that can be any security to them. In short, they have no refuge, nothing to take hold of, all that preserves them every moment is the meer arbitrary will, and uncovenanted unobliged forbearance of an incensed God.

Application

The use may be of awakening to unconverted persons in this congregation. This that you have heard is the case of every one of you that are out of Christ. That world of misery, that lake of burning brimstone is extended abroad under you. There is the dreadful pit of the glowing flames of the wrath of God; there is hell's wide gaping mouth open; and you have nothing to stand upon, nor any thing to take hold of; there is nothing between you and Hell but the air; 'tis only the power and meer pleasure of God that holds you up.

You probably are not sensible of this; you find you are kept out of Hell, but don't see the hand of God in it, but look at other things, as the good state of your bodily constitution, your care of your own life, and the means you use for your own preservation. But indeed these things are nothing; if God should withdraw his hand, they would avail no more to keep you from falling, than the thin air to hold up a person that is suspended in it.

Your wickedness makes you as it were heavy as lead, and to tend downwards with great weight and pressure towards Hell; and if God should let you go, you would immediately sink and swiftly descend & plunge into the bottomless gulf, and your healthy constitution, and your own care and prudence, and best contrivance, and all your righteousness, would have no more influence to uphold you and keep you out of hell, than a spider's web would have to stop a falling rock. Were it not that so is the sovereign pleasure of God, the earth would not bear you one moment; for you are a burden to it; the creation groans with you; the creature is made subject to the bondage of your corruption, not willingly; the sun don't willingly shine upon you to give you light to serve sin and Satan; the earth don't willingly yield her increase to satisfy your lusts; nor is it willingly a stage for your wickedness to be acted upon; the air don't willingly serve you for breath to maintain the flame of life in your vitals, while you spend your life in the service of God's enemies. God's creatures are good, and were made for men to serve God with, and don't willingly subserve to any other purpose, and groan when they are abused to purposes so directly contrary to their nature and end. And the world would spew you out, were it not for the sovereign hand of him who hath subjected it in hope. There are the black clouds of God's wrath now hanging directly over your heads, full of the dreadful storm, and big with thunder; and were it not for the restraining hand of God, it would immediately burst forth upon you. The sovereign pleasure of God for the present, stays his rough wind; otherwise it would come with fury, and your destruction would come like a whirlwind, and you would be like the chaff on the summer threshing floor.

The wrath of God is like great waters that are dammed for the present; they increase more and more, & rise higher and higher, till an outlet is given, and the longer the stream is stop'd, the more rapid and mighty is its course, when once it is let loose. 'Tis that judgment against your evil works has not been executed hitherto; the floods of God's vengeance have been withheld; but your guilt in the mean time is constantly increasing, and you are every day treasuring up more wrath; the waters are constantly rising and waxing more and more mighty; and there is nothing but the meer pleasure of God that holds the waters back that are unwilling to be stopped, and press hard to go forward; if God should only withdraw his hand from the flood-gate, it would immediately fly open, and the fiery floods of the fierceness and wrath of God would rush forth with inconceivable fury, and would come upon you with omnipotent power; and if your strength were ten thousand times greater than it is, yea, ten thousand times greater than the strength of the stoutest, sturdiest Devil in Hell, it would be nothing to withstand or endure it.

The bow of God's wrath is bent, and the arrow made ready on the string, and justice bends the arrow at your heart, and strains the bow, and it is nothing but the meer pleasure of God, and that of an angry God, without any promise or obligation at all, that keeps the arrow one moment from being made drunk with your blood.

Thus are all you that never passed under a great change of heart, by the mighty power of the Spirit of God upon your souls; all that were never born again, and made new creatures, and raised from being dead in sin, to a state of new, and before altogether unexperienced light and life, (however you may have reformed your life in many things, and may have had religious affections, and may keep up a form of religion in your families and closets, and in the house of God, and may be strict in it,) you are thus in the hands of an angry God; 'tis nothing but his meer pleasure that keeps you from being this moment swallowed up in everlasting destruction.

However unconvinced you may now be of the truth of what you hear, by & by you will be fully convinced of it. Those that are gone from being in the like circumstances with you, see that it was so with them; for destruction came suddenly upon most of them, when they expected nothing of it, and while they were saying, peace and safety: now they see, that those things that they depended on for peace and safety, were nothing but thin air and empty shadows.

The God that holds you over the pit of Hell, much as one holds a spider, or some loathsome insect, over the fire, abhors you, and is dreadfully provoked; his wrath towards you burns like fire; he looks upon you as worthy of nothing else, but to be cast into the fire; he is of purer eyes than to bear to have you in his sight; you are ten thousand times more abominable in his eyes as the most hateful venomous serpent is in ours. You have offended him infinitely more than ever a stubborn rebel did his prince: and yet 'tis nothing but his hand that holds you from falling into the fire every moment: 'Tis to be ascribed to nothing else, that you did not go to Hell the last night; that you was suffer'd to awake again in this world, after you closed your eyes to sleep: and there is no other reason to be given why you have not dropped into hell since you arose in the morning, but that God's hand has held you up: There is no other reason to be given why you han't gone to Hell since you have sat here in the house of God, provoking his pure eyes by your sinful wicked manner of attending his solemn worship: Yea, there is nothing else that is to be given as a reason why you don't this very moment drop down into Hell.

O sinner! Consider the fearful danger you are in: 'tis a great furnace of wrath, a wide and bottomless pit, full of the fire of wrath, that you are held over in the hand of that God, whose wrath is provoked and incensed as much against you as against many of the damned in Hell. You hang by a slender thread, with the flames of divine wrath flashing about it, and ready every moment to singe it, and burn it asunder; and you have no interest in any Mediator, and nothing to lay hold of to save yourself, nothing to keep off the flames of wrath, nothing of your own, nothing that you ever have done, nothing that you can do, to induce God to spare you one moment.

And consider here more particularly several things concerning that wrath that you are in such danger of.

1. Whose wrath it is: it is the wrath of the infinite God. If it were only the wrath of man, tho' it were of the most potent prince, it would be comparatively little to be regarded. The wrath of kings is very much dreaded, especially of absolute monarchs, that have the possessions and lives of their subjects wholly in their power, to be disposed of at their meer will. Prov. 20. 2. *The fear of a king is as the roaring of a lion: whoso provoketh him to anger, sinneth against his own soul.* The subject that very much enrages an arbitrary prince, is liable to suffer the most extream torments, that human art can invent or human power can inflict. But the greatest earthly potentates, in their greatest majesty and strength, and when clothed in their greatest terrors, are but feeble despicable worms of the dust, in comparison of the great and almighty Creator and King of Heaven and Earth: It is but little that they can do, when most enraged, and when they have exerted the utmost of their fury. All the kings of the earth before God are as grasshoppers, they are nothing and less than nothing: both their love and their hatred is to be despised. The wrath of the great King of Kings is as much more terrible than their's, as his majesty is greater. Luke 12. 4, 5. *And I say unto you, my friends, be not afraid of them that kill the body, and after that have no more that they can do: But I will forewarn you whom you shall fear; fear him, which after he hath killed, hath power to cast into Hell: yea I say unto you, fear him.*

2. 'Tis the fierceness of his wrath that you are exposed to. We often read of the fury of God; as in Isai. 59:18. *According to their deeds, accordingly he will repay fury to his adversaries.* So Isai. 66. 15. *For behold, the Lord will come with fire, and with chariots like a whirlwind, to render his anger with fury, and his rebukes with flames of fire.* And so in many other places. So we read of God's fierceness Rev. 19:15 we read of the wine press of the fierceness and wrath of Almighty God. The words are exceeding terrible. There 'tis not only said so, but if it had only been said, *the wrath of God,* the words would have implied that which is infinitely dreadful: but 'tis the fierceness and wrath of God: the fury of God! the fierceness of Jehovah! Oh how dreadful that must be! Who can utter or conceive what such expressions carry in them! But it is not only said so, but the fierceness and wrath of almighty God. As tho' there would be a very great manifestation of his almighty power, in what the fierceness of his wrath should inflict, as tho' omnipotence

should be as it were enraged, and excited, as men are wont to exert their strength in the fierceness of their wrath. Oh! then, what will be the consequence! What will become of the poor worms that shall suffer it! Whose hands can be strong? And whose heart can endure? To what a dreadful, inexpressible, inconceivable depth of misery must the poor creature be sunk, who shall be the subject of this!

Consider this, you that are here present, that yet remain in an unregenerate state. That God will execute the fierceness of his anger, implies that he will inflict wrath without any pity: when God beholds the ineffable extremity of your case, and sees your torment to be so vastly disproportion'd to your strength, and sees how your poor soul is crushed and sinks down, as it were into an infinite gloom, he will have no compassion upon you, he will not forbear the executions of his wrath, or in the least lighten his hand; there shall be no moderation or mercy, nor will God then at all stay his rough wind; he will have no regard to your welfare, nor be at all careful lest you should suffer too much, in any other sense than only that you shall not suffer beyond what strict justice requires: nothing shall be with held, because it's so hard for you to bear. Ezek. 8. 18. *Therefore will I also deal in fury; mine eye shall not spare, neither will I have pity; and tho' they cry in mine ears with a loud voice, yet I will not hear them.* Now God stands ready to pity you; this is a day of mercy; you may cry now with some encouragement of obtaining mercy, but when once the day of mercy is past, your most lamentable and dolorous cries and shrieks will be in vain; you will be wholly lost and thrown away of God as to any regard to your welfare; God will have no other use to put you to but to suffer misery; you shall be continued in being to no other end; for you will be a vessel of wrath fitted to destruction; and there will be no other use of this vessel but to be filled full of wrath. God will be so far from pitying you when you cry to him, that 'tis said he will only *laugh and mock,* Prov. 1. 25, 26, &c.

How awful are those words, Isai. 63:3, which are the words of the great God, *I will tread them in mine anger, and will trample them in my fury, and their blood shall be sprinkled upon my garments, and I will stain all my raiment.* 'Tis perhaps impossible to conceive of words that carry in them greater manifestations of these three things, viz. contempt, and hatred, and fierceness of indignation. If you cry to God to pity you, he will be so far from pitying you in your doleful case, or shewing you the least regard or favour, that instead of that, he'll only tread you under foot: And tho' he will know that you can't bear the weight of omnipotence treading upon you, yet he won't regard that, but he will crush you under his feet without mercy; he'll crush out your blood, and make it fly, and it shall be sprinkled on his garments, so as to stain all his raiment. He will not only hate you, but he will have you in the utmost contempt; no place shall be thought fit for you, but under his feet, to be trodden down as the mire of the streets.

3. The misery you are exposed to is that which God will inflict to that end, that he might shew what that wrath of Jehovah is. God hath had it on his heart to shew to angels and men, both how excellent his love is, and also how terrible his wrath is. Sometimes earthly kings have a mind to shew how terrible their wrath is, by the extream punishments they would execute on those that provoke 'em. Nebuchadnezzar, that mighty and haughty monarch of the Chaldean empire, was willing to shew his wrath when enraged with Shadrach, Meshach, and Abednego; and accordingly gave orders that the burning fiery furnace should be het seven times hotter than it was before; doubtless it was raised to the utmost degree of fierceness that humane art could raise it: But the great God is also willing to shew his wrath, and magnify his awful majesty and mighty power in the extream sufferings of his enemies. Rom. 9:22. *What if God, willing to show his wrath, and to make his power known, endured with much long-suffering the vessels of wrath fitted to destruction?* And seeing this is his design, and what he has determined, even to shew how terrible the unmixed, unrestrained wrath, the fury and fierceness of Jehovah is, he will do it to effect. There will be something accomplished and brought to pass, that will be dreadful with a witness. When the great and angry God hath risen up and executed his awful vengeance on the poor sinner, and the wretch is actually suffering the infinite weight and power of his indignation, then will God call upon the whole universe to behold that awful majesty, and mighty power that is to be seen in it. Isai. 33. 12, 13, 14. *And the people shall be as the burning of lime, as thorns cut up shall they be burnt in the fire. Hear ye that are far off what I have done; and ye that are near acknowledge my might. The sinners in Zion are afraid, fearfulness hath surprized the hypocrites, &c.*

Thus it will be with you that are in an unconverted state, if you continue in it; the infinite might, and majesty and terribleness of the OMNIPOTENT GOD shall be magnified upon you, in the ineffable strength of your torments: You shall be tormented in the presence of the holy angels, and in the presence of the Lamb; and when you shall be in this state of suffering, the glorious inhabitants of heaven shall go forth and look on the awful spectacle, that they may see what the wrath and fierceness of the Almighty is, and when they have seen it, they will fall down and adore that great power and majesty. Isai. 66. 23, 24. *And it shall come to pass, that from one new moon to another, and from one sabbath to another, shall all flesh come to worship before me, saith the Lord; and they shall go forth and look upon the carcasses of the men that have transgressed against me; for their worm shall not die, neither shall their fire be quenched, and they shall be an abhorring unto all flesh.*

4. 'Tis everlasting wrath. It would be dreadful to suffer this fierceness and wrath of Almighty God one moment; but you must suffer it to all eternity: there will be no end to this exquisite horrible misery: When you look forward, you shall see a long forever, a boundless duration before you, which will swallow up your thoughts, and amaze your soul; and you will absolutely despair of ever having any deliverance, any end, any mitigation, any rest at all; you will know certainly that you must wear out long ages, millions of millions of ages, in wrestling and conflicting with this almighty merciless vengeance; and then when you have so done, when so many ages have actually been spent by you in this manner, you will know that all is but a point to what remains. So that your punishment will indeed be infinite. Oh who can express what the state of a soul in such circumstances is! All that we can possibly say about it, gives but a very feeble, faint representation of it; 'tis inexpressible and inconceivable: For who knows the power of God's anger?

How dreadful is the state of those that are daily and hourly in the danger of this great wrath, and infinite misery! But this is the dismal case of every soul in this congregation, that has not been born again, however moral and strict, sober and religious, they may otherwise be. Oh that you would consider it, whether you be young or old. There is reason to think, that there are many in this congregation now hearing this discourse, that will actually be the subjects of this very misery to all eternity. We know not who they are, or in what seats they sit, or what thoughts they now have: it may be they are now at ease, and hear all these things without much disturbance, and are now flattering themselves that they are not the persons, promising themselves that they shall escape. If we knew that there was one person, and but one, in the whole congregation, that was to be the subject of this misery, what an awful thing it would be to think of! If we knew who it was, what an awful sight it would be to see such a person! How might all the rest of the congregation lift up a lamentable and bitter cry over him! But, alas! instead of one, how many is it likely will remember this discourse in Hell? And it would be a wonder, if some that are now present, should not be in Hell in a very short time, before this year is out. And it would be no wonder if some person that now sits here in some seat of this meeting-house in health, and quiet & secure, should be there before tomorrow morning. Those of you that finally continue in a natural condition, that shall keep out of Hell longest, will be there in a little time! your damnation don't slumber; it will come swiftly, and, in all probability very suddenly upon many of you. You have reason to wonder, that you are not already in Hell. 'Tis doubtless the case of some that you have seen and known, that never deserved Hell more than you, and that heretofore appeared as likely to have been now alive as you: Their case is past all hope; they are crying in extream misery and perfect despair; but here you are in the land of the living, and in the house of God, and have an opportunity to obtain salvation. What would not those poor damned, hopeless souls give for one day's opportunity such as you now enjoy!

And now you have an extraordinary opportunity, a day wherein Christ has thrown the door of mercy wide open, and stands in the door calling and crying with a loud voice to poor sinners; a day wherein many are flocking to him, and pressing into the kingdom of God; many are daily coming from the East, West, North and South; many that were very lately in the same miserable condition that you are in, are now in an happy state, with their hearts filled with love to him who has loved them and washed them from their sins in his own blood, and rejoicing in hope of the glory of God. How awful is it to be left behind at such a day! To see so many others feasting, while you are pining and perishing! To see so many rejoicing and singing for joy of heart, while you have cause to mourn for sorrow of heart, and howl for vexation of spirit! How can you rest one moment in such a condition? Are not your souls as precious as the souls of the people at Suffield, where they are flocking from day to day to Christ?

Are there not many here who have lived long in the world, that are not to this day born again, and so are aliens from the commonwealth of Israel, and have done nothing ever since they have lived, but treasure up wrath against the day of wrath? Oh sirs, your case, in an especial manner, is extreamly dangerous; your guilt and hardness of heart is extreamly great. Don't you see how generally persons of your years are pass'd over and left, in the present remarkable & wonderful dispensation of God's mercy? You had need to consider your selves, and wake thoroughly out of sleep; you cannot bear the fierceness and wrath of the infinite God.

And you that are young men, and young women, will you neglect this precious season which you now enjoy, when so many others of your age are renouncing all youthful vanities, and flocking to CHRIST? You especially have now an extraordinary opportunity; but if you neglect it, it will soon be with you as with those persons who spent all the precious days of youth in sin, and are now come to such a dreadful pass in blindness and hardness.

And you children that are unconverted, don't you know that you are going down to Hell, to bear the dreadful wrath of that God that is now angry with you every day, and every night? Will you be content to be the children of the Devil, when so many other children in the land are converted, and are become the holy and happy children of the King of Kings?

And let every one that is yet out of Christ, and hanging over the pit of Hell, whether they be old men and women, or middle aged, or young people, or little children, now hearken to the loud calls of God's word and providence. This acceptable year of the LORD, that is a day of such great favour to some, will doubtless be a day of as remarkable vengeance to others. Men's hearts harden, and their guilt increases apace at such a day as this, if they neglect their souls: and never was there so great danger of such persons being given up to hardness of heart and blindness of mind. God seems now to be hastily gathering in his elect in all parts of the land; and probably the greater part of adult persons that ever shall be saved, will be brought in now in a little time, and that it will be as it was on the great out-pouring of the Spirit upon the Jews in the apostles' days, the election will obtain, and the rest will be blinded. If this should be the case with you, you will eternally curse this day, and will curse the day that ever you was born, to see such a season of the pouring out of God's spirit, and will wish that you had died and gone to Hell before you had seen it. Now undoubtedly it is, as it was in the days of John the Baptist, the axe is in an extraordinary manner laid at the root of the trees, that every tree which brings not forth good fruit, may be hewen down and cast into the fire.

Therefore, let every one that is out of CHRIST, now awake and fly from the wrath to come. The wrath of Almighty God is now undoubtedly hanging over great part of this congregation. Let every one fly out of Sodom: *Haste and escape for your lives, look not behind you, escape to the mountain, least you be consumed.*

SOURCE: Jonathan Edwards and Others. *Sinners in the Hands of an Angry God and Other Puritan Sermons*. Mineola, New York: Dover Publications, 2005.

PHILLIS WHEATLEY

The first African American woman to publish a book of poetry, Phillis Wheatley (1753?–1784) was born in Africa, and enslaved and brought to America in 1761. She was freed from slavery in 1778 while living in Boston.

On Being Brought from Africa to America (1773)

'Twas mercy brought me from my pagan land,
Taught my benighted soul to understand
That there's a God, that there's a savior too:
Once I redemption neither sought nor knew.
Some view our sable race with scornful eye,
"Their color is a diabolic dye."
Remember, Christians, Negroes, black as Cain,
May be refin'd, and join th' angelic train.

On Imagination (1773)

Thy various works, imperial queen, we see,
How bright their forms! how decked with pomp by thee!
Thy wond'rous acts in beauteous order stand,
And all attest how potent is thine hand.

From *Helicon*'s refulgent heights attend,
Ye sacred choir, and my attempts befriend:
To tell her glories with a faithful tongue,
Ye blooming graces, triumph in my song.

Now here, now there, the roving *Fancy* flies,
Till some loved object strikes her wand'ring eyes,
Whose silken fetters all the senses bind,
And soft captivity involves the mind.

Imagination! who can sing thy force?
Or who describe the swiftness of thy course?
Soaring through air to find the bright abode,
Th' empyreal palace of the thund'ring God,
We on thy pinions can surpass the wind,
And leave the rolling universe behind:
From star to star the mental optics rove,
Measure the skies, and range the realms above.
There in one view we grasp the mighty whole,
Or with new worlds amaze th' unbounded soul.

Though *Winter* frowns to *Fancy's* raptured eyes
The fields may flourish, and gay scenes arise;
The frozen deeps may break their iron bands,
And bid their waters murmur o'er the sands.
Fair *Flora* may resume her fragrant reign,
And with her flow'ry riches deck the plain;
Sylvanus may diffuse his honors round,
And all the forest may with leaves be crowned:
Show'rs may descend, and dews their gems disclose,
And nectar sparkle on the blooming rose.

Such is thy pow'r, nor are thine orders vain,
O thou the leader of the mental train:
In full perfection all thy works are wrought,
And thine the sceptre o'er the realms of thought.
Before thy throne the subject passions bow,
Of subject-passions sov'reign ruler Thou,
At thy command joy rushes on the heart,
And through the glowing veins the spirits dart.

Fancy might now her silken pinions try
To rise from earth, and sweep th' expanse on high;
From *Tithon's* bed now might *Aurora* rise,
Her cheeks all glowing with celestial dyes,
While a pure stream of light o'erflows the skies.

The monarch of the day I might behold
And all the mountains tipt with radiant gold,
But I reluctant leave the pleasing views,
Which *Fancy* dresses to delight the *Muse*;
Winter austere forbids me to aspire,
And northern tempests damp the rising fire;
They chill the tides of *Fancy's* flowing sea,
Cease then, my song, cease the unequal lay.

To S. M., a Young African Painter, on Seeing His Works (1773)

To show the lab'ring bosom's deep intent,
And thought in living characters to paint,
When first thy pencil did those beauties give,
And breathing figures learnt from thee to live,
How did those prospects give my soul delight,
A new creation rushing on my sight?
Still, wond'rous youth! each noble path pursue,
On deathless glories fix thine ardent view:
Still may the painter's and the poet's fire
To aid thy pencil, and thy verse conspire!
And may the charms of each seraphic theme
Conduct thy footsteps to immortal fame!
High to the blissful wonders of the skies
Elate thy soul, and raise thy wishful eyes.
Thrice happy, when exalted to survey
That splendid city, crown'd with endless day,
Whose twice six gates on radiant hinges ring:
Celestial *Salem* blooms in endless spring.

Calm and serene thy moments glide along,
And may the muse inspire each future song!
Still, with the sweets of contemplation bless'd,
May peace with balmy wings your soul invest!
But when these shades of time are chas'd away,
And darkness ends in everlasting day,
On what seraphic pinions shall we move,
And view the landscapes in the realms above?
There shall thy tongue in heav'nly murmurs flow,

And there my muse with heav'nly transport glow:
No more to tell of *Damon*'s tender sighs,
Or rising radiance of *Aurora*'s eyes,
For nobler themes demand a nobler strain,
And purer language on th' ethereal plain.
Cease, gentle muse! the solemn gloom of night
Now seals the fair creation from my sight.

SOURCE: Phillis Wheatley, Negro Servant to Mr. John Wheatley, of Boston, in New England. *Poems on Various Subjects Religious and Moral.* London and Boston, 1773. [Setting edition: W. H. Lawrence and Company. Denver, 1886.]

THOMAS PAINE

We present the introduction to and first part of the second edition of Thomas Paine's pamphlet Common Sense *(the first edition was published only a month before). When he wrote the manifesto that helped inspire the successful revolution against Great Britain, the British-born author (1737–1809) had been in America only a year and a half (he had been encouraged to emigrate from England by Benjamin Franklin). "Writing, for him," his twentieth-century admirer John Dos Passos reminds us, "was the direct putting down of plain speech."*[1]

From *Common Sense* (1776)

ADDRESSED TO THE INHABITANTS OF AMERICA

"Man knows no Master save creating HEAVEN,
Or those whom Choice and common Good ordain."
—THOMSON.[2]

February 14, 1776

Introduction

PERHAPS THE SENTIMENTS contained in the following pages, are not *yet* sufficiently fashionable to procure them general favor; a long habit of not thinking a thing *wrong*, gives it a superficial appearance of being *right*, and raises at first a formidable outcry in defence of custom. But the tumult soon subsides. Time makes more converts than reason.

1. John Dos Passos. *The Essential Thomas Paine.* Mineola, New York: Dover Publications, 2008. 2.
2. James Thomson, from *Liberty: A Poem*, 1736

As a long and violent abuse of power, is generally the Means of calling the right of it in question (and in Matters too which might never have been thought of, had not the Sufferers been aggravated into the inquiry) and as the King of England hath undertaken in his *own Right*, to support the Parliament in what he calls *Theirs*, and as the good people of this country are grievously oppressed by the combination, they have an undoubted privilege to inquire into the pretensions of both, and equally to reject the usurpation of either.

In the following sheets, the author hath studiously avoided every thing which is personal among ourselves. Compliments as well as censure to individuals make no part thereof. The wise, and the worthy, need not the triumph of a pamphlet; and those whose sentiments are injudicious, or unfriendly, will cease of themselves unless too much pains is bestowed upon their conversion.

The cause of America is in a great measure the cause of all mankind. Many circumstances hath, and will arise, which are not local, but universal, and through which the principles of all Lovers of Mankind are affected, and in the Event of which, their Affections are interested. The laying a Country desolate with Fire and Sword, declaring War against the natural rights of all Mankind, and extirpating the Defenders thereof from the Face of the Earth, is the Concern of every Man to whom Nature hath given the Power of feeling; of which Class, regardless of Party Censure, is the

AUTHOR

P.S. . . . Who the Author of this Production is, is wholly unnecessary to the Public, as the Object for Attention is the *Doctrine itself*, not the *Man*. Yet it may not be unnecessary to say, That he is unconnected with any Party, and under no sort of Influence public or private, but the influence of reason and principle.

Philadelphia, February 14, 1776.

COMMON SENSE

Of the Origin and Design of Government in General. With concise Remarks on the English Constitution

Some writers have so confounded society with government, as to leave little or no distinction between them; whereas they are not only different, but have different origins. Society is produced by our wants, and government by our wickedness; the former promotes our happiness *positively* by uniting our affections, the latter *negatively* by restraining our vices. The one encourages intercourse, the other creates distinctions. The first is a patron, the last a punisher.

Society in every state is a blessing, but government even in its best state is but a necessary evil; in its worst state an intolerable one; for when we suffer, or are exposed to the same miseries *by a government*, which we might expect in a country *without government*, our calamity is heightened by reflecting that we furnish the means by which we suffer. Government, like dress, is the badge of lost innocence; the palaces of kings are built on the ruins of the bowers of paradise. For were the impulses of conscience clear, uniform, and irresistibly obeyed, man would need no other lawgiver; but that not being the case, he finds it necessary to surrender up a part of his property to furnish means for the protection of the rest; and this he is induced to do by the same prudence which in every other case advises him out of two evils to choose the least. *Wherefore*, security being the true design and end of government, it unanswerably follows that whatever *form* thereof appears most likely to ensure it to us, with the least expence and greatest benefit, is preferable to all others.

In order to gain a clear and just idea of the design and end of government, let us suppose a small number of persons settled in some sequestered part of the earth, unconnected with the rest, they will then represent the first peopling of any country, or of the world. In this state of natural liberty, society will be their first thought. A thousand motives will excite them thereto, the strength of one man is so unequal to his wants, and his mind so unfitted for perpetual solitude, that he is soon obliged to seek assistance and relief of another, who in his turn requires the same. Four or five united would be able to raise a tolerable dwelling in the midst of a wilderness, but *one* man might labour out the common period of life without accomplishing any thing; when he had felled his timber he could not remove it, nor erect it after it was removed; hunger in the mean time would urge him from his work, and every different want call him a different way. Disease, nay even misfortune would be death, for though neither might be mortal, yet either would disable him from living, and reduce him to a state in which he might rather be said to perish than to die.

Thus necessity, like a gravitating power, would soon form our newly arrived emigrants into society, the reciprocal blessings of which, would supersede, and render the obligations of law and government unnecessary while they remained perfectly just to each other; but as nothing but heaven is impregnable to vice, it will unavoidably happen, that in proportion as they surmount the first difficulties of emigration, which bound them together in a common cause, they will begin to relax in their duty and attachment to each other; and this remissness, will point out the necessity, of establishing some form of government to supply the defect of moral virtue.

Some convenient tree will afford them a State-House, under the branches of which, the whole colony may assemble to deliberate on public matters. It is more than probable that their first laws will have the title only of REGULATIONS, and be enforced by no other penalty than public disesteem. In this first parliament every man, by natural right, will have a seat.

But as the colony increases, the public concerns will increase likewise, and the distance at which the members may be separated, will render it too inconvenient for all of them to meet on every occasion as at first, when their number was small, their habitations near, and the public concerns few and trifling. This will point out the convenience of their consenting to leave the legislative part to be managed by a select number chosen from the whole body, who are supposed to have the same concerns at stake which those have who appointed them, and who will act in the same manner as the whole body would act were they present. If the colony continue increasing, it will become necessary to augment the number of the representatives, and that the interest of every part of the colony may be attended to, it will be found best to divide the whole into convenient parts, each part sending its proper number; and that the *elected* might never form to themselves an interest separate from the *electors*, prudence will point out the propriety of having elections often; because as the *elected* might by that means return and mix again with the general body of the *electors* in a few months, their fidelity to the public will be secured by the prudent reflexion of not making a rod for themselves. And as this frequent interchange will establish a common interest with every part of the community, they will mutually and naturally support each other, and on this (not on the unmeaning name of king) depends the *strength of government, and the happiness of the governed.*

Here then is the origin and rise of government; namely, a mode rendered necessary by the inability of moral virtue to govern the world; here too is the design and end of government, viz. freedom and security. And however our eyes may be dazzled with show, or our ears deceived by sound; however prejudice may warp our wills, or interest darken our understanding, the simple voice of nature and of reason will say, it is right.

I draw my idea of the form of government from a principle in nature, which no art can overturn, viz. that the more simple any thing is, the less liable it is to be disordered, and the easier repaired when disordered; and with this maxim in view, I offer a few remarks on the so much boasted constitution of England. That it was noble for the dark and slavish times in which it was erected, is granted. When the world was over run with tyranny the least remove therefrom was a glorious rescue. But that it is imperfect, subject to convulsions, and incapable of producing what it seems to promise, is easily demonstrated.

Absolute governments (tho' the disgrace of human nature) have this advantage with them, that they are simple; if the people suffer, they know the head from which their suffering springs, know likewise the remedy, and are not bewildered by a variety of causes and cures. But the constitution of England is so exceedingly complex, that the nation may suffer for years together without being able to discover in which part the fault lies, some will say in one and some in another, and every political physician will advise a different medicine.

I know it is difficult to get over local or long standing prejudices, yet if we will suffer ourselves to examine the component parts of the English constitution, we shall find them to be the base remains of two ancient tyrannies, compounded with some new republican materials.

First.—The remains of monarchical tyranny in the person of the king.

Secondly.—The remains of aristocratical tyranny in the persons of the peers.

Thirdly.—The new republican materials, in the persons of the commons, on whose virtue depends the freedom of England.

The two first, by being hereditary, are independent of the people; wherefore in a *constitutional sense* they contribute nothing towards the freedom of the state.

To say that the constitution of England is a *union* of three powers reciprocally *checking* each other, is farcical, either the words have no meaning, or they are flat contradictions.

To say that the commons is a check upon the king, presupposes two things.

First.—That the king is not to be trusted without being looked after, or in other words, that a thirst for absolute power is the natural disease of monarchy.

Secondly.—That the commons, by being appointed for that purpose, are either wiser or more worthy of confidence than the crown.

But as the same constitution which gives the commons a power to check the king by withholding the supplies, gives afterwards the king a power to check the commons, by empowering him to reject their other bills; it again supposes that the king is wiser than those whom it has already supposed to be wiser than him. A mere absurdity!

There is something exceedingly ridiculous in the composition of monarchy; it first excludes a man from the means of information, yet empowers him to act in cases where the highest judgment is required. The state of a king shuts him from the world, yet the business of a king requires him to know it thoroughly; wherefore the different parts, by unnaturally opposing and destroying each other, prove the whole character to be absurd and useless.

Some writers have explained the English constitution thus; the king, say they, is one, the people another; the peers are an house in behalf of the king; the commons in behalf of the people; but this hath all the distinctions of an house divided against itself; and though the expressions be pleasantly arranged, yet when examined they appear idle and ambiguous; and it will always happen, that the nicest construction that words are capable of, when applied to the description of something which either cannot exist, or is too incomprehensible to be within the compass of description, will be words of sound only, and though they may amuse the ear, they cannot inform the mind, for this explanation includes a previous question, viz. *How came the king by a power which the people are afraid to trust, and always obliged to check?* Such a power could not be the gift of a wise people, neither can any power, *which needs checking*, be from God; yet the provision, which the constitution makes, supposes such a power to exist.

But the provision is unequal to the task; the means either cannot or will not accomplish the end, and the whole affair is a felo de se[3]; for as the greater weight will always carry up the less, and as all the

3. *felo de se*: an act of deliberate self-destruction.

wheels of a machine are put in motion by one, it only remains to know which power in the constitution has the most weight, for that will govern; and though the others, or a part of them, may clog, or, as the phrase is, check the rapidity of its motion, yet so long as they cannot stop it, their endeavors will be ineffectual; the first moving power will at last have its way, and what it wants in speed is supplied by time.

That the crown is this overbearing part in the English constitution needs not be mentioned, and that it derives its whole consequence merely from being the giver of places and pensions is self-evident, wherefore, though we have been wise enough to shut and lock a door against absolute monarchy, we at the same time have been foolish enough to put the crown in possession of the key.

The prejudice of Englishmen, in favour of their own government by king, lords and commons, arises as much or more from national pride than reason. Individuals are undoubtedly safer in England than in some other countries, but the *will* of the king is as much the *law* of the land in Britain as in France, with this difference, that instead of proceeding directly from his mouth, it is handed to the people under the most formidable shape of an act of parliament. For the fate of Charles the first, hath only made kings more subtle—not more just.

Wherefore, laying aside all national pride and prejudice in favour of modes and forms, the plain truth is, that *it is wholly owing to the constitution of the people, and not to the constitution of the government* that the crown is not as oppressive in England as in Turkey.

An inquiry into the *constitutional errors* in the English form of government is at this time highly necessary, for as we are never in a proper condition of doing justice to others, while we continue under the influence of some leading partiality, so neither are we capable of doing it to ourselves while we remain fettered by any obstinate prejudice. And as a man, who is attached to a prostitute, is unfitted to choose or judge of a wife, so any prepossession in favour of a rotten constitution of government will disable us from discerning a good one.

SOURCE: Thomas Paine. *Common Sense.* Philadelphia: William and Thomas Bradford, 1776.

J. HECTOR ST. JOHN DE CRÈVECOEUR

J. Hector St. John de Crèvecoeur (1735–1813) moved from France to America in 1759, where he married and then cultivated his farm along the Hudson River in New York. His book consists of twelve "letters," excited topical essays on various aspects of the experiment of American life: "He is an American, who leaving behind him all his ancient prejudices and manners, receives new ones from the new mode of life he has embraced, the new government he obeys, and the new rank he holds." Some of his remarks on general characteristics of particular immigrant or geographical groups may offend, but Crèvecoeur himself reminds us, "There is no tracing observations of this kind, without making at the same time very great allowances, as there are everywhere to be found, a great many exceptions. The Irish themselves, from different parts of that kingdom, are very different. It is difficult to account for this surprising locality, one would think on so small an island an Irishman must be an Irishman: yet it is not so, they are different in their aptitude to, and in their love of labour." His writing inspired many Americans with an appreciation of their new identity. Unfortunately, shortly after his book's publication, while he was traveling abroad, Crèvecoeur's farm was destroyed and his wife died. In 1790 he returned to France, where he lived until his death.

Letters from an American Farmer
Letter III: "What Is an American" (1782)

I WISH I could be acquainted with the feelings and thoughts which must agitate the heart and present themselves to the mind of an enlightened Englishman, when he first lands on this continent. He must greatly rejoice that he lived at a time to see this fair country discovered and settled; he must necessarily feel a share of national pride, when he views the chain of settlements which embellishes these extended shores. When he says to himself, this is the work of my countrymen, who, when convulsed by factions, afflicted by a variety of miseries and wants, restless and impatient, took refuge here. They brought along with them their national genius, to which they principally owe what liberty they enjoy, and what substance they possess. Here he sees the industry of his native country displayed in a new manner, and traces in their works the embryos of all the arts, sciences, and ingenuity which flourish in Europe. Here he beholds fair cities, substantial villages, extensive fields, an immense country filled with decent houses, good roads, orchards, meadows, and bridges, where an hundred years ago all was wild, woody, and uncultivated! What a train of pleasing ideas this fair spectacle must suggest; it is a prospect which must inspire a good citizen with the most heartfelt pleasure. The difficulty consists in the manner of viewing so extensive a scene. He is arrived on a new continent; a modern society offers itself to his contemplation, different from what he had hitherto seen. It is not composed, as in Europe, of great lords who possess everything and of a herd of people who have nothing. Here are no aristocratical families, no courts, no kings, no bishops, no ecclesiastical dominion, no invisible power giving to a few a very visible one; no great manufacturers employing thousands, no great refinements of luxury. The rich and the poor are not so far removed from each other as they are in Europe. Some few towns excepted, we are all tillers of the earth, from Nova Scotia to West Florida. We are a people of cultivators, scattered over an immense territory communicating with each other by means of good roads and navigable rivers, united by the silken bands of mild government, all respecting the laws, without dreading their power, because they are equitable. We are all animated with the spirit of an industry which is unfettered and unrestrained, because each person works for himself. If he travels through our rural districts he views not the hostile castle, and the haughty mansion, contrasted with the clay-built hut and miserable cabin, where cattle and men help to keep each other warm, and dwell in meanness, smoke, and indigence. A pleasing uniformity of decent competence appears throughout our habitations. The meanest of our log-houses is a dry and comfortable habitation. Lawyer or merchant are the fairest titles our towns afford; that of a farmer is the only appellation of the rural inhabitants of our country. It must take some time ere he can reconcile himself to our dictionary, which is but short in words of dignity, and names of honour. There, on a Sunday, he sees a congregation of respectable farmers and their wives, all clad in neat homespun, well mounted, or riding in their own humble waggons. There is not among them an esquire, saving the unlettered magistrate. There he sees a parson as simple as his flock, a farmer who does not riot on the labour of others. We have no princes, for whom we toil, starve, and bleed: we are the most perfect society now existing in the world. Here man is free; as he ought to be; nor is this pleasing equality so transitory as many others are. Many ages will not see the shores of our great lakes replenished with inland nations, nor the unknown bounds of North America entirely peopled. Who can tell how far it extends? Who can tell the millions of men whom it will feed and contain? for no European foot has as yet travelled half the extent of this mighty continent!

The next wish of this traveller will be to know whence came all these people? they are a mixture of English, Scotch, Irish, French, Dutch, Germans, and Swedes. From this promiscuous breed, that race now called Americans have arisen. The eastern provinces must indeed be excepted, as being the unmixed descendants of Englishmen. I have heard many wish that they had been more intermixed also: for my part, I am no wisher, and think it much better as it has happened. They exhibit a most conspicuous figure in this great and variegated picture; they too enter for a great share in the pleasing perspective displayed in these thirteen provinces. I know it is fashionable to reflect on them, but I respect them for what they have done; for the accuracy and wisdom with which they have settled their territory; for the decency of their manners; for their early love of letters; their ancient college, the first in this hemisphere; for their industry; which to me who am but a farmer, is the criterion of everything. There never was a people, situated as they are, who with so ungrateful a soil have done more in so short a time. Do you think that the monarchical ingredients which are more prevalent in other governments, have purged them from all foul stains? Their histories assert the contrary.

In this great American asylum, the poor of Europe have by some means met together, and in consequence of various causes; to what purpose should they ask one another what countrymen they are? Alas, two thirds of them had no country. Can a wretch who wanders about, who works and starves, whose life is a continual scene of sore affliction or pinching penury; can that man call England or any other kingdom his country? A country that had no bread for him, whose fields procured him no harvest, who met with nothing but the frowns of the rich, the severity of the laws, with jails and punishments; who owned not a single foot of the extensive surface of this planet? No! urged by a variety of motives, here they came. Everything has tended to regenerate them; new laws, a new mode of living, a new social system; here they are become men: in Europe they were as so many useless plants, wanting vegetative mould, and refreshing showers; they withered, and were mowed down by want, hunger, and war; but now by the power of transplantation, like all other plants they have taken root and flourished! Formerly they were not numbered in any civil lists of their country, except in those of the poor; here they rank as citizens. By what invisible power has this surprising metamorphosis been performed? By that of the laws and that of their industry. The laws, the indulgent laws, protect them as they arrive, stamping on them the symbol of adoption; they receive ample rewards for their labours; these accumulated rewards procure them lands; those lands confer on them the title of freemen, and to that title every benefit is affixed which men can possibly require. This is the great operation daily performed by our laws. From whence proceed these laws? From our government. Whence the government? It is derived from the original genius and strong desire of the people ratified and confirmed by the crown. This is the great chain which links us all, this is the picture which every province exhibits, Nova Scotia excepted. There the crown has done all; either there were no people who had genius, or it was not much attended to: the consequence is, that the province is very thinly inhabited indeed; the power of the crown in conjunction with the musketos has prevented men from settling there. Yet some parts of it flourished once, and it contained a mild harmless set of people. But for the fault of a few leaders, the whole were banished. The greatest political error the crown ever committed in America, was to cut off men from a country which wanted nothing but men!

What attachment can a poor European emigrant have for a country where he had nothing? The knowledge of the language, the love of a few kindred as poor as himself, were the only cords that tied him: his country is now that which gives him land, bread, protection, and consequence: *Ubi panis ibi patria*,[1] is the motto of all emigrants. What then is the American, this new man? He is either an European, or the descendant of an European, hence that strange mixture of blood, which you will find in no other country.

1. This is apparently Crèvecoeur's own coined Latin, meaning: "Where the bread is my country is."

I could point out to you a family whose grandfather was an Englishman, whose wife was Dutch, whose son married a French woman, and whose present four sons have now four wives of different nations. *He* is an American, who leaving behind him all his ancient prejudices and manners, receives new ones from the new mode of life he has embraced, the new government he obeys, and the new rank he holds. He becomes an American by being received in the broad lap of our great *Alma Mater*. Here individuals of all nations are melted into a new race of men, whose labours and posterity will one day cause great changes in the world. Americans are the western pilgrims, who are carrying along with them that great mass of arts, sciences, vigour, and industry which began long since in the east; they will finish the great circle. The Americans were once scattered all over Europe; here they are incorporated into one of the finest systems of population which has ever appeared, and which will hereafter become distinct by the power of the different climates they inhabit. The American ought therefore to love this country much better than that wherein either he or his forefathers were born. Here the rewards of his industry follow with equal steps the progress of his labour; his labour is founded on the basis of nature, *self-interest*; can it want a stronger allurement? Wives and children, who before in vain demanded of him a morsel of bread, now, fat and frolicsome, gladly help their father to clear those fields whence exuberant crops are to arise to feed and to clothe them all; without any part being claimed, either by a despotic prince, a rich abbot, or a mighty lord. Here religion demands but little of him; a small voluntary salary to the minister, and gratitude to God; can he refuse these? The American is a new man, who acts upon new principles; he must therefore entertain new ideas, and form new opinions. From involuntary idleness, servile dependence, penury, and useless labour, he has passed to toils of a very different nature, rewarded by ample subsistence.—This is an American.

British America is divided into many provinces, forming a large association, scattered along a coast 1500 miles extent and about 200 wide. This society I would fain examine, at least such as it appears in the middle provinces; if it does not afford that variety of tinges and gradations which may be observed in Europe, we have colours peculiar to ourselves. For instance, it is natural to conceive that those who live near the sea, must be very different from those who live in the woods; the intermediate space will afford a separate and distinct class.

Men are like plants; the goodness and flavour of the fruit proceeds from the peculiar soil and exposition in which they grow. We are nothing but what we derive from the air we breathe, the climate we inhabit, the government we obey, the system of religion we profess, and the nature of our employment. Here you will find but few crimes; these have acquired as yet no root among us. I wish I were able to trace all my ideas; if my ignorance prevents me from describing them properly, I hope I shall be able to delineate a few of the outlines, which are all I propose.

Those who live near the sea, feed more on fish than on flesh, and often encounter that boisterous element. This renders them more bold and enterprising; this leads them to neglect the confined occupations of the land. They see and converse with a variety of people; their intercourse with mankind becomes extensive. The sea inspires them with a love of traffic, a desire of transporting produce from one place to another; and leads them to a variety of resources which supply the place of labour. Those who inhabit the middle settlements, by far the most numerous, must be very different; the simple cultivation of the earth purifies them, but the indulgences of the government, the soft remonstrances of religion, the rank of independent freeholders, must necessarily inspire them with sentiments, very little known in Europe among people of the same class. What do I say? Europe has no such class of men; the early knowledge they acquire, the early bargains they make, give them a great degree of sagacity. As freemen they will be litigious; pride and obstinacy are often the cause of law suits; the nature of our laws and governments may be another. As citizens it is easy to imagine, that they will carefully read the newspapers, enter into every political disquisition, freely blame or censure governors and others. As farmers they will be careful and anxious to get as much as they can, because what they get is their own. As northern men they will love the cheerful cup. As Christians, religion curbs them not in their opinions; the general indulgence leaves every one to think for themselves in spiritual matters; the laws inspect our actions, our thoughts are left to God. Industry, good living, selfishness, litigiousness, country politics, the pride of freemen, religious indifference, are their characteristics. If you recede still farther from the sea, you will come into more modern settlements; they exhibit the same strong lineaments, in a ruder appearance. Religion seems to have still less influence, and their manners are less improved.

Now we arrive near the great woods, near the last inhabited districts; there men seem to be placed still farther beyond the reach of government, which in some measure leaves them to themselves. How can it pervade every corner; as they were driven there by misfortunes, necessity of beginnings, desire of acquiring large tracks of land, idleness, frequent want of economy, ancient debts; the re-union of such people does not afford a very pleasing spectacle. When discord, want of unity and friendship; when either drunkenness or idleness prevail in such remote districts; contention, inactivity, and wretchedness must ensue. There are not the same remedies to these evils as in a long established community. The few magistrates they have, are in general little better than the rest; they are often in a perfect state of war; that of man against man, sometimes decided by blows, sometimes by means of the law; that of man against every wild inhabitant of these venerable woods, of which they are come to dispossess them. There men appear to be no better than carnivorous animals of a superior rank, living on the flesh of wild animals when they can catch them, and when they are not able, they subsist on grain. He who would wish to see America in its proper light, and have a true idea of its feeble beginnings and barbarous rudiments, must visit our extended line of frontiers where the last settlers dwell, and where he may see the first labours of the mode of clearing the earth, in their different appearances; where men are wholly left dependent on their native tempers, and on the spur of uncertain industry, which often fails when not sanctified by the efficacy of a few moral rules. There, remote from the power of example, and check of shame, many families exhibit the most hideous parts of our society. They are a kind of forlorn hope, preceding by ten or twelve years the most respectable army of veterans which come after them. In that space, prosperity will polish some, vice and the law will drive off the rest, who uniting again with others like themselves will recede still farther; making room for more industrious people, who will finish their improvements, convert the loghouse into a convenient habitation, and rejoicing that the first heavy labours are finished, will change in a few years that hitherto barbarous country into a fine fertile, well regulated district. Such is our progress, such is the march of the Europeans toward the interior parts of this continent. In all societies there are off-casts; this impure part serves as our precursors or pioneers; my father himself was one of that class, but he came upon honest principles, and was therefore one of the few who held fast; by good conduct and temperance, he transmitted to me his fair inheritance, when not above one in fourteen of his contemporaries had the same good fortune.

Forty years ago this smiling country was thus inhabited; it is now purged, a general decency of manners prevails throughout, and such has been the fate of our best countries.

Exclusive of those general characteristics, each province has its own, founded on the government, climate, mode of husbandry, customs, and peculiarity of circumstances. Europeans submit insensibly to these great powers, and become, in the course of a few generations, not only Americans in general, but either Pennsylvanians, Virginians, or provincials under some other name. Whoever traverses the continent must easily observe those strong differences, which will grow more evident in time. The inhabitants of Canada, Massachusetts, the middle provinces, the southern ones will be as different as their climates; their only points of unity will be those of religion and language.

As I have endeavoured to show you how Europeans become Americans; it may not be disagreeable to show you likewise how the various Christian sects introduced, wear out, and how religious indifference becomes prevalent. When any considerable number of a particular sect happen to dwell contiguous to each other, they immediately erect a temple, and there worship the Divinity agreeably to their own peculiar ideas. Nobody disturbs them. If any new sect springs up in Europe, it may happen that many of its professors will come and settle in America. As they bring their zeal with them, they are at liberty to make proselytes if they can, and to build a meeting and to follow the dictates of their consciences; for neither the government nor any other power interferes. If they are peaceable subjects, and are industrious, what is it to their neighbours how and in what manner they think fit to address their prayers to the Supreme Being? But if the sectaries are not settled close together, if they are mixed with other denominations, their zeal will cool for want of fuel, and will be extinguished in a little time. Then the Americans become as to religion, what they are as to country, allied to all. In them the name of Englishman, Frenchman, and European is lost, and in like manner, the strict modes of Christianity as practised in Europe are lost also. This effect will extend itself still farther hereafter, and though this may appear to you as a strange idea, yet it is a very true one. I shall be able perhaps hereafter to explain myself better; in the meanwhile, let the following example serve as my first justification.

Let us suppose you and I to be travelling; we observe that in this house, to the right, lives a Catholic, who prays to God as he has been taught, and believes in transubstantiation; he works and raises wheat, he has a large family of children, all hale and robust; his belief, his prayers offend nobody. About one mile farther on the same road, his next neighbour may be a good honest plodding German Lutheran, who addresses himself to the same God, the God of all, agreeably to the modes he has been educated in, and believes in consubstantiation; by so doing he scandalizes nobody; he also works in his fields, embellishes the earth, clears swamps, &c. What has the world to do with his Lutheran principles? He persecutes nobody, and nobody persecutes him, he visits his neighbours, and his neighbours visit him. Next to him lives a seceder, the most enthusiastic of all sectaries; his zeal is hot and fiery, but separated as he is from others of the same complexion, he has no congregation of his own to resort to, where he might cabal and mingle religious pride with worldly obstinacy. He likewise raises good crops, his house is handsomely painted, his orchard is one of the fairest in the neighbourhood. How does it concern the welfare of the country, or of the province at large, what this man's religious sentiments are, or really whether he has any at all? He is a good farmer, he is a sober, peaceable, good citizen: William Penn himself would not wish for more. This is the visible character, the invisible one is only guessed at, and is nobody's business. Next again lives a Low Dutchman, who implicitly believes the rules laid down by the synod of Dort. He conceives no other idea of a clergyman than that of an hired man; if he does his work well he will pay him the stipulated sum; if not he will dismiss him, and do without his sermons, and let his church be shut up for years. But notwithstanding this coarse idea, you will find his house and farm to be the neatest in all the country; and you will judge by his waggon and fat horses, that he thinks more of the affairs of this world than of those of the next. He is sober and laborious, therefore he is all he ought to be as to the affairs of this life; as for those of the next, he must trust to the great Creator. Each of these people instruct their children as well as they can, but these instructions are feeble compared to those which are given to the youth of the poorest class in Europe. Their children will therefore grow up less zealous and more indifferent in matters of religion than their parents. The foolish vanity, or rather the fury of making Proselytes, is unknown here; they have no time, the seasons call for all their attention, and thus in a few years, this mixed neighbourhood will exhibit a strange religious medley, that will be neither pure Catholicism nor pure Calvinism. A very perceptible indifference even in the first generation, will become apparent; and it may happen that the daughter of the Catholic will marry the son of the seceder, and settle by themselves at a distance from their parents. What religious education will they give their children? A very imperfect one. If there happens to be in the neighbourhood any place of worship, we will suppose a Quaker's meeting; rather than not show their fine clothes, they will go to it, and some of them may perhaps attach themselves to that society. Others will remain in a perfect state of indifference; the children of these zealous parents will not be able to tell what their religious principles are, and their grandchildren still less. The neighborhood of a place of worship generally leads them to it, and the action of going thither, is the strongest evidence they can give of their attachment to any sect. The Quakers are the only people who retain a fondness for their own mode of worship; for be they ever so far separated from each other, they hold a sort of communion with the society, and seldom depart from its rules, at least in this country. Thus all sects are mixed as well as all nations; thus religious indifference is imperceptibly disseminated from one end of the continent to the other; which is at present one of the strongest characteristics of the Americans. Where this will reach no one can tell, perhaps it may leave a vacuum fit to receive other systems. Persecution, religious pride, the love of contradiction, are the food of what the world commonly calls religion. These motives have ceased here: zeal in Europe is confined; here it evaporates in the great distance it has to travel; there it is a grain of powder inclosed, here it burns away in the open air, and consumes without effect.

But to return to our back settlers. I must tell you, that there is something in the proximity of the woods, which is very singular. It is with men as it is with the plants and animals that grow and live in the forests; they are entirely different from those that live in the plains. I will candidly tell you all my thoughts but you are not to expect that I shall advance any reasons. By living in or near the woods, their actions are regulated by the wildness of the neighbourhood. The deer often come to eat their grain, the wolves to destroy their sheep, the bears to kill their hogs, the foxes to catch their poultry. This surrounding hostility immediately puts the gun into their hands; they watch these animals, they kill some; and thus by defending their property, they soon become professed hunters; this is the progress; once hunters, farewell to the plough. The chase renders them ferocious, gloomy, and unsociable; a hunter wants no neighbour, he rather hates them, because he dreads the competition. In a little time their success in the woods makes them neglect their tillage. They trust to the natural fecundity of the earth, and therefore do little; carelessness in fencing often exposes what little they sow to destruction; they are not at home to watch; in order therefore to make up the deficiency, they go oftener to the woods. That new mode of life brings along with it a new set of manners, which I cannot easily describe. These new manners being grafted on the old stock, produce a strange sort of lawless profligacy, the impressions of which are indelible. The manners of the Indian natives are respectable, compared with this European medley. Their wives and children live in sloth and inactivity; and having no proper pursuits, you may judge what education the latter receive. Their tender minds have nothing else to contemplate but the example of their parents; like them they grow up a mongrel breed, half civilized, half savage, except nature stamps on them some constitutional propensities. That rich, that voluptuous sentiment is gone that struck them so forcibly; the possession of their freeholds no longer conveys to their minds the same pleasure and pride. To all these reasons you must add, their lonely situation, and you cannot imagine what an effect on manners the great distances they live from each other has! Consider one of the last settlements in its first view: of what is it composed? Europeans who have not that sufficient share of knowledge they ought to have, in order to prosper; people who have suddenly passed from oppression, dread of government, and fear of laws, into the unlimited freedom of the woods. This sudden change must have a very great effect on most men, and on that class particularly. Eating of wild meat, what ever you may think, tends to alter their temper though all the proof I can adduce, is, that I have seen it: and having no place of worship to resort to, what little society this might afford, is denied them. The Sunday meetings, exclusive of religious benefits, were the only social bonds that might have inspired them with some degree of emulation in neatness. Is it then surprising to see men thus situated, immersed in great and heavy labours, degenerate a little? It is rather a wonder the effect is not more diffusive. The Moravians and the Quakers are the only instances in exception to what I have advanced. The first never settle singly, it is a colony of the society which emigrates; they carry with them their forms, worship, rules, and decency: the others never begin so hard, they are always able to buy improvements, in which there is a great advantage, for by that time the country is recovered from its first barbarity. Thus our bad people are those who are half cultivators and half hunters; and the worst of them are those who have degenerated altogether into the hunting state. As old ploughmen and new men of the woods, as Europeans and new made Indians, they contract the vices of both; they adopt the moroseness and ferocity of a native, without his mildness, or even his industry at home. If manners are not refined, at least they are rendered simple and inoffensive by tilling the earth; all our wants are supplied by it, our time is divided between labour and rest, and leaves none for the commission of great misdeeds. As hunters it is divided between the toil of the chase, the idleness of repose, or the indulgence of inebriation. Hunting is but a licentious idle life, and if it does not always pervert good dispositions; yet, when it is united with bad luck, it leads to want: want stimulates that propensity to rapacity and injustice, too natural to needy men, which is the fatal gradation. After this explanation of the effects which follow by living in the woods, shall we yet vainly flatter ourselves with the hope of converting the Indians? We should rather begin with converting our back-settlers; and now if I dare mention the name of religion, its sweet accents would be lost in the immensity of these woods. Men thus placed, are not fit either to receive or remember its mild instructions; they want temples and ministers, but as soon as men cease to remain at home, and begin to lead an erratic life, let them be either tawny or white, they cease to be its disciples.

Thus have I faintly and imperfectly endeavoured to trace our society from the sea to our woods! yet you must not imagine that every person who moves back, acts upon the same principles, or falls into the same degeneracy. Many families carry with them all their decency of conduct, purity of morals, and respect of religion; but these are scarce, the power of example is sometimes irresistible. Even among these back-settlers, their depravity is greater or less, according to what nation or province they belong. Were I to adduce proofs of this, I might be accused of partiality. If there happens to be some rich intervals, some fertile bottoms, in those remote districts, the people will there prefer tilling the land to hunting, and will attach themselves to it; but even on these fertile spots you may plainly perceive the inhabitants to acquire a great degree of rusticity and selfishness.

It is in consequence of this straggling situation, and the astonishing power it has on manners, that the back-settlers of both the Carolinas, Virginia, and many other parts, have been long a set of lawless people; it has been even dangerous to travel among them. Government can do nothing in so extensive a country, better it should wink at these irregularities, than that it should use means inconsistent with its usual mildness. Time will efface those stains: in proportion as the great body of population approaches them they will reform, and become polished and subordinate. Whatever has been said of the four New England provinces, no such degeneracy of manners has ever tarnished their annals; their back-settlers have been kept within the bounds of decency, and government, by means of wise laws, and by the influence of religion. What a detestable idea such people must have given to the natives of the Europeans! They trade with them, the worst of people are permitted to do that which none but persons of the best characters should be employed in. They get drunk with them, and often defraud the Indians. Their avarice, removed from the eyes of their superiors, knows no bounds; and aided by a little superiority of knowledge, these traders deceive them, and even sometimes shed blood. Hence those shocking violations, those sudden devastations which have so often stained our frontiers, when hundreds of innocent people have been sacrificed for the crimes of a few. It was in consequence of such behaviour, that the Indians took the hatchet against the Virginians in 1774. Thus are our first steps trod, thus are our first trees felled, in general, by the most vicious of our people and thus the path is opened for the arrival of a second and better class, the true American freeholders; the most respectable set of people in this part of the world: respectable for their industry, their happy independence, the great share of freedom they possess, the good regulation of their families, and for extending the trade and the dominion of our mother country.

Europe contains hardly any other distinctions but lords and tenants; this fair country alone is settled by freeholders, the possessors of the soil they cultivate, members of the government they obey, and the framers of their own laws, by means of their representatives. This is a thought which you have taught me to cherish; our difference from Europe, far from diminishing, rather adds to our usefulness and consequence as men and subjects. Had our forefathers remained there, they would only have crowded it, and perhaps prolonged those convulsions which had shook it so long. Every industrious European who transports himself here may be compared to a sprout growing at the foot of a great tree; it enjoys and draws but a little portion of sap; wrench it from the parent roots, transplant it, and it will become a tree bearing fruit also. Colonists are therefore entitled to the consideration due to the most useful subjects; a hundred families barely existing in some parts of Scotland, will here in six years, cause an annual exportation of 10,000 bushels of wheat: 100 bushels being but a common quantity for an industrious family to sell, if they cultivate good land. It is here then that the idle may be employed, the useless become useful, and the poor become rich; but by riches I do not mean gold and silver, we have but little of those metals; I mean a better sort of wealth, cleared lands, cattle, good houses, good clothes, and an increase of people to enjoy them.

It is no wonder that this country has so many charms, and presents to Europeans so many temptations to remain in it. A traveller in Europe becomes a stranger as soon as he quits his own kingdom; but it is otherwise here. We know, properly speaking, no strangers; this is every person's country; the variety of our soils, situations, climates, governments, and produce, hath something which must please every body. No sooner does an European arrive, no matter of what condition, than his eyes are opened upon the fair prospect; he hears his language spoke, he retraces many of his own country manners, he perpetually hears the names of families and towns with which he is acquainted; he sees happiness and prosperity in all places disseminated; he meets with hospitality, kindness, and plenty everywhere; he beholds hardly any poor, he seldom hears of punishments and executions; and he wonders at the elegance of our towns, those miracles of industry and freedom. He cannot admire enough our rural districts, our convenient roads, good taverns, and our many accommodations; he involuntarily loves a country where everything is so lovely. When in England, he was a mere Englishman; here he stands on a larger portion of the globe, not less than its fourth part, and may see the productions of the north, in iron and naval stores; the provisions of Ireland, the grain of Egypt, the indigo, the rice of China. He does not find, as in Europe, a crowded society, where every place is over-stocked; he does not feel that perpetual collision of parties, that difficulty of beginning, that contention which oversets so many. There is room for everybody in America; has he any particular talent, or industry? he exerts it in order to procure a livelihood, and it succeeds. Is he a merchant? the avenues of trade are infinite; is he eminent in any respect? he will be employed and respected. Does he love a country life? pleasant farms present themselves; he may purchase what he wants, and thereby become an American farmer. Is he a labourer, sober and industrious? he need not go many miles, nor receive many informations before he will be hired, well fed at the table of his employer, and paid four or five times more than he can get in Europe. Does he want uncultivated lands? Thousands of acres present themselves, which he may purchase cheap. Whatever be his talents or inclinations, if they are moderate, he may satisfy them. I do not mean that every one who comes will grow rich in a little time; no, but he may procure an easy, decent maintenance, by his industry. Instead of starving he will be fed, instead of being idle he will have employment; and these are riches enough for such men as come over here. The rich stay in Europe, it is only the middling and the poor that emigrate. Would you wish to travel in independent idleness, from north to south, you will find easy access, and the most chearful reception at every house; society without ostentation, good cheer without pride, and every decent diversion which the country affords, with little expence. It is no wonder that the European who has lived here a few years, is desirous to remain; Europe with all its pomp, is not to be compared to this continent, for men of middle stations, or labourers.

An European, when he first arrives, seems limited in his intentions, as well as in his views; but he very suddenly alters his scale; two hundred miles formerly appeared a very great distance, it is now but a trifle; he no sooner breathes our air than he forms schemes, and embarks in designs he never would have thought of in his own country. There the plenitude of society confines many useful ideas, and often extinguishes the most laudable schemes which here ripen into maturity. Thus Europeans become Americans.

But how is this accomplished in that crowd of low, indigent people, who flock here every year from all parts of Europe? I will tell you; they no sooner arrive than they immediately feel the good effects of that plenty of provisions we possess: they fare on our best food, and they are kindly entertained; their talents, character, and peculiar industry are immediately inquired into; they find countrymen everywhere disseminated, let them come from whatever part of Europe. Let me select one as an epitome of the rest; he is hired, he goes to work, and works moderately; instead of being employed by a haughty person, he finds himself with his equal, placed at the substantial table of the farmer, or else at an inferior one as good; his wages are high, his bed is not like that bed of sorrow on which he used to lie: if he behaves with propriety, and is faithful, he is caressed, and becomes as it were a member of the family. He begins to feel the effects of a sort of resurrection; hitherto he had not lived, but simply vegetated; he now feels himself a man, because he is treated as such; the laws of his own country had overlooked him in his insignificancy; the laws of this cover him with their mantle. Judge what an alteration there must arise in the mind and thoughts of this man; he begins to forget his former servitude and dependence, his heart involuntarily swells and glows; this first swell inspires him with those new thoughts which constitute an American. What love can he entertain for a country where his existence was a burthen to him; if he is a generous good man, the love of this new adoptive parent will sink deep into his heart. He looks around, and sees many a prosperous person, who but a few years before was as poor as himself. This encourages him much, he begins to form some little scheme, the first, alas, he ever formed in his life. If he is wise he thus spends two or three years, in which time he acquires knowledge, the use of tools, the modes of working the lands, felling trees, etc. This prepares the foundation of a good name, the most useful acquisition he can make. He is encouraged, he has gained friends; he is advised and directed, he feels bold, he purchases some land; he gives all the money he has brought over, as well as what he has earned, and trusts to the God of harvests for the discharge of the rest. His good name procures him credit. He is now possessed of the deed, conveying to him and his posterity the fee simple and absolute property of two hundred acres of land, situated on such a river. What an epocha in this man's life! He is become a freeholder, from perhaps a German boor—he is now an American, a Pennsylvanian, an English subject. He is naturalized, his name is enrolled with those of the other citizens of the province. Instead of being a vagrant, he has a place of residence; he is called the inhabitant of such a county, or of such a district, and for the first time in his life counts for something; for hitherto he has been a cypher. I only repeat what I have heard many say, and no wonder their hearts should glow, and be agitated with a multitude of feelings, not easy to describe. From nothing to start into being; from a servant to the rank of a master; from being the slave of some despotic prince, to become a free man, invested with lands, to which every municipal blessing is annexed! What a change indeed! It is in consequence of that change that he becomes an American. This great metamorphosis has a double effect, it extinguishes all his European prejudices, he forgets that mechanism of subordination, that servility of disposition which poverty had taught him; and sometimes he is apt to forget too much, often passing from one extreme to the other. If he is a good man, he forms schemes of future prosperity, he proposes to educate his children better than he has been educated himself; he thinks of future modes of conduct, feels an ardour to labour he never felt before. Pride steps in and leads him to everything that the laws do not forbid: he respects them; with a heart-felt gratitude he looks toward the east, toward that insular government from whose wisdom all his new felicity is derived, and under whose wings and protection he now lives. These reflections constitute him the good man and the good subject. Ye poor Europeans, ye, who sweat, and work for the great—ye, who are obliged to give so many sheaves to the church, so many to your lords, so many to your government, and have hardly any left for yourselves—ye, who are held in less estimation than favourite hunters or useless lap-dogs—ye, who only breathe the air of nature, because it cannot be withheld from you; it is here that ye can conceive the possibility of those feelings I have been describing; it is here the laws of naturalization invite every one to partake of our great labours and felicity, to till unrented untaxed lands! Many, corrupted beyond the power of amendment, have brought with them all their vices, and disregarding the advantages held to them, have gone on in their former career of iniquity, until they have been overtaken and punished by our laws. It is not every emigrant who succeeds; no, it is only the sober, the honest, and industrious: happy those to whom this transition has served as a powerful spur to labour, to prosperity, and to the good establishment of children, born in the days of their poverty; and who had no other portion to expect but the rags of their parents, had it not been for their happy emigration. Others again, have been led astray by this enchanting scene; their new pride, instead of leading them to the fields, has kept them in idleness; the idea of possessing lands is all that satisfies them—though surrounded with fertility, they have mouldered away their time in inactivity, misinformed husbandry, and ineffectual endeavours. How much wiser, in general, the honest Germans than almost all other Europeans; they hire themselves to some of their wealthy landsmen, and in that apprenticeship learn everything that is necessary. They attentively consider the prosperous industry of others, which imprints in their minds a strong desire of possessing the same advantages. This forcible idea never quits them, they launch forth, and by dint of sobriety, rigid parsimony, and the most persevering industry, they commonly succeed. Their astonishment at their first arrival from Germany is very great—it is to them a dream; the contrast must be powerful indeed; they observe their countrymen flourishing in every place; they travel through whole counties where not a word of English is spoken; and in the names and the language of the people, they retrace Germany. They have been an useful acquisition to this continent, and to Pennsylvania in particular; to them it owes some share of its prosperity: to their mechanical knowledge and patience it owes the finest mills in all America, the best teams of horses, and many other advantages. The recollection of their former poverty and slavery never quits them as long as they live.

The Scotch and the Irish might have lived in their own country perhaps as poor, but enjoying more civil advantages, the effects of their new situation do not strike them so forcibly, nor has it so lasting an effect. From whence the difference arises I know not, but out of twelve families of emigrants of each country, generally seven Scotch will succeed, nine German, and four Irish. The Scotch are frugal and laborious, but their wives cannot work so hard as German women, who on the contrary vie with their husbands, and often share with them the most severe toils of the field, which they understand better. They have therefore nothing to struggle against, but the common casualties of nature. The Irish do not prosper so well; they love to drink and to quarrel; they are litigious, and soon take to the gun, which is the ruin of everything; they seem beside to labour under a greater degree of ignorance in husbandry than the others; perhaps it is that their industry had less scope, and was less exercised at home. I have heard many relate, how the land was parcelled out in that kingdom; their ancient conquest has been a great detriment to them, by over-setting their landed property. The lands possessed by a few, are leased down *ad infinitum*, and the occupiers often pay five guineas an acre. The poor are worse lodged there than anywhere else in Europe; their potatoes, which are easily raised, are perhaps an inducement to laziness: their ages are too low and their whisky too cheap.

There is no tracing observations of this kind, without making at the same time very great allowances, as there are everywhere to be found, a great many exceptions. The Irish themselves, from different parts of that kingdom, are very different. It is difficult to account for this surprising locality, one would think on so small an island an Irishman must be an Irishman: yet it is not so, they are different in their aptitude to, and in their love of labour.

The Scotch on the contrary are all industrious and saving; they want nothing more than a field to exert themselves in, and they are commonly sure of succeeding. The only difficulty they labour under is, that technical American knowledge which requires some time to obtain; it is not easy for those who seldom saw a tree, to conceive how it is to be felled, cut up, and split into rails and posts.

As I am fond of seeing and talking of prosperous families, I intend to finish this letter by relating to you the history of an honest Scotch Hebridean, who came here in 1774, which will show you in epitome, what the Scotch can do, wherever they have room for the exertion of their industry. Whenever I hear of any new settlement, I pay it a visit once or twice a year, on purpose to observe the different steps each settler takes, the gradual improvements, the different tempers of each family, on which their prosperity in a great nature depends; their different modifications of industry, their ingenuity, and contrivance; for being all poor, their life requires sagacity and prudence. In an evening I love to hear them tell their stories, they furnish me with new ideas; I sit still and listen to their ancient misfortunes, observing in many of them a strong degree of gratitude to God, and the government. Many a well-meant sermon have I preached to some of them. When I found laziness and inattention to prevail, who could refrain from wishing well to these new countrymen after having undergone so many fatigues. Who could withhold good advice? What a happy change it must be, to descend from the high, sterile, bleak lands of Scotland, where everything is barren and cold, to rest on some fertile farms in these middle provinces! Such a transition must have afforded the most pleasing satisfaction.

The following dialogue passed at an out-settlement, where I lately paid a visit:

"Well, friend, how do you do now; I am come fifty odd miles on purpose to see you; how do you go on with your new cutting and slashing?" "Very well, good Sir, we learn the use of the axe bravely, we shall make it out; we have a belly full of victuals every day, our cows run about, and come home full of milk, our hogs get fat of themselves in the woods: Oh, this is a good country! God bless the king, and William Penn; we shall do very well by and by, if we keep our healths." "Your loghouse looks neat and light, where did you get these shingles?" "One of our neighbours is a New-England man, and he showed us how to split them out of chestnut-trees. Now for a barn, but all in good time, here are fine trees to build with." "Who is to frame it, sure you don't understand that work yet?" "A countryman of ours who has been in America these ten years, offers to wait for his money until the second crop is lodged in it." "What did you give for your land?" "Thirty-five shillings per acre, payable in seven years." "How many acres have you got?" "An hundred and fifty." "That is enough to begin with; is not your land pretty hard to clear?" "Yes, Sir, hard enough, but it would be harder still if it was ready cleared, for then we should have no timber, and I love the woods much; the land is nothing without them." "Have not you found out any bees yet?" "No, Sir; and if we had we should not know what to do with them." "I will tell you by and by." "You are very kind." "Farewell, honest man, God prosper you; whenever you travel toward ——, enquire for J. S. He will entertain you kindly, provided you bring him good tidings from your family and farm."

In this manner I often visit them, and carefully examine their houses, their modes of ingenuity, their different ways; and make them all relate all they know, and describe all they feel. These are scenes which I believe you would willingly share with me. I well remember your philanthropic turn of mind. Is it not better to contemplate under these humble roofs, the rudiments of future wealth and population, than to behold the accumulated bundles of litigious papers in the office of a lawyer? To examine how the world is gradually settled, how the howling swamp is converted into a pleasing meadow, the rough ridge into a fine field; and to hear the chearful whistling, the rural song, where there was no sound heard before, save the yell of the savage, the screech of the owl, or the hissing of the snake? Here an European, fatigued with luxury, riches, and pleasures, may find a sweet relaxation in a series of interesting scenes, as affecting as they are new. England, which now contains so many domes, so many castles, was once like this; a place woody and marshy; its inhabitants, now the favourite nation for arts and commerce, were once painted like our neighbours. The country will flourish in its turn, and the same observations will be made which I have just delineated. Posterity will look back with avidity and pleasure, to trace, if possible, the era of this or that particular settlement.

Pray, what is the reason that the Scots are in general more religious, more faithful, more honest, and industrious than the Irish? I do not mean to insinuate national reflections, God forbid! It ill becomes any man, and much less an American; but as I know men are nothing of themselves, and that they owe all their different modifications either to government or other local circumstances, there must be some powerful causes which constitute this great national difference.

Agreeable to the account which several Scotchmen have given me of the north of Britain, of the Orkneys, and the Hebride Islands, they seem, on many accounts, to be unfit for the habitation of men; they appear to be calculated only for great sheep pastures. Who then can blame the inhabitants of these countries for transporting themselves hither? This great continent must in time absorb the poorest part of Europe; and this will happen in proportion as it becomes better known; and as war, taxation, oppression, and misery increase there. The Hebrides appear to be fit only for the residence of malefactors, and it would be much better to send felons there than either to Virginia or Maryland. What a strange compliment has our mother country paid to two of the finest provinces in America! England has entertained in that respect very mistaken ideas; what was intended as a punishment, is become the good fortune of several; many of those who have been transported as felons, are now rich, and strangers to the stings of those wants that urged them to violations of the law: they are become industrious, exemplary, and useful citizens. The English government should purchase the most northern and barren of those islands; it should send over to us the honest, primitive Hebrideans, settle them here on good lands, as a reward for their virtue and ancient poverty; and replace them with a colony of her wicked sons. The severity of the climate, the inclemency of the seasons, the sterility of the soil, the tempestuousness of the sea, would afflict and punish enough. Could there be found a spot better adapted to retaliate the injury it had received by their crimes? Some of those islands might be considered as the hell of Great Britain, where all evil spirits should be sent. Two essential ends would be answered by this simple operation. The good people, by emigration, would be rendered happier; the bad ones would be placed where they ought to be. In a few years the dread of being sent to that wintry region would have a much stronger effect than that of transportation. This is no place of punishment; were I a poor hopeless, breadless Englishman, and not restrained by the power of shame, I should be very thankful for the passage. It is of very little importance how, and in what manner an indigent man arrives; for if he is but sober, honest, and industrious, he has nothing more to ask of heaven. Let him go to work, he will have opportunities enough to earn a comfortable support, and even the means of procuring some land; which ought to be the utmost wish of every person who has health and hands to work. I knew a man who came to this country, in the literal sense of the expression, stark naked; I think he was a Frenchman and a sailor on board an English man of war. Being discontented, he had stripped himself and swam ashore; where finding clothes and friends, he settled afterwards at Maraneck, in the county of Chester, in the province of New York: he married and left a good farm to each of his sons. I knew another person who was but twelve years old when he was taken on the frontiers of Canada, by the Indians; at his arrival at Albany he was purchased by a gentleman, who generously bound him apprentice to a tailor. He lived to the age of ninety, and left behind him a fine estate and a numerous family, all well settled; many of them I am acquainted with. Where is then the industrious European who ought to despair?

After a foreigner from any part of Europe is arrived, and become a citizen, let him devoutly listen to the voice of our great parent, which says to him, "Welcome to my shores, distressed European; bless the hour in which thou didst see my verdant fields, my fair navigable rivers, and my green mountains! If thou wilt work, I have bread for thee; if thou wilt be honest, sober, and industrious, I have greater rewards to confer on thee—ease and independence. I will give thee fields to feed and clothe thee; a comfortable fireside to sit by, and tell thy children by what means thou hast prospered; and a decent bed to repose on. I shall endow thee beside with the immunities of a freeman. If thou wilt carefully educate thy children, teach them gratitude to God, and reverence to that government, that philanthropic government, which has collected here so many men and made them happy. I will also provide for thy progeny; and to every good man this ought to be the most holy, the most powerful, the most earnest wish he can possibly form, as well as the most consolatory prospect when he dies. Go thou and work and till; thou shalt prosper, provided thou be just, grateful, and industrious."

SOURCE: J. Hector St. John de Crèvecoeur. *Letters from an American Farmer.* Reprinted from the original ed., with a prefatory note by W. P. Trent and an introduction by Ludwig Lewisohn. New York: Fox, Duffield, 1904.

SARAH WENTWORTH MORTON

Sarah Wentworth Morton (1759–1846) was a native of Boston; in the midst of her popularity as a poet in the 1790s, her pen name was Philenia. "The African Chief," about an enslaved man who was killed in Santa Domingo in 1791, inspired anti-slavery advocates for the next several decades, among them the poet John Greenleaf Whittier. Morton based the story upon newspaper accounts: "Taken in arms, fighting for his freedom, and inhumanly butchered by his conquerors! This affecting event was fully delineated in the various Gazettes of that period." We have used her 1823 setting of the poem.

The African Chief (1792)

See how the black ship cleaves the main,
High bounding o'er the dark blue wave,
Remurmuring with the groans of pain,
Deep freighted with the princely slave!

Did all the Gods of Afric sleep,
Forgetful of their guardian love,
When the white tyrants of the deep,
Betrayed him in the palmy grove.

A Chief of *Gambia's* golden shore,
Whose arm the band of warriors led,
Or more—the lord of generous power,
By whom the foodless poor were fed.

Does not the voice of reason cry,
Claim the first right that nature gave,
From the red scourge of bondage fly,
Nor deign to live a burdened slave.

Has not his suffering offspring clung,
  Desponding round his fettered knee;
On his worn shoulder, weeping hung,
  And urged one effort to be free!

His wife by nameless wrongs subdued,
  His bosom's friend to death resigned;
The flinty path-way drenched in blood;
  He saw with cold and phrenzied mind.

Strong in despair, then sought the plain,
  To heaven was raised his stedfast eye,
Resolved to burst the crushing chain,
  Or mid the battle's blast to die.

First of his race, he led the band,
  Guardless of danger, hurling round,
Till by his red avenging hand,
  Full many a despot stained the ground.

When erst *Messenia's* sons oppressed,
  Flew desperate to the sanguine field,
With iron cloathed each injured breast,
  And saw the cruel Spartan yield.

Did not the soul to heaven allied,
  With the proud heart as greatly swell,
As when the *Roman Decius* died,
  Or when the *Grecian victim* fell.

Do later deeds quick rapture raise,
  The boon *Batavia's William* won,
Paoli's time-enduring praise,
  Or the yet greater *Washington!*

If these exalt thy sacred zeal,
  To hate oppression's mad controul,
For bleeding *Afric* learn to feel,
  Whose Chieftain claimed a kindred soul.

Ah, mourn the last disastrous hour,
Lift the full eye of bootless grief,
While victory treads the sultry shore,
And tears from hope the captive Chief.

While the hard race of *pallid hue,*
Unpracticed in the power to feel,
Resign him to the murderous crew,
The horrors of the quivering wheel.

Let sorrow bathe each blushing cheek,
Bend piteous o'er the tortured slave,
Whose wrongs compassion cannot speak,
Whose only refuge was the grave.

SOURCE: Sarah Wentworth Morton. *My Mind and Its Thoughts, in Sketches, Fragments, and Essays.* Boston: Wells and Lilly, 1823.

MERIWETHER LEWIS AND WILLIAM CLARK

Captain Meriwether Lewis (1774–1809) and Captain William Clark (1770–1838) led the expedition President Thomas Jefferson commissioned through the War Department. His stated purposes were, among others, to explore the Missouri River to its source, and "to establish trade with the Native American people of the West and find a water route to the Pacific." They were to collect information about the western part of the continent, about which Jefferson had so much curiosity. This excerpt from the original journals of the Lewis and Clark expedition covers their trek from Three Forks (in today's Montana) to Beaver's Head (also in Montana), July 28–August 10, 1805. Along the way, they met Toussaint Charbonneau, a French-Canadian trader, and his now famous wife, Sacagawea, a Shoshone woman whose familiarity with native tribes and ability to communicate with them helped the expedition cross the Rocky Mountains and reach the Oregon coast in November. Lewis is a clear-eyed and clearheaded observer and excellent journal-keeper. Clark, for all his intelligence, was a note-taker and summarizer at best, and was at this point in his career a bewildered speller also unfamiliar with the proper use of punctuation. We have added capitalization after periods, silently added a dozen or two punctuation marks, but have otherwise left the writing just as it appears in Thwaites's superb 1904 edition.

From *Original Journals of the Lewis and Clark Expedition* (1804–1806)

[LEWIS:] *Sunday July* 28th, 1805.

MY FRIEND CAPT. Clark was very sick all last night but feels himself somewhat better this morning since his medicine has opperated. I dispatched two men early this morning up the S.E. Fork to examine the river; and permitted sundry others to hunt in the neighbourhood of this place. Both Capt. C. and myself corrisponded in opinon with rispect to the impropriety of calling either of these streams the Missouri and accordingly agreed to name them after the President of the United States and the Secretaries of the Treasury and state having previously named one river in honour of the Secretaries of War and Navy. In pursuance of this resolution we called the S.W. fork, that which we meant to ascend, Jefferson's River in honor of that illustrious personage Thomas Jefferson. [*the author of our enterprize.*] The Middle fork we called Madison's River in honor of James Madison, and the S.E. Fork we called Gallitin's River in honor of Albert Gallitin. The two first are 90 yards wide and the last is 70 yards. All of them run with great volocity and throw out large bodies of water. Gallitin's River is reather more rapid than either of the others, is not quite as deep but from all appearances may be navigated to a considerable distance. Capt. C. who came down Madison's river yesterday and has also seen Jefferson's some distance thinks Madison's reather the most rapid, but it is not as much so by any means as Gallitin's. The beds of all these streams are formed of smooth pebble and gravel, and their waters perfectly transparent; in short they are three noble streams.

There is timber enough here to support an establishment, provided it be erected with brick or stone either of which would be much cheaper than wood as all the materials for such a work are immediately at the spot. There are several small sand-bars along the shores at no great distance of very pure sand and the earth appears as if it would make good brick.

I had all our baggage spread out to dry this morning; and the day proving warm, I had a small bower or booth erected for the comfort of Capt. C. Our leather lodge when exposed to the sun is excessively hot.

I observe large quantities of the sand rush in these bottoms which grow in many places as high as a man's breast and stand as thick as the stalks of wheat usually do. This affords one of the best winter pastures on earth for horses or cows, and of course will be much in favour of an establishment should it ever be thought necessary to fix one at this place. The grass is also luxouriant and would afford a fine swarth of hay at this time in parsels of ma[n]y acres together. All those who are not hunting altho' much fatiegued are busily engaged in dressing their skins, making mockersons lexing [leggings] &c to make themselves comfortable.

The Musquetoes are more than usually troublesome, the knats are not as much so. In the evening about 4 O'Ck the wind blew hard from South West and after some little time brought on a Cloud attended with thunder and Lightning from which we had a fine refreshing shower which cooled the air considerably; the showers continued with short intervals untill after dark.

In the evening the hunters all returned[;] they had killed 8 deer and 2 Elk, some of the deer were in excellent order.

Those whome I had sent up Gallitin's river reported that after it passed the point to which I had seen it yesterday that it turned more to the East to a considerable distance or as far as they could discover the opening of the Mountains formed by it's valley which was many miles. The bottoms were tolerably wide but not as much so as at or near it's mouth. It's current is rappid and the stream much divided with islands but is sufficiently deep for canoe navigation.

Our present camp is precisely on the spot that the Snake Indians were encamped at the time the Minnetares of the Knife R. first came in sight of them five years since. From hence they retreated about three miles up Jeffersons river and concealed themselves in the woods, the Minnetares pursued, attacked them, killed 4 men 4 women a number of boys, and mad[e] prisoners of all the females and four boys, *Sah-cah-gar-we-ah*[1] o[u]r Indian woman was one of the female prisoners taken at that time; tho' I cannot discover that she shews any immotion of sorrow in recollecting this event, or of joy in being again restored to her native country; if she has enough to eat and a few trinkets to wear I beleive she would be perfectly content anywhere.

Point of observation No. 39.

At our encampment on Camp Island, near the junction of the three forks of the Missouri. . . . {Lewis recorded "observed equal altitudes" with a sextant and the "latitude deduced from this observation."}

[Clark:] *July* 28th *Sunday* 1805

I was verry unwell all night, Something better this morning, a very worm day untill 4 oClock when the wind rose & blew hard from the SW. and was Cloudy. The Thermomet Stood at 90° above 0'.

In the evening a heavy thunder Shower from the SW. which continued at intervales untill after dark. Several deer killed to day. Men all employed dressing Skins for Clothes & Mockersons. Two

1. That is, the woman later known to history as Sacagawea (c.1788–1812).

men went up the East fork & reports that it is nearly the Size of the N. fork, verry rapid & has maney Islands.

Our present Camp is the prosize Spot the Snake Indians were Camped at the time the *Minetarries* came in Sight, attacked & killed 4 men 4 women & a number of boys, & made prisoners of all the females & 4 boys.

[LEWIS:] *Monday July* 29th 1805.

This morning some of the hunters turned out and returned in a few hours with four fat bucks, the venison is now very fine. We have killed no mule deer since we lay here, they are all of the longtailed red deer which appear qu[i]te as large as those of the United States.

The hunters brought in a living young sandhill crain; it has nearly obtained it's growth but cannot fly; they had pursued it and caught it in the meadows. It's colour is precisely that of the red deer. We see a number of the old or full grown crains of this species feeding in these meadows. This young animal is very f[i]erce and strikes a severe blow with his beak; after amusing myself with it I had it set at liberty and it moved off apparently much pleased with being releived from his captivity.

The men have been busily engaged all day in dising [dressing] skins and making them into various garments. All are leather dressers and taylors. We see a great abundance of fish in the stream some of which we take to be trout but they will not bite at any bate we can offer them. The King fisher is common on the river since we have left the falls of the Missouri. We have not seen the summer duck since we left that place, nor do I beleive that it is an inhabitant of the Rocky mountains. The Duckanmallard were first seen with their young on the 20th inst. and I forgot to note it; they are now abundant with their young but do not breed in the Missouri below the mountains.

The grasshopers and crickets are abundant in the plains as are also the small birds frequently mentioned. There is also in these plains a large ant with a redish brown body and legs, and a black head and abdomen; they construct little perimids of small gravel in a conic shape, about 10 or 12 inches high without a mixture of sticks and with but little earth.

Capt. Clark is much better today, is perfectly clear of fever but still very languid and complains of a general soarness in all his limbs. I prevailed on him to take the barks which he has done and eate tolerably freely of our good venison.

Today I continued my observations [of altitude and latitude]. . . .

[CLARK:] *July* 29 *Monday* 1805

A fair morning wind from the North. I feel my Self something better to day, made some Celestial observations took two Merdn. altitudes . . . Men all dressing skins &c.

[LEWIS:] *Tuesday July* 30th 1805.

Capt. Clark being much better this morning and having completed my observations we reloaded our canoes and set out, ascending Jeffersons river. Sharbono, his woman two invalleds and myself walked through the bottom on the Lar[boar]d. side of the river about 4 1/2 miles when we again struck it at the place the woman informed us that she was taken prisoner. Here we halted untill Capt. Clark arrived which was not untill after one P.M. the water being strong and the river extreemly crooked.

We dined and again proceeded on; as the river now passed through the woods the invalleds got on board together with Sharbono and the Indian woman; I passed the river and continued my walk on the Stard. side. Saw a vast number of beaver in many large dams which they had maid in various bayoes of the river which are distributed to the distance of three or four miles on this side of the river over an extensive bottom of timbered and meadow lands intermixed. In order to avoid these bayoes and beaver dams which I fou[n]d difficult to pass I directed my course to the high plain to the right which I gained after some time with much difficulty and waiding many beaver dams to my waist in mud and water. I would willingly have joined the canoes but the brush were so thick, the river crooked and bottoms intercepted in such manner by the beaver dams, that I found it uceless to attempt to find them, and therefore proceeded on up the river in order to intersept it where it came near the plain and woult be more collected into one channel.

At length about sunset I arrived at the river only about six miles from my calculation on a direct line from the place I had left the canoes but I thought they were still below me. I found the river was divided where I reached it by an Island and was therefore fearfull that they might pass without my seeing them, and went down to the lower point of the large island; here I discovered a small Island, close under the shore on which I was; I passed the narrow channel to the small island and examined the gravly bar along the edge of the river for the tracks of the men, knowing from the appearance of the river at this place that if they had passed they would have used the cord on the side where I was. I saw no tracks and was then fully convinced that they were below me. I fired my gun and hallooed but counld hear nothing of them.

By this time it was getting nearly dark and a duck lit on the shore in about 40 steps of me and I killed it; having now secured my supper I looked our [out?] for a suitable place to amuse myself in combating the musquetoes for the ballance of the evening. I found a parsel of drift wood at the head of the little Island on which I was and immediately set it on fire and collected some willow brush to lye on. I cooked my duck which I found very good and after eating it layed down and should have had a comfortable nights lodge but for the musquetoes which infested me all night.

Late at night I was awakened by the nois of some animal runing over the stoney bar on which I lay but did not see it; from the weight with which it ran I supposed it to be either an Elk or a brown bear. The latter are very abundant in this neighbourhood. The night was cool but I felt very little inconvenience from it as I had a large fire all night. Capt. Clark had proceeded on after I seperated from him and encamped on a island only about 2 miles below me but did not hear the report of my gun nor of my hooping. I saw some deer and antelopes. . . .

[LEWIS:] *Wednesday July* 31st 1805.

This morning I waited at my camp very impatiently for the arrival of Capt. Clark and party; I observed by my watch that it was 7. A. M. and they had not come in sight. I now became very uneasy and determined to wait until 8 and if they did not arrive by that time to proceed on up the river taking it as a fact that they had passed my camp some miles last evening. Just as I set out to pursue my plan I discovered Charbono walking up shore some distance below me and waited untill [he] arrived.

I now learnt that the canoes were behind, they arrived shortly after. Their detention had been caused by the rapidity of the water and the circuitous rout of the river. They halted and breakfasted after which we all set out again and I continued my walk on the Stard. shore. . . .

. . . This evening just before we encamped Drewyer discovered a brown bear enter a small cops of bushes on the Lard. side; we surrounded the place an[d] surched the brush but he had escaped in some manner unperceived but how we could not discover. Nothing killed today and our fresh meat is out. When we have a plenty of fresh meat I find it impossible to make the men take any care of it, or use it with the least frugallity. Tho' I expect that necessity will shortly teach them this art.

The mountiains on both sides of the river at no great distance are very lofty. We have a lame crew just now, two with tumers or bad boils on various parts of them, one with a bad stone bruise, one with his arm accedently dislocated but fortunately well replaced, and a fifth has streigned his back by sliping and falling backwards on the gunwall of the canoe. The latter is Sergt. Gass. It gives him great pain to work in the canoe in his present situation, but he thinks he can walk with convenience, I therefore scelected him as one of the party to accompany me to-morrow, being determined to go in quest of the Snake Indians. I also directed Drewyer and Charbono to hold themselves in readiness. Charbono thinks that his ankle is sufficiently recovered to stand the march but I entertain my doubts of the fact; he is very anxious to accompany me and I therefore indulge him. . . .

[Lewis:] *Thursday August* 1st 1805.

This morning we set out early and proceeded on tolerably well untill 8 OC'k by which time we had arrived within a few miles of a mountain through which the river passes. We halted on the Stard. side and took breakfast. After which or at *1/2* after 8.A.M. as had been previously concerted betwe[e]n Capt. Clark and myself I set out with three men in surch of the Snake Indians or Sosonees. Our rout lay over a high range of mountains on the North side of the river. Capt C. recommended this rout to me no doubt from a beleif that the river as soon as it passed this chain of mountains boar to the N. of W. he having on the 26th ult. ascended these mountains to a position from whence he discovered a large valley passing between the mountains which boar to the N.W. and presumed that the river passed in that direction; this however proved to be the passage of a large creek which discharged itself into the river just above this range of mountains, the river bearing to the S.W. We were therefore thrown several miles out of our rout. As soon as we discovered our error we directed our course to the river which we at length gained about 2 P.M. much exhausted by the heat of the day, the roughness of the road and the want of water.

The mountains are extreemly bare of timber, and our rout lay through the steep and narrow hollows of the mountains exposed to the intense heat of the midday sun without shade or scarcely a breath of air: to add to my fatiegue in this walk of about 11 milles, I had taken a doze of glauber salts in the morning in consequence of a slight disentary with which I had been afflicted for several days. Being weakened by the disorder and the operation of the medicine I found myself almost exhausted before we reached the river.

I felt my sperits much revived on our near approach to the river at the sight of a herd of Elk, of which Drewyer and myself soon killed a couple. We then hurryed to the river and allayed our thirst. I ordered two of the men to skin the Elk and bring the meat to the river, while myself and the other prepared a fire and cooked some of the meat for our dinner. We made a comfortable meal on the Elk, and left the ballance of the meat and skins on the bank of the river for Capt. Clark and party. This supply will no doubt be acceptable to them, as they had had no fresh meat when I left them for almost 2 days except one beaver; game being very scarce and shy above the forks. We had seen a few deer and antelopes but had not been fortunate enough to kill any of them.

As I passed these mountains I saw a flock of the black or dark brown phesants; the young phesant is almost grown. We killed one of them. This bird is fully a third larger than the common phesant of the Atlantic states. It's form is much the same. It is booted nearly to the toes and the male has not the tufts of long black feathers on the sides of the neck which are so conspicuous in those of the Atlantic. Their colour is a uniform dark brown with a small mixture of yellow or yelloish brown specks on some of the feathers particularly those of the tail, tho' the extremities of these are perfectly black for about one inch. The eye is nearly black, the iris has a small dash of yellowish brown. The feathers of the tail are reather longer than that of our phesant or partridge as they are Called in the Eastern States; are the same in number or eighteen and all nearly of the same length, those in the intermediate part being somewhat longest. The flesh of this bird is white and agreeably flavored.

I also saw near the top of the mountain among some scattering pine a blue bird about the size of the common robbin. It's action and form is somewhat that of the jay bird and never rests long in any one position but constantly flying or hoping from sprey to sprey. I shot at one of them but missed it. Their note is loud and frequently repeated both flying and when at rest and is char ah', cha'r-ah, char-ah', as nearly as letters can express it.

After dinner we resumed our march and my pack felt much lighter than it had done about 2 hours before. We traveled about six miles further and encamped on the stard bank of the river, making a distance of 17 miles for this day. The Musquetoes were troublesome but I had taken the precaution of bringing my bier. . . .

[CLARK:] *August* 1st *Wednesday* 1805

A fine day. Capt. Lewis left me at 8 oClock. Just below the place I entered a verrey high mountain which jutted its treme[n]-dious Clifts on either Side for 9 Miles. The rocks ragide, Some verry dark & other part verry light rock; the light rocks is Sand Stone. The water Swift & very Sholey. I killed a *Ibix* on which the whole party Dined. After passing through the Mountain we entered a wide exte[n]sive Vallie of from 4 to 8 Miles, wide verry leavell. A Creek falls in at the Commencement of this Vallie on the Lard Side, the river widens & spreds into Small Chanels. W[e] encamped on the Lard Side opposit a large Creek. I sent out Jo. & R Fields to hunt this evening. They killed 5 Deer. I saw a large Bear eateing Currents this evining. The river so rapid that the greatest exertion is required by all to get the boats on. . . .

[LEWIS:] *Friday August* 2nd 1805.

We resumed our march this morning at sunrise; the [day] was fair and wind from N.W. Finding that the river still boar to the South I determined to pass it if possible in order to shorten our rout; this we effected by wading the river about 5 miles above our encampment of the last evening. We found the current very rapid waist deep and about 90 yds. wide. Bottom smooth pebble with a small mixture of coarse gravel. This is the first time that I ever dared to wade the river, tho' there are many places between this and the forks where I presume it might be attempted with equal success.

The valley along which we passed today, and through which the river winds it's meandering course is from 6 to 8 miles wide and consists of a bea[u]tifull level plain with but little timber and that confined to the verge of the river; the land is tolerably fertile, and is either black or a dark yellow loam, covered with grass from 9 inches to 2 feet high. The plain ascends gradually on either side of the river to the bases of two ranges of high mountains, which lye parallel to the river and prescribe the limits of the plains. The tops of these mountains are yet covered partially with snow, while we in the valley are nearly suffocated with the intense heat of the mid-day sun; the nights are so cold that two blankets are not more than sufficient covering.

Soon after passing the river this morning Sergt. Gass lost my tommahawk in the thick brush and we were unable to find it, I regret the loss of this usefull implement, however accedents will happen in the best families, and I consoled myself with the recollection that it was not the only one we had with us.

The bones of the buffaloe and their excrement of an old date are to be met with in every part of this valley but we have long since lost all hope of meeting with that animal in these mountains. We met with great quantities of currants today, two species of which were red, others yellow, deep perple and black; also black goosberries and serviceberries now ripe and in great perfection. We feasted sumptuously on our wild fruits, particularly the yellow currant and the deep perple serviceberries, which I found to be excellent. The serviceberry grows on a small bush and differs from ours only in colour size and superior excellence of it's flavour. It is somewhat larger than ours.

On our way we saw an abundance of deer (and) Antelopes, of the former we killed 2. We also saw many tracks of the Elk and bear.

No recent appearance of Indians. The Indians in this part of the country appear to construct their lodges with the willow boughs and brush; they are small of a conic figure and have a small aperture on one side through which they enter.

We continued our rout up this valley on the Lard. side of the river untill sunset, at which time we encamped on the Lard. bank of the river having traveled 24 miles. We had brought with us a good stock of venison of which we eat a hearty supper. I feel myself perfectly recovered of my indisposition, and do not doubt being able to pursue my rout tomorrow with the same comfort I have done today.

We saw some very large beaver dams today in the bottoms of the river several of which wer five feet high and overflowed several acres of land; these dams are formed of willow brush mud and gravel and are closely interwoven that they resist the water perfectly. The base of this work is thick and rises nearly perpendicularly on the lower side while the upper side or that within the dam is gently sloped. The brush appear to be laid in no regular order yet acquires a strength by the irregularity with which they are placed by the beaver that it would puzzle the engenuity of man to give them. . . .

[CLARK:] *August* 2nd *Friday* 1805

A fine day, set out early. The river has much the Same kind of banks, Chanel, Current &c. as it had in the last Vallie. I walked out this morning on Shore & Saw Several rattle Snakes in the plain. The wind from the NW we proceeded on with great dificuelty from the rapidity of the current & rapids abt 15 miles and Encamped on the Lard Side. Saw a large Gangue of Elk at Sunset to the SW. Passed a Small Creek on the Stard. Side called Birth Creek and maney large and Small Islands. Saw a number of young Ducks as we have also Seen everry Day, Some geese. I saw Black woodpeckers. I have either got my foot bitten by Some poisonous insect or a tumer is riseing on the inner bone of my ankle which is painfull.

[LEWIS:] *Saturday August* 3rd 1805.

Set out early this morning, or before sunrise; still continued our march through the level valley on the lard. side of the river. The valley much as yesterday only reather wider; I think it 12 Miles wide, tho' the plains near the mountains rise higher and are more broken with some scattering pine near the mountain. In the leaveler parts of the plain and river bottoms which are very extensive there is no timber except a scant proportion of cottonwood near the river. The under wood consists of the narrow leafed or small willow, the small honeysuckle, rosebushes, currant, serviceberry, and goosbery bushes; also a small species of berch in but small quantities, the leaf of which is oval, finely indented, small and of a deep green colour. The stem is simple ascending and branching, and seldom rises higher than 10 or 12 feet. The Mountains continue high on either side of the valley, and are but scantily supplyed with timber; small pine apears to be the prevalent growth; it is of the pi[t]ch kind, with a short leaf.

At 11 A.M. Drewyer killed a doe and we halted about 2 hours and breakfasted, and then continued our rout untill night without halting, when we arrived at the river in a level bottom which appeared to spread to greater extent than usual. From the appearance of the timber I supposed that the river forked above us and resolved to examine this part of the river minutely tomorrow.

This evening we passed through a high plain for about 8 miles covered with prickley pears and bearded grass, tho' we found this even better walking than the wide bottoms of the river, which we passed in the evening; these altho' apparently level, from some cause which I know not, were formed into meriads of deep holes as if rooted up by hogs; these the grass covered so thick that it was impossible to walk without the risk of falling down at every step. Some parts of these bottoms also possess excellent terf or peat, I beleive of many feet deep. The mineral salts also frequently mentioned on the Missouri we saw this evening in these uneven bottoms.

We saw many deer, Antelopes, ducks, gees, some beaver and great appearance of their work. Also a small bird and the Curlooe as usual. We encamped on the river bank on Lard. side having traveled by estimate 23 Miles.

The fish of this part of the river are trout and a species of scale fish of a white colour and a remarkable small long mouth which one of our men inform us are the same with the species called in the Eastern states *bottlenose*.

The snowey region of the mountains and for some distance below has no timber or herbage of any kind; the timber is confined to the lower and middle regions.

. . . The men wer compelled to be a great proportion of their time in the water today; they have had a severe days labour and are much fortiegued. . . .

[CLARK:] *August 3rd Saturday* 1805

A fine morning, wind from the NE. I walked on Shore & killed a Deer. In my walk I saw a fresh track which I took to be an Indian from the Shape of the foot as the toes turned in, I think it probable that this Indian Spied our fires and Came to a Situation to view us from the top of a Small knob on the Lard Side.

The river more rapid and Sholey than yesterday. One man R. F. killed a large *Panthor* on the Shore.

We are oblige to haul over the Sholes [the] Canoes in maney places where the Islands are noumerous and bottom Sholey, in the evening the river more rapid and Sholey we encamped on an Island above a part of the river which passed thro a rockey bed enclosed on both sides with thick willow Current & red buries &c. &c.

Passed a bold Stream which heads in the mountains to our right and the drean of the monting Snow in the Montn on that side ar in View. At 4 oClock passed a bold Stream which falls from a Mountn in three Channels to our left. The Greater portion of the Snow on this mountain is melted, but little remaining near us.

Some Deer Elk & antelopes & Bear in the bottoms. But fiew trees and they Small. The Mountains on our left Contain pine. those on our right but verry partially Supplied and what pine & cedar it has is on the Lower region, no wood being near the Snow. Great numbers of Beaver Otter &c. Some fish, trout & bottle nose. Birds as usial. Geese young Ducks & Curlows.

[CLARK:] *August* 4th *Sunday*. 1805.

A fine morning, cool. Proceeded on verry early and Brackfast at the Camp. Capt. Lewis left yesterday morning. At this Camp he left a note informing that he discovered no fresh Sign of Indians &c. The river continued to be crouded with Islands, Sholey rapid & clear. I could not walk on Shore to day as my ankle was sore from a tumer on that part. The method we are compelled to take to get on is fatigueing & laborious in the extreen, haul the Canoes over the rapids, which Suckceed each other every two or three hundred yards and between the water rapid oblige to tow & walke on stones the whole day except when we have poleing. Men wet all day, sore feet &c. &c. . . .

[LEWIS:] *Monday August* 5th 1805.

As Charbono complained of being unable to march far today I ordered him and Sergt. Gass to pass the rappid river near our camp and proceed at their leasure through the level bottom to a point of high timber about seven miles distant on the middle fork which was in view; I gave them my pack, that of Drewyer and the meat which we had, directing them to remain at that place untill we joined them. I took Drewyer with me and continued my rout up the stard. side of the river about 4 miles and then waded it; found it so rapid and shallow that it was impossible to navigate it. Continued up it on the Lard. side about 1 ½ miles further, when the mountains put in close on both sides and arrose to great hight, partially covered with snow. From hence the course of the river was to the East of North.

I took the advantage of a high projecting spur of the mountain which with some difficulty we ascended to its summit in about half an hour. From this emmance I had a pleasing view of the valley through which I had passed many miles below and the continuation of the middle fork through the valley equally wide above me to the distance of about 20 miles when that also appeared to enter the mountains and disappeared to my view; however the mountains which termineate the valley in this direction appeared much lower than those up either of the other forks. On the rapid fork they appeared still to rise, the one range towering above another as far as I could perceive them. The middle fork as I suspected dose bear considerably to the West of South and the gap formed by it in the mountains after the valley terminates is in the same direction. Under these circumstances I did not hesitate in beleiving the middle fork the most proper for us to ascend. About South from me, the middle fork approached within about 5 miles.

I resolved to pass across the plains to it and return to Gass and Charbòno, accordingly we set out and decended the mountain among some steep and difficult precipices of rocks. Here Drewyer missed his step and had a very dangerous fall, he sprained one of his fingers and hirt his leg very much. In fifteen or 20 minutes he was able to proceed and we continued our rout to the river where we had desighned to interscept it. I quenched my thirst and rested a few minutes examined the river and found it still very navigable.

An old indian road very large and plain leads up this fork, but I could see no tracks except those of horses which appeared to have passed early in the spring. As the river mad[e] a great bend to the South East we again ascended the high plain and steered our course as streight as we could to the point where I had directed Gass and Sharbono to remain. We passed the plain, regained the bottom and struck the river about 3 miles above them; by this time it was perfectly dark & we hooped but could hear no tidings of them. We had struck the river at the point of timber to which I had directed them, but [they] having mistaken a point of woods lower down, had halted short of the place. We continued our rout after dark down the bottom through thick brush of the pulppy leafed thorn and prickly pears for about 2 hours when we arrived at their camp.

They had a small quantity of meat left which Drewyer and myself eat it being the first we had taisted today. We had traveled about 25 miles. I soon laid down and slept very soundly untill morning.

I saw no deer today nor any game except a few Antelopes which were very shy. . . .

[CLARK:] *August* 5th *Monday* 1805

A cold clear morning, the wind from the S. E. The river Streight & much more rapid than yesterday, I sent out Jo. & R. Fields to kill some meat; they killed two Deer & we brackfast on one of them and proceeded on with great dificuelity from the rapidity of the Current, and [in]numerable rapids we had to encounter.

At 4 o'Clock PM Murcery 49 . . . , passed the mouth of principal fork which falls in on the Lard. Side, this fork is about the size of the Stard. one, less water reather not to rapid, its Course as far as can be seen is S.E. & appear to pass through between two mountains, the NW. fork being the one most in our course i. e. S. 25 W. as far as I can See, deturmind me to take this fork as the principal and the one most proper the S E fork is of a Greenish Colour & contains but little timber. The SW fork contains more timber than is below for some distance, we assended this fork about one mile and Encamped on an Island which had been laterly overflown & was wet. We raised our bead on bushes. We passed a part of the river above the forks which was divided and Scattered thro' the willows in such a manner as to render it dificuelt to pass through for a 1/4 of a mile, we were oblige to Cut our way thro' the willows.

Men much fatigued from their excessive labours in hauling the Canoes over the rapids &c. Verry weak being in the water all day. My foot verry painfull.

[LEWIS:] *Tuesday August* 6th 1805.

We set out this morning very early on our return to the forks. Having nothing to eat I se[n]t Drewyer to the woodlands to my left in order to kill a deer, sent Sergt. Gass to the right with orders to keep sufficiently near to discover Capt. C and the party should they be on their way up that stream, and with Sharbono I directed my course to the main forks through the bottom directing the others to meet us there. About five miles above the forks I hea[r]d the hooping of the party to my left and changed my rout towards them; on my arrival found that they had taken the rapid fork and learnt from Capt. Clark that he had not found the note which I had left for him at that place and the reasons which had induced him to ascend this stream. It was easeist & more in our direction, and apd to contain as much water. He had however previously to my comeing up with him, met Drewyer who informed him of the state of the two rivers and was on his return. One of their canoes had just overset and all the baggage wet, the medecine box among other articles and several articles lost a shot pouch and horn with all the implements for one rifle lost and never recovered. I walked down to the point where I waited their return.

On their arrival found that two other canoes had filled with water and wet their cargoes completely. Whitehouse had been thrown out of one of the canoes as she swing in a rapid current and the canoe had rubed him and pressed him to the bottom as she passed over him and had the water been 2 inches shallower must inevitably have crushed him to death. Our parched meal, corn, Indian preasents, and a great part of our most valuable stores were wet and much damaged on this ocasion. To examine, dry and arrange our stores was the first object; we therefore passed over to the lard. side opposite to the entrance of the rapid fork where there was a large gravly bar that answered our purposes; wood was also convenient and plenty. Here we fixed our camp, and unloaded all our canoes and opened and exposed to dry such articles as had been wet. A part of the load of each canoe consisted of the leaden canestirs of powder which were not in least injured, tho' some of them had remained upwards of an hour under water. About 20 lbs. of powder which we had in a tight Keg or at l[e]ast one which we thought sufficiently so got wet and intirely spoiled. This would have been the case with the other had it not have been for the expedient which I had fallen on of securing the powder by means of the lead having the latter formed into canesters which were filled with the necessary proportion of po[w]der to discharge the lead when used, and those canesters well secured with corks and wax. In this country the air is so pure and dry that any vessel however well seasoned the timber may be will give way or shrink unless it is kept full of some liquid.

We found that three deer skins which we had left at a considerable hight on a tree were taken off which we supposed had been done by a panther. We sent out some men to hunt this evening, they killed 3 deer and four Elk which gave us a plentifull supply of meat once more. Shannon had been dispatched up the rapid fork this morning to hunt, by Capt Clark before he met with Drewyer or learnt his mistake in the rivers. When he returned he sent Drewyer in surch of him, but he rejoined us this evening and reported that he had been several miles up the river and could find nothing of him. We had the trumpet sounded and fired several guns but he did not join us this evening. I am fearful he is lost again. This is the same man who was seperated from us 15 days as we came up the Missouri and subsisted 9 days of that time on grapes only.

Whitehouse is in much pain this evening with the injury one of his legs sustained from the canoe today at the time it upset and swing over him. Capt Clarks ankle is also very painfull to him. We should have given the party a days rest some where near this place had not this accedent happened, as I had determined to take some observations to fix the Latitude and longitude of these forks.

Our merchandize medecine &c are not sufficiently dry this evening; we covered them securely for the evening. . . .

[Lewis:] *Wednesday August* 7th 1805

The morning being fair we spread our stores to dry at an early hour. Dispatched Reubin Fields in surch of Shannon. Our stores were now so much exhausted that we found we could proceed with one canoe less, we therefore drew out one of them into a thicket of brush and secured her in such manner that the water could not take her off should the river rise to the hight where she is. The creek which falls in above us we called *turf creek* from the cercu[m]stance of it's bottoms being composed of excellent turf.

My air gun was out of order and her sights had been removed by some accedent I put her in order and regulated her. She shot again as well as she ever did. The clouds last night prevented my taking any lunar observations. This day I took Equal Altitudes . . . with Sextant. . . .

At one oclock all our baggage was dry; we therefore packed it up reloaded the canoes and the party proceeded with Capt. Clark up Jefferson's river. I remained with Sergt. Gass to complete the observation of equal altitudes and joined them in the evening at their camp on the Lard. side just above the entance of turf creek.

We had a shower of rain which continued about 40 minutes attended with thunder and lightning. This shower wet me perfectly before I reached the camp. The clouds continued during the night in such manner that I was unable to obtain any lunar observations. This evening Drewyer brought in a deer which he had killed. We have not heard any thing from Shannon yet, we expect that he has pursued Wisdom river upwards for som[e] distance probably killed some heavy animal and is waiting our arrival.

The large biteing fly or hare fly as they [are] sometimes called are very troublesome to us. I observe two kinds of them a large black species and a small brown species with a green head. The musquetoes are not as troublesome as they were below, but are still in considerable quantities. The eye knats have disappeared. The green or blowing flies are still in swarms. . . .

[LEWIS:] *Thursday August* 8th 1805.

We had a heavy dew this morning. As one canoe had been left we had now more ha[n]ds to spear for the chase; game being scarce it requires more hunters to supply us. We therefore dispatched four this morning. We set out at sunrise and continued our rout up the river which we find much more gentle and deep than below the entrance of Wisdom river. It is from 35 to 45 yards wide very crooked many short bends constituteing large and general bends; insomuch that altho' we travel briskly and a considerable distance yet it takes us only a few miles on our general course or rout. . . .

At Noon Reubin Fields arrived and reported that he had been up Wisdom river some miles above where it entered the mountain and could find nothing of Shannon, he had killed a deer and an Antelope. Great quantity of beaver Otter and musk-rats in these rivers. Two of the hunters we sent out this morning returned at noon had killed each a deer and an Antelope. . . .

The hunters brought in another deer this evening. The tumor on Capt. Clarks ankle has discharged a considerable quantity of matter but is still much swolen and inflamed and gives him considerable pain.

Saw a number of Gees ducks and some Crains today. The former begin to fly. The evening again proved cloudy much to my mortification and prevented my making any lunar observations.

The Indian woman {Sacagawea} recognized the point of a high plain to our right which she informed us was not very distant from the summer retreat of her nation on a river beyond the mountains which runs to the west. This hill she says her nation calls the beaver's head from a conceived re[se]mblance of it's figure to the head of that animal.[2] She assures us that we shall either find her people on this river or on the river immediately west of it's source; which from it's present size cannot be very distant. As it is now all important with us to meet with those people as soon as possible I determined to proceed tomorrow with a small party to the source of the principal stream of this river and pass the mountains to the Columbia; and down that river untill I found the Indians; in short it is my resolusion to find them or some others, who have horses if it should cause me a trip of one month. For without horses we shall be obliged to leave a great part of our stores, of which, it appears to me that we have a stock already sufficiently small for the length of the voyage before us.[3]

[LEWIS:] *Friday August* 9th 1805.

The morning was fair and fine; we set out at an early hour and proceeded on very well. Some parts of the river more rapid than yesterday. I walked on shore across the land to a point which I presumed they would reach by 8. A. M. our usual time of halting. By this means I acquired leasure to accomplish some wrightings which I conceived from the nature of my instructions necessary

2. "The Beaverhead lies about twelve miles south from Twin Bridges and eighteen miles north (by road) from Dillon, Mont.; but it is generally known as the Point of Rocks. Less than thirty miles from it is the 'Rattlesnake Cliff' of Lewis and Clark, which in shape bears as striking a resemblance to a beaver's head as does the other cliffs and it is accordingly known in that region as the Beaverhead." [Note by O.D. Wheeler.]

3. The historian John Bakeless reminds us here that "This is the first hint of what Sacagawea's real service was to be. Again she gives a little geographical information. But the important problem now is horses; and it was the meeting with Sacagawea's own band [of Shoshone]—a meeting she now predicts and at which she would serve as translator—that provided the horses with which to cross the Rockies." (*The Journals of Lewis and Clark: A New Selection.* New York: Mentor, 1964. 221.)

lest any accedent should befall me on the long and reather hazardous rout I was now about to take.

The party did not arrive and I returned about a mile and met them, here they halted and we breakfasted; I had killed two fine gees on my return. While we halted here Shannon arrived, and informed us that having missed the party the day on which he set out he had returned the next morning to the place from whence he had set out or furst left them and not finding [them] that he had supposed that they wer above him; that he then set out and marched one day up wisdom river, by which time he was convinced that they were not above him as the river could not be navigated; he then returned to the forks and had pursued us up this river. He brought the skins of three deer which he had killed which he said were in good order. He had lived very plentifully this trip but looked a good deel worried with his march. . . .

[LEWIS:] *Saturday August* 10th 1805.

We set out very early this morning and continued our rout through the wide bottom on the Lard. side of the river. After passing a large creek at about 5 miles we fel in with a plain Indian road which led towards the point that the river entered the mountain we therefore pursued the road. I sent Drewyer to the wright to kill a deer which we saw feeding and halted on the river under an immencely high perpendicular clift of rocks where it entered the mountain; here we kindled a fire and waited for Drewyer. He arrived in about an hour and a half or at noon with three deer skins and the flesh of one of the best of them; we cooked and eat a haisty meal and departed, returning a short distance to the Indian road which led us the best way over the mountains, which are not very high but are ruggid and approach the river closely on both sides.

Just below these mountains I saw several bald Eagles and two large white headed fishinghawks; boath these birds were the same common to our country. From the number of rattle snakes about the Clifts at which we halted we called them the rattle snake clifts. This serpent is the same before discribed with oval spots of yellowish brown. The river below the mountains is rapid rocky, very crooked, much divided by islands and withal shallow. After it enters the mountains it's bends are not so circuetous and it's general course more direct, but it is equally shallow les[s] divided more rocky and rapid.

We continued our rout along the Indian road which led us sometimes over the hills and again in the narrow bottoms of the river till at the distance of fifteen Mf from the rattle snake Clifts we arrived in a ha[n]dsome open and leavel vally where the river divided itself nearly into two equal branches; here I halted and examined those streams and readily discovered from their size that it would be vain to attempt the navigation of either any further.[4] . . .

There is scarcely any timber on the river above the Rt. Snake Clifts, nor is there anything larger than willow brush in sight of these forks. Immediately in the level plain between the forks and about ½ a mile distance from them stands a high rocky mountain, the base of which is surrounded by the level plain; it has a singular appearance. The mountains do not appear very high in any direction tho' the tops of some of them are partially covered with snow. This convinces me that we have ascended to a great hight since we have entered the rocky Mountains, yet the ascent has been so gradual along the vallies that it was scarcely perceptable by land. I do not beleive that the world can furnish an example of a river runing to the extent which the Missouri and Jefferson's rivers do through such a mountainous country and at the same time so navigable as they are. If the Columbia furnishes us such another example, a communication across the continent by water will be practicable and safe. But this I can scarcely hope from a knowledge of its having in it[s] comparitively short course to the ocean the same number of feet to decend which the Missouri and Mississippi have from this point to the Gulph of Mexico. . . .

SOURCE: *Original Journals of the Lewis and Clark Expedition: 1804–1806.* Vol. 2. Edited by Reuben Gold Thwaites. New York; Dodd, Mead and Company, 1904.

4. "The southeast fork is the true Jefferson or Missouri River; the western branch is the present Prairie Creek. Their junction is very nearly on the parallel of 45 degrees N. latitude, and in the neighborhood of Grayling, Montana." [Note by Reuben Gold Thwaites.]

RED JACKET, SAGOYEWATHA

The foremost embodiment of the tradition of Iroquois oratory and probably the greatest of orators in Native American history, Red Jacket (c. 1751–1830) was—unlike, for instance, Pontiac, Tecumseh, Black Hawk or Sitting Bull—no warrior. His fiery, incisive eloquence, however, inspired cultural pride and tribal resistance, and sometimes even affected the behavior of his non-Indian auditors. He understood English, but determinedly refused to speak it in public. His Seneca name, Sagoyewatha, means "He is prepared." In the following speech, he answered a young missionary named Cram who had come to convert the Senecas to Christianity.

You Have Got Our Country, but Are Not Satisfied (1805)

FRIEND AND BROTHER; it was the will of the Great Spirit that we should meet together this day. He orders all things, and he has given us a fine day for our council. He has taken his garment from before the sun, and caused it to shine with brightness upon us; our eyes are opened, that we see clearly; our ears are unstopped, that we have been able to hear distinctly the words that you have spoken; for all these favors we thank the Great Spirit, and him only.

Brother, this council fire was kindled by you; it was at your request that we came together at this time; we have listened with attention to what you have said. You requested us to speak our minds freely; this gives us great joy, for we now consider that we stand upright before you, and can speak what we think; all have heard your voice, and all speak to you as one man; our minds are agreed.

Brother, you say you want an answer to your talk before you leave this place. It is right you should have one, as you are a great distance from home, and we do not wish to detain you; but we will first look back a little, and tell you what our fathers have told us, and what we have heard from the white people.

Brother, listen to what we say. There was a time when our forefathers owned this great island. Their seats extended from the rising to the setting sun. The Great Spirit had made it for the use of Indians. He had created the buffalo, the deer, and other animals for food. He made the bear and the beaver, and their skins served us for clothing. He had scattered them over the country, and taught us how to take them. He had caused the earth to produce corn for bread. All this he had done for his red children because he loved them. If we had any disputes about hunting grounds, they were generally settled without the shedding of much blood. But an evil day came upon us; your forefathers crossed the great waters, and landed on this island. Their numbers were small; they found friends, and not enemies; they told us they had fled from their own country for fear of wicked men, and come here to enjoy their religion. They asked for a small seat; we took pity on them, granted their request, and they sat down amongst us; we gave them corn and meat; they gave us poison in return. The white people had now found our country; tidings were carried back, and more came amongst us; yet we did not fear them, we took them to be friends; they called us brothers; we believed them, and gave them a larger seat. At length, their numbers had greatly increased; they wanted more land; they wanted our country. Our eyes were opened, and our minds became uneasy. Wars took place; Indians were hired to fight against Indians, and many of our people were destroyed. They also brought strong liquor among us; it was strong and powerful, and has slain thousands.

Brother, our seats were once large, and yours were very small; you have now become a great people, and we have scarcely a place left to spread our blankets; you have got our country, but are not satisfied; you want to force your religion upon us.

Brother, continue to listen. You say you are sent to instruct us how to worship the Great Spirit agreeably to his mind, and if we do not take hold of the religion which you white people teach, we shall be unhappy hereafter. You say that you are right, and we are lost; how do we know this to be true? We understand that your religion is written in a book; if it was intended for us as well as you, why has not the Great Spirit given it to us, and not only to us, but why did he not give to our forefathers the knowledge of that book, with the means of understanding it rightly? We only know what you tell us about it. How shall we know when to believe, being so often deceived by the white people?

Brother, you say there is but one way to worship and serve the Great Spirit; if there is but one religion, why do you white people differ so much about it? Why not all agree, as you can all read the book?

Brother, we do not understand these things. We are told that your religion was given to your forefathers, and has been handed down from father to son. We also have a religion which was given to our forefathers, and has been handed down to us their children. We worship that way. It teacheth us to be thankful for all the favors we receive; to love each other, and to be united. We never quarrel about religion.

Brother, the Great Spirit has made us all; but he has made a great difference between his white and red children; he has given us a different complexion, and different customs; to you he has given the arts; to these he has not opened our eyes; we know these things to be true. Since he has made so great a difference between us in other things, why may we not conclude that he has given us a different religion according to our understanding. The Great Spirit does right; he knows what is best for his children; we are satisfied.

Brother, we do not wish to destroy your religion, or take it from you; we only want to enjoy our own.

Brother, you say you have not come to get our land or our money, but to enlighten our minds. I will now tell you that I have been at your meetings, and saw you collecting money from the meeting. I cannot tell what this money was intended for, but suppose it was for your minister; and if we should conform to your way of thinking, perhaps you may want some from us.

Brother, we are told that you have been preaching to the white people in this place. These people are our neighbors; we are acquainted with them; we will wait a little while, and see what effect your preaching has upon them. If we find it does them good, makes them honest and less disposed to cheat Indians, we will then consider again what you have said.

Brother, you have now heard our answer to your talk, and this is all we have to say at present. As we are going to part, we will come and take you by the hand, and hope the Great Spirit will protect you on your journey, and return you safe to your friends.

SOURCE: Daniel Drake. *Lives of Celebrated American Indians.* Boston: Bradbury, Soden & Co., 1843.

We Are Determined Not to Sell Our Lands
(1811)

Introducing this speech, the biographer William L. Stone writes: "In the Spring of 1811 an attempt was made by the New-York Company holding the pre-emptive title to the reservations within the Morris, or Holland Purchase, to divest the Indians of their rights by negotiation and purchase. The agent employed by the Company was a Mr. Richardson. He met the chiefs in council at Buffalo Creek [in present-day New York State], in May, and after opening his business, awaited their reply, which was made by Red-Jacket, a few days afterward . . ."[1]

BROTHER: WE OPENED our ears to the talk you lately delivered to us, at our Council fire. In doing important business it is best not to tell long stories, but to come to it in a few words. We therefore shall not repeat your talk, which is fresh in our minds. We have well considered it, and the advantages and disadvantages of your offers. We request your attention to our answer, which is not from the speaker alone, but from all the Sachems and Chiefs now around our Council fire.

Brother: We know that great men as well as great nations, having different interests have different minds, and do not see the same subject in the same light,—but we hope our answer will be agreeable to you and to your employers.

Brother: Your application for the purchase of our lands is to our minds very extraordinary. It has been made in a crooked manner,—you have not walked in the straight path pointed out by the great Council of your nation. You have no writings from our great father the President.

Brother: In making up our minds we have looked back, and remembered how the Yorkers purchased our lands in former times. They bought them piece after piece for a little money paid to a few men in our nation, and not to all our brethren; our planting and hunting grounds have become very small, and if we sell these we know not where to spread our blankets.

Brother: You tell us your employers have purchased of the Council of Yorkers a right to buy our lands,—we do not understand how this can be,—the lands do not belong to the Yorkers; they are ours, and were given to us by the Great Spirit.

---

1. William L. Stone. *Life and Times of Red-Jacket, Or Sa-go-ye-wat-ha: Being the Sequel to the History of the Six Nations.* New York: Wiley and Putnam, 1841.

Brother: We think it strange that you should jump over the lands of our brethren in the East, to come to our Council fire so far off, to get our lands. When we sold our lands in the East to the white people, we determined never to sell those we kept, which are as small as we can live comfortably on.

Brother: You want us to travel with you, and look for other lands. If we should sell our lands and move off into a distant country, towards the setting sun, we should be looked upon in the country to which we go as foreigners, and strangers, and be despised by the red as well as the white men, and we should soon be surrounded by the white men, who will there also kill our game, come upon our lands, and try to get them from us.

Brother: We are determined not to sell our lands, but to continue on them,—we like them,—they are fruitful and produce us corn in abundance, for the support of our women and children, and grass and herbs for our cattle.

Brother: At the treaties held for the purchase of our lands, the white men with sweet voices and smiling faces told us they loved us, and that they would not cheat us, but that the king's children on the other side the lake would cheat us. When we go on the other side the lake the king's children tell us your people will cheat us, but with sweet voices and smiling faces assure us of their love and that they will not cheat us. These things puzzle our heads, and we believe that the Indians must take care of themselves, and not trust either in your people or in the king's children.

Brother: At a late Council we requested our agents to tell you that we would not sell our lands, and we think you have not spoken to our agents, or they would have informed you so, and we should not have met you at our Council fire at this time.

Brother: The white people buy and sell false rights to our lands; your employers have, you say, paid a great price for their right; they must have plenty of money, to spend it in buying false rights to lands belonging to Indians; the loss of it will not hurt them, but our lands are of great value to us, and we wish you to go back with your talk to your employers, and to tell them and the Yorkers that they have no right to buy and sell false rights to our lands.

Brother: We hope you clearly understand the words we have spoken. This is all we have to say.

[**William L. Stone:**] *Thus, as in the great majority of their speeches, the Indians were still endeavoring to brace themselves against what they* *considered to be the inordinate rapacity of the whites, in the acquisition of their lands. This disposition of the white man to grasp at all their property, with a view, as it appeared, of driving them from the face of the earth, was then, as it is now, and probably ever will be until the race becomes extinct, the source of their jealousy, and the burden of their complaint. Notwithstanding the rapid diminution of their numbers, and their increasingly depressed condition, they still felt that they were independent nations, and they were tenacious of that character. They believed that they had been placed on "this island" by the Great Spirit, and that he had created it for their sole benefit, and they held that nobody could have a right to dispossess them. Hence nothing could have been more inopportune than an effort made at this very council, by a missionary society in the city of New-York, to establish a Christian mission among them. The former attempts had left no favorable impression upon the mind of Red-Jacket, now their principal civil chief. On the contrary, he had imbibed a fixed and deep-rooted hatred to the system, countenancing, as he supposed, a course of policy on the part of its professors that would eventually sap the foundations of the happiness, and work the ruin of his people. Least of all was it an auspicious moment to strive farther to persuade them to change their religion, at the very time when those who called themselves Christians were renewing their efforts to dispossess them of their few remaining roods of ground. Hence the following reply, by Red-Jacket, to the advances of the Rev. Mr. Alexander, the agent of the Missionary Society on that occasion:—*

Brother: We listened to the talk you delivered to us from the Council of Black Coats in New-York. We have fully considered your talk, and the offers you have made us: we perfectly understand them, and we return an answer which we wish you also to understand. In making up our minds we have looked back and remembered what has been done in our days, and what our fathers have told us was done in old times.

Brother: Great numbers of black coats have been amongst the Indians, and with sweet voices, and smiling faces, have offered to teach them the religion of the white people. Our brethren in the East listened to the black coats,—turned from the religion of their fathers, and took up the religion of the white people. What good has it done them? Are they more happy and more friendly one to another than we are? No, brother, they are a divided people,—we are united; they quarrel about religion,—we live in love and friendship; they drink strong water,—have learnt how to cheat,—and to practice all the vices of the white men, which disgrace

Indians, without imitating the virtues of the white men. Brother, if you are our well wisher, keep away and do not disturb us.

Brother: We do not worship the Great Spirit as the white men do, but we believe that forms of worship are indifferent to the Great Spirit,—it is the offering of a sincere heart that pleases him, and we worship him in this manner. According to your religion we must believe in a Father and a Son, or we shall not be happy hereafter. We have always believed in a Father, and we worship him, as we were taught by our fathers. Your book says the Son was sent on earth by the Father,—did all the people who saw the Son believe in him? No, they did not, and the consequences must be known to you, if you have read the book.

Brother: You wish us to change our religion for yours,—we like our religion and do not want another. Our friends (pointing to Mr. Granger, the Agent of the United States for Indian affairs, who was present, Mr. Parish, the Indian interpreter, and Mr. Taylor), do us great good,—they counsel us in our troubles, and instruct us how to make ourselves comfortable. Our friends the Quakers do more than this,—they give us ploughs, and show us how to use them. They tell us we are accountable beings, but do not say we must change our religion. We are satisfied with what they do.

Brother: For these reasons we cannot receive your offers—we have other things to do, and beg you to make your mind easy, and not trouble us, lest our heads should be too much loaded, and by and by burst.

[**William L. Stone:**] *It is a fact that cannot be sufficiently deplored, that men boasting of their civilization, and calling themselves Christians, not only in this but in other lands, have by their own vicious examples interposed the greatest obstacles to the efforts of those who are earnestly laboring for the moral, social and religious improvement of the heathen. . . . The total neglect of all religion prevailing too generally in frontier settlements, even among many who have at some time professed to be the followers of Christ,—the public and bare-faced profanation of the Sabbath,—the avarice, lying and cozening which characterize their dealings, sometimes with each other, and most shamefully often in their commerce with the Indians,—the drunkenness, loose morals, and hardness of heart, in daily illustration all around them, have in but too many instances steeled the Indian's soul against Christianity. However earnestly the missionaries may be preaching to him the excellencies of Christianity and civilization, he doubts if they have any of the former, and scoffs at the latter. He cannot* *think well of a system, the professed adherents of which pay so little regard to God, to truth, and to duty. Hence the tone of Red-Jacket's speeches to Mr. Cram and Mr. Alexander; hence also the kindred character of the following outline of another of the Seneca orator's philippics against Christianity, delivered on a similar occasion, at about the same period of his life with his last mentioned address:—*

Brother:—I rise to return you the thanks of this nation, and to return them back to our ancient friends,—if any such we have,—for their good wishes toward us in attempting to teach us your religion. Inform them we will look well into this matter. We have well weighed your exertions, and find your success not to answer our expectations. But instead of producing that happy effect which you so long promised us, its introduction so far has rendered us uncomfortable and miserable. You have taken a number of our young men to your schools. You have educated them and taught them your religion. They have returned to their kindred and color, neither white men nor Indians. The arts they have learned are incompatible with the chase, and ill adapted to our customs. They have been taught that which is useless to us. They have been made to feel artificial wants, which never entered the minds of their brothers. They have imbibed, in your great towns, the seeds of vices which were unknown in the forest. They become discouraged and dissipated,—despised by the Indians, neglected by the whites, and without value to either,—less honest than the former, and *perhaps* more knavish than the latter.

Brother:—We were told that the failure of these first attempts was attributable to miscalculation, and we were invited to try again, by sending others of our young men to different schools, to be taught by different instructors. Brother, the result has been invariably the same. We believe it wrong for you to attempt further to promote your religion among us, or to introduce your arts, manners, habits, and feelings. We believe that it is wrong for us to encourage you in so doing. We believe that the Great Spirit made the whites and the Indians, but for different purposes.

Brother:—In attempting to pattern your example, the Great Spirit is angry,—for you see he does not bless or crown your exertions.

[**William L. Stone:**] *Here, according to the manuscript, Red-Jacket painted in the most glowing and descriptive colors the curse that seemed to* *have descended upon all those Indians who had been made the objects of pious but mistaken missions,—how imbecile, poor, effeminate, contemptible, drunken, lying, thieving, cheating, malicious, meddlesome, backbiting, quarrelsome, degraded and despised, the poor victims of civilized instruction had become,—having lost all the noble qualities of the savage, and acquired all the ignoble vices of the whites,—without one solitary exception where the Indian had been bettered. He then proceeded:—*

But, Brother, on the other hand we know that the Great Spirit is pleased that we follow the traditions and customs of our forefathers,—for in so doing we receive his blessing,—we have received strength and vigor for the chase. The Great Spirit has provided abundance,—when we are hungry we find the forest filled with game,—when thirsty, we slake our thirst at the pure streams and springs that spread around us. When weary, the leaves of the trees are our bed,—we retire with contentment to rest,—we rise with gratitude to the Great Preserver. Renovated strength in our limbs, and bounding joy in our hearts, we feel blessed and happy. No luxuries, no vices, no disputed titles, no avaricious desires, shake the foundations of our society, or disturb our peace and happiness. We know the Great Spirit is better pleased with his red children, than with his white, when he bestows upon us a hundred fold more blessings than upon you.

Perhaps, Brother, you are right in your religion:—it may be peculiarly adapted to your condition. You say that you destroyed the Son of the Great Spirit. Perhaps this is the merited cause of all your troubles and misfortunes. But, Brothers, bear in mind that we had no participation in this murder. We disclaim it,—we love the Great Spirit,—and as we never had any agency in so unjust, so merciless an outrage, he therefore continues to smile upon us, and to give us peace, joy and plenty.

Brother:—We pity you,—we wish you to bear to our good friends our best wishes. Inform them that in compassion toward them, we are willing to send them missionaries to teach them our religion, habits and customs. We would be willing they should be as happy as we are, and assure them that if they should follow our example, they would be more, far more happy than they are now. We cannot embrace your religion. It renders us divided and unhappy,—but by your embracing ours, we believe that you would be more happy and more acceptable to the Great Spirit. Here, (pointing his finger to several whites present who had been captured when children, and been brought up among them,) here, Brother, (with an animation and exulting triumph which cannot be described,) here is the living evidence before you. Those young men have been brought up with us. They are contented and happy. Nothing would be an inducement with them to abandon their enjoyments and adopt yours,—for they are too well aware of the blessings of our society, and the evils of yours. But as you have our good will, we would gladly know that you have relinquished your religion, productive of so much disagreement and inquietude among yourselves, and instead thereof that you should follow ours.

Accept of this advice, Brother, and take it back to your friends, as the best pledge of our wishes for your welfare. Perhaps you think we are ignorant and uninformed. Go, then, and teach the whites. Select, for example, the people of Buffalo. We will be spectators, and remain silent. Improve their morals and refine their habits,—make them less disposed to cheat Indians. Make the whites generally less inclined to make Indians drunk, and to take from them their lands. Let us know the tree by the blossoms, and the blossoms by the fruit. When this shall be made clear to our minds we may be more willing to listen to you. But until then we must be allowed to follow the religion of our ancestors.

Brother:—Farewell!

[William L. Stone:] *A bitter satire! Humanity weeps that the conduct of civilized men puts arguments like these into the mouths of the heathen, against their own best good. It is a striking coincidence that the Iroquois Indians were first unhappily made acquainted with their two greatest enemies, RUM and GUNPOWDER, by the rival discoverers, Hudson and Champlain, during the same week of the same year, 1609. While Henry Hudson was cautiously feeling his way, as he supposed, into the northern ocean, through the channel of the river which bears his name, Champlain was accompanying a war-party of the Hurons against the Iroquois, upon the lake receiving its name from him. Hudson discovered a company of the Iroquois upon the bank of the river, whom he regaled with rum. Champlain discovered a body of Iroquois warriors upon the coast of the lake, near the spot afterward selected for the site of Ticonderoga, and there first taught them the fatal power of gunpowder.*

SOURCE: William L. Stone. *Life and Times of Red-Jacket, or Sa-go-ye-wat-ha: Being the Sequel to the History of the Six Nations*. New York: Wiley and Putnam, 1841.

TECUMSEH

Tecumseh (c. 1768–1813), a far-seeing and brave leader of the Shawnee tribe, a dynamo of war and oratory, respected and feared by whites and Native Americans alike, was indefatigable in trying to organize a confederation of resistance to encroachment on Native American lands by the United States. He traveled from present-day Indiana to Florida, to Missouri, to the Plains, and into Canada in his efforts to galvanize a union of tribes. In spite of his charisma and persuasiveness, he was not always successful.

"I wish it was in my power to do justice to the eloquence of this distinguished man," writes John D. Hunter, who recorded the following speech made to the Osages in Missouri in the winter of 1811–1812, "but it is utterly impossible. The richest colours, shaded with a master's pencil, would fall infinitely short of the glowing finish of the original. The occasion and subject were peculiarly adapted to call into action all the powers of genuine patriotism; and such language, such gestures, and such feelings and fulness of soul contending for utterance, were exhibited by this untutored native of the forest in the central wilds of America, as no audience, I am persuaded, either in ancient or modern times ever before witnessed. . . . The unlettered Te-cum-seh gave extemporaneous utterance only to what he felt; it was a simple, but vehement narration of the wrongs imposed by the white people on the Indians, and an exhortation for the latter to resist them. The whole addressed to an audience composed of individuals who had been educated to prefer almost any sacrifice to that of personal liberty, and even death to the degradation of their nation; and who, on this occasion, felt the portraiture of Te-cum-seh but too strikingly identified with their own condition, wrongs, and sufferings."

We All Belong to One Family (1811)

BROTHERS,—WE ALL BELONG to one family; we are all children of the Great Spirit; we walk in the same path; slake our thirst at the same spring; and now affairs of the greatest concern lead us to smoke the pipe around the same council fire!

Brothers,—We are friends; we must assist each other to bear our burdens. The blood of many of our fathers and brothers has run like water on the ground, to satisfy the avarice of the white men. We, ourselves, are threatened with a great evil; nothing will pacify them but the destruction of all the red men.

Brothers,—When the white men first set foot on our grounds, they were hungry; they had no place on which to spread their blankets, or to kindle their fires. They were feeble; they could do nothing for themselves. Our fathers commiserated their distress, and shared freely with them whatever the Great Spirit had given his red children. They gave them food when hungry, medicine when sick, spread skins for them to sleep on, and gave them grounds, that they might hunt and raise corn.

Brothers,—The white people are like poisonous serpents: when chilled, they are feeble and harmless; but invigorate them with warmth, and they sting their benefactors to death. The white people came among us feeble; and now we have made them strong, they wish to kill us, or drive us back, as they would wolves and panthers.

Brothers,—The white men are not friends to the Indians: at first, they only asked for land sufficient for a wigwam; now, nothing will satisfy them but the whole of our hunting grounds, from the rising to the setting sun.

Brothers,—The white men want more than our hunting grounds; they wish to kill our warriors; they would even kill our old men, women, and little ones.

Brothers,—Many winters ago, there was no land; the sun did not rise and set: all was darkness. The Great Spirit made all things. He gave the white people a home beyond the great waters. He supplied these grounds with game, and gave them to his red children; and he gave them strength and courage to defend them.

Brothers,—My people wish for peace; the red men all wish for peace: but where the white people are, there is no peace for them, except it be on the bosom of our mother.

Brothers,—The white men despise and cheat the Indians; they abuse and insult them; they do not think the red men sufficiently good to live. The red men have borne many and great injuries; they ought to suffer them no longer. My people will not; they are determined on vengeance; they have taken up the tomahawk; they will make it fat with blood; they will drink the blood of the white people.

Brothers,—My people are brave and numerous; but the white people are too strong for them alone. I wish you to take up the tomahawk with them. If we all unite, we will cause the rivers to stain the great waters with their blood.

Brothers,—If you do not unite with us, they will first destroy us, and then you will fall an easy prey to them. They have destroyed many nations of red men because they were not united, because they were not friends to each other.

Brothers,—The white people send runners amongst us; they wish to make us enemies, that they may sweep over and desolate our hunting grounds, like devastating winds, or rushing waters.

Brothers,—Our Great Father, over the great waters, is angry with the white people, our enemies. He will send his brave warriors against them; he will send us rifles, and whatever else we want—he is our friend, and we are his children.

Brothers,—Who are the white people that we should fear them? They cannot run fast, and are good marks to shoot at: they are only men; our fathers have killed many of them: we are not squaws, and we will stain the earth red with their blood.

Brothers,—The Great Spirit is angry with our enemies; he speaks in thunder, and the earth swallows up villages, and drinks up the Mississippi. The great waters will cover their lowlands; their corn cannot grow; and the Great Spirit will sweep those who escape to the hills from the earth with his terrible breath.

Brothers,—We must be united; we must smoke the same pipe; we must fight each other's battles; and more than all, we must love the Great Spirit: he is for us; he will destroy our enemies, and make all his red children happy.

[John D. Hunter:] . . . *I looked upon war as inevitable; and in its consequences contemplated the destruction of our enemies, and the restoration of the Indians to their primitive rights, power, and happiness. There was nothing I then so ardently desired as that of being a warrior, and I even envied those who were to achieve these important objects the fame and glory that would redound as a necessary result. In a short time afterwards, however, the Osages rejected Te-cum-seh's proposals, and all these brilliant prospects vanished.*

SOURCE: John D. Hunter. *Memoirs of a Captivity among the Indians of North America, from Childhood to the Age of Seventeen: With Anecdotes Descriptive of Their Manners and Customs.* London: Longman, Hurst, Rees, Orme, and Brown, 1823.

Father!—Listen to Your Children! (1813)

When the United States declared war on England in 1812, Tecumseh saw that with the help of the British, who were less interested in settlement than in trade, he would have his best chance of forcing the U.S. to accept the establishment of a wholly independent Native American nation. But then, after a series of triumphs, which included the Native American-British capture of Detroit, a British general named Henry Proctor, lacking Tecumseh's nerve and passion, made plans to withdraw into eastern Ontario. In the following speech, made on September 18, 1813, Tecumseh scolded Proctor for his deceit and cowardice. Proctor's hasty retreat left Tecumseh's warriors to fight an overwhelming U.S. force. Two weeks after this speech, on October 5, Tecumseh was killed by William Henry Harrison's soldiers.

FATHER!—LISTEN TO your children! You have them now all before you. The war before this our British father gave the hatchet to his red children, when our old chiefs were alive. They are now dead. In that war our father was thrown flat on his back by the Americans, and our father took them by the hand without our knowledge. We are afraid that our father will do so again at this time. Summer before last, when I came forward with my red brethren, and was ready to take up the hatchet in favor of our British father, we were told not to be in a hurry—that he had not yet determined to fight the Americans.

Listen!—When war was declared, our father stood up and gave us the tomahawk, and told us that he was then ready to strike the Americans, that he wanted our assistance—and that he would certainly get us our lands back, which the Americans had taken from us.

Listen!—You told us, at that time, to bring forward our families to this place, and we did so. You also promised to take care of them—they should want for nothing, while the men would go and fight the enemy—that we need not trouble ourselves about the enemy's garrisons—that we knew nothing about them—and that our father would attend to that part of the business. You also told your red children that you would take good care of your garrison here, which made our hearts glad.

Listen!—When we were last at the Rapids, it is true we gave you little assistance. It is hard to fight people who live like ground-hogs.

Father, listen!—Our fleet has gone out; we know they have fought; we have heard the great guns; but we know nothing of what has happened to our father with one arm. Our ships have gone one way, and we are much astonished to see our father tying up everything and preparing to run away the other, without letting his red children know what his intentions are. You always told us to remain here and take care of our lands; it made our hearts glad to hear that was your wish. Our great father, the king, is the head, and you represent him: You always told us that you would never draw your foot off British ground. But now, father, we see you are drawing back, and we are sorry to see our father doing so without seeing the enemy. We must compare our father's conduct to a fat animal that carries its tail upon its back, but when affrighted, it drops it between its legs and runs off.

Father, listen!—The Americans have not yet defeated us by land—neither are we sure that they have done so by water—we therefore wish to remain here and fight our enemy, should they make their appearance. If they defeat us, we will then retreat with our father. At the battle of the Rapids, last war, the Americans certainly defeated us; and when we retreated to our father's fort, at that place the gates were shut against us. We were afraid that it would now be the case; but instead of that, we now see our British father preparing to march out of his garrison.

Father!—You have got the arms and ammunition which our great father sent for his red children. If you have an idea of going away, give them to us, and you may go and welcome for us. Our lives are in the hands of the Great Spirit. We are determined to defend our lands, and if it be his will, we wish to leave our bones upon them.

SOURCE: B. B. Thatcher. *Indian Life and Battles*. Akron: New Werner Co., 1910.

WASHINGTON IRVING

Born in New York, Washington Irving (1783–1859) was educated to become a lawyer but instead became famous for his satirical A History of New York *(1809). "Rip Van Winkle" appeared in Irving's* The Sketch Book of Geoffrey Crayon, Gent., *and while its story line is well known, the tale itself is seldom read in its entirety.*

Rip Van Winkle: A Posthumous Tale of Diedrich Knickerbocker (1819–1820)

NOTE: The following Tale was found among the papers of the late Diedrich Knickerbocker, an old gentleman of New York, who was very curious in the Dutch history of the province, and the manners of the descendants from its primitive settlers. His historical researches, however, did not lie so much among books as among men; for the former are lamentably scanty on his favorite topics; whereas he found the old burghers, and still more their wives, rich in that legendary lore so invaluable to true history. Whenever, therefore, he happened upon a genuine Dutch family, snugly shut up in its low-roofed farmhouse, under a spreading sycamore, he looked upon it as a little clasped volume of black-letter, and studied it with the zeal of a book-worm.

The result of all these researches was a history of the province during the reign of the Dutch governors, which he published some years since. There have been various opinions as to the literary character of his work, and, to tell the truth, it is not a whit better than it should be. Its chief merit is its scrupulous accuracy, which indeed was a little questioned, on its first appearance, but has since been completely established; and it is now admitted into all historical collections as a book of unquestionable authority.

The old gentleman died shortly after the publication of his work; and now that he is dead and gone, it cannot do much harm to his memory to say that his time might have been much better employed in weightier labors. He, however, was apt to ride his hobby his own way; and though it did now and then kick up the dust a little in the eyes of his neighbors, and grieve the spirit of some friends, for whom he felt the truest deference and affection, yet his errors and follies are remembered "more in sorrow than in anger," and it begins to be suspected that he never intended to injure or offend. But however his memory may be appreciated by critics, it is still held dear by many folk whose good opinion is well worth having; particularly by certain biscuit-bakers, who have gone so far as to imprint his likeness on their new-year cakes; and have thus given him a chance for immortality, almost equal to the being stamped on a Waterloo Medal, or a Queen Anne's Farthing.

WHOEVER HAS MADE a voyage up the Hudson must remember the Kaatskill Mountains. They are a dismembered branch of the great Appalachian family, and are seen away to the west of the river, swelling up to a noble height, and lording it over the surrounding country. Every change of season, every change of weather, indeed, every hour of the day, produces some change in the magical hues and shapes of these mountains, and they are regarded by all the good wives, far and near, as perfect barometers. When the weather is fair and settled, they are clothed in blue and purple, and print their bold outlines on the clear evening sky; but, sometimes, when the rest of the landscape is cloudless, they will gather a hood of gray vapors about their summits, which, in the last rays of the setting sun, will glow and light up like a crown of glory.

At the foot of these fairy mountains, the voyager may have descried the light smoke curling up from a village, whose shingle-roofs gleam among the trees, just where the blue tints of the upland melt away into the fresh green of the nearer landscape. It is a little village of great antiquity, having been founded by some of the Dutch colonists, in the early times of the province, just about the beginning of the government of the good Peter Stuyvesant (may he rest in peace!), and there were some of the houses of the original settlers standing within a few years, built of small yellow bricks brought from Holland, having latticed windows and gable fronts, surmounted with weather-cocks.

In that same village, and in one of these very houses (which, to tell the precise truth, was sadly time-worn and weather-beaten), there lived many years since, while the country was yet a province of Great Britain, a simple good-natured fellow of the name of Rip Van Winkle. He was a descendant of the Van Winkles who figured so gallantly in the chivalrous days of Peter Stuyvesant, and accompanied him to the siege of Fort Christina. He inherited, however, but little of the martial character of his ancestors. I have observed that he was a simple, good-natured man; he was, moreover, a kind neighbor, and an obedient, hen-pecked husband. Indeed, to the latter circumstance might be owing that meekness of spirit which gained him such universal popularity; for those men are most apt to be obsequious and conciliating abroad, who are under the discipline of shrews at home. Their tempers, doubtless, are rendered pliant and malleable in the fiery furnace of domestic tribulation; and a curtain lecture is worth all the sermons in the world for teaching the virtues of patience and long-suffering. A termagant wife may, therefore, in some respects, be considered a tolerable blessing; and if so, Rip Van Winkle was thrice blessed.

Certain it is that he was a great favorite among all the good wives of the village, who, as usual with the amiable sex, took his part in all family squabbles, and never failed, whenever they talked those matters over in their evening gossipings, to lay all the blame on Dame Van Winkle. The children of the village, too, would shout with joy whenever he approached. He assisted at their sports, made their playthings, taught them to fly kites and shoot marbles, and told them long stories of ghosts, witches and Indians. Whenever he went dodging about the village, he was surrounded by a troop of them, hanging on his skirts, clambering on his back, and playing a thousand tricks on him with impunity; and not a dog would bark at him throughout the neighborhood.

The great error in Rip's composition was an insuperable aversion to all kinds of profitable labor. It could not be from the want of assiduity or perseverance; for he would sit on a wet rock, with a rod as long and heavy as a Tartar's lance, and fish all day without a murmur, even though he should not be encouraged by a single nibble. He would carry a fowling-piece on his shoulder for hours together, trudging through woods and swamps, and up hill and down dale, to shoot a few squirrels or wild pigeons. He would never refuse to assist a neighbor even in the roughest toil, and was a foremost man at all country frolics for husking Indian corn, or building stone-fences; the women of the village, too, used to employ him to run their errands, and to do such little odd jobs as their less obliging husbands would not do for them. In a word, Rip was ready to attend to anybody's business but his own; but as to doing family duty, and keeping his farm in order, he found it impossible.

In fact, he declared it was of no use to work on his farm: it was the most pestilent little piece of ground in the whole country; everything about it went wrong, and would go wrong, in spite of him. His fences were continually falling to pieces; his cow would either go astray, or get among the cabbages; weeds were sure to grow quicker in his fields than anywhere else; the rain always made a point of setting in just as he had some out-door work to do; so that, though his patrimonial estate had dwindled away under his management, acre by acre, until there was little more left than a mere patch of Indian corn and potatoes, yet it was the worst conditioned farm in the neighborhood.

His children, too, were as ragged and wild as if they belonged to nobody. His son Rip, an urchin begotten in his own likeness, promised to inherit the habits with the old clothes of his father. He was generally seen trooping like a colt at his mother's heels, equipped in a pair of his father's cast-off galligaskins, which he had much ado to hold up with one hand, as a fine lady does her train in bad weather.

Rip Van Winkle, however, was one of those happy mortals, of foolish, well-oiled dispositions, who take the world easy, eat white bread or brown, whichever can be got with least thought or trouble, and would rather starve on a penny than work for a pound. If left to himself, he would have whistled life away in perfect contentment; but his wife kept continually dinning in his ears about his idleness, his carelessness and the ruin he was bringing on his family. Morning, noon and night her tongue was incessantly going, and everything he said or did was sure to produce a torrent of household eloquence. Rip had one way of replying to all lectures of the kind, and that, by frequent use, had grown into a habit. He shrugged his shoulders, shook his head, cast up his eyes, but said nothing. This, however, always provoked a fresh volley from his wife; so that he was fain to draw off his forces, and take to the outside of the house—the only side which, in truth, belongs to a hen-pecked husband.

Rip's old domestic adherent was his dog Wolf, who was as much hen-pecked as his master; for Dame Van Winkle regarded them as companions in idleness, and even looked upon Wolf with an evil eye, as the cause of his master's going so often astray. True it is, in all points of spirit befitting an honorable dog, he was as courageous an animal as ever scoured the woods—but what courage can withstand the ever-during and all-besetting terrors of a woman's tongue? The moment Wolf entered the house his crest fell, his tail dropped to the ground, or curled between his legs, he sneaked about with a gallows air, casting many a sidelong glance at Dame Van Winkle, and at the least flourish of a broom-stick or ladle, he would fly to the door with yelping precipitation.

Times grew worse and worse with Rip Van Winkle as years of matrimony rolled on; a tart temper never mellows with age, and a sharp tongue is the only edged tool that grows keener with constant use. For a long while he used to console himself, when driven from home, by frequenting a kind of perpetual club of the sages, philosophers, and other idle personages of the village; which held its sessions on a bench before a small inn, designated by a rubicund portrait of His Majesty George the Third. Here they used to sit in the shade through a long lazy summer's day, talking listlessly over village gossip, or telling endless sleepy stories about nothing. But it would have been worth any statesman's money to have heard the profound discussions that sometimes took place, when by chance an old newspaper fell into their hands from some passing traveler. How solemnly they would listen to the contents, as drawled out by Derrick Van Bummel, the schoolmaster, a dapper, learned little man, who was not to be daunted by the most gigantic word in the dictionary; and how sagely they would deliberate upon public events some months after they had taken place.

The opinions of this junto were completely controlled by Nicholas Vedder, a patriarch of the village, and landlord of the inn, at the door of which he took his seat from morning till night, just moving sufficiently to avoid the sun and keep in the shade of a large tree; so that the neighbors could tell the hour by his movements as accurately as by a sun-dial. It is true he was rarely heard to speak, but smoked his pipe incessantly. His adherents, however (for every great man has his adherents), perfectly understood him, and knew how to gather his opinions. When anything that was read or related displeased him, he was observed to smoke his pipe vehemently, and to send forth short, frequent and angry puffs; but when pleased, he would inhale the smoke slowly and tranquilly, and emit it in light and placid clouds; and sometimes, taking the pipe from his mouth, and letting the fragrant vapor curl about his nose, would gravely nod his head in token of perfect approbation.

From even this stronghold the unlucky Rip was at length routed by his termagant wife, who would suddenly break in upon the tranquility of the assemblage and call the members all to naught; nor was that august personage, Nicholas Vedder himself, sacred from the daring tongue of this terrible virago, who charged him outright with encouraging her husband in habits of idleness.

Poor Rip was at last reduced almost to despair; and his only alternative, to escape from the labor of the farm and clamor of his wife, was to take gun in hand and stroll away into the woods. Here he would sometimes seat himself at the foot of a tree, and share the contents of his wallet with Wolf, with whom he sympathized as a fellow-sufferer in persecution. "Poor Wolf," he would say, "thy mistress leads thee a dog's life of it; but never mind, my lad, whilst I live thou shalt never want a friend to stand by thee!" Wolf would wag his tail, look wistfully in his master's face, and if dogs can feel pity, I verily believe he reciprocated the sentiment with all his heart.

In a long ramble of the kind on a fine autumnal day, Rip had unconsciously scrambled to one of the highest parts of the Kaatskill Mountains. He was after his favorite sport of squirrel shooting, and the still solitudes had echoed and re-echoed with the reports of his gun. Panting and fatigued, he threw himself, late in the afternoon, on a green knoll, covered with mountain herbage, that crowned the brow of a precipice. From an opening between the trees he could overlook all the lower country for many a mile of rich woodland. He saw at a distance the lordly Hudson, far, far below him, moving on its silent but majestic course, with the reflection of a purple cloud, or the sail of a lagging bark, here and there sleeping on its grassy bosom, and at last losing itself in the blue highlands.

On the other side he looked down into a deep mountain glen, wild, lonely and shagged, the bottom filled with fragments from the impending cliffs, and scarcely lighted by the reflected rays of the setting sun. For some time Rip lay musing on this scene; evening was gradually advancing; the mountains began to throw their long blue shadows over the valleys; he saw that it would be dark long before he could reach the village, and he heaved a heavy sigh when he thought of encountering the terrors of Dame Van Winkle.

As he was about to descend, he heard a voice from a distance hallooing, "Rip Van Winkle! Rip Van Winkle!" He looked round, but could see nothing but a crow winging its solitary flight across the mountain. He thought his fancy must have deceived him, and turned again to descend, when he heard the same cry ring through the still evening air; "Rip Van Winkle! Rip Van Winkle!"—at the same time Wolf bristled up his back, and giving a low growl, skulked to his master's side, looking fearfully down into the glen. Rip now felt a vague apprehension stealing over him; he looked anxiously in the same direction, and perceived a strange figure slowly toiling up the rocks, and bending under the weight of something he carried on his back. He was surprised to see any human being in this lonely and unfrequented place, but supposing it to be some one of the neighborhood in need of his assistance, he hastened down to yield it.

On nearer approach he was still more surprised at the singularity of the stranger's appearance. He was a short, square-built old fellow, with thick bushy hair, and a grizzled beard. His dress was of the antique Dutch fashion—a cloth jerkin strapped round the waist—several pair of breeches, the outer one of ample volume, decorated with rows of buttons down the sides, and bunches at the knees. He bore on his shoulder a stout keg, that seemed full of liquor, and made signs for Rip to approach and assist him with the load. Though rather shy and distrustful of this new acquaintance, Rip complied with his usual alacrity; and mutually relieving one another, they clambered up a narrow gully, apparently the dry bed of a mountain torrent. As they ascended, Rip every now and then heard long rolling peals like distant thunder, that seemed to issue out of a deep ravine, or, rather, cleft, between lofty rocks, toward which their rugged path conducted. He paused for an instant, but supposing it to be the muttering of one of those transient thunder-showers which often take place in mountain heights, he proceeded. Passing through the ravine they came to a hollow, like a small amphitheatre, surrounded by perpendicular precipices, over the brinks of which impending trees shot their branches, so that you only caught glimpses of the azure sky and the bright evening cloud. During the whole time Rip and his companion had labored on in silence; for though the former marveled greatly what could be the object of carrying a keg of liquor up this wild mountain, yet there was something strange and incomprehensible about the unknown, that inspired awe and checked familiarity.

On entering the amphitheatre, new objects of wonder presented themselves. On a level spot in the center was a company of odd-looking personages playing at nine-pins. They were dressed in a quaint outlandish fashion; some wore short doublets, others jerkins, with long knives in their belts, and most of them had enormous breeches, of similar style with that of the guide's. Their visages, too, were peculiar: one had a large beard, broad face, and small piggish eyes: the face of another seemed to consist entirely of nose, and was surmounted by a white sugar-loaf hat set off with a little red cock's tail. They all had beards, of various shapes and colors. There was one who seemed to be the commander. He was a stout old gentleman, with a weather-beaten countenance; he wore a laced doublet, broad belt and hanger, high-crowned hat and feather, red stockings and high-heeled shoes, with roses in them. The whole group reminded Rip of the figures in an old Flemish painting, in the parlor of Dominie Van Shaick, the village parson, and which had been brought over from Holland at the time of the settlement.

What seemed particularly odd to Rip was, that though these folks were evidently amusing themselves, yet they maintained the gravest faces, the most mysterious silence, and were, withal, the most melancholy party of pleasure he had ever witnessed. Nothing interrupted the stillness of the scene but the noise of the balls, which, whenever they were rolled, echoed along the mountains like rumbling peals of thunder.

As Rip and his companion approached them, they suddenly desisted from their play, and stared at him with such fixed statue-like gaze, and such strange, uncouth, lack-lustre countenances, that his heart turned within him, and his knees smote together. His companion now emptied the contents of the keg into large flagons, and made signs to him to wait upon the company. He obeyed with fear and trembling; they quaffed the liquor in profound silence, and then returned to their game.

By degrees Rip's awe and apprehension subsided. He even ventured, when no eye was fixed upon him, to taste the beverage, which he found had much of the flavor of excellent Hollands. He was naturally a thirsty soul, and was soon tempted to repeat the draught. One taste provoked another; and he reiterated his visits to the flagon so often that at length his senses were overpowered, his eyes swam in his head, his head gradually declined, and he fell into a deep sleep.

On waking, he found himself on the green knoll whence he had first seen the old man of the glen. He rubbed his eyes—it was a bright sunny morning. The birds were hopping and twittering among the bushes, and the eagle was wheeling aloft, and breasting the pure mountain breeze. "Surely," thought Rip, "I have not slept here all night." He recalled the occurrences before he fell asleep: the strange man with a keg of liquor—the mountain ravine—the wild retreat among the rocks—the woebegone party at nine-pins—the flagon—"Oh! that flagon! that wicked flagon!" thought Rip—"what excuse shall I make to Dame Van Winkle!"

He looked round for his gun, but in place of the clean, well-oiled fowling-piece, he found an old firelock lying by him, the barrel encrusted with rust, the lock falling off, and the stock worm-eaten. He now suspected that the grave roisters of the mountain had put a trick upon him, and, having dosed him with liquor, had robbed him of his gun. Wolf, too, had disappeared, but he might have strayed away after a squirrel or partridge. He whistled after him and shouted his name, but all in vain; the echoes repeated his whistle and shout, but no dog was to be seen.

He determined to revisit the scene of the last evening's gambol, and if he met with any of the party, to demand his dog and gun. As he rose to walk, he found himself stiff in the joints, and wanting in his usual activity. "These mountain beds do not agree with me," thought Rip, "and if this frolic should lay me up with a fit of the rheumatism, I shall have a blessed time with Dame Van Winkle." With some difficulty he got down into the glen: he found the gully up which he and his companion had ascended the preceding evening; but to his astonishment a mountain stream was now foaming down it, leaping from rock to rock, and filling the glen with babbling murmurs. He, however, made a shift to scramble up its sides, working his toilsome way through thickets of birch, sassafras and witch-hazel, and sometimes tripped up or entangled by the wild grapevines that twisted their coils or tendrils from tree to tree, and spread a kind of network in his path.

At length he reached to where the ravine had opened through the cliffs to the amphitheatre; but no traces of such opening remained. The rocks presented a high impenetrable wall over which the torrent came tumbling in a sheet of feathery foam, and fell into a broad deep basin, black from the shadows of the surrounding forest. Here, then, poor Rip was brought to a stand.

He again called and whistled after his dog; he was only answered by the cawing of a flock of idle crows, sporting high in air about a dry tree that overhung a sunny precipice; and who, secure in their elevation, seemed to look down and scoff at the poor man's perplexities. What was to be done? the morning was passing away, and Rip felt famished for want of his breakfast. He grieved to give up his dog and gun; he dreaded to meet his wife; but it would not do to starve among the mountains. He shook his head, shouldered the rusty firelock, and, with a heart full of trouble and anxiety, turned his steps homeward.

As he approached the village he met a number of people, but none whom he knew, which somewhat surprised him, for he had thought himself acquainted with every one in the country round. Their dress, too, was of a different fashion from that to which he was accustomed. They all stared at him with equal marks of surprise, and, whenever they cast their eyes upon him, invariably stroked their chins. The constant recurrence of this gesture induced Rip, involuntarily, to do the same, when, to his astonishment, he found his beard had grown a foot long!

He had now entered the skirts of the village. A troop of strange children ran at his heels, hooting after him, and pointing at his gray beard. The dogs, too, not one of which he recognized for an old acquaintance, barked at him as he passed. The very village was altered; it was larger and more populous. There were rows of houses which he had never seen before, and those which had been his familiar haunts had disappeared. Strange names were over the doors—strange faces at the windows—everything was strange. His mind now misgave him; he began to doubt whether both he and the world around him were not bewitched. Surely this was his native village, which he had left but the day before. There stood the Kaatskill Mountains—there ran the silver Hudson at a distance—there was every hill and dale precisely as it had always been—Rip was sorely perplexed—"That flagon last night," thought he, "has addled my poor head sadly!"

It was with some difficulty that he found the way to his own house, which he approached with silent awe, expecting every moment to hear the shrill voice of Dame Van Winkle. He found the house gone to decay—the roof had fallen in, the windows shattered, and the doors off the hinges. A half-starved dog that looked like Wolf was skulking about it. Rip called him by name, but the cur snarled, showed his teeth, and passed on. This was an unkind cut indeed—"My very dog," sighed poor Rip, "has forgotten me!"

He entered the house, which, to tell the truth, Dame Van Winkle had always kept in neat order. It was empty, forlorn, and apparently abandoned. This desolateness overcame all his connubial fears—he called loudly for his wife and children—the lonely chambers rang for a moment with his voice, and then all again was silence.

He now hurried forth, and hastened to his old resort, the village inn—but it too was gone. A large rickety wooden building stood in its place, with great gaping windows, some of them broken and mended with old hats and petticoats, and over the door was painted, "The Union Hotel, by Jonathan Doolittle." Instead of the great tree that used to shelter the quiet little Dutch inn of yore, there now was reared a tall naked pole, with something on the top that looked like a red night-cap, and from it was fluttering a flag, on which was a singular assemblage of stars and stripes—all this was strange and incomprehensible. He recognized on the sign, however, the ruby face of King George, under which he had smoked so many a peaceful pipe; but even this was singularly metamorphosed. The red coat was changed for one of blue and buff, a sword was held in the hand instead of a scepter, the head was decorated with a cocked hat, and underneath was painted in large characters, GENERAL WASHINGTON.

There was, as usual, a crowd of folk about the door, but none that Rip recollected. The very character of the people seemed changed. There was a busy, bustling, disputatious tone about it, instead of the accustomed phlegm and drowsy tranquility. He looked in vain for the sage Nicholas Vedder, with his broad face, double chin, and fair long pipe, uttering clouds of tobacco-smoke instead of idle speeches; or Van Bummel, the schoolmaster, doling forth the contents of an ancient newspaper. In place of these, a lean, bilious-looking fellow, with his pockets full of handbills, was haranguing vehemently about rights of citizens—elections—members of Congress—liberty—Bunker's Hill—heroes of seventy-six—and other words, which were a perfect Babylonish jargon to the bewildered Van Winkle.

The appearance of Rip, with his long grizzled beard, his rusty fowling-piece, his uncouth dress, and an army of women and children at his heels, soon attracted the attention of the tavern politicians. They crowded round him, eyeing him from head to foot with great curiosity. The orator bustled up to him, and, drawing him partly aside, inquired "on which side he voted?" Rip stared in vacant stupidity. Another short but busy little fellow pulled him by the arm, and, rising on tiptoe, inquired in his ear, "Whether he was Federal or Democrat?" Rip was equally at a loss to comprehend the question; when a knowing, self-important old gentleman, in a sharp cocked hat, made his way through the crowd, putting them to the right and left with his elbows as he passed, and planting himself before Van Winkle, with one arm akimbo, the other resting on his cane, his keen eyes and sharp hat penetrating, as it were, into his very soul, demanded in an austere tone, "what brought him to the election with a gun on his shoulder, and a mob at his heels, and whether he meant to breed a riot in the village?"—"Alas!" gentlemen," cried Rip, somewhat dismayed, "I am a poor quiet man, a native of the place, and a loyal subject of the king, God bless him!"

Here a general shout burst from the by-standers—"a Tory! a Tory! a spy! a refugee! hustle him! away with him!" It was with great difficulty that the self-important man in the cocked hat restored order; and, having assumed a tenfold austerity of brow, demanded again of the unknown culprit what he came there for, and whom he was seeking? The poor man humbly assured him that he meant no harm, but merely came there in search of some of his neighbors, who used to keep about the tavern.

"Well—who are they?—name them."

Rip bethought himself a moment, and inquired, "Where's Nicholas Vedder?"

There was a silence for a little while, when an old man replied, in a thin piping voice, "Nicholas Vedder! why, he is dead and gone these eighteen years! There was a wooden tombstone in the church-yard that used to tell all about him, but that's rotten and gone too."

"Where's Brom Dutcher?"

"Oh, he went off to the army in the beginning of the war; some say he was killed at the storming of Stony Point—others say he was drowned in a squall at the foot of Antony's Nose—I don't know—he never came back again."

"Where's Van Bummel, the schoolmaster?"

"He went off to the wars too, was a great militia general, and is now in Congress."

Rip's heart died away at hearing of these sad changes in his home and friends, and finding himself thus alone in the world. Every answer puzzled him too, by treating of such enormous lapses of time, and of matters which he could not understand: war—Congress—Stony Point—he had no courage to ask after any more friends, but cried out in despair, "Does nobody here know Rip Van Winkle?"

"Oh, Rip Van Winkle!" exclaimed two or three, "Oh, to be sure! that's Rip Van Winkle yonder, leaning against the tree."

Rip looked, and beheld a precise counterpart of himself, as he went up the mountain: apparently as lazy, and certainly as ragged. The poor fellow was now completely confounded. He doubted his own identity, and whether he was himself or another man. In the midst of his bewilderment, the man in the cocked hat demanded who he was, and what was his name?

"God knows," exclaimed he, at his wit's end; "I'm not myself—I'm somebody else—that's me yonder—no—that's somebody else got into my shoes—I was myself last night, but I fell asleep on the mountain, and they've changed my gun, and every thing's changed, and I'm changed, and I can't tell what's my name, or who I am!"

The by-standers began now to look at each other, nod, wink significantly, and tap their fingers against their foreheads. There was a whisper, also, about securing the gun, and keeping the old fellow from doing mischief, at the very suggestion of which the self-important man in the cocked hat retired with some precipitation. At this critical moment a fresh, comely woman pressed through the throng to get a peep at the gray-bearded man. She had a chubby child in her arms, which, frightened at his looks, began to cry. "Hush, Rip," cried she, "hush, you little fool; the old man won't hurt you." The name of the child, the air of the mother, the tone of her voice, all awakened a train of recollections in his mind. "What is your name, my good woman?" asked he.

"Judith Gardenier."

"And your father's name?"

"Ah, poor man, Rip Van Winkle was his name, but it's twenty years since he went away from home with his gun, and never has been heard of since—his dog came home without him; but whether he shot himself, or was carried away by the Indians, nobody can tell. I was then but a little girl."

Rip had but one question more to ask; but he put it with a faltering voice:

"Where's your mother?"

"Oh, she too had died but a short time since; she broke a blood-vessel in a fit of passion at a New-England peddler."

There was a drop of comfort, at least, in this intelligence. The honest man could contain himself no longer. He caught his daughter and her child in his arms. "I am your father!" cried he—"Young Rip Van Winkle once—old Rip Van Winkle now! Does nobody know poor Rip Van Winkle?"

All stood amazed, until an old woman, tottering out from among the crowd, put her hand to her brow, and peering under it in his face for a moment, exclaimed, "Sure enough! It is Rip Van Winkle—it is himself! Welcome home again, old neighbor—why, where have you been these twenty long years?"

Rip's story was soon told, for the whole twenty years had been to him as one night. The neighbors stared when they heard it; some were seen to wink at each other, and put their tongues in their cheeks: and the self-important man in the cocked hat, who, when the alarm was over, had returned to the field, screwed down the corners of his mouth, and shook his head, upon which there was a general shaking of the head throughout the assemblage.

It was determined, however, to take the opinion of old Peter Vanderdonk, who was seen slowly advancing up the road. He was a descendant of the historian of that name, who wrote one of the earliest accounts of the province. Peter was the most ancient inhabitant of the village, and well versed in all the wonderful events and traditions of the neighborhood. He recollected Rip at once, and corroborated his story in the most satisfactory manner. He assured the company that it was a fact, handed down from his ancestor the historian, that the Kaatskill Mountains had always been haunted by strange beings. That it was affirmed that the great Hendrick Hudson, the first discoverer of the river and country, kept a kind of vigil there every twenty years, with his crew of the Half-Moon, being permitted in this way to revisit the scenes of his enterprise, and keep a guardian eye upon the river, and the great city called by his name. That his father had once seen them in their old Dutch dresses playing at nine-pins in a hollow of the mountain; and that he himself had heard, one summer afternoon, the sound of their balls, like distant peals of thunder.

To make a long story short, the company broke up, and returned to the more important concerns of the election. Rip's daughter took him home to live with her; she had a snug, well-furnished house, and a stout cheery farmer for a husband, whom Rip recollected for one of the urchins that used to climb upon his back. As to Rip's son and heir, who was the ditto of himself, seen leaning against the tree, he was employed to work on the farm; but evinced an hereditary disposition to attend to anything else but his business.

Rip now resumed his old walks and habits; he soon found many of his former cronies, though all rather the worse for the wear and tear of time; and preferred making friends among the rising generation, with whom he soon grew into great favor.

Having nothing to do at home, and being arrived at that happy age when a man can be idle with impunity, he took his place once more on the bench at the inn door, and was reverenced as one of the patriarchs of the village, and a chronicle of the old times "before the war." It was some time before he could get into the regular track of gossip, or could be made to comprehend the strange events that had taken place during his torpor. How that there had been a revolutionary war—that the country had thrown off the yoke of old England—and that, instead of being a subject of his Majesty George the Third, he was now a free citizen of the United States. Rip, in fact, was no politician; the changes of states and empires made but little impression on him; but there was one species of despotism under which he had long groaned, and that was—petticoat government. Happily that was at an end; he had got his neck out of the yoke of matrimony, and could go in and out whenever he pleased, without dreading the tyranny of Dame Van Winkle. Whenever her name was mentioned, however, he shook his head, shrugged his shoulders, and cast up his eyes; which might pass either for an expression of resignation to his fate, or joy at his deliverance.

He used to tell his story to every stranger that arrived at Mr. Doolittle's hotel. He was observed, at first, to vary on some points every time he told it, which was, doubtless, owing to his having so recently awakened. It at last settled down precisely to the tale I have related, and not a man, woman or child in the neighborhood, but knew it by heart. Some always pretended to doubt the reality of it, and insisted that Rip had been out of his head, and that this was one point on which he always remained flighty. The old Dutch inhabitants, however, almost universally gave it full credit. Even to this day they never hear a thunderstorm of a summer afternoon about the Kaatskill, but they say Hendrick Hudson and his crew are at their game of nine-pins; and it is a common wish of all hen-pecked husbands in the neighborhood, when life hangs heavy on their hands, that they might have a quieting draught out of Rip Van Winkle's flagon.

SOURCE: Washington Irving. *The Sketch Book of Geoffrey Crayon, Gent.* New York: George P. Putnam, 1848.

JAMES FENIMORE COOPER

James Fenimore Cooper (1789–1851) became one of America's most popular novelists despite not having shown any interest in writing until his thirties. He relied on his love of the outdoors in upstate New York for the settings in this novel. His characterization reveals a most peculiar fascination with his hero, Natty Bumppo, a scout known in these passages as Hawkeye or La Longue Carabine. The other characters, from romantic or hardy young women, to sublimely virtuous or absurdly villainous Native Americans, seem to have been based on romantic ideas about independence, virtue, race and nature. Through their popularity, Cooper's novels created various pervasive stereotypes of Native American life. Despite the novel's title, the Mohicans (or Mohegans) survived. The writing is sometimes cramped and convoluted, and yet as the scenes awkwardly unfold, we realize we have distinctly envisioned them.

The novel takes place in 1757 during the French and Indian War, which occurred in upper New York between the French and the English. British Major Duncan Heyward is relying on the help of Hawkeye and the Mohican father and son, Chingachgook and Uncas, to restore General Munro's beautiful daughters to his fort, and later to rescue them from Magua, the energetic Huron villain fighting for the Iroquois and the French.

Chapters from *The Last of the Mohicans* (1826)

Chapter 3

Chapter 3 introduces Hawkeye, Chingachgook and Uncas.

"Before these fields were shorn and till'd,
Full to the brim our rivers flow'd;
The melody of waters fill'd
The fresh and boundless wood;
And torrents dash'd, and rivulets play'd,
And fountains spouted in the shade."

BRYANT

LEAVING THE UNSUSPECTING Heyward and his confiding companions to penetrate still deeper into a forest that contained such treacherous inmates, we must use an author's privilege, and shift the scene a few miles to the westward of the place where we have last seen them.

On that day, two men were lingering on the banks of a small but rapid stream, within an hour's journey of the encampment of Webb, like those who awaited the appearance of an absent person, or the approach of some expected event. The vast canopy of woods spread itself to the margin of the river, overhanging the water, and shadowing its dark current with a deeper hue. The rays of the sun were beginning to grow less fierce, and the intense heat of the day was lessened, as the cooler vapors of the springs and fountains rose above their leafy beds, and rested in the atmosphere. Still that breathing silence, which marks the drowsy sultriness of an American landscape in July, pervaded the secluded spot, interrupted only by the low voices of the men, the occasional and lazy tap of a woodpecker, the discordant cry of some gaudy jay, or a swelling on the ear, from the dull roar of a distant waterfall.

These feeble and broken sounds were, however, too familiar to the foresters to draw their attention from the more interesting matter of their dialogue. While one of these loiterers showed the red skin and wild accounterments of a native of the woods, the other exhibited, through the mask of his rude and nearly savage equipments, the brighter, though sun-burned and long-faced complexion of one who might claim descent from a European parentage. The former was seated on the end of a mossy log, in a posture that permitted him to heighten the effect of his earnest language, by the calm but expressive gestures of an Indian engaged in debate. His body, which was nearly naked, presented a terrific emblem of death, drawn in intermingled colors of white and black. His closely-shaved head, on which no other hair than the well-known and chivalrous scalping tuft[1] was preserved, was without ornament of any kind, with the exception of a solitary eagle's

1. [Cooper's note:] The North American warrior caused the hair to be plucked from his whole body; a small tuft was left on the crown of his head, in order that his enemy might avail himself of it, in wrenching off the scalp in the event of his fall. The scalp was the only admissible trophy of victory. Thus, it was deemed more important to obtain the scalp than to kill the man. Some tribes lay great stress on the honor of striking a dead body. These practices have nearly disappeared among the Indians of the Atlantic states.

plume, that crossed his crown, and depended over the left shoulder. A tomahawk and scalping knife, of English manufacture, were in his girdle; while a short military rifle, of that sort with which the policy of the whites armed their savage allies, lay carelessly across his bare and sinewy knee. The expanded chest, full formed limbs, and grave countenance of this warrior, would denote that he had reached the vigor of his days, though no symptoms of decay appeared to have yet weakened his manhood.

The frame of the white man, judging by such parts as were not concealed by his clothes, was like that of one who had known hardships and exertion from his earliest youth. His person, though muscular, was rather attenuated than full; but every nerve and muscle appeared strung and indurated by unremitted exposure and toil. He wore a hunting shirt of forest-green, fringed with faded yellow,[2] and a summer cap of skins which had been shorn of their fur. He also bore a knife in a girdle of wampum, like that which confined the scanty garments of the Indian, but no tomahawk. His moccasins were ornamented after the gay fashion of the natives, while the only part of his under-dress which appeared below the hunting-frock, was a pair of buckskin leggings, that laced at the sides, and which were gartered above the knees, with the sinews of a deer. A pouch and horn completed his personal accouterments, though a rifle of great length,[3] which the theory of the more ingenious whites had taught them was the most dangerous of all firearms, leaned against a neighboring sapling. The eye of the hunter, or scout, whichever he might be, was small, quick, keen, and restless, roving while he spoke, on every side of him, as if in quest of game, or distrusting the sudden approach of some lurking enemy. Notwithstanding the symptoms of habitual suspicion, his countenance was not only without guile, but at the moment at which he is introduced, it was charged with an expression of sturdy honesty.

"Even your traditions make the case in my favor, Chingachgook," he said, speaking in the tongue which was known to all the natives

2. [Cooper's note:] The hunting-shirt is a picturesque smock-frock, being shorter, and ornamented with fringes and tassels. The colors are intended to imitate the hues of the wood, with a view to concealment. Many corps of American riflemen have been thus attired, and the dress is one of the most striking of modern times. The hunting-shirt is frequently white.

3. [Cooper's note:] The rifle of the army is short; that of the hunter is always long.

who formerly inhabited the country between the Hudson and the Potomac, and of which we shall give a free translation for the benefit of the reader; endeavoring, at the same time, to preserve some of the peculiarities, both of the individual and of the language. "Your fathers came from the setting sun, crossed the big river,[4] fought the people of the country, and took the land, and mine came from the red sky of the morning, over the salt lake, and did their work much after the fashion that had been set them by yours; then let God judge the matter between us, and friends spare their words!"

"My fathers fought with the naked red man!" returned the Indian, sternly, in the same language. "Is there no difference, Hawkeye, between the stone-headed arrow of the warrior, and the leaden bullet with which you kill?"

"There is reason in an Indian, though nature has made him with a red skin!" said the white man, shaking his head like one on whom such an appeal to his justice was not thrown away. For a moment he appeared to be conscious of having the worst of the argument, then, rallying again, he answered the objection of his antagonist in the best manner his limited information would allow: "I am no scholar, and I care not who knows it; but, judging from what I have seen, at deer chases and squirrel hunts, of the sparks below, I should think a rifle in the hands of their grandfathers was not so dangerous as a hickory bow and a good flint-head might be, if drawn with Indian judgment, and sent by an Indian eye."

"You have the story told by your fathers," returned the other, coldly waving his hand. "What say your old men? Do they tell the young warriors that the pale faces met the red men, painted for war and armed with the stone hatchet and wooden gun?"

"I am not a prejudiced man, nor one who vaunts himself on his natural privileges, though the worst enemy I have on earth, and he is an Iroquois, daren't deny that I am genuine white," the scout replied, surveying, with secret satisfaction, the faded color of his bony and sinewy hand, "and I am willing to own that my people have many ways, of which, as an honest man, I can't approve. It is one of their customs to write in books what they have done and seen, instead of telling them in their villages, where the lie can be

4. [Cooper's note:] The Mississippi. The scout alludes to a tradition which is very popular among the tribes of the Atlantic states. Evidence of their Asiatic origin is deduced from the circumstances, though great uncertainty hangs over the whole history of the Indians.

given to the face of a cowardly boaster, and the brave soldier can call on his comrades to witness for the truth of his words. In consequence of this bad fashion, a man, who is too conscientious to misspend his days among the women, in learning the names of black marks, may never hear of the deeds of his fathers, nor feel a pride in striving to outdo them. For myself, I conclude the Bumppos could shoot, for I have a natural turn with a rifle, which must have been handed down from generation to generation, as, our holy commandments tell us, all good and evil gifts are bestowed; though I should be loath to answer for other people in such a matter. But every story has its two sides; so I ask you, Chingachgook, what passed, according to the traditions of the red men, when our fathers first met?"

A silence of a minute succeeded, during which the Indian sat mute; then, full of the dignity of his office, he commenced his brief tale, with a solemnity that served to heighten its appearance of truth.

"Listen, Hawkeye, and your ear shall drink no lie. 'Tis what my fathers have said, and what the Mohicans have done." He hesitated a single instant, and bending a cautious glance toward his companion, he continued, in a manner that was divided between interrogation and assertion. "Does not this stream at our feet run toward the summer, until its waters grow salt, and the current flows upward?"

"It can't be denied that your traditions tell you true in both these matters," said the white man; "for I have been there, and have seen them, though why water, which is so sweet in the shade, should become bitter in the sun, is an alteration for which I have never been able to account."

"And the current!" demanded the Indian, who expected his reply with that sort of interest that a man feels in the confirmation of testimony, at which he marvels even while he respects it; "the fathers of Chingachgook have not lied!"

"The Holy Bible is not more true, and that is the truest thing in nature. They call this up-stream current the tide, which is a thing soon explained, and clear enough. Six hours the waters run in, and six hours they run out, and the reason is this: when there is higher water in the sea than in the river, they run in until the river gets to be highest, and then it runs out again."

"The waters in the woods, and on the great lakes, run downward until they lie like my hand," said the Indian, stretching the limb horizontally before him, "and then they run no more."

"No honest man will deny it," said the scout, a little nettled at the implied distrust of his explanation of the mystery of the tides; "and I grant that it is true on the small scale, and where the land is level. But everything depends on what scale you look at things. Now, on the small scale, the 'arth is level; but on the large scale it is round. In this manner, pools and ponds, and even the great fresh-water lakes, may be stagnant, as you and I both know they are, having seen them; but when you come to spread water over a great tract, like the sea, where the earth is round, how in reason can the water be quiet? You might as well expect the river to lie still on the brink of those black rocks a mile above us, though your own ears tell you that it is tumbling over them at this very moment."

If unsatisfied by the philosophy of his companion, the Indian was far too dignified to betray his unbelief. He listened like one who was convinced, and resumed his narrative in his former solemn manner.

"We came from the place where the sun is hid at night, over great plains where the buffaloes live, until we reached the big river. There we fought the Alligewi, till the ground was red with their blood. From the banks of the big river to the shores of the salt lake, there was none to meet us. The Maquas followed at a distance. We said the country should be ours from the place where the water runs up no longer on this stream, to a river twenty sun's journey toward the summer. We drove the Maquas into the woods with the bears. They only tasted salt at the licks; they drew no fish from the great lake; we threw them the bones."

"All this I have heard and believe," said the white man, observing that the Indian paused; "but it was long before the English came into the country."

"A pine grew then where this chestnut now stands. The first pale faces who came among us spoke no English. They came in a large canoe, when my fathers had buried the tomahawk with the red men around them. Then, Hawkeye," he continued, betraying his deep emotion, only by permitting his voice to fall to those low, guttural tones, which render his language, as spoken at times, so very musical; "then, Hawkeye, we were one people, and we were happy. The salt lake gave us its fish, the wood its deer, and the air its birds. We took wives who bore us children; we worshipped the Great Spirit; and we kept the Maquas beyond the sound of our songs of triumph."

"Know you anything of your own family at that time?" demanded the white. "But you are just a man, for an Indian; and as I suppose you hold their gifts, your fathers must have been brave warriors, and wise men at the council-fire."

"My tribe is the grandfather of nations, but I am an unmixed man. The blood of chiefs is in my veins, where it must stay forever. The Dutch landed, and gave my people the fire-water; they drank until the heavens and the earth seemed to meet, and they foolishly thought they had found the Great Spirit. Then they parted with their land. Foot by foot, they were driven back from the shores, until I, that am a chief and a Sagamore, have never seen the sun shine but through the trees, and have never visited the graves of my fathers."

"Graves bring solemn feelings over the mind," returned the scout, a good deal touched at the calm suffering of his companion; "and they often aid a man in his good intentions; though, for myself, I expect to leave my own bones unburied, to bleach in the woods, or to be torn asunder by the wolves. But where are to be found those of your race who came to their kin in the Delaware country, so many summers since?"

"Where are the blossoms of those summers!—fallen, one by one; so all of my family departed, each in his turn, to the land of spirits. I am on the hilltop and must go down into the valley; and when Uncas follows in my footsteps there will no longer be any of the blood of the Sagamores, for my boy is the last of the Mohicans."

"Uncas is here," said another voice, in the same soft, guttural tones, near his elbow; "who speaks to Uncas?"

The white man loosened his knife in his leathern sheath, and made an involuntary movement of the hand toward his rifle, at this sudden interruption; but the Indian sat composed, and without turning his head at the unexpected sounds.

At the next instant, a youthful warrior passed between them, with a noiseless step, and seated himself on the bank of the rapid stream. No exclamation of surprise escaped the father, nor was any question asked, or reply given, for several minutes; each appearing to await the moment when he might speak, without betraying womanish curiosity or childish impatience. The white man seemed to take counsel from their customs, and, relinquishing his grasp of the rifle, he also remained silent and reserved. At length Chingachgook turned his eyes slowly toward his son, and demanded:

"Do the Maquas dare to leave the print of their moccasins in these woods?"

"I have been on their trail," replied the young Indian, "and know that they number as many as the fingers of my two hands; but they lie hid like cowards."

"The thieves are outlying for scalps and plunder," said the white man, whom we shall call Hawkeye, after the manner of his companions. "That busy Frenchman, Montcalm, will send his spies into our very camp, but he will know what road we travel!"

" 'Tis enough," returned the father, glancing his eye toward the setting sun; "they shall be driven like deer from their bushes. Hawkeye, let us eat to-night, and show the Maquas that we are men to-morrow."

"I am as ready to do the one as the other; but to fight the Iroquois 'tis necessary to find the skulkers; and to eat, 'tis necessary to get the game—talk of the devil and he will come; there is a pair of the biggest antlers I have seen this season, moving the bushes below the hill! Now, Uncas," he continued, in a half whisper, and laughing with a kind of inward sound, like one who had learned to be watchful, "I will bet my charger three times full of powder, against a foot of wampum, that I take him atwixt the eyes, and nearer to the right than to the left."

"It cannot be!" said the young Indian, springing to his feet with youthful eagerness; "all but the tips of his horns are hid!"

"He's a boy!" said the white man, shaking his head while he spoke, and addressing the father. "Does he think when a hunter sees a part of the creatur', he can't tell where the rest of him should be!"

Adjusting his rifle, he was about to make an exhibition of that skill on which he so much valued himself, when the warrior struck up the piece with his hand, saying:

"Hawkeye! will you fight the Maquas?"

"These Indians know the nature of the woods, as it might be by instinct!" returned the scout, dropping his rifle, and turning away like a man who was convinced of his error. "I must leave the buck to your arrow, Uncas, or we may kill a deer for them thieves, the Iroquois, to eat."

The instant the father seconded this intimation by an expressive gesture of the hand, Uncas threw himself on the ground, and approached the animal with wary movements. When within a few yards of the cover, he fitted an arrow to his bow with the utmost care, while the antlers moved, as if their owner snuffed an enemy in the tainted air. In another moment the twang of the cord was heard, a white streak was seen glancing into the bushes, and the wounded buck plunged from the cover, to the very feet of his hidden enemy. Avoiding the horns of the infuriated animal, Uncas darted to his side, and passed his knife across the throat, when bounding to the edge of the river it fell, dyeing the waters with its blood.

"'Twas done with Indian skill," said the scout laughing inwardly, but with vast satisfaction; "and 'twas a pretty sight to behold! Though an arrow is a near shot, and needs a knife to finish the work."

"Hugh!" ejaculated his companion, turning quickly, like a hound who scented game.

"By the Lord, there is a drove of them!" exclaimed the scout, whose eyes began to glisten with the ardor of his usual occupation; "if they come within range of a bullet I will drop one, though the whole Six Nations should be lurking within sound! What do you hear, Chingachgook? for to my ears the woods are dumb."

"There is but one deer, and he is dead," said the Indian, bending his body till his ear nearly touched the earth. "I hear the sounds of feet!"

"Perhaps the wolves have driven the buck to shelter, and are following on his trail."

"No. The horses of white men are coming!" returned the other, raising himself with dignity, and resuming his seat on the log with his former composure. "Hawkeye, they are your brothers; speak to them."

"That I will, and in English that the king needn't be ashamed to answer," returned the hunter, speaking in the language of which he boasted; "but I see nothing, nor do I hear the sounds of man or beast; 'tis strange that an Indian should understand white sounds better than a man who, his very enemies will own, has no cross in his blood, although he may have lived with the red skins long enough to be suspected! Ha! there goes something like the cracking of a dry stick, too—now I hear the bushes move—yes, yes, there is a trampling that I mistook for the falls—and—but here they come themselves; God keep them from the Iroquois!"

Chapter 17

In this chapter, after the French victory led by General Montcalm at Fort Henry we meet Magua, or "Le Renard Subtil."

"Weave we the woof. The thread is spun.
The web is wove. The work is done."
Gray

The hostile armies, which lay in the wilds of the Horican, passed the night of the ninth of August, 1757, much in the manner they would, had they encountered on the fairest field of Europe. While the conquered were still, sullen, and dejected, the victors triumphed. But there are limits alike to grief and joy; and long before the watches of the morning came the stillness of those boundless woods was only broken by a gay call from some exulting young Frenchman of the advanced pickets, or a menacing challenge from the fort, which sternly forbade the approach of any hostile footsteps before the stipulated moment. Even these occasional threatening sounds ceased to be heard in that dull hour which precedes the day, at which period a listener might have sought in vain any evidence of the presence of those armed powers that then slumbered on the shores of the "holy lake."

It was during these moments of deep silence that the canvas which concealed the entrance to a spacious marquee in the French encampment was shoved aside, and a man issued from beneath the drapery into the open air. He was enveloped in a cloak that might have been intended as a protection from the chilling damps of the woods, but which served equally well as a mantle to conceal his person. He was permitted to pass the grenadier, who watched over the slumbers of the French commander, without interruption, the man making the usual salute which betokens military deference, as the other passed swiftly through the little city of tents, in the direction of William Henry. Whenever this unknown individual encountered one of the numberless sentinels who crossed his path, his answer was prompt, and, as it appeared, satisfactory; for he was uniformly allowed to proceed without further interrogation.

With the exception of such repeated but brief interruptions, he had moved silently from the center of the camp to its most advanced outposts, when he drew nigh the soldier who held his watch nearest to the works of the enemy. As he approached he was received with the usual challenge:

"Qui vive?"

"France," was the reply.

"Le mot d'ordre?"

"La victorie," said the other, drawing so nigh as to be heard in a loud whisper.

"C'est bien," returned the sentinel, throwing his musket from the charge to his shoulder; "vous promenez bien matin, monsieur!"

"Il est nécessaire d'être vigilant, mon enfant," the other observed, dropping a fold of his cloak, and looking the soldier close in the face as he passed him, still continuing his way toward the British fortification. The man started; his arms rattled heavily as he threw them forward in the lowest and most respectful salute; and when he had again recovered his piece, he turned to walk his post, muttering between his teeth:

"Il faut être vigilant, en vérité! je crois que nous avons là, un caporal qui ne dort jamais!"

The officer proceeded, without affecting to hear the words which escaped the sentinel in his surprise; nor did he again pause until he had reached the low strand, and in a somewhat dangerous vicinity to the western water bastion of the fort. The light of an obscure moon was just sufficient to render objects, though dim, perceptible in their outlines. He, therefore, took the precaution to place himself against the trunk of a tree, where he leaned for many minutes, and seemed to contemplate the dark and silent mounds of the English works in profound attention. His gaze at the ramparts was not that of a curious or idle spectator; but his looks wandered from point to point, denoting his knowledge of military usages, and betraying that his search was not unaccompanied by distrust. At length he appeared satisfied; and having cast his eyes impatiently upward toward the summit of the eastern mountain, as if anticipating the approach of the morning, he was in the act of turning on his footsteps, when a light sound on the nearest angle of the bastion caught his ear, and induced him to remain.

Just then a figure was seen to approach the edge of the rampart, where it stood, apparently contemplating in its turn the distant tents of the French encampment. Its head was then turned toward the east, as though equally anxious for the appearance of light, when the form leaned against the mound, and seemed to gaze upon the glassy expanse of the waters, which, like a submarine firmament, glittered with its thousand mimic stars. The melancholy air, the hour, together with the vast frame of the man who thus leaned, musing, against the English ramparts, left no doubt as to his person in the mind of the observant spectator. Delicacy, no less than prudence, now urged him to retire; and he had moved cautiously round the body of the tree for that purpose, when another sound drew his attention, and once more arrested his footsteps. It was a low and almost inaudible movement of the water, and was succeeded by a grating of pebbles one against the other. In a moment he saw a dark form rise, as it were, out of the lake, and steal without further noise to the land, within a few feet of the place where he himself stood. A rifle next slowly rose between his eyes and the watery mirror; but before it could be discharged his own hand was on the lock.

"Hugh!" exclaimed the savage, whose treacherous aim was so singularly and so unexpectedly interrupted.

Without making any reply, the French officer laid his hand on the shoulder of the Indian, and led him in profound silence to a distance from the spot, where their subsequent dialogue might have proved dangerous, and where it seemed that one of them, at least, sought a victim. Then throwing open his cloak, so as to expose his uniform and the cross of St. Louis which was suspended at his breast, Montcalm sternly demanded:

"What means this? Does not my son know that the hatchet is buried between the English and his Canadian Father?"

"What can the Hurons do?" returned the savage, speaking also, though imperfectly, in the French language. "Not a warrior has a scalp, and the pale faces make friends!"

"Ha, Le Renard Subtil! Methinks this is an excess of zeal for a friend who was so late an enemy! How many suns have set since Le Renard struck the war-post of the English?"

"Where is that sun?" demanded the sullen savage. "Behind the hill; and it is dark and cold. But when he comes again, it will be bright and warm. Le Subtil is the sun of his tribe. There have been clouds, and many mountains between him and his nation; but now he shines and it is a clear sky!"

"That Le Renard has power with his people, I well know," said Montcalm; "for yesterday he hunted for their scalps, and to-day they hear him at the council-fire."

"Magua is a great chief."

"Let him prove it, by teaching his nation how to conduct themselves toward our new friends."

"Why did the chief of the Canadas bring his young men into the woods, and fire his cannon at the earthen house?" demanded the subtle Indian.

"To subdue it. My master owns the land, and your father was ordered to drive off these English squatters. They have consented to go, and now he calls them enemies no longer."

"'Tis well. Magua took the hatchet to color it with blood. It is now bright; when it is red, it shall be buried."

"But Magua is pledged not to sully the lilies of France. The enemies of the great king across the salt lake are his enemies; his friends, the friends of the Hurons."

"Friends!" repeated the Indian in scorn. "Let his father give Magua a hand."

Montcalm, who felt that his influence over the warlike tribes he had gathered was to be maintained by concession rather than by power, complied reluctantly with the other's request. The savage placed the fingers of the French commander on a deep scar in his bosom, and then exultingly demanded:

"Does my father know that?"

"What warrior does not? 'Tis where a leaden bullet has cut."

"And this?" continued the Indian, who had turned his naked back to the other, his body being without its usual calico mantle.

"This!—my son has been sadly injured here; who has done this?"

"Magua slept hard in the English wigwams, and the sticks have left their mark," returned the savage, with a hollow laugh, which did not conceal the fierce temper that nearly choked him. Then, recollecting himself, with sudden and native dignity, he added: "Go; teach your young men it is peace. Le Renard Subtil knows how to speak to a Huron warrior."

Without deigning to bestow further words, or to wait for any answer, the savage cast his rifle into the hollow of his arm, and moved silently through the encampment toward the woods where his own tribe was known to lie. Every few yards as he proceeded he was challenged by the sentinels; but he stalked sullenly onward, utterly disregarding the summons of the soldiers, who only spared his life because they knew the air and tread no less than the obstinate daring of an Indian.

Montcalm lingered long and melancholy on the strand where he had been left by his companion, brooding deeply on the temper which his ungovernable ally had just discovered. Already had his fair fame been tarnished by one horrid scene, and in circumstances fearfully resembling those under which he now found himself. As he mused he became keenly sensible of the deep responsibility they assume who disregard the means to attain the end, and of all the danger of setting in motion an engine which it exceeds human power to control. Then shaking off a train of reflections that he accounted a weakness in such a moment of triumph, he retraced his steps toward his tent, giving the order as he passed to make the signal that should arouse the army from its slumbers.

The first tap of the French drums was echoed from the bosom of the fort, and presently the valley was filled with the strains of martial music, rising long, thrilling and lively above the rattling accompaniment. The horns of the victors sounded merry and cheerful flourishes, until the last laggard of the camp was at his post; but the instant the British fifes had blown their shrill signal, they became mute. In the meantime the day had dawned, and when the line of the French army was ready to receive its general, the rays of a brilliant sun were glancing along the glittering array. Then that success, which was already so well known, was officially announced; the favored band who were selected to guard the gates of the fort were detailed, and defiled before their chief; the signal of their approach was given, and all the usual preparations for a change of masters were ordered and executed directly under the guns of the contested works.

A very different scene presented itself within the lines of the Anglo-American army. As soon as the warning signal was given, it exhibited all the signs of a hurried and forced departure. The sullen soldiers shouldered their empty tubes and fell into their places, like men whose blood had been heated by the past contest, and who only desired the opportunity to revenge an indignity which was still wounding to their pride, concealed as it was under the observances of military etiquette.

Women and children ran from place to place, some bearing the scanty remnants of their baggage, and others searching in the ranks for those countenances they looked up to for protection.

Munro appeared among his silent troops firm but dejected. It was evident that the unexpected blow had struck deep into his heart, though he struggled to sustain his misfortune with the port of a man.

Duncan was touched at the quiet and impressive exhibition of his grief. He had discharged his own duty, and he now pressed to the side of the old man, to know in what particular he might serve him.

"My daughters," was the brief but expressive reply.

"Good heavens! are not arrangements already made for their convenience?"

"To-day I am only a soldier, Major Heyward," said the veteran. "All that you see here, claim alike to be my children."

Duncan had heard enough. Without losing one of those moments which had now become so precious, he flew toward the quarters of Munro, in quest of the sisters. He found them on the threshold of the low edifice, already prepared to depart, and surrounded by a clamorous and weeping assemblage of their own sex, that had gathered about the place, with a sort of instinctive consciousness that it was the point most likely to be protected. Though the cheeks of Cora were pale and her countenance anxious, she had lost none of her firmness; but the eyes of Alice were inflamed, and betrayed how long and bitterly she had wept. They both, however, received the young man with undisguised pleasure; the former, for a novelty, being the first to speak.

"The fort is lost," she said, with a melancholy smile; "though our good name, I trust, remains."

" 'Tis brighter than ever. But, dearest Miss Munro, it is time to think less of others, and to make some provision for yourself. Military usage—pride—that pride on which you so much value yourself, demands that your father and I should for a little while continue with the troops. Then where to seek a proper protector for you against the confusion and chances of such a scene?"

"None is necessary," returned Cora; "who will dare to injure or insult the daughter of such a father, at a time like this?"

"I would not leave you alone," continued the youth, looking about him in a hurried manner, "for the command of the best regiment in the pay of the king. Remember, our Alice is not gifted with all your firmness, and God only knows the terror she might endure."

"You may be right," Cora replied, smiling again, but far more sadly than before. "Listen! chance has already sent us a friend when he is most needed."

Duncan did listen, and on the instant comprehended her meaning. The low and serious sounds of the sacred music, so well known to the eastern provinces, caught his ear, and instantly drew him to an apartment in an adjacent building, which had already been deserted by its customary tenants. There he found David, pouring out his pious feelings through the only medium in which he ever indulged. Duncan waited, until, by the cessation of the movement of the hand, he believed the strain was ended, when, by touching his shoulder, he drew the attention of the other to himself, and in a few words explained his wishes.

"Even so," replied the single-minded disciple of the King of Israel, when the young man had ended; "I have found much that is comely and melodious in the maidens, and it is fitting that we who have consorted in so much peril, should abide together in peace. I will attend them, when I have completed my morning praise, to which nothing is now wanting but the doxology. Wilt thou bear a part, friend? The meter is common, and the tune 'Southwell.'"

Then, extending the little volume, and giving the pitch of the air anew with considerate attention, David recommenced and finished his strains, with a fixedness of manner that it was not easy to interrupt. Heyward was fain to wait until the verse was ended; when, seeing David relieving himself from the spectacles, and replacing the book, he continued.

"It will be your duty to see that none dare to approach the ladies with any rude intention, or to offer insult or taunt at the misfortune of their brave father. In this task you will be seconded by the domestics of their household."

"Even so."

"It is possible that the Indians and stragglers of the enemy may intrude, in which case you will remind them of the terms of the capitulation, and threaten to report their conduct to Montcalm. A word will suffice."

"If not, I have that here which shall," returned David, exhibiting his book, with an air in which meekness and confidence were singularly blended. Here are words which, uttered, or rather thundered, with proper emphasis, and in measured time, shall quiet the most unruly temper:

"'Why rage the heathen furiously'?"

"Enough," said Heyward, interrupting the burst of his musical invocation; "we understand each other; it is time that we should now assume our respective duties."

Gamut cheerfully assented, and together they sought the females. Cora received her new and somewhat extraordinary protector courteously, at least; and even the pallid features of Alice lighted again with some of their native archness as she thanked Heyward for his care. Duncan took occasion to assure them he had done the best that circumstances permitted, and, as he believed, quite enough for the security of their feelings; of danger there was none. He then spoke gladly of his intention to rejoin them the moment he had led the advance a few miles toward the Hudson, and immediately took his leave.

By this time the signal for departure had been given, and the head of the English column was in motion. The sisters started at the sound, and glancing their eyes around, they saw the white uniforms of the French grenadiers, who had already taken possession of the gates of the fort. At that moment an enormous cloud seemed to pass suddenly above their heads, and, looking upward, they discovered that they stood beneath the wide folds of the standard of France.

"Let us go," said Cora; "this is no longer a fit place for the children of an English officer."

Alice clung to the arm of her sister, and together they left the parade, accompanied by the moving throng that surrounded them.

As they passed the gates, the French officers, who had learned their rank, bowed often and low, forbearing, however, to intrude those attentions which they saw, with peculiar tact, might not be agreeable. As every vehicle and each beast of burden was occupied by the sick and wounded, Cora had decided to endure the fatigues of a foot march, rather than interfere with their comforts. Indeed, many a maimed and feeble soldier was compelled to drag his exhausted limbs in the rear of the columns, for the want of the necessary means of conveyance in that wilderness. The whole, however, was in motion; the weak and wounded, groaning and in suffering; their comrades silent and sullen; and the women and children in terror, they knew not of what.

As the confused and timid throng left the protecting mounds of the fort, and issued on the open plain, the whole scene was at once presented to their eyes. At a little distance on the right, and somewhat in the rear, the French army stood to their arms, Montcalm having collected his parties, so soon as his guards had possession of the works. They were attentive but silent observers of the proceedings of the vanquished, failing in none of the stipulated military honors, and offering no taunt or insult, in their success, to their less fortunate foes. Living masses of the English, to the amount, in the whole, of near three thousand, were moving slowly across the plain, toward the common center, and gradually approached each other, as they converged to the point of their march, a vista cut through the lofty trees, where the road to the Hudson entered the forest. Along the sweeping borders of the woods hung a dark cloud of savages, eyeing the passage of their enemies, and hovering at a distance, like vultures who were only kept from swooping on their prey by the presence and restraint of a superior army. A few had straggled among the conquered columns, where they stalked in sullen discontent; attentive, though, as yet, passive observers of the moving multitude.

The advance, with Heyward at its head, had already reached the defile, and was slowly disappearing, when the attention of Cora was drawn to a collection of stragglers by the sounds of contention. A truant provincial was paying the forfeit of his disobedience, by being plundered of those very effects which had caused him to desert his place in the ranks. The man was of powerful frame, and too avaricious to part with his goods without a struggle. Individuals from either party interfered; the one side to prevent and the other to aid in the robbery. Voices grew loud and angry, and a hundred savages appeared, as it were, by magic, where a dozen only had been seen a minute before. It was then that Cora saw the form of Magua gliding among his countrymen, and speaking with his fatal and artful eloquence. The mass of women and children stopped, and hovered together like alarmed and fluttering birds. But the cupidity of the Indian was soon gratified, and the different bodies again moved slowly onward.

The savages now fell back, and seemed content to let their enemies advance without further molestation. But, as the female crowd approached them, the gaudy colors of a shawl attracted the eyes of a wild and untutored Huron. He advanced to seize it without the least hesitation. The woman, more in terror than through love of the ornament, wrapped her child in the coveted article, and folded both more closely to her bosom. Cora was in the act of speaking, with an intent to advise the woman to abandon the trifle, when the savage relinquished his hold of the shawl, and tore the screaming infant from her arms. Abandoning everything to the greedy grasp of those around her, the mother darted, with distraction in her mien, to reclaim her child. The Indian smiled grimly, and extended one hand, in sign of a willingness to exchange, while, with the other, he flourished the babe over his head, holding it by the feet as if to enhance the value of the ransom.

"Here—here—there—all—any—everything!" exclaimed the breathless woman, tearing the lighter articles of dress from her person with ill-directed and trembling fingers; "take all, but give me my babe!"

The savage spurned the worthless rags, and perceiving that the shawl had already become a prize to another, his bantering but sullen smile changing to a gleam of ferocity, he dashed the head of the infant against a rock, and cast its quivering remains to her very feet. For an instant the mother stood, like a statue of despair, looking wildly down at the unseemly object, which had so lately nestled in her bosom and smiled in her face; and then she raised her eyes and countenance toward heaven, as if calling on God to curse the perpetrator of the foul deed. She was spared the sin of such a prayer for, maddened at his disappointment, and excited at the sight of blood, the Huron mercifully drove his tomahawk into her own brain. The mother sank under the blow, and fell, grasping at her child, in death, with the same engrossing love that had caused her to cherish it when living.

At that dangerous moment, Magua placed his hands to his mouth, and raised the fatal and appalling whoop. The scattered Indians started at the well-known cry, as coursers bound at the signal to quit the goal; and directly there arose such a yell along the plain, and through the arches of the wood, as seldom burst from human lips before. They who heard it listened with a curdling horror at the heart, little inferior to that dread which may be expected to attend the blasts of the final summons.

More than two thousand raving savages broke from the forest at the signal, and threw themselves across the fatal plain with instinctive alacrity. We shall not dwell on the revolting horrors that succeeded. Death was everywhere, and in his most terrific and disgusting aspects. Resistance only served to inflame the murderers, who inflicted their furious blows long after their victims were beyond the power of their resentment. The flow of blood might be likened to the outbreaking of a torrent; and as the natives became heated and maddened by the sight, many among them even kneeled to the earth, and drank freely, exultingly, hellishly, of the crimson tide.

The trained bodies of the troops threw themselves quickly into solid masses, endeavoring to awe their assailants by the imposing appearance of a military front. The experiment in some measure succeeded, though far too many suffered their unloaded muskets to be torn from their hands, in the vain hope of appeasing the savages.

In such a scene none had leisure to note the fleeting moments. It might have been ten minutes (it seemed an age) that the sisters had stood riveted to one spot, horror-stricken and nearly helpless. When the first blow was struck, their screaming companions had pressed upon them in a body, rendering flight impossible; and now that fear or death had scattered most, if not all, from around them, they saw no avenue open, but such as conducted to the tomahawks of their foes.

On every side arose shrieks, groans, exhortations and curses. At this moment, Alice caught a glimpse of the vast form of her father, moving rapidly across the plain, in the direction of the French army. He was, in truth, proceeding to Montcalm, fearless of every danger, to claim the tardy escort for which he had before conditioned. Fifty glittering axes and barbed spears were offered unheeded at his life, but the savages respected his rank and calmness, even in their fury. The dangerous weapons were brushed aside by the still nervous arm of the veteran, or fell of themselves, after menacing an act that it would seem no one had courage to perform. Fortunately, the vindictive Magua was searching for his victim in the very band the veteran had just quitted.

"Father—father—we are here!" shrieked Alice, as he passed, at no great distance, without appearing to heed them. "Come to us, father, or we die!"

The cry was repeated, and in terms and tones that might have melted a heart of stone, but it was unanswered. Once, indeed, the old man appeared to catch the sound, for he paused and listened; but Alice had dropped senseless on the earth, and Cora had sunk at her side, hovering in untiring tenderness over her lifeless form. Munro shook his head in disappointment, and proceeded, bent on the high duty of his station.

"Lady," said Gamut, who, helpless and useless as he was, had not yet dreamed of deserting his trust, "it is the jubilee of the devils, and this is not a meet place for Christians to tarry in. Let us up and fly."

"Go," said Cora, still gazing at her unconscious sister; "save thyself. To me thou canst not be of further use."

David comprehended the unyielding character of her resolution, by the simple but expressive gesture that accompanied her words. He gazed for a moment at the dusky forms that were acting their hellish rites on every side of him, and his tall person grew more erect while his chest heaved, and every feature swelled, and seemed to speak with the power of the feelings by which he was governed.

"If the Jewish boy might tame the great spirit of Saul by the sound of his harp, and the words of sacred song, it may not be amiss," he said, "to try the potency of music here."

Then raising his voice to its highest tone, he poured out a strain so powerful as to be heard even amid the din of that bloody field. More than one savage rushed toward them, thinking to rifle the unprotected sisters of their attire, and bear away their scalps; but when they found this strange and unmoved figure riveted to his post, they paused to listen. Astonishment soon changed to admiration, and they passed on to other and less courageous victims, openly expressing their satisfaction at the firmness with which the white warrior sang his death song. Encouraged and deluded by his success, David exerted all his powers to extend what he believed so holy an influence. The unwonted sounds caught the ears of a distant savage, who flew raging from group to group, like one who, scorning to touch the vulgar herd, hunted for some victim more worthy of his renown. It was Magua, who uttered a yell of pleasure when he beheld his ancient prisoners again at his mercy.

"Come," he said, laying his soiled hands on the dress of Cora, "the wigwam of the Huron is still open. Is it not better than this place?"

"Away!" cried Cora, veiling her eyes from his revolting aspect.

The Indian laughed tauntingly, as he held up his reeking hand, and answered: "It is red, but it comes from white veins!"

"Monster! there is blood, oceans of blood, upon thy soul; thy spirit has moved this scene."

"Magua is a great chief!" returned the exulting savage, "will the dark-hair go to his tribe?"

"Never! strike if thou wilt, and complete thy revenge." He hesitated a moment, and then catching the light and senseless form of Alice in his arms, the subtle Indian moved swiftly across the plain toward the woods.

"Hold!" shrieked Cora, following wildly on his footsteps; "release the child! wretch! what is't you do?"

But Magua was deaf to her voice; or, rather, he knew his power, and was determined to maintain it.

"Stay—lady—stay," called Gamut, after the unconscious Cora. "The holy charm is beginning to be felt, and soon shalt thou see this horrid tumult stilled."

Perceiving that, in his turn, he was unheeded, the faithful David followed the distracted sister, raising his voice again in sacred song, and sweeping the air to the measure, with his long arm, in diligent accompaniment. In this manner they traversed the plain, through the flying, the wounded and the dead. The fierce Huron was, at any time, sufficient for himself and the victim that he bore; though Cora would have fallen more than once under the blows of her savage enemies, but for the extraordinary being who stalked in her rear, and who now appeared to the astonished natives gifted with the protecting spirit of madness.

Magua, who knew how to avoid the more pressing dangers, and also to elude pursuit, entered the woods through a low ravine, where he quickly found the Narragansetts, which the travelers had abandoned so shortly before, awaiting his appearance, in custody of a savage as fierce and malign in his expression as himself. Laying Alice on one of the horses, he made a sign to Cora to mount the other.

Notwithstanding the horror excited by the presence of her captor, there was a present relief in escaping from the bloody scene enacting on the plain, to which Cora could not be altogether insensible. She took her seat, and held forth her arms for her sister, with an air of entreaty and love that even the Huron could not deny. Placing Alice, then, on the same animal with Cora, he seized the bridle, and commenced his route by plunging deeper into the forest. David, perceiving that he was left alone, utterly disregarded as a subject too worthless even to destroy, threw his long limb across the saddle of the beast they had deserted, and made such progress in the pursuit as the difficulties of the path permitted.

They soon began to ascend; but as the motion had a tendency to revive the dormant faculties of her sister, the attention of Cora was too much divided between the tenderest solicitude in her behalf, and in listening to the cries which were still too audible on the plain, to note the direction in which they journeyed. When, however, they gained the flattened surface of the mountain-top, and approached the eastern precipice, she recognized the spot to which she had once before been led under the more friendly auspices of the scout. Here Magua suffered them to dismount; and notwithstanding their own captivity, the curiosity which seems inseparable from horror, induced them to gaze at the sickening sight below.

The cruel work was still unchecked. On every side the captured were flying before their relentless persecutors, while the armed columns of the Christian king stood fast in an apathy which has never been explained, and which has left an immovable blot on the otherwise fair escutcheon of their leader. Nor was the sword of death stayed until cupidity got the mastery of revenge. Then, indeed, the shrieks of the wounded, and the yells of their murderers grew less frequent, until, finally, the cries of horror were lost to their ear, or were drowned in the loud, long and piercing whoops of the triumphant savages.

Chapter 29

This characteristic chapter includes a shooting contest and a dramatic plea by the heroine Cora Munro.

> "The assembly seated, rising o'er the rest,
> Achilles thus the king of men addressed."
>
> POPE'S *ILIAD*

CORA STOOD FOREMOST among the prisoners, entwining her arms in those of Alice, in the tenderness of sisterly love. Notwithstanding the fearful and menacing array of savages on every side of her, no apprehension on her own account could prevent the nobler-minded maiden from keeping her eyes fastened on the pale and anxious features of the trembling Alice. Close at their side stood Heyward, with an interest in both, that, at such a moment of intense uncertainty, scarcely knew a preponderance in favor of her whom he most loved. Hawkeye had placed himself a little in the rear, with a deference to the superior rank of his companions, that no similarity in the state of their present fortunes could induce him to forget. Uncas was not there.

When perfect silence was again restored, and after the usual long, impressive pause, one of the two aged chiefs who sat at the side of the patriarch arose, and demanded aloud, in very intelligible English:

"Which of my prisoners is La Longue Carabine?"

Neither Duncan nor the scout answered. The former, however, glanced his eyes around the dark and silent assembly, and recoiled a pace, when they fell on the malignant visage of Magua. He saw, at once, that this wily savage had some secret agency in their present arraignment before the nation, and determined to throw every possible impediment in the way of the execution of his sinister plans. He had witnessed one instance of the summary punishments of the Indians, and now dreaded that his companion was to be selected for a second. In this dilemma, with little or no time for reflection, he suddenly determined to cloak his invaluable friend, at any or every hazard to himself. Before he had time, however, to speak, the question was repeated in a louder voice, and with a clearer utterance.

"Give us arms," the young man haughtily replied, "and place us in yonder woods. Our deeds shall speak for us!"

"This is the warrior whose name has filled our ears!" returned the chief, regarding Heyward with that sort of curious interest which seems inseparable from man, when first beholding one of his fellows to whom merit or accident, virtue or crime, has given notoriety. "What has brought the white man into the camp of the Delawares?"

"My necessities. I come for food, shelter, and friends."

"It cannot be. The woods are full of game. The head of a warrior needs no other shelter than a sky without clouds; and the Delawares are the enemies, and not the friends of the Yengeese. Go, the mouth has spoken, while the heart said nothing."

Duncan, a little at a loss in what manner to proceed, remained silent; but the scout, who had listened attentively to all that passed, now advanced steadily to the front.

"That I did not answer to the call for La Longue Carabine, was not owing either to shame or fear," he said, "for neither one nor the other is the gift of an honest man. But I do not admit the right of the Mingoes to bestow a name on one whose friends have been mindful of his gifts, in this particular; especially as their title is a lie, 'killdeer' being a grooved barrel and no carabyne. I am the man, however, that got the name of Nathaniel from my kin; the compliment of Hawkeye from the Delawares, who live on their own river; and whom the Iroquois have presumed to style the 'Long Rifle,' without any warranty from him who is most concerned in the matter."

The eyes of all present, which had hitherto been gravely scanning the person of Duncan, were now turned, on the instant, toward the upright iron frame of this new pretender to the distinguished appellation. It was in no degree remarkable that there should be found two who were willing to claim so great an honor, for imposters, though rare, were not unknown among the natives; but it was altogether material to the just and severe intentions of the Delawares, that there should be no mistake in the matter. Some of their old men consulted together in private, and then, as it would seem, they determined to interrogate their visitor on the subject.

"My brother has said that a snake crept into my camp," said the chief to Magua; "which is he?"

The Huron pointed to the scout.

"Will a wise Delaware believe the barking of a wolf?" exclaimed Duncan, still more confirmed in the evil intentions of his ancient enemy: "a dog never lies, but when was a wolf known to speak the truth?"

The eyes of Magua flashed fire; but suddenly recollecting the necessity of maintaining his presence of mind, he turned away in silent disdain, well assured that the sagacity of the Indians would not fail to extract the real merits of the point in controversy. He was not deceived; for, after another short consultation, the wary Delaware turned to him again, and expressed the determination of the chiefs, though in the most considerate language.

"My brother has been called a liar," he said, "and his friends are angry. They will show that he has spoken the truth. Give my prisoners guns, and let them prove which is the man."

Magua affected to consider the expedient, which he well knew proceeded from distrust of himself, as a compliment, and made a gesture of acquiescence, well content that his veracity should be supported by so skillful a marksman as the scout. The weapons were instantly placed in the hands of the friendly opponents, and they were bid to fire, over the heads of the seated multitude, at an earthen vessel, which lay, by accident, on a stump, some fifty yards from the place where they stood.

Heyward smiled to himself at the idea of a competition with the scout, though he determined to persevere in the deception, until apprised of the real designs of Magua.

Raising his rifle with the utmost care, and renewing his aim three several times, he fired. The bullet cut the wood within a few inches of the vessel; and a general exclamation of satisfaction announced that the shot was considered a proof of great skill in the use of a weapon. Even Hawkeye nodded his head, as if he would say, it was better than he expected. But, instead of manifesting an intention to contend with the successful marksman, he stood leaning on his rifle for more than a minute, like a man who was completely buried in thought. From this reverie, he was, however, awakened by one of the young Indians who had furnished the arms, and who now touched his shoulder, saying in exceedingly broken English:

"Can the pale face beat it?"

"Yes, Huron!" exclaimed the scout, raising the short rifle in his right hand, and shaking it at Magua, with as much apparent ease as if it were a reed; "yes, Huron, I could strike you now, and no power on earth could prevent the deed! The soaring hawk is not more certain of the dove than I am this moment of you, did I choose to send a bullet to your heart! Why should I not? Why!—because the gifts of my color forbid it, and I might draw down evil on tender and innocent heads. If you know such a being as God, thank Him, therefore, in your inward soul; for you have reason!"

The flushed countenance, angry eye and swelling figure of the scout, produced a sensation of secret awe in all that heard him. The Delawares held their breath in expectation; but Magua himself, even while he distrusted the forbearance of his enemy, remained immovable and calm, where he stood wedged in by the crowd, as one who grew to the spot.

"Beat it," repeated the young Delaware at the elbow of the scout.

"Beat what, fool!—what?" exclaimed Hawkeye, still flourishing the weapon angrily above his head, though his eye no longer sought the person of Magua.

"If the white man is the warrior he pretends," said the aged chief, "let him strike nigher to the mark."

The scout laughed aloud—a noise that produced the startling effect of an unnatural sound on Heyward; then dropping the piece, heavily, into his extended left hand, it was discharged, apparently by the shock, driving the fragments of the vessel into the air, and scattering them on every side. Almost at the same instant, the rattling sound of the rifle was heard, as he suffered it to fall, contemptuously, to the earth.

The first impression of so strange a scene was engrossing admiration. Then a low, but increasing murmur, ran through the multitude, and finally swelled into sounds that denoted a lively opposition in the sentiments of the spectators. While some openly testified their satisfaction at so unexampled dexterity, by far the larger portion of the tribe were inclined to believe the success of the shot was the result of accident. Heyward was not slow to confirm an opinion that was so favorable to his own pretensions.

"It was chance!" he exclaimed; "none can shoot without an aim!"

"Chance!" echoed the excited woodsman, who was now stubbornly bent on maintaining his identity at every hazard, and on whom the secret hints of Heyward to acquiesce in the deception were entirely lost. "Does yonder lying Huron, too, think it chance? Give him another gun, and place us face to face, without cover or dodge, and let Providence, and our own eyes, decide the matter atween us! I do not make the offer, to you, major; for our blood is of a color, and we serve the same master."

"That the Huron is a liar, is very evident," returned Heyward, coolly; "you have yourself heard him assert you to be La Longue Carabine."

It were impossible to say what violent assertion the stubborn Hawkeye would have next made, in his headlong wish to vindicate his identity, had not the aged Delaware once more interposed.

"The hawk which comes from the clouds can return when he will," he said; "give them the guns."

This time the scout seized the rifle with avidity; nor had Magua, though he watched the movements of the marksman with jealous eyes, any further cause for apprehension.

"Now let it be proved, in the face of this tribe of Delawares, which is the better man," cried the scout, tapping the butt of his piece with that finger which had pulled so many fatal triggers.

"You see that gourd hanging against yonder tree, major; if you are a marksman fit for the borders, let me see you break its shell!"

Duncan noted the object, and prepared himself to renew the trial. The gourd was one of the usual little vessels used by the Indians, and it was suspended from a dead branch of a small pine, by a thong of deerskin, at the full distance of a hundred yards. So strangely compounded is the feeling of self-love, that the young soldier, while he knew the utter worthlessness of the suffrages of his savage umpires, forgot the sudden motives of the contest in a wish to excel. It had been seen, already, that his skill was far from being contemptible, and he now resolved to put forth its nicest qualities. Had his life depended on the issue, the aim of Duncan could not have been more deliberate or guarded. He fired; and three or four young Indians, who sprang forward at the report, announced with a shout, that the ball was in the tree, a very little on one side of the proper object. The warriors uttered a common ejaculation of pleasure, and then turned their eyes, inquiringly, on the movements of his rival.

"It may do for the Royal Americans!" said Hawkeye, laughing once more in his own silent, heartfelt manner; "but had my gun often turned so much from the true line, many a marten, whose skin is now in a lady's muff, would still be in the woods; ay, and many a bloody Mingo, who has departed to his final account, would be acting his deviltries at this very day, atween the provinces. I hope the squaw who owns the gourd has more of them in her wigwam, for this will never hold water again!"

The scout had shook his priming, and cocked his piece, while speaking; and, as he ended, he threw back a foot, and slowly raised the muzzle from the earth: the motion was steady, uniform, and in one direction. When on a perfect level, it remained for a single moment, without tremor or variation, as though both man and rifle were carved in stone. During that stationary instant, it poured forth its contents, in a bright, glancing sheet of flame. Again the young Indians bounded forward; but their hurried search and disappointed looks announced that no traces of the bullet were to be seen.

"Go!" said the old chief to the scout, in a tone of strong disgust; "thou art a wolf in the skin of a dog. I will talk to the 'Long Rifle' of the Yengeese."

"Ah! had I that piece which furnished the name you use, I would obligate myself to cut the thong, and drop the gourd without breaking it!" returned Hawkeye, perfectly undisturbed by the other's manner. "Fools, if you would find the bullet of a sharpshooter in these woods, you must look *in* the object, and not around it!"

The Indian youths instantly comprehended his meaning—for this time he spoke in the Delaware tongue—and tearing the gourd from the tree, they held it on high with an exulting shout, displaying a hole in its bottom, which had been cut by the bullet, after passing through the usual orifice in the center of its upper side. At this unexpected exhibition, a loud and vehement expression of pleasure burst from the mouth of every warrior present. It decided the question, and effectually established Hawkeye in the possession of his dangerous reputation. Those curious and admiring eyes which had been turned again on Heyward, were finally directed to the weather-beaten form of the scout, who immediately became the principal object of attention to the simple and unsophisticated beings by whom he was surrounded. When the sudden and noisy commotion had a little subsided, the aged chief resumed his examination.

"Why did you wish to stop my ears?" he said, addressing Duncan; "are the Delawares fools that they could not know the young panther from the cat?"

"They will yet find the Huron a singing-bird," said Duncan, endeavoring to adopt the figurative language of the natives.

"It is good. We will know who can shut the ears of men. Brother," added the chief turning his eyes on Magua, "the Delawares listen."

Thus singled, and directly called on to declare his object, the Huron arose; and advancing with great deliberation and dignity into the very center of the circle, where he stood confronted by the prisoners, he placed himself in an attitude to speak. Before opening his mouth, however, he bent his eyes slowly along the whole living boundary of earnest faces, as if to temper his expressions to the capacities of his audience. On Hawkeye he cast a glance of respectful enmity; on Duncan, a look of inextinguishable hatred; the shrinking figure of Alice he scarcely deigned to notice; but when his glance met the firm, commanding, and yet lovely form of Cora, his eye lingered a moment, with an expression that it might have been difficult to define. Then, filled with his own dark intentions, he spoke in the language of the Canadas, a tongue that he well knew was comprehended by most of his auditors.

"The Spirit that made men colored them differently," commenced the subtle Huron. "Some are blacker than the sluggish bear. These He said should be slaves; and He ordered them to work forever, like the beaver. You may hear them groan, when the south wind blows, louder than the lowing buffaloes, along the shores of the great salt lake, where the big canoes come and go with them in droves. Some He made with faces paler than the ermine of the forests; and these He ordered to be traders; dogs to their women, and wolves to their slaves. He gave this people the nature of the pigeon; wings that never tire; young, more plentiful than the leaves on the trees, and appetites to devour the earth. He gave them tongues like the false call of the wildcat; hearts like rabbits; the cunning of the hog (but none of the fox), and arms longer than the legs of the moose. With his tongue he stops the ears of the Indians; his heart teaches him to pay warriors to fight his battles; his cunning tells him how to get together the goods of the earth; and his arms inclose the land from the shores of the salt-water to the islands of the great lake. His gluttony makes him sick. God gave him enough, and yet he wants all. Such are the pale faces.

"Some the Great Spirit made with skins brighter and redder than yonder sun," continued Magua, pointing impressively upward to the lurid luminary, which was struggling through the misty atmosphere of the horizon; "and these did He fashion to His own mind. He gave them this island as He had made it, covered with trees, and filled with game. The wind made their clearings; the sun and rain ripened their fruits; and the snows came to tell them to be thankful. What need had they of roads to journey by! They saw through the hills! When the beavers worked, they lay in the shade, and looked on. The winds cooled them in summer; in winter, skins kept them warm. If they fought among themselves, it was to prove that they were men. They were brave; they were just; they were happy."

Here the speaker paused, and again looked around him to discover if his legend had touched the sympathies of his listeners. He met everywhere, with eyes riveted on his own, heads erect and nostrils expanded, as if each individual present felt himself able and willing, singly, to redress the wrongs of his race.

"If the Great Spirit gave different tongues to his red children," he continued, in a low, still melancholy voice, "it was that all animals might understand them. Some He placed among the snows, with their cousin, the bear. Some he placed near the setting sun, on the road to the happy hunting grounds. Some on the lands around the great fresh waters; but to His greatest, and most beloved, He gave the sands of the salt lake. Do my brothers know the name of this favored people?"

"It was the Lenape!" exclaimed twenty eager voices in a breath.

"It was the Lenni Lenape," returned Magua, affecting to bend his head in reverence to their former greatness. "It was the tribes of the Lenape! The sun rose from water that was salt, and set in water that was sweet, and never hid himself from their eyes. But why should I, a Huron of the woods, tell a wise people their own traditions? Why remind them of their injuries; their ancient greatness; their deeds; their glory; their happiness; their losses; their defeats; their misery? Is there not one among them who has seen it all, and who knows it to be true? I have done. My tongue is still for my heart is of lead. I listen."

As the voice of the speaker suddenly ceased, every face and all eyes turned, by a common movement, toward the venerable Tamenund. From the moment that he took his seat, until the present instant, the lips of the patriarch had not severed, and scarcely a sign of life had escaped him. He sat bent in feebleness, and apparently unconscious of the presence he was in, during the whole of that opening scene, in which the skill of the scout had been so clearly established. At the nicely graduated sound of Magua's voice, however, he betrayed some evidence of consciousness, and once or twice he even raised his head, as if to listen. But when the crafty Huron spoke of his nation by name, the eyelids of the old man raised themselves, and he looked out upon the multitude with that sort of dull, unmeaning expression which might be supposed to belong to the countenance of a specter. Then he made an effort to rise, and being upheld by his supporters, he gained his feet, in a posture commanding by its dignity, while he tottered with weakness.

"Who calls upon the children of the Lenape?" he said, in a deep, guttural voice, that was rendered awfully audible by the breathless silence of the multitude; "who speaks of things gone? Does not the egg become a worm—the worm a fly, and perish? Why tell the Delawares of good that is past? Better thank the Manitou for that which remains."

"It is a Wyandot," said Magua, stepping nigher to the rude platform on which the other stood; "a friend of Tamenund."

"A friend!" repeated the sage, on whose brow a dark frown settled, imparting a portion of that severity which had rendered his eye so terrible in middle age. "Are the Mingoes rulers of the earth? What brings a Huron in here?"

"Justice. His prisoners are with his brothers, and he comes for his own."

Tamenund turned his head toward one of his supporters, and listened to the short explanation the man gave.

Then, facing the applicant, he regarded him a moment with deep attention; after which he said, in a low and reluctant voice:

"Justice is the law of the great Manitou. My children, give the stranger food. Then, Huron, take thine own and depart."

On the delivery of this solemn judgment, the patriarch seated himself, and closed his eyes again, as if better pleased with the images of his own ripened experience than with the visible objects of the world. Against such a decree there was no Delaware sufficiently hardy to murmur, much less oppose himself. The words were barely uttered when four or five of the younger warriors, stepping behind Heyward and the scout, passed thongs so dexterously and rapidly around their arms, as to hold them both in instant bondage. The former was too much engrossed with his precious and nearly insensible burden, to be aware of their intentions before they were executed; and the latter, who considered even the hostile tribes of the Delawares a superior race of beings, submitted without resistance. Perhaps, however, the manner of the scout would not have been so passive, had he fully comprehended the language in which the preceding dialogue had been conducted.

Magua cast a look of triumph around the whole assembly before he proceeded to the execution of his purpose. Perceiving that the men were unable to offer any resistance, he turned his looks on her he valued most. Cora met his gaze with an eye so calm and firm, that his resolution wavered. Then, recollecting his former artifice, he raised Alice from the arms of the warrior against whom she leaned, and beckoning Heyward to follow, he motioned for the encircling crowd to open. But Cora, instead of obeying the impulse he had expected, rushed to the feet of the patriarch, and, raising her voice, exclaimed aloud:

"Just and venerable Delaware, on thy wisdom and power we lean for mercy! Be deaf to yonder artful and remorseless monster, who poisons thy ears with falsehoods to feed his thirst for blood. Thou that hast lived long, and that hast seen the evil of the world, should know how to temper its calamities to the miserable."

The eyes of the old man opened heavily, and he once more looked upward at the multitude. As the piercing tones of the suppliant swelled on his ears, they moved slowly in the direction of her person, and finally settled there in a steady gaze. Cora had cast herself to her knees; and, with hands clenched in each other and pressed upon her bosom, she remained like a beauteous and breathing model of her sex, looking up in his faded but majestic countenance, with a species of holy reverence. Gradually the expression of Tamenund's features changed, and losing their vacancy in admiration, they lighted with a portion of that intelligence which a century before had been wont to communicate his youthful fire to the extensive bands of the Delawares. Rising without assistance, and seemingly without an effort, he demanded, in a voice that startled its auditors by its firmness:

"What art thou?"

"A woman. One of a hated race, if thou wilt—a Yengee. But one who has never harmed thee, and who cannot harm thy people, if she would; who asks for succor."

"Tell me, my children," continued the patriarch, hoarsely, motioning to those around him, though his eyes still dwelt upon the kneeling form of Cora, "where have the Delawares camped?"

"In the mountains of the Iroquois, beyond the clear springs of the Horican."

"Many parching summers are come and gone," continued the sage, "since I drank of the water of my own rivers. The children of Minquon[5] are the justest white men, but they were thirsty and they took it to themselves. Do they follow us so far?"

"We follow none, we covet nothing," answered Cora. "Captives against our wills, have we been brought amongst you; and we ask but permission to depart to our own in peace. Art thou not Tamenund—the father, the judge, I had almost said, the prophet—of this people?"

"I am Tamenund of many days."

"'Tis now some seven years that one of thy people was at the mercy of a white chief on the borders of this province. He claimed to be of the blood of the good and just Tamenund. 'Go,' said the white man, 'for thy parent's sake thou art free.' Dost thou remember the name of that English warrior?"

"I remember, that when a laughing boy," returned the patriarch, with the peculiar recollection of vast age, "I stood upon the sands of the sea shore, and saw a big canoe, with wings whiter than the swan's, and wider than many eagles, come from the rising sun."

"Nay, nay; I speak not of a time so very distant, but of favor shown to thy kindred by one of mine, within the memory of thy youngest warrior."

---

5. [Cooper's note:] William Penn was termed Minquon by the Delawares, and, as he never used violence or injustice in his dealings with them, his reputation for probity passed into a proverb. The American is justly proud of the origin of his nation, which is perhaps unequaled in the history of the world; but the Pennsylvanian and Jerseyman have more reason to value themselves in their ancestors than the natives of any other state, since no wrong was done the original owners of the soil.

"Was it when the Yengeese and the Dutchmanne fought for the hunting-grounds of the Delawares? Then Tamenund was a chief, and first laid aside the bow for the lightning of the pale faces——"

"Not yet then," interrupted Cora, "by many ages; I speak of a thing of yesterday. Surely, surely, you forget it not."

"It was but yesterday," rejoined the aged man, with touching pathos, "that the children of the Lenape were masters of the world. The fishes of the salt lake, the birds, the beasts, and the Mengee of the woods, owned them for Sagamores."

Cora bowed her head in disappointment, and, for a bitter moment struggled with her chagrin. Then, elevating her rich features and beaming eyes, she continued, in tones scarcely less penetrating than the unearthly voice of the patriarch himself:

"Tell me, is Tamenund a father?"

The old man looked down upon her from his elevated stand, with a benignant smile on his wasted countenance, and then casting his eyes slowly over the whole assemblage, he answered:

"Of a nation."

"For myself I ask nothing. Like thee and thine, venerable chief," she continued, pressing her hands convulsively on her heart, and suffering her head to droop until her burning cheeks were nearly concealed in the maze of dark, glossy tresses that fell in disorder upon her shoulders, "the curse of my ancestors has fallen heavily on their child. But yonder is one who has never known the weight of Heaven's displeasure until now. She is the daughter of an old and failing man, whose days are near their close. She has many, very many, to love her, and delight in her; and she is too good, much too precious, to become the victim of that villain."

"I know that the pale faces are a proud and hungry race. I know that they claim not only to have the earth, but that the meanest of their color is better than the Sachems of the red man. The dogs and crows of their tribes," continued the earnest old chieftain, without heeding the wounded spirit of his listener, whose head was nearly crushed to the earth in shame, as he proceeded, "would bark and caw before they would take a woman to their wigwams whose blood was not of the color of snow. But let them not boast before the face of the Manitou too loud. They entered the land at the rising, and may yet go off at the setting sun. I have often seen the locusts strip the leaves from the trees, but the season of blossoms has always come again."

"It is so," said Cora, drawing a long breath, as if reviving from a trance, raising her face, and shaking back her shining veil, with a kindling eye, that contradicted the death-like paleness of her countenance; "but why—it is not permitted us to inquire. There is yet one of thine own people who has not been brought before thee; before thou lettest the Huron depart in triumph, hear him speak."

Observing Tamenund to look about him doubtingly, one of his companions said:

"It is a snake—a red-skin in the pay of the Yengeese. We keep him for the torture."

"Let him come," returned the sage.

Then Tamenund once more sank into his seat, and a silence so deep prevailed while the young man prepared to obey his simple mandate, that the leaves, which fluttered in the draught of the light morning air, were distinctly heard rustling in the surrounding forest.

Chapter 32

The exciting conclusion of the action of the novel follows. An additional chapter, not excerpted here, serves as an epilogue.

> "But plagues shall spread, and funeral fires increase,
> Till the great king, without a ransom paid,
> To her own Chrysa send the black-eyed maid."
>
> Pope

During the time Uncas was making this disposition of his forces, the woods were as still, and, with the exception of those who had met in council, apparently as much untenanted as when they came fresh from the hands of their Almighty Creator. The eye could range, in every direction, through the long and shadowed vistas of the trees; but nowhere was any object to be seen that did not properly belong to the peaceful and slumbering scenery.

Here and there a bird was heard fluttering among the branches of the beeches, and occasionally a squirrel dropped a nut, drawing the startled looks of the party for a moment to the place; but the instant the casual interruption ceased, the passing air was heard murmuring above their heads, along that verdant and undulating surface of forest, which spread itself unbroken, unless by stream or lake, over such a vast region of country. Across the tract of wilderness which lay between the Delawares and the village of their enemies, it seemed as if the foot of man had never trodden, so breathing and deep was the silence in which it lay. But Hawkeye, whose duty led him foremost in the adventure, knew the character of those with whom he was about to contend too well to trust the treacherous quiet.

When he saw his little band collected, the scout threw "killdeer" into the hollow of his arm, and making a silent signal that he would be followed, he led them many rods toward the rear, into the bed of a little brook which they had crossed in advancing. Here he halted, and after waiting for the whole of his grave and attentive warriors to close about him, he spoke in Delaware, demanding:

"Do any of my young men know whither this run will lead us?"

A Delaware stretched forth a hand, with the two fingers separated, and indicating the manner in which they were joined at the root, he answered:

"Before the sun could go his own length, the little water will be in the big." Then he added, pointing in the direction of the place he mentioned, "the two make enough for the beavers."

"I thought as much," returned the scout, glancing his eye upward at the opening in the tree-tops, "from the course it takes, and the bearings of the mountains. Men, we will keep within the cover of its banks till we scent the Hurons."

His companions gave the usual brief exclamation of assent, but, perceiving that their leader was about to lead the way in person, one or two made signs that all was not as it should be. Hawkeye, who comprehended their meaning glances, turned and perceived that his party had been followed thus far by the singing-master.

"Do you know, friend," asked the scout, gravely, and perhaps with a little of the pride of conscious deserving in his manner, "that this is a band of rangers chosen for the most desperate service, and put under the command of one who, though another might say it with a better face, will not be apt to leave them idle. It may not be five, it cannot be thirty minutes, before we tread on the body of a Huron, living or dead."

"Though not admonished of your intentions in words," returned David, whose face was a little flushed, and whose ordinarily quiet and unmeaning eyes glimmered with an expression of unusual fire, "your men have reminded me of the children of Jacob going out to battle against the Shechemites, for wickedly aspiring to wedlock with a woman of a race that was favored of the Lord. Now, I have journeyed far, and sojourned much in good and evil with the maiden ye seek; and, though not a man of war, with my loins girded and my sword sharpened, yet would I gladly strike a blow in her behalf."

The scout hesitated, as if weighing the chances of such a strange enlistment in his mind before he answered:

"You know not the use of any we'pon. You carry no rifle; and believe me, what the Mingoes take they will freely give again."

"Though not a vaunting and bloodily disposed Goliath," returned David, drawing a sling from beneath his parti-colored and uncouth attire, "I have not forgotten the example of the Jewish boy. With this ancient instrument of war have I practised much in my youth, and peradventure the skill has not entirely departed from me."

"Ay!" said Hawkeye, considering the deer-skin thong and apron, with a cold and discouraging eye; "the thing might do its work among arrows, or even knives; but these Mengwe have been furnished by the Frenchers with a good grooved barrel a man. However, it seems to be your gift to go unharmed amid fire; and as you have hitherto been favored—major, you have left your rifle at a cock; a single shot before the time would be just twenty scalps lost to no purpose—singer, you can follow; we may find use for you in the shoutings."

"I thank you, friend," returned David, supplying himself, like his royal namesake, from among the pebbles of the brook; "though not given to the desire to kill, had you sent me away my spirit would have been troubled."

"Remember," added the scout, tapping his own head significantly on that spot where Gamut was yet sore, "we come to fight, and not to musickate. Until the general whoop is given, nothing speaks but the rifle."

David nodded, as much to signify his acquiescence with the terms; and then Hawkeye, casting another observant glance over his followers made the signal to proceed.

Their route lay, for the distance of a mile, along the bed of the water-course. Though protected from any great danger of observation by the precipitous banks, and the thick shrubbery which skirted the stream, no precaution known to an Indian attack was neglected. A warrior rather crawled than walked on each flank so as to catch occasional glimpses into the forest; and every few minutes the band came to a halt, and listened for hostile sounds, with an acuteness of organs that would be scarcely conceivable to a man in a less natural state. Their march was, however, unmolested, and they reached the point where the lesser stream was lost in the greater, without the smallest evidence that their progress had been noted. Here the scout again halted, to consult the signs of the forest.

"We are likely to have a good day for a fight," he said, in English, addressing Heyward, and glancing his eyes upward at the clouds, which began to move in broad sheets across the firmament; "a bright sun and a glittering barrel are no friends to true sight. Everything is favorable; they have the wind, which will bring down their noises and their smoke, too, no little matter in itself; whereas, with us it will be first a shot, and then a clear view. But here is an end to our cover; the beavers have had the range of this stream for hundreds of years, and what atween their food and their dams, there is, as you see, many a girdled stub, but few living trees."

Hawkeye had, in truth, in these few words, given no bad description of the prospect that now lay in their front. The brook was irregular in its width, sometimes shooting through narrow fissures in the rocks, and at others spreading over acres of bottom land, forming little areas that might be termed ponds. Everywhere along its banks were the moldering relics of dead trees, in all the stages of decay, from those that groaned on their tottering trunks to such as had recently been robbed of those rugged coats that so mysteriously contain their principle of life. A few long, low, and moss-covered piles were scattered among them, like the memorials of a former and long-departed generation.

All these minute particulars were noted by the scout, with a gravity and interest that they probably had never before attracted. He knew that the Huron encampment lay a short half mile up the brook; and, with the characteristic anxiety of one who dreaded a hidden danger, he was greatly troubled at not finding the smallest trace of the presence of his enemy. Once or twice he felt induced to give the order for a rush, and to attempt the village by surprise; but his experience quickly admonished him of the danger of so useless an experiment. Then he listened intently, and with painful uncertainty, for the sounds of hostility in the quarter where Uncas was left; but nothing was audible except the sighing of the wind, that began to sweep over the bosom of the forest in gusts which threatened a tempest. At length, yielding rather to his unusual impatience than taking counsel from his knowledge, he determined to bring matters to an issue, by unmasking his force, and proceeding cautiously, but steadily, up the stream.

The scout had stood, while making his observations, sheltered by a brake, and his companions still lay in the bed of the ravine, through which the smaller stream debouched; but on hearing his low, though intelligible, signal the whole party stole up the bank, like so many dark specters, and silently arranged themselves around him. Pointing in the direction he wished to proceed, Hawkeye advanced, the band breaking off in single files, and following so accurately in his footsteps, as to leave it, if we except Heyward and David, the trail of but a single man.

The party was, however, scarcely uncovered before a volley from a dozen rifles was heard in their rear; and a Delaware leaping high in to the air, like a wounded deer, fell at his whole length, dead.

"Ah, I feared some deviltry like this!" exclaimed the scout, in English, adding, with the quickness of thought, in his adopted tongue: "To cover, men, and charge!"

The band dispersed at the word, and before Heyward had well recovered from his surprise, he found himself standing alone with David. Luckily the Hurons had already fallen back, and he was safe from their fire. But this state of things was evidently to be of short continuance; for the scout set the example of pressing on their retreat, by discharging his rifle, and darting from tree to tree as his enemy slowly yielded ground.

It would seem that the assault had been made by a very small party of the Hurons, which, however, continued to increase in numbers, as it retired on its friends, until the return fire was very nearly, if not quite, equal to that maintained by the advancing Delawares. Heyward threw himself among the combatants, and imitating the necessary caution of his companions, he made quick discharges with his own rifle. The contest now grew warm and stationary. Few were injured, as both parties kept their bodies as much protected as possible by the trees; never, indeed, exposing any part of their persons except in the act of taking aim. But the chances were gradually growing unfavorable to Hawkeye and his band. The quick-sighted scout perceived his danger without knowing how to remedy it. He saw it was more dangerous to retreat than to maintain his ground; while he found his enemy throwing out men on his flank, which rendered the task of keeping themselves covered so very difficult to the Delawares, as nearly to silence their fire. At this embarrassing moment, when they began to think the whole of the hostile tribe was gradually encircling them, they heard the yell of combatants and the rattling of arms echoing under the arches of the wood at the place where Uncas was posted, a bottom which, in a manner, lay beneath the ground on which Hawkeye and his party were contending.

The effects of this attack were instantaneous, and to the scout and his friends greatly relieving. It would seem that, while his own surprise had been anticipated, and had consequently failed, the enemy, in their turn, having been deceived in its object and in his numbers, had left too small a force to resist the impetuous onset of the young Mohican. This fact was doubly apparent, by the rapid manner in which the battle in the forest rolled upward toward the village, and by an instant falling off in the number of their assailants, who rushed to assist in maintaining the front, and, as it now proved to be, the principal point of defense.

Animating his followers by his voice, and his own example, Hawkeye then gave the word to bear down upon their foes.

The charge, in that rude species of warfare, consisted merely in pushing from cover to cover, nigher to the enemy; and in this maneuver he was instantly and successfully obeyed. The Hurons were compelled to withdraw, and the scene of the contest rapidly changed from the more open ground, on which it had commenced, to a spot where the assailed found a thicket to rest upon. Here the struggle was protracted, arduous and seemingly of doubtful issue; the Delawares, though none of them fell, beginning to bleed freely, in consequence of the disadvantage at which they were held.

In this crisis, Hawkeye found means to get behind the same tree as that which served for a cover to Heyward; most of his own combatants being within call, a little on his right, where they maintained rapid, though fruitless, discharges on their sheltered enemies.

"You are a young man, major," said the scout, dropping the butt of "killdeer" to the earth, and leaning on the barrel, a little fatigued with his previous industry; "and it may be your gift to lead armies, at some future day, ag'in these imps, the Mingoes. You may here see the philosophy of an Indian fight. It consists mainly in ready hand, a quick eye and a good cover. Now, if you had a company of the Royal Americans here, in what manner would you set them to work in this business?"

"The bayonet would make a road."

"Ay, there is white reason in what you say; but a man must ask himself, in this wilderness, how many lives he can spare. No—horse,"[6] continued the scout, shaking his head, like one who mused; "horse, I am ashamed to say must sooner or later decide these scrimmages. The brutes are better than men, and to horse must we come at last. Put a shodden hoof on the moccasin of a red-skin, and, if his rifle be once emptied, he will never stop to load it again."

"This is a subject that might better be discussed at another time," returned Heyward; "shall we charge?"

"I see no contradiction to the gifts of any man in passing his breathing spells in useful reflections," the scout replied. "As to rush, I little relish such a measure; for a scalp or two must be thrown away in the attempt. And yet," he added, bending his head aside, to catch the sounds of the distant combat, "if we are to be of use to Uncas, these knaves in our front must be got rid of."

Then, turning with a prompt and decided air, he called aloud to his Indians, in their own language. His words were answered by a shout; and, at a given signal, each warrior made a swift movement around his particular tree. The sight of so many dark bodies, glancing before their eyes at the same instant, drew a hasty and consequently an ineffectual fire from the Hurons. Without stopping to breathe, the Delawares leaped in long bounds toward the wood, like so many panthers springing upon their prey. Hawkeye was in front, brandishing his terrible rifle and animating his followers by his example. A few of the older and more cunning Hurons, who had not been deceived by the artifice which had been practiced to draw their fire, now made a close and deadly discharge of their pieces and justified the apprehensions of the scout by felling three of his foremost warriors. But the shock was insufficient to repel the impetus of the charge. The Delawares broke into the cover with

6. [Cooper's note:] The American forest admits of the passage of horses, there being little underbrush, and few tangled brakes. The plan of Hawkeye is the one which has always proved the most successful in the battles between the whites and the Indians. Wayne, in his celebrated campaign on the Miami, received the fire of his enemies in line; and then causing his dragoons to wheel round his flanks, the Indians were driven from their covers before they had time to load. One of the most conspicuous of the chiefs who fought in the battle of Miami assured the writer, that the red men could not fight the warriors with "long knives and leather stockings"; meaning the dragoons with their sabers and boots.

the ferocity of their natures and swept away every trace of resistance by the fury of the onset.

The combat endured only for an instant, hand to hand, and then the assailed yielded ground rapidly, until they reached the opposite margin of the thicket, where they clung to the cover, with the sort of obstinacy that is so often witnessed in hunted brutes. At this critical moment, when the success of the struggle was again becoming doubtful, the crack of a rifle was heard behind the Hurons, and a bullet came whizzing from among some beaver lodges, which were situated in the clearing, in their rear, and was followed by the fierce and appalling yell of the war-whoop.

"There speaks the Sagamore!" shouted Hawkeye, answering the cry with his own stentorian voice; "we have them now in face and back!"

The effect on the Hurons was instantaneous. Discouraged by an assault from a quarter that left them no opportunity for cover, the warriors uttered a common yell of disappointment, and breaking off in a body, they spread themselves across the opening, heedless of every consideration but flight. Many fell, in making the experiment, under the bullets and the blows of the pursuing Delawares.

We shall not pause to detail the meeting between the scout and Chingachgook, or the more touching interview that Duncan held with Munro. A few brief and hurried words served to explain the state of things to both parties; and then Hawkeye, pointing out the Sagamore to his band, resigned the chief authority into the hands of the Mohican chief. Chingachgook assumed the station to which his birth and experience gave him so distinguished a claim, with the grave dignity that always gives force to the mandates of a native warrior. Following the footsteps of the scout, he led the party back through the thicket, his men scalping the fallen Hurons and secreting the bodies of their own dead as they proceeded, until they gained a point where the former was content to make a halt.

The warriors, who had breathed themselves freely in the preceding struggle, were now posted on a bit of level ground, sprinkled with trees in sufficient numbers to conceal them. The land fell away rather precipitately in front, and beneath their eyes stretched, for several miles, a narrow, dark, and wooded vale. It was through this dense and dark forest that Uncas was still contending with the main body of the Hurons.

The Mohican and his friends advanced to the brow of the hill, and listened, with practised ears, to the sounds of the combat. A few birds hovered over the leafy bosom of the valley, frightened from their secluded nests; and here and there a light vapory cloud, which seemed already blending with the atmosphere, arose above the trees, and indicated some spot where the struggle had been fierce and stationary.

"The fight is coming up the ascent," said Duncan, pointing in the direction of a new explosion of firearms; "we are too much in the center of their line to be effective."

"They will incline into the hollow, where the cover is thicker," said the scout, "and that will leave us well on their flank. Go, Sagamore; you will hardly be in time to give the whoop, and lead on the young men. I will fight this scrimmage with warriors of my own color. You know me, Mohican; not a Huron of them all shall cross the swell, into your rear, without the notice of 'killdeer.'"

The Indian chief paused another moment to consider the signs of the contest, which was now rolling rapidly up the ascent, a certain evidence that the Delawares triumphed; nor did he actually quit the place until admonished of the proximity of his friends, as well as enemies, by the bullets of the former, which began to patter among the dried leaves on the ground, like the bits of falling hail which precede the bursting of the tempest. Hawkeye and his three companions withdrew a few paces to a shelter, and awaited the issue with calmness that nothing but great practise could impart in such a scene.

It was not long before the reports of the rifles began to lose the echoes of the woods, and to sound like weapons discharged in the open air. Then a warrior appeared, here and there, driven to the skirts of the forest, and rallying as he entered the clearing, as at the place where the final stand was to be made. These were soon joined by others, until a long line of swarthy figures was to be seen clinging to the cover with the obstinacy of desperation. Heyward began to grow impatient, and turned his eyes anxiously in the direction of Chingachgook. The chief was seated on a rock, with nothing visible but his calm visage, considering the spectacle with an eye as deliberate as if he were posted there merely to view the struggle.

"The time has come for the Delaware to strike!" said Duncan.

"Not so, not so," returned the scout; "when he scents his friends, he will let them know that he is here. See, see; the knaves are getting in that clump of pines, like bees settling after their flight. By the Lord, a squaw might put a bullet into the center of such a knot of dark skins!"

At that instant the whoop was given, and a dozen Hurons fell by a discharge from Chingachgook and his band. The shout that followed was answered by a single war-cry from the forest, and a yell passed through the air that sounded as if a thousand throats were united in a common effort. The Hurons staggered, deserting the center of their line, and Uncas issued from the forest through the opening they left, at the head of a hundred warriors.

Waving his hands right and left, the young chief pointed out the enemy to his followers, who separated in pursuit. The war now divided, both wings of the broken Hurons seeking protection in the woods again, hotly pressed by the victorious warriors of the Lenape. A minute might have passed, but the sounds were already receding in different directions, and gradually losing their distinctness beneath the echoing arches of the woods. One little knot of Hurons, however, had disdained to seek a cover, and were retiring, like lions at bay, slowly and sullenly up the acclivity which Chingachgook and his band had just deserted, to mingle more closely in the fray. Magua was conspicuous in this party, both by his fierce and savage mien, and by the air of haughty authority he yet maintained.

In his eagerness to expedite the pursuit, Uncas had left himself nearly alone; but the moment his eye caught the figure of Le Subtil, every other consideration was forgotten. Raising his cry of battle, which recalled some six or seven warriors, and reckless of the disparity of their numbers, he rushed upon his enemy. Le Renard, who watched the movement, paused to receive him with secret joy. But at the moment when he thought the rashness of his impetuous young assailant had left him at his mercy, another shout was given, and La Longue Carabine was seen rushing to the rescue, attended by all his white associates. The Huron instantly turned, and commenced a rapid retreat up the ascent.

There was no time for greetings or congratulations; for Uncas, though unconscious of the presence of his friends, continued the pursuit with the velocity of the wind. In vain Hawkeye called to him to respect the covers; the young Mohican braved the dangerous fire of his enemies, and soon compelled them to a flight as swift as his own headlong speed. It was fortunate that the race was of short continuance, and that the white men were much favored by their position, or the Delaware would soon have outstripped all his companions, and fallen a victim to his own temerity. But, ere such a calamity could happen, the pursuers and pursued entered the Wyandot village, within striking distance of each other.

Excited by the presence of their dwellings, and tired of the chase, the Hurons now made a stand, and fought around their council-lodge with the fury of despair. The onset and the issue were like the passage and destruction of a whirlwind. The tomahawk of Uncas, the blows of Hawkeye, and even the still nervous arm of Munro were all busy for that passing moment, and the ground was quickly strewed with their enemies. Still Magua, though daring and much exposed, escaped from every effort against his life, with that sort of fabled protection that was made to overlook the fortunes of favored heroes in the legends of ancient poetry. Raising a yell that spoke volumes of anger and disappointment, the subtle chief, when he saw his comrades fallen, darted away from the place, attended by his two only surviving friends, leaving the Delawares engaged in stripping the dead of the bloody trophies of their victory.

But Uncas, who had vainly sought him in the mêlée, bounded forward in pursuit; Hawkeye, Heyward and David still pressing on his footsteps. The utmost that the scout could effect, was to keep the muzzle of his rifle a little in advance of his friend, to whom, however, it answered every purpose of a charmed shield. Once Magua appeared disposed to make another and a final effort to revenge his losses; but, abandoning his intention as soon as demonstrated, he leaped into a thicket of bushes, through which he was followed by his enemies, and suddenly entered the mouth of the cave already known to the reader. Hawkeye, who had only forborne to fire in tenderness to Uncas, raised a shout of success, and proclaimed aloud that now they were certain of their game. The pursuers dashed into the long and narrow entrance, in time to catch a glimpse of the retreating forms of the Hurons. Their passage through the natural galleries and subterraneous apartments of the cavern was preceded by the shrieks and cries of hundreds of women and children. The place, seen by its dim and uncertain light, appeared like the shades of the infernal regions, across which unhappy ghosts and savage demons were flitting in multitudes.

Still Uncas kept his eye on Magua, as if life to him possessed but a single object. Heyward and the scout still pressed on his rear, actuated, though possibly in a less degree, by a common feeling. But their way was becoming intricate, in those dark and gloomy passages, and the glimpses of the retiring warriors less distinct and frequent; and for a moment the trace was believed to be lost, when a white robe was seen fluttering in the further extremity of a passage that seemed to lead up the mountain.

"'Tis Cora!" exclaimed Heyward, in a voice in which horror and delight were wildly mingled.

"Cora! Cora!" echoed Uncas, bounding forward like a deer.

"'Tis the maiden!" shouted the scout. "Courage, lady; we come! we come!"

The chase was renewed with a diligence rendered tenfold encouraging by this glimpse of the captive. But the way was rugged, broken, and in spots nearly impassable. Uncas abandoned his rifle, and leaped forward with headlong precipitation. Heyward rashly imitated his example, though both were, a moment afterward, admonished of his madness by hearing the bellowing of a piece, that the Hurons found time to discharge down the passage in the rocks, the bullet from which even gave the young Mohican a slight wound.

"We must close!" said the scout, passing his friends by a desperate leap; "the knaves will pick us all off at this distance; and see, they hold the maiden so as to shield themselves!"

Though his words were unheeded, or rather unheard, his example was followed by his companions, who, by incredible exertions, got near enough to the fugitives to perceive that Cora was borne along between the two warriors while Magua prescribed the direction and manner of their flight. At this moment the forms of all four were strongly drawn against an opening in the sky, and they disappeared. Nearly frantic with disappointment, Uncas and Heyward increased efforts that already seemed superhuman, and they issued from the cavern on the side of the mountain, in time to note the route of the pursued. The course lay up the ascent, and still continued hazardous and laborious.

Encumbered by his rifle, and, perhaps, not sustained by so deep an interest in the captive as his companions, the scout suffered the latter to precede him a little, Uncas, in his turn, taking the lead of Heyward. In this manner, rocks, precipices and difficulties were surmounted in an incredibly short space, that at another time, and under other circumstances, would have been deemed almost insuperable. But the impetuous young men were rewarded by finding that, encumbered with Cora, the Hurons were losing ground in the race.

"Stay, dog of the Wyandots!" exclaimed Uncas, shaking his bright tomahawk at Magua; "a Delaware girl calls stay!"

"I will go no further!" cried Cora, stopping unexpectedly on a ledge of rock, that overhung a deep precipice, at no great distance from the summit of the mountain. "Kill me if thou wilt, detestable Huron; I will go no further."

The supporters of the maiden raised their ready tomahawks with the impious joy that fiends are thought to take in mischief, but Magua stayed the uplifted arms. The Huron chief, after casting the weapons he had wrested from his companions over the rock, drew his knife, and turned to his captive, with a look in which conflicting passions fiercely contended.

"Woman," he said, "choose; the wigwam or the knife of Le Subtil!"

Cora regarded him not, but dropping on her knees, she raised her eyes and stretched her arms toward heaven, saying in a meek and yet confiding voice:

"I am thine; do with me as thou seest best!"

"Woman," repeated Magua, hoarsely, and endeavoring in vain to catch a glance from her serene and beaming eye, "choose!"

But Cora neither heard nor heeded his demand. The form of the Huron trembled in every fibre, and he raised his arm on high, but dropped it again with a bewildered air, like one who doubted. Once more he struggled with himself and lifted the keen weapon again; but just then a piercing cry was heard above them, and Uncas appeared, leaping frantically, from a fearful height, upon the ledge. Magua recoiled a step; and one of his assistants, profiting by the chance, sheathed his own knife in the bosom of Cora.

The Huron sprang like a tiger on his offending and already retreating country man, but the falling form of Uncas separated the unnatural combatants. Diverted from his object by this interruption, and maddened by the murder he had just witnessed, Magua buried his weapon in the back of the prostrate Delaware, uttering an unearthly shout as he committed the dastardly deed. But Uncas arose from the blow, as the wounded panther turns upon his foe, and struck the murderer of Cora to his feet, by an effort in which the last of his failing strength was expended. Then, with a stern and steady look, he turned to Le Subtil, and indicated by the expression of his eye all that he would do had not the power deserted him. The latter seized the nerveless arm of the unresisting Delaware, and passed his knife into his bosom three several times, before his victim, still keeping his gaze riveted on his enemy, with a look of inextinguishable scorn, fell dead at his feet.

"Mercy! mercy! Huron," cried Heyward, from above, in tones nearly choked by horror; "give mercy, and thou shalt receive from it!"

Whirling the bloody knife up at the imploring youth, the victorious Magua uttered a cry so fierce, so wild, and yet so joyous, that it conveyed the sounds of savage triumph to the ears of those who fought in the valley, a thousand feet below. He was answered by a burst from the lips of the scout, whose tall person was just then seen moving swiftly toward him, along those dangerous crags, with steps as bold and reckless as if he possessed the power to move in air. But when the hunter reached the scene of the ruthless massacre, the ledge was tenanted only by the dead.

His keen eye took a single look at the victims, and then shot its glances over the difficulties of the ascent in his front. A form stood at the brow of the mountain, on the very edge of the giddy height, with uplifted arms, in an awful attitude of menace. Without stopping to consider his person, the rifle of Hawkeye was raised; but a rock, which fell on the head of one of the fugitives below, exposed the indignant and glowing countenance of the honest Gamut. Then Magua issued from a crevice, and, stepping with calm indifference over the body of the last of his associates, he leaped a wide fissure, and ascended the rocks at a point where the arm of David could not reach him. A single bound would carry him to the brow of the precipice, and assure his safety. Before taking the leap, however, the Huron paused, and shaking his hand at the scout, he shouted:

"The pale faces are dogs! the Delawares women! Magua leaves them on the rocks, for the crows!"

Laughing hoarsely, he made a desperate leap, and fell short of his mark, though his hands grasped a shrub on the verge of the height. The form of Hawkeye had crouched like a beast about to take its spring, and his frame trembled so violently with eagerness that the muzzle of the half-raised rifle played like a leaf fluttering in the wind. Without exhausting himself with fruitless efforts, the cunning Magua suffered his body to drop to the length of his arms, and found a fragment for his feet to rest on. Then, summoning all his powers, he renewed the attempt, and so far succeeded as to draw his knees on the edge of the mountain. It was now, when the body of his enemy was most collected together, that the agitated weapon of the scout was drawn to his shoulder. The surrounding rocks themselves were not steadier than the piece became, for the single instant that it poured out its contents. The arms of the Huron relaxed, and his body fell back a little, while his knees still kept their position. Turning a relentless look on his enemy, he shook a hand in grim defiance. But his hold loosened, and his dark person was seen cutting the air with its head downward, for a fleeting instant, until it glided past the fringe of shrubbery which clung to the mountain, in its rapid flight to destruction.

SOURCE: James Fenimore Cooper. *The Last of the Mohicans: A Narrative of 1757*. Philadelphia: H. C. Carey and I. Lea, 1826.

CATHARINE MARIA SEDGWICK

Catharine Maria Sedgwick (1789–1867) was from western Massachusetts, the setting for her historical romance, Hope Leslie, *in the aftermath of the Pequot War of 1637, a war in which the Puritan settlers almost completely killed off the native tribe. Sedgwick's heroine, Hope Leslie, an English orphan whose arrival in the village in the Massachusetts Bay Colony in 1638 is anticipated in these two chapters, is a determined, clever, sensitive and willful adolescent. She will have her way, breaking laws in the cause of ultimate moral (and, Sedgwick suggests, divine) justice. In these two early chapters from Part I, Mrs. Fletcher (the wife of Hope's new guardian) and the Fletchers' children are all killed or captured by the few surviving members of the Pequots (spelled "Pequod" by Sedgwick). The novel, less well-known than any of James Fenimore Cooper's, is just as melodramatic but, for the most part, certainly more realistic in its depictions of psychology. "It is," as Professor John Matteson notes, "arguably the first novel to deal successfully with the American Puritans and their complicated relation with the native peoples of New England."*[1]

Everell Fletcher is the teenaged boy who tries to save his mother and siblings from the Pequot attack. Magawisca, a Pequot survivor, is the foster child of the Fletchers and beloved by Everell; Digby is the Fletchers' faithful working-hand. Nelema is an old Pequot woman who has never reconciled herself to life under Puritan rule. In Chapter 4, Magawisca relates to Everell the story, which Sedgwick based on historical sources, of the Christians' slaughter of her tribe and the execution of her brother. In Chapter 5, Sedgwick presents the scene of Magawisca's father's revenge on the Fletcher family, which immediately precedes Hope Leslie's arrival.

---

1. Catharine Maria Sedgwick. *Hope Leslie or Early Times in Massachusetts.* Introduction to the Dover Edition by John Matteson. Mineola, New York: Dover Publications, 2011. Page iv.

Chapters from *Hope Leslie; or Early Times in Massachusetts* (1827)

Volume 1: Chapter 4

"It would have been happy if they had converted some before they had killed any."

—Robinson

The house at Bethel had, both in front and in rear, a portico, or, as it was more humbly, and therefore more appropriately named, a shed; that in the rear was a sort of adjunct to the kitchen, and one end of it was enclosed for the purpose of a bedroom, and occupied by Magawisca. Everell found Digby sitting at the other extremity of this portico; his position was prudently chosen. The moon was high and the heavens clear, and there, concealed and sheltered by the shadow of the roof, he could, without being seen, command the whole extent of cleared ground that bordered on the forest, whence the foe would come, if he came at all.

Everell, like a good knight, had carefully inspected his arms, and just taken his position beside Digby, when they heard Magawisca's window cautiously opened, and saw her spring through it. Everell would have spoken to her, but Digby made a signal of silence; and she, without observing them, hastened with a quick and light step towards the wood, and entered it, taking the path that led to Nelema's hut.

"Confound her!" exclaimed Digby, "she is in a plot with the old woman."

"No, no. On my life she is not, Digby."

"Some mischief—some mischief," said Digby, shaking his head. "They are a treacherous race. Let's follow her. No, we had best keep clear of the wood. Do you call after her; she will hearken to you."

Everell hesitated. "Speak quickly, Mr. Everell," urged Digby; "she will be beyond the reach of your voice. It is no light matter that could take her to Nelema's hut at this time of the night."

"She has good reason for going, Digby. I am sure of it; and I will not call her back."

"Reason," muttered Digby; "reason is but a jack-o'-lantern light in most people's minds. You trust her too far, Mr. Everell; but there, she is returning! See how she looks all around her, like a frightened bird that hears an enemy in every rustling leaf. Stand close; observe her; see, she lays her ear to the earth—it is their crafty way of listening; there, she is gone again!" he exclaimed, as Magawisca darted away into the wood. "It is past doubt she holds communication with some one. God send us a safe deliverance. I had rather meet a legion of Frenchmen than a company of these savages. They are a kind of beast we don't comprehend—out of the range of God's creatures—neither angel, man, nor yet quite devil. I would have sent to the fort for a guard to-night, but I liked not being driven hither and yon by that old hag's tokens, nor yet quite to take counsel from your good mother's fears, she being but a woman."

"I think you have caught the fear, Digby, without taking its counsel," said Everell, "which does little credit to your wisdom; the only use of fear being to provide against danger."

"That is true, Mr. Everell; but don't think I am afraid. It is one thing to know what danger is, and wish to shun it, and another thing to feel like you fear-naught lads, that have never felt a twinge of pain, and have scarce a sense of your own mortality. You would be the boldest at an attack, Mr. Everell, and I should stand a siege best. A boy's courage is a keen weapon that wants temper."

"Apt to break at the first stroke from the enemy, you mean, Digby?" Digby nodded assent. "Well, I should like, at any rate, to prove it," added Everell.

"Time enough this half dozen years yet, my young master. I should be loath to see that fair skin of thine stained with blood; and, besides, you have yet to get a little more worldly prudence than to trust a young Indian girl just because she takes your fancy."

"And why does she take my fancy, Digby? because she is true and noble-minded. I am certain, that if she knows of any danger approaching us, she is seeking to avert it."

"I don't know that, Mr. Everell; she'll be first true to her own people. The old proverb holds fast with these savages, as well as with the rest of the world—'hawks won't pick out hawks' eyes.' Like to like, throughout all nature. I grant you, she hath truly a fair seeming."

"And all that's foul is our own suspicion, is it not, Digby?"

"Not exactly; there's plainly some mystery between Magawisca and the old woman, and we know these Pequods were famed above all the Indian tribes for their cunning."

"And what is superior cunning among savages but superior sense?"

"You may out-talk me, Mr. Everell," replied Digby, with the impatience that a man feels when he is sure he is right, without being able to make it appear. "You may out-talk me, but you will never convince me. Was not I in the Pequod war? I ought to know, I think."

"Yes, and I think you have told me they showed more resolution than cunning there; in particular, that the brother of Magawisca, whom she so piteously bemoans to this day, fought like a young lion."

"Yes, he did, poor dog!—and he was afterward cruelly cut off; and it is this that makes me think they will take some terrible revenge for his death. I often hear Magawisca talking to Oneco of her brother, and I think it is to stir his spirit; but this boy is no more like to him than a spaniel to a bloodhound."

Nothing Digby said had any tendency to weaken Everell's confidence in Magawisca.

The subject of the Pequod war once started, Digby and Everell were in no danger of sleeping at their post. Digby loved, as well as another man, and particularly those who have had brief military experience, to fight his battles o'er again; and Everell was at an age to listen with delight to tales of adventure and danger. They thus wore away the time till the imaginations of both relater and listener were at that pitch when every shadow is imbodied, and every passing sound bears a voice to the quickened sense.

"Hark!" said Digby; "did you not hear footsteps?"

"I hear them now," replied Everell; "they seem not very near. Is it not Magawisca returning?"

"No, there is more than one; and it is the heavy, though cautious, tread of men. Ha! Argus scents them." The old house-dog now sprang from his rest on a mat at the door-stone, and gave one of those loud, inquiring barks, by which this animal first hails the approach of a strange footstep. "Hush, Argus, hush!" cried Everell; and the dog, having obeyed his instinct, seemed satisfied to submit to his master's voice, and crept lazily back to his place of repose.

"You have hushed Argus, and the footsteps too," said Digby; "but it is well, perhaps, if there really is an enemy near, that he should know we are on guard."

"If there really is, Digby!" said Everell, who, terrific as the apprehended danger was, felt the irrepressible thirst of youth of adventure; "do you think we could both have been deceived?"

"Nothing easier, Mr. Everell, than to deceive senses on the watch for alarm. We heard something, but it might have been the wolves that even now prowl about the very clearing here at night. Ha!" he exclaimed, "there they are;"—and, starting forward, he levelled his musket towards the wood.

"You are mad," said Everell, striking down Digby's musket with the butt end of his own. "It is Magawisca." Magawisca at that moment emerged from the wood.

Digby appeared confounded. "Could I have been so deceived?" he said; "could it have been her shadow? I thought I saw an Indian beyond that birch-tree; you see the white bark? well, just beyond in the shade. It could not have been Magawisca, nor her shadow, for you see there are trees between the footpath and that place; and yet how should he have vanished without motion or sound?"

"Our senses deceive us, Digby," said Everell, reciprocating Digby's own argument.

"In this tormenting moonlight they do; but my senses have been well schooled in their time, and should have learned to know a man from a woman, and a shadow from a substance."

Digby had not a very strong conviction of the actual presence of an enemy, as was evident from his giving no alarm to his auxiliaries in the house; and he believed that if there were hostile Indians prowling about them, they were few in number; still he deemed it prudent to persevere in their precautionary measures. "I will remain here," he said, "Mr. Everell, and do you follow Magawisca; sift what you can from her. Depend on't, there's something wrong. Why should she have turned away on seeing us? and did you not observe her hide something beneath her mantle?"

Everell acceded to Digby's proposition, not with the expectation of confirming his suspicions, but in the hope that Magawisca would show they were groundless. He followed her to the front of the house, to which she seemed involuntarily to have bent her steps on perceiving him.

"You have taken the most difficult part of our duty on yourself, Magawisca," he said, on coming up to her. "You have acted as vidette, while I have been quiet at my post."

Perhaps Magawisca did not understand him; at any rate, she made no reply.

"Have you met an enemy in your reconnoitring? Digby and I fancied that we both heard and saw the foe."

"When and where?" exclaimed Magawisca, in a hurried, alarmed tone.

"Not many minutes since, and just at the very edge of the wood."

"What! when Digby raised his gun? I thought that had been in sport, to startle me."

"No—Magawisca; sporting does not suit our present case. My mother and her little ones are in peril, and Digby is a faithful servant."

"Faithful!" echoed Magawisca, as if there were more in Everell's expression than met the ear; "he surely may walk straight who hath nothing to draw him aside. Digby hath but one path, and that is plain before him; but one voice from his heart, and why should he not obey it?" The girl's voice faltered as she spoke, and as she concluded she burst into tears. Everell had never before witnessed this expression of feeling from her. She had an habitual self-command, that hid the emotions of her heart from common observers, and veiled them even from those who most narrowly watched her. Everell's confidence in Magawisca had not been in the least degree weakened by all the appearances against her. He did not mean to imply suspicion by his commendation of Digby, but merely to throw out a leading observation, which she might follow if she would.

He felt reproached and touched by her distress; but, struck by the clew which, as he thought, her language afforded to the mystery of her conduct, and confident that she would in no way aid or abet any mischief that her own people might be contriving against them, he followed the natural bent of his generous temper, and assured her, again and again, of his entire trust in her. This seemed rather to aggravate than abate her distress. She threw herself on the ground, drew her mantle over her face, and wept convulsively. He found he could not allay the storm he had raised, and he seated himself beside her. After a little while, either exhausted by the violence of her emotion, or comforted by Everell's silent sympathy, she became composed, and raised her face from her mantle, and as she did so, something fell from beneath its folds. She hastily recovered and replaced it, but not till Everell had perceived it was an eagle's feather. He knew this was the badge of her tribe, and he had heard her say that "a tuft from the wing of the monarch bird was her father's crest." A suspicion flashed through his mind, and was conveyed to Magawisca's by one bright glance of inquiry. She said nothing, but her responding look was rather sorrowful than confused; and Everell, anxious to believe what he wished to be true, came, after a little consideration, to the conclusion that the feather had been dropped in her path by a passing bird. He did not scrutinize her motive in concealing it; he could not think her capable of evil; and, anxious to efface from her mind the distrust his countenance might have expressed—"This beautiful moon and her train of stars," he said, "look as if they were keeping their watch over our dwelling. There are those, Magawisca, who believe the stars have a mysterious influence on human destiny. I know nothing of the grounds of their faith, and my imagination is none of the brightest; but I can almost fancy they are stationed there as guardian angels, and I feel quite sure that nothing evil can walk abroad in their light."

"They do look peaceful," she replied, mournfully; "but ah! Everell, man is ever breaking the peace of nature. It was such a night as this, so bright and still, when your English came upon our quiet homes."

"You have never spoken to me of that night, Magawisca."

"No, Everell, for our hands have taken hold of the chain of friendship, and I feared to break it by speaking of the wrongs your people did to mine."

"You need not fear it; I can honour noble deeds, though done by our enemies, and see that cruelty is cruelty, though inflicted by our friends."

"Then listen to me; and when the hour of vengeance comes, if it should come, remember it was provoked."

She paused for a few moments, sighed deeply, and then began the recital of the last acts in the tragedy of her people, the principal circumstances of which are detailed in the chronicles of the times by the witnesses of the bloody scenes. "You know," she said, "our fortress-homes were on the level summit of a hill. Thence we could see, as far as the eye could stretch, our hunting-grounds and our gardens, which lay beneath us on the borders of a stream that glided around our hill, and so near to it that in the still nights we could hear its gentle voice. Our fort and wigwams were encompassed with a palisade, formed of young trees, and branches interwoven and sharply pointed. No enemy's foot had ever approached this nest, which the eagles of the tribe had built for their mates and their young. Sassacus and my father were both away on that dreadful night. They had called a council of our chiefs and old men; our young men had been out in their canoes, and when they returned they had danced and feasted, and were now in deep sleep. My mother was in her hut with her children—not sleeping, for my brother Samoset had lingered behind his companions, and had not yet returned from the watersport. The warning spirit, that ever keeps its station at a mother's pillow, whispered that some evil was near; and my mother, bidding me lie still with the little ones, went forth in quest of my brother. All the servants of the Great Spirit spoke to my mother's ear and eye of danger and death. The moon, as she sunk behind the hills, appeared a ball of fire; strange lights darted through the air; to my mother's eye they seemed fiery arrows; to her ear the air was filled with death-sighs.

"She had passed the palisade, and was descending the hill, when she met old Cushmakin. 'Do you know aught of my boy?' she asked.

" 'Your boy is safe, and sleeps with his companions; he returned by the Sassafras knoll; that way can only be trodden by the strong-limbed and lightfooted.'

" 'My boy is safe,' said my mother; 'then tell me, for thou art wise, and canst see quite through the dark future, tell me, what evil is coming to our tribe?' She then described the omens she had seen. 'I know not,' said Cushmakin: 'of late darkness hath spread over my soul, and all is black there, as before these eyes, that the arrows of death have pierced; but tell me, Monoco, what see you now in the fields of heaven?'

" 'Oh, now,' said my mother, 'I see nothing but the blue depths and the watching stars. The spirits of the air have ceased their moaning, and steal over my cheek like an infant's breath. The waterspirits are rising, and will soon spread their soft wings around the nest of our tribe.'

" 'The boy sleeps safely,' muttered the old man, 'and I have listened to the idle fear of a doting mother.'

" 'I come not of a fearful race,' said my mother.

" 'Nay, that I did not mean,' replied Cushmakin; 'but the panther watching her young is fearful as a doe.' The night was far spent, and my mother bade him go home with her, for our powwows have ever a mat in the wigwam of their chief. 'Nay,' he said, 'the day is near, and I am always abroad at the rising of the sun.' It seemed that the first warm touch of the sun opened the eye of the old man's soul, and he saw again the flushed hills and the shaded valleys, the sparkling waters, the green maize, and the gray old rocks of our home. They were just passing the little gate of the palisade, when the old man's dog sprang from him with a fearful bark. A rushing sound was heard. 'Owanox! Owanox! (the English! the English!') cried Cushmakin. My mother joined her voice to his, and in an instant the cry of alarm spread through the wigwams. The enemy were indeed upon us. They had surrounded the palisade, and opened their fire."

"Was it so sudden? Did they so rush on sleeping women and children?" asked Everell, who was unconsciously lending all his interest to the party of the narrator.

"Even so; they were guided to us by the traitor Wequash; he from whose bloody hand my mother had shielded the captive English maidens; he who had eaten from my father's dish, and slept on his mat. They were flanked by the cowardly Narragansetts, who shrunk from the sight of our tribe; who were pale as white men at the thought of Sassacus, and so feared him, that when his name was spoken they were like an unstrung bow, and they said, 'He is all one God—no man can kill him.' These cowardly allies waited for the prey they dared not attack."

"Then," said Everell, "as I have heard, our people had all the honour of the fight."

"Honour! was it, Everell?—ye shall hear. Our warriors rushed forth to meet the foe; they surrounded the huts of their mothers, wives, sisters, children; they fought as if each man had a hundred lives, and would give each and all to redeem their homes. Oh! the dreadful fray even now rings in my ears! Those fearful guns that we had never heard before—the shouts of your people—our own battle yell—the piteous cries of the little children—the groans of our mothers; and oh! worse, worse than all, the silence of those that could not speak.—The English fell back; they were driven to the palisade, some beyond it, when their leader gave the cry to fire our huts, and led the way to my mother's. Samoset, the noble boy, defended the entrance like a stag at bay till they struck him down; prostrate and bleeding, he again bent his bow, and had taken deadly aim at the English leader, when a sabre-blow severed his bowstring. Then was taken from our hearth-stone, where the English had been so often warmed and cherished, the brand to consume our dwellings. They were covered with mats, and burned like dried straw. The enemy retreated without the palisade. In vain did our warriors fight for a path in which we might escape from the consuming fire; they were beaten back; the fire gained on us; the Narragansetts pressed on the English, howling like wolves for their prey. Some of our people threw themselves into the midst of the crackling flames, and their courageous souls parted with one shout of triumph; others mounted the palisade, but they were shot, and dropped like a flock of birds smitten by the hunter's arrows. Thus did the strangers destroy, in our own homes, hundreds of our tribe."

"And how did you escape in that dreadful hour, Magawisca? you were not, then, taken prisoners?"

"No; there was a rock at one extremity of our hut, and beneath it a cavity into which my mother crept, with Oneco, myself, and the two little ones that afterward perished. Our simple habitations were soon consumed; we heard the foe retiring, and when the last sound had died away, we came forth to a sight that made us lament to be among the living. The sun was scarce an hour from his rising, and yet in this brief space our homes had vanished. The bodies of our people were strewn about the smouldering ruin, and all around the palisade lay the strong and valiant warriors, cold, silent, powerless as the unformed clay."

Magawisca paused; she was overcome with the recollection of this scene of desolation. She looked upward with an intent gaze, as if she held communion with an invisible being. "Spirit of my mother!" burst from her lips; "oh! that I could follow thee to that blessed land, where I should no more dread the war-cry nor the death-knife." Everell dashed the gathering tears from his eyes, and Magawisca proceeded in her narrative.

"While we all stood silent and motionless, we heard footsteps and cheerful voices. They came from my father and Sassacus, and their band, returning from the friendly council. They approached on the side of the hill that was covered with a thicket of oaks, and their ruined homes at once burst upon their view. Oh! what horrid sounds then pealed on the air! shouts of wailing, and cries for vengeance. Every eye was turned with suspicion and hatred on my father. *He* had been the friend of the English; *he* had counselled peace and alliance with them; *he* had protected their traders; delivered the captives taken from them, and restored them to their people: now *his* wife and children alone were living, and they called him traitor. I heard an angry murmur, and many hands were lifted to strike the deathblow. He moved not—'Nay, nay,' cried Sassacus, beating them off, 'touch him not; his soul is bright as the sun; sooner shall you darken that than find treason in his breast. If he hath shown the dove's heart to the English when he believed them friends, he will show himself the fierce eagle now he knows them enemies. Touch him not, warriors; remember my blood runneth in his veins.'

"From that moment my father was a changed man. He neither spoke nor looked at his wife or children; but, placing himself at the head of one band of the young men, he shouted his war-cry, and then silently pursued the enemy. Sassacus went forth to assemble the tribe, and we followed my mother to one of our villages."

"You did not tell me, Magawisca," said Everell, "how Samoset perished; was he consumed in the flames, or shot from the palisade?"

"Neither—neither. He was reserved to whet my father's revenge to a still keener edge. He had forced a passage through the English, and, hastily collecting a few warriors, they pursued the enemy, sprung upon them from a covert, and did so annoy them that the English turned and gave them battle. All fled save my brother, and him they took prisoner. They told him they would spare his life if he would guide them to our strongholds; he refused. He had, Everell, lived but sixteen summers; he loved the light of the sun even as we love it; his manly spirit was tamed by wounds and weariness; his limbs were like a bending reed, and his heart beat like a woman's; but the fire of his soul burned clear. Again they pressed him with offers of life and reward; he faithfully refused, and with one sabre-stroke they severed his head from his body."

Magawisca paused—she looked at Everell, and said with a bitter smile, "You English tell us, Everell, that the book of your law is better than that written on our hearts; for ye say it teaches mercy, compassion, forgiveness—if ye had such a law, and believed it, would ye thus have treated a captive boy?"

Magawisca's reflecting mind suggested the most serious obstacle to the progress of the Christian religion, in all ages and under all circumstances: the contrariety between its divine principles and the conduct of its professors; which, instead of always being a medium for the light that emanates from our Holy Law, is too often the darkest cloud that obstructs the passage of its rays to the hearts of heathen men. Everell had been carefully instructed in the principles of his religion, and he felt Magawisca's relation to be an awkward comment on them, and her inquiry natural; but, though he knew not what answer to make, he was sure there must be a good one, and mentally resolving to refer the case to his mother, he begged Magawisca to proceed with her narrative.

"The fragments of our broken tribe," she said, "were collected, and some other small dependent tribes persuaded to join us. We were obliged to flee from the open grounds, and shelter ourselves in a dismal swamp. The English surrounded us; they sent in to us a messenger, and offered life and pardon to all who had not shed the blood of Englishmen. Our allies listened, and fled from us as frightened birds fly from a falling tree. My father looked upon his warriors; they answered that look with their battle-shout. 'Tell your people,' said my father to the messenger, 'that we have shed and drank English blood, and that we will take nothing from them but death.'

"The messenger departed, and again returned with offers of pardon if we would come forth, and lay our arrows and our tomahawks at the feet of the English. 'What say you, warriors?' cried my father—'shall we take *pardon* from those who have burned your wives and children, and given your homes to the beasts of prey; who have robbed you of your hunting-grounds, and driven your canoes from their waters?' A hundred arrows were pointed to the messenger. 'Enough—you have your answer,' said my father; and the messenger returned to announce the fate we had chosen."

"Where was Sassacus?—had he abandoned his people?" asked Everell.

"Abandoned them! No—his life was in theirs; but, accustomed to attack and victory, he could not bear to be thus driven, like a fox, to his hole. His soul was sick within him, and he was silent, and left all to my father. All day we heard the strokes of the English axes felling the trees that defended us, and when night came they had approached so near that we could see the glimmering of their watchlights through the branches of the trees. All night they were pouring in their bullets, alike on warriors, women, and children. Old Cushmakin was lying at my mother's feet when he received a death-wound. Gasping for breath, he called on Sassacus and my father—'Stay not here,' he said; 'look not on your wives and children, but burst your prison bound; sound through the nations the cry of revenge! Linked together, ye shall drive the English into the sea. I speak the word of the Great Spirit—obey it!' While he was yet speaking he stiffened in death, 'Obey him, warriors,' cried my mother; 'see,' she said, pointing to the mist that was now wrapping itself around the wood like a thick curtain—'see, our friends have come from the spirit-land to shelter you. Nay, look not on us—our hearts have been tender in the wigwam, but we can die before our enemies without a groan. Go forth and avenge us.'

"'Have we come to the counsel of old men and old women?' said Sassacus, in the bitterness of his spirit.

"'When women put down their womanish thoughts and counsel like men, they should be obeyed,' said my father. 'Follow me, warriors!'

"They burst through the enclosure. We saw nothing more, but we heard the shout from the foe as they issued from the wood—the momentary fierce encounter—and the cry, 'They have escaped!' Then it was that my mother, who had listened with breathless silence, threw herself down on the mossy stones, and, laying her hot cheek to mine—'Oh, my children—my children!' she said, 'would that I could die for you! But fear not death—the blood of a hundred chieftains, that never knew fear, runneth in your veins. Hark, the enemy comes nearer and nearer. Now lift up your heads, my children, and show them that even the weak ones of our tribe are strong in soul.'

"We rose from the ground—all about sat women and children in family clusters, awaiting unmoved their fate. The English had penetrated the forest-screen, and were already on the little rising ground where we had been intrenched. Death was dealt freely. None resisted—not a movement was made—not a voice lifted—not a sound escaped, save the wailings of the dying children.

"One of your soldiers knew my mother, and a command was given that her life and that of her children should be spared. A guard was stationed round us.

"You know that, after our tribe was thus cut off, we were taken, with a few other captives, to Boston. Some were sent to the Islands of the Sun, to bend their free limbs to bondage like your beasts of burden. There are among your people those who have not put out the light of the Great Spirit; they can remember a kindness, albeit done by an Indian; and when it was known to your sachems that the wife of Mononotto, once the protector and friend of your people, was a prisoner, they treated her with honour and gentleness. But her people were extinguished; her husband driven to distant forests—forced on earth to the misery of wicked souls—to wander without a home; her children were captives, and her heart was broken. You know the rest."

This war, so fatal to the Pequods, had transpired the preceding year [1637]. It was an important event to the infant colonies, and its magnitude probably somewhat heightened to the imaginations of the English by the terror this resolute tribe had inspired. All the circumstances attending it were still fresh in men's minds, and Everell had heard them detailed with the interest and particularity that belongs to recent adventures; but he had heard them in the language of the enemies and conquerors of the Pequods, and from Magawisca's lips they took a new form and hue; she seemed to him to imbody nature's best gifts, and her feelings to be the inspiration of heaven. This new version of an old story reminded him of the man and the lion in the fable. But here it was not merely changing sculptors to give the advantage to one or the other of the artist's subjects, but it was putting the chisel into the hands of truth, and giving it to whom it belonged.

He had heard this destruction of the original possessors of the soil described, as we find it in the history of the times, where we are told "the number destroyed was about four hundred;" and "it was a fearful sight to see them thus frying in the fire, and the streams of blood quenching the same, and the horrible scent thereof; but the victory seemed a sweet sacrifice, and they gave the praise thereof to God."

In the relations of their enemies, the courage of the Pequods was distorted into ferocity, and their fortitude in their last extremity thus set forth: "many were killed in the swamp, like sullen dogs, that would rather, in their self-willedness and madness, sit still to be shot or cut in pieces, than receive their lives for asking at the hands of those into whose power they had now fallen."

Everell's imagination, touched by the wand of feeling, presented a very different picture of those defenceless families of savages, pent in the recesses of their native forests, and there exterminated, not by superior natural force, but by the adventitious circumstances of arms, skill, and knowledge, from that offered by those who, "then living and worthy of credit, did affirm, that in the morning, entering into the swamp, they saw several heaps of them (the Pequods) sitting close together, upon whom they discharged their pieces, laden with ten or twelve pistol-bullets at a time, putting the muzzles of their pieces under the boughs within a few yards of them."

Everell did not fail to express to Magawisca, with all the eloquence of a heated imagination, his sympathy and admiration of her heroic and suffering people. She listened with a mournful pleasure, as one listens to the praise of a departed friend. Both seemed to have forgotten the purpose of their vigil, which they had marvellously kept without apprehension or heaviness, when they were roused from their romantic abstraction by Digby's voice: "Now to your beds, children," he said; "the family is stirring, and the day is at hand. See the morning star hanging just over those trees, like a single watchlight in all the wide canopy. As you have not to look in a prayer-book for it, Master Everell, don't forget to thank the Lord for keeping us safe, as your mother, God bless her, would say, through the night watches. Stop one moment," added Digby, lowering his voice, to Everell, as he rose to follow Magawisca; "did she tell you?"

"Tell me! what?"

"What! Heaven's mercy! what ails the boy? Why, did she tell you what brought her out to-night? Did she explain all the mysterious actions we have seen? Are you crazy? Did not you ask her?"

Everell hesitated—fortunately for him, the light was too dim to expose to Digby's eye the blushes that betrayed his consciousness that he had forgotten his duty. "Magawisca did not tell me," he said; "but I am sure, Digby, that—"

"That she can do no wrong—hey, Master Everell; well, that may be very satisfactory to you, but it does not content me. I like not her secret ways—'it's bad ware that needs a dark store.'"

Everell had tried the force of his own convictions on Digby, and knew it to be unavailing; therefore, having no reply to make, he very discreetly retreated without attempting any.

Magawisca crept to her bed, but not to repose—neither watching nor weariness procured sleep for her. Her mind was racked with apprehensions and conflicting duties, the cruellest rack to an honourable mind.

Nelema had communicated to her, the preceding day, the fact which she had darkly intimated to Mrs. Fletcher, that Mononotto, with one or two associates, was lurking in the forest, and watching an opportunity to make an attack on Bethel. How far his purpose extended, whether simply to the recovery of his children or to the destruction of the family, she knew not. The latter was most probable, for hostile Indians always left blood on their trail. In reply to Magawisca's eager inquiries, Nelema said she had, again and again, assured her father of the kind treatment his children had received at the hands of Mrs. Fletcher; but he seemed scarcely to hear what she said, and precipitately left her, telling her that she would not again see him till his work was done.

Magawisca's first impulse had been to reveal all to Mrs. Fletcher; but by doing this she would jeopard her father's life. Her natural sympathies—her strong affections—her pride, were all enlisted on the side of her people; but she shrunk, as if her own life were menaced, from the blow that was about to fall on her friends. She would have done or suffered anything to avert it—any thing but betray her father. The hope of meeting him explains all that seemed mysterious to Digby. She did go to Nelema's hut, but all was quiet there. In returning she found an eagle's feather in the path—she believed it must have just been dropped there by her father, and this circumstance determined her to remain watching through the night, that, if her father should appear, she might avert his vengeance.

She did not doubt that Digby had really seen and heard him; and believing that her father would not shrink from a single armed man, she hoped against hope, that his sole object was to recover his children; hoped against hope, we say, for her reason told her that, if that were his only purpose, it might easily have been accomplished by the intervention of Nelema.

Magawisca had said truly to Everell, that her father's nature had been changed by the wrongs he had received. When the Pequods were proud and prosperous, he was more noted for his humane virtues than his warlike spirit. The supremacy of his tribe was acknowledged, and it seemed to be his noble nature, as it is sometimes the instinct of the most powerful animals, to protect and defend rather than attack and oppress. The ambitious spirit of his brother chieftain, Sassacus, had ever aspired to dominion over the allied tribes; and, immediately after the appearance of the English, the same temper was manifest in a jealousy of their encroachments. He employed all his art, and influence, and authority, to unite the tribes for the extirpation of the dangerous invaders. Mononotto, on the contrary, averse to all hostility, and foreseeing no danger from them, was the advocate of an hospitable reception and pacific conduct.

This difference of feeling between the two chiefs may account for the apparent treachery of the Pequods, who, as the influence of one or the other prevailed, received the English traders with favour and hospitality, or, violating their treaties of friendship, inflicted on them cruelties and death.

The stories of the murders of Stone, Norton, and Oldham are familiar to every reader of our early annals; and the anecdote of the two English girls who were captured at Wethersfield, and protected and restored to their friends by the wife of Mononotto, has already been illustrated by a sister labourer, and is precious to all those who would accumulate proofs that the image of God is never quite effaced from the souls of his creatures, and that, in their darkest ignorance and deepest degradation, there are still to be found traits of mercy and benevolence. These will be gathered and treasured in the memory with that fond feeling with which Mungo Park describes himself to have culled and cherished in his bosom the single flower that bloomed in his melancholy track over the African desert.

The chieftain of a savage race is the depository of the honour of his tribe; and their defeat is a disgrace to him, that can only be effaced by the blood of his conquerors. It is a common case with the unfortunate, to be compelled to endure the reproach of inevitable evils; and Mononotto was often reminded by the remnant of his tribe, in the bitterness of their spirit, of his former kindness to the English. This reproach sharpened too keenly the edge of his adversity.

He had seen his people slaughtered, or driven from their homes and hunting-grounds into shameful exile; his wife had died in captivity, and his children lived in servile dependence in the house of his enemies.

Sassacus perished by treachery, and Mononotto alone remained to endure this accumulated misery. In this extremity, he determined on the rescue of his children, and the infliction of some signal deed of vengeance, by which he hoped to revive the spirit of the natives, and reinstate himself as the head of his broken and dispersed people: in his most sanguine moments, he meditated a combination and unity that should eventually expel the invaders.

Volume 1: Chapter 5

"There have been sweet singing voices
In your walks that now are still;
There are seats left void in your earthly homes,
Which none again may fill."

—MRS. HEMANS

MAGAWISCA ROSE FROM her sleepless pillow to join the family at prayers, her mind distracted with opposing fears, which her face, the mirror of her soul, too truly reflected.

Mrs. Fletcher observed her narrowly; and, confirmed in her forebodings by the girl's apprehensive countenance, and still farther by Digby's report of her behaviour during the night, she resolved to dispatch him to Mr. Pynchon for his advice and assistance touching her removal to the fort, or the appointment of a guard for Bethel. Her servant (who prudently kept his alarm to himself, knowing, as he said, that a woman's fears were always ahead of danger) applauded her decision, and was on the point of proceeding to act upon it, when a messenger arrived with the joyful tidings that Mr. Fletcher was within a few hours' ride of Bethel; and the intelligence, no less joyful to Dame Grafton, that with his luggage, already arrived at the village, was a small box of millinery which she had ordered from London.

Mrs. Fletcher, feeling, as good wives do, a sense of safety from the proximity of her husband, bade Digby defer any new arrangement till he had the benefit of his master's counsel. The whole house was thrown into the commotion so common in a retired family when an arrival is about to interrupt the equable current of life. Whatever unexpressed and superior happiness some others might have felt, no individual made such bustling demonstrations as Mrs. Grafton. It was difficult to say which excited her most, the anticipation of seeing her niece, Hope Leslie, or of inspecting the box of millinery.

Immediately after dinner, two of the men-servants were dispatched to the village to transport their master's luggage. They had hardly gone, when Mrs. Grafton recollected that her box contained a present for Madam Holioke, which it would be a thousand pities to have brought to Bethel, and lie there perhaps a week before it would be sent to her, and "she would like of all things, if Mrs. Fletcher saw no objection, to have the pony saddled and ride to the village herself, where the present could be made forthwith."

Mrs. Fletcher was too happy to throw a shadow across anyone's path, and wearied too, perhaps, with Mrs. Grafton's fidgeting (for the good dame had all day been wondering whether her confidential agent had matched her orange satin; how she had trimmed her cap, &c. &c. &c.), she ordered a horse to be saddled and brought to the door. The animal proved a little restive, and Mrs. Grafton, not excelling in horsemanship, became alarmed, and begged that Digby might be allowed to attend her.

Digby's cleverness was felt by all the household, and his talents were always in requisition for the miscellaneous wants of the family; but Digby, like good servants in every age, was aware of his importance, and was not more willing than a domestic of the present day to be worked like a machine. He muttered something of "old women making fools of themselves with new top-knots," and saying aloud that "Mistress Grafton knew it was his master's order that all the men-servants should not be away from the place at the same time," he was turning off, when Mrs. Fletcher, who was standing at the door observing him, requested him, with more authority than was usual in her manner, to comply with Mrs. Grafton's request.

"I would not wish," said Digby, still hesitating, "to disoblige Mrs. Grafton—if it were a matter of life and death," he added, lowering his voice; "but to get more furbelows for the old lady, when, with what she has already, she makes such a fool of herself, that our young witlings, Master Everell and Oneco, garnish out our old Yorkshire hen with peacock's feathers and dandelions, and then call her 'Dame Grafton in a flurry.'"

"Hush, Digby!" said Mrs. Fletcher; "it ill befits you to laugh at such fooleries in the boys—they shall be corrected; and do you learn to treat your master's friend with respect."

"Come—come, Digby!" screamed Mrs. Grafton.

"Shall I go and break my master's orders?" asked Digby, still bent on having his own way.

"For this once you shall, Digby," answered Mrs. Fletcher; "and if you need any apology to your master, I shall not fail to make it."

"But if anything should happen to you, Mistress Fletcher—"

"Nothing will happen, my good Digby. Is not your master at hand? and an hour or two will be the extent of your absence. So get thee along, without more ado."

Digby could not resist any farther the authority of his gentle mistress, and he walked by the side of Mrs. Grafton's pony with slow, unwilling steps.

All was joy in Mrs. Fletcher's dwelling. "My dear mother," said Everell, "it is now quite time to look out for father and Hope Leslie. I have turned the hour-glass three times since dinner, and counted all the sands, I think. Let us all go on the front portico, where we can catch the first glimpse of them as they come past the elm-trees. Here, Oneco," he continued, as he saw assent in his mother's smile, "help me out with mother's rocking-chair—rather rough rocking," he added, as he adjusted the rockers lengthwise with the logs that served for the flooring—"but mother won't mind trifles just now. Ah! blessed baby brother," he continued, taking in his arms the beautiful infant, "you shall come too, even though you cheat me out of my birthright, and get the first kiss from father." Thus saying, he placed the laughing infant in his go-cart beside his mother. He then aided his little sisters in their arrangement of the playthings they had brought forth to welcome and astonish Hope; and, finally, he made an elevated position for Faith Leslie, where she might, he said, as she ought, catch the very first glimpse of her sister.

"Thank, thank you, Everell," said the little girl, as she mounted her pinnacle; "if you knew Hope, you would want to see her first too—every body loves Hope. We shall always have pleasant times when Hope gets here."

It was one of the most beautiful afternoons at the close of the month of May. The lagging spring had at last come forth in all her power; her "work of gladness" was finished, and forests, fields, and meadows were bright with renovated life. The full Connecticut swept triumphantly on, as if still exulting in its release from the fetters of winter. Every gushing rill had the spring-note of joy. The meadows were for the first time enriched with patches of English grain, which the new settlers had sown scantily by way of experiment, prudently occupying the greatest portion of their rich mould with the native Indian corn. This product of our soil is beautiful in all its progress, from the moment when, as now, it studded the meadow with hillocks, shooting its bright-pointed spear from its mother earth, to its maturity, when the long golden ear bursts from the rustling leaf.

The grounds about Mrs. Fletcher's house had been prepared with the neatness of English taste, and a rich bed of clover, that overspread the lawn immediately before the portico, already rewarded the industry of the cultivators. Over this delicate carpet, the domestic fowls, the first civilized inhabitants of the country of their tribe, were now treading, picking their food here and there like dainty little epicures.

The scene had also its minstrels; the birds, those ministers and worshippers of nature, were on the wing, filling the air with melody; while, like diligent little housewives, they ransacked forest and field for materials for their housekeeping.

A mother encircled by healthful sporting children is always a beautiful spectacle—a spectacle that appeals to nature in every human breast. Mrs. Fletcher, in obedience to matrimonial duty, or, it may be, from some lingering of female vanity, had on this occasion dressed herself with extraordinary care. What woman does not wish to look handsome—in the eyes of her husband?

"Mother," said Everell, putting aside the exquisitely fine lace that shaded her cheek, "I do not believe you looked more beautiful than you do to-day when, as I have heard, they called you 'the rose of the wilderness'—our little Mary's cheek is as round and as bright as a peach, but it is not so handsome as yours, mother. Your heart has sent this colour here," he continued, kissing her tenderly—"it seems to have come forth to tell us that our father is near."

"It would shame me, Everell," replied his mother, embracing him with a feeling that the proudest drawing-room belle might have envied, "to take such flattery from any lips but thine."

"Oh, do not call it flattery, mother—look, Magawisca—for Heaven's sake, cheer up—look, would you know mother's eye? Just turn it, mother, one minute from that road—and her pale cheek too, with this rich colour."

"Alas! alas!" replied Magawisca, glancing her eye at Mrs. Fletcher, and then, as if heart-struck, withdrawing them, "how soon the flush of the setting sun fades away."

"Oh, Magawisca," said Everell, impatiently, "why are you so dismal? Your voice is too sweet for a bird of ill omen. I shall begin to think, as Jennet says—though Jennet is no text-book for me—I shall begin to think old Nelema has really bewitched you."

"You call me a bird of ill omen," replied Magawisca, half proud, half sorrowful, "and you call the owl a bird of ill omen, but we hold him sacred—he is our sentinel, and when danger is near he cries awake! awake!"

"Magawisca, you are positively unkind—Jeremiah's lamentations on a holiday would not be more out of time than your croaking is now—the very skies, earth, and air seem to partake our joy at my father's return, and you only make a discord. Do you think, if your father was near, I would not share your joy?"

Tears fell fast from Magawisca's eye, but she made no reply; and Mrs. Fletcher, observing and compassionating her emotion, and thinking it probably arose from comparing her orphan state to that of the merry children about her, called her and said, "Magawisca, you are neither a stranger nor a servant, will you not share our joy? Do you not love us?"

"Love you!" she exclaimed, clasping her hands; "love you! I would give my life for you."

"We do not ask your life, my good girl," replied Mrs. Fletcher, kindly smiling on her, "but a light heart and a cheerful look. A sad countenance doth not become this joyful hour. Go and help Oneco—he is quite out of breath blowing those soap-bubbles for the children."

Oneco smiled and shook his head, and continued to send off one after another of the prismatic globes; and as they rose and floated on the air, and brightened with the many-coloured ray, the little girls clapped their hands, and the baby stretched his to grasp the brilliant vapour.

"Oh!" said Magawisca, impetuously covering her eyes, "I do not like to see any thing so beautiful pass so quickly away."

Scarcely had she uttered these words, when suddenly, as if the earth had opened on them, three Indian warriors darted from the forest, and pealed on the air their horrible yells.

"My father! my father!" burst from the lips of Magawisca and Oneco.

Faith Leslie sprang towards the Indian boy, and clung fast to him—and the children clustered about their mother—she instinctively caught her infant, and held it close within her arms, as if their ineffectual shelter were a rampart.

Magawisca uttered a cry of agony, and springing forward with her arms uplifted, as if deprecating his approach, she sunk down at her father's feet, and clasping her hands, "Save them! save them!" she cried, "the mother—the children—oh, they are all good—take vengeance on your enemies—but spare—spare our friends, our benefactors—I bleed when they are struck—oh, command them to stop!" she screamed, looking to the companions of her father, who, unchecked by her cries, were pressing on to their deadly work.

Mononotto was silent and motionless; his eye glanced wildly from Magawisca to Oneco. Magawisca replied to the glance of fire—"Yes, they have sheltered us—they have spread the wing of love over us—save them—save them—oh, it will be too late," she cried, springing from her father, whose silence and fixedness showed that, if his better nature rebelled against the work of revenge, there was no relenting of purpose. Magawisca darted before the Indian who was advancing towards Mrs. Fletcher with an uplifted hatchet. "You shall hew me to pieces ere you touch her," she said, and planted herself as a shield before her benefactress.

The warrior's obdurate heart, untouched by the sight of the helpless mother and her little ones, was thrilled by the courage of the heroic girl—he paused and grimly smiled on her, when his companion, crying, "Hasten, the dogs will be on us!" leveled a deadly blow at Mrs. Fletcher—but his uplifted arm was penetrated by a musket shot, and the hatchet fell harmless to the floor.

"Courage, mother!" cried Everell, reloading the piece; but neither courage nor celerity could avail—the second Indian sprang upon him, threw him on the floor, wrested his musket from him, and brandishing his tomahawk over his head, he would have aimed the fatal stroke, when a cry from Mononotto arrested his arm.

Everell extricated himself from his grasp, and one hope flashing into his mind, he seized a bugle-horn which hung beside the door, and winded it. This was the conventional signal of alarm—and he sent forth a blast—long and loud—a death-cry.

Mrs. Grafton and her attendants were just mounting their horses to return home. Digby listened for a moment—then exclaiming, "It comes from our master's dwelling! Ride for your life, Hutton!" he tossed away a bandbox that encumbered him, and spurred his horse to its utmost speed.

The alarm was spread through the village, and in a brief space Mr. Pynchon, with six armed men, were pressing towards the fatal scene.

In the mean time the tragedy was proceeding at Bethel. Mrs. Fletcher's senses had been stunned with terror. She had neither spoken nor moved after she grasped her infant. Everell's gallant interposition restored a momentary consciousness; she screamed to him—"Fly, Everell, my son, fly; for your father's sake, fly."

"Never," he replied, springing to his mother's side.

The savages, always rapid in their movements, were now aware that their safety depended on despatch. "Finish your work, warriors," cried Mononotto. Obedient to the command, and infuriated by his bleeding wound, the Indian, who, on receiving the shot, had staggered back and leaned against the wall, now sprang forward and tore the infant from its mother's breast. She shrieked, and in that shriek passed the agony of death. She was unconscious that her son, putting forth a strength beyond nature, for a moment kept the Indian at bay; she neither saw nor felt the knife struck at her own heart. She felt not the arms of her defenders, Everell and Magawisca, as they met around her neck. She fainted and fell to the floor, dragging her impotent protectors with her.

The savage, in his struggle with Everell, had tossed the infant boy to the ground; he fell quite unharmed on the turf at Mononotto's feet. There, raising his head, and looking up into the chieftain's face, he probably perceived a gleam of mercy, for, with the quick instinct of infancy, that with unerring sagacity directs its appeal, he clasped the naked leg of the savage with one arm, and stretched the other towards him with a piteous supplication that no words could have expressed.

Mononotto's heart melted within him; he stooped to raise the sweet suppliant, when one of the Mohawks fiercely seized him, tossed him wildly around his head, and dashed him on the door-stone. But the silent prayer—perhaps the celestial inspiration—of the innocent creature was not lost. "We have had blood enough," cried Mononotto, "you have well avenged me, brothers."

Then looking at Oneco, who had remained in one corner of the portico, clasping Faith Leslie in his arms, he commanded him to follow him with the child. Everell was torn from the lifeless bodies of his mother and sisters, and dragged into the forest. Magawisca uttered one cry of agony and despair as she looked for the last time on the bloody scene, and then followed her father.

As they passed the boundary of the cleared ground, Mononotto tore from Oneco his English dress, and casting it from him—"Thus perish," he said, "every mark of the captivity of my children. Thou shalt return to our forests," he continued, wrapping a skin around him, "with the badge of thy people."

SOURCE: Catharine Maria Sedgwick. *Hope Leslie; or Early Times in the Massachusetts.* New York: White, Gallaher, and White, 1827.

WILLIAM LLOYD GARRISON

William Lloyd Garrison (1805–1879) was the most public and one of America's most radical abolitionists for the three decades before the nation's Civil War. His Boston-based weekly newspaper, The Liberator, *began publication with this passionate announcement on January 1, 1831.*

To the Public (1831)

IN THE MONTH, of August, I issued proposals for publishing "THE LIBERATOR" in Washington City; but the enterprise, though hailed in different sections of the country, was palsied by public indifference. Since that time, the removal of the *Genius of Universal Emancipation* to the Seat of Government has rendered less imperious the establishment of a similar periodical in that quarter.

During my recent tour for the purpose of exciting the minds of the people by a series of discourses on the subject of slavery, every place that I visited gave fresh evidence of the fact, that a greater revolution in public sentiment was to be effected in the free States—*and particularly in New-England*—than at the South. I found contempt more bitter, opposition more active, detraction more relentless, prejudice more stubborn, and apathy more frozen, than among slave-owners themselves. Of course, there were individual exceptions to the contrary. This state of things afflicted, but did not dishearten me. I determined, at every hazard, to lift up the standard of emancipation in the eyes of the nation, *within sight of Bunker Hill and in the birthplace of liberty*. That standard is now unfurled; and long may it float, unhurt by the spoliations of time or the missiles of a desperate foe—yea, till every chain be broken, and every bondman set free! Let Southern oppressors tremble—let their secret abettors tremble—let their Northern apologists tremble—let all the enemies of the persecuted blacks tremble.

I deem the publication of my original Prospectus unnecessary, as it has obtained a wide circulation. The principles therein inculcated will be steadily pursued in this paper, excepting that I shall not array myself as the political partisan of any man. In defending the great cause of human rights, I wish to derive the assistance of all religions and of all parties.

Assenting to the "self-evident truth" maintained in the American Declaration of Independence, "that all men are created equal, and endowed by their Creator with certain inalienable rights—among which are life, liberty and the pursuit of happiness," I shall strenuously contend for the immediate enfranchisement of our slave population. In Park-Street Church, on the Fourth of July, 1829, in an address on slavery, I unreflectingly assented to the popular but pernicious doctrine of *gradual* abolition. I seize this opportunity to make a full and unequivocal recantation, and thus publicly to ask pardon of my God, of my country, and of my brethren the poor slaves, for having uttered a sentiment so full of timidity, injustice, and absurdity. A similar recantation, from my pen, was published in the *Genius of Universal Emancipation* at Baltimore, in September, 1829. My conscience is now satisfied.

I am aware that many object to the severity of my language; but is there not cause for severity? I *will be* as harsh as truth, and as uncompromising as justice. On this subject, I do not wish to think, or speak, or write, with moderation. No! no! Tell a man whose house is on fire to give a moderate alarm; tell him to moderately rescue his wife from the hands of the ravisher; tell the mother to gradually extricate her babe from the fire into which it has fallen;—but urge me not to use moderation in a cause like the present. I am in earnest—I will not equivocate—I will not excuse—I will not retreat a single inch—AND I WILL BE HEARD. The apathy of the people is enough to make every statue leap from its pedestal, and to hasten the resurrection of the dead.

It is pretended, that I am retarding the cause of emancipation by the coarseness of my invective and the precipitancy of my measures. *The charge is not true.* On this question my influence,—humble as it is,—is felt at this moment to a considerable extent, and shall be felt in coming years—not perniciously, but beneficially—not as a curse, but as a blessing; and posterity will bear testimony that I was right. I desire to thank God, that he enables me to disregard "the fear of man which bringeth a snare," and to speak his truth in its simplicity and power. And here I close with this fresh dedication:

"Oppression! I have seen thee, face to face,
And met thy cruel eye and cloudy brow;
But thy soul-withering glance I fear not now—
For dread to prouder feelings doth give place
Of deep abhorrence! Scorning the disgrace
Of slavish knees that at thy footstool bow,
I also kneel—but with far other vow
Do hail thee and thy herd of hirelings base:—
I swear, while life-blood warms my throbbing veins,
Still to oppose and thwart, with heart and hand.
Thy brutalising sway—till Afric's chains
Are burst, and Freedom rules the rescued land,—
Trampling Oppression and his iron rod:
Such is the vote I take—so HELP ME GOD!"[1]

SOURCE: Wendell Phillips Garrison, Francis Jackson Garrison. *William Lloyd Garrison, 1805–1879: The Story of His Life Told by His Children.* New York: The Century Company, 1885.

1. The author of this sonnet was Thomas Pringle, the Scottish poet, 1789–1834, one of the founders of *Blackwood's Magazine,* and Secretary of the London Society for the Abolition of Slavery throughout the British Dominions. [Note by Garrison's children.]

BLACK HAWK

Black Hawk (c. 1770–1838; his tribal name was Makataimeshekiakiak) allied himself with Tecumseh in the War of 1812 and was the energetic warrior spirit of the Sauks. He resented the broken treaties that continually pushed the tribes westward. After his campaign of revenge on settlers in the so-called Black Hawk War of 1832, Black Hawk, his braves, tribespeople and allies were hunted down and killed or taken prisoner by U.S. soldiers and Sioux. Black Hawk surrendered at Prairie du Chien and made the following speech on August 27.

Farewell to Black Hawk (1832)

You have taken me prisoner with all my warriors. I am much grieved, for I expected, if I did not defeat you, to hold out much longer, and give you more trouble before I surrendered. I tried hard to bring you into ambush, but your last general understands Indian fighting. The first one was not so wise. When I saw that I could not beat you by Indian fighting, I determined to rush on you, and fight you face to face. I fought hard. But your guns were well aimed. The bullets flew like birds in the air, and whizzed by our ears like the wind through the trees in the winter. My warriors fell around me; it began to look dismal. I saw my evil day at hand. The sun rose dim on us in the morning, and at night it sunk in a dark cloud, and looked like a ball of fire. That was the last sun that shone on Black Hawk. His heart is dead, and no longer beats quick in his bosom.—He is now a prisoner to the white men; they will do with him as they wish. But he can stand torture, and is not afraid of death. He is no coward. Black Hawk is an Indian.

He has done nothing for which an Indian ought to be ashamed. He has fought for his countrymen, the squaws and papooses, against white men, who came, year after year, to cheat them and take away their lands. You know the cause of our making war. It is known to all white men. They ought to be ashamed of it. The white men despise the Indians, and drive them from their homes. But the Indians are not deceitful. The white men speak bad of the Indian, and look at him spitefully. But the Indian does not tell lies; Indians do not steal.

An Indian who is as bad as the white men, could not live in our nation; he would be put to death, and eat up by the wolves. The white men are bad schoolmasters, they carry false looks, and deal in false actions; they smile in the face of the poor Indian to cheat him; they shake them by the hand to gain their confidence, to make them drunk, to deceive them, and ruin our wives. We told them to let us alone, and keep away from us; but they followed on, and beset our paths, and they coiled themselves among us, like the snake. They poisoned us by their touch. We were not safe. We lived in danger. We were becoming like them, hypocrites and liars, adulterers, lazy drones, all talkers, and no workers.

We looked up to the Great Spirit. We went to our great father. We were encouraged. His great council gave us fair words and big promises; but we got no satisfaction. Things were growing worse. There were no deer in the forest. The opossum and beaver were fled; the springs were drying up, and our squaws and papooses without victuals to keep them from starving; we called a great council, and built a large fire. The spirit of our fathers arose and spoke to us to avenge our wrongs or die. We all spoke before the council fire. It was warm and pleasant. We set up the war-whoop, and dug up the tomahawk; our knives were ready, and the heart of Black Hawk swelled high in his bosom when he led his warriors to battle. He is satisfied. He will go to the world of spirits contented. He has done his duty. His father will meet him there, and commend him.

Black Hawk is a true Indian, and disdains to cry like a woman. He feels for his wife, his children and friends. But he does not care for himself. He cares for his nation and the Indians. They will suffer. He laments their fate. The white men do not scalp the head; but they do worse—they poison the heart; it is not pure with them.—His countrymen will not be scalped, but they will, in a few years, become like the white men, so that you can't trust them, and there must be, as in the white settlements, nearly as many officers as men to take care of them and keep them in order.

Farewell, my nation! Black Hawk tried to save you, and avenge your wrongs. He drank the blood of some of the whites. He has been taken prisoner, and his plans are stopped. He can do no more. He is near his end. His sun is setting, and he will rise no more. Farewell to Black Hawk.

SOURCE: Samuel Gardner Drake. *Biography and History of the Indians of North America.* Volume 3. Boston: O. L. Perkins, 1834.

NATHANIEL HAWTHORNE

Nathaniel Hawthorne (1804–1864), in his most famous works of fiction, seemed intent on exposing the hypocrisy of the pious and describing the allure of evil. In "Young Goodman Brown" he narrates a story about a young husband's awakening of consciousness to "the mystery of sin" in the days of the Puritans in seventeenth-century Salem.

Young Goodman Brown (1835)

YOUNG GOODMAN BROWN came forth at sunset into the street at Salem village; but put his head back, after crossing the threshold, to exchange a parting kiss with his young wife. And Faith, as the wife was aptly named, thrust her own pretty head into the street, letting the wind play with the pink ribbons of her cap while she called to Goodman Brown.

"Dearest heart," whispered she, softly and rather sadly, when her lips were close to his ear, "prithee put off your journey until sunrise and sleep in your own bed to-night. A lone woman is troubled with such dreams and such thoughts that she's afeard of herself sometimes. Pray tarry with me this night, dear husband, of all nights in the year."

"My love and my Faith," replied young Goodman Brown, "of all nights in the year, this one night must I tarry away from thee. My journey, as thou callest it, forth and back again, must needs be done 'twixt now and sunrise. What, my sweet, pretty wife, dost thou doubt me already, and we but three months married?"

"Then God bless you!" said Faith, with the pink ribbons; "and may you find all well when you come back."

"Amen!" cried Goodman Brown. "Say thy prayers, dear Faith, and go to bed at dusk, and no harm will come to thee."

So they parted; and the young man pursued his way until, being about to turn the corner by the meeting-house, he looked back and saw the head of Faith still peeping after him with a melancholy air, in spite of her pink ribbons.

"Poor little Faith!" thought he, for his heart smote him. "What a wretch am I to leave her on such an errand! She talks of dreams, too. Methought as she spoke there was trouble in her face, as if a dream had warned her what work is to be done to-night. But no, no; 't would kill her to think it. Well, she's a blessed angel on earth; and after this one night I'll cling to her skirts and follow her to heaven."

With this excellent resolve for the future, Goodman Brown felt himself justified in making more haste on his present evil purpose. He had taken a dreary road, darkened by all the gloomiest trees of the forest, which barely stood aside to let the narrow path creep through, and closed immediately behind. It was all as lonely as could be; and there is this peculiarity in such a solitude, that the traveller knows not who may be concealed by the innumerable trunks and the thick boughs overhead; so that with lonely footsteps he may yet be passing through an unseen multitude.

"There may be a devilish Indian behind every tree," said Goodman Brown to himself; and he glanced fearfully behind him as he added, "What if the Devil himself should be at my very elbow!"

His head being turned back, he passed a crook of the road, and, looking forward again, beheld the figure of a man, in grave and decent attire, seated at the foot of an old tree. He arose at Goodman Brown's approach and walked onward side by side with him.

"You are late, Goodman Brown," said he. "The clock of the Old South was striking as I came through Boston; and that is full fifteen minutes agone."

"Faith kept me back a while," replied the young man, with a tremor in his voice, caused by the sudden appearance of his companion, though not wholly unexpected.

It was now deep dusk in the forest, and deepest in that part of it where these two were journeying. As nearly as could be discerned, the second traveller was about fifty years old, apparently in the same rank of life as Goodman Brown, and bearing a considerable resemblance to him, though perhaps more in expression than features. Still they might have been taken for father and son. And yet, though the elder person was as simply clad as the younger and as simple in manner too, he had an indescribable air of one who knew the world, and who would not have felt abashed at the governor's dinner-table or in King William's court, were it possible that his affairs should call him thither. But the only thing about him that could be fixed upon as remarkable was his staff, which bore the likeness of a great black snake, so curiously wrought that it might almost be seen to twist and wriggle itself like a living serpent. This, of course, must have been an ocular deception, assisted by the uncertain light.

"Come, Goodman Brown," cried his fellow-traveller, "this is a dull pace for the beginning of a journey. Take my staff, if you are so soon weary."

"Friend," said the other, exchanging his slow pace for a full stop, "having kept covenant by meeting thee here, it is my purpose now to return whence I came. I have scruples touching the matter thou wot'st of."

"Sayest thou so?" replied he of the serpent, smiling apart. "Let us walk on, nevertheless, reasoning as we go; and if I convince thee not, thou shalt turn back. We are but a little way in the forest yet."

"Too far! too far!" exclaimed the goodman, unconsciously resuming his walk. "My father never went into the woods on such an errand, nor his father before him. We have been a race of honest men and good Christians since the days of the martyrs; and shall I be the first of the name of Brown that ever took this path and kept—"

"Such company, thou wouldst say," observed the elder person, interpreting his pause. "Well said, Goodman Brown! I have been as well acquainted with your family as with ever a one among the Puritans; and that's no trifle to say. I helped your grandfather, the constable, when he lashed the Quaker woman so smartly through the streets of Salem; and it was I that brought your father a pitch-pine knot, kindled at my own hearth, to set fire to an Indian village, in King Philip's war. They were my good friends both; and many a pleasant walk have we had along this path, and returned merrily after midnight. I would fain be friends with you for their sake."

"If it be as thou sayest," replied Goodman Brown, "I marvel they never spoke of these matters; or, verily, I marvel not, seeing that the least rumor of the sort would have driven them from New England. We are a people of prayer, and good works to boot, and abide no such wickedness."

"Wickedness or not," said the traveller with the twisted staff, "I have a very general acquaintance here in New England. The deacons of many a church have drunk the communion wine with me; the selectmen of divers towns make me their chairman; and a majority of the Great and General Court are firm supporters of my interest. The governor and I, too—But these are state secrets."

"Can this be so?" cried Goodman Brown, with a stare of amazement at his undisturbed companion. "Howbeit, I have nothing to do with the governor and council; they have their own ways, and are no rule for a simple husbandman like me. But, were I to go on with thee, how should I meet the eye of that good old man, our minister, at Salem village? O, his voice would make me tremble both Sabbath day and lecture day!"

Thus far the elder traveller had listened with due gravity; but now burst into a fit of irrepressible mirth, shaking himself so violently that his snake-like staff actually seemed to wriggle in sympathy.

"Ha! ha! ha!" shouted he again and again; then composing himself, "Well, go on, Goodman Brown, go on; but, prithee, don't kill me with laughing."

"Well, then, to end the matter at once," said Goodman Brown, considerably nettled, "there is my wife, Faith. It would break her dear little heart; and I'd rather break my own."

"Nay, if that be the case," answered the other, "e'en go thy ways, Goodman Brown. I would not for twenty old women like the one hobbling before us that Faith should come to any harm."

As he spoke, he pointed his staff at a female figure on the path, in whom Goodman Brown recognized a very pious and exemplary dame, who had taught him his catechism in youth, and was still his moral and spiritual adviser, jointly with the minister and Deacon Gookin.

"A marvel, truly, that Goody Cloyse should be so far in the wilderness at nightfall," said he. "But, with your leave, friend, I shall take a cut through the woods until we have left this Christian woman behind. Being a stranger to you, she might ask whom I was consorting with and whither I was going."

"Be it so," said his fellow-traveller. "Betake you to the woods, and let me keep the path."

Accordingly the young man turned aside, but took care to watch his companion, who advanced softly along the road until he had come within a staff's length of the old dame. She, meanwhile, was making the best of her way, with singular speed for so aged a woman, and mumbling some indistinct words—a prayer, doubtless—as she went. The traveller put forth his staff and touched her withered neck with what seemed the serpent's tail.

"The Devil!" screamed the pious old lady.

"Then Goody Cloyse knows her old friend?" observed the traveller, confronting her and leaning on his writhing stick.

"Ah, forsooth, and is it your worship indeed?" cried the good dame. "Yea, truly is it, and in the very image of my old gossip, Goodman Brown, the grandfather of the silly fellow that now is. But—would your worship believe it?—my broomstick hath strangely disappeared, stolen, as I suspect, by that unhanged witch, Goody Cory, and that, too, when I was all anointed with the juice of smallage, and cinquefoil, and wolf's bane—"

"Mingled with fine wheat and the fat of a new-born babe," said the shape of old Goodman Brown.

"Ah, your worship knows the recipe," cried the old lady, cackling aloud. "So, as I was saying, being all ready for the meeting, and no horse to ride on, I made up my mind to foot it; for they tell me there is a nice young man to be taken into communion to-night. But now your good worship will lend me your arm, and we shall be there in a twinkling."

"That can hardly be," answered her friend. "I may not spare you my arm, Goody Cloyse; but here is my staff, if you will."

So saying, he threw it down at her feet, where, perhaps, it assumed life, being one of the rods which its owner had formerly lent to the Egyptian magi. Of this fact, however, Goodman Brown could not take cognizance. He had cast up his eyes in astonishment, and, looking down again, beheld neither Goody Cloyse nor the serpentine staff, but his fellow-traveller alone, who waited for him as calmly as if nothing had happened.

"That old woman taught me my catechism," said the young man; and there was a world of meaning in this simple comment.

They continued to walk onward, while the elder traveller exhorted his companion to make good speed and persevere in the path, discoursing so aptly that his arguments seemed rather to spring up in the bosom of his auditor than to be suggested by himself. As they went, he plucked a branch of maple to serve for a walking stick, and began to strip it of the twigs and little boughs, which were wet with evening dew. The moment his fingers touched them they became strangely withered and dried up as with a week's sunshine. Thus the pair proceeded, at a good free pace, until suddenly, in a gloomy hollow of the road, Goodman

Brown sat himself down on the stump of a tree and refused to go any farther.

"Friend," said he, stubbornly, "my mind is made up. Not another step will I budge on this errand. What if a wretched old woman do choose to go to the Devil when I thought she was going to heaven: is that any reason why I should quit my dear Faith and go after her?"

"You will think better of this by and by," said his acquaintance, composedly. "Sit here and rest yourself awhile; and when you feel like moving again, there is my staff to help you along."

Without more words, he threw his companion the maple-stick, and was as speedily out of sight as if he had vanished into the deepening gloom. The young man sat a few moments by the roadside, applauding himself greatly, and thinking with how clear a conscience he should meet the minister in his morning walk, nor shrink from the eye of good old Deacon Gookin. And what calm sleep would be his that very night, which was to have been spent so wickedly, but so purely and sweetly now, in the arms of Faith! Amidst these pleasant and praiseworthy meditations, Goodman Brown heard the tramp of horses along the road, and deemed it advisable to conceal himself within the verge of the forest, conscious of the guilty purpose that had brought him thither, though now so happily turned from it.

On came the hoof-tramps and the voices of the riders, two grave old voices, conversing soberly as they drew near. These mingled sounds appeared to pass along the road, within a few yards of the young man's hiding-place; but, owing doubtless to the depth of the gloom at that particular spot, neither the travellers nor their steeds were visible. Though their figures brushed the small boughs by the wayside, it could not be seen that they intercepted, even for a moment, the faint gleam from the strip of bright sky athwart which they must have passed. Goodman Brown alternately crouched and stood on tiptoe, pulling aside the branches and thrusting forth his head as far as he durst without discerning so much as a shadow. It vexed him the more, because he could have sworn, were such a thing possible, that he recognized the voices of the minister and Deacon Gookin, jogging along quietly, as they were wont to do, when bound to some ordination or ecclesiastical council. While yet within hearing, one of the riders stopped to pluck a switch.

"Of the two, reverend sir," said the voice like the deacon's, "I had rather miss an ordination dinner than to-night's meeting. They tell me that some of our community are to be here from Falmouth and beyond, and others from Connecticut and Rhode Island, besides several of the Indian powwows, who, after their fashion, know almost as much deviltry as the best of us. Moreover, there is a goodly young woman to be taken into communion."

"Mighty well, Deacon Gookin!" replied the solemn old tones of the minister. "Spur up, or we shall be late. Nothing can be done, you know, until I get on the ground."

The hoofs clattered again; and the voices, talking so strangely in the empty air, passed on through the forest, where no church had ever been gathered or solitary Christian prayed. Whither, then, could these holy men be journeying so deep into the heathen wilderness? Young Goodman Brown caught hold of a tree for support, being ready to sink down on the ground, faint and overburdened with the heavy sickness of his heart. He looked up to the sky, doubting whether there really was a heaven above him. Yet there was the blue arch, and the stars brightening in it.

"With heaven above and Faith below, I will yet stand firm against the Devil!" cried Goodman Brown.

While he still gazed upward into the deep arch of the firmament and had lifted his hands to pray, a cloud, though no wind was stirring, hurried across the zenith and hid the brightening stars. The blue sky was still visible except directly overhead, where this black mass of cloud was sweeping swiftly northward. Aloft in the air, as if from the depths of the cloud, came a confused and doubtful sound of voices. Once the listener fancied that he could distinguish the accents of townspeople of his own, men and women, both pious and ungodly, many of whom he had met at the communion-table, and had seen others rioting at the tavern. The next moment, so indistinct were the sounds, he doubted whether he had heard aught but the murmur of the old forest, whispering without a wind. Then came a stronger swell of those familiar tones, heard daily in the sunshine at Salem village, but never until now from a cloud of night. There was one voice, of a young woman, uttering lamentations, yet with an uncertain sorrow, and entreating for some favor, which, perhaps, it would grieve her to obtain; and all the unseen multitude, both saints and sinners, seemed to encourage her onward.

"Faith!" shouted Goodman Brown, in a voice of agony and desperation; and the echoes of the forest mocked him, crying, "Faith! Faith!" as if bewildered wretches were seeking her all through the wilderness.

The cry of grief, rage, and terror was yet piercing the night, when the unhappy husband held his breath for a response. There was a scream, drowned immediately in a louder murmur of voices, fading into far-off laughter, as the dark cloud swept away, leaving the clear and silent sky above Goodman Brown. But something fluttered lightly down through the air and caught on the branch of a tree. The young man seized it, and beheld a pink ribbon.

"My Faith is gone!" cried he, after one stupefied moment. "There is no good on earth; and sin is but a name. Come, Devil; for to thee is this world given."

And, maddened with despair, so that he laughed loud and long, did Goodman Brown grasp his staff and set forth again, at such a rate that he seemed to fly along the forest path rather than to walk or run. The road grew wilder and drearier and more faintly traced, and vanished at length, leaving him in the heart of the dark wilderness, still rushing onward with the instinct that guides mortal man to evil. The whole forest was peopled with frightful sounds,—the creaking of the trees, the howling of wild beasts, and the yell of Indians; while sometimes the wind tolled like a distant church-bell, and sometimes gave a broad roar around the traveller, as if all Nature were laughing him to scorn. But he was himself the chief horror of the scene, and shrank not from its other horrors.

"Ha! ha! ha!" roared Goodman Brown when the wind laughed at him. "Let us hear which will laugh loudest. Think not to frighten me with your deviltry. Come witch, come wizard, come Indian powwow, come Devil himself, and here comes Goodman Brown. You may as well fear him as he fear you."

In truth, all through the haunted forest there could be nothing more frightful than the figure of Goodman Brown. On he flew among the black pines, brandishing his staff with frenzied gestures, now giving vent to an inspiration of horrid blasphemy, and now shouting forth such laughter as set all the echoes of the forest laughing like demons around him. The fiend in his own shape is less hideous than when he rages in the breast of man. Thus sped the demoniac on his course, until, quivering among the trees, he saw a red light before him, as when the felled trunks and branches of a clearing have been set on fire, and throw up their lurid blaze against the sky, at the hour of midnight. He paused, in a lull of the tempest that had driven him onward, and heard the swell of what seemed a hymn rolling solemnly from a distance with the weight of many voices. He knew the tune; it was a familiar one in the choir of the village meeting-house. The verse died heavily away, and was lengthened by a chorus, not of human voices, but of all the sounds of the benighted wilderness pealing in awful harmony together. Goodman Brown cried out; and his cry was lost to his own ear by its unison with the cry of the desert.

In the interval of silence he stole forward until the light glared full upon his eyes. At one extremity of an open space, hemmed in by the dark wall of the forest, arose a rock, bearing some rude, natural resemblance either to an alter or a pulpit, and surrounded by four blazing pines, their tops aflame, their stems untouched, like candles at an evening meeting. The mass of foliage that had overgrown the summit of the rock was all on fire, blazing high into the night and fitfully illuminating the whole field. Each pendent twig and leafy festoon was in a blaze. As the red light arose and fell, a numerous congregation alternately shone forth, then disappeared in shadow, and again grew, as it were, out of the darkness, peopling the heart of the solitary woods at once.

"A grave and dark-clad company," quoth Goodman Brown.

In truth they were such. Among them, quivering to and fro between gloom and splendor, appeared faces that would be seen next day at the council board of the province, and others which, Sabbath after Sabbath, looked devoutly heavenward, and benignantly over the crowded pews, from the holiest pulpits in the land. Some affirm that the lady of the governor was there. At least there were high dames well known to her, and wives of honored husbands, and widows, a great multitude, and ancient maidens, all of excellent repute, and fair young girls, who trembled lest their mothers should espy them. Either the sudden gleams of light flashing over the obscure field bedazzled Goodman Brown, or he recognized a score of the church members of Salem village famous for their especial sanctity. Good old Deacon Gookin had arrived, and waited at the skirts of that venerable saint, his revered pastor. But, irreverently consorting with these grave, reputable, and pious people, these elders of the church, these chaste dames and dewy virgins, there were men of dissolute lives and women of spotted fame, wretches given over to all mean and filthy vice, and suspected even of horrid crimes. It was strange to see that the good shrank not from the wicked, nor were the sinners abashed by the saints. Scattered also among their pale-faced enemies were the Indian priests, or powwows, who had often scared their native forest with more hideous incantations than any known to English witchcraft.

"But where is Faith?" thought Goodman Brown; and, as hope came into his heart, he trembled.

Another verse of the hymn arose, a slow and mournful strain, such as the pious love, but joined to words which expressed all that our nature can conceive of sin, and darkly hinted at far more. Unfathomable to mere mortals is the lore of fiends. Verse after verse was sung; and still the chorus of the desert swelled between like the deepest tone of a mighty organ; and with the final peal of that dreadful anthem there came a sound, as if the roaring wind, the rushing streams, the howling beasts, and every other voice of the unconcerted wilderness were mingling and according with the voice of guilty man in homage to the prince of all. The four blazing pines threw up a loftier flame, and obscurely discovered shapes and visages of horror on the smoke-wreaths above the impious assembly. At the same moment the fire on the rock shot redly forth and formed a glowing arch above its base, where now appeared a figure. With reverence be it spoken, the figure bore no slight similitude, both in garb and manner, to some grave divine of the New England churches.

"Bring forth the converts!" cried a voice that echoed through the field and rolled into the forest.

At the word, Goodman Brown stepped forth from the shadow of the trees and approached the congregation, with whom he felt a loathful brotherhood by the sympathy of all that was wicked in his heart. He could have well-nigh sworn that the shape of his own dead father beckoned him to advance, looking downward from a smoke-wreath, while a woman, with dim features of despair, threw out her hand to warn him back. Was it his mother? But he had no power to retreat one step, nor to resist, even in thought, when the minister and good old Deacon Gookin seized his arms and led him to the blazing rock. Thither came also the slender form of a veiled female, led between Goody Cloyse, that pious teacher of the catechism, and Martha Carrier, who had received the Devil's promise to be queen of hell. A rampant hag was she. And there stood the proselytes beneath the canopy of fire.

"Welcome, my children," said the dark figure, "to the communion of your race. Ye have found thus young your nature and your destiny. My children, look behind you!"

They turned; and flashing forth, as it were, in a sheet of flame, the fiend worshippers were seen; the smile of welcome gleamed darkly on every visage.

"There," resumed the sable form, "are all whom ye have reverenced from youth. Ye deemed them holier than yourselves, and shrank from your own sin, contrasting it with their lives of righteousness and prayerful aspirations heavenward. Yet here are they all in my worshipping assembly. This night it shall be granted you to know their secret deeds; how hoary-bearded elders of the church have whispered wanton words to the young maids of their households; how many a woman, eager for widows' weeds, has given her husband a drink at bedtime and let him sleep his last sleep in her bosom; how beardless youths have made haste to inherit their fathers' wealth; and how fair damsels—blush not, sweet ones—have dug little graves in the garden, and bidden me, the sole guest, to an infant's funeral. By the sympathy of your human hearts for sin ye shall scent out all the places—whether in church, bedchamber, street, field, or forest—where crime has been committed, and shall exult to behold the whole earth one stain of guilt, one mighty blood spot. Far more than this. It shall be yours to penetrate, in every bosom, the deep mystery of sin, the fountain of all wicked arts, and which inexhaustibly supplies more evil impulses than human power—than my power at its utmost—can make manifest in deeds. And now, my children, look upon each other."

They did so; and, by the blaze of the hell-kindled torches, the wretched man beheld his Faith, and the wife her husband, trembling before that unhallowed altar.

"Lo, there ye stand, my children," said the figure, in a deep and solemn tone, almost sad with its despairing awfulness, as if his once angelic nature could yet mourn for our miserable race. "Depending upon one another's hearts, ye had still hoped that virtue were not all a dream. Now are ye undeceived. Evil is the nature of mankind. Evil must be your only happiness. Welcome again, my children, to the communion of your race."

"Welcome," repeated the fiend worshippers, in one cry of despair and triumph.

And there they stood, the only pair, as it seemed, who were yet hesitating on the verge of wickedness in this dark world. A basin was hollowed, naturally, in the rock. Did it contain water, reddened by the lurid light? or was it blood? or, perchance, a liquid flame? Herein did the shape of evil dip his hand and prepare to lay the mark of baptism upon their foreheads, that they might be partakers of the mystery of sin, more conscious of the secret guilt of others, both in deed and thought, than they could now be of their own. The husband cast one look at his pale wife, and Faith at him. What polluted wretches would the next glance show them to each other, shuddering alike at what they disclosed and what they saw!

"Faith! Faith!" cried the husband, "look up to Heaven, and resist the wicked one."

Whether Faith obeyed he knew not. Hardly had he spoken, when he found himself amid calm night and solitude, listening to a roar of the wind which died heavily away through the forest. He staggered against the rock, and felt it chill and damp; while a hanging twig, that had been all on fire, besprinkled his cheek with the coldest dew.

The next morning young Goodman Brown came slowly into the street of Salem village, staring around him like a bewildered man. The good old minister was taking a walk along the graveyard to get an appetite for breakfast and meditate his sermon, and bestowed a blessing, as he passed, on Goodman Brown. He shrank from the venerable saint as if to avoid an anathema. Old Deacon Gookin was at domestic worship, and the holy words of his prayer were heard through the open window. "What God doth the wizard pray to?" quoth Goodman Brown. Goody Cloyse, that excellent old Christian, stood in the early sunshine at her own lattice, catechising a little girl who had brought her a pint of morning's milk. Goodman Brown snatched away the child as from the grasp of the fiend himself. Turning the corner by the meeting-house, he spied the head of Faith, with the pink ribbons, gazing anxiously forth, and bursting into such joy at sight of him that she skipped along the street and almost kissed her husband before the whole village. But Goodman Brown looked sternly and sadly into her face, and passed on without a greeting.

Had Goodman Brown fallen asleep in the forest and only dreamed a wild dream of a witch-meeting?

Be it so if you will; but, alas! it was a dream of evil omen for young Goodman Brown. A stern, a sad, a darkly meditative, a distrustful, if not a desperate man did he become from the night of that fearful dream. On the Sabbath day, when the congregation were singing a holy psalm, he could not listen, because an anthem of sin rushed loudly upon his ear and drowned all the blessed strain. When the minister spoke from the pulpit, with power and fervid eloquence, and with his hand on the open Bible, of the sacred truths of our religion, and of saint-like lives and triumphant deaths, and of future bliss or misery unutterable, then did Goodman Brown turn pale, dreading lest the roof should thunder down upon the gray blasphemer and his hearers. Often, waking suddenly at midnight, he shrank from the bosom of Faith; and at morning or eventide, when the family knelt down at prayer, he scowled, and muttered to himself, and gazed sternly at his wife, and turned away. And when he had lived long, and was borne to his grave, a hoary corpse, followed by Faith, an aged woman, and children and grandchildren, a goodly procession, besides neighbors not a few, they carved no hopeful verse upon his tombstone, for his dying hour was gloom.

SOURCE: Nathaniel Hawthorne. *Mosses from an Old Manse.* Boston: Ticknor and Fields, 1854.

Dr. Heidegger's Experiment (1837)

In this fantastical story, Hawthorne plays with the idea of longing for youth.

THAT VERY SINGULAR man, old Dr. Heidegger, once invited four venerable friends to meet him in his study. There were three white-bearded gentlemen, Mr. Medbourne, Colonel Killigrew, and Mr. Gascoigne, and a withered gentlewoman, whose name was the Widow Wycherly. They were all melancholy old creatures, who had been unfortunate in life, and whose greatest misfortune it was that they were not long ago in their graves. Mr. Medbourne, in the vigor of his age, had been a prosperous merchant, but had lost his all by a frantic speculation, and was now little better than a mendicant. Colonel Killigrew had wasted his best years, and his health and substance, in the pursuit of sinful pleasures, which had given birth to a brood of pains, such as the gout, and divers other torments of soul and body. Mr. Gascoigne was a ruined politician, a man of evil fame, or at least had been so till time had buried him from the knowledge of the present generation, and made him obscure instead of infamous. As for the Widow Wycherly, tradition tells us that she was a great beauty in her day; but, for a long while past, she had lived in deep seclusion, on account of certain scandalous stories which had prejudiced the gentry of the town against her. It is a circumstance worth mentioning that each of these three old gentlemen, Mr. Medbourne, Colonel Killigrew, and Mr. Gascoigne, were early lovers of the Widow Wycherly, and had once been on the point of cutting each other's throats for her sake. And, before proceeding further, I will merely hint that Dr. Heidegger and all his foul guests were sometimes thought to be a little beside themselves,—as is not unfrequently the case with old people, when worried either by present troubles or woful recollections.

"My dear old friends," said Dr. Heidegger, motioning them to be seated, "I am desirous of your assistance in one of those little experiments with which I amuse myself here in my study."

If all stories were true, Dr. Heidegger's study must have been a very curious place. It was a dim, old-fashioned chamber, festooned with cobwebs, and besprinkled with antique dust. Around the walls stood several oaken bookcases, the lower shelves of which were filled with rows of gigantic folios and black-letter quartos, and the upper with little parchment-covered duodecimos. Over the central bookcase was a bronze bust of Hippocrates, with which, according to some authorities, Dr. Heidegger was accustomed to hold consultations, in all difficult cases of his practice. In the obscurest corner of the room stood a tall and narrow oaken closet, with its door ajar, within which doubtfully appeared a skeleton. Between two of the bookcases hung a looking-glass, presenting its high and dusty plate within a tarnished gilt frame. Among many wonderful stories related of this mirror, it was fabled that the spirits of all the doctor's deceased patients dwelt within its verge, and would stare him in the face whenever he looked thitherward. The opposite side of the chamber was ornamented with the full-length portrait of a young lady, arrayed in the faded magnificence of silk, satin, and brocade, and with a visage as faded as her dress. Above half a century ago, Dr. Heidegger had been on the point of marriage with this young lady; but, being affected with some slight disorder, she had swallowed one of her lover's prescriptions, and died on the bridal evening. The greatest curiosity of the study remains to be mentioned; it was a ponderous folio volume, bound in black leather, with massive silver clasps. There were no letters on the back, and nobody could tell the title of the book. But it was well known to be a book of magic; and once, when a chambermaid had lifted it, merely to brush away the dust, the skeleton had rattled in its closet, the picture of the young lady had stepped one foot upon the floor, and several ghastly faces had peeped forth from the mirror; while the brazen head of Hippocrates frowned, and said, "Forbear!"

Such was Dr. Heidegger's study. On the summer afternoon of our tale a small round table, as black as ebony, stood in the centre of the room, sustaining a cut-glass vase of beautiful form and elaborate workmanship. The sunshine came through the window, between the heavy festoons of two faded damask curtains, and fell directly across this vase; so that a mild splendor was reflected from it on the ashen visages of the five old people who sat around. Four champagne glasses were also on the table.

"My dear old friends," repeated Dr. Heidegger, "may I reckon on your aid in performing an exceedingly curious experiment?"

Now Dr. Heidegger was a very strange old gentleman, whose eccentricity had become the nucleus for a thousand fantastic stories. Some of these fables, to my shame be it spoken, might possibly be traced back to mine own veracious self; and if any passages of the present tale should startle the reader's faith, I must be content to bear the stigma of a fiction-monger.

When the doctor's four guests heard him talk of his proposed experiment, they anticipated nothing more wonderful than the murder of a mouse in an air-pump, or the examination of a cobweb by the microscope, or some similar nonsense, with which he was constantly in the habit of pestering his intimates. But without waiting for a reply, Dr. Heidegger hobbled across the chamber, and returned with the same ponderous folio, bound in black leather, which common report affirmed to be a book of magic. Undoing the silver clasps, he opened the volume, and took from among its black-letter pages a rose, or what was once a rose, though now the green leaves and crimson petals had assumed one brownish hue, and the ancient flower seemed ready to crumble to dust in the doctor's hands.

"This rose," said Dr. Heidegger, with a sigh, "this same withered and crumbling flower, blossomed five-and-fifty years ago. It was given me by Sylvia Ward, whose portrait hangs yonder; and I meant to wear it in my bosom at our wedding. Five-and-fifty years it has been treasured between the leaves of this old volume. Now, would you deem it possible that this rose of half a century could ever bloom again?"

"Nonsense!" said the Widow Wycherly, with a peevish toss of her head. "You might as well ask whether an old woman's wrinkled face could ever bloom again."

"See!" answered Dr. Heidegger.

He uncovered the vase, and threw the faded rose into the water which it contained. At first, it lay lightly on the surface of the fluid, appearing to imbibe none of its moisture. Soon, however, a singular change began to be visible. The crushed and dried petals stirred, and assumed a deepening tinge of crimson, as if the flower were reviving from a death-like slumber; the slender stalk and twigs of foliage became green; and there was the rose of half a century, looking as fresh as when Sylvia Ward had first given it to her lover. It was scarcely full blown; for some of its delicate red leaves curled modestly around its moist bosom, within which two or three dewdrops were sparkling.

"That is certainly a very pretty deception," said the doctor's friends; carelessly, however, for they had witnessed greater miracles at a conjurer's show; "pray how was it effected?"

"Did you never hear of the 'Fountain of Youth?'" asked Dr. Heidegger, "which Ponce de Leon, the Spanish adventurer, went in search of, two or three centuries ago?"

"But did Ponce de Leon ever find it?" said the Widow Wycherly.

"No," answered Dr. Heidegger, "for he never sought it in the right place. The famous Fountain of Youth, if I am rightly informed, is situated in the southern part of the Floridian peninsula, not far from Lake Macaco. Its source is overshadowed by several gigantic magnolias, which, though numberless centuries old, have been kept as fresh as violets, by the virtues of this wonderful water. An acquaintance of mine, knowing my curiosity in such matters, has sent me what you see in the vase."

"Ahem!" said Colonel Killigrew, who believed not a word of the doctor's story; "and what may be the effect of this fluid on the human frame?"

"You shall judge for yourself, my dear Colonel," replied Dr. Heidegger; "and all of you, my respected friends, are welcome to so much of this admirable fluid as may restore to you the bloom of youth. For my own part, having had much trouble in growing old,

I am in no hurry to grow young again. With your permission, therefore, I will merely watch the progress of the experiment."

While he spoke, Dr. Heidegger had been filling the four champagne glasses with the water of the Fountain of Youth. It was apparently impregnated with an effervescent gas, for little bubbles were continually ascending from the depths of the glasses, and bursting in silvery spray at the surface. As the liquor diffused a pleasant perfume, the old people doubted not that it possessed cordial and comfortable properties; and, though utter sceptics as to its rejuvenescent power, they were inclined to swallow it at once. But Dr. Heidegger besought them to stay a moment.

"Before you drink, my respectable old friends," said he, "it would be well that, with the experience of a lifetime to direct you, you should draw up a few general rules for your guidance, in passing a second time through the perils of youth. Think what a sin and shame it would be, if, with your peculiar advantages, you should not become patterns of virtue and wisdom to all the young people of the age."

The doctor's four venerable friends made him no answer, except by a feeble and tremulous laugh; so very ridiculous was the idea, that, knowing how closely repentance treads behind the steps of error, they should ever go astray again.

"Drink, then," said the doctor, bowing. "I rejoice that I have so well selected the subjects of my experiment."

With palsied hands, they raised the glasses to their lips. The liquor, if it really possessed such virtues as Dr. Heidegger imputed to it, could not have been bestowed on four human beings who needed it more wofully. They looked as if they had never known what youth or pleasure was, but had been the offspring of Nature's dotage, and always the gray, decrepit, sapless, miserable creatures who now sat stooping round the doctor's table, without life enough in their souls or bodies to be animated even by the prospect of growing young again. They drank off the water, and replaced their glasses on the table.

Assuredly there was an almost immediate improvement in the aspect of the party, not unlike what might have been produced by a glass of generous wine, together with a sudden glow of cheerful sunshine brightening over all their visages at once. There was a healthful suffusion on their cheeks, instead of the ashen hue that had made them look so corpse-like. They gazed at one another, and fancied that some magic power had really begun to smooth away the deep and sad inscriptions which Father Time had been so long engraving on their brows. The Widow Wycherly adjusted her cap, for she felt almost like a woman again.

"Give us more of this wondrous water!" cried they, eagerly. "We are younger,—but we are still too old! Quick,—give us more!"

"Patience, patience!" quoth Dr. Heidegger, who sat watching the experiment with philosophic coolness. "You have been a long time growing old. Surely, you might be content to grow young in half an hour! But the water is at your service."

Again he filled their glasses with the liquor of youth, enough of which still remained in the vase to turn half the old people in the city to the age of their own grandchildren. While the bubbles were yet sparkling on the brim, the doctor's four guests snatched their glasses from the table, and swallowed the contents at a single gulp. Was it delusion? even while the draught was passing down their throats, it seemed to have wrought a change on their whole systems. Their eyes grew clear and bright; a dark shade deepened among their silvery locks; they sat around the table, three gentlemen of middle age, and a woman, hardly beyond her buxom prime.

"My dear widow, you are charming!" cried Colonel Killigrew, whose eyes had been fixed upon her face, while the shadows of age were flitting from it like darkness from the crimson daybreak.

The fair widow knew, of old, that Colonel Killigrew's compliments were not always measured by sober truth; so she started up and ran to the mirror, still dreading that the ugly visage of an old woman would meet her gaze. Meanwhile, the three gentlemen behaved in such a manner, as proved that the water of the Fountain of Youth possessed some intoxicating qualities; unless, indeed, their exhilaration of spirits were merely a lightsome dizziness, caused by the sudden removal of the weight of years. Mr. Gascoigne's mind seemed to run on political topics, but whether relating to the past, present, or future, could not easily be determined, since the same ideas and phrases have been in vogue these fifty years. Now he rattled forth full-throated sentences about patriotism, national glory, and the people's right; now he muttered some perilous stuff or other, in a sly and doubtful whisper, so cautiously that even his own conscience could scarcely catch the secret; and now, again, he spoke in measured accents, and a deeply deferential tone, as if a royal ear were listening to his well-turned periods. Colonel Killigrew all this time had been trolling forth a jolly bottle song, and ringing his glass in symphony with the chorus, while his eyes wandered toward the buxom figure of the Widow Wycherly. On the other side of the table, Mr. Medbourne was involved in a calculation of dollars and cents, with which was strangely intermingled a project for supplying the East Indies with ice, by harnessing a team of whales to the polar icebergs.

As for the Widow Wycherly, she stood before the mirror courtseying and simpering to her own image, and greeting it as the friend whom she loved better than all the world beside. She thrust her face close to the glass, to see whether some long-remembered wrinkle or crow's-foot had indeed vanished. She examined whether the snow had so entirely melted from her hair, that the venerable cap could be safely thrown aside. At last, turning briskly away, she came with a sort of dancing step to the table.

"My dear old doctor," cried she, "pray favor me with another glass!"

"Certainly, my dear madam, certainly!" replied the complaisant doctor; "see! I have already filled the glasses."

There, in fact, stood the four glasses, brimful of this wonderful water, the delicate spray of which, as it effervesced from the surface, resembled the tremulous glitter of diamonds. It was now so nearly sunset, that the chamber had grown duskier than ever; but a mild and moonlike splendor gleamed from within the vase, and rested alike on the four guests, and on the doctor's venerable figure. He sat in a high-backed, elaborately carved, oaken arm-chair, with a gray dignity of aspect that might have well befitted that very Father Time, whose power had never been disputed, save by this fortunate company. Even while quaffing the third draught of the Fountain of Youth, they were almost awed by the expression of his mysterious visage.

But, the next moment, the exhilarating gush of young life shot through their veins. They were now in the happy prime of youth. Age, with its miserable train of cares, and sorrows, and diseases, was remembered only as the trouble of a dream, from which they had joyously awoke. The fresh gloss of the soul, so early lost, and without which the world's successive scenes had been but a gallery of faded pictures, again threw its enchantment over all their prospects. They felt like new-created beings, in a new-created universe.

"We are young! We are young!" they cried exultingly.

Youth, like the extremity of age, had effaced the strongly marked characteristics of middle life, and mutually assimilated them all. They were a group of merry youngsters, almost maddened with the exuberant frolicsomeness of their years. The most singular effect of their gayety was an impulse to mock the infirmity and decrepitude of which they had so lately been the victims. They laughed loudly at their old-fashioned attire, the wide-skirted coats and flapped waistcoats of the young men, and the ancient cap and gown of the blooming girl. One limped across the floor like a gouty grandfather; one set a pair of spectacles astride of his nose, and pretended to pore over the black-letter pages of the book of magic; a third seated himself in an arm-chair, and strove to imitate the venerable dignity of Dr. Heidegger. Then all shouted mirthfully, and leaped about the room. The Widow Wycherly—if so fresh a damsel could be called a widow—tripped up to the doctor's chair, with a mischievous merriment in her rosy face.

"Doctor, you dear old soul," cried she, "get up and dance with me!" And then the four young people laughed louder than ever, to think what a queer figure the poor old doctor would cut.

"Pray excuse me," answered the doctor, quietly. "I am old and rheumatic, and my dancing days were over long ago. But either of these gay young gentlemen will be glad of so pretty a partner."

"Dance with me, Clara!" cried Colonel Killigrew.

"No, no, I will be her partner!" shouted Mr. Gascoigne.

"She promised me her hand, fifty years ago!" exclaimed Mr. Medbourne.

They all gathered round her. One caught both her hands in his passionate grasp,—another threw his arm about her waist,—the third buried his hand among the glossy curls that clustered beneath the widow's cap. Blushing, panting, struggling, chiding, laughing, her warm breath fanning each of their faces by turns, she strove to disengage herself, yet still remained in their triple embrace. Never was there a livelier picture of youthful rivalship, with bewitching beauty for the prize. Yet, by a strange deception, owing to the duskiness of the chamber, and the antique dresses which they still wore, the tall mirror is said to have reflected the figures of the three old, gray, withered grandsires, ridiculously contending for the skinny ugliness of a shrivelled grandam.

But they were young: their burning passions proved them so. Inflamed to madness by the coquetry of the girl-widow, who neither granted nor quite withheld her favors, the three rivals began to interchange threatening glances. Still keeping hold of the fair prize, they grappled fiercely at one another's throats. As they struggled to and fro, the table was over-turned, and the vase dashed into a thousand fragments. The precious Water of Youth flowed in a bright stream across the floor, moistening the wings of a butterfly, which, grown old in the decline of summer, had alighted there to die. The insect fluttered lightly through the chamber, and settled on the snowy head of Dr. Heidegger.

"Come, come, gentlemen!—come, Madam Wycherly," exclaimed the doctor, "I really must protest against this riot."

They stood still and shivered; for it seemed as if gray Time were calling them back from their sunny youth, far down into the chill and darksome vale of years. They looked at old Dr. Heidegger, who sat in his carved arm-chair, holding the rose of half a century, which he had rescued from among the fragments of the shattered vase. At the motion of his hand, the four rioters resumed their seats; the more readily, because their violent exertions had wearied them, youthful though they were.

"My poor Sylvia's rose!" ejaculated Dr. Heidegger, holding it in the light of the sunset clouds; "it appears to be fading again."

And so it was. Even while the party were looking at it, the flower continued to shrivel up, till it became as dry and fragile as when the doctor had first thrown it into the vase. He shook off the few drops of moisture which clung to its petals.

"I love it as well thus, as in its dewy freshness," observed he, pressing the withered rose to his withered lips. While he spoke, the butterfly fluttered down from the doctor's snowy head, and fell upon the floor.

His guests shivered again. A strange chillness, whether of the body or spirit they could not tell, was creeping gradually over them all. They gazed at one another, and fancied that each fleeting moment snatched away a charm, and left a deepening furrow where none had been before. Was it an illusion? Had the changes of a lifetime been crowded into so brief a space, and were they now four aged people, sitting with their old friend, Dr. Heidegger?

"Are we grown old again, so soon?" cried they, dolefully.

In truth, they had. The Water of Youth possessed merely a virtue more transient than that of wine. The delirium which it created had effervesced away. Yes! they were old again. With a shuddering impulse, that showed her a woman still, the widow clasped her skinny hands before her face, and wished that the coffin-lid were over it, since it could be no longer beautiful.

"Yes, friends, ye are old again," said Dr. Heidegger, "and lo! the Water of Youth is all lavished on the ground. Well, I bemoan it not; for if the fountain gushed at my very doorstep, I would not stoop to bathe my lips in it; no, though its delirium were for years instead of moments. Such is the lesson ye have taught me!"

But the doctor's four friends had taught no such lesson to themselves. They resolved forthwith to make a pilgrimage to Florida, and quaff at morning, noon, and night, from the Fountain of Youth.[1]

SOURCE: Nathaniel Hawthorne. *Twice-told Tales*. Boston: Ticknor, Reed, and Fields, 1851.

Chapters from *The Scarlet Letter* (1850)

This "romance of seventeenth-century Salem," writes Stanley Appelbaum, "is a critique and a tragedy. It concerns sin and the attempt of societies to purge themselves of it, as well as the blundering nature of many of these attempts. Compassionately articulating the distinctions between shame and guilt, righteousness and brutality, it is a novel that shows us the less than obvious forms of human dignity. Its heroine, Hester Prynne, is a classical figure in American literature."[2] Even more unusual and impressive is Pearl, the living symbol of Hester's "sin," the daughter for whom Hester is forced to wear a scarlet A (for "Adultress"): "that little creature, whose innocent life had sprung, by the inscrutable decree of Providence, a lovely and immortal flower, out of the rank luxuriance of a guilty passion."

Chapter 5: Hester at Her Needle

HESTER PRYNNE'S TERM of confinement was now at an end. Her prison-door was thrown open, and she came forth into the sunshine, which, falling on all alike, seemed, to her sick and morbid heart, as if meant for no other purpose than to reveal the scarlet

1. [Hawthorne's note, from 1860:] In an English review, not long since, I have been accused of plagiarizing the idea of this story from a chapter in one of the novels of Alexandre Dumas. There has undoubtedly been a plagiarism on one side or the other; but as my story was written a good deal more than twenty years ago, and as the novel is of considerably more recent date, I take pleasure in thinking that M. Dumas has done me the honor to appropriate one of the fanciful conceptions of my earlier days. He is heartily welcome to it; nor is it the only instance, by many, in which the great French romancer has exercised the privilege of commanding genius by confiscating the intellectual property of less famous people to his own use and behoof.
2. Nathaniel Hawthorne. *The Scarlet Letter*. Edited by Stanley Appelbaum. New York: Dover Publications, 1994. Page v.

letter on her breast. Perhaps there was a more real torture in her first unattended footsteps from the threshold of the prison, than even in the procession and spectacle that have been described, where she was made the common infamy, at which all mankind was summoned to point its finger. Then, she was supported by an unnatural tension of the nerves, and by all the combative energy of her character, which enabled her to convert the scene into a kind of lurid triumph. It was, moreover, a separate and insulated event, to occur but once in her lifetime, and to meet which, therefore, reckless of economy, she might call up the vital strength that would have sufficed for many quiet years. The very law that condemned her—a giant of stern features, but with vigor to support, as well as to annihilate, in his iron arm—had held her up, through the terrible ordeal of her ignominy. But now, with this unattended walk from her prison-door, began the daily custom, and she must either sustain and carry it forward by the ordinary resources of her nature, or sink beneath it. She could no longer borrow from the future, to help her through the present grief. To-morrow would bring its own trial with it; so would the next day, and so would the next; each its own trial, and yet the very same that was now so unutterably grievous to be borne. The days of the far-off future would toil onward, still with the same burden for her to take up, and bear along with her, but never to fling down; for the accumulating days, and added years, would pile up their misery upon the heap of shame. Throughout them all, giving up her individuality, she would become the general symbol at which the preacher and moralist might point, and in which they might vivify and embody their images of woman's frailty and sinful passion. Thus the young and pure would be taught to look at her, with the scarlet letter flaming on her breast,—at her, the child of honorable parents,—at her, the mother of a babe, that would hereafter be a woman,—at her, who had once been innocent,—as the figure, the body, the reality of sin. And over her grave, the infamy that she must carry thither would be her only monument.

It may seem marvellous, that, with the world before her,—kept by no restrictive clause of her condemnation within the limits of the Puritan settlement, so remote and so obscure,—free to return to her birthplace, or to any other European land, and there hide her character and identity under a new exterior, as completely as if emerging into another state of being,—and having also the passes of the dark, inscrutable forest open to her, where the wildness of her nature might assimilate itself with a people whose customs and life were alien from the law that had condemned her,—it may seem marvellous, that this woman should still call that place her home, where, and where only, she must needs be the type of shame. But there is a fatality, a feeling so irresistible and inevitable that it has the force of doom, which almost invariably compels human beings to linger around and haunt, ghost-like, the spot where some great and marked event has given the color to their lifetime; and still the more irresistibly, the darker the tinge that saddens it. Her sin, her ignominy, were the roots which she had struck into the soil. It was as if a new birth, with stronger assimilations than the first, had converted the forest-land, still so uncongenial to every other pilgrim and wanderer, into Hester Prynne's wild and dreary, but life-long home. All other scenes of earth—even that village of rural England, where happy infancy and stainless maidenhood seemed yet to be in her mother's keeping, like garments put off long ago—were foreign to her, in comparison. The chain that bound her here was of iron links, and galling to her inmost soul, but could never be broken.

It might be, too,—doubtless it was so, although she hid the secret from herself, and grew pale whenever it struggled out of her heart, like a serpent from its hole,—it might be that another feeling kept her within the scene and pathway that had been so fatal. There dwelt, there trode the feet of one with whom she deemed herself connected in a union, that, unrecognized on earth, would bring them together before the bar of final judgment, and make that their marriage-altar, for a joint futurity of endless retribution. Over and over again, the tempter of souls had thrust this idea upon Hester's contemplation, and laughed at the passionate and desperate joy with which she seized, and then strove to cast it from her. She barely looked the idea in the face, and hastened to bar it in its dungeon. What she compelled herself to believe,—what, finally, she reasoned upon, as her motive for continuing a resident of New England—was half a truth, and half a self-delusion. Here, she said to herself, had been the scene of her guilt, and here should be the scene of her earthly punishment; and so, perchance, the torture of her daily shame would at length purge her soul, and work out another purity than that which she had lost; more saint-like, because the result of martyrdom.

Hester Prynne, therefore, did not flee. On the outskirts of the town, within the verge of the peninsula, but not in close vicinity to any other habitation, there was a small thatched cottage. It had been built by an earlier settler, and abandoned, because the soil about it was too sterile for cultivation, while its comparative remoteness put it out of the sphere of that social activity which already marked the habits of the emigrants. It stood on the shore, looking across a basin of the sea at the forest-covered hills, towards the west. A clump of scrubby trees, such as alone grew on the peninsula, did not so much conceal the cottage from view, as seem to denote that here was some object which would fain have been, or at least ought to be, concealed. In this little, lonesome dwelling, with some slender means that she possessed, and by the license of the magistrates, who still kept an inquisitorial watch over her, Hester established herself, with her infant child. A mystic shadow of suspicion immediately attached itself to the spot. Children, too young to comprehend wherefore this woman should be shut out from the sphere of human charities, would creep nigh enough to behold her plying her needle at the cottage-window, or standing in the doorway, or laboring in her little garden, or coming forth along the pathway that led townward; and, discerning the scarlet letter on her breast, would scamper off with a strange, contagious fear.

Lonely as was Hester's situation, and without a friend on earth who dared to show himself, she, however, incurred no risk of want. She possessed an art that sufficed, even in a land that afforded comparatively little scope for its exercise, to supply food for her thriving infant and herself. It was the art—then, as now, almost the only one within a woman's grasp—of needlework. She bore on her breast, in the curiously embroidered letter, a specimen of her delicate and imaginative skill, of which the dames of a court might gladly have availed themselves, to add the richer and more spiritual adornment of human ingenuity to their fabrics of silk and gold. Here, indeed, in the sable simplicity that generally characterized the Puritanic modes of dress, there might be an infrequent call for the finer productions of her handiwork. Yet the taste of the age, demanding whatever was elaborate in compositions of this kind, did not fail to extend its influence over our stern progenitors, who had cast behind them so many fashions which it might seem harder to dispense with. Public ceremonies, such as ordinations, the installation of magistrates, and all that could give majesty to the forms in which a new government manifested itself to the people, were, as a matter of policy, marked by a stately and well-conducted ceremonial, and a sombre, but yet a studied magnificence. Deep ruffs, painfully wrought bands, and gorgeously embroidered gloves, were all deemed necessary to the official state of men assuming the reins of power; and were readily allowed to individuals dignified by rank or wealth, even while sumptuary laws forbade these and similar extravagances to the plebeian order. In the array of funerals, too,—whether for the apparel of the dead body, or to typify, by manifold emblematic devices of sable cloth and snowy lawn, the sorrow of the survivors,—there was a frequent and characteristic demand for such labor as Hester Prynne could supply. Baby-linen—for babies then wore robes of state—afforded still another possibility of toil and emolument.

By degrees, nor very slowly, her handiwork became what would now be termed the fashion. Whether from commiseration for a woman of so miserable a destiny; or from the morbid curiosity that gives a fictitious value even to common or worthless things; or by whatever other intangible circumstance was then, as now, sufficient to bestow, on some persons, what others might seek in vain; or because Hester really filled a gap which must otherwise have remained vacant; it is certain that she had ready and fairly requited employment for as many hours as she saw fit to occupy with her needle. Vanity, it may be, chose to mortify itself, by putting on, for ceremonials of pomp and state, the garments that had been wrought by her sinful hands. Her needle-work was seen on the ruff of the Governor; military men wore it on their scarfs, and the minister on his band; it decked the baby's little cap; it was shut up, to be mildewed and moulder away, in the coffins of the dead. But it is not recorded that, in a single instance, her skill was called in aid to embroider the white veil which was to cover the pure blushes of a bride. The exception indicated the ever-relentless rigor with which society frowned upon her sin.

Hester sought not to acquire anything beyond a subsistence, of the plainest and most ascetic description, for herself, and a simple abundance for her child. Her own dress was of the coarsest materials and the most sombre hue; with only that one ornament,—the scarlet letter,—which it was her doom to wear. The child's attire, on the other hand, was distinguished by a fanciful, or, we might rather say, a fantastic ingenuity, which served, indeed, to heighten the airy charm that early began to develop itself in the little girl, but which appeared to have also a deeper meaning. We may speak further of it hereafter. Except for that small expenditure in the decoration of her infant, Hester bestowed all her superfluous means in charity, on wretches less miserable than herself, and who not unfrequently insulted the hand that fed them. Much of the time, which she might readily have applied to the better efforts of her art, she employed in making coarse garments for the poor. It is probable that there was an idea of penance in this mode of occupation, and that she offered up a real sacrifice of enjoyment, in devoting so many hours to such rude handiwork. She had in her nature a rich, voluptuous, Oriental characteristic,—a taste for the gorgeously beautiful, which, save in the exquisite productions of her needle, found nothing else, in all the possibilities of her life, to exercise itself upon. Women derive a pleasure, incomprehensible to the other sex, from the delicate toil of the needle. To Hester Prynne it might have been a mode of expressing, and therefore soothing, the passion of her life. Like all other joys, she rejected it as sin. This morbid meddling of conscience with an immaterial matter betokened, it is to be feared, no genuine and steadfast penitence, but something doubtful, something that might be deeply wrong, beneath.

In this manner, Hester Prynne came to have a part to perform in the world. With her native energy of character, and rare capacity, it could not entirely cast her off, although it had set a mark upon her, more intolerable to a woman's heart than that which branded the brow of Cain. In all her intercourse with society, however, there was nothing that made her feel as if she belonged to it. Every gesture, every word, and even the silence of those with whom she came in contact, implied, and often expressed, that she was banished, and as much alone as if she inhabited another sphere, or communicated with the common nature by other organs and senses than the rest of human kind. She stood apart from moral interests, yet close beside them, like a ghost that revisits the familiar fireside, and can no longer make itself seen or felt; no more smile with the household joy, nor mourn with the kindred sorrow; or, should it succeed in manifesting its forbidden sympathy, awakening only terror and horrible repugnance. These emotions, in fact, and its bitterest scorn besides, seemed to be the sole portion that she retained in the universal heart. It was not an age of delicacy; and her position, although she understood it well, and was in little danger of forgetting it, was often brought before her vivid self-perception, like a new anguish, by the rudest touch upon the tenderest spot. The poor, as we have already said, whom she sought out to be the objects of her bounty, often reviled the hand that was stretched forth to succor them. Dames of elevated rank, likewise, whose doors she entered in the way of her occupation, were accustomed to distil drops of bitterness into her heart; sometimes through that alchemy of quiet malice, by which women can concoct a subtile poison from ordinary trifles; and sometimes, also, by a coarser expression, that fell upon the sufferer's defenceless breast like a rough blow upon an ulcerated wound. Hester had schooled herself long and well; she never responded to these attacks, save by a flush of crimson that rose irrepressibly over her pale cheek, and again subsided into the depths of her bosom. She was patient,—a martyr, indeed,—but she forbore to pray for her enemies; lest, in spite of her forgiving aspirations, the words of the blessing should stubbornly twist themselves into a curse.

Continually, and in a thousand other ways, did she feel the innumerable throbs of anguish that had been so cunningly contrived for her by the undying, the ever-active sentence of the Puritan tribunal. Clergymen paused in the street to address words of exhortation, that brought a crowd, with its mingled grin and frown, around the poor, sinful woman. If she entered a church, trusting to share the Sabbath smile of the Universal Father, it was often her mishap to find herself the text of the discourse. She grew to have a dread of children; for they had imbibed from their parents a vague idea of something horrible in this dreary woman, gliding silently through the town, with never any companion but one only child. Therefore, first allowing her to pass, they pursued her at a distance with shrill cries, and the utterance of a word that had no distinct purport to their own minds, but was none the less terrible to her, as proceeding from lips that babbled it unconsciously. It seemed to argue so wide a diffusion of her shame, that all nature knew of it; it could have caused her no deeper pang, had the leaves of the trees whispered the dark story among themselves,—had the summer breeze murmured about it—had the wintry blast shrieked it aloud! Another peculiar torture was felt in the gaze of a new eye. When strangers looked curiously at the scarlet letter,—and none ever failed to do so,—they branded it afresh into Hester's soul; so that, oftentimes, she could scarcely refrain, yet always did refrain, from covering the symbol with her hand. But then, again, an accustomed eye had likewise its own anguish to inflict. Its cool stare of familiarity was intolerable. From first to last, in short, Hester Prynne had always this dreadful agony in feeling a human eye upon the token; the spot never grew callous; it seemed, on the contrary, to grow more sensitive with daily torture.

But sometimes, once in many days, or perchance in many months, she felt an eye—a human eye—upon the ignominious brand, that seemed to give a momentary relief, as if half of her agony were shared. The next instant, back it all rushed again, with still a deeper throb of pain; for, in that brief interval, she had sinned anew. Had Hester sinned alone?

Her imagination was somewhat affected, and, had she been of a softer moral and intellectual fibre, would have been still more so, by the strange and solitary anguish of her life. Walking to and fro, with those lonely footsteps, in the little world with which she was outwardly connected, it now and then appeared to Hester,—if altogether fancy, it was nevertheless too potent to be resisted,—she felt or fancied, then, that the scarlet letter had endowed her with a new sense. She shuddered to believe, yet could not help believing, that it gave her a sympathetic knowledge of the hidden sin in other hearts. She was terror-stricken by the revelations that were thus made. What were they? Could they be other than the insidious whispers of the bad angel, who would fain have persuaded the struggling woman, as yet only half his victim, that the outward guise of purity was but a lie, and that, if truth were everywhere to be shown, a scarlet letter would blaze forth on many a bosom besides Hester Prynne's? Or, must she receive those intimations—so obscure, yet so distinct—as truth? In all her miserable experience, there was nothing else so awful and so loathsome as this sense. It perplexed, as well as shocked her, by the irreverent inopportuneness of the occasions that brought it into vivid action. Sometimes the red infamy upon her breast would give a sympathetic throb, as she passed near a venerable minister or magistrate, the model of piety and justice, to whom that age of antique reverence looked up, as to a mortal man in fellowship with angels. "What evil thing is at hand?" would Hester say to herself. Lifting her reluctant eyes, there would be nothing human within the scope of view, save the form of this earthly saint! Again, a mystic sisterhood would contumaciously assert itself, as she met the sanctified frown of some matron, who, according to the rumor of all tongues, had kept cold snow within her bosom throughout life. That unsunned snow in the matron's bosom, and the burning shame on Hester Prynne's,—what had the two in common? Or, once more, the electric thrill would give her warning,—"Behold, Hester, here is a companion!"—and, looking up, she would detect the eyes of a young maiden glancing at the scarlet letter, shyly and aside, and quickly averted, with a faint, chill crimson in her cheeks; as if her purity were somewhat sullied by that momentary glance. O Fiend, whose talisman was that fatal symbol, wouldst thou leave nothing, whether in youth or age, for this poor sinner to revere?—such loss of faith is ever one of the saddest results of sin. Be it accepted as a proof that all was not corrupt in this poor victim of her own frailty, and man's hard law, that Hester Prynne yet struggled to believe that no fellow-mortal was guilty like herself.

The vulgar, who, in those dreary old times, were always contributing a grotesque horror to what interested their imaginations, had a story about the scarlet letter which we might readily work up into a terrific legend. They averred, that the symbol was not mere scarlet cloth, tinged in an earthly dye-pot, but was red-hot with infernal fire, and could be seen glowing all alight, whenever Hester Prynne walked abroad in the night-time. And we must needs say, it seared Hester's bosom so deeply, that perhaps there was more truth in the rumor than our modern incredulity may be inclined to admit.

Chapter 6: Pearl

We have as yet hardly spoken of the infant; that little creature, whose innocent life had sprung, by the inscrutable decree of Providence, a lovely and immortal flower, out of the rank luxuriance of a guilty passion. How strange it seemed to the sad woman, as she watched the growth, and the beauty that became every day more brilliant, and the intelligence that threw its quivering sunshine over the tiny features of this child! Her Pearl!—For so had Hester called her; not as a name expressive of her aspect, which had nothing of the calm, white, unimpassioned lustre that would be indicated by the comparison. But she named the infant "Pearl," as being of great price,—purchased with all she had,—her mother's only treasure! How strange, indeed! Man had marked this woman's sin by a scarlet letter, which had such potent and disastrous efficacy that no human sympathy could reach her, save it were sinful like herself. God, as a direct consequence of the sin which man thus punished, had given her a lovely child, whose place was on that same dishonored bosom, to connect her parent forever with the race and descent of mortals, and to be finally a blessed soul in heaven! Yet these thoughts affected Hester Prynne less with hope than apprehension. She knew that her deed had been evil; she could have no faith, therefore, that its result would be good. Day after day, she looked fearfully into the child's expanding nature, ever dreading to detect some dark and wild peculiarity, that should correspond with the guiltiness to which she owed her being.

Certainly, there was no physical defect. By its perfect shape, its vigor, and its natural dexterity in the use of all its untried limbs, the infant was worthy to have been brought forth in Eden; worthy to have been left there, to be the plaything of the angels, after the world's first parents were driven out. The child had a native grace which does not invariably coexist with faultless beauty; its attire, however simple, always impressed the beholder as if it were the very garb that precisely became it best. But little Pearl was not clad in rustic weeds. Her mother, with a morbid purpose that may be better understood hereafter, had bought the richest tissues that could be procured, and allowed her imaginative faculty its full play in the arrangement and decoration of the dresses which the child wore, before the public eye. So magnificent was the small figure, when thus arrayed, and such was the splendor of Pearl's own proper beauty, shining through the gorgeous robes which might have extinguished a paler loveliness, that there was an absolute circle of radiance around her, on the darksome cottage floor. And yet a russet gown, torn and soiled with the child's rude play, made a picture of her just as perfect. Pearl's aspect was imbued with a spell of infinite variety; in this one child there were many children, comprehending the full scope between the wild-flower prettiness of a peasant-baby, and the pomp, in little, of an infant princess. Throughout all, however, there was a trait of passion, a certain depth of hue, which she never lost; and if, in any of her changes, she had grown fainter or paler, she would have ceased to be herself;—it would have been no longer Pearl!

This outward mutability indicated, and did not more than fairly express, the various properties of her inner life. Her nature appeared to possess depth, too, as well as variety; but—or else Hester's fears deceived her—it lacked reference and adaptation to the world into which she was born. The child could not be made amenable to rules. In giving her existence, a great law had been broken; and the result was a being whose elements were perhaps beautiful and brilliant, but all in disorder; or with an order peculiar to themselves, amidst which the point of variety and arrangement was difficult or impossible to be discovered. Hester could only account for the child's character—and even then most vaguely and imperfectly—by recalling what she herself had been, during that momentous period while Pearl was imbibing her soul from the spiritual world, and her bodily frame from its material of earth. The mother's impassioned state had been the medium through which were transmitted to the unborn infant the rays of its moral life; and, however white and clear originally, they had taken the deep stains of crimson and gold, the fiery lustre, the black shadow, and the untempered light, of the intervening substance. Above all, the warfare of Hester's spirit, at that epoch, was perpetuated in Pearl. She could recognize her wild, desperate, defiant mood, the flightiness of her temper, and even some of the very cloud-shapes of gloom and despondency that had brooded in her heart. They were now illuminated by the morning radiance of a young child's disposition, but, later in the day of earthly existence, might be prolific of the storm and whirlwind.

The discipline of the family, in those days, was of a far more rigid kind than now. The frown, the harsh rebuke, the frequent application of the rod, enjoined by Scriptural authority, were used, not merely in the way of punishment for actual offences, but as a wholesome regimen for the growth and promotion of all childish virtues. Hester Prynne, nevertheless, the lonely mother of this one child, ran little risk of erring on the side of undue severity. Mindful, however, of her own errors and misfortunes, she early sought to impose a tender, but strict control over the infant immortality that was committed to her charge. But the task was beyond her skill. After testing both smiles and frowns, and proving that neither mode of treatment possessed any calculable influence, Hester was ultimately compelled to stand aside, and permit the child to be swayed by her own impulses. Physical compulsion or restraint was effectual, of course, while it lasted. As to any other kind of discipline, whether addressed to her mind or heart, little Pearl might or might not be within its reach, in accordance with the caprice that ruled the moment. Her mother, while Pearl was yet an infant, grew acquainted with a certain peculiar look, that warned her when it would be labor thrown away to insist, persuade, or plead. It was a look so intelligent, yet inexplicable, so perverse, sometimes so malicious, but generally accompanied by a wild flow of spirits, that Hester could not help questioning, at such moments, whether Pearl was a human child. She seemed rather an airy sprite, which, after playing its fantastic sports for a little while upon the cottage-floor, would flit away with a mocking smile. Whenever that look appeared in her wild, bright, deeply black eyes, it invested her with a strange remoteness and intangibility; it was as if she were hovering in the air and might vanish, like a glimmering light, that comes we know not whence, and goes we know not whither. Beholding it, Hester was constrained to rush towards the child,—to pursue the little elf in the flight which she invariably began,—to snatch her to her bosom, with a close pressure and earnest kisses,—not so much from overflowing love, as to assure herself that Pearl was flesh and blood, and not utterly delusive. But Pearl's laugh, when she was caught, though full of merriment and music, made her mother more doubtful than before.

Heart-smitten at this bewildering and baffling spell, that so often came between herself and her sole treasure, whom she had bought so dear, and who was all her world, Hester sometimes burst into passionate tears. Then, perhaps,—for there was no foreseeing how it might affect her,—Pearl would frown, and clench her little fist, and harden her small features into a stern, unsympathizing look of discontent. Not seldom, she would laugh anew, and louder than before, like a thing incapable and unintelligent of human sorrow. Or—but this more rarely happened—she would be convulsed with a rage of grief, and sob out her love for her mother, in broken words, and seem intent on proving that she had a heart, by breaking it. Yet Hester was hardly safe in confiding herself to that gusty tenderness; it passed, as suddenly as it came. Brooding over all these matters, the mother felt like one who has evoked a spirit, but, by some irregularity in the process of conjuration, has failed to win the master-word that should control this new and incomprehensible intelligence. Her only real comfort was when the child lay in the placidity of sleep. Then she was sure of her, and tasted hours of quiet, sad, delicious happiness; until—perhaps with that perverse expression glimmering from beneath her opening lids—little Pearl awoke!

How soon—with what strange rapidity, indeed!—did Pearl arrive at an age that was capable of social intercourse, beyond the mother's ever-ready smile and nonsense-words! And then what a happiness would it have been, could Hester Prynne have heard her clear, bird-like voice mingling with the uproar of other childish voices, and have distinguished and unravelled her own darling's tones, amid all the entangled outcry of a group of sportive children! But this could never be. Pearl was a born outcast of the infantile world. An imp of evil, emblem and product of sin, she had no right among christened infants. Nothing was more remarkable than the instinct, as it seemed, with which the child comprehended her loneliness; the destiny that had drawn an inviolable circle round about her; the whole peculiarity, in short, of her position in respect to other children. Never, since her release from prison, had Hester met the public gaze without her. In all her walks about the town, Pearl, too, was there; first as the babe in arms, and afterwards as the little girl, small companion of her mother, holding a forefinger with her whole grasp, and tripping along at the rate of three or four footsteps to one of Hester's. She saw the children of the settlement, on the grassy margin of the street, or at the domestic thresholds, disporting themselves in such grim fashion as the Puritanic nurture would permit; playing at going to church, perchance; or at scourging Quakers; or taking scalps in a sham-fight with the Indians; or scaring one another with freaks of imitative witchcraft. Pearl saw, and gazed intently, but never sought to make acquaintance. If spoken to, she would not speak again. If the children gathered about her, as they sometimes did, Pearl would grow positively terrible in her puny wrath, snatching up stones to fling at them, with shrill, incoherent exclamations, that made her mother tremble, because they had so much the sound of a witch's anathemas in some unknown tongue.

The truth was, that the little Puritans, being of the most intolerant brood that ever lived, had got a vague idea of something outlandish, unearthly, or at variance with ordinary fashions, in the mother and child; and therefore scorned them in their hearts, and not unfrequently reviled them with their tongues. Pearl felt the sentiment, and requited it with the bitterest hatred that can be supposed to rankle in a childish bosom. These outbreaks of a fierce temper had a kind of value, and even comfort, for her mother; because there was at least an intelligible earnestness in the mood, instead of the fitful caprice that so often thwarted her in the child's manifestations. It appalled her, nevertheless, to discern here, again, a shadowy reflection of the evil that had existed in herself. All this enmity and passion had Pearl inherited, by inalienable right, out of Hester's heart. Mother and daughter stood together in the same circle of seclusion from human society; and in the nature of the child seemed to be perpetuated those unquiet elements that had distracted Hester Prynne before Pearl's birth, but had since begun to be soothed away by the softening influences of maternity.

At home, within and around her mother's cottage, Pearl wanted not a wide and various circle of acquaintance. The spell of life went forth from her ever-creative spirit, and communicated itself to a thousand objects, as a torch kindles a flame wherever it may be applied. The unlikeliest materials—a stick, a bunch of rags, a flower—were the puppets of Pearl's witchcraft, and, without undergoing any outward change, became spiritually adapted to whatever drama occupied the stage of her inner world. Her one baby-voice served a multitude of imaginary personages, old and young, to talk withal. The pine-trees, aged, black and solemn, and flinging groans and other melancholy utterances on the breeze, needed little transformation to figure as Puritan elders; the ugliest weeds of the garden were their children, whom Pearl smote down and uprooted, most unmercifully. It was wonderful, the vast variety of forms into which she threw her intellect, with no continuity, indeed, but darting up and dancing, always in a state of preternatural activity,—soon sinking down, as if exhausted by so rapid and feverish a tide of life,—and succeeded by other shapes of a similar wild energy. It was like nothing so much as the phantasmagoric play of the northern lights. In the mere exercise of the fancy, however, and the sportiveness of a growing mind, there might be little more than was observable in other children of bright faculties; except as Pearl, in the dearth of human playmates, was thrown more upon the visionary throng which she created. The singularity lay in the hostile feelings with which the child regarded all these offspring of her own heart and mind. She never created a friend, but seemed always to be sowing broadcast the dragon's teeth, whence sprung a harvest of armed enemies, against whom she rushed to battle. It was inexpressibly sad—then what depth of sorrow to a mother, who felt in her own heart the cause!—to observe, in one so young, this constant recognition of an adverse world, and so fierce a training of the energies that were to make good her cause, in the contest that must ensue.

Gazing at Pearl, Hester Prynne often dropped her work upon her knees, and cried out with an agony which she would fain have hidden, but which made utterance for itself, betwixt speech and a groan,—"O Father in Heaven,—if Thou art still my Father,—what is this being which I have brought into the world!" And Pearl, overhearing the ejaculation, or aware, through some more subtile channel, of those throbs of anguish, would turn her vivid and beautiful little face upon her mother, smile with sprite-like intelligence, and resume her play.

One peculiarity of the child's deportment remains yet to be told. The very first thing which she had noticed, in her life was—what?—not the mother's smile, responding to it, as other babies do, by that faint, embryo smile of the little mouth, remembered so doubtfully afterwards, and with such fond discussion whether it were indeed a smile. By no means! But that first object of which Pearl seemed to become aware was—shall we say it?—the scarlet letter on Hester's bosom! One day, as her mother stooped over the cradle, the infant's eyes had been caught by the glimmering of the gold embroidery about the letter; and, putting up her little hand, she grasped at it, smiling, not doubtfully, but with a decided gleam, that gave her face the look of a much older child. Then, gasping for breath, did Hester Prynne clutch the fatal token, instinctively endeavoring to tear it away; so infinite was the torture inflicted by the intelligent touch of Pearl's baby-hand. Again, as if her mother's agonized gesture were meant only to make sport for her, did little Pearl look into her eyes, and smile! From that epoch, except when the child was asleep, Hester had never felt a moment's safety; not a moment's calm enjoyment of her. Weeks, it is true, would sometimes elapse, during which Pearl's gaze might never once be fixed upon the scarlet letter; but then, again, it would come at unawares, like the stroke of sudden death, and always with that peculiar smile, and odd expression of the eyes.

Once, this freakish, elvish cast came into the child's eyes, while Hester was looking at her own image in them, as mothers are fond of doing; and, suddenly,—for women in solitude, and with troubled hearts, are pestered with unaccountable delusions,—she fancied that she beheld, not her own miniature portrait, but another face, in the small black mirror of Pearl's eye. It was a face, fiend-like, full of smiling malice, yet bearing the semblance of features that she had known full well, though seldom with a smile, and never with malice in them. It was as if an evil spirit possessed the child, and had just then peeped forth in mockery. Many a time afterwards had Hester been tortured, though less vividly, by the same illusion.

In the afternoon of a certain summer's day, after Pearl grew big enough to run about, she amused herself with gathering handfuls of wild-flowers, and flinging them, one by one, at her mother's bosom; dancing up and down, like a little elf, whenever she hit the scarlet letter. Hester's first motion had been to cover her bosom with her clasped hands. But, whether from pride or resignation, or a feeling that her penance might best be wrought out by this unutterable pain, she resisted the impulse, and sat erect, pale as death, looking sadly into little Pearl's wild eyes. Still came the battery of flowers, almost invariably hitting the mark, and covering the mother's breast with hurts for which she could find no balm in this world, nor knew how to seek it in another. At last, her shot being all expended, the child stood still and gazed at Hester, with that little, laughing image of a fiend peeping out—or, whether it peeped or no, her mother so imagined it—from the unsearchable abyss of her black eyes.

"Child, what art thou?" cried the mother.

"O, I am your little Pearl!" answered the child.

But, while she said it, Pearl laughed, and began to dance up and down, with the humorsome gesticulation of a little imp, whose next freak might be to fly up the chimney.

"Art thou my child, in very truth?" asked Hester.

Nor did she put the question altogether idly, but, for the moment, with a portion of genuine earnestness; for, such was Pearl's wonderful intelligence, that her mother half doubted whether she were not acquainted with the secret spell of her existence, and might not now reveal herself.

"Yes; I am little Pearl!" repeated the child, continuing her antics.

"Thou art not my child! Thou art no Pearl of mine!" said the mother, half playfully; for it was often the case that a sportive impulse came over her, in the midst of her deepest suffering. "Tell me, then, what thou art, and who sent thee hither?"

"Tell me, mother!" said the child, seriously, coming up to Hester, and pressing herself close to her knees. "Do thou tell me!"

"Thy Heavenly Father sent thee!" answered Hester Prynne.

But she said it with a hesitation that did not escape the acuteness of the child. Whether moved only by her ordinary freakishness, or because an evil spirit prompted her, she put up her small forefinger, and touched the scarlet letter.

"He did not send me!" cried she, positively. "I have no Heavenly Father!"

"Hush, Pearl, hush! Thou must not talk so!" answered the mother, suppressing a groan. "He sent us all into this world. He sent even me, thy mother. Then, much more, thee! Or, if not, thou strange and elfish child, whence didst thou come?"

"Tell me! Tell me!" repeated Pearl, no longer seriously, but laughing, and capering about the floor. "It is thou that must tell me!"

But Hester could not resolve the query, being herself in a dismal labyrinth of doubt. She remembered—betwixt a smile and a shudder—the talk of the neighboring townspeople; who, seeking vainly elsewhere for the child's paternity, and observing some of her odd attributes, had given out that poor little Pearl was a demon offspring; such as, ever since old Catholic times, had occasionally been seen on earth, through the agency of their mother's sin, and to promote some foul and wicked purpose. Luther, according to the scandal of his monkish enemies, was a brat of that hellish breed; nor was Pearl the only child to whom this inauspicious origin was assigned, among the New England Puritans.

SOURCE: Nathaniel Hawthorne. *The Scarlet Letter.* Boston: Ticknor, Reed, and Fields, 1850.

RALPH WALDO EMERSON

In his time, the poet, lecturer and essayist Ralph Waldo Emerson (1803–1882) was America's most well-regarded man of letters. Though his fame has diminished, his essays on the natural world, Transcendentalism and on practical philosophy remain exciting and exuberant: "Crossing a bare common, in snow puddles, at twilight, under a clouded sky, without having in my thoughts any occurrence of special good fortune, I have enjoyed a perfect exhilaration. Almost I fear to think how glad I am. In the woods too, a man casts off his years, as the snake his slough, and at what period soever of life, is always a child. In the woods, is perpetual youth."

Nature (1836)

"Nature" is the first chapter from the booklength work of the same name.

TO GO INTO solitude, a man needs to retire as much from his chamber as from society. I am not solitary whilst I read and write, though nobody is with me. But if a man would be alone, let him look at the stars. The rays that come from those heavenly worlds, will separate between him and vulgar things. One might think the atmosphere was made transparent with this design, to give man, in the heavenly bodies, the perpetual presence of the sublime. Seen in the streets of cities, how great they are! If the stars should appear one night in a thousand years, how would men believe and adore; and preserve for many generations the remembrance of the city of God which had been shown! But every night come out these preachers of beauty, and light the universe with their admonishing smile.

The stars awaken a certain reverence, because though always present, they are always inaccessible; but all natural objects make a kindred impression, when the mind is open to their influence.

Nature never wears a mean appearance. Neither does the wisest man extort all her secret, and lose his curiosity by finding out all her perfection. Nature never became a toy to a wise spirit. The flowers, the animals, the mountains, reflected all the wisdom of his best hour, as much as they had delighted the simplicity of his childhood.

When we speak of nature in this manner, we have a distinct but most poetical sense in the mind. We mean the integrity of impression made by manifold natural objects. It is this which distinguishes the stick of timber of the wood-cutter, from the tree of the poet. The charming landscape which I saw this morning, is indubitably made up of some twenty or thirty farms. Miller owns this field, Locke that, and Manning the woodland beyond. But none of them owns the landscape. There is a property in the horizon which no man has but he whose eye can integrate all the parts, that is, the poet. This is the best part of these men's farms, yet to this their land-deeds give them no title.

To speak truly, few adult persons can see nature. Most persons do not see the sun. At least they have a very superficial seeing. The sun illuminates only the eye of the man, but shines into the eye and the heart of the child. The lover of nature is he whose inward and outward senses are still truly adjusted to each other; who has retained the spirit of infancy even into the era of manhood. His intercourse with heaven and earth, becomes part of his daily food. In the presence of nature, a wild delight runs through the man, in spite of real sorrows. Nature says,—he is my creature, and maugre [in spite of] all his impertinent griefs, he shall be glad with me. Not the sun or the summer alone, but every hour and season yields its tribute of delight; for every hour and change corresponds to and authorizes a different state of the mind, from breathless noon to grimmest midnight. Nature is a setting that fits equally well a comic or a mourning piece. In good health, the air is a cordial of incredible virtue. Crossing a bare common, in snow puddles, at twilight, under a clouded sky, without having in my thoughts any occurrence of special good fortune, I have enjoyed a perfect exhilaration. Almost I fear to think how glad I am. In the woods too, a man casts off his years, as the snake his slough, and at what period soever of life, is always a child. In the woods, is perpetual youth. Within these plantations of God, a decorum and sanctity reign, a perennial festival is dressed, and the guest sees not how he should tire of them in a thousand years. In the woods, we return to reason and faith. There I feel that nothing can befall me in life,—no disgrace, no calamity, (leaving me my eyes,) which nature cannot repair. Standing on the bare ground,—my head bathed by the blithe air, and uplifted into infinite space,—all mean egotism vanishes. I become a transparent eye-ball. I am nothing. I see all. The currents of the Universal Being circulate through me; I am part or particle of God. The name of the nearest friend sounds then foreign and accidental. To be brothers, to be acquaintances,—master or servant, is then a trifle and a disturbance. I am the lover of uncontained and immortal beauty. In the wilderness, I find something more dear and connate than in streets or villages. In the tranquil landscape, and especially in the distant line of the horizon, man beholds somewhat as beautiful as his own nature.

The greatest delight which the fields and woods minister, is the suggestion of an occult relation between man and the vegetable. I am not alone and unacknowledged. They nod to me and I to them. The waving of the boughs in the storm, is new to me and old. It takes me by surprise, and yet is not unknown. Its effect is like that of a higher thought or a better emotion coming over me, when I deemed I was thinking justly or doing right.

Yet it is certain that the power to produce this delight, does not reside in nature, but in man, or in a harmony of both. It is necessary to use these pleasures with great temperance. For, nature is not always tricked in holiday attire, but the same scene which yesterday breathed perfume and glittered as for the frolic of the nymphs, is overspread with melancholy today. Nature always wears the colors of the spirit. To a man laboring under calamity, the heat of his own fire hath sadness in it. Then, there is a kind of contempt of the landscape felt by him who has just lost by death a dear friend. The sky is less grand as it shuts down over less worth in the population.

SOURCE: Ralph Waldo Emerson. *Nature.* Boston: James Munroe and Company, 1836.

Self-Reliance (1841)

In one of the great philosophical essays of nineteenth-century literature, Emerson preaches and meditates upon the self-awareness and self-confidence required for "Self-Reliance." We have relied on the first version published in book form, which, discounting the changes in punctuation, has a sharper, fresher edge.

I READ THE other day some verses written by an eminent painter, which were original and not conventional. Always the soul hears an admonition in such lines, let the subject be what it may. The sentiment they instil is of more value than any thought they may contain. To believe your own thought, to believe that what is true for you in your private heart, is true for all men,—that is genius. Speak your latent conviction, and it shall be the universal sense; for always the inmost becomes the outmost,—and our first thought is rendered back to us by the trumpets of the Last Judgment. Familiar as the voice of the mind is to each, the highest merit we ascribe to Moses, Plato, and Milton, is that they set at naught books and traditions, and spoke not what men, but what they thought. A man should learn to detect and watch that gleam of light which flashes across his mind from within, more than the lustre of the firmament of bards and sages. Yet he dismisses without notice his thought, because it is his. In every work of genius we recognise our own rejected thoughts: they come back to us with a certain alienated majesty. Great works of art have no more affecting lesson for us than this. They teach us to abide by our spontaneous impression with good humored inflexibility then most when the whole cry of voices is on the other side. Else, to-morrow a stranger will say with masterly good sense precisely what we have thought and felt all the time, and we shall be forced to take with shame our own opinion from another.

There is a time in every man's education when he arrives at the conviction that envy is ignorance; that imitation is suicide; that he must take himself for better, for worse, as his portion; that though the wide universe is full of good, no kernel of nourishing corn can come to him but through his toil bestowed on that plot of ground which is given to him to till. The power which resides in him is new in nature, and none but he knows what that is which he can do, nor does he know until he has tried. Not for nothing one face, one character, one fact makes much impression on him, and another none. It is not without preestablished harmony, this sculpture in the memory. The eye was placed where one ray should fall, that it might testify of that particular ray. Bravely let him speak the utmost syllable of his confession. We but half express ourselves, and are ashamed of that divine idea which each of us represents. It may be safely trusted as proportionate and of good issues, so it be faithfully imparted, but God will not have his work made manifest by cowards. A man is relieved and gay when he has put his heart into his work and done his best; but what he has said or done otherwise, shall give him no peace. It is a deliverance which does not deliver. In the attempt, his genius deserts him; no muse befriends—no invention, no hope.

Trust thyself: every heart vibrates to that iron string. Accept the place the Divine Providence has found for you; the society of your contemporaries, the connexion of events. Great men have always done so, and confided themselves childlike to the genius of their age, betraying their perception that the Eternal was stirring at their heart, working through their hands, predominating in all their being. And we are now men, and must accept in the highest mind the same transcendent destiny; and not pinched in a corner, not cowards fleeing before a revolution, but redeemers and benefactors, pious aspirants to be noble clay plastic under the Almighty effort, let us advance, and advance on Chaos and the Dark.

What pretty oracles nature yields us on this text, in the face and behavior of children, babes and even brutes. That divided and rebel mind, that distrust of a sentiment because our arithmetic has computed the strength and means opposed to our purpose, these have not. Their mind being whole, their eye is as yet unconquered; and when we look in their faces, we are disconcerted. Infancy conforms to nobody: all conform to it, so that one babe commonly makes four or five out of the adults who prattle and play to it. So God has armed youth and puberty and manhood no less with its own piquancy and charm, and made it enviable and gracious, and its claims not to be put by, if it will stand by itself. Do not think the youth has no force because he cannot speak to you and me. Hark! in the next room, who spoke so clear and emphatic? Good heaven! it is he! it is that very lump of bashfulness and phlegm which for weeks has done nothing but eat when you were by, that now rolls out these words like bell-strokes. It seems he knows how to speak to his contemporaries. Bashful or bold, then, he will know how to make us seniors very unnecessary.

The nonchalance of boys who are sure of a dinner, and would disdain as much as a lord to do or say aught to conciliate one, is the healthy attitude of human nature. How is a boy the master of society! independent, irresponsible, looking out from his corner on such people and facts as pass by, he tries and sentences them on their merits, in the swift summary way of boys, as good, bad, interesting, silly, eloquent, troublesome. He cumbers himself never about consequences, about interests; he gives an independent, genuine verdict. You must court him; he does not court you. But the man is, as it were, clapped into jail by his consciousness. As soon as he has once acted or spoken with eclat, he is a committed person, watched by the sympathy or the hatred of hundreds, whose affections must now enter into his account. There is no Lethe for this. Ah, that he could pass again into his neutral, godlike independence! Who can thus lose all pledge, and having observed, observe again from the same unaffected, unbiased, unbribable, unaffrighted innocence, must always be formidable, must always engage the poet's and the man's regards. Of such an immortal youth the force would be felt. He would utter opinions on all passing affairs, which being seen to be not private but necessary, would sink like darts into the ear of men, and put them in fear.

These are the voices which we hear in solitude, but they grow faint and inaudible as we enter into the world. Society everywhere is in conspiracy against the manhood of every one of its members. Society is a joint-stock company in which the members agree, for the better securing of his bread to each shareholder, to surrender the liberty and culture of the eater. The virtue in most request is conformity. Self-reliance is its aversion. It loves not realities and creators, but names and customs.

Whoso would be a man must be a nonconformist. He who would gather immortal palms must not be hindered by the name of goodness, but must explore if it be goodness. Nothing is at last sacred but the integrity of your own mind. Absolve you to yourself, and you shall have the suffrage of the world. I remember an answer which when quite young I was prompted to make to a valued adviser who was wont to importune me with the dear old doctrines of the church. On my saying, What have I to do with the sacredness of traditions, if I live wholly from within? my friend suggested—"But these impulses may be from below, not from above." I replied, "They do not seem to me to be such; but if I am the devil's child, I will live then from the devil." No law can be sacred to me but that of my nature. Good and bad are but names very readily transferable to that or this; the only right is what is after my constitution, the only wrong what is against it. A man is to carry himself in the presence of all opposition as if every thing were titular and ephemeral but he. I am ashamed to think how easily we capitulate to badges and names, to large societies and dead institutions. Every decent and well-spoken individual affects and sways me more than is right. I ought to go upright and vital, and speak the rude truth in all ways. If malice and vanity wear the coat of philanthropy, shall that pass? If an angry bigot assumes this bountiful cause of Abolition, and comes to me with his last news from Barbadoes, why should I not say to him, "Go love thy infant; love thy wood-chopper; be good-natured and modest; have that grace; and never varnish your hard, uncharitable ambition with this incredible tenderness for black folk a thousand miles off. Thy love afar is spite at home." Rough and graceless would be such greeting, but truth is handsomer than the affectation of love. Your goodness must have some edge to it—else it is none. The doctrine of hatred must be preached as the counteraction of the doctrine of love, when that pules and whines. I shun father and mother and wife and brother, when my genius calls me. I would write on the lintels of the door-post, *Whim*. I hope it is somewhat better than whim at last, but we cannot spend the day in explanation. Expect me not to show cause why I seek or why I exclude company. Then, again, do not tell me, as a good man did to-day, of my obligation to put all poor men in good situations. Are they *my* poor? I tell thee, thou foolish philanthropist, that I grudge the dollar, the dime, the cent I give to such men as do not belong to me and to whom I do not belong. There is a class of persons to whom by all spiritual affinity I am bought and sold; for them I will go to prison, if need be; but your miscellaneous popular charities; the education at college of fools; the building of meeting-houses to the vain end to which many now stand; alms to sots; and the thousandfold Relief Societies;—though I confess with shame I sometimes succumb and give the dollar, it is a wicked dollar which by-and-by I shall have the manhood to withhold.

Virtues are, in the popular estimate, rather the exception than the rule. There is the man *and* his virtues. Men do what is called a good action, as some piece of courage or charity, much as they would pay a fine in expiation of daily non-appearance on parade. Their works are done as an apology or extenuation of their living in the world,—as invalids and the insane pay a high board. Their virtues are penances. I do not wish to expiate, but to live. My life is not an apology, but a life. It is for itself, and not for a spectacle. I much prefer that it should be of a lower strain, so it be genuine and equal, than that it should be glittering and unsteady. I wish it to be sound and sweet, and not to need diet and bleeding. My life should be unique; it should be an alms, a battle, a conquest, a medicine. I ask primary evidence that you are a man, and refuse this appeal from the man to his actions. I know that for myself it makes no difference whether I do or forbear those actions which are reckoned excellent. I cannot consent to pay for a privilege where I have intrinsic right. Few and mean as my gifts may be, I actually am, and do not need for my own assurance or the assurance of my fellows any secondary testimony.

What I must do, is all that concerns me, not what the people think. This rule, equally arduous in actual and in intellectual life, may serve for the whole distinction between greatness and meanness. It is the harder, because you will always find those who think they know what is your duty better than you know it. It is easy in the world to live after the world's opinion; it is easy in solitude to live after our own; but the great man is he who in the midst of the crowd keeps with perfect sweetness the independence of solitude.

The objection to conforming to usages that have become dead to you, is, that it scatters your force. It loses your time and blurs the impression of your character. If you maintain a dead church, contribute to a dead Bible-Society, vote with a great party either for the Government or against it, spread your table like base housekeepers,—under all these screens, I have difficulty to detect the precise man you are. And, of course, so much force is withdrawn from your proper life. But do your thing, and I shall know you. Do your work, and you shall reinforce yourself. A man must consider what a blindman's-buff is this game of conformity. If I know your sect, I anticipate your argument. I hear a preacher announce for his text and topic the expediency of one of the institutions of his church. Do I not know beforehand that not possibly can he say a new and spontaneous word? Do I not know that with all this ostentation of examining the grounds of the institution, he will do no such thing? Do I not know that he is pledged to himself not to look but at one side, the permitted side, not as a man, but as a parish minister? He is a retained attorney, and these airs of the bench are the emptiest affectation. Well, most men have bound their eyes with one or another handkerchief, and attached themselves to some one of these communities of opinion. This conformity makes them not false in a few particulars, authors of a few lies, but false in all particulars. Their every truth is not quite true. Their two is not the real two, their four not the real four; so that every word they say chagrins us, and we know not where to begin to set them right. Meantime nature is not slow to equip us in the prison-uniform of the party to which we adhere. We come to wear one cut of face and figure, and acquire by degrees the gentlest asinine expression. There is a mortifying experience in particular which does not fail to wreak itself also in the general history; I mean "the foolish face of praise," the forced smile which we put on in company where we do not feel at ease, in answer to conversation which does not interest us. The muscles, not spontaneously moved, but moved by a low usurping wilfulness, grow tight about the outline of the face with the most disagreeable sensation, a sensation of rebuke and warning which no brave young man will suffer twice.

For non-conformity the world whips you with its displeasure. And therefore a man must know how to estimate a sour face. The bystanders look askance on him in the public street or in the friend's parlor. If this aversation had its origin in contempt and resistance like his own, he might well go home with a sad countenance; but the sour faces of the multitude, like their sweet faces, have no deep cause,—disguise no god, but are put on and off as the wind blows, and a newspaper directs. Yet is the discontent of the multitude more formidable than that of the senate and the college. It is easy enough for a firm man who knows the world to brook the rage of the cultivated classes. Their rage is decorous and prudent, for they are timid as being very vulnerable themselves. But when to their feminine rage the indignation of the people is added, when the ignorant and the poor are aroused, when the unintelligent brute force that lies at the bottom of society is made to growl and mow, it needs the habit of magnanimity and religion to treat it godlike as a trifle of no concernment.

The other terror that scares us from self-trust is our consistency; a reverence for our past act or word, because the eyes of others have no other data for computing our orbit than our past acts, and we are loath to disappoint them.

But why should you keep your head over your shoulder? Why drag about this monstrous corpse of your memory, lest you contradict somewhat you have stated in this or that public place? Suppose you should contradict yourself; what then? It seems to be a rule of wisdom never to rely on your memory alone, scarcely even in acts of pure memory, but to bring the past for judgment into the thousand-eyed present, and live ever in a new day. In your metaphysics you have denied personality to the Deity; yet when the devout motions of the soul come, yield to them heart and life, though they should clothe God with shape and color. Leave your theory, as Joseph his coat in the hand of the harlot, and flee.

A foolish consistency is the hobgoblin of little minds, adored by little statesmen and philosophers and divines. With consistency a great soul has simply nothing to do. He may as well concern himself with his shadow on the wall. Out upon your guarded lips! Sew them up with packthread, do. Else, if you would be a man, speak what you think to-day in words as hard as cannon balls, and to-morrow speak what to-morrow thinks in hard words again, though it contradict everything you said to-day. Ah, then, exclaim the aged ladies, you shall be sure to be misunderstood. Misunderstood! It is a right fool's word. Is it so bad then to be misunderstood? Pythagoras was misunderstood, and Socrates, and Jesus, and Luther, and Copernicus, and Galileo, and Newton, and every pure and wise spirit that ever took flesh. To be great is to be misunderstood.

I suppose no man can violate his nature. All the sallies of his will are rounded in by the law of his being as the inequalities of Andes and Himmaleh are insignificant in the curve of the sphere. Nor does it matter how you gauge and try him. A character is like an acrostic or Alexandrian stanza;—read it forward, backward, or across, it still spells the same thing. In this pleasing contrite wood-life which God allows me, let me record day by day my honest thought without prospect or retrospect, and, I cannot doubt, it will be found symmetrical, though I mean it not, and see it not. My book should smell of pines and resound with the hum of insects. The swallow over my window should interweave that thread or straw he carries in his bill into my web also. We pass for what we are. Character teaches above our wills. Men imagine that they communicate their virtue or vice only by overt actions and do not see that virtue or vice emit a breath every moment.

Fear never but you shall be consistent in whatever variety of actions, so they be each honest and natural in their hour. For of one will, the actions will be harmonious, however unlike they seem. These varieties are lost sight of when seen at a little distance, at a little height of thought. One tendency unites them all. The voyage of the best ship is a zigzag line of a hundred tacks. See the line from a sufficient distance, and it straightens itself to the average tendency. Your genuine action will explain itself and will explain your other genuine actions. Your conformity explains nothing. Act singly, and what you have already done singly, will justify you now. Greatness appeals to the future. If I can be great enough now to do right and scorn eyes, I must have done so much right before, as to defend me now. Be it how it will, do right now. Always scorn appearances, and you always may. The force of character is cumulative. All the foregone days of virtue work their health into this. What makes the majesty of the heroes of the senate and the field, which so fills the imagination? The consciousness of a train of great days and victories behind. There they all stand and shed an united light on the advancing actor. He is attended as by a visible escort of angels to every man's eye. That is it which throws thunder into Chatham's voice, and dignity into Washington's port, and America into Adams's eye. Honor is venerable to us because it is no ephemeris. It is always ancient virtue. We worship it to-day, because it is not of to-day. We love it and pay it homage, because it is not a trap for our love and homage, but is self-dependent, self-derived, and therefore of an old immaculate pedigree, even if shown in a young person.

I hope in these days we have heard the last of conformity and consistency. Let the words be gazetted and ridiculous henceforward. Instead of the gong for dinner, let us hear a whistle from the Spartan fife. Let us never bow and apologize more. A great man is coming to eat at my house. I do not wish to please him: I wish that he should wish to please me. I will stand here for humanity, and though I would make it kind, I would make it true. Let us affront and reprimand the smooth mediocrity and squalid contentment of the times, and hurl in the face of custom, and trade, and office, the fact which is the upshot of all history, that there is a great responsible Thinker and Actor moving wherever moves a man; that a true man belongs to no other time or place, but is the centre of things. Where he is, there is nature. He measures you, and all men, and all events. Ordinarily every body in society reminds us of somewhat else, or of some other person. Character, reality, reminds you of nothing else. It takes place of the whole creation. The man must be so much that he must make all circumstances indifferent,—put all means into the shade. This all great men are and do. Every true man is a cause, a country, and an age; requires infinite spaces and numbers and time fully to accomplish his thought;—and posterity seem to follow his steps as a procession. A man Caesar is born, and for ages after, we have a Roman Empire. Christ is born, and millions of minds so grow and cleave to his genius, that he is confounded with virtue and the possible of man. An institution is the lengthened shadow of one man: as the

Reformation, of Luther; Quakerism, of Fox; Methodism, of Wesley; Abolition, of Clarkson. Scipio, Milton called "the height of Rome;" and all history resolves itself very easily into the biography of a few stout and earnest persons.

Let a man then know his worth, and keep things under his feet. Let him not peep or steal, or skulk up and down with the air of a charity-boy, a bastard, or an interloper, in the world which exists for him. But the man in the street finding no worth in himself which corresponds to the force which built a tower or sculptured a marble god, feels poor when he looks on these. To him a palace, a statue, or a costly book have an alien and forbidding air, much like a gay equipage, and seem to say like that, "Who are you, sir?" Yet they all are his, suitors for his notice, petitioners to his faculties that they will come out and take possession. The picture waits for my verdict; it is not to command me, but I am to settle its claims to praise. That popular fable of the sot who was picked up dead drunk in the street, carried to the duke's house, washed and dressed and laid in the duke's bed, and, on his waking, treated with all obsequious ceremony like the duke, and assured that he had been insane, owes its popularity to the fact, that it symbolizes so well the state of man, who is in the world a sort of sot, but now and then wakes up, exercises his reason, and finds himself a true prince.

Our reading is mendicant and sycophantic. In history, our imagination makes fools of us, plays us false. Kingdom and lordship, power and estate are a gaudier vocabulary than private John and Edward in a small house and common day's work: but the things of life are the same to both; the sum total of both is the same. Why all this deference to Alfred, and Scanderbeg, and Gustavus? Suppose they were virtuous—did they wear out virtue? As great a stake depends on your private act to-day, as followed their public and renowned steps. When private men shall act with vast views, the lustre will be transferred from the actions of kings to those of gentlemen.

The world has been instructed by its kings, who have so magnetized the eyes of nations. It has been taught by this colossal symbol the mutual reverence that is due from man to man. The joyful loyalty with which men have everywhere suffered the king, the noble, or the great proprietor to walk among them by a law of his own, make his own scale of men and things, and reverse theirs, pay for benefits not with money but with honor, and represent the Law in his person, was the hieroglyphic by which they obscurely signified their consciousness of their own right and comeliness, the right of every man.

The magnetism which all original action exerts is explained when we inquire the reason of self-trust. Who is the Trustee? What is the aboriginal Self on which a universal reliance may be grounded? What is the nature and power of that science-baffling star, without parallax, without calculable elements, which shoots a ray of beauty even into trivial and impure actions, if the least mark of independence appear? The inquiry leads us to that source, at once the essence of genius, the essence of virtue, and the essence of life, which we call Spontaneity or Instinct. We denote this primary wisdom as Intuition, whilst all later teachings are tuitions. In that deep force, the last fact behind which analysis cannot go, all things find their common origin. For the sense of being which in calm hours rises, we know not how, in the soul, is not diverse from things, from space, from light, from time, from man, but one with them, and proceedeth obviously from the same source whence their life and being also proceedeth. We first share the life by which things exist, and afterwards see them as appearances in nature, and forget that we have shared their cause. Here is the fountain of action and of thought. Here are the lungs of that inspiration which giveth man wisdom, of that inspiration of man which cannot be denied without impiety and atheism. We lie in the lap of immense intelligence, which makes us organs of its activity and receivers of its truth. When we discern justice, when we discern truth, we do nothing of ourselves, but allow a passage to its beams. If we ask whence this comes, if we seek to pry into the soul that causes,—all metaphysics, all philosophy is at fault. Its presence or its absence is all we can affirm. Every man discerns between the voluntary acts of his mind, and his involuntary perceptions. And to his involuntary perceptions, he knows a perfect respect is due. He may err in the expression of them, but he knows that these things are so, like day and night, not to be disputed. All my wilful actions and acquisitions are but roving;—the most trivial reverie, the faintest native emotion, are domestic and divine. Thoughtless people contradict as readily the statement of perceptions as of opinions, or rather much more readily; for, they do not distinguish between perception and notion. They fancy that I choose to see this or that thing. But perception is not whimsical, but fatal. If I see a trait, my children will see it after me, and in course of time, all mankind,—although it may chance that no one has seen it before me. For my perception of it is as much a fact as the sun.

The relations of the soul to the Divine Spirit are so pure that it is profane to seek to interpose helps. It must be that when God speaketh, he should communicate not one thing, but all things; should fill the world with his voice; should scatter forth light, nature, time, souls, from the centre of the present thought; and new date and new create the whole. Whenever a mind is simple, and receives a Divine wisdom, then old things pass away,—means, teachers, texts, temples fall; it lives now and absorbs past and future into the present hour. All things are made sacred by relation to it,—one as much as another. All things are dissolved to their centre by their cause, and in the universal miracle petty and particular miracles disappear. This is and must be. If, therefore, a man claims to know and speak of God, and carries you backward to the phraseology of some old mouldered nation in another country, in another world, believe him not. Is the acorn better than the oak which is its fulness and completion? Is the parent better than the child into whom he has cast his ripened being? Whence then this worship of the past? The centuries are conspirators against the sanity and authority of the soul. Time and space are but physiological colors which the eye maketh: but the soul is light; where it is, is day; where it was, is night; and history is an impertinence and an injury, if it be anything more than a cheerful apologue or parable of my being and becoming.

Man is timid and apologetic. He is no longer upright. He dares not say "I think," "I am," but quotes some saint or sage. He is ashamed before the blade of grass or the blowing rose. These roses under my window make no reference to former roses or to better ones; they are for what they are; they exist with God to-day. There is no time to them. There is simply the rose; it is perfect in every moment of its existence. Before a leaf-bud has burst, its whole life acts; in the full-blown flower, there is no more; in the leafless root, there is no less. Its nature is satisfied, and it satisfies nature, in all moments alike. There is no time to it. But man postpones or remembers; he does not live in the present, but with reverted eye laments the past, or, heedless of the riches that surround him, stands on tiptoe to foresee the future. He cannot be happy and strong until he too lives with nature in the present, above time.

This should be plain enough. Yet see what strong intellects dare not yet hear God himself, unless he speak the phraseology of I know not what David, or Jeremiah, or Paul. We shall not always set so great a price on a few texts, on a few lives. We are like children who repeat by rote the sentences of grandames and tutors, and, as they grow older, of the men of talents and character they chance to see,—painfully recollecting the exact words they spoke; afterwards, when they come into the point of view which those had who uttered these sayings, they understand them, and are willing to let the words go; for, at any time, they can use words as good, when occasion comes. So was it with us, so will it be, if we proceed. If we live truly, we shall see truly. It is as easy for the strong man to be strong, as it is for the weak to be weak. When we have new perception, we shall gladly disburden the memory of its hoarded treasures as old rubbish. When a man lives with God, his voice shall be as sweet as the murmur of the brook and the rustle of the corn.

And now at last the highest truth on this subject remains unsaid; probably, cannot be said; for all that we say is the far off remembering of the intuition. That thought, by what I can now nearest approach to say it, is this. When good is near you, when you have life in yourself,—it is not by any known or appointed way; you shall not discern the foot-prints of any other; you shall not see the face of man; you shall not hear any name;—the way, the thought, the good shall be wholly strange and new. It shall exclude all other being. You take the way from man, not to man. All persons that ever existed are its fugitive ministers. There shall be no fear in it. Fear and hope are alike beneath it. It asks nothing. There is somewhat low even in hope. We are then in vision. There is nothing that can be called gratitude nor properly joy. The soul is raised over passion. It seeth identity and eternal causation. It is a perceiving that Truth and Right are. Hence it becomes a Tranquillity out of the knowing that all things go well. Vast spaces of nature; the Atlantic Ocean, the South Sea; vast intervals of time, years, centuries, are of no account. This which I think and feel, underlay that former state of life and circumstances, as it does underlie my present, and will always all circumstance, and what is called life, and what is called death.

Life only avails, not the having lived. Power ceases in the instant of repose; it resides in the moment of transition from a past to a new state; in the shooting of the gulf; in the darting to an aim. This one fact the world hates, that the soul *becomes*; for, that forever degrades the past; turns all riches to poverty; all reputation to a shame; confounds the saint with the rogue; shoves Jesus and Judas equally aside. Why then do we prate of self-reliance? Inasmuch as the soul is present, there will be power not confident but agent. To talk of reliance is a poor external way of speaking. Speak rather of that which relies, because it works and is. Who has more soul than I, masters me, though he should not raise his finger. Round him I must revolve by the gravitation of spirits; who has less, I rule with like facility. We fancy it rhetoric when we speak of eminent virtue. We do not yet see that virtue is Height, and that a man or a company of men plastic and permeable to principles, by the law of nature must overpower and ride all cities, nations, kings, rich men, poets, who are not.

This is the ultimate fact which we so quickly reach on this as on every topic, the resolution of all into the ever-blessed ONE. Virtue is the governor, the creator, the reality. All things real are so by so much of virtue as they contain. Hardship, husbandry, hunting, whaling, war, eloquence, personal weight, are somewhat, and engage my respect as examples of the soul's presence and impure action. I see the same law working in nature for conservation and growth. The poise of a planet, the bended tree recovering itself from the strong wind, the vital resources of every animal and vegetable, are also demonstrations of the self-sufficing, and therefore self-relying soul. All history from its highest to its trivial passages is the various record of this power.

Thus all concentrates; let us not rove; let us sit at home with the cause. Let us stun and astonish the intruding rabble of men and books and institutions by a simple declaration of the divine fact. Bid them take the shoes from off their feet, for God is here within. Let our simplicity judge them, and our docility to our own law demonstrate the poverty of nature and fortune beside our native riches.

But now we are a mob. Man does not stand in awe of man, nor is the soul admonished to stay at home, to put itself in communication with the internal ocean, but it goes abroad to beg a cup of water of the urns of men. We must go alone. Isolation must precede true society. I like the silent church before the service begins, better than any preaching. How far off, how cool, how chaste the persons look, begirt each one with a precinct or sanctuary. So let us always sit. Why should we assume the faults of our friend, or wife, or father, or child, because they sit around our hearth, or are said to have the same blood? All men have my blood, and I have all men's. Not for that will I adopt their petulance or folly, even to the extent of being ashamed of it. But your isolation must not be mechanical, but spiritual, that is, must be elevation. At times the whole world seems to be in conspiracy to importune you with emphatic trifles. Friend, client, child, sickness, fear, want, charity, all knock at once at thy closet door, and say, "Come out unto us."—Do not spill thy soul; do not descend; keep thy state; stay at home in thine own heaven; come not for a moment into their facts, into their hubbub of conflicting appearances, but let in the light of thy law on their confusion. The power men possess to annoy me, I give them by a weak curiosity. No man can come near me but through my act. "What we love that we have, but by desire we bereave ourselves of the love."

If we cannot at once rise to the sanctities of obedience and faith, let us at least resist our temptations, let us enter into the state of war, and wake Thor and Woden, courage and constancy in our Saxon breasts. This is to be done in our smooth times by speaking the truth. Check this lying hospitality and lying affection. Live no longer to the expectation of these deceived and deceiving people with whom we converse. Say to them, O father, O mother, O wife, O brother, O friend, I have lived with you after appearances hitherto. Henceforward I am the truth's. Be it known unto you that henceforward I obey no law less than the eternal law. I will have no covenants but proximities. I shall endeavour to nourish my parents, to support my family, to be the chaste husband of one wife,—but these relations I must fill after a new and unprecedented way. I appeal from your customs. I must be myself. I cannot break myself any longer for you, or you. If you can love me for what I am, we shall be the happier. If you cannot, I will still seek to deserve that you should. I must be myself. I will not hide my tastes or aversions. I will so trust that what is deep is holy, that I will do strongly before the sun and moon whatever inly rejoices me, and the heart appoints. If you are noble, I will love you; if you are not, I will not hurt you and myself by hypocritical attentions. If you are true, but not in the same truth with me, cleave to your companions; I will seek my own. I do this not selfishly, but humbly and truly. It is alike your interest and mine and all men's, however long we have dwelt in lies, to live in truth. Does this sound harsh today? You will soon love what is dictated by your nature as well as mine, and, if we follow the truth, it will bring us out safe at last.—But so you may give these friends pain. Yes, but I cannot sell my liberty and my power, to save their sensibility. Besides, all persons have their moments of reason when they look out into the region of absolute truth; then will they justify me and do the same thing.

The populace think that your rejection of popular standards is a rejection of all standard, and mere antinomianism; and the bold sensualist will use the name of philosophy to gild his crimes. But the law of consciousness abides. There are two confessionals, in one or the other of which we must be shriven. You may fulfil your round of duties by clearing yourself in the *direct*, or, in the *reflex* way. Consider whether you have satisfied your relations to father, mother, cousin, neighbor, town, cat, and dog; whether any of these can upbraid you. But I may also neglect this reflex standard, and absolve me to myself. I have my own stern claims and perfect circle. It denies the name of duty to many offices that are called duties. But if I can discharge its debts, it enables me to dispense with the popular code. If any one imagines that this law is lax, let him keep its commandment one day.

And truly it demands something godlike in him who has cast off the common motives of humanity, and has ventured to trust himself for a taskmaster. High be his heart, faithful his will, clear his sight, that he may in good earnest be doctrine, society, law to himself, that a simple purpose may be to him as strong as iron necessity is to others.

If any man consider the present aspects of what is called by distinction *society*, he will see the need of these ethics. The sinew and heart of man seem to be drawn out, and we are become timorous, desponding whimperers. We are afraid of truth, afraid of fortune, afraid of death, and afraid of each other. Our age yields no great and perfect persons. We want men and women who shall renovate life and our social state, but we see that most natures are insolvent; cannot satisfy their own wants, have an ambition out of all proportion to their practical force, and so do lean and beg day and night continually. Our housekeeping is mendicant, our arts, our occupations, our marriages, our religion we have not chosen, but society has chosen for us. We are parlor soldiers. The rugged battle of fate, where strength is born, we shun.

If our young men miscarry in their first enterprizes, they lose all heart. If the young merchant fails, men say he is *ruined*. If the finest genius studies at one of our colleges, and is not installed in an office within one year afterwards in the cities or suburbs of Boston or New York, it seems to his friends and to himself that he is right in being disheartened and in complaining the rest of his life. A sturdy lad from New Hampshire or Vermont, who in turn tries all the professions, who *teams it, farms it, peddles*, keeps a school, preaches, edits a newspaper, goes to Congress, buys a township, and so forth, in successive years, and always, like a cat, falls on his feet, is worth a hundred of these city dolls. He walks abreast with his days, and feels no shame in not "studying a profession," for he does not postpone his life, but lives already. He has not one chance, but a hundred chances. Let a stoic arise who shall reveal the resources of man, and tell men they are not leaning willows, but can and must detach themselves; that with the exercise of self-trust, new powers shall appear; that a man is the word made flesh, born to shed healing to the nations, that he should be ashamed of our compassion, and that the moment he acts from himself, tossing the laws, the books, idolatries, and customs out of the window,—we pity him no more but thank and revere him,—and that teacher shall restore the life of man to splendor, and make his name dear to all History.

It is easy to see that a greater self-reliance,—a new respect for the divinity in man,—must work a revolution in all the offices and relations of men; in their religion; in their education; in their pursuits; their modes of living; their association; in their property; in their speculative views.

1. In what prayers do men allow themselves! That which they call a holy office, is not so much as brave and manly. Prayer looks abroad and asks for some foreign addition to come through some foreign virtue, and loses itself in endless mazes of natural and supernatural, and mediatorial and miraculous. Prayer that craves a particular commodity,—anything less than all good, is vicious. Prayer is the contemplation of the facts of life from the highest point of view. It is the soliloquy of a beholding and jubilant soul. It is the spirit of God pronouncing his works good. But prayer as a means to effect a private end, is theft and meanness. It supposes dualism and not unity in nature and consciousness. As soon as the man is at one with God, he will not beg. He will then see prayer in all action. The prayer of the farmer kneeling in his field to weed it, the prayer of the rower kneeling with the stroke of his oar, are true prayers heard throughout nature, though for cheap ends. Caratach, in Fletcher's *Bonduca*, when admonished to inquire the mind of the god Audate, replies,

> "His hidden meaning lies in our endeavours,
> Our valors are our best gods."

Another sort of false prayers are our regrets. Discontent is the want of self-reliance: it is infirmity of will. Regret calamities, if you can thereby help the sufferer; if not, attend your own work, and already the evil begins to be repaired. Our sympathy is just as base. We come to them who weep foolishly, and sit down and cry for company, instead of imparting to them truth and health in rough electric shocks, putting them once more in communication with the soul. The secret of fortune is joy in our hands. Welcome evermore to gods and men is the self-helping man. For him all doors are flung wide. Him all tongues greet, all honors crown, all eyes follow with desire. Our love goes out to him and embraces him, because he did not need it. We solicitously and apologetically caress and celebrate him, because he held on his way and scorned our disapprobation. The gods love him because men hated him. "To the persevering mortal," said Zoroaster, "the blessed Immortals are swift."

As men's prayers are a disease of the will, so are their creeds a disease of the intellect. They say with those foolish Israelites, "Let not God speak to us, lest we die. Speak thou, speak any man with us, and we will obey." Everywhere I am bereaved of meeting God in my brother, because he has shut his own temple doors, and recites fables merely of his brother's, or his brother's brother's God. Every new mind is a new classification. If it prove a mind of uncommon activity and power, a Locke, a Lavoisier, a Hutton, a Bentham, a Spurzheim, it imposes its classification on other men, and lo! a new system. In proportion always to the depth of the thought, and so to the number of the objects it touches and brings within reach of the pupil, is his complacency. But chiefly is this apparent in creeds and churches, which are also classifications of some powerful mind acting on the elemental thought of Duty, and man's relation to the Highest. Such is Calvinism, Quakerism, Swedenborgianism. The pupil takes the same delight in subordinating everything to the new terminology as a girl who has just learned botany, in seeing a new earth and new seasons thereby. It will happen for a time, that the pupil will feel a real debt to the teacher,—will find his intellectual power has grown by the study of his writings. This will continue until he has exhausted his master's mind. But in all unbalanced minds, the classification is idolized, passes for the end, and not for a speedily exhaustible means, so that the walls of the system blend to their eye in the remote horizon with the walls of the universe; the luminaries of heaven seem to them hung on the arch their master built. They cannot imagine how you aliens have any right to see,—how you can see: "It must be somehow that you stole the light from us." They do not yet perceive, that light, unsystematic, indomitable, will break into any cabin, even into theirs. Let them chirp awhile and call it their own. If they are honest and do well, presently their neat new pinfold will be too strait and low, will crack, will lean, will rot and vanish, and the immortal light, all young and joyful, million-orbed, million-colored, will beam over the universe as on the first morning.

2. It is for want of self-culture that the idol of Travelling, the idol of Italy, of England, of Egypt, remains for all educated Americans. They who made England, Italy, or Greece venerable in the imagination, did so not by rambling round creation as a moth round a lamp, but by sticking fast where they were, like an axis of the earth. In manly hours, we feel that duty is our place, and that the merrymen of circumstance should follow as they may. The soul is no traveler: the wise man stays at home with the soul, and when his necessities, his duties, on any occasion call him from his house, or into foreign lands, he is at home still, and is not gadding abroad from himself, and shall make men sensible by the expression of his countenance, that he goes the missionary of wisdom and virtue, and visits cities and men like a sovereign, and not like an interloper or a valet.

I have no churlish objection to the circumnavigation of the globe, for the purposes of art, of study, and benevolence, so that the man is first domesticated, or does not go abroad with the hope of finding somewhat greater than he knows. He who travels to be amused, or to get somewhat which he does not carry, travels away from himself, and grows old even in youth among old things. In Thebes, in Palmyra, his will and mind have become old and dilapidated as they. He carries ruins to ruins.

Travelling is a fool's paradise. We owe to our first journeys the discovery that place is nothing. At home I dream that at Naples, at Rome, I can be intoxicated with beauty, and lose my sadness. I pack my trunk, embrace my friends, embark on the sea, and at last wake up in Naples, and there beside me is the stern Fact, the sad self, unrelenting, identical, that I fled from. I seek the Vatican, and the palaces. I affect to be intoxicated with sights and suggestions, but I am not intoxicated. My giant goes with me wherever I go.

3. But the rage of travelling is itself only a symptom of a deeper unsoundness affecting the whole intellectual action. The

intellect is vagabond, and the universal system of education fosters restlessness. Our minds travel when our bodies are forced to stay at home. We imitate; and what is imitation but the travelling of the mind? Our houses are built with foreign taste; our shelves are garnished with foreign ornaments; our opinions, our tastes, our whole minds lean, and follow the Past and the Distant, as the eyes of a maid follow her mistress. The soul created the arts wherever they have flourished. It was in his own mind that the artist sought his model. It was an application of his own thought to the thing to be done and the conditions to be observed. And why need we copy the Doric or the Gothic model? Beauty, convenience, grandeur of thought, and quaint expression are as near to us as to any, and if the American artist will study with hope and love the precise thing to be done by him, considering the climate, the soil, the length of the day, the wants of the people, the habit and form of the government, he will create a house in which all these will find themselves fitted, and taste and sentiment will be satisfied also.

Insist on yourself; never imitate. Your own gift you can present every moment with the cumulative force of a whole life's cultivation; but of the adopted talent of another, you have only an extemporaneous, half possession. That which each can do best, none but his Maker can teach him. No man yet knows what it is, nor can, till that person has exhibited it. Where is the master who could have taught Shakspeare? Where is the master who could have instructed Franklin, or Washington, or Bacon, or Newton? Every great man is an unique. The Scipionism of Scipio is precisely that part he could not borrow. If any body will tell me whom the great man imitates in the original crisis when he performs a great act, I will tell him who else than himself can teach him. Shakspeare will never be made by the study of Shakspeare. Do that which is assigned thee, and thou canst not hope too much or dare too much. There is at this moment, there is for me an utterance bare and grand as that of the colossal chisel of Phidias, or trowel of the Egyptians, or the pen of Moses, or Dante, but different from all these. Not possibly will the soul all rich, all eloquent, with thousand-cloven tongue, deign to repeat itself; but if you can hear what these patriarchs say, surely I can reply to them in the same pitch of voice: for the ear and the tongue are two organs of one nature. Dwell up there in the simple and noble regions of thy life, obey thy heart, and thou shalt reproduce the Foreworld again.

4. As our Religion, our Education, our Art look abroad, so does our spirit of society. All men plume themselves on the improvement of society, and no man improves.

Society never advances. It recedes as fast on one side as it gains on the other. Its progress is only apparent, like the workers of a treadmill. It undergoes continual changes: it is barbarous, it is civilized, it is christianized, it is rich, it is scientific; but this change is not amelioration. For everything that is given, something is taken. Society acquires new arts and loses old instincts. What a contrast between the well-clad, reading, writing, thinking American, with a watch, a pencil, and a bill of exchange in his pocket, and the naked New Zealander, whose property is a club, a spear, a mat, and an undivided twentieth of a shed to sleep under. But compare the health of the two men, and you shall see that his aboriginal strength the white man has lost. If the traveller tell us truly, strike the savage with a broad axe, and in a day or two the flesh shall unite and heal as if you struck the blow into soft pitch, and the same blow shall send the white to his grave.

The civilized man has built a coach, but has lost the use of his feet. He is supported on crutches, but lacks so much support of muscle. He has a fine Geneva watch, but he has lost the skill to tell the hour by the sun. A Greenwich nautical almanac he has, and so being sure of the information when he wants it, the man in the street does not know a star in the sky. The solstice he does not observe; the equinox he knows as little; and the whole bright calendar of the year is without a dial in his mind. His note-books impair his memory; his libraries overload his wit; the insurance office increases the number of accidents; and it may be a question whether machinery does not encumber; whether we have not lost by refinement some energy, by a Christianity entrenched in establishments and forms, some vigor of wild virtue. For every Stoic was a Stoic; but in Christendom where is the Christian?

There is no more deviation in the moral standard than in the standard of height or bulk. No greater men are now than ever were. A singular equality may be observed between the great men of the first and of the last ages; nor can all the science, art, religion, and philosophy of the nineteenth century avail to educate greater men than Plutarch's heroes, three or four and twenty centuries ago. Not in time is the race progressive. Phocion, Socrates, Anaxagoras, Diogenes, are great men, but they leave no class. He who is really of their class will not be called by their name, but will be his own man, and, in his turn the founder of a sect. The arts and inventions of each period are only its costume, and do not invigorate men. The harm of the improved machinery may compensate its good. Hudson and Behring accomplished so much in their fishing-boats, as to astonish Parry and Franklin, whose equipment exhausted the resources of science and art. Galileo, with an opera-glass, discovered a more splendid series of facts than any one since. Columbus found the New World in an undecked boat. It is curious to see the periodical disuse and perishing of means and machinery which were introduced with loud laudation, a few years or centuries before. The great genius returns to essential man. We reckoned the improvements of the art of war among the triumphs of science, and yet Napoleon conquered Europe by the bivouac, which consisted of falling back on naked valor, and disencumbering it of all aids. The emperor held it impossible to make a perfect army, says Las Casas, "without abolishing our arms, magazines, commissaries, and carriages, until, in imitation of the Roman custom, the soldier should receive his supply of corn, grind it in his hand-mill, and bake his bread himself."

Society is a wave. The wave moves onward, but the water of which it is composed, does not. The same particle does not rise from the valley to the ridge. Its unity is only phenomenal. The persons who make up a nation to-day, next year die, and their experience with them.

And so the reliance on Property, including the reliance on governments which protect it, is the want of self-reliance. Men have looked away from themselves and at things so long, that they have come to esteem what they call the soul's progress, namely, the religious, learned, and civil institutions, as guards of property, and they deprecate assaults on these, because they feel them to be assaults on property. They measure their esteem of each other by what each has, and not by what each is. But a cultivated man becomes ashamed of his property, out of new respect for his being. Especially he hates what he has, if he see that it is accidental,—came to him by inheritance, or gift, or crime; then he feels that it is not having; it does not belong to him, has no root in him, and merely lies there, because no revolution or no robber takes it away. But that which a man is, does always by necessity acquire, and what the man acquires is permanent and living property, which does not wait the beck of rulers, or mobs, or revolutions, or fire, or storm, or bankruptcies, but perpetually renews itself wherever the man breathes. "Thy lot or portion of life," said the Caliph Ali, "is seeking after thee; therefore be at rest from seeking after it." Our dependence on these foreign goods leads us to our slavish respect for numbers. The political parties meet in numerous conventions; the greater the concourse, and with each new uproar of announcement—the Delegation from Essex! The Democrats from New Hampshire! The Whigs of Maine!—the young patriot feels himself stronger than before by a new thousand of eyes and arms. In like manner the reformers summon conventions, and vote and resolve in multitude. But not so, O friends! will the God deign to enter and inhabit you, but by a method precisely the reverse. It is only as a man puts off from himself all external support, and stands alone, that I see him to be strong and to prevail. He is weaker by every recruit to his banner. Is not a man better than a town? Ask nothing of men, and in the endless mutation, thou only firm column must presently appear the upholder of all that surrounds thee. He who knows that power is in the soul, that he is weak only because he has looked for good out of him and elsewhere, and so perceiving, throws himself unhesitatingly on his thought, instantly rights himself, stands in the erect position, commands his limbs, works miracles; just as a man who stands on his feet is stronger than a man who stands on his head.

So use all that is called Fortune. Most men gamble with her, and gain all, and lose all, as her wheel rolls. But do thou leave as unlawful these winnings, and deal with Cause and Effect, the chancellors of God. In the Will work and acquire, and thou hast chained the wheel of Chance, and shalt always drag her after thee. A political victory, a rise of rents, the recovery of your sick, or the return of your absent friend, or some other quiet external event, raises your spirits, and you think good days are preparing for you. Do not believe it. Nothing can bring you peace but yourself. Nothing can bring you peace but the triumph of principles.

SOURCE: Ralph Waldo Emerson. *Essays*. Boston: James Munroe and Company, 1841.

HENRY WADSWORTH LONGFELLOW

Henry Wadsworth Longfellow (1807–1882) was the most popular poet in America during the nineteenth century; though he has since been surpassed in popularity by Walt Whitman and Emily Dickinson, his steady rhythms, dramatic topics and catchy phrasings have remained part of American culture.

A Psalm of Life (1838)

WHAT THE HEART OF THE YOUNG MAN
SAID TO THE PSALMIST

Tell me not, in mournful numbers,
  Life is but an empty dream!—
For the soul is dead that slumbers,
  And things are not what they seem.

Life is real! Life is earnest!
  And the grave is not its goal;
Dust thou art, to dust returnest,
  Was not spoken of the soul.

Not enjoyment, and not sorrow,
  Is our destined end or way;
But to act, that each to-morrow
  Find us farther than to-day.

Art is long, and Time is fleeting,
  And our hearts, though stout and brave,
Still, like muffled drums, are beating
  Funeral marches to the grave.

In the world's broad field of battle,
    In the bivouac of Life,
Be not like dumb, driven cattle!
    Be a hero in the strife!

Trust no Future, howe'er pleasant!
    Let the dead Past bury its dead!
Act,—act in the living Present!
    Heart within, and God o'erhead!

Lives of great men all remind us
    We can make our lives sublime,
And, departing, leave behind us
    Footprints on the sands of time;

Footprints, that perhaps another,
    Sailing o'er life's solemn main,
A forlorn and shipwrecked brother,
    Seeing, shall take heart again.

Let us, then, be up and doing,
    With a heart for any fate;
Still achieving, still pursuing,
    Learn to labor and to wait.

The Wreck of the Hesperus (1839)

It was the schooner Hesperus,
    That sailed the wintry sea;
And the skipper had taken his little daughtèr,
    To bear him company.

Blue were her eyes as the fairy-flax,
    Her cheeks like the dawn of day,
And her bosom white as the hawthorn buds,
    That ope in the month of May.

The skipper he stood beside the helm,
    His pipe was in his mouth,
And he watched how the veering flaw did blow
    The smoke now West, now South.

Then up and spake an old Sailòr,
    Had sailed the Spanish Main,
"I pray thee put into yonder port,
    For I fear a hurricane.

"Last night, the moon had a golden ring,
    And to-night no moon we see!"
The skipper, he blew a whiff from his pipe,
    And a scornful laugh laughed he.

Colder and louder blew the wind,
    A gale from the Northeast,
The snow fell hissing in the brine,
    And the billows frothed like yeast.

Down came the storm, and smote amain
    The vessel in its strength;
She shuddered and paused, like a frighted steed,
    Then leaped her cable's length.

"Come hither! come hither! my little daughtèr,
    And do not tremble so;
For I can weather the roughest gale
    That ever wind did blow."

He wrapped her warm in his seaman's coat
    Against the stinging blast;
He cut a rope from a broken spar,
    And bound her to the mast.

"O father! I hear the church-bells ring,
    Oh say, what may it be?"
"'T is a fog-bell on a rock-bound coast!"—
    And he steered for the open sea.

"O father! I hear the sound of guns,
    Oh say, what may it be?"
"Some ship in distress, that cannot live
    In such an angry sea!"

"O father! I see a gleaming light,
Oh say, what may it be?"
But the father answered never a word,
A frozen corpse was he.

Lashed to the helm, all stiff and stark,
With his face turned to the skies,
The lantern gleamed through the gleaming snow
On his fixed and glassy eyes.

Then the maiden clasped her hands and prayed
That savèd she might be;
And she thought of Christ, who stilled the wave,
On the Lake of Galilee.

And fast through the midnight dark and drear,
Through the whistling sleet and snow,
Like a sheeted ghost, the vessel swept
Tow'rds the reef of Norman's Woe.

And ever the fitful gusts between
A sound came from the land;
It was the sound of the trampling surf,
On the rocks and the hard sea-sand.

The breakers were right beneath her bows,
She drifted a dreary wreck,
And a whooping billow swept the crew
Like icicles from her deck.

She struck where the white and fleecy waves
Looked soft as carded wool,
But the cruel rocks, they gored her side
Like the horns of an angry bull.

Her rattling shrouds, all sheathed in ice,
With the masts went by the board;
Like a vessel of glass, she stove and sank,
Ho! ho! the breakers roared!

At daybreak, on the bleak sea-beach,
A fisherman stood aghast,
To see the form of a maiden fair
Lashed close to a drifting mast.

The salt sea was frozen on her breast,
The salt tears in her eyes;
And he saw her hair, like the brown sea-weed,
On the billows fall and rise.

Such was the wreck of the Hesperus,
In the midnight and the snow!
Christ save us all from a death like this,
On the reef of Norman's Woe!

Beware! (1839)

(TRANSLATED FROM THE ANONYMOUS GERMAN "HÜT DU DICH!")

I know a maiden fair to see,
Take care!
She can both false and friendly be,
Beware! Beware!
Trust her not,
She is fooling thee!

She has two eyes, so soft and brown,
Take care!
She gives a side-glance and looks down,
Beware! Beware!
Trust her not,
She is fooling thee!

And she has hair of a golden hue,
Take care!
And what she says, it is not true,
Beware! Beware!
Trust her not,
She is fooling thee!

She has a bosom as white as snow,
Take care!
She knows how much it is best to show,
Beware! Beware!
Trust her not,
She is fooling thee!

She gives thee a garland woven fair,
Take care!
It is a fool's-cap for thee to wear,
Beware! Beware!
Trust her not,
She is fooling thee!

The Rainy Day (1841)

The day is cold, and dark, and dreary;
It rains, and the wind is never weary;
The vine still clings to the mouldering wall,
But at every gust the dead leaves fall,
And the day is dark and dreary.

My life is cold, and dark, and dreary;
It rains, and the wind is never weary;
My thoughts still cling to the mouldering Past,
But the hopes of youth fall thick in the blast,
And the days are dark and dreary.

Be still, sad heart! and cease repining;
Behind the clouds is the sun still shining;
Thy fate is the common fate of all,
Into each life some rain must fall,
Some days must be dark and dreary.

The Slave's Dream (1842)

Beside the ungathered rice he lay,
His sickle in his hand;
His breast was bare, his matted hair

Was buried in the sand.
Again, in the mist and shadow of sleep,
He saw his Native Land.

Wide through the landscape of his dreams
The lordly Niger flowed;
Beneath the palm-trees on the plain
Once more a king he strode;
And heard the tinkling caravans
Descend the mountain road.

He saw once more his dark-eyed queen
Among her children stand;
They clasped his neck, they kissed his cheeks,
They held him by the hand!—
A tear burst from the sleeper's lids
And fell into the sand.

And then at furious speed he rode
Along the Niger's bank;
His bridle-reins were golden chains,
And, with a martial clank,
At each leap he could feel his scabbard of steel
Smiting his stallion's flank.

Before him, like a blood-red flag,
The bright flamingoes flew;
From morn till night he followed their flight,
O'er plains where the tamarind grew,
Till he saw the roofs of Caffre huts,
And the ocean rose to view.

At night he heard the lion roar,
And the hyena scream,
And the river-horse, as he crushed the reeds
Beside some hidden stream;
And it passed, like a glorious roll of drums,
Through the triumph of his dream.

The forests, with their myriad tongues,
Shouted of liberty;

And the Blast of the Desert cried aloud,
  With a voice so wild and free,
That he started in his sleep and smiled
  At their tempestuous glee.

He did not feel the driver's whip,
  Nor the burning heat of day;
For Death had illumined the Land of Sleep,
  And his lifeless body lay
A worn-out fetter, that the soul
  Had broken and thrown away!

The Day Is Done (1844)

The day is done, and the darkness
  Falls from the wings of Night,
As a feather wafted downward
  From an eagle in his flight.

I see the lights of the village
  Gleam through the rain and the mist,
And a feeling of sadness comes o'er me
  That my soul cannot resist:

A feeling of sadness and longing,
  That is not akin to pain,
And resembles sorrow only
  As the mist resembles the rain.

Come, read to me some poem,
  Some simple and heartfelt lay,
That shall soothe this restless feeling,
  And banish the thoughts of day.

Not from the grand old masters,
  Not from the bards sublime,
Whose distant footsteps echo
  Through the corridors of Time.

For, like the strains of martial music,
Their mighty throughts suggest
Life's endless toil and endeavor;
And to-night I long for rest.

Read from the humbler poet,
Whose songs gushed from his heart,
As showers from the clouds of summer,
Or tears from the eyelids start;

Who, through long days of labor,
And nights devoid of ease,
Still heard in his soul the music
Of wonderful melodies.

Such songs have power to quiet
The restless pulse of care,
And come like the benediction
That follows after prayer.

Then read the treasured volume
The poem of thy choice,
And lend to the rhyme of the poet
The beauty of thy voice.

And the night shall be filled with music,
And the cares, that infest the day,
Shall fold their tents, like the Arabs,
And as silently steal away.

The Arrow and the Song (1845)

I shot an arrow into the air,
It fell to earth, I knew not where;
For, so swiftly it flew, the sight
Could not follow it in its flight.

I breathed a song into the air,
It fell to earth, I knew not where;

For who has sight so keen and strong,
That it can follow the flight of song?

Long, long afterward, in an oak
I found the arrow, still unbroke;
And the song, from beginning to end,
I found again in the heart of a friend.

The Ladder of Saint Augustine (1850)

Saint Augustine! well hast thou said,
  That of our vices we can frame
A ladder, if we will but tread
  Beneath our feet each deed of shame!

All common things, each day's events,
  That with the hour begin and end,
Our pleasures and our discontents,
  Are rounds by which we may ascend.

The low desire, the base design,
  That makes another's virtues less;
The revel of the ruddy wine,
  And all occasions of excess;

The longing for ignoble things;
  The strife for triumph more than truth;
The hardening of the heart, that brings
  Irreverence for the dreams of youth;

All thoughts of ill; all evil deeds,
  That have their root in thoughts of ill;
Whatever hinders or impedes
  The action of the nobler will;—

All these must first be trampled down
  Beneath our feet, if we would gain
In the bright fields of fair renown
  The right of eminent domain.

We have not wings, we cannot soar;
But we have feet to scale and climb
By slow degrees, by more and more,
The cloudy summits of our time.

The mighty pyramids of stone
That wedge-like cleave the desert airs,
When nearer seen, and better known,
Are but gigantic flights of stairs.

The distant mountains, that uprear
Their solid bastions to the skies,
Are crossed by pathways, that appear
As we to higher levels rise.

The heights by great men reached and kept
Were not attained by sudden flight,
But they, while their companions slept,
Were toiling upward in the night.

Standing on what too long we bore
With shoulders bent and downcast eyes,
We may discern—unseen before—
A path to higher destinies,

Nor deem the irrevocable Past,
As wholly wasted, wholly vain,
If, rising on its wrecks, at last
To something nobler we attain.

The Children's Hour (1859)

Between the dark and the daylight,
When the night is beginning to lower,
Comes a pause in the day's occupations,
That is known as the Children's Hour.

I hear in the chamber above me
The patter of little feet,
The sound of a door that is opened,
And voices soft and sweet.

From my study I see in the lamplight,
 Descending the broad hall stair,
Grave Alice, and laughing Allegra,
 And Edith with golden hair.

A whisper, and then a silence:
 Yet I know by their merry eyes
They are plotting and planning together
 To take me by surprise.

A sudden rush from the stairway,
 A sudden raid from the hall!
By three doors left unguarded
 They enter my castle wall!

They climb up into my turret
 O'er the arms and back of my chair;
If I try to escape, they surround me;
 They seem to be everywhere.

They almost devour me with kisses,
 Their arms about me entwine,
Till I think of the Bishop of Bingen
 In his Mouse-Tower on the Rhine!

Do you think, O blue-eyed banditti,
 Because you have scaled the wall,
Such an old mustache as I am
 Is not a match for you all!

I have you fast in my fortress,
 And will not let you depart,
But put you down into the dungeon
 In the round-tower of my heart.

And there will I keep you forever,
 Yes, forever and a day,
Till the walls shall crumble to ruin,
 And moulder in dust away!

Paul Revere's Ride (1860)

(THE LANDLORD'S TALE IN PART FIRST
OF *TALES OF A WAYSIDE INN*)

Listen, my children, and you shall hear
Of the midnight ride of Paul Revere,
On the eighteenth of April, in Seventy-five;
Hardly a man is now alive
Who remembers that famous day and year.

He said to his friend, "If the British march
By land or sea from the town to-night,
Hang a lantern aloft in the belfry arch
Of the North Church tower as a signal light,—
One, if by land, and two, if by sea;
And I on the opposite shore will be,
Ready to ride and spread the alarm
Through every Middlesex village and farm,
For the country folk to be up and to arm."

Then he said, "Good night!" and with muffled oar
Silently rowed to the Charlestown shore,
Just as the moon rose over the bay,
Where swinging wide at her moorings lay
The Somerset, British man-of-war;
A phantom ship, with each mast and spar
Across the moon like a prison bar,
And a huge black hulk, that was magnified
By its own reflection in the tide.

Meanwhile, his friend, through alley and street,
Wanders and watches with eager ears,
Till in the silence around him he hears
The muster of men at the barrack door,
The sound of arms, and the tramp of feet,
And the measured tread of the grenadiers,
Marching down to their boats on the shore.

Then he climbed the tower of the Old North Church,
By the wooden stairs, with stealthy tread,
To the belfry-chamber overhead,

And startled the pigeons from their perch
On the sombre rafters, that round him made
Masses and moving shapes of shade,—
By the trembling ladder, steep and tall,
To the highest window in the wall,
Where he paused to listen and look down
A moment on the roofs of the town,
And the moonlight flowing over all.

Beneath, in the churchyard, lay the dead,
In their night-encampment on the hill,
Wrapped in silence so deep and still
That he could hear, like a sentinel's tread,
The watchful night-wind, as it went
Creeping along from tent to tent,
And seeming to whisper, "All is well!"
A moment only he feels the spell
Of the place and the hour, and the secret dread
Of the lonely belfry and the dead;
For suddenly all his thoughts are bent
On a shadowy something far away,
Where the river widens to meet the bay,—
A line of black that bends and floats
On the rising tide, like a bridge of boats.

Meanwhile, impatient to mount and ride,
Booted and spurred, with a heavy stride
On the opposite shore walked Paul Revere.
Now he patted his horse's side,
Now gazed at the landscape far and near,
Then, impetuous, stamped the earth,
And turned and tightened his saddle-girth;
But mostly he watched with eager search
The belfry-tower of the Old North Church,
As it rose above the graves on the hill,
Lonely and spectral and sombre and still.
And lo! as he looks, on the belfry's height
A glimmer, and then a gleam of light!
He springs to the saddle, the bridle he turns,
But lingers and gazes, till full on his sight
A second lamp in the belfry burns!

A hurry of hoofs in a village street,
A shape in the moonlight, a bulk in the dark,
And beneath, from the pebbles, in passing, a spark
Struck out by a steed flying fearless and fleet:
That was all! And yet, through the gloom and the light,
The fate of a nation was riding that night;
And the spark struck out by that steed, in his flight,
Kindled the land into flame with its heat.

He has left the village and mounted the steep,
And beneath him, tranquil and broad and deep,
Is the Mystic, meeting the ocean tides;
And under the alders that skirt its edge,
Now soft on the sand, now loud on the ledge,
Is heard the tramp of his steed as he rides.

It was twelve by the village clock,
When he crossed the bridge into Medford town.
He heard the crowing of the cock,
And the barking of the farmer's dog,
And felt the damp of the river fog,
That rises after the sun goes down.

It was one by the village clock,
When he galloped into Lexington.
He saw the gilded weathercock
Swim in the moonlight as he passed,
And the meeting-house windows, blank and bare,
Gaze at him with a spectral glare,
As if they already stood aghast
At the bloody work they would look upon.

It was two by the village clock,
When he came to the bridge in Concord town.
He heard the bleating of the flock,
And the twitter of birds among the trees,
And felt the breath of the morning breeze
Blowing over the meadows brown.
And one was safe and asleep in his bed
Who at the bridge would be first to fall,
Who that day would be lying dead,
Pierced by a British musket-ball.

You know the rest. In the books you have read,
How the British Regulars fired and fled,—
How the farmers gave them ball for ball,
From behind each fence and farm-yard wall,
Chasing the red-coats down the lane,
Then crossing the fields to emerge again
Under the trees at the turn of the road,
And only pausing to fire and load.

So through the night rode Paul Revere;
And so through the night went his cry of alarm
To every Middlesex village and farm,—
A cry of defiance and not of fear,
A voice in the darkness, a knock at the door,
And a word that shall echo forevermore!
For, borne on the night-wind of the Past,
Through all our history, to the last,
In the hour of darkness and peril and need,
The people will waken and listen to hear
The hurrying hoof-beats of that steed,
And the midnight message of Paul Revere.

SOURCE: Henry Wadsworth Longfellow. *Favorite Poems*. Edited by Stanley Appelbaum. New York: Dover Publications, 1992.

Killed at the Ford (1866)

This poem was published shortly after the conclusion of the Civil War; Longfellow said it was not based on an actual event.

He is dead, the beautiful youth,
The heart of honor, the tongue of truth,
He, the life and light of us all,
Whose voice was blithe as a bugle-call,
Whom all eyes followed with one consent,
The cheer of whose laugh, and whose pleasant word,
Hashed all murmurs of discontent.

Only last night, as we rode along,
Down the dark of the mountain gap,
To visit the picket-guard at the ford,

Little dreaming of any mishap,
He was humming the words of some old song:
"Two red roses he had on his cap
And another he bore at the point of his sword."

Sudden and swift a whistling ball
Came out of a wood, and the voice was still;
Something I heard in the darkness fall,
And for a moment my blood grew chill;
I spake in a whisper, as he who speaks
In a room where some one is lying dead;
But he made no answer to what I said.

We lifted him up to his saddle again,
And through the mire and the mist and the rain
Carried him back to the silent camp,
And laid him as if asleep on his bed;
And I saw by the light of the surgeon's lamp
Two white roses upon his cheeks,
And one, just over his heart, blood-red!

And I saw in a vision how far and fleet
That fatal bullet went speeding forth,
Till it reached a town in the distant North,
Till it reached a house in a sunny street,
Till it reached a heart that ceased to beat
Without a murmur, without a cry;
And a bell was tolled, in that far-off town,
For one who had passed from cross to crown,
And the neighbors wondered that she should die.

SOURCE: *The Atlantic Monthly*. April 1866.

EDGAR ALLAN POE

Born in 1809 in Boston, Edgar Allan Poe, who lived a difficult and impoverished life, has become one of the most popular of American authors, particularly for his mystery stories, which were written in a peculiar literary voice all his own. The narrator of "William Wilson" is an English ne'er-do-well who recounts the torments he has faced from a contemporary with the same name.

William Wilson (1839)

What say of it? what say CONSCIENCE *grim,*
That spectre in my path?
—CHAMBERLAYNE'S *PHARRONIDA*

LET ME CALL myself, for the present, William Wilson. The fair page now lying before me need not be sullied with my real appellation. This has been already too much an object for the scorn—for the horror—for the detestation of my race. To the uttermost regions of the globe have not the indignant winds bruited its unparalleled infamy? Oh, outcast of all outcasts most abandoned!—to the earth art thou not forever dead? to its honors, to its flowers, to its golden aspirations?—and a cloud, dense, dismal, and limitless, does it not hang eternally between thy hopes and heaven?

I would not, if I could, here or to-day, embody a record of my later years of unspeakable misery, and unpardonable crime. This epoch—these later years—took unto themselves a sudden elevation in turpitude, whose origin alone it is my present purpose to assign. Men usually grow base by degrees. From me, in an instant, all virtue dropped bodily as a mantle. From comparatively trivial wickedness I passed, with the stride of a giant, into more than the enormities of an Elah-Gabalus. What chance—what one event brought this evil thing to pass, bear with me while I relate. Death approaches; and the shadow which foreruns him has thrown a softening influence over my spirit. I long, in passing through the dim valley, for the sympathy—I had nearly said for the pity—of my fellow men. I would fain have them believe that I have been, in some measure, the slave of circumstances beyond human control. I would wish them to seek out for me, in the details I am about to give, some little oasis of *fatality* amid a wilderness of error. I would have them allow—what they cannot refrain from allowing—that, although temptation may have erewhile existed as great, man was never *thus*, at least, tempted before—certainly, never *thus* fell. And is it therefore that he has never thus suffered? Have I not indeed been living in a dream? And am I not now dying a victim to the horror and the mystery of the wildest of all sublunary visions?

I am the descendant of a race whose imaginative and easily excitable temperament has at all times rendered them remarkable; and, in my earliest infancy, I gave evidence of having fully inherited the family character. As I advanced in years it was more strongly developed; becoming, for many reasons, a cause of serious disquietude to my friends, and of positive injury to myself. I grew self-willed, addicted to the wildest caprices, and a prey to the most ungovernable passions. Weak-minded, and beset with constitutional infirmities akin to my own, my parents could do but little to check the evil propensities which distinguished me. Some feeble and ill-directed efforts resulted in complete failure on their part, and, of course, in total triumph on mine. Thenceforward my voice was a household law; and at an age when few children have abandoned their leading-strings, I was left to the guidance of my own will, and became, in all but name, the master of my own actions.

My earliest recollections of a school-life, are connected with a large, rambling, Elizabethan house, in a misty-looking village of England, where were a vast number of gigantic and gnarled trees, and where all the houses were excessively ancient. In truth, it was a dream-like and spirit-soothing place, that venerable old town. At this moment, in fancy, I feel the refreshing chilliness of its deeply-shadowed avenues, inhale the fragrance of its thousand shrubberies, and thrill anew with undefinable delight, at the deep hollow note of the church-bell, breaking, each hour, with sullen and sudden roar, upon the stillness of the dusky atmosphere in which the fretted Gothic steeple lay imbedded and asleep.

It gives me, perhaps, as much of pleasure as I can now in any manner experience, to dwell upon minute recollections of the school and its concerns. Steeped in misery as I am—misery, alas! only too real—I shall be pardoned for seeking relief, however slight and temporary, in the weakness of a few rambling details. These, moreover, utterly trivial, and even ridiculous in themselves, assume, to my fancy, adventitious importance, as connected with a period and a locality when and where I recognise the first ambiguous monitions of the destiny which afterwards so fully overshadowed me. Let me then remember.

The house, I have said, was old and irregular. The grounds were extensive, and a high and solid brick wall, topped with a bed of mortar and broken glass, encompassed the whole. This prison-like rampart formed the limit of our domain; beyond it we saw but thrice a week—once every Saturday afternoon, when, attended by two ushers, we were permitted to take brief walks in a body through some of the neighbouring fields—and twice during Sunday, when we were paraded in the same formal manner to the morning and evening service in the one church of the village. Of this church the principal of our school was pastor. With how deep a spirit of wonder and perplexity was I wont to regard him from our remote pew in the gallery, as, with step solemn and slow, he ascended the pulpit! This reverend man, with countenance so demurely benign, with robes so glossy and so clerically flowing, with wig so minutely powdered, so rigid and so vast,—-could this be he who, of late, with sour visage, and in snuffy habiliments, administered, ferule in hand, the Draconian laws of the academy? Oh, gigantic paradox, too utterly monstrous for solution!

At an angle of the ponderous wall frowned a more ponderous gate. It was riveted and studded with iron bolts, and surmounted with jagged iron spikes. What impressions of deep awe did it inspire! It was never opened save for the three periodical egressions and ingressions already mentioned; then, in every creak of its mighty hinges, we found a plenitude of mystery—a world of matter for solemn remark, or for more solemn meditation.

The extensive enclosure was irregular in form, having many capacious recesses. Of these, three or four of the largest constituted the play-ground. It was level, and covered with fine hard gravel. I well remember it had no trees, nor benches, nor any thing similar within it. Of course it was in the rear of the house. In front lay a small parterre, planted with box and other shrubs; but through this sacred division we passed only upon rare occasions indeed—such as a first advent to school or final departure thence, or perhaps, when a parent or friend having called for us, we joyfully took our way home for the Christmas or Midsummer holydays.

But the house!—how quaint an old building was this!—to me how veritably a palace of enchantment! There was really no end to its windings—to its incomprehensible subdivisions. It was difficult, at any given time, to say with certainty upon which of its two stories one happened to be. From each room to every other there were sure to be found three or four steps either in ascent or descent. Then the lateral branches were innumerable—inconceivable—and so returning in upon themselves, that our most exact ideas in regard to the whole mansion were not very far different from those with which we pondered upon infinity. During the five years of my residence here, I was never able to ascertain with precision, in what remote locality lay the little sleeping apartment assigned to myself and some eighteen or twenty other scholars.

The school-room was the largest in the house—I could not help thinking, in the world. It was very long, narrow, and dismally low, with pointed Gothic windows and a ceiling of oak. In a remote and terror-inspiring angle was a square enclosure of eight or ten feet, comprising the *sanctum*, "during hours," of our principal, the Reverend Dr. Bransby. It was a solid structure, with massy door, sooner than open which in the absence of the "Dominic," we would all have willingly perished by the *peine forte et dure.*[1] In other angles were two other similar boxes, far less reverenced, indeed, but still greatly matters of awe. One of these was the pulpit of the "classical" usher, one of the "English and mathematical." Interspersed about the room, crossing and recrossing in endless irregularity, were innumerable benches and desks, black, ancient, and time-worn, piled desperately with much-bethumbed books, and so beseamed with initial letters, names at full length, grotesque figures, and other multiplied efforts of the knife, as to have entirely lost what little of original form might have been their portion in days long departed. A huge bucket with water stood at one extremity of the room, and a clock of stupendous dimensions at the other.

Encompassed by the massy walls of this venerable academy, I passed, yet not in tedium or disgust, the years of the third lustrum

1. *peine forte et dure:* being pressed to death

of my life. The teeming brain of childhood requires no external world of incident to occupy or amuse it; and the apparently dismal monotony of a school was replete with more intense excitement than my riper youth has derived from luxury, or my full manhood from crime. Yet I must believe that my first mental development had in it much of the uncommon—even much of the *outré*. Upon mankind at large the events of very early existence rarely leave in mature age any definite impression. All is gray shadow—a weak and irregular remembrance—an indistinct regathering of feeble pleasures and phantasmagoric pains. With me this is not so. In childhood I must have felt with the energy of a man what I now find stamped upon memory in lines as vivid, as deep, and as durable as the *exergues*[2] of the Carthaginian medals.

Yet in fact—in the fact of the world's view—how little was there to remember! The morning's awakening, the nightly summons to bed; the connings, the recitations; the periodical half-holidays, and perambulations; the play-ground, with its broils, its pastimes, its intrigues;—these, by a mental sorcery long forgotten, were made to involve a wilderness of sensation, a world of rich incident, an universe of varied emotion, of excitement the most passionate and spirit-stirring. *"Oh, le bon temps, que ce siècle de fer!"*[3]

In truth, the ardor, the enthusiasm, and the imperiousness of my disposition, soon rendered me a marked character among my schoolmates, and by slow, but natural gradations, gave me an ascendancy over all not greatly older than myself;—over all with a single exception. This exception was found in the person of a scholar, who, although no relation, bore the same Christian and surname as myself;—a circumstance, in fact, little remarkable; for, notwithstanding a noble descent, mine was one of those everyday appellations which seem, by prescriptive right, to have been, time out of mind, the common property of the mob. In this narrative I have therefore designated myself as William Wilson,—a fictitious title not very dissimilar to the real. My namesake alone, of those who in school phraseology constituted "our set," presumed to compete with me in the studies of the class—in the sports and broils of the play-ground—to refuse implicit belief in my assertions, and submission to my will—indeed, to interfere with my arbitrary dictation in any respect whatsoever. If there is on earth a supreme

2. *exergues:* inscriptions

3. *"Oh, le bon temps, que ce siècle de fer!"*: "Oh, what a good time that iron age was!"

and unqualified despotism, it is the despotism of a master mind in boyhood over the less energetic spirits of its companions.

Wilson's rebellion was to me a source of the greatest embarrassment;—the more so as, in spite of the bravado with which in public I made a point of treating him and his pretensions, I secretly felt that I feared him, and could not help thinking the equality which he maintained so easily with myself, a proof of his true superiority; since not to be overcome cost me a perpetual struggle. Yet this superiority—even this equality—was in truth acknowledged by no one but myself; our associates, by some unaccountable blindness, seemed not even to suspect it. Indeed, his competition, his resistance, and especially his impertinent and dogged interference with my purposes, were not more pointed than private. He appeared to be destitute alike of the ambition which urged, and of the passionate energy of mind which enabled me to excel. In his rivalry he might have been supposed actuated solely by a whimsical desire to thwart, astonish, or mortify myself; although there were times when I could not help observing, with a feeling made up of wonder, abasement, and pique, that he mingled with his injuries, his insults, or his contradictions, a certain most inappropriate, and assuredly most unwelcome *affectionateness* of manner. I could only conceive this singular behavior to arise from a consummate self-conceit assuming the vulgar airs of patronage and protection.

Perhaps it was this latter trait in Wilson's conduct, conjoined with our identity of name, and the mere accident of our having entered the school upon the same day, which set afloat the notion that we were brothers, among the senior classes in the academy. These do not usually inquire with much strictness into the affairs of their juniors. I have before said, or should have said, that Wilson was not, in the most remote degree, connected with my family. But assuredly if we *had* been brothers we must have been twins; for, after leaving Dr. Bransby's, I casually learned that my namesake was born on the nineteenth of January, 1813—and this is a somewhat remarkable coincidence; for the day is precisely that of my own nativity.

It may seem strange that in spite of the continual anxiety occasioned me by the rivalry of Wilson, and his intolerable spirit of contradiction, I could not bring myself to hate him altogether. We had, to be sure, nearly every day a quarrel in which, yielding me publicly the palm of victory, he, in some manner, contrived to make me feel that it was he who had deserved it; yet a sense of pride on my part, and a veritable dignity on his own, kept us always upon what are called "speaking terms," while there were many points of strong congeniality in our tempers, operating to awake me in a sentiment which our position alone, perhaps, prevented from ripening into friendship. It is difficult, indeed, to define, or even to describe, my real feelings towards him. They formed a motley and heterogeneous admixture;—some petulant animosity, which was not yet hatred, some esteem, more respect, much fear, with a world of uneasy curiosity. To the moralist it will be unnecessary to say, in addition, that Wilson and myself were the most inseparable of companions.

It was no doubt the anomalous state of affairs existing between us, which turned all my attacks upon him, (and they were many, either open or covert) into the channel of banter or practical joke (giving pain while assuming the aspect of mere fun) rather than into a more serious and determined hostility. But my endeavours on this head were by no means uniformly successful, even when my plans were the most wittily concocted; for my namesake had much about him, in character, of that unassuming and quiet austerity which, while enjoying the poignancy of its own jokes, has no heel of Achilles in itself, and absolutely refuses to be laughed at. I could find, indeed, but one vulnerable point, and that, lying in a personal peculiarity, arising, perhaps, from constitutional disease, would have been spared by any antagonist less at his wit's end than myself;—my rival had a weakness in the faucial or guttural organs, which precluded him from raising his voice at any time *above a very low whisper*. Of this defect I did not fail to take what poor advantage lay in my power.

Wilson's retaliations in kind were many; and there was one form of his practical wit that disturbed me beyond measure. How his sagacity first discovered at all that so petty a thing would vex me, is a question I never could solve; but, having discovered, he habitually practised the annoyance. I had always felt aversion to my uncourtly patronymic, and its very common, if not plebeian praenomen. The words were venom in my ears; and when, upon the day of my arrival, a second William Wilson came also to the academy, I felt angry with him for bearing the name, and doubly disgusted with the name because a stranger bore it, who would be the cause of its twofold repetition, who would be constantly in my presence, and whose concerns, in the ordinary routine of the school business, must inevitably, on account of the detestable coincidence, be often confounded with my own.

The feeling of vexation thus engendered grew stronger with every circumstance tending to show resemblance, moral or physical, between my rival and myself. I had not then discovered the remarkable fact that we were of the same age; but I saw that we were of the same height, and I perceived that we were even singularly alike in general contour of person and outline of feature. I was galled, too, by the rumor touching a relationship, which had grown current in the upper forms. In a word, nothing could more seriously disturb me, (although I scrupulously concealed such disturbance,) than any allusion to a similarity of mind, person, or condition existing between us. But, in truth, I had no reason to believe that (with the exception of the matter of relationship, and in the case of Wilson himself,) this similarity had ever been made a subject of comment, or even observed at all by our schoolfellows. That *he* observed it in all its bearings, and as fixedly as I, was apparent; but that he could discover in such circumstances so fruitful a field of annoyance, can only be attributed, as I said before, to his more than ordinary penetration.

His cue, which was to perfect an imitation of myself, lay both in words and in actions; and most admirably did he play his part. My dress it was an easy matter to copy; my gait and general manner were, without difficulty, appropriated; in spite of his constitutional defect, even my voice did not escape him. My louder tones were, of course, unattempted, but then the key, it was identical; *and his singular whisper, it grew the very echo of my own.*

How greatly this most exquisite portraiture harassed me, (for it could not justly be termed a caricature,) I will not now venture to describe. I had but one consolation—in the fact that the imitation, apparently, was noticed by myself alone, and that I had to endure only the knowing and strangely sarcastic smiles of my namesake himself. Satisfied with having produced in my bosom the intended effect, he seemed to chuckle in secret over the sting he had inflicted, and was characteristically disregardful of the public applause which the success of his witty endeavours might have so easily elicited. That the school, indeed, did not feel his design, perceive its accomplishment, and participate in his sneer, was, for many anxious months, a riddle I could not resolve. Perhaps the *gradation* of his copy rendered it not so readily perceptible; or, more possibly, I owed my security to the master air of the copyist, who, disdaining the letter, (which in a painting is all the obtuse can see,) gave but the full spirit of his original for my individual contemplation and chagrin.

I have already more than once spoken of the disgusting air of patronage which he assumed toward me, and of his frequent officious interference with my will. This interference often took the ungracious character of advice; advice not openly given, but hinted or insinuated. I received it with a repugnance which gained strength as I grew in years. Yet, at this distant day, let me do him the simple justice to acknowledge that I can recall no occasion when the suggestions of my rival were on the side of those errors or follies so usual to his immature age and seeming inexperience; that his moral sense, at least, if not his general talents and worldly wisdom, was far keener than my own; and that I might, to-day, have been a better, and thus a happier man, had I less frequently rejected the counsels embodied in those meaning whispers which I then but too cordially hated and too bitterly despised.

As it was, I at length grew restive in the extreme under his distasteful supervision, and daily resented more and more openly what I considered his intolerable arrogance. I have said that, in the first years of our connexion as schoolmates, my feelings in regard to him might have been easily ripened into friendship; but, in the latter months of my residence at the academy, although the intrusion of his ordinary manner had, beyond doubt, in some measure, abated, my sentiments, in nearly similar proportion, partook very much of positive hatred. Upon one occasion he saw this, I think, and afterwards avoided, or made a show of avoiding me.

It was about the same period, if I remember aright, that, in an altercation of violence with him, in which he was more than usually thrown off his guard, and spoke and acted with an openness of demeanor rather foreign to his nature, I discovered, or fancied I discovered, in his accent, his air, and general appearance, a something which first startled, and then deeply interested me, by bringing to mind dim visions of my earliest infancy—wild, confused and thronging memories of a time when memory herself was yet unborn. I cannot better describe the sensation which oppressed me than by saying that I could with difficulty shake off the belief of my having been acquainted with the being who stood before me, at some epoch very long ago—some point of the past even infinitely remote. The delusion, however, faded rapidly as it came;

and I mention it at all but to define the day of the last conversation I there held with my singular namesake.

The huge old house, with its countless subdivisions, had several large chambers communicating with each other, where slept the greater number of the students. There were, however, (as must necessarily happen in a building so awkwardly planned,) many little nooks or recesses, the odds and ends of the structure; and these the economic ingenuity of Dr. Bransby had also fitted up as dormitories; although, being the merest closets, they were capable of accommodating but a single individual. One of these small apartments was occupied by Wilson.

One night, about the close of my fifth year at the school, and immediately after the altercation just mentioned, finding every one wrapped in sleep, I arose from bed, and, lamp in hand, stole through a wilderness of narrow passages from my own bedroom to that of my rival. I had long been plotting one of those ill-natured pieces of practical wit at his expense in which I had hitherto been so uniformly unsuccessful. It was my intention, now, to put my scheme in operation, and I resolved to make him feel the whole extent of the malice with which I was imbued. Having reached his closet, I noiselessly entered, leaving the lamp, with a shade over it, on the outside. I advanced a step, and listened to the sound of his tranquil breathing. Assured of his being asleep, I returned, took the light, and with it again approached the bed. Close curtains were around it, which, in the prosecution of my plan, I slowly and quietly withdrew, when the bright rays fell vividly upon the sleeper, and my eyes, at the same moment, upon his countenance. I looked;—and a numbness, an iciness of feeling instantly pervaded my frame. My breast heaved, my knees tottered, my whole spirit became possessed with an objectless yet intolerable horror. Gasping for breath, I lowered the lamp in still nearer proximity to the face. Were these—*these* the lineaments of William Wilson? I saw, indeed, that they were his, but I shook as if with a fit of the ague in fancying they were not. What *was* there about them to confound me in this manner? I gazed;—while my brain reeled with a multitude of incoherent thoughts. Not thus he appeared—assuredly not *thus*—in the vivacity of his waking hours. The same name! the same contour of person! the same day of arrival at the academy! And then his dogged and meaningless imitation of my gait, my voice, my habits, and my manner! Was it, in truth, within the bounds of human possibility, that *what I now saw* was the result, merely, of the habitual practice of this sarcastic imitation? Awe-stricken, and with a creeping shudder, I extinguished the lamp, passed silently from the chamber, and left, at once, the halls of that old academy, never to enter them again.

After a lapse of some months, spent at home in mere idleness, I found myself a student at Eton. The brief interval had been sufficient to enfeeble my remembrance of the events at Dr. Bransby's, or at least to effect a material change in the nature of the feelings with which I remembered them. The truth—the tragedy—of the drama was no more. I could now find room to doubt the evidence of my senses; and seldom called up the subject at all but with wonder at the extent of human credulity, and a smile at the vivid force of the imagination which I hereditarily possessed. Neither was this species of scepticism likely to be diminished by the character of the life I led at Eton. The vortex of thoughtless folly into which I there so immediately and so recklessly plunged, washed away all but the froth of my past hours, engulfed at once every solid or serious impression, and left to memory only the veriest levities of a former existence.

I do not wish, however, to trace the course of my miserable profligacy here—a profligacy which set at defiance the laws, while it eluded the vigilance of the institution. Three years of folly, passed without profit, had but given me rooted habits of vice, and added, in a somewhat unusual degree, to my bodily stature, when, after a week of soulless dissipation, I invited a small party of the most dissolute students to a secret carousal in my chambers. We met at a late hour of the night; for our debaucheries were to be faithfully protracted until morning. The wine flowed freely, and there were not wanting other and perhaps more dangerous seductions; so that the gray dawn had already faintly appeared in the east, while our delirious extravagance was at its height. Madly flushed with cards and intoxication, I was in the act of insisting upon a toast of more than wonted profanity, when my attention was suddenly diverted by the violent, although partial unclosing of the door of the apartment, and by the eager voice of a servant from without. He said that some person, apparently in great haste, demanded to speak with me in the hall.

Wildly excited with wine, the unexpected interruption rather delighted than surprised me. I staggered forward at once, and a few steps brought me to the vestibule of the building. In this low and small room there hung no lamp; and now no light at all was admitted, save that of the exceedingly feeble dawn which made its way through the semi-circular window. As I put my foot over the threshold, I became aware of the figure of a youth about my own height, and habited in a white kerseymere morning frock, cut in the novel fashion of the one I myself wore at the moment. This the faint light enabled me to perceive; but the features of his face I could not distinguish. Upon my entering he strode hurriedly up to me, and, seizing me by the arm with a gesture of petulant impatience, whispered the words "William Wilson!" in my ear.

I grew perfectly sober in an instant.

There was that in the manner of the stranger, and in the tremulous shake of his uplifted finger, as he held it between my eyes and the light, which filled me with unqualified amazement; but it was not this which had so violently moved me. It was the pregnancy of solemn admonition in the singular, low, hissing utterance; and, above all, it was the character, the tone, *the key,* of those few, simple, and familiar, yet *whispered* syllables, which came with a thousand thronging memories of bygone days, and struck upon my soul with the shock of a galvanic battery. Ere I could recover the use of my senses he was gone.

Although this event failed not of a vivid effect upon my disordered imagination, yet was it evanescent as vivid. For some weeks, indeed, I busied myself in earnest inquiry, or was wrapped in a cloud of morbid speculation. I did not pretend to disguise from my perception the identity of the singular individual who thus perseveringly interfered with my affairs, and harassed me with his insinuated counsel. But who and what was this Wilson?—and whence came he?—and what were his purposes? Upon neither of these points could I be satisfied; merely ascertaining, in regard to him, that a sudden accident in his family had caused his removal from Dr. Bransby's academy on the afternoon of the day in which I myself had eloped. But in a brief period I ceased to think upon the subject; my attention being all absorbed in a contemplated departure for Oxford. Thither I soon went; the uncalculating vanity of my parents furnishing me with an outfit, and annual establishment, which would enable me to indulge at will in the luxury already so dear to my heart,—to vie in profuseness of expenditure with the haughtiest heirs of the wealthiest earldoms in Great Britain.

Excited by such appliances to vice, my constitutional temperament broke forth with redoubled ardor, and I spurned even the common restraints of decency in the mad infatuation of my revels. But it were absurd to pause in the detail of my extravagance. Let it suffice, that among spendthrifts I out-Heroded Herod, and that, giving name to a multitude of novel follies, I added no brief appendix to the long catalogue of vices then usual in the most dissolute university of Europe.

It could hardly be credited, however, that I had, even here, so utterly fallen from the gentlemanly estate, as to seek acquaintance with the vilest arts of the gambler by profession, and, having become an adept in his despicable science, to practise it habitually as a means of increasing my already enormous income at the expense of the weak-minded among my fellow collegians. Such, nevertheless, was the fact. And the very enormity of this offence against all manly and honourable sentiment proved, beyond doubt, the main if not the sole reason of the impunity with which it was committed. Who, indeed, among my most abandoned associates, would not rather have disputed the clearest evidence of his senses, than have suspected of such courses, the gay, the frank, the generous William Wilson—the noblest and most liberal commoner at Oxford—him whose follies (said his parasites) were but the follies of youth and unbridled fancy—whose errors but inimitable whim—whose darkest vice but a careless and dashing extravagance?

I had been now two years successfully busied in this way, when there came to the university a young parvenu nobleman, Glendinning—rich, said report, as Herodes Atticus—his riches, too, as easily acquired. I soon found him of weak intellect, and, of course, marked him as a fitting subject for my skill. I frequently engaged him in play, and contrived, with the gambler's usual art, to let him win considerable sums, the more effectually to entangle him in my snares. At length, my schemes being ripe, I met him (with the full intention that this meeting should be final and decisive) at the chambers of a fellow-commoner, (Mr. Preston,) equally intimate with both, but who, to do him justice, entertained not even a remote suspicion of my design. To give to this a better colouring, I had contrived to have assembled a party of some eight or ten, and was solicitously careful that the introduction of cards should appear accidental, and originate in the proposal of my contemplated dupe himself. To be brief upon a vile topic, none of the low finesse was omitted, so customary upon similar occasions that it is a just matter for wonder how any are still found so besotted as to fall its victim.

We had protracted our sitting far into the night, and I had at length effected the manoeuvre of getting Glendinning as my sole antagonist. The game, too, was my favorite *écarté*. The rest of the company, interested in the extent of our play, had abandoned their own cards, and were standing around us as spectators. The parvenu, who had been induced by my artifices in the early part of the evening, to drink deeply, now shuffled, dealt, or played, with a wild nervousness of manner for which his intoxication, I thought, might partially, but could not altogether account. In a very short period he had become my debtor to a large amount, when, having taken a long draught of port, he did precisely what I had been coolly anticipating—he proposed to double our already extravagant stakes. With a well-feigned show of reluctance, and not until after my repeated refusal had seduced him into some angry words which gave a color of *pique* to my compliance, did I finally comply. The result, of course, did but prove how entirely the prey was in my toils; in less than an hour he had quadrupled his debt. For some time his countenance had been losing the florid tinge lent it by the wine; but now, to my astonishment, I perceived that it had grown to a pallor truly fearful. I say to my astonishment. Glendinning had been represented to my eager inquiries as immeasurably wealthy; and the sums which he had as yet lost, although in themselves vast, could not, I supposed, very seriously annoy, much less so violently affect him. That he was overcome by the wine just swallowed, was the idea which most readily presented itself; and, rather with a view to the preservation of my own character in the eyes of my associates, than from any less interested motive, I was about to insist, peremptorily, upon a discontinuance of the play, when some expressions at my elbow from among the company, and an ejaculation evincing utter despair on the part of Glendinning, gave me to understand that I had effected his total ruin under circumstances which, rendering him an object for the pity of all, should have protected him from the ill offices even of a fiend.

What now might have been my conduct it is difficult to say. The pitiable condition of my dupe had thrown an air of embarrassed gloom over all; and, for some moments, a profound silence was maintained, during which I could not help feeling my cheeks tingle with the many burning glances of scorn or reproach cast upon me by the less abandoned of the party. I will even own that an intolerable weight of anxiety was for a brief instant lifted from my bosom by the sudden and extraordinary interruption which ensued. The wide, heavy folding doors of the apartment were all at once thrown open, to their full extent, with a vigorous and rushing impetuosity that extinguished, as if by magic, every candle in the room. Their light, in dying, enabled us just to perceive that a stranger had entered, about my own height, and closely muffled in a cloak. The darkness, however, was now total; and we could only feel that he was standing in our midst. Before any one of us could recover from the extreme astonishment into which this rudeness had thrown all, we heard the voice of the intruder.

"Gentlemen," he said, in a low, distinct, and never-to-be-forgotten *whisper* which thrilled to the very marrow of my bones, "Gentlemen, I make no apology for this behaviour, because in thus behaving, I am but fulfilling a duty. You are, beyond doubt, uninformed of the true character of the person who has to-night won at *écarté* a large sum of money from Lord Glendinning. I will therefore put you upon an expeditious and decisive plan of obtaining this very necessary information. Please to examine, at your leisure, the inner linings of the cuff of his left sleeve, and the several little packages which may be found in the somewhat capacious pockets of his embroidered morning wrapper."

While he spoke, so profound was the stillness that one might have heard a pin drop upon the floor. In ceasing, he departed at once, and as abruptly as he had entered. Can I—shall I describe my sensations?—must I say that I felt all the horrors of the damned? Most assuredly I had little time given for reflection. Many hands roughly seized me upon the spot, and lights were immediately reprocured. A search ensued. In the lining of my sleeve were found all the court cards essential in *écarté*, and, in the pockets of my wrapper, a number of packs, facsimiles of those used at our sittings, with the single exception that mine were of the species called, technically, *arrondées*;[4] the honours being slightly convex at the ends, the lower cards slightly convex at the sides. In this disposition, the dupe who cuts, as customary, at the length of the pack, will invariably find that he cuts his antagonist an honor; while the gambler, cutting at the breadth, will, as certainly, cut nothing for his victim which may count in the records of the game.

4. *arrondées:* Probably an error for *arrondies*, "rounded off."

Any burst of indignation upon this discovery would have affected me less than the silent contempt, or the sarcastic composure, with which it was received.

"Mr. Wilson," said our host, stooping to remove from beneath his feet an exceedingly luxurious cloak of rare furs, "Mr. Wilson, this is your property." (The weather was cold; and, upon quitting my own room, I had thrown a cloak over my dressing wrapper, putting it off upon reaching the scene of play.) "I presume it is supererogatory to seek here (eyeing the folds of the garment with a bitter smile) for any farther evidence of your skill. Indeed, we have had enough. You will see the necessity, I hope, of quitting Oxford—at all events, of quitting instantly my chambers."

Abased, humbled to the dust as I then was, it is probable that I should have resented this galling language by immediate personal violence, had not my whole attention been at the moment arrested by a fact of the most startling character. The cloak which I had worn was of a rare description of fur; how rare, how extravagantly costly, I shall not venture to say. Its fashion, too, was of my own fantastic invention; for I was fastidious to an absurd degree of coxcombry, in matters of this frivolous nature. When, therefore, Mr. Preston reached me that which he had picked up upon the floor, and near the folding doors of the apartment, it was with an astonishment nearly bordering upon terror, that I perceived my own already hanging on my arm, (where I had no doubt unwittingly placed it,) and that the one presented me was but its exact counterpart in every, in even the minutest possible particular. The singular being who had so disastrously exposed me, had been muffled, I remembered, in a cloak; and none had been worn at all by any of the members of our party with the exception of myself. Retaining some presence of mind, I took the one offered me by Preston; placed it, unnoticed, over my own; left the apartment with a resolute scowl of defiance; and, next morning ere dawn of day, commenced a hurried journey from Oxford to the continent, in a perfect agony of horror and of shame.

I fled in vain. My evil destiny pursued me as if in exultation, and proved, indeed, that the exercise of its mysterious dominion had as yet only begun. Scarcely had I set foot in Paris ere I had fresh evidence of the detestable interest taken by this Wilson in my concerns. Years flew, while I experienced no relief. Villain!—at Rome, with how untimely, yet with how spectral an officiousness, stepped he in between me and my ambition! At Vienna, too—at

Berlin—and at Moscow! Where, in truth, had I *not* bitter cause to curse him within my heart? From his inscrutable tyranny did I at length flee, panic-stricken, as from a pestilence; and to the very ends of the earth *I fled in vain.*

And again, and again, in secret communion with my own spirit, would I demand the questions "Who is he?—whence came he?—and what are his objects?" But no answer was there found. And then I scrutinized, with a minute scrutiny, the forms, and the methods, and the leading traits of his impertinent supervision. But even here there was very little upon which to base a conjecture. It was noticeable, indeed, that, in no one of the multiplied instances in which he had of late crossed my path, had he so crossed it except to frustrate those schemes, or to disturb those actions, which, if fully carried out, might have resulted in bitter mischief. Poor justification this, in truth, for an authority so imperiously assumed! Poor indemnity for natural rights of self-agency so pertinaciously, so insultingly denied!

I had also been forced to notice that my tormentor, for a very long period of time, (while scrupulously and with miraculous dexterity maintaining his whim of an identity of apparel with myself,) had so contrived it, in the execution of his varied interference with my will, that I saw not, at any moment, the features of his face. Be Wilson what he might, *this*, at least, was but the veriest of affectation, or of folly. Could he, for an instant, have supposed that, in my admonisher at Eton—in the destroyer of my honor at Oxford,—in him who thwarted my ambition at Rome, my revenge at Paris, my passionate love at Naples, or what he falsely termed my avarice in Egypt,—that in this, my arch-enemy and evil genius, could fail to recognise the William Wilson of my school boy days,—the namesake, the companion, the rival,—the hated and dreaded rival at Dr. Bransby's? Impossible!—But let me hasten to the last eventful scene of the drama.

Thus far I had succumbed supinely to this imperious domination. The sentiment of deep awe with which I habitually regarded the elevated character, the majestic wisdom, the apparent omnipresence and omnipotence of Wilson, added to a feeling of even terror, with which certain other traits in his nature and assumptions inspired me, had operated, hitherto, to impress me with an idea of my own utter weakness and helplessness, and to suggest an implicit, although bitterly reluctant submission to his arbitrary will. But, of late days, I had given myself up entirely to wine; and its maddening influence upon my hereditary temper rendered me more and more impatient of control. I began to murmur,—to hesitate,—to resist. And was it only fancy which induced me to believe that, with the increase of my own firmness, that of my tormentor underwent a proportional diminution? Be this as it may, I now began to feel the inspiration of a burning hope, and at length nurtured in my secret thoughts a stern and desperate resolution that I would submit no longer to be enslaved.

It was at Rome, during the Carnival of 18—, that I attended a masquerade in the palazzo of the Neapolitan Duke Di Broglio. I had indulged more freely than usual in the excesses of the wine-table; and now the suffocating atmosphere of the crowded rooms irritated me beyond endurance. The difficulty, too, of forcing my way through the mazes of the company contributed not a little to the ruffling of my temper; for I was anxiously seeking, (let me not say with what unworthy motive) the young, the gay, the beautiful wife of the aged and doting Di Broglio. With a too unscrupulous confidence she had previously communicated to me the secret of the costume in which she would be habited, and now, having caught a glimpse of her person, I was hurrying to make my way into her presence.—At this moment I felt a light hand placed upon my shoulder, and that ever-remembered, low, damnable *whisper* within my ear.

In an absolute phrenzy of wrath, I turned at once upon him who had thus interrupted me, and seized him violently by the collar. He was attired, as I had expected, in a costume altogether similar to my own; wearing a Spanish cloak of blue velvet, begirt about the waist with a crimson belt sustaining a rapier. A mask of black silk entirely covered his face.

"Scoundrel!" I said, in a voice husky with rage, while every syllable I uttered seemed as new fuel to my fury, "scoundrel! impostor! accursed villain! you shall not—you *shall not* dog me unto death! Follow me, or I stab you where you stand!"—and I broke my way from the ball-room into a small ante-chamber adjoining—dragging him unresistingly with me as I went.

Upon entering, I thrust him furiously from me. He staggered against the wall, while I closed the door with an oath, and commanded him to draw. He hesitated but for an instant; then, with a slight sigh, drew in silence, and put himself upon his defence.

The contest was brief indeed. I was frantic with every species of wild excitement, and felt within my single arm the energy and power of a multitude. In a few seconds I forced him by sheer strength against the wainscoting, and thus, getting him at mercy, plunged my sword, with brute ferocity, repeatedly through and through his bosom.

At that instant some person tried the latch of the door. I hastened to prevent an intrusion, and then immediately returned to my dying antagonist. But what human language can adequately portray *that* astonishment, *that* horror which possessed me at the spectacle then presented to view? The brief moment in which I averted my eyes had been sufficient to produce, apparently, a material change in the arrangements at the upper or farther end of the room. A large mirror,—so at first it seemed to me in my confusion—now stood where none had been perceptible before; and, as I stepped up to it in extremity of terror, mine own image, but with features all pale and dabbled in blood, advanced to meet me with a feeble and tottering gait.

Thus it appeared, I say, but was not. It was my antagonist—it was Wilson, who then stood before me in the agonies of his dissolution. His mask and cloak lay, where he had thrown them, upon the floor. Not a thread in all his raiment—not a line in all the marked and singular lineaments of his face which was not, even in the most absolute identity, *mine own!*

It was Wilson; but he spoke no longer in a whisper, and I could have fancied that I myself was speaking while he said:

"You have conquered, and I yield. Yet, henceforward art thou also dead—dead to the World, to Heaven and to Hope! In me didst thou exist—and, in my death, see by this image, which is thine own, how utterly thou hast murdered thyself."

SOURCE: Edgar Allan Poe. "William Wilson. A Tale" in *The Gift*. Philadelphia: Carey and Hart, 1839.

The Tell-Tale Heart (1843)

This story has inspired countless imitations. Poe "tapped his own compulsive anxieties—aggravated by illness, family sorrows and alcoholism—as source material for his famous tales of suspense, horror and loathing," notes the editor of the Dover edition, Stanley Appelbaum.

TRUE!—NERVOUS—VERY, very dreadfully nervous I had been and am; but why *will* you say that I am mad? The disease had sharpened my senses—not destroyed—not dulled them. Above all was the sense of hearing acute. I heard all things in the heaven and in the earth. I heard many things in hell. How, then, am I mad? Hearken! and observe how healthily—how calmly I can tell you the whole story.

It is impossible to say how first the idea entered my brain; but once conceived, it haunted me day and night. Object there was none. Passion there was none. I loved the old man. He had never wronged me. He had never given me insult. For his gold I had no desire. I think it was his eye! yes, it was this! He had the eye of a vulture—a pale blue eye, with a film over it. Whenever it fell upon me, my blood ran cold; and so by degrees—very gradually—I made up my mind to take the life of the old man, and thus rid myself of the eye forever.

Now this is the point. You fancy me mad. Madmen know nothing. But you should have seen me. You should have seen how wisely I proceeded—with what caution—with what foresight—with what dissimulation I went to work! I was never kinder to the old man than during the whole week before I killed him. And every night, about midnight, I turned the latch of his door and opened it—oh, so gently! And then, when I had made an opening sufficient for my head, I put in a dark lantern, all closed, closed, that no light shone out, and then I thrust in my head. Oh, you would have laughed to see how cunningly I thrust it in! I moved it slowly—very, very slowly, so that I might not disturb the old man's sleep. It took me an hour to place my whole head within the opening so far that I could see him as he lay upon his bed. Ha! would a madman have been so wise as this? And then, when my head was well in the room, I undid the lantern cautiously—oh, so cautiously—cautiously (for the hinges creaked)—I undid it just so much that a single thin ray fell upon the vulture eye. And this I did for seven long nights—every night just at midnight—but I found the eye always closed; and so it was impossible to do the work; for it was not the old man who vexed me, but his Evil Eye. And every morning, when the day broke, I went boldly into the chamber, and spoke courageously to him, calling him by name in a hearty tone, and inquiring how he had passed the night. So you see he would have been a very profound old man, indeed, to suspect that every night, just at twelve, I looked in upon him while he slept.

Upon the eighth night I was more than usually cautious in opening the door. A watch's minute hand moves more quickly than did mine. Never before that night had I *felt* the extent of my own powers—of my sagacity. I could scarcely contain my feelings of triumph. To think that there I was, opening the door, little by little, and he not even to dream of my secret deeds or thoughts. I fairly chuckled at the idea; and perhaps he heard me; for he moved on the bed suddenly, as if startled. Now you may think that I drew back—but no. His room was as black as pitch with the thick darkness (for the shutters were close fastened, through fear of robbers), and so I knew that he could not see the opening of the door, and I kept pushing it on steadily, steadily.

I had my head in, and was about to open the lantern, when my thumb slipped upon the tin fastening, and the old man sprang up in bed, crying out—"Who's there?"

I kept quite still and said nothing. For a whole hour I did not move a muscle, and in the meantime I did not hear him lie down. He was still sitting up in the bed listening;—just as I have done, night after night, hearkening to the death watches in the wall.

Presently I heard a slight groan, and I knew it was the groan of mortal terror. It was not a groan of pain or of grief—oh, no!—it was the low stifled sound that arises from the bottom of the soul when overcharged with awe. I knew the sound well. Many a night, just at midnight, when all the world slept, it has welled up from my own bosom, deepening, with its dreadful echo, the terrors that distracted me. I say I knew it well. I knew what the old man felt, and pitied him, although I chuckled at heart. I knew that he had been lying awake ever since the first slight noise, when he had turned in the bed. His fears had been ever since growing upon him. He had been trying to fancy them causeless, but could not. He had been saying to himself—"It is nothing but the wind in the chimney—it is only a mouse crossing the floor," or "It is merely a cricket which has made a single chirp." Yes, he had been trying to comfort himself with these suppositions: but he had found all in vain. *All in vain;* because Death, in approaching him, had stalked with his black shadow before him, and enveloped the victim. And it was the mournful influence of the unperceived shadow that caused him to feel—although he neither saw nor heard—to *feel* the presence of my head within the room.

When I had waited a long time, very patiently, without hearing him lie down, I resolved to open a little—a very, very little crevice in the lantern. So I opened it—you cannot imagine how stealthily, stealthily—until, at length a simple dim ray, like the thread of the spider, shot from out the crevice and fell full upon the vulture eye.

It was open—wide, wide open—and I grew furious as I gazed upon it. I saw it with perfect distinctness—all a dull blue, with a hideous veil over it that chilled the very marrow in my bones; but I could see nothing else of the old man's face or person: for I had directed the ray as if by instinct, precisely upon the damned spot.

And have I not told you that what you mistake for madness is but over-acuteness of the sense?—now, I say, there came to my ears a low, dull, quick sound, such as a watch makes when enveloped in cotton. I knew *that* sound well, too. It was the beating of the old man's heart. It increased my fury, as the beating of a drum stimulates the soldier into courage.

But even yet I refrained and kept still. I scarcely breathed. I held the lantern motionless. I tried how steadily I could maintain the ray upon the eve. Meantime the hellish tattoo of the heart increased. It grew quicker and quicker, and louder and louder every instant. The old man's terror must have been extreme! It grew louder, I say, louder every moment!—do you mark me well I have told you that I am nervous: so I am. And now at the dead hour of the night, amid the dreadful silence of that old house, so strange a noise as this excited me to uncontrollable terror. Yet, for some minutes longer I refrained and stood still. But the beating grew louder, louder! I thought the heart must burst. And now a new anxiety seized me—the sound would be heard by a neighbour! The old man's hour had come! With a loud yell, I threw open the lantern and leaped into the room. He shrieked once—once only. In an instant I dragged him to the floor, and pulled the heavy bed over him. I then smiled gaily, to find the deed so far done. But, for many minutes, the heart beat on with a muffled sound. This, however, did not vex me; it would not be heard through the wall. At length it ceased. The old man was dead. I removed the bed and examined the corpse. Yes, he was stone, stone dead. I placed my hand upon the heart and held it there many minutes. There was no pulsation. He was stone dead. His eye would trouble me no more.

If still you think me mad, you will think so no longer when I describe the wise precautions I took for the concealment of the body. The night waned, and I worked hastily, but in silence. First of all I dismembered the corpse. I cut off the head and the arms and the legs.

I then took up three planks from the flooring of the chamber, and deposited all between the scantlings. I then replaced the boards so cleverly, so cunningly, that no human eye—not even his—could have detected any thing wrong. There was nothing to wash out—no stain of any kind—no blood-spot whatever. I had been too wary for that. A tub had caught all—ha! ha!

When I had made an end of these labors, it was four o'clock—still dark as midnight. As the bell sounded the hour, there came a knocking at the street door. I went down to open it with a light heart,—for what had I now to fear? There entered three men, who introduced themselves, with perfect suavity, as officers of the police. A shriek had been heard by a neighbour during the night; suspicion of foul play had been aroused; information had been lodged at the police office, and they (the officers) had been deputed to search the premises.

I smiled,—for *what* had I to fear? I bade the gentlemen welcome. The shriek, I said, was my own in a dream. The old man, I mentioned, was absent in the country. I took my visitors all over the house. I bade them search—search *well*. I led them, at length, to *his* chamber. I showed them his treasures, secure, undisturbed. In the enthusiasm of my confidence, I brought chairs into the room, and desired them *here* to rest from their fatigues, while I myself, in the wild audacity of my perfect triumph, placed my own seat upon the very spot beneath which reposed the corpse of the victim.

The officers were satisfied. My *manner* had convinced them. I was singularly at ease. They sat, and while I answered cheerily, they chatted of familiar things. But, ere long, I felt myself getting pale and wished them gone. My head ached, and I fancied a ringing in my ears: but still they sat and still chatted. The ringing became more distinct:—It continued and became more distinct: I talked more freely to get rid of the feeling: but it continued and gained definiteness—until, at length, I found that the noise was not within my ears.

No doubt I now grew *very* pale;—but I talked more fluently, and with a heightened voice. Yet the sound increased—and what could I do? It was *a low, dull, quick sound—much such a sound as a watch makes when enveloped in cotton*. I gasped for breath—and yet the officers heard it not. I talked more quickly—more vehemently; but the noise steadily increased. I arose and argued about trifles, in a high key and with violent gesticulations; but the noise steadily increased. Why *would* they not be gone? I paced the floor to and fro with heavy strides, as if excited to fury by the observations of the men—but the noise steadily increased. Oh God! what *could* I do? I foamed—I raved—I swore! I swung the chair upon which I had been sitting, and grated it upon the boards, but the noise arose over all and continually increased. It grew louder—louder—*louder!* And still the men chatted pleasantly, and smiled. Was it possible they heard not? Almighty God!—no, no! They heard!—they suspected!—they *knew!*—they were making a mockery of my horror!—this I thought, and this I think. But any thing was better than this agony! Any thing was more tolerable than this derision! I could bear those hypocritical smiles no longer! I felt that I must scream or die! and now—again!—hark! louder! louder! louder! *louder!*—

"Villains!" I shrieked, "dissemble no more! I admit the deed!—tear up the planks!—here, here!—it is the beating of his hideous heart!"

SOURCE: Edgar Allan Poe. "The Tell-Tale Heart" in *The Pioneer*. Boston: Leland and Whiting, January 1843.

The Raven (1845–1849)

Poe thought of himself primarily as a poet, and was known to have diligently revised this poem after its first publication.

Once upon a midnight dreary, while I pondered, weak and weary,
Over many a quaint and curious volume of forgotten lore—
While I nodded, nearly napping, suddenly there came a tapping,
As of some one gently rapping, rapping at my chamber door.
"'Tis some visitor," I muttered, "tapping at my chamber door—
    Only this and nothing more."

Ah, distinctly I remember it was in the bleak December;
And each separate dying ember wrought its ghost upon the floor.
Eagerly I wished the morrow;—vainly I had sought to borrow
From my books surcease of sorrow—sorrow for the lost Lenore—
For the rare and radiant maiden whom the angels name Lenore—
    Nameless *here* for evermore.

And the silken, sad, uncertain rustling of each purple curtain
Thrilled me—filled me with fantastic terrors never felt before;
So that now, to still the beating of my heart, I stood repeating

"'Tis some visitor entreating entrance at my chamber door—
Some late visitor entreating entrance at my chamber door;—
    This it is and nothing more."

Presently my soul grew stronger; hesitating then no longer,
"Sir," said I, "or Madam, truly your forgiveness I implore;
But the fact is I was napping, and so gently you came rapping,
And so faintly you came tapping, tapping at my chamber door,
That I scarce was sure I heard you"—here I opened wide the door;—
    Darkness there and nothing more.

Deep into that darkness peering, long I stood there wondering,
  fearing,
Doubting, dreaming dreams no mortal ever dared to dream
  before;
But the silence was unbroken, and the stillness gave no token,
And the only word there spoken was the whispered word,
  "Lenore!"
This I whispered, and an echo murmured back the word "Lenore!"
    Merely this and nothing more.

Back into the chamber turning, all my soul within me burning,
Soon again I heard a tapping somewhat louder than before.
"Surely," said I, "surely that is something at my window lattice;
Let me see, then, what thereat is, and this mystery explore—
Let my heart be still a moment and this mystery explore;—
    'Tis the wind and nothing more!"

Open here I flung the shutter, when, with many a flirt and
  flutter,
In there stepped a stately Raven of the saintly days of yore.
Not the least obeisance made he; not a minute stopped or stayed
  he;
But, with mien of lord or lady, perched above my chamber door—
Perched upon a bust of Pallas just above my chamber door—
    Perched, and sat, and nothing more.

Then this ebony bird beguiling my sad fancy into smiling,
By the grave and stern decorum of the countenance it wore,
"Though thy crest be shorn and shaven, thou," I said, "art sure
  no craven,

Ghastly grim and ancient Raven wandering from the Nightly shore—
Tell me what thy lordly name is on the Night's Plutonian shore!"
Quoth the Raven, "Nevermore."

Much I marvelled this ungainly fowl to hear discourse so plainly,
Though its answer little meaning—little relevancy bore;
For we cannot help agreeing that no living human being
Ever yet was blessed with seeing bird above his chamber door—
Bird or beast upon the sculptured bust above his chamber door,
With such name as "Nevermore."

But the Raven, sitting lonely on the placid bust, spoke only
That one word, as if his soul in that one word he did outpour.
Nothing farther then he uttered—not a feather then he fluttered—
Till I scarcely more than muttered, "Other friends have flown before—
On the morrow *he* will leave me, as my Hopes have flown before."
Then the bird said, "Nevermore."

Startled at the stillness broken by reply so aptly spoken,
"Doubtless," said I, "what it utters is its only stock and store
Caught from some unhappy master whom unmerciful Disaster
Followed fast and followed faster till his songs one burden bore—
Till the dirges of his Hope that melancholy burden bore
Of 'Never—nevermore.'"

But the Raven still beguiling all my fancy into smiling,
Straight I wheeled a cushioned seat in front of bird, and bust and door;
Then, upon the velvet sinking, I betook myself to linking
Fancy unto fancy, thinking what this ominous bird of yore—
What this grim, ungainly, ghastly, gaunt, and ominous bird of yore
Meant in croaking "Nevermore."

This I sat engaged in guessing, but no syllable expressing
To the fowl whose fiery eyes now burned into my bosom's core;
This and more I sat divining, with my head at ease reclining

On the cushion's velvet lining that the lamp-light gloated o'er,
But whose velvet violet lining with the lamp-light gloating o'er,
She shall press, ah, nevermore!

Then, methought, the air grew denser, perfumed from an unseen censer
Swung by Seraphim whose foot-falls tinkled on the tufted floor.
"Wretch," I cried, "thy God hath lent thee—by these angels he hath sent thee
Respite—respite and nepenthe from thy memories of Lenore;
Quaff, oh quaff this kind nepenthe and forget this lost Lenore!"
Quoth the Raven "Nevermore."

"Prophet!" said I, "thing of evil!—prophet still, if bird or devil!—
Whether Tempter sent, or whether tempest tossed thee here ashore,
Desolate yet all undaunted, on this desert land enchanted—
On this home by Horror haunted—tell me truly, I implore—
Is there—*is* there balm in Gilead?—tell me—tell me, I implore!"
Quoth the Raven "Nevermore."

"Prophet!" said I, "thing of evil!—prophet still, if bird or devil!
By that Heaven that bends above us—by that God we both adore—
Tell this soul with sorrow laden if, within the distant Aidenn,
It shall clasp a sainted maiden whom the angels name Lenore—
Clasp a rare and radiant maiden whom the angels name Lenore."
Quoth the Raven "Nevermore."

"Be that word our sign of parting, bird or fiend!" I shrieked, upstarting—
"Get thee back into the tempest and the Night's Plutonian shore!
Leave no black plume as a token of that lie thy soul hath spoken!
Leave my loneliness unbroken!—quit the bust above my door!
Take thy beak from out my heart, and take thy form from off my door!"
Quoth the Raven "Nevermore."

And the Raven, never flitting, still is sitting, *still* is sitting
On the pallid bust of Pallas just above my chamber door;
And his eyes have all the seeming of a demon's that is dreaming,

And the lamp-light o'er him streaming throws his shadow on the floor;
And my soul from out that shadow that lies floating on the floor
Shall be lifted—nevermore!

SOURCE: Edgar Allan Poe. *The Raven and Other Poems.* New York: Wiley and Putnam, 1845.

Annabel Lee (1849–1850)

It was many and many a year ago,
In a kingdom by the sea,
That a maiden there lived whom you may know
By the name of ANNABEL LEE;
And this maiden she lived with no other thought
Than to love and be loved by me.

I was a child and *she* was a child,
In this kingdom by the sea:
But we loved with a love that was more than love—
I and my ANNABEL LEE;
With a love that the winged seraphs of heaven
Coveted her and me.

And this was the reason that, long ago,
In this kingdom by the sea,
A wind blew out of a cloud, chilling
My beautiful ANNABEL LEE;
So that her high-born kinsman came
And bore her away from me,
To shut her up in a sepulchre
In this kingdom by the sea.

The angels, not half so happy in heaven,
Went envying her and me—
Yes!—that was the reason (as all men know,
In this kingdom by the sea)
That the wind came out of the cloud by night,
Chilling and killing my ANNABEL LEE.

But our love it was stronger by far than the love
  Of those who were older than we—
  Of many far wiser than we—
And neither the angels in heaven above,
  Nor the demons down under the sea,
Can ever dissever my soul from the soul
  Of the beautiful ANNABEL LEE:

For the moon never beams, without bringing me dreams
  Of the beautiful ANNABEL LEE;
And the stars never rise, but I feel the bright eyes
  Of the beautiful ANNABEL LEE;
And so, all the night-tide, I lie down by the side
Of my darling—my darling—my life and my bride,
  In the sepulchre there by the sea,
  In her tomb by the sounding sea.

SOURCE: Edgar Allan Poe. *Sartain's Union Magazine of Literature and Art.* Philadelphia: John Sartain, 1849. [First published in book form in 1850.]

FREDERICK DOUGLASS

Frederick Douglass (1818–1895) was born a slave in Maryland. After he escaped the South in 1838, he soon became—as a result of his enthralling orations and extraordinary writings on the topic of the abolition of slavery—the most famous black man in the world. In these chapters from the most read classic of American autobiography, Douglass tells of his first great revelation: "From that moment, I understood the pathway from slavery to freedom. It was just what I wanted, and I got it at a time when I the least expected it. . . . Though conscious of the difficulty of learning without a teacher, I set out with high hope, and a fixed purpose, at whatever cost of trouble, to learn how to read."

Chapters from *Narrative of the Life of Frederick Douglass, an American Slave. Written by Himself* (1845)

Chapter 6

MY NEW MISTRESS proved to be all she appeared when I first met her at the door,—a woman of the kindest heart and finest feelings. She had never had a slave under her control previously to myself, and prior to her marriage she had been dependent upon her own industry for a living. She was by trade a weaver; and by constant application to her business, she had been in a good degree preserved from the blighting and dehumanizing effects of slavery. I was utterly astonished at her goodness. I scarcely knew how to behave towards her. She was entirely unlike any other white woman I had ever seen. I could not approach her as I was accustomed to approach other white ladies. My early instruction was all out of place. The crouching servility, usually so acceptable a quality in a slave, did not answer when manifested toward her. Her favor was not gained by it; she seemed to be disturbed by it. She did not deem it impudent or unmannerly for a slave to look her in the face. The meanest slave was put fully at ease in her presence, and none left without feeling better for having seen her. Her face was made of heavenly smiles, and her voice of tranquil music.

But, alas! this kind heart had but a short time to remain such. The fatal poison of irresponsible power was already in her hands, and soon commenced its infernal work. That cheerful eye, under the influence of slavery, soon became red with rage; that voice, made all of sweet accord, changed to one of harsh and horrid discord; and that angelic face gave place to that of a demon.

Very soon after I went to live with Mr. and Mrs. Auld, she very kindly commenced to teach me the A, B, C. After I had learned this, she assisted me in learning to spell words of three or four letters. Just at this point of my progress, Mr. Auld found out what was going on, and at once forbade Mrs. Auld to instruct me further, telling her, among other things, that it was unlawful, as well as unsafe, to teach a slave to read. To use his own words, further, he said, "If you give a nigger an inch, he will take an ell. A nigger should know nothing but to obey his master—to do as he is told to do. Learning would *spoil* the best nigger in the world. Now," said he, "if you teach that nigger (speaking of myself) how to read, there would be no keeping him. It would forever unfit him to be a slave. He would at once become unmanageable, and of no value to his master. As to himself, it could do him no good, but a great deal of harm. It would make him discontented and unhappy." These words sank deep into my heart, stirred up sentiments within that lay slumbering, and called into existence an entirely new train of thought. It was a new and special revelation, explaining dark and mysterious things, with which my youthful understanding had struggled, but struggled in vain. I now understood what had been to me a most perplexing difficulty—to wit, the white man's power to enslave the black man. It was a grand achievement, and I prized it highly. From that moment, I understood the pathway from slavery to freedom. It was just what I wanted, and I got it at a time when I the least expected it. Whilst I was saddened by the thought of losing the aid of my kind mistress, I was gladdened by the invaluable instruction which, by the merest accident, I had gained from my master. Though conscious of the difficulty of learning without a teacher, I set out with high hope, and a fixed purpose, at whatever cost of trouble, to learn how to read. The very decided manner with which he spoke, and strove to impress his wife with the evil consequences of giving me instruction, served to convince me that he was deeply sensible of the truths he was uttering. It gave me the best assurance that I might rely with the utmost confidence on the results which, he said, would flow from teaching me to read. What he most dreaded, that I most desired. What he most loved, that I most hated. That which to him was a great evil, to be carefully shunned, was to me a great good, to be diligently sought; and the argument which he so warmly urged, against my learning to read, only served to inspire me with a desire and determination to learn. In learning to read, I owe almost as much to the bitter opposition of my master, as to the kindly aid of my mistress. I acknowledge the benefit of both.

I had resided but a short time in Baltimore before I observed a marked difference, in the treatment of slaves, from that which I had witnessed in the country. A city slave is almost a freeman, compared with a slave on the plantation. He is much better fed and clothed, and enjoys privileges altogether unknown to the slave on the plantation. There is a vestige of decency, a sense of shame, that does much to curb and check those outbreaks of atrocious cruelty so commonly enacted upon the plantation. He is a desperate slave-holder, who will shock the humanity of his non-slaveholding neighbors with the cries of his lacerated slave. Few are willing to incur the odium attaching to the reputation of being a cruel master; and above all things, they would not be known as not giving a slave enough to eat. Every city slaveholder is anxious to have it known of him, that he feeds his slaves well; and it is due to them to say, that most of them do give their slaves enough to eat. There are, however, some painful exceptions to this rule. Directly opposite to us, on Philpot Street, lived Mr. Thomas Hamilton. He owned two slaves. Their names were Henrietta and Mary. Henrietta was about twenty-two years of age, Mary was about fourteen; and of all the mangled and emaciated creatures I ever looked upon, these two were the most so. His heart must be harder than stone, that could look upon these unmoved. The head, neck, and shoulders of Mary were literally cut to pieces. I have frequently felt her head, and found it nearly covered with festering sores, caused by the lash of her cruel mistress. I do not know that her master ever whipped her, but I have been an eye-witness to the cruelty of Mrs. Hamilton. I used to be in Mr. Hamilton's house nearly every day. Mrs. Hamilton used to sit in a large chair in the middle of the room, with a heavy cowskin always by her side, and scarce an hour passed during the day but was marked by the blood of one of these slaves. The girls seldom passed her without her saying, "Move faster, you *black gip!*" at the same time giving them a blow with the cowskin over the head or shoulders, often drawing the blood. She would then say, "Take that, you *black gip!*"—continuing, "If you don't move faster, I'll move you!" Added to the cruel lashings to which these slaves were subjected, they were kept nearly half-starved. They seldom knew what it was to eat a full meal. I have seen Mary contending with the pigs for the offal thrown into the street. So much was Mary kicked and cut to pieces, that she was oftener called "*pecked*" than by her name.

Chapter 7

I LIVED IN Master Hugh's family about seven years. During this time, I succeeded in learning to read and write. In accomplishing this, I was compelled to resort to various stratagems. I had no regular teacher. My mistress, who had kindly commenced to instruct me, had, in compliance with the advice and direction of her husband, not only ceased to instruct, but had set her face against my being instructed by any one else. It is due, however, to my mistress to say of her, that she did not adopt this course of treatment immediately. She at first lacked the depravity indispensable to shutting me up in mental darkness. It was at least necessary for her to have some training in the exercise of irresponsible power, to make her equal to the task of treating me as though I were a brute.

My mistress was, as I have said, a kind and tender-hearted woman; and in the simplicity of her soul she commenced, when I first went to live with her, to treat me as she supposed one human being ought to treat another. In entering upon the duties of a slaveholder, she did not seem to perceive that I sustained to her the relation of a mere chattel, and that for her to treat me as a human being was not only wrong, but dangerously so. Slavery proved as injurious to her as it did to me. When I went there, she was a pious, warm, and tender-hearted woman. There was no sorrow or suffering for which she had not a tear. She had bread for the hungry, clothes for the naked, and comfort for every mourner that came within her reach. Slavery soon proved its ability to divest her of these heavenly qualities. Under its influence, the tender heart became stone, and the lamblike disposition gave way to one of tiger-like fierceness. The first step in her downward course was in her ceasing to instruct me. She now commenced to practise her husband's precepts. She finally became even more violent in her opposition than her husband himself. She was not satisfied with simply doing as well as he had commanded; she seemed anxious to do better. Nothing seemed to make her more angry than to see me with a newspaper. She seemed to think that here lay the danger. I have had her rush at me with a face made all up of fury, and snatch from me a newspaper, in a manner that fully revealed her apprehension. She was an apt woman; and a little experience soon demonstrated, to her satisfaction, that education and slavery were incompatible with each other.

From this time I was most narrowly watched. If I was in a separate room any considerable length of time, I was sure to be suspected of having a book, and was at once called to give an account of myself. All this, however, was too late. The first step had been taken. Mistress, in teaching me the alphabet, had given me the *inch*, and no precaution could prevent me from taking the *ell*.

The plan which I adopted, and the one by which I was most successful, was that of making friends of all the little white boys whom I met in the street. As many of these as I could, I converted into teachers. With their kindly aid, obtained at different times and in different places, I finally succeeded in learning to read. When I was sent of errands, I always took my book with me, and by going one part of my errand quickly, I found time to get a lesson before my return. I used also to carry bread with me, enough of which was always in the house, and to which I was always welcome; for I was much better off in this regard than many of the poor white children in our neighborhood. This bread I used to bestow upon the hungry little urchins, who, in return, would give me that more valuable bread of knowledge. I am strongly tempted to give the names of two or three of those little boys, as a testimonial of the gratitude and affection I bear them; but prudence forbids;—not that it would injure me, but it might embarrass them; for it is almost an unpardonable offence to teach slaves to read in this Christian country. It is enough to say of the dear little fellows, that they lived on Philpot Street, very near Durgin and Bailey's shipyard. I used to talk this matter of slavery over with them. I would sometimes say to them, I wished I could be as free as they would be when they got to be men. "You will be free as soon as you are twenty-one, *but I am a slave for life*! Have not I as good a right to be free as you have?" These words used to trouble them; they would express for me the liveliest sympathy, and console me with the hope that something would occur by which I might be free.

I was now about twelve years old, and the thought of being *a slave for life* began to bear heavily upon my heart. Just about this time, I got hold of a book entitled "The Columbian Orator." Every opportunity I got, I used to read this book. Among much of other interesting matter, I found in it a dialogue between a master and his slave. The slave was represented as having run away from his master three times. The dialogue represented the conversation which took place between them, when the slave was retaken the third time. In this dialogue, the whole argument in behalf of slavery was brought forward by the master, all of which was disposed of by the slave. The slave was made to say some very smart as well as impressive things in reply to his master—things which had the desired though unexpected effect; for the conversation resulted in the voluntary emancipation of the slave on the part of the master.

In the same book, I met with one of Sheridan's mighty speeches on and in behalf of Catholic emancipation. These were choice documents to me. I read them over and over again with unabated interest. They gave tongue to interesting thoughts of my own soul, which had frequently flashed through my mind, and died away for want of utterance. The moral which I gained from the dialogue was the power of truth over the conscience of even a slaveholder. What I got from Sheridan was a bold denunciation of slavery, and a powerful vindication of human rights. The reading of these documents enabled me to utter my thoughts, and to meet the arguments brought forward to sustain slavery; but while they relieved me of one difficulty, they brought on another even more painful than the one of which I was relieved. The more I read, the more I was led to abhor and detest my enslavers. I could regard them in no other light than a band of successful robbers, who had left their homes, and gone to Africa, and stolen us from our homes, and in a strange land reduced us to slavery. I loathed them as being the meanest as well as the most wicked of men. As I read and contemplated the subject, behold! that very discontentment which Master Hugh had predicted would follow my learning to read had already come, to torment and sting my soul to unutterable anguish. As I writhed under it, I would at times feel that learning to read had been a curse rather than a blessing. It had given me a view of my wretched condition, without the remedy. It opened my eyes to the horrible pit, but to no ladder upon which to get out. In moments of agony, I envied my fellow-slaves for their stupidity. I have often wished myself a beast. I preferred the condition of the meanest reptile to my own. Any thing, no matter what, to get rid of thinking! It was this everlasting thinking of my condition that tormented me. There was no getting rid of it. It was pressed upon me by every object within sight or hearing, animate or inanimate. The silver trump of freedom had roused my soul to eternal wakefulness. Freedom now appeared, to disappear no more forever. It was heard in every sound, and seen in every thing. It was ever present to torment me with a sense of my wretched condition. I saw nothing without seeing it, I heard nothing without hearing it, and felt nothing without feeling it. It looked from every star, it smiled in every calm, breathed in every wind, and moved in every storm.

I often found myself regretting my own existence, and wishing myself dead; and but for the hope of being free, I have no doubt but that I should have killed myself, or done something for which I should have been killed. While in this state of mind, I was eager to hear any one speak of slavery. I was a ready listener. Every little while, I could hear something about the abolitionists. It was some time before I found what the word meant. It was always used in such connections as to make it an interesting word to me. If a slave ran away and succeeded in getting clear, or if a slave killed his master, set fire to a barn, or did any thing very wrong in the mind of a slaveholder, it was spoken of as the fruit of *abolition*. Hearing the word in this connection very often, I set about learning what it meant. The dictionary afforded me little or no help. I found it was "the act of abolishing;" but then I did not know what was to be abolished. Here I was perplexed. I did not dare to ask any one about its meaning, for I was satisfied that it was something they wanted me to know very little about. After a patient waiting, I got one of our city papers, containing an account of the number of petitions from the north, praying for the abolition of slavery in the District of Columbia, and of the slave trade between the States. From this time I understood the words *abolition* and *abolitionist*, and always drew near when that word was spoken, expecting to hear something of importance to myself and fellow-slaves. The light broke in upon me by degrees. I went one day down on the wharf of Mr. Waters; and seeing two Irishmen unloading a scow of stone, I went, unasked, and helped them. When we had finished, one of them came to me and asked me if I were a slave. I told him I was. He asked, "Are ye a slave for life?" I told him that I was. The good Irishman seemed to be deeply affected by the statement. He said to the other that it was a pity so fine a little fellow as myself should be a slave for life. He said it was a shame to hold me. They both advised me to run away to the north; that I should find friends there, and that I should be free. I pretended not to be interested in what they said, and treated them as if I did not understand them; for I feared they might be treacherous. White men have been known to encourage slaves to escape, and then, to get the reward, catch them and return them to their masters. I was afraid that these seemingly good men might use me so; but I nevertheless remembered their advice, and from that time I resolved to run away. I looked forward to a time at which it would be safe for me to escape. I was too young to think of doing so immediately; besides, I wished to learn how to write, as I might have occasion to write my own pass. I consoled myself with the hope that I should one day find a good chance. Meanwhile, I would learn to write.

The idea as to how I might learn to write was suggested to me by being in Durgin and Bailey's ship-yard, and frequently seeing the ship carpenters, after hewing, and getting a piece of timber ready for use, write on the timber the name of that part of the ship for which it was intended. When a piece of timber was intended for the larboard side, it would be marked thus—"L." When a piece was for the starboard side, it would be marked thus—"S." A piece for the larboard side forward, would be marked thus—"L. F." When a piece was for starboard side forward, it would be marked thus—"S. F." For larboard aft, it would be marked thus—"L. A." For starboard aft, it would be marked thus—"S. A." I soon learned the names of these letters, and for what they were intended when placed upon a piece of timber in the ship-yard. I immediately commenced copying them, and in a short time was able to make the four letters named. After that, when I met with any boy who I knew could write, I would tell him I could write as well as he. The next word would be, "I don't believe you. Let me see you try it." I would then make the letters which I had been so fortunate as to learn, and ask him to beat that. In this way I got a good many lessons in writing, which it is quite possible I should never have gotten in any other way. During this time, my copy-book was the board fence, brick wall, and pavement; my pen and ink was a lump of chalk. With these, I learned mainly how to write. I then commenced and continued copying the Italics in Webster's Spelling Book, until I could make them all without looking on the book. By this time, my little Master Thomas had gone to school, and learned how to write, and had written over a number of copy-books. These had been brought home, and shown to some of our near neighbors, and then laid aside. My mistress used to go to class meeting at the Wilk Street meeting house every Monday afternoon, and leave me to take care of the house. When left thus, I used to spend the time in writing in the spaces left in Master Thomas's copy-book, copying what he had written. I continued to do this until I could write a hand very similar to that of Master Thomas. Thus, after a long, tedious effort for years, I finally succeeded in learning how to write.

SOURCE: Frederick Douglass. *Narrative of the Life of Frederick Douglass.* Boston: The Anti-Slavery Office, 1845.

MARGARET FULLER

Margaret Fuller (1810–1850) was the author of the renowned Woman in the Nineteenth Century *(1845), a book-length essay. She was a poet, Transcendentalist, women's rights activist, editor and journalist. She, her husband and her child died when the ship on which they were returning to America sank off Fire Island, New York. The first essay, similar in topic and manner to the writing in* Woman in the Nineteenth Century, *was found among her papers after her death by her brother, Arthur Buckminster Fuller, and included in "Miscellanies" in an 1855 edition of her work.*

Educate Men and Women as Souls (c. 1845)

HAD CHRISTENDOM BUT been true to its standard, while accommodating its modes of operation to the calls of successive times, Woman would now have not only equal *power* with Man,—for of that omnipotent nature will never suffer her to be defrauded,—but a *chartered* power, too fully recognized to be abused. Indeed, all that is wanting is, that Man should prove his own freedom by making her free. Let him abandon conventional restriction, as a vestige of that Oriental barbarity which confined Woman to a seraglio. Let him trust her entirely, and give her every privilege already acquired for himself,—elective franchise, tenure of property, liberty to speak in public assemblies, &c.

Nature has pointed out her ordinary sphere by the circumstances of her physical existence. She cannot wander far. If here and there the gods send their missives through women as through men, let them speak without remonstrance. In no age have men been able wholly to hinder them. A Deborah must always be a spiritual mother in Israel. A Corinna may be excluded from the Olympic games, yet all men will hear her song, and a Pindar sit at her feet. It is Man's fault that there ever were Aspasias and Ninons. These exquisite forms were intended for the shrines of virtue.

Neither need men fear to lose their domestic deities. Woman is born for love, and it is impossible to turn her from seeking it. Men should deserve her love as an inheritance, rather than seize and guard it like a prey. Were they noble, they would strive rather not to be loved too much, and to turn her from idolatry to the true, the only Love. Then, children of one Father, they could not err nor misconceive one another.

Society is now so complex, that it is no longer possible to educate Woman merely as Woman; the tasks which come to her hand are so various, and so large a proportion of women are thrown entirely upon their own resources. I admit that this is not their state of perfect development; but it seems as if Heaven, having so long issued its edict in poetry and religion without securing intelligent obedience, now commanded the world in prose to take a high and rational view. The lesson reads to me thus:—

Sex, like rank, wealth, beauty, or talent, is but an accident of birth. As you would not educate a soul to be an aristocrat, so do not to be a woman. A general regard to her usual sphere is dictated in the economy of nature. You need never enforce these provisions rigorously. Achilles had long plied the distaff as a princess; yet, at first sight of a sword, he seized it. So with Woman; one hour of love would teach her more of her proper relations than all your formulas and conventions. Express your views, men, of what you *seek* in women; thus best do you give them laws. Learn, women, what you should *demand* of men; thus only can they become themselves. Turn both from the contemplation of what is merely phenomenal in your existence, to your permanent life as souls. Man, do not prescribe how the Divine shall display itself in Woman. Woman, do not expect to see all of God in Man. Fellow-pilgrims and helpmeets are ye, Apollo and Diana, twins of one heavenly birth, both beneficent, and both armed. Man, fear not to yield to Woman's hand both the quiver and the lyre; for if her urn be filled with light, she will use both to the glory of God. There is but one doctrine for ye both, and that is the doctrine of the SOUL.

Woman in Poverty (1846)

This piece was first published in the New-York Daily Tribune *on March 25, 1846.*

WOMAN, EVEN LESS than Man, is what she should be as a whole. She is not that self-centred being, full of profound intuitions, angelic love, and flowing poesy, that she should be. Yet there are circumstances in which the native force and purity of her being teach her how to conquer where the restless impatience of Man brings defeat, and leaves him crushed and bleeding on the field.

Images rise to mind of calm strength, of gentle wisdom learning from every turn of adverse fate,—of youthful tenderness and faith undimmed to the close of life, which redeem humanity and make the heart glow with fresh courage as we write. They are mostly from obscure corners and very private walks. There was nothing shining, nothing of an obvious and sounding heroism to make their conduct doubtful, by tainting their motives with vanity. Unknown they lived, untrumpeted they died. Many hearts were warmed and fed by them, but perhaps no mind but our own ever consciously took account of their virtues.

Had Art but the power adequately to tell their simple virtues, and to cast upon them the light which, shining through those marked and faded faces, foretold the glories of a second spring! The tears of holy emotion which fell from those eyes have seemed to us pearls beyond all price; or rather, whose price will be paid only when, beyond the grave, they enter those better spheres in whose faith they felt and acted here.

From this private gallery we will, for the present, bring forth but one picture. That of a Black Nun was wont to fetter the eyes of visitors in the royal galleries of France, and my Sister of Mercy, too, is of that complexion. The old woman was recommended as a laundress by my friend, who had long prized her. I was immediately struck with the dignity and propriety of her manner. In the depth of winter she brought herself the heavy baskets through the slippery streets; and, when I asked her why she did not employ some younger person to do what was so entirely disproportioned to her strength, simply said, "she lived alone, and could not afford to hire an errand-boy." "It was hard for her?" "No, she was fortunate in being able to get work at her age, when others could do it better. Her friends were very good to procure it for her." "Had she a comfortable home?" "Tolerably so,—she should not need one long." "Was that a thought of joy to her?" "Yes, for she hoped to see again the husband and children from whom she had long been separated."

Thus much in answer to the questions, but at other times the little she said was on general topics. It was not from her that I learnt how the great idea of Duty had held her upright through a life of incessant toil, sorrow, bereavement; and that not only she had remained upright, but that her character had been constantly progressive. Her latest act had been to take home a poor sick girl who had no home of her own, and could not bear the idea of dying in a hospital, and maintain and nurse her through the last weeks of her life. "Her eyesight was failing, and she should not be able to work much longer,—but, then, God would provide. *Somebody* ought to see to the poor, motherless girl."

It was not merely the greatness of the act, for one in such circumstances, but the quiet matter-of-course way in which it was done, that showed the habitual tone of the mind, and made us feel that life could hardly do more for a human being than to make him or her the *somebody* that is daily so deeply needed, to represent the right, to do the plain right thing.

"God will provide." Yes, it is the poor who feel themselves near to the God of love. Though he slay them, still do they trust him.

"I hope," said I to a poor apple-woman, who had been drawn on to disclose a tale of distress that, almost in the mere hearing, made me weary of life, "I hope I may yet see you in a happier condition." "With God's help," she replied, with a smile that Raphael would have delighted to transfer to his canvas; a Mozart, to strains of angelic sweetness. All her life she had seemed an outcast child; still she leaned upon a Father's love.

The dignity of a state like this may vary its form in more or less richness and beauty of detail, but here is the focus of what makes life valuable. It is this spirit which makes poverty the best servant to the ideal of human nature. I am content with this type, and will only quote, in addition, a ballad I found in a foreign periodical, translated from Chamisso, and which forcibly recalled my own laundress as an equally admirable sample of the same class, the Ideal Poor, which we need for our consolation, so long as there must be real poverty.

The Old Washerwoman

Among yon lines her hands have laden,
    A laundress with white hair appears,
Alert as many a youthful maiden,
    Spite of her five-and-seventy years;
Bravely she won those white hairs, still
    Eating the bread hard toil obtained her,
And laboring truly to fulfil
    The duties to which God ordained her.

Once she was young and full of gladness,
  She loved and hoped,—was wooed and won;
Then came the matron's cares,—the sadness
  No loving heart on earth may shun.
Three babes she bore her mate; she prayed
  Beside his sick-bed,—he was taken;
She saw him in the church-yard laid,
  Yet kept her faith and hope unshaken.

The task her little ones of feeding
  She met unfaltering from that hour;
She taught them thrift and honest breeding.
  Her virtues were their worldly dower.
To seek employment, one by one,
  Forth with her blessing they departed,
And she was in the world alone—
  Alone and old, but still high-hearted.

With frugal forethought, self-denying,
  She gathered coin, and flax she bought,
And many a night her spindle plying,
  Good store of fine-spun thread she wrought.
The thread was fashioned in the loom;
  She brought it home, and calmly seated
To work, with not a thought of gloom,
  Her decent grave-clothes she completed.

She looks on them with fond elation;
  They are her wealth, her treasure rare,
Her age's pride and consolation,
  Hoarded with all a miser's care.
She dons the sark each Sabbath day,
  To hear the Word that faileth never;
Well-pleased she lays it then away
  Till she shall sleep in it forever!

Would that my spirit witness bore me
  That, like this woman, I had done
The work my Master put before me
  Duly from morn till set of sun!
Would that life's cup had been by me

Quaffed in such wise and happy measure,
And that I too might finally
Look on my shroud with such meek pleasure!

Such are the noble of the earth. They do not repine, they do not chafe, even in the inmost heart. They feel that, whatever else may be denied or withdrawn, there remains the better part, which cannot be taken from them. This line exactly expresses the woman I knew:—

"Alone and old, but still high-hearted."

Will any, poor or rich, fail to feel that the children of such a parent were rich when

"Her virtues were their worldly dower?"

Will any fail to bow the heart in assent to the aspiration,

"Would that my spirit witness bore me
That, like this woman, I had done
The work my Master put before me
Duly from morn till set of sun!"

May not that suffice to any man's ambition?

SOURCE: Margaret Fuller Ossoli. *Woman in the Nineteenth Century and Kindred Papers Relating to the Sphere, Condition, and Duties of Woman.* Edited by Arthur B. Fuller. Boston: Brown, Taggard and Chase, 1860.

FRANCIS PARKMAN

The historian Francis Parkman (1823–1893) reworked this piece, The Oregon Trail, *originally published in* Knickerbocker's Magazine, *into chapters 24 and 25 of one of the nineteenth century's classic books of travel and adventure—"The California and Oregon Trail" (1849). Among the curious and striking details in this narrative, the Harvard graduate dared his readers to express any misgivings about his accounts of his regular slaughter of buffalo: ". . . this boundless scene was often a wild and animated one; for twice a day, at sunrise and at noon, the buffalo came issuing from the hills, slowly advancing in their grave processions to drink at the river. All our amusements were to be at their expense. It may be that after the fashion of the day, some one of our New-England reformers may incline to denounce such sport as repugnant to his notions of humanity. I need only beg him, if he knows how to ride and use a gun, to mount a good horse and place himself within sight of a band of buffalo. If he has red blood in his veins he will inevitably forget his principles and attack them no less eagerly than if they were human antagonists who had opposed his measures or called in question the truth of his theories; and when he has slain his shaggy enemy and has leisure to contemplate him, he will take credit to himself for having rid the earth of a hideous and brutish monster."*

The Oregon Trail: The Buffalo Camp (1848)

In pastures measureless as air,
The bison is my noble game.
—BRYANT

NO ONE IN the camp was more active than Jim Gurney, and no one half so lazy as Ellis. Between these two there was a great antipathy. Ellis never stirred in the morning until he was compelled to, but Jim was always on his feet before day break; and this morning as usual the sound of his voice awakened the party.

"Get up, you booby! up with you now, you're fit for nothing but eating and sleeping. Stop your grumbling and come out of that buffalo-robe or I'll pull it on for you."

Jim's words were interspersed with numerous expletives, which gave them great additional effect. Ellis drawled out something in a nasal tone from among the folds of his buffalo-robe; then slowly disengaged himself, rose into a sitting posture, stretched his long powerful arms, yawned hideously and finally raising his tall person erect, stood staring round him to all the four quarters of the horizon. Delorier's fire was soon blazing, and the horses and mules loosened from their pickets, were feeding on the neighboring meadow. When we sat down to breakfast the prairie was still in the dusky light of morning; and as the sun rose we were mounted and on our way again.

"A white buffalo!" exclaimed Munroe.

"I'll have that fellow," said Shaw, "if I run my horse to death after him."

He threw the cover of his gun to Delorier and galloped out upon the prairie.

"Stop, Mr. Shaw, stop!" called out Henry Chatillon, "you'll run down your horse for nothing; it's only a white ox."

But Shaw was already out of hearing. The ox who had no doubt strayed away from some of the government wagon trains, was standing beneath some low hills which bounded the plain in the distance. Not far from him a band of veritable buffalo bulls were grazing; and startled at Shaw's approach, they all broke into a run and went scrambling up the hill-sides to gain the high prairie above. One of them in his haste and terror involved himself in a fatal catastrophe. Along the foot of the hills was a narrow strip of deep marshy soil, into which the bull plunged and hopelessly entangled himself. We all rode up to the spot. The huge carcass was half sunk in the mud which flowed to his very chin and his shaggy mane was outspread upon the surface. As we came near the bull began to struggle with convulsive strength; he writhed to and fro and in the energy of his fright and desperation would lift himself for a moment half out of the slough, while the reluctant mire returned a sucking sound as he strained to drag his limbs from its tenacious depths. We stimulated his exertions by getting behind him and twisting his tail; nothing would do. There was clearly no hope for him. After every effort his heaving sides were more deeply imbedded and the mire almost overflowed his nostrils; he lay still at length, and looking round at us with a furious eye seemed to resign himself to his fate. Ellis slowly dismounted from his horse and deliberately levelling his boasted yager, shot the old bull through the heart; then he lazily climbed back again to his seat, pluming himself no doubt on having actually killed a buffalo. That day the invincible yager drew blood for the first and last time during the whole journey.

The morning was a bright and gay one, and the air so clear that on the farthest horizon the outline of the pale blue prairie was sharply drawn against the sky. Shaw felt in the mood for hunting; he rode in advance of the party, and before long we saw a file of bulls galloping at full speed upon a vast green swell of the prairie at some distance in front. Shaw came scouring along behind them arrayed in his red shirt which looked very well in the distance; he gained fast on the fugitives, and as the foremost bull was disappearing behind the summit of the swell we saw him in the act of assaulting the hindmost; a smoke sprang from the muzzle of his gun and floated away before the wind like a little white cloud; the bull turned upon him, and just then the rising ground concealed them both from view.

We were moving forward until about noon, when we stopped by the side of the Arkansas. At that moment Shaw appeared riding slowly down the side of a distant hill; his horse was tired and jaded and when he threw his saddle upon the ground I observed that the tails of two bulls were dangling behind it. No sooner were the horses turned loose to feed than Henry asking Munroe to go with him, took his rifle and walked quietly away. Shaw, Tête Rouge and I, sat down by the side of the cart to discuss the dinner which Delorier placed before us; we had scarcely finished when we saw Munroe walking toward us along the river bank. Henry, he said, had killed four fat cows and had sent him back for horses to bring in the meat. Shaw took a horse for himself and another for Henry, and he and Munroe left the camp together. After a short absence all three of them came back, their horses loaded with the choicest parts of the meat; we kept two of the cows for ourselves and gave the others to Munroe and his companions. Delorier seated himself on the grass before the pile of meat and worked industriously for some time to cut it into thin, broad sheets for drying. This is no easy matter, but Delorier had all the skill of an Indian squaw. Long before night, cords of raw hide were stretched around the camp and the meat was hung upon them to dry in the sunshine and pure air of the prairie. Our California companions were less successful at the work; but they accomplished it after their own fashion, and their side of the camp was soon garnished in the same manner as our own.

We meant to remain at this place long enough to prepare provisions for our journey to the frontier, which as we supposed might occupy about a month. Had the distance been twice as great and the party ten times as large, the unerring rifle of Henry Chatillon would have supplied meat enough for the whole within two days; we were obliged to remain, however, until it should be dry enough for transportation; so we erected our tent and made the other arrangements for a permanent camp. The California men, who had no such shelter, contented themselves with arranging their packs on the grass around their fire. In the meantime we had nothing to do but amuse ourselves. Our tent was within a rod of the river, if the broad sand-beds with a scanty stream of water coursing here and there along their surface, deserve to be dignified with the name of river. The vast flat plains on either side were almost on a level with the sand-beds, and they were bounded in the distance by low, monotonous hills, parallel to the course of the Arkansas. All was one vast expanse of grass; there was no wood in view except some trees and stunted bushes upon two islands which rose from amid the wet sands of the river. Yet far from being dull and tame this boundless scene was often a wild and animated one; for twice a day, at sunrise and at noon, the buffalo came issuing from the hills, slowly advancing in their grave processions to drink at the river. All our amusements were to be at their expense. It may be that after the fashion of the day, some one of our New-England reformers may incline to denounce such sport as repugnant to his notions of humanity. I need only beg him, if he knows how to ride and use a gun, to mount a good horse and place himself within sight of a band of buffalo. If he has red blood in his veins he will inevitably forget his principles and attack them no less eagerly than if they were human antagonists who had opposed his measures or called in question the truth of his theories; and when he has slain his shaggy enemy and has leisure to contemplate him, he will take credit to himself for having rid the earth of a hideous and brutish monster. Except an elephant, I have seen no animal that can surpass a buffalo bull in size and strength, and the world may be searched in vain to find any thing of a more ugly and ferocious aspect. At first sight of him every feeling of sympathy vanishes; no man who has not experienced it, can understand with what keen relish one inflicts his death wound, with what profound contentment of mind he beholds the gigantic savage fall. The cows are much smaller and of a gentler appearance, as becomes their sex. While in this camp we forbore to attack them, leaving to Henry Chatillon, who could better judge their fatness and good quality, the task of killing such as we wanted for use; but against the bulls we waged an unrelenting war. Thousands of them might be slaughtered without causing any detriment to the species, for their numbers greatly exceed those of the cows; it is the hides of the latter alone which are used for the purpose of commerce and for making the lodges of the Indians; and the destruction among them is therefore altogether disproportioned.

Our horses were tired, and we now usually hunted on foot by the method called "approaching." The chase on horseback which goes by the name of "running" is the more violent and dashing mode of the two. Indeed, of all American wild sports this is the wildest. Once among the buffalo, the hunter, unless long use has made him familiar with the situation, dashes forward in utter recklessness and self-abandonment. He thinks of nothing, cares for nothing but the game; his mind is stimulated to the highest pitch yet intensely concentrated on one object. In the midst of the flying herd where the uproar and the dust are thickest it never wavers for a moment; he drops the rein and abandons his horse to his furious career; he levels his gun, the report sounds faint amid the thunder of the buffalo; and when his wounded enemy leaps in vain fury upon him, his heart thrills with a feeling like the fierce delight of the battle-field. A practised and skilful hunter well mounted, will sometimes kill five or six cows in a single chase, loading his gun again and again as his horse rushes through the tumult. An exploit like this is quite beyond the capacities of a novice. In attacking a small band of buffalo, or in separating a single animal from the herd and assailing it apart from the rest there is less excitement and less danger. With a bold and well-trained horse the hunter may ride so close to the buffalo that as they gallop side by side he may reach over and touch him with his hand; nor is there much danger in this as long as the buffalo's strength and breath continue unabated; but when he becomes tired and can no longer run with ease, when his tongue lolls out and the foam flies from his jaws, then the hunter had better keep a more respectful distance; the distressed brute may turn upon him at any instant; and at the moment when he fires his gun he will often be attacked in a similar manner; the wounded buffalo springs at his enemy; the horse leaps violently aside; and then the hunter has need of a tenacious seat in the saddle, for if he is thrown to the ground there is no hope for him. When he sees his attack defeated the buffalo resumes his flight, but if the shot be well directed he soon stops; for a few moments he stands still, then totters and falls heavily upon the prairie.

The chief difficulty in running buffalo, as it seems to me, is that of loading the gun or pistol at full gallop. Many hunters for convenience sake carry three or four bullets in the mouth; the powder is poured down the muzzle of the piece, the bullet dropped in after it, the stock struck hard upon the pommel of the saddle and the work is done. The danger of this method is obvious, should the blow on the pommel fail to send the bullet home, or should the latter in the act of aiming, start from its place and roll toward the muzzle, the gun would probably burst in discharging. Many a shattered hand and worse casualties beside have been the result of such an accident. To obviate it, some hunters make use of a ramrod, usually hung by a string from the neck, but this materially increases the difficulty of loading. The bows and arrows which the Indians use in running buffalo have many advantages over fire-arms, and even white men occasionally employ them.

The danger of the chase arises not so much from the onset of the wounded animal as from the nature of the ground which the hunter must ride over. The prairie does not always present a smooth, level and uniform surface; very often it is broken with hills and hollows, intersected by ravines, and in the remoter parts studded by the stiff wild sage bushes. The most formidable obstructions, however, are the burrows of wild animals, wolves, badgers and particularly prairie-dogs; the ground for a very great extent is frequently honey-combed with the holes of the latter. In the blindness of the chase the hunter rushes over it unconscious of danger; his horse at full career, thrusts his leg deep into one of the burrows; the bone snaps like a pipe-stem, the rider is hurled forward to the ground and probably killed. Yet accidents in buffalo running happen less frequently than one would suppose; in the recklessness of the chase, the hunter enjoys all the impunity of a drunken man, and may ride in safety over gullies and declivities, where, should he attempt to pass in his sober senses he would infallibly break his neck.

The method of "approaching" has many advantages over that of "running;" in the former, one neither breaks down his horse nor endangers his own life; instead of yielding to excitement he must be cool, collected and watchful; he must understand the buffalo, observe the features of the country and the course of the wind, and be well skilled moreover in using the rifle. The buffalo are strange animals; sometimes they are so stupid and infatuated that a man may walk up to them in full sight on the open prairie, and even shoot several of their number before the rest will think it necessary to retreat. Again at another moment they will be so shy and wary, that in order to approach them the utmost skill, experience and judgment are necessary. Kit Carson, I believe, stands preëminent in running buffalo; in approaching, no man living can bear away the palm from Henry Chatillon.

The wide, flat sand-beds of the Arkansas, as the reader will remember, lay close by the side of our camp. While we were lying on the grass after dinner, smoking, conversing, or laughing at Tête Rouge, one of us would look up and observe, far out on the plains beyond the river, certain black objects slowly approaching. He would inhale a parting whiff from the pipe, then rising lazily, take his rifle, which leaned against the cart, throw over his shoulder the strap of his pouch and powder-horn, and with his moccasins in his hand, walk quietly across the sand toward the opposite side of the river. This was very easy; for though the sands were about a quarter of a mile wide, the water was nowhere more than two feet deep. The farther bank was about four or five feet high, and quite perpendicular, being cut away by the water in spring; tall grass grew along its edge. Putting it aside with his hand, and cautiously looking through it, the hunter can discern the huge shaggy back of the buffalo slowly swaying to and fro, as with his clumsy swinging gait he advances towards the water. The buffalo have regular paths by which they come down to drink. Seeing at a glance along which of these his intended victim is moving, the hunter crouches under the bank to within fifteen or twenty yards, it may be, of the point where the path enters the river. Here he sits down quietly on the sand. Listening intently, he hears the heavy, monotonous tread of the approaching bull. He sets the hair-trigger of his rifle. The moment after, he sees a motion among the long weeds and grass just at the spot where the path is channelled through the bank. A huge black head is thrust out, the horns just visible amid the mass of shaggy and tangled mane. Half sliding, half plunging, down comes the buffalo upon the river-bed below. He steps out in full sight upon the sands. Just before him a runnel of water is gliding, and he bends his head to drink. You may hear the water as it gurgles with hollow sound down his capacious throat. He raises his head, and the drops trickle from his wet beard. He stands with an air of stupid abstraction, unconscious of the lurking danger. Noiselessly the hunter cocks his rifle. As he sits upon the sand, his knee is raised, and his elbow rests upon it, that he may level his heavy weapon with a steadier aim. The stock is at his shoulder; his eye ranges along the barrel. Still he is in no haste to fire. Now the bull, with slow deliberation, begins his march over the sands to the other side. He advances his fore-leg, and as he does so he exposes to view a small spot, denuded of hair, just behind the point of his shoulder; upon this the hunter brings the sights of his rifle to bear; lightly and delicately his finger presses the hair-trigger. Quick as thought the spiteful crack of the rifle responds to his slight touch, and instantly in the middle of the bare spot appears a small red dot. The buffalo shivers; death has overtaken him, he cannot tell from whence; still he does not fall, but walks heavily forward, as if nothing had happened. Yet before he has advanced half a dozen rods out upon the sand, you see him stop; he totters; his knees bend under him, and his head sinks forward to the ground. Scarcely has he done so, when his whole vast bulk sways to one side; he rolls over on the sand, and with a scarcely perceptible struggle yields up his life. The hunter steps forward and looks upon the inanimate pile of flesh and bones, hides, tendons and matted hair. At the slightest touch of his fore-finger those gigantic limbs were paralyzed, that mountain of flesh reeled and fell prostrate.

Waylaying the buffalo in this manner, and shooting them as they come to water, is the easiest and laziest method of hunting them. They may also be approached by crawling up ravines or behind hills, or even over the open prairie. This is often surprisingly easy; but at other times, and under other circumstances, it requires the utmost skill of the most experienced hunter. Henry Chatillon was a man of extraordinary strength and hardihood; but I have seen him return to camp quite exhausted with his efforts, his limbs scratched and wounded, and his buck-skin dress stuck full of the thorns of the prickly-pear, among which he had been crawling. Sometimes he would lay flat upon his face, and drag himself along in this position for many rods together.

On the second day of our stay at this place, Henry went out for an afternoon hunt. Shaw and I remained in camp, until, observing some bulls approaching the water upon the other side of the river, we crossed over to attack them. They were so near, however, that before we could get under cover of the bank our appearance as we walked over the sands alarmed them. Turning round before coming within gun-shot, they began to move off to the right in a direction parallel to the river. I climbed up the bank and ran after them. They were walking swiftly, and before I could come within gun-shot distance they slowly wheeled about and faced toward me. Before they had turned far enough to see me I had fallen flat on my face. For a moment they stood and stared at the strange object upon the grass; then turning away, again they walked on as before; and I rising immediately, ran once more in pursuit. Again they wheeled about, and again I fell prostrate. Repeating this three or four times, I came at length within a hundred yards of the fugitives, and as I saw them turning again, I sat down and levelled my rifle. The one in the centre was the largest I had ever seen. I shot him behind the shoulder. His two companions ran off. He attempted to follow, but soon came to a stand, and at length lay down as quietly as an ox chewing the cud. Cautiously approaching him, I saw by his dull and jelly-like eye that he was dead.

When I began the chase, the prairie was almost tenantless; but a great multitude of buffalo had suddenly thronged upon it, and looking up, I saw within fifty rods a heavy, dark column stretching to the right and left as far as I could see. I walked toward them. My approach did not alarm them in the least. The column itself consisted almost entirely of cows and calves, but a great many old bulls were ranging about the prairie on its flank, and as I drew near they faced toward me with such a shaggy and ferocious look that I thought it best to proceed no farther. Indeed I was already within close rifle-shot of the column, and I sat down on the ground to watch their movements. Sometimes the whole would stand still, their heads all facing one way; then they would trot forward, as if by a common impulse, their hoofs and horns clattering together as they moved. I soon began to hear at a distance on the left the sharp reports of a rifle, again and again repeated; and not long after, dull and heavy sounds succeeded, which I recognised as the familiar voice of Shaw's double-barreled gun. When Henry's rifle was at work there was always meat to be brought in. I went back across the river for a horse, and returning, I reached the spot where the hunters were standing. A dark mass of buffalo were visible on the distant prairie. The living had retreated from the ground, but about a dozen carcases were scattered in various directions. Henry, knife in hand, was stooping over a dead cow, cutting away the best and fattest of the meat.

When Shaw left me he had walked down for some distance under the river-bank to find another bull. At length he saw the plains covered with a host of buffalo, and soon after he heard the crack of Henry's rifle. Ascending the bank, he crawled through the grass, which for a rod or two from the river was very high and rank. He had not crawled far before to his astonishment he saw Henry standing erect upon the prairie, almost surrounded by the buffalo. Henry was in his appropriate element. Nelson on the deck of the "Victory," Bonaparte at the head of his army, hardly felt a prouder sense of mastery than he. Quite unconscious that any one was looking at him, he stood at the full height of his tall, strong figure, one hand resting upon his side, and the other arm leaning carelessly on the muzzle of his rifle. His eye was ranging over the singular assemblage around him. Now and then he would select such a cow as suited him, level his rifle, and shoot her dead; then quietly reloading his piece, he would resume his former position. The buffalo seemed no more to regard his presence than if he were one of themselves; the bulls were bellowing and butting at each other, or else rolling about in the dust. A dozen buffalo would gather about the carcass of a dead cow, snuffing at her wounds; and sometimes they would come behind those that had not yet fallen, and endeavor to push them from the spot. Now and then some old bull would face toward Henry with an air of stupid amazement, but none seemed inclined to attack or fly from him. For some time Shaw lay among the grass, looking in surprise at this extraordinary sight; at length he crawled cautiously forward, and spoke in a low voice to Henry, who told him to rise and come on. Still the buffalo showed no sign of fear; they remained gathered about their dead companions. Henry had already killed as many cows as we wanted for use, and Shaw, kneeling behind one of the carcasses, shot five bulls before the rest thought it necessary to disperse.

The frequent stupidity and infatuation of the buffalo seems the more remarkable from the contrast it offers to their wildness and wariness at other times. Henry knew all their peculiarities; he had studied them as a scholar studies his books, and he derived quite as much pleasure from the occupation. The buffalo were a kind of companions to him, and, as he said, he never felt alone when they were about him. He took great pride in his skill in hunting. Henry was one of the most modest men living; yet in the manly simplicity and frankness of his character it was quite clear that he looked upon his preëminence in this respect as a thing too palpable and well-established ever to be disputed; whatever may have been his estimate of his own skill, it was rather below than above that which others placed upon it. The only time that I ever saw a shade of scorn darken his open countenance was when two volunteer soldiers, who had just killed a buffalo for the first time, undertook to instruct him as to the best method of "approaching." To borrow an illustration from an opposite side of life, an Eton-boy might as well have sought to enlighten Porson on the formation of a Greek verb, or a Fleet-street shop-keeper to instruct Beau Brummel concerning a point of etiquette. Henry always seemed to think that he had a sort of prescriptive right to the buffalo and to look upon them as something belonging peculiarly to himself. Nothing excited his indignation so much as any wanton destruction committed among the cows, and in his view shooting a calf was a cardinal sin.

Henry Chatillon and Tête Rouge were of the same age; that is, about thirty. Henry was twice as large and fully six times as strong as Tête Rouge. Henry's face was roughened by winds and storms; Tête Rouge's was bloated by sherry-cobblers and brandy-toddy. Henry talked of Indians and buffalo; Tête Rouge of theatres and oyster-cellars. Henry had led a life of hardship and privation; Tête Rouge never had a whim which he would not gratify at the first moment he was able. Henry moreover was the most disinterested man I ever saw; while Tête Rouge, though equally good-natured in his way, cared for nobody but himself. Yet we would not have lost him on any account; he admirably served the purpose of a jester in a feudal castle; our camp would have been lifeless without him. For the past week he had fattened in a most amazing manner; and, indeed, this was not at all surprising, since his appetite was most inordinate. He was eating from morning till night; half the time he would be at work cooking some private repast for himself, and he paid a visit to the coffee-pot eight or ten times a day. His rueful and disconsolate face became jovial and rubicund, his eyes stood out like a lobster's, and his spirits, which before were sunk to the depths of despondency, were now elated in proportion; all day he was singing, whistling, laughing and telling stories. Being mortally afraid of Jim Gurney, he kept close in the neighborhood of our tent. As he had seen an abundance of low dissipated life, and had a considerable fund of humor, his anecdotes were extremely amusing, especially since he never hesitated to place himself in a ludicrous point of view, provided he could raise a laugh by doing so. Tête Rouge, however, was sometimes rather troublesome; he had an inveterate habit of pilfering provisions at all times of the day. He set ridicule at utter defiance; and being without a particle of self-respect, he would never have given over his tricks, even if they had drawn upon him the scorn of the whole party. Now and then, indeed, something worse than laughter fell to his share; on these occasions he would exhibit much contrition, but half an hour after we would generally observe him stealing round to the box at the back of the cart and slyly making off with the provisions which Delorier had laid by for supper. He was very fond of smoking; but having no tobacco of his own, we used to provide him with as much as he wanted, a small piece at a time. At first we gave him half a pound together; but this experiment proved an entire failure, for he invariably lost not only the tobacco, but the knife entrusted to him for cutting it, and a few minutes after he would come to us with many apologies and beg for more.

We had been two days at this camp, and some of the meat was nearly fit for transportation, when a tremendous storm came suddenly upon us. About sunset the whole sky grew as black as ink, and the long grass at the river's edge bent and rose mournfully with the first gusts of the approaching hurricane. Munroe and his two companions brought their guns and placed them under cover of our tent. Having no shelter for themselves, they built a fire of driftwood that might have defied a cataract, and wrapped in their buffalo-robes, sat down on the ground around it to bide the fury of the storm. Delorier ensconced himself under the cover of the cart. Shaw and I, together with Henry and Tête Rouge, crowded into the little tent; but first of all the dried meat was piled together and well protected by buffalo-robes pinned firmly to the ground. About nine o'clock the storm broke, amid absolute darkness; it blew a gale, and torrents of rain roared over the boundless expanse of open prairie. Our tent was filled with mist and spray, beating through the canvass and saturating every thing within. We could only distinguish each other at short intervals by the dazzling flash of lightning which displayed the whole wild waste around us with its momentary glare. We had our fears for the tent; but for an hour or two it stood fast; until at length the cap gave way before a furious blast; the pole tore through the top, and in an instant we were half suffocated by the cold and dripping folds of the canvass, which fell down upon us. Seizing upon our guns, we placed them erect, in order to lift the saturated cloth above our heads. In this agreeable situation, involved among wet blankets and buffalo-robes, we spent many hours of the night, during which the storm would not abate for a moment, but pelted down above our heads with merciless fury. Before long the ground beneath us became saturated with moisture, and the water gathered there in a pool two or three inches deep; so that for a considerable part of the night we were partially immersed in a cold bath. In spite of all this, Tête Rouge's flow of spirits did not desert him for an instant; he laughed, whistled and sung in defiance of the storm, and that night he paid off the long arrears of laughter which he owed us. While we lay in silence, enduring the infliction with what philosophy we could muster, Tête Rouge, who was intoxicated with animal spirits, was cracking jokes at our expense by the hour together. At about three o'clock in the morning, preferring the tyranny of the open night to such a wretched shelter, we crawled out from beneath the fallen canvass. The wind had abated, but the rain fell steadily. The fire of the California men still blazed amid the darkness, and we joined them as they sat around it. We made ready some hot coffee by way of refreshment; but when some of the party sought to replenish their cups, it was found that Tête Rouge, having disposed of his own share, had privately abstracted the coffee-pot and drank up the rest of the contents out of the spout.

In the morning to our great joy, an unclouded sun rose upon the prairie. We presented a rather laughable appearance, for the cold and clammy buckskin saturated with water, clung fast to every man's limbs; the light wind and the warm sunshine soon dried them again, and then we were all encased in armor of intolerable rigidity. Roaming all day over the prairie and shooting two or three bulls were scarcely enough to restore the stiffened leather to its usual pliancy.

Beside Henry Chatillon, Shaw and I were the only hunters in the party; Munroe this morning made an attempt to run a buffalo, but his horse could not come up to the game; Shaw went out with him, and being better mounted soon found himself in the midst of the herd. Seeing nothing but cows and calves around him, he checked his horse; an old bull came galloping on the open prairie at some distance behind, and turning his horse, Shaw rode across his path in front of him, levelling his gun as he passed and shooting him through the shoulder into the heart. The heavy bullets of Shaw's double-barrelled gun made wild work wherever they struck.

A great flock of buzzards were usually soaring about a few trees that stood on the island just below our camp. Throughout the whole of yesterday we had noticed an eagle among them, to-day he was still there; and Tête Rouge declaring that he would kill the bird of America, borrowed Delorier's gun and set out on his unpatriotic mission. As might have been expected the eagle suffered no great harm at his hands; he soon returned, saying that he could not find him, but had shot a buzzard instead. Being required to produce the bird in proof of his assertion, he said he believed that he was not quite dead, but he must be hurt from the swiftness with which he flew off.

"If you want," said Tête Rouge, "I'll go and get one of his feathers, I knocked off plenty of them when I shot him."

Just opposite our camp, was another island covered with bushes, and behind it was a deep pool of water while two or three considerable streams coursed over the sand not far off. I was bathing at this place in the afternoon when a white wolf, larger than the largest Newfoundland dog, ran out from behind the point of the island and galloped leisurely over the sand not half a stone's throw distant. I could plainly see his red eyes and the bristles about his snout; he was an ugly scoundrel with a bushy tail, large head and a most repulsive countenance. Having neither rifle to shoot nor stone to pelt him with, I was looking eagerly after some missile for his benefit, when the report of a gun came from the camp and the ball threw up the sand just beyond him; at this he gave a slight jump and stretched away so swiftly that he soon dwindled into a mere speck on the distant sand-beds. The number of carcasses that by this time were lying about the prairie all round us, summoned the wolves from every quarter; the spot where Shaw and Henry had hunted together soon became their favorite resort, for here about a dozen dead buffalo were fermenting under the hot sun. I used often to go over the river and watch them at their meal; by lying under the bank it was easy to get a full view of them. Three different kinds were present; there were the white wolves and the grey wolves, both extremely large, and beside these the small prairie wolves, not much bigger than spaniels. They would howl and fight a dozen at a time around a single carcass, yet they were so watchful, and their senses so acute, that I never was able to crawl within a fair shooting distance; whenever I attempted it, they would all scatter at once and glide silently away through the tall grass. The air above this spot was always full of buzzards or black vultures; whenever the wolves left a carcass they would descend upon it and cover it so densely that a rifle bullet shot at random among the gormandizing crowd would generally strike down two or three of them. These birds would now be sailing by scores just above our camp, their broad black wings seeming half transparent as they expanded them against the bright sky. The wolves and the buzzards thickened about us with every hour, and two or three eagles also came in to the feast. I killed a bull within rifle-shot of the camp; that night the wolves made a fearful howling close at hand, and in the morning the carcass was completely hollowed out by these voracious feeders.

After we had remained four days at this camp we prepared to leave it. We had for our own part about five hundred pounds of dried meat, and the California men had prepared some three hundred more; this consisted of the fattest and choicest parts of eight or nine cows, a very small quantity only being taken from each and the rest abandoned to the wolves. The pack animals were laden, the horses were saddled and the mules harnessed to the cart. Even Tête Rouge was ready at last, and slowly moving from the ground, we resumed our journey eastward. When we had advanced about a mile Shaw missed a valuable hunting-knife and turned back in search of it, thinking that he had left it at the camp. He approached the place cautiously, fearful that Indians might be lurking about, for a deserted camp is dangerous to return to. He saw no enemy, but the scene was a wild and dreary one; the prairie was overshadowed by dull, leaden clouds, for the day was dark and lowering. The ashes of the fires were still smoking by the river side; the grass around them was trampled down by men and horses, and strewn with bones, pieces of meat, fragments of hide and all the litter of a camp. Our departure had been a gathering signal to the birds and beasts of prey; Shaw assured me that literally dozens of wolves were prowling about the smouldering fires while multitudes more were roaming over the prairie around; they all fled as he approached, some running over the sand-beds and some over the grassy plains. The vultures in great clouds were soaring overhead and the dead bull near the camp was completely blackened by the flock that had alighted upon it; they flapped their broad wings and stretched upward their crested heads and long skinny necks, fearing to remain, yet reluctant to leave their disgusting feast. As he searched about the fires he saw the wolves seated on the distant hills waiting for his departure. Having looked in vain for his knife, he mounted again and left the wolves and the vultures to banquet freely upon the carrion of the hunting-camp.

Source: "The Oregon Trail: The Buffalo Hunt." *The Knickerbocker, Or, New-York Monthly Magazine* (New York, December 1848).

HENRY DAVID THOREAU

There has been no one like Henry David Thoreau (1817–1862), yet, along with Benjamin Franklin, Abraham Lincoln, Frederick Douglass and Mark Twain, he has typified for the world and the United States a particularly American kind of man. "He is a singular character—a young man with much of wild original nature still remaining in him; and so far as he is sophisticated, it is in a way and method of his own,"[1] *the novelist Nathaniel Hawthorne wrote in his journal of Thoreau. "Civil Disobedience," Thoreau's essay that began its public life as a lecture in 1848 called "The Rights and Duties of the Individual in Relation to Government," was revised and published in 1849 as "Resistance to Civil Government"; after its final renaming in 1866 as "Civil Disobedience," its ideas influenced the philosophies and actions of, among others, Leo Tolstoy, Mahatma Gandhi and Martin Luther King, Jr.*

Civil Disobedience (1849)

I HEARTILY ACCEPT the motto,—"That government is best which governs least"; and I should like to see it acted up to more rapidly and systematically. Carried out, it finally amounts to this, which also I believe,—"That government is best which governs not at all;" and when men are prepared for it, that will be the kind of government which they will have. Government is at best but an expedient; but most governments are usually, and all governments are sometimes, inexpedient. The objections which have been brought against a standing army, and they are many and weighty, and deserve to prevail, may also at last be brought against a standing government. The standing army is only an arm of the standing government. The government itself, which is only the mode which the people have

1. As cited by Michael Sims in *The Adventures of Henry Thoreau: A Young Man's Unlikely Path to Walden Pond* (New York: Bloomsbury, 2014).

chosen to execute their will, is equally liable to be abused and perverted before the people can act through it. Witness the present Mexican war, the work of comparatively a few individuals using the standing government as their tool; for, in the outset, the people would not have consented to this measure.

This American government—what is it but a tradition, though a recent one, endeavoring to transmit itself unimpaired to posterity, but each instant losing some of its integrity? It has not the vitality and force of a single living man; for a single man can bend it to his will. It is a sort of wooden gun to the people themselves; and, if ever they should use it in earnest as a real one against each other, it will surely split. But it is not the less necessary for this; for the people must have some complicated machinery or other, and hear its din, to satisfy that idea of government which they have. Governments show thus how successfully men can be imposed on, even impose on themselves, for their own advantage. It is excellent, we must all allow; yet this government never of itself furthered any enterprise, but by the alacrity with which it got out of its way. *It* does not keep the country free. *It* does not settle the West. *It* does not educate. The character inherent in the American people has done all that has been accomplished; and it would have done somewhat more, if the government had not sometimes got in its way. For government is an expedient by which men would fain succeed in letting one another alone; and, as has been said, when it is most expedient, the governed are most let alone by it. Trade and commerce, if they were not made of India rubber, would never manage to bounce over the obstacles which legislators are continually putting in their way; and, if one were to judge these men wholly by the effects of their actions, and not partly by their intentions, they would deserve to be classed and punished with those mischievous persons who put obstructions on the railroads.

But, to speak practically and as a citizen, unlike those who call themselves no-government men, I ask for, not at once no government, but *at once* a better government. Let every man make known what kind of government would command his respect, and that will be one step toward obtaining it.

After all, the practical reason why, when the power is once in the hands of the people, a majority are permitted, and for a long period continue, to rule, is not because they are most likely to be in the right, nor because this seems fairest to the minority, but because they are physically the strongest. But a government in which the majority rule in all cases cannot be based on justice, even as far as men understand it. Can there not be a government in which majorities do not virtually decide right and wrong, but conscience?—in which majorities decide only those questions to which the rule of expediency is applicable? Must the citizen ever for a moment, or in the least degree, resign his conscience to the legislator? Why has every man a conscience, then? I think that we should be men first, and subjects afterward. It is not desirable to cultivate a respect for the law, so much as for the right. The only obligation which I have a right to assume, is to do at any time what I think right. It is truly enough said, that a corporation has no conscience; but a corporation of conscientious men is a corporation *with* a conscience. Law never made men a whit more just; and, by means of their respect for it, even the well-disposed are daily made the agents of injustice. A common and natural result of an undue respect for law is, that you may see a file of soldiers, colonel, captain, corporal, privates, powder-monkeys and all, marching in admirable order over hill and dale to the wars, against their wills, aye, against their common sense and consciences, which makes it very steep marching indeed, and produces a palpitation of the heart. They have no doubt that it is a damnable business in which they are concerned; they are all peaceably inclined. Now, what are they? Men at all? or small moveable forts and magazines, at the service of some unscrupulous man in power? Visit the Navy Yard, and behold a marine, such a man as an American government can make, or such as it can make a man with its black arts, a mere shadow and reminiscence of humanity, a man laid out alive and standing, and already, as one may say, buried under arms with funeral accompaniments, though it may be

> "Not a drum was heard, not a funeral note,
> As his corse to the rampart we hurried;
> Not a soldier discharged his farewell shot
> O'er the grave where our hero we buried."

The mass of men serve the State thus, not as men mainly, but as machines, with their bodies. They are the standing army, and the militia, jailers, constables, *posse comitatus*, &c. In most cases there is no free exercise whatever of the judgment or of the moral sense; but they put themselves on a level with wood and earth and stones; and wooden men can perhaps be manufactured that will serve the purpose as well. Such command no more respect than men of straw, or a lump of dirt. They have the same sort of worth only as horses and dogs. Yet such as these even are commonly esteemed good citizens. Others, as most legislators, politicians, lawyers, ministers, and office-holders, serve the State chiefly with their heads; and, as they rarely make any moral distinctions, they are as likely to serve the devil, without intending it, as God. A very few, as heroes, patriots, martyrs, reformers in the great sense, and *men*, serve the State with their consciences also, and so necessarily resist it for the most part; and they are commonly treated by it as enemies. A wise man will only be useful as a man, and will not submit to be "clay," and "stop a hole to keep the wind away," but leave that office to his dust at least:—

> "I am too high-born to be propertied,
> To be a secondary at control,
> Or useful serving-man and instrument
> To any sovereign state throughout the world."

He who gives himself entirely to his fellow-men appears to them useless and selfish; but he who gives himself partially to them is pronounced a benefactor and philanthropist.

How does it become a man to behave toward this American government to-day? I answer that he cannot without disgrace be associated with it. I cannot for an instant recognize that political organization as *my* government which is the *slave's* government also.

All men recognize the right of revolution; that is, the right to refuse allegiance to and to resist the government, when its tyranny or its inefficiency are great and unendurable. But almost all say that such is not the case now. But such was the case, they think, in the Revolution of '75. If one were to tell me that this was a bad government because it taxed certain foreign commodities brought to its ports, it is most probable that I should not make an ado about it, for I can do without them: all machines have their friction; and possibly this does enough good to counterbalance the evil. At any rate, it is a great evil to make a stir about it. But when the friction comes to have its machine, and oppression and robbery are organized, I say, let us not have such a machine any longer. In other words, when a sixth of the population of a nation which has undertaken to be the refuge of liberty are slaves, and a whole country is unjustly overrun and conquered by a foreign army, and subjected to military law, I think that it is not too soon for honest men to rebel and revolutionize. What makes this duty the more urgent is the fact, that the country so overrun is not our own, but ours is the invading army.

Paley, a common authority with many on moral questions, in his chapter on the "Duty of Submission to Civil Government," resolves all civil obligation into expediency; and he proceeds to say, "that so long as the interest of the whole society requires it, that is, so long as the established government cannot be resisted or changed without public inconveniency, it is the will of God that the established government be obeyed, and no longer."—"This principle being admitted, the justice of every particular case of resistance is reduced to a computation of the quantity of the danger and grievance on the one side, and of the probability and expense of redressing it on the other." Of this, he says, every man shall judge for himself. But Paley appears never to have contemplated those cases to which the rule of expediency does not apply, in which a people, as well as an individual, must do justice, cost what it may. If I have unjustly wrested a plank from a drowning man, I must restore it to him though I drown myself. This, according to Paley, would be inconvenient. But he that would save his life, in such a case, shall lose it. This people must cease to hold slaves, and to make war on Mexico, though it cost them their existence as a people.

In their practice, nations agree with Paley; but does any one think that Massachusetts does exactly what is right at the present crisis?

> "A drab of state, a cloth-o'-silver slut,
> To have her train borne up, and her soul trail in the dirt."

Practically speaking, the opponents to a reform in Massachusetts are not a hundred thousand politicians at the South, but a hundred thousand merchants and farmers here, who are more interested in commerce and agriculture than they are in humanity, and are not prepared to do justice to the slave and to Mexico, *cost what it may*. I quarrel not with far-off foes, but with those who, near at home, co-operate with, and do the bidding of those far away, and without whom the latter would be harmless. We are accustomed to say, that the mass of men are unprepared; but improvement is slow, because the few are not materially wiser or better than the many. It is not so important that many should be as good as you, as that there be some absolute goodness somewhere; for that will leaven the whole lump. There are thousands who are *in opinion* opposed to slavery and to the war, who yet in effect do nothing to put an end to them; who, esteeming themselves children of Washington and Franklin, sit down with their hands in their pockets, and say that they know not what to do, and do nothing; who even postpone the question of freedom to the question of free-trade, and quietly read the prices-current along with the latest advices from Mexico, after dinner, and, it may be, fall asleep over them both. What is the price-current of an honest man and patriot to-day? They hesitate, and they regret, and sometimes they petition; but they do nothing in earnest and with effect. They will wait, well disposed, for others to remedy the evil, that they may no longer have it to regret. At most, they give only a cheap vote, and a feeble countenance and Godspeed, to the right, as it goes by them. There are nine hundred and ninety-nine patrons of virtue to one virtuous man; but it is easier to deal with the real possessor of a thing than with the temporary guardian of it.

All voting is a sort of gaming, like chequers or backgammon, with a slight moral tinge to it, a playing with right and wrong, with moral questions; and betting naturally accompanies it. The character of the voters is not staked. I cast my vote, perchance, as I think right; but I am not vitally concerned that that right should prevail. I am willing to leave it to the majority. Its obligation, therefore, never exceeds that of expediency. Even voting *for the right* is *doing* nothing for it. It is only expressing to men feebly your desire that it should prevail. A wise man will not leave the right to the mercy of chance, nor wish it to prevail through the power of the majority. There is but little virtue in the action of masses of men. When the majority shall at length vote for the abolition of slavery, it will be because they are indifferent to slavery, or because there is but little slavery left to be abolished by their vote. *They* will then be the only slaves. Only *his* vote can hasten the abolition of slavery who asserts his own freedom by his vote.

I hear of a convention to be held at Baltimore, or elsewhere, for the selection of a candidate for the Presidency, made up chiefly of editors, and men who are politicians by profession; but I think, what is it to any independent, intelligent, and respectable man what decision they may come to, shall we not have the advantage of his wisdom and honesty, nevertheless? Can we not count upon some independent votes? Are there not many individuals in the country who do not attend conventions? But no: I find that the respectable man, so called, has immediately drifted from his position, and despairs of his country, when his country has more reason to despair of him. He forthwith adopts one of the candidates thus selected as the only *available* one, thus proving that he is himself *available* for any purposes of the demagogue. His vote is of no more worth than that of any unprincipled foreigner or hireling native, who may have been bought. Oh for a man who is a *man*, and, as my neighbor says, has a bone in his back which you cannot pass your hand through! Our statistics are at fault: the population has been returned too large. How many *men* are there to a square thousand miles in this country? Hardly one. Does not America offer any inducement for men to settle here? The American has dwindled into an Odd Fellow,—one who may be known by the development of his organ of gregariousness, and a manifest lack of intellect and cheerful self-reliance; whose first and chief concern, on coming into the world, is to see that the almshouses are in good repair; and, before yet he has lawfully donned the virile garb, to collect a fund for the support of the widows and orphans that may be; who, in short, ventures to live only by the aid of the mutual insurance company, which has promised to bury him decently.

It is not a man's duty, as a matter of course, to devote himself to the eradication of any, even the most enormous wrong; he may still properly have other concerns to engage him; but it is his duty, at least, to wash his hands of it, and, if he gives it no thought longer, not to give it practically his support. If I devote myself to other pursuits and contemplations, I must first see, at least, that I do not pursue them sitting upon another man's shoulders. I must get off him first, that he may pursue his contemplations too. See what gross inconsistency is tolerated. I have heard some of my townsmen say, "I should like to have them order me out to help put down an insurrection of the slaves, or to march to Mexico,—see if I would go;" and yet these very men have each, directly by their allegiance, and so indirectly, at least, by their money, furnished a substitute. The soldier is applauded who refuses to serve in an unjust war by those who do not refuse to sustain the unjust government which makes the war; is applauded by those whose own act and authority he disregards and sets at nought; as if the State were penitent to that degree that it hired one to scourge it while it sinned; but not to that degree that it left off sinning for a moment. Thus, under the name of Order and Civil Government, we are all made at last to pay homage to and support our own meanness. After the first blush of sin, comes its indifference; and from immoral it becomes, as it were, *un*moral, and not quite unnecessary to that life which we have made.

The broadest and most prevalent error requires the most disinterested virtue to sustain it. The slight reproach to which the virtue of patriotism is commonly liable, the noble are most likely to incur. Those who, while they disapprove of the character and measures of a government, yield to it their allegiance and support, are undoubtedly its most conscientious supporters, and so frequently the most serious obstacles to reform. Some are petitioning the State to dissolve the Union, to disregard the requisitions of the President. Why do they not dissolve it themselves,—the union between themselves and the State,—and refuse to pay their quota into its treasury? Do not they stand in the same relation to the State, that the State does to the Union? And have not the same reasons prevented the State from resisting the Union, which have prevented them from resisting the State?

How can a man be satisfied to entertain an opinion merely, and enjoy *it?* Is there any enjoyment in it, if his opinion is that he is aggrieved? If you are cheated out of a single dollar by your neighbor, you do not rest satisfied with knowing that you are cheated, or with saying that you are cheated, or even with petitioning him to pay you your due; but you take effectual steps at once to obtain the full amount, and see that you are never cheated again. Action from principle,—the perception and the performance of right,—changes things and relations; it is essentially revolutionary, and does not consist wholly with anything which was. It not only divides states and churches, it divides families; aye, it divides the *individual*, separating the diabolical in him from the divine.

Unjust laws exist: shall we be content to obey them, or shall we endeavor to amend them, and obey them until we have succeeded, or shall we transgress them at once? Men generally, under such a government as this, think that they ought to wait until they have persuaded the majority to alter them. They think that, if they should resist, the remedy would be worse than the evil. But it is the fault of the government itself that the remedy *is* worse than the evil. *It* makes it worse. Why is it not more apt to anticipate and provide for reform? Why does it not cherish its wise minority? Why does it cry and resist before it is hurt? Why does it not encourage its citizens to be on the alert to point out its faults, and *do* better than it would have them? Why does it always crucify Christ, and excommunicate Copernicus and Luther, and pronounce Washington and Franklin rebels?

One would think, that a deliberate and practical denial of its authority was the only offence never contemplated by government; else, why has it not assigned its definite, its suitable and proportionate penalty? If a man who has no property refuses but once to earn nine shillings for the State, he is put in prison for a period unlimited by any law that I know, and determined only by the discretion of those who placed him there; but if he should steal ninety times nine shillings from the State, he is soon permitted to go at large again.

If the injustice is part of the necessary friction of the machine of government, let it go, let it go: perchance it will wear smooth,—certainly the machine will wear out. If the injustice has a spring, or a pulley, or a rope, or a crank, exclusively for itself, then perhaps you may consider whether the remedy will not be worse than the evil; but if it is of such a nature that it requires you to be the agent of injustice to another, then, I say, break the law. Let your life be a counter friction to stop the machine. What I have to do is to see, at any rate, that I do not lend myself to the wrong which I condemn.

As for adopting the ways which the State has provided for remedying the evil, I know not of such ways. They take too much time, and a man's life will be gone. I have other affairs to attend to. I came into this world, not chiefly to make this a good place to live in, but to live in it, be it good or bad. A man has not everything to do, but something; and because he cannot do *every thing*, it is not necessary that he should do *something* wrong. It is not my business to be petitioning the governor or the legislature any more than it is theirs to petition me; and, if they should not hear my petition, what should I do then? But in this case the State has provided no way: its very Constitution is the evil. This may seem to be harsh and stubborn and unconciliatory; but it is to treat with the utmost kindness and consideration the only spirit that can appreciate or deserves it. So is all change for the better, like birth and death which convulse the body.

I do not hesitate to say, that those who call themselves abolitionists should at once effectually withdraw their support, both in person and property, from the government of Massachusetts, and not wait till they constitute a majority of one, before they suffer the right to prevail through them. I think that it is enough if they have God on their side, without waiting for that other one. Moreover, any man more right than his neighbors, constitutes a majority of one already.

I meet this American government, or its representative the State government, directly, and face to face, once a year, no more, in the person of its tax-gatherer; this is the only mode in which a man situated as I am necessarily meets it; and it then says distinctly, Recognize me; and the simplest, the most effectual, and, in the present posture of affairs, the indispensablest mode of treating with it on this head, of expressing your little satisfaction with and love for it, is to deny it then. My civil neighbor, the tax-gatherer, is the very man I have to deal with,—for it is, after all, with men and not with parchment that I quarrel,—and he has voluntarily chosen to be an agent of the government. How shall he ever know well what he is and does as an officer of the government, or as a man, until he is obliged to consider whether he shall treat me, his neighbor, for whom he has respect, as a neighbor and well-disposed man, or as a maniac and disturber of the peace, and see if he can get over this obstruction to his neighborliness without a ruder and more impetuous thought or speech corresponding with his action? I know this well, that if one thousand, if one hundred, if ten men whom I could name,—if ten *honest* men only,—aye, if *one* HONEST man, in this State of Massachusetts, *ceasing to hold slaves*, were actually to withdraw from this copartnership, and be locked up in the county jail therefor, it would be the abolition of slavery in America. For it matters not how small the beginning may seem to be: what is once well done is done forever. But we love better to talk about it: that we say is our mission. Reform keeps many scores of newspapers in its service, but not one man. If my esteemed neighbor, the State's ambassador, who will devote his days to the settlement of the question of human rights in the Council Chamber, instead of being threatened with the prisons of Carolina, were to sit down the prisoner of Massachusetts, that State which is so anxious to foist the sin of slavery upon her sister,—though at present she can discover only an act of inhospitality to be the ground of a quarrel with her,—the Legislature would not wholly waive the subject the following winter.

Under a government which imprisons any unjustly, the true place for a just man is also a prison. The proper place to-day, the only place which Massachusetts has provided for her freer and less desponding spirits, is in her prisons, to be put out and locked out of the State by her own act, as they have already put themselves out by their principles. It is there that the fugitive slave, and the Mexican prisoner on parole, and the Indian come to plead the wrongs of his race, should find them; on that separate, but more free and honorable ground, where the State places those who are not *with* her, but *against* her,—the only house in a slave-state in which a free man can abide with honor. If any think that their influence would be lost there, and their voices no longer afflict the ear of the State, that they would not be as an enemy within its walls, they do not know by how much truth is stronger than error, nor how much more eloquently and effectively he can combat injustice who has experienced a little in his own person. Cast your whole vote, not a strip of paper merely, but your whole influence. A minority is powerless while it conforms to the majority; it is not even a minority then; but it is irresistible when it clogs by its whole weight. If the alternative is to keep all just men in prison, or give up war and slavery, the State will not hesitate which to choose. If a thousand men were not to pay their tax-bills this year, that would not be a violent and bloody measure, as it would be to pay them, and enable the State to commit violence and shed innocent blood. This is, in fact, the definition of a peaceable revolution, if any such is possible. If the tax-gatherer, or any other public officer, asks me, as one has done, "But what shall I do?" my answer is, "If you really wish to do any thing, resign your office." When the subject has refused allegiance, and the officer has resigned his office, then the revolution is accomplished. But even suppose blood should flow. Is there not a sort of blood shed when the conscience is wounded? Through this wound a man's real manhood and immortality flow out, and he bleeds to an everlasting death. I see this blood flowing now.

I have contemplated the imprisonment of the offender, rather than the seizure of his goods,—though both will serve the same purpose,—because they who assert the purest right, and consequently are most dangerous to a corrupt State, commonly have not spent much time in accumulating property. To such the State renders comparatively small service, and a slight tax is wont to appear exorbitant, particularly if they are obliged to earn it by special labor with their hands. If there were one who lived wholly without the use of money, the State itself would hesitate to demand it of him. But the rich man—not to make any invidious comparison—is always sold to the institution which makes him rich. Absolutely speaking, the more money, the less virtue; for money comes between a man and his objects, and obtains them for him; and it was certainly no great virtue to obtain it. It puts to rest many questions which he would otherwise be taxed to answer; while the only new question which it puts is the hard but superfluous one, how to spend it. Thus his moral ground is taken from under his feet. The opportunities of living are diminished in proportion as what are called the "means" are increased. The best thing a man can do for his culture when he is rich is to endeavor to carry out those schemes which he entertained when he was poor. Christ answered the Herodians according to their condition. "Show me the tribute-money," said he;—and one took a penny out of his pocket;—if you use money which has the image of Cæsar on it, and which he has made current and valuable, that is, *if you are men of the State*, and gladly enjoy the advantages of Cæsar's government, then pay him back some of his own when he demands it; "Render therefore to Cæsar that which is Cæsar's, and to God those things which are God's,"—leaving them no wiser than before as to which was which; for they did not wish to know.

When I converse with the freest of my neighbors, I perceive that, whatever they may say about the magnitude and seriousness of the question, and their regard for the public tranquillity, the long and the short of the matter is, that they cannot spare the protection of the existing government, and they dread the consequences of disobedience to it to their property and families. For my own part, I should not like to think that I ever rely on the protection of the State. But, if I deny the authority of the State when it presents its tax-bill, it will soon take and waste all my property, and so harass me and my children without end. This is hard. This makes it impossible for a man to live honestly and at the same time comfortably in outward respects. It will not be worth the while to accumulate property; that would be sure to go again. You must hire or squat somewhere, and raise but a small crop, and eat that soon. You must live within yourself, and depend upon yourself, always tucked up and ready for a start, and not have many affairs. A man may grow rich in Turkey even, if he will be in all respects a good subject of the Turkish government. Confucius said,—"If a State is governed by the principles of reason, poverty and misery are subjects of shame; if a State is not governed by the principles of reason, riches and honors are the subjects of shame."

No: until I want the protection of Massachusetts to be extended to me in some distant southern port, where my liberty is endangered, or until I am bent solely on building up an estate at home by peaceful enterprise, I can afford to refuse allegiance to Massachusetts, and her right to my property and life. It costs me less in every sense to incur the penalty of disobedience to the State, than it would to obey. I should feel as if I were worth less in that case.

Some years ago, the State met me in behalf of the Church, and commanded me to pay a certain sum toward the support of a clergyman whose preaching my father attended, but never I myself. "Pay," it said, "or be locked up in the jail." I declined to pay. But, unfortunately, another man saw fit to pay it. I did not see why the schoolmaster should be taxed to support the priest, and not the priest the schoolmaster; for I was not the State's schoolmaster, but I supported myself by voluntary subscription. I did not see why the lyceum should not present its tax-bill, and have the State to back its demand, as well as the church. However, at the request of the selectmen, I condescended to make some such statement as this in writing:—"Know all men by these presents, that I, Henry Thoreau, do not wish to be regarded as a member of any incorporated society which I have not joined." This I gave to the town-clerk; and he has it. The State, having thus learned that I did not wish to be regarded as a member of that church, has never made a like demand on me since; though it said that it must adhere to its original presumption that time. If I had known how to name them, I should then have signed off in detail from all the societies which I never signed on to; but I did not know where to find a complete list.

I have paid no poll-tax for six years. I was put into a jail once on this account, for one night; and, as I stood considering the walls of solid stone, two or three feet thick, the door of wood and iron, a foot thick, and the iron grating which strained the light, I could not help being struck with the foolishness of that institution which treated me as if I were mere flesh and blood and bones, to be locked up. I wondered that it should have concluded at length that this was the best use it could put me to, and had never thought to avail itself of my services in some way. I saw that, if there was a wall of stone between me and my townsmen, there was a still more difficult one to climb or break through, before they could get to be as free as I was. I did not for a moment feel confined, and the walls seemed a great waste of stone and mortar. I felt as if I alone of all my townsmen had paid my tax. They plainly did not know how to treat me, but behaved like persons who are underbred. In every threat and in every compliment there was a blunder; for they thought that my chief desire was to stand the other side of that stone wall. I could not but smile to see how industriously they locked the door on my meditations, which followed them out again without let or hinderance, and *they* were really all that was dangerous. As they could not reach me, they had resolved to punish my body; just as boys, if they cannot come at some person against whom they have a spite, will abuse his dog. I saw that the State was half-witted, that it was timid as a lone woman with her silver spoons, and that it did not know its friends from its foes, and I lost all my remaining respect for it, and pitied it.

Thus the State never intentionally confronts a man's sense, intellectual or moral, but only his body, his senses. It is not armed with superior wit or honesty, but with superior physical strength. I was not born to be forced. I will breathe after my own fashion. Let us see who is the strongest. What force has a multitude? They only can force me who obey a higher law than I. They force me to become like themselves. I do not hear of *men* being *forced* to have this way or that by masses of men. What sort of life were that to live? When I meet a government which says to me, "Your money or your life," why should I be in haste to give it my money? It may be in a great strait, and not know what to do: I cannot help that. It must help itself; do as I do. It is not worth the while to snivel about it. I am not responsible for the successful working of the machinery of society. I am not the son of the engineer. I perceive that, when an acorn and a chestnut fall side by side, the one does not remain inert to make way for the other, but both obey their own laws, and spring and grow and flourish as best they can, till one, perchance, overshadows and destroys the other. If a plant cannot live according to its nature, it dies; and so a man.

The night in prison was novel and interesting enough. The prisoners in their shirt-sleeves were enjoying a chat and the evening air in the door-way, when I entered. But the jailer said, "Come, boys, it is time to lock up;" and so they dispersed, and I heard the sound of their steps returning into the hollow apartments. My room-mate was introduced to me by the jailer as "a first-rate fellow and a clever man." When the door was locked, he showed me where to hang my hat, and how he managed matters there. The rooms were whitewashed once a month; and this one, at least, was the whitest, most simply furnished, and probably the neatest apartment in the town. He naturally wanted to know where I came from, and what brought me there; and, when I had told him, I asked him in my turn how he came there, presuming him to be an honest man, of course; and, as the world goes, I believe he was. "Why," said he, "they accuse me of burning a barn; but I never did it." As near as I could discover, he had probably gone to bed in a barn when drunk, and smoked his pipe there; and so a barn was burnt. He had the reputation of being a clever man, had been there some three months waiting for his trial to come on, and would have to wait as much longer; but he was quite domesticated and contented, since he got his board for nothing, and thought that he was well treated.

He occupied one window, and I the other; and I saw, that, if one stayed there long, his principal business would be to look out the window. I had soon read all the tracts that were left there, and examined where former prisoners had broken out, and where a grate had been sawed off, and heard the history of the various occupants of that room; for I found that even here there was a history and a gossip which never circulated beyond the walls of the jail. Probably this is the only house in the town where verses are composed, which are afterward printed in a circular form, but not published. I was shown quite a long list of verses which were composed by some young men who had been detected in an attempt to escape, who avenged themselves by singing them.

I pumped my fellow-prisoner as dry as I could, for fear I should never see him again; but at length he showed me which was my bed, and left me to blow out the lamp.

It was like travelling into a far country, such as I had never expected to behold, to lie there for one night. It seemed to me that I never had heard the town-clock strike before, nor the evening sounds of the village; for we slept with the windows open, which were inside the grating. It was to see my native village in the light of the middle ages, and our Concord was turned into a Rhine stream, and visions of knights and castles passed before me. They were the voices of old burghers that I heard in the streets. I was an involuntary spectator and auditor of whatever was done and said in the kitchen of the adjacent village-inn,—a wholly new and rare experience to me. It was a closer view of my native town. I was fairly inside of it. I never had seen its institutions before. This is one of its peculiar institutions; for it is a shire town. I began to comprehend what its inhabitants were about.

In the morning, our breakfasts were put through the hole in the door, in small oblong-square tin pans, made to fit, and holding a pint of chocolate, with brown bread, and an iron spoon. When they called for the vessels again, I was green enough to return what bread

I had left; but my comrade seized it, and said that I should lay that up for lunch or dinner. Soon after he was let out to work at haying in a neighboring field, whither he went every day, and would not be back till noon; so he bade me good-day, saying that he doubted if he should see me again.

When I came out of prison,—for some one interfered, and paid that tax,—I did not perceive that great changes had taken place on the common, such as he observed who went in a youth, and emerged a tottering and gray-headed man; and yet a change had to my eyes come over the scene,—the town, and State, and country,—greater than any that mere time could effect. I saw yet more distinctly the State in which I lived. I saw to what extent the people among whom I lived could be trusted as good neighbors and friends; that their friendship was for summer weather only; that they did not greatly purpose to do right; that they were a distinct race from me by their prejudices and superstitions, as the Chinamen and Malays are; that, in their sacrifices to humanity, they ran no risks, not even to their property; that, after all, they were not so noble but they treated the thief as he had treated them, and hoped, by a certain outward observance and a few prayers, and by walking in a particular straight though useless path from time to time, to save their souls. This may be to judge my neighbors harshly; for I believe that many of them are not aware that they have such an institution as the jail in their village.

It was formerly the custom in our village, when a poor debtor came out of jail, for his acquaintances to salute him, looking through their fingers, which were crossed to represent the grating of a jail window, "How do ye do?" My neighbors did not thus salute me, but first looked at me, and then at one another, as if I had returned from a long journey. I was put into jail as I was going to the shoemaker's to get a shoe which was mended. When I was let out the next morning, I proceeded to finish my errand, and, having put on my mended shoe, joined a huckleberry party, who were impatient to put themselves under my conduct; and in half an hour,—for the horse was soon tackled,—was in the midst of a huckleberry field, on one of our highest hills, two miles off; and then the State was nowhere to be seen.

This is the whole history of "My Prisons."

I have never declined paying the highway tax, because I am as desirous of being a good neighbor as I am of being a bad subject; and, as for supporting schools, I am doing my part to educate my fellow-countrymen now. It is for no particular item in the tax-bill that I refuse to pay it. I simply wish to refuse allegiance to the

State, to withdraw and stand aloof from it effectually. I do not care to trace the course of my dollar, if I could, till it buys a man, or a musket to shoot one with,—the dollar is innocent,—but I am concerned to trace the effects of my allegiance. In fact, I quietly declare war with the State, after my fashion, though I will still make what use and get what advantage of her I can, as is usual in such cases.

If others pay the tax which is demanded of me, from a sympathy with the State, they do but what they have already done in their own case, or rather they abet injustice to a greater extent than the State requires. If they pay the tax from a mistaken interest in the individual taxed, to save his property or prevent his going to jail, it is because they have not considered wisely how far they let their private feelings interfere with the public good.

This, then, is my position at present. But one cannot be too much on his guard in such a case, lest his action be biassed by obstinacy, or an undue regard for the opinions of men. Let him see that he does only what belongs to himself and to the hour.

I think sometimes, Why, this people mean well; they are only ignorant; they would do better if they knew how: why give your neighbors this pain to treat you as they are not inclined to? But I think, again, this is no reason why I should do as they do, or permit others to suffer much greater pain of a different kind. Again, I sometimes say to myself, When many millions of men, without heat, without ill-will, without personal feeling of any kind, demand of you a few shillings only, without the possibility, such is their constitution, of retracting or altering their present demand, and without the possibility, on your side, of appeal to any other millions, why expose yourself to this overwhelming brute force? You do not resist cold and hunger, the winds and the waves, thus obstinately; you quietly submit to a thousand similar necessities. You do not put your head into the fire. But just in proportion as I regard this as not wholly a brute force, but partly a human force, and consider that I have relations to those millions as to so many millions of men, and not of mere brute or inanimate things, I see that appeal is possible, first and instantaneously, from them to the Maker of them, and, secondly, from them to themselves. But, if I put my head deliberately into the fire, there is no appeal to fire or to the Maker of fire, and I have only myself to blame. If I could convince myself that I have any right to be satisfied with men as they are, and to treat them accordingly, and not according, in some respects, to my requisitions and expectations of what they and I ought to be, then, like a good Mussulman and fatalist, I should endeavor to be satisfied with things as they are, and say it is the will of God. And, above all, there is this difference between resisting this and a purely brute or natural force, that I can resist this with some effect; but I cannot expect, like Orpheus, to change the nature of the rocks and trees and beasts.

I do not wish to quarrel with any man or nation. I do not wish to split hairs, to make fine distinctions, or set myself up as better than my neighbors. I seek rather, I may say, even an excuse for conforming to the laws of the land. I am but too ready to conform to them. Indeed, I have reason to suspect myself on this head; and each year, as the tax-gatherer comes round, I find myself disposed to review the acts and position of the general and state governments, and the spirit of the people, to discover a pretext for conformity. I believe that the State will soon be able to take all my work of this sort out of my hands, and then I shall be no better a patriot than my fellow-countrymen. Seen from a lower point of view, the Constitution, with all its faults, is very good; the law and the courts are very respectable; even this State and this American government are, in many respects, very admirable and rare things, to be thankful for, such as a great many have described them; but seen from a point of view a little higher, they are what I have described them; seen from a higher still, and the highest, who shall say what they are, or that they are worth looking at or thinking of at all?

However, the government does not concern me much, and I shall bestow the fewest possible thoughts on it. It is not many moments that I live under a government, even in this world. If a man is thought-free, fancy-free, imagination-free, that which *is not* never for a long time appearing *to be* to him, unwise rulers or reformers cannot fatally interrupt him.

I know that most men think differently from myself; but those whose lives are by profession devoted to the study of these or kindred subjects, content me as little as any. Statesmen and legislators, standing so completely within the institution, never distinctly and nakedly behold it. They speak of moving society, but have no resting-place without it. They may be men of a certain experience and discrimination, and have no doubt invented ingenious and even useful systems, for which we sincerely thank them; but all their wit and usefulness lie within certain not very wide limits. They are wont to forget that the world is not governed by policy and expediency. Webster never goes behind government, and so cannot speak with authority about it. His words are wisdom to those legislators who contemplate no essential reform in the existing government; but for thinkers, and those who legislate for all time, he never once glances at the subject. I know of those whose serene and wise speculations on this theme would soon reveal the limits of his mind's range and hospitality. Yet, compared with the cheap professions of most reformers, and the still cheaper wisdom and eloquence of politicians in general, his are almost the only sensible and valuable words, and we thank Heaven for him. Comparatively, he is always strong, original, and, above all, practical. Still, his quality is not wisdom, but prudence. The lawyer's truth is not Truth, but consistency, or a consistent expediency. Truth is always in harmony with herself, and is not concerned chiefly to reveal the justice that may consist with wrong-doing. He well deserves to be called, as he has been called, the Defender of the Constitution. There are really no blows to be given by him but defensive ones. He is not a leader, but a follower. His leaders are the men of '87. "I have never made an effort," he says, "and never propose to make an effort; I have never countenanced an effort, and never mean to countenance an effort, to disturb the arrangement as originally made, by which the various States came into the Union." Still thinking of the sanction which the Constitution gives to slavery, he says, "Because it was a part of the original compact,—let it stand." Notwithstanding his special acuteness and ability, he is unable to take a fact out of its merely political relations, and behold it as it lies absolutely to be disposed of by the intellect,—what, for instance, it behooves a man to do here in America to-day with regard to slavery, but ventures, or is driven, to make some such desperate answer as the following, while professing to speak absolutely, and as a private man,—from which what new and singular code of social duties might be inferred?—"The manner," says he, "in which the governments of those States where slavery exists are to regulate it, is for their own consideration, under their responsibility to their constituents, to the general laws of propriety, humanity, and justice, and to God. Associations formed elsewhere, springing from a feeling of humanity, or any other cause, have nothing whatever to do with it. They have never received any encouragement from me, and they never will."[2]

They who know of no purer sources of truth, who have traced up its stream no higher, stand, and wisely stand, by the Bible and the Constitution, and drink at it there with reverence and humility; but they who behold where it comes trickling into this lake or that pool, gird up their loins once more, and continue their pilgrimage toward its fountain-head.

No man with a genius for legislation has appeared in America. They are rare in the history of the world. There are orators, politicians, and eloquent men, by the thousand; but the speaker has not yet opened his mouth to speak, who is capable of settling the much-vexed questions of the day. We love eloquence for its own sake, and not for any truth which it may utter, or any heroism it may inspire. Our legislators have not yet learned the comparative value of free-trade and of freedom, of union, and of rectitude, to a nation. They have no genius or talent for comparatively humble questions of taxation and finance, commerce and manufacturers and agriculture. If we were left solely to the wordy wit of legislators in Congress for our guidance, uncorrected by the seasonable experience and the effectual complaints of the people, America would not long retain her rank among the nations. For eighteen hundred years, though perchance I have no right to say it, the New Testament has been written; yet where is the legislator who has wisdom and practical talent enough to avail himself of the light which it sheds on the science of legislation?

The authority of government, even such as I am willing to submit to,—for I will cheerfully obey those who know and can do better than I, and in many things even those who neither know nor can do so well,—is still an impure one: to be strictly just, it must have the sanction and consent of the governed. It can have no pure right over my person and property but what I concede to it. The progress from an absolute to a limited monarchy, from a limited monarchy to a democracy, is a progress toward a true respect for the individual. Even the Chinese philosopher was wise enough to regard the individual as the basis of the empire. Is a democracy, such as we know it, the last improvement possible in government? Is it not possible to take a step further towards

2. Thoreau's note: These extracts [from Webster] have been inserted since the Lecture was read.

recognizing and organizing the rights of man? There will never be a really free and enlightened State, until the State comes to recognize the individual as a higher and independent power, from which all its own power and authority are derived, and treats him accordingly. I please myself with imagining a State at last which can afford to be just to all men, and to treat the individual with respect as a neighbor; which even would not think it inconsistent with its own repose, if a few were to live aloof from it, not meddling with it, nor embraced by it, who fulfilled all the duties of neighbors and fellow-men. A State which bore this kind of fruit, and suffered it to drop off as fast as it ripened, would prepare the way for a still more perfect and glorious State, which also I have imagined, but not yet anywhere seen.

SOURCE: Henry David Thoreau. "Resistance to Civil Government" in *Æsthetic Papers*. Edited by Elizabeth P. Peabody. New York: G. P. Putnam, 1849.

From *Walden; or, Life in the Woods* (1854)

Walden *is Thoreau's odd-hewn, unforgettable memoir about his two years, two months and two days of experiences while living in a simple dwelling he built beside Walden Pond, a lake in Concord, Massachusetts. These excerpts from Chapter 1, "Economy," introduce us to Thoreau's experiment, which he so thoroughly described and which made "Walden" a byword for simple, plain living.*

WHEN I WROTE the following pages, or rather the bulk of them, I lived alone, in the woods, a mile from any neighbor, in a house which I had built myself, on the shore of Walden Pond, in Concord, Massachusetts, and earned my living by the labor of my hands only. I lived there two years and two months. At present I am a sojourner in civilized life again.

I should not obtrude my affairs so much on the notice of my readers if very particular inquiries had not been made by my townsmen concerning my mode of life, which some would call impertinent, though they do not appear to me at all impertinent, but, considering the circumstances, very natural and pertinent. Some have asked what I got to eat; if I did not feel lonesome; if I was not afraid; and the like. Others have been curious to learn what portion of my income I devoted to charitable purposes; and some, who have large families, how many poor children I maintained. I will therefore ask those of my readers who feel no particular interest in me to pardon me if I undertake to answer some of these questions in this book. In most books, the I, or first person, is omitted; in this it will be retained; that, in respect to egotism, is the main difference. We commonly do not remember that it is, after all, always the first person that is speaking. I should not talk so much about myself if there were anybody else whom I knew as well. Unfortunately, I am confined to this theme by the narrowness of my experience. Moreover, I, on my side, require of every writer, first or last, a simple and sincere account of his own life, and not merely what he has heard of other men's lives; some such account as he would send to his kindred from a distant land; for if he has lived sincerely, it must have been in a distant land to me. Perhaps these pages are more particularly addressed to poor students. As for the rest of my readers, they will accept such portions as apply to them. I trust that none will stretch the seams in putting on the coat, for it may do good service to him whom it fits.

I would fain say something, not so much concerning the Chinese and Sandwich Islanders as you who read these pages, who are said to live in New England; something about your condition, especially your outward condition or circumstances in this world, in this town, what it is, whether it is necessary that it be as bad as it is, whether it cannot be improved as well as not. I have travelled a good deal in Concord; and everywhere, in shops, and offices, and fields, the inhabitants have appeared to me to be doing penance in a thousand remarkable ways. What I have heard of Bramins sitting exposed to four fires and looking in the face of the sun; or hanging suspended, with their heads downward, over flames; or looking at the heavens over their shoulders "until it becomes impossible for them to resume their natural position, while from the twist of the neck nothing but liquids can pass into the stomach;" or dwelling, chained for life, at the foot of a tree; or measuring with their bodies, like caterpillars, the breadth of vast empires; or standing on one leg on the tops of pillars—even these forms of conscious penance are hardly more incredible and astonishing than the scenes which I daily witness. The twelve labors of Hercules were trifling in comparison with those which my neighbors have undertaken; for they were only twelve, and had an end; but I could never see that these men slew or captured any monster or finished any labor. They have no friend Iolas to burn with a hot iron the root of the hydra's head, but as soon as one head is crushed, two spring up.

I see young men, my townsmen, whose misfortune it is to have inherited farms, houses, barns, cattle, and farming tools; for these are more easily acquired than got rid of. Better if they had been born in the open pasture and suckled by a wolf, that they might have seen with clearer eyes what field they were called to labor in. Who made them serfs of the soil? Why should they eat their sixty acres, when man is condemned to eat only his peck of dirt? Why should they begin digging their graves as soon as they are born? They have got to live a man's life, pushing all these things before them, and get on as well as they can. How many a poor immortal soul have I met well-nigh crushed and smothered under its load, creeping down the road of life, pushing before it a barn seventy-five feet by forty, its Augean stables never cleansed, and one hundred acres of land, tillage, mowing, pasture, and woodlot! The portionless, who struggle with no such unnecessary inherited encumbrances, find it labor enough to subdue and cultivate a few cubic feet of flesh.

But men labor under a mistake. The better part of the man is soon plowed into the soil for compost. By a seeming fate, commonly called necessity, they are employed, as it says in an old book, laying up treasures which moth and rust will corrupt and thieves break through and steal. It is a fool's life, as they will find when they get to the end of it, if not before. It is said that Deucalion and Pyrrha created men by throwing stones over their heads behind them:—

> Inde genus durum sumus, experiensque laborum,
> Et documenta damus quâ simus origine nati.

Or, as Raleigh rhymes it in his sonorous way,—

> "From thence our kind hard-hearted is, enduring pain and care,
> Approving that our bodies of a stony nature are."

So much for a blind obedience to a blundering oracle, throwing the stones over their heads behind them, and not seeing where they fell.

Most men, even in this comparatively free country, through mere ignorance and mistake, are so occupied with the factitious cares and superfluously coarse labors of life that its finer fruits cannot be plucked by them. Their fingers, from excessive toil, are too clumsy and tremble too much for that. Actually, the laboring man has not leisure for a true integrity day by day; he cannot afford to sustain the manliest relations to men; his labor would be depreciated in the market. He has no time to be anything but a machine. How can he remember well his ignorance—which his growth requires—who has so often to use his knowledge? We should feed and clothe him gratuitously sometimes, and recruit him with our cordials, before we judge of him. The finest qualities of our nature, like the bloom on fruits, can be preserved only by the most delicate handling. Yet we do not treat ourselves nor one another thus tenderly.

Some of you, we all know, are poor, find it hard to live, are sometimes, as it were, gasping for breath. I have no doubt that some of you who read this book are unable to pay for all the dinners which you have actually eaten, or for the coats and shoes which are fast wearing or are already worn out, and have come to this page to spend borrowed or stolen time, robbing your creditors of an hour. It is very evident what mean and sneaking lives many of you live, for my sight has been whetted by experience; always on the limits, trying to get into business and trying to get out of debt, a very ancient slough, called by the Latins *aes alienum*, another's brass, for some of their coins were made of brass; still living, and dying, and buried by this other's brass; always promising to pay, promising to pay, tomorrow, and dying today, insolvent; seeking to curry favor, to get custom, by how many modes, only not state-prison offenses; lying, flattering, voting, contracting yourselves into a nutshell of civility or dilating into an atmosphere of thin and vaporous generosity, that you may persuade your neighbor to let you make his shoes, or his hat, or his coat, or his carriage, or import his groceries for him; making yourselves sick, that you may lay up something against a sick day, something to be tucked away in an old chest, or in a stocking behind the plastering, or, more safely, in the brick bank; no matter where, no matter how much or how little.

I sometimes wonder that we can be so frivolous, I may almost say, as to attend to the gross but somewhat foreign form of servitude called Negro Slavery, there are so many keen and subtle masters that enslave both North and South. It is hard to have a Southern overseer; it is worse to have a Northern one; but worst of all when you are the slave-driver of yourself. Talk of a divinity in man! Look at the teamster on the highway, wending to market by day or night; does any divinity stir within him? His highest duty to fodder and water his horses! What is his destiny to him compared with the shipping interests? Does not he drive for Squire Make-a-stir? How godlike, how immortal, is he? See how he cowers and sneaks, how vaguely all the day he fears, not being immortal nor divine, but the slave and prisoner of his own opinion of himself, a fame won by his own deeds. Public opinion is a weak tyrant compared with our own private opinion. What a man thinks of himself, that it is which determines, or rather indicates, his fate. Self-emancipation even in the West Indian provinces of the fancy and imagination—what Wilberforce is there to bring that about? Think, also, of the ladies of the land weaving toilet cushions against the last day, not to betray too green an interest in their fates! As if you could kill time without injuring eternity.

The mass of men lead lives of quiet desperation. What is called resignation is confirmed desperation. From the desperate city you go into the desperate country, and have to console yourself with the bravery of minks and muskrats. A stereotyped but unconscious despair is concealed even under what are called the games and amusements of mankind. There is no play in them, for this comes after work. But it is a characteristic of wisdom not to do desperate things.

When we consider what, to use the words of the catechism, is the chief end of man, and what are the true necessaries and means of life, it appears as if men had deliberately chosen the common mode of living because they preferred it to any other. Yet they honestly think there is no choice left. But alert and healthy natures remember that the sun rose clear. It is never too late to give up our prejudices. No way of thinking or doing, however ancient, can be trusted without proof. What everybody echoes or in silence passes by as true to-day may turn out to be falsehood to-morrow, mere smoke of opinion, which some had trusted for a cloud that would sprinkle fertilizing rain on their fields. What old people say you cannot do, you try and find that you can. Old deeds for old people, and new deeds for new. Old people did not know enough once, perchance, to fetch fresh fuel to keep the fire a-going; new people put a little dry wood under a pot, and are whirled round the globe with the speed of birds, in a way to kill old people, as the phrase is. Age is no better, hardly so well, qualified for an instructor as youth, for it has not profited so much as it has lost. One may almost doubt if the wisest man has learned anything of absolute value by living. Practically, the old have no very important advice to give the young, their own experience has been so partial, and their lives have been such miserable failures, for private reasons, as they must believe; and it may be that they have some faith left which belies that experience, and they are only less young than they were. I have lived some thirty years on this planet, and I have yet to hear the first syllable of valuable or even earnest advice from my seniors. They have told me nothing, and probably cannot tell me anything to the purpose. Here is life, an experiment to a great extent untried by me; but it does not avail me that they have tried it. If I have any experience which I think valuable, I am sure to reflect that this my Mentors said nothing about.

One farmer says to me, "You cannot live on vegetable food solely, for it furnishes nothing to make bones with;" and so he religiously devotes a part of his day to supplying his system with the raw material of bones; walking all the while he talks behind his oxen, which, with vegetable-made bones, jerk him and his lumbering plow along in spite of every obstacle. Some things are really necessaries of life in some circles, the most helpless and diseased, which in others are luxuries merely, and in others still are entirely unknown.

The whole ground of human life seems to some to have been gone over by their predecessors, both the heights and the valleys, and all things to have been cared for. According to Evelyn, "the wise Solomon prescribed ordinances for the very distances of trees; and the Roman praetors have decided how often you may go into your neighbor's land to gather the acorns which fall on it without trespass, and what share belongs to that neighbor." Hippocrates has even left directions how we should cut our nails; that is, even with the ends of the fingers, neither shorter nor longer. Undoubtedly the very tedium and ennui which presume to have exhausted the variety and the joys of life are as old as Adam. But man's capacities have never been measured; nor are we to judge of what he can do by any precedents, so little has been tried. Whatever have been thy failures hitherto, "be not afflicted, my child, for who shall assign to thee what thou hast left undone?"

We might try our lives by a thousand simple tests; as, for instance, that the same sun which ripens my beans illumines at once a system of earths like ours. If I had remembered this it would have prevented some mistakes. This was not the light in which I hoed them. The stars are the apexes of what wonderful triangles! What distant and different beings in the various mansions of the universe are contemplating the same one at the same moment! Nature and human life are as various as our several constitutions. Who shall say what prospect life offers to another? Could a greater miracle take place than for us to look through each other's eyes for an instant? We should live in all the ages of the world in an hour; ay, in all the worlds of the ages. History, Poetry, Mythology!—I know of no reading of another's experience so startling and informing as this would be.

The greater part of what my neighbors call good I believe in my soul to be bad, and if I repent of anything, it is very likely to be my good behavior. What demon possessed me that I behaved so well? You may say the wisest thing you can, old man—you who have lived seventy years, not without honor of a kind—I hear an irresistible voice which invites me away from all that. One generation abandons the enterprises of another like stranded vessels.

I think that we may safely trust a good deal more than we do. We may waive just so much care of ourselves as we honestly bestow elsewhere. Nature is as well adapted to our weakness as to our strength. The incessant anxiety and strain of some is a well-nigh incurable form of disease. We are made to exaggerate the importance of what work we do; and yet how much is not done by us! or, what if we had been taken sick? How vigilant we are! determined not to live by faith if we can avoid it; all the day long on the alert, at night we unwillingly say our prayers and commit ourselves to uncertainties. So thoroughly and sincerely are we compelled to live, reverencing our life, and denying the possibility of change. This is the only way, we say; but there are as many ways as there can be drawn radii from one centre. All change is a miracle to contemplate; but it is a miracle which is taking place every instant. Confucius said, "To know that we know what we know, and that we do not know what we do not know, that is true knowledge." When one man has reduced a fact of the imagination to be a fact to his understanding, I foresee that all men at length establish their lives on that basis.

Let us consider for a moment what most of the trouble and anxiety which I have referred to is about, and how much it is necessary that we be troubled, or at least careful. It would be some advantage to live a primitive and frontier life, though in the midst of an outward civilization, if only to learn what are the gross necessaries of life and what methods have been taken to obtain them; or even to look over the old day-books of the merchants, to see what it was that men most commonly bought at the stores, what they stored, that is, what are the grossest groceries. For the improvements of ages have had but little influence on the essential laws of man's existence; as our skeletons, probably, are not to be distinguished from those of our ancestors.

By the words, *necessary of life,* I mean whatever, of all that man obtains by his own exertions, has been from the first, or from long use has become, so important to human life that few, if any, whether from savageness, or poverty, or philosophy, ever attempt to do without it. To many creatures there is in this sense but one necessary of life, Food. To the bison of the prairie it is a few inches of palatable grass, with water to drink; unless he seeks the Shelter of the forest or the mountain's shadow. None of the brute creation requires more than Food and Shelter. The necessaries of life for man in this climate may, accurately enough, be distributed under the several heads of Food, Shelter, Clothing, and Fuel; for not till we have secured these are we prepared to entertain the true problems of life with freedom and a prospect of success. Man has invented, not only houses, but clothes and cooked food; and possibly from the accidental discovery of the warmth of fire, and the consequent use of it, at first a luxury, arose the present necessity to sit by it. We observe cats and dogs acquiring the same second nature. By proper Shelter and Clothing we legitimately retain our own internal heat; but with an excess of these, or of Fuel, that is, with an external heat greater than our own internal, may not cookery properly be said to begin? Darwin, the naturalist, says of the inhabitants of Tierra del Fuego, that while his own party, who were well clothed and sitting close to a fire, were far from too warm, these naked savages, who were farther off, were observed, to his great surprise, "to be streaming with perspiration at undergoing such a roasting." So, we are told, the New Hollander goes naked with impunity, while the European shivers in his clothes. Is it impossible to combine the hardiness of these savages with the intellectualness of the civilized man? According to Liebig, man's body is a stove, and food the fuel which keeps up the internal combustion in the lungs. In cold weather we eat more, in warm less. The animal heat is the result of a slow combustion, and disease and death take place when this is too rapid; or for want of fuel, or from some defect in the draught, the fire goes out. Of course the vital heat is not to be confounded with fire; but so much for analogy. It appears, therefore, from the above list, that the expression, *animal life,* is nearly synonymous with the expression, *animal heat;* for while Food may be regarded as the Fuel which keeps up the fire within us—and Fuel serves only to prepare that Food or to increase the warmth of our bodies by addition from without—Shelter and Clothing also serve only to retain the heat thus generated and absorbed.

The grand necessity, then, for our bodies, is to keep warm, to keep the vital heat in us. What pains we accordingly take, not only with our Food, and Clothing, and Shelter, but with our beds, which are our night-clothes, robbing the nests and breasts of birds to prepare this shelter within a shelter, as the mole has its bed of grass and leaves at the end of its burrow! The poor man is wont to complain that this is a cold world; and to cold, no less physical than social, we refer directly a great part of our ails. The summer, in some climates, makes possible to man a sort of Elysian life. Fuel, except to cook his Food, is then unnecessary; the sun is his fire, and many of the fruits are sufficiently cooked by its rays; while Food generally is more various, and more easily obtained, and Clothing and Shelter are wholly or half unnecessary. At the present day, and in this country, as I find by my own experience, a few implements, a knife, an axe, a spade, a wheelbarrow, &c., and for the studious, lamplight, stationery, and access to a few books, rank next to necessaries, and can all be obtained at a trifling cost. Yet some, not wise, go to the other side of the globe, to barbarous and unhealthy regions, and devote themselves to trade for ten or twenty years, in order that they may live—that is, keep comfortably warm—and die in New England at last. The luxuriously rich are not simply kept comfortably warm, but unnaturally hot; as I implied before, they are cooked, of course *à la mode.*

Most of the luxuries, and many of the so-called comforts of life, are not only not indispensable, but positive hindrances to the elevation of mankind. With respect to luxuries and comforts, the wisest have ever lived a more simple and meagre life than the poor. The ancient philosophers, Chinese, Hindoo, Persian, and Greek, were a class than which none has been poorer in outward riches, none so rich in inward. We know not much about them. It is remarkable that we know so much of them as we do. The same is true of the more modern reformers and benefactors of their race. None can be an impartial or wise observer of human life but from the vantage ground of what we should call voluntary poverty. Of a life of luxury the fruit is luxury, whether in agriculture, or commerce, or literature, or art. There are nowadays professors of philosophy, but not philosophers. Yet it is admirable to profess because it was once admirable to live. To be a philosopher is not merely to have subtle thoughts, nor even to found a school, but so to love wisdom as to live according to its dictates, a life of simplicity, independence, magnanimity, and trust. It is to solve some of the problems of life, not only theoretically, but practically. The success of great scholars and thinkers is commonly a courtier-like success, not kingly, not manly. They make shift to live merely by conformity, practically as their fathers did, and are in no sense the progenitors of a noble race of men. But why do men degenerate ever? What makes families run out? What is the nature of the luxury which enervates and destroys nations? Are we sure that there is none of it in our own lives? The philosopher is in advance of his age even in the outward form of his life. He is not fed, sheltered, clothed, warmed, like his contemporaries. How can a man be a philosopher and not maintain his vital heat by better methods than other men?

When a man is warmed by the several modes which I have described, what does he want next? Surely not more warmth of the same kind, as more and richer food, larger and more splendid houses, finer and more abundant clothing, more numerous, incessant, and hotter fires, and the like. When he has obtained those things which are necessary to life, there is another alternative than to obtain the superfluities; and that is, to adventure on life now, his vacation from humbler toil having commenced. The soil, it appears, is suited to the seed, for it has sent its radicle downward, and it may now send its shoot upward also with confidence. Why has man rooted himself thus firmly in the earth, but that he may rise in the same proportion into the heavens above?—for the nobler plants are valued for the fruit they bear at last in the air and light, far from the ground, and are not treated like the humbler esculents, which, though they may be biennials, are cultivated only till they have perfected their root, and often cut down at top for this purpose, so that most would not know them in their flowering season.

I do not mean to prescribe rules to strong and valiant natures, who will mind their own affairs whether in heaven or hell, and perchance build more magnificently and spend more lavishly than the richest, without ever impoverishing themselves, not knowing how they live—if, indeed, there are any such, as has been dreamed;

nor to those who find their encouragement and inspiration in precisely the present condition of things, and cherish it with the fondness and enthusiasm of lovers—and, to some extent, I reckon myself in this number; I do not speak to those who are well employed, in whatever circumstances, and they know whether they are well employed or not;—but mainly to the mass of men who are discontented, and idly complaining of the hardness of their lot or of the times, when they might improve them. There are some who complain most energetically and inconsolably of any, because they are, as they say, doing their duty. I also have in my mind that seemingly wealthy, but most terribly impoverished class of all, who have accumulated dross, but know not how to use it, or get rid of it, and thus have forged their own golden or silver fetters.

If I should attempt to tell how I have desired to spend my life in years past, it would probably surprise those of my readers who are somewhat acquainted with its actual history; it would certainly astonish those who know nothing about it. I will only hint at some of the enterprises which I have cherished.

In any weather, at any hour of the day or night, I have been anxious to improve the nick of time, and notch it on my stick too; to stand on the meeting of two eternities, the past and future, which is precisely the present moment; to toe that line. You will pardon some obscurities, for there are more secrets in my trade than in most men's, and yet not voluntarily kept, but inseparable from its very nature. I would gladly tell all that I know about it, and never paint "No Admittance" on my gate.

I long ago lost a hound, a bay horse, and a turtle dove, and am still on their trail. Many are the travellers I have spoken concerning them, describing their tracks and what calls they answered to. I have met one or two who had heard the hound, and the tramp of the horse, and even seen the dove disappear behind a cloud, and they seemed as anxious to recover them as if they had lost them themselves.

To anticipate, not the sunrise and the dawn merely, but, if possible, Nature herself! How many mornings, summer and winter, before yet any neighbor was stirring about his business, have I been about mine! No doubt, many of my townsmen have met me returning from this enterprise, farmers starting for Boston in the twilight, or woodchoppers going to their work. It is true, I never assisted the sun materially in his rising, but, doubt not, it was of the last importance only to be present at it.

So many autumn, ay, and winter days, spent outside the town, trying to hear what was in the wind, to hear and carry it express! I well-nigh sunk all my capital in it, and lost my own breath into the bargain, running in the face of it. If it had concerned either of the political parties, depend upon it, it would have appeared in the Gazette with the earliest intelligence. At other times watching from the observatory of some cliff or tree, to telegraph any new arrival; or waiting at evening on the hill-tops for the sky to fall, that I might catch something, though I never caught much, and that, manna-wise, would dissolve again in the sun.

For a long time I was reporter to a journal, of no very wide circulation, whose editor has never yet seen fit to print the bulk of my contributions, and, as is too common with writers, I got only my labor for my pains. However, in this case my pains were their own reward.

For many years I was self-appointed inspector of snow-storms and rain-storms, and did my duty faithfully; surveyor, if not of highways, then of forest paths and all across-lot routes, keeping them open, and ravines bridged and passable at all seasons, where the public heel had testified to their utility.

I have looked after the wild stock of the town, which give a faithful herdsman a good deal of trouble by leaping fences; and I have had an eye to the unfrequented nooks and corners of the farm; though I did not always know whether Jonas or Solomon worked in a particular field to-day; that was none of my business. I have watered the red huckleberry, the sand cherry and the nettle-tree, the red pine and the black ash, the white grape and the yellow violet, which might have withered else in dry seasons.

In short, I went on thus for a long time (I may say it without boasting), faithfully minding my business, till it became more and more evident that my townsmen would not after all admit me into the list of town officers, nor make my place a sinecure with a moderate allowance. My accounts, which I can swear to have kept faithfully, I have, indeed, never got audited, still less accepted, still less paid and settled. However, I have not set my heart on that.

Not long since, a strolling Indian went to sell baskets at the house of a well-known lawyer in my neighborhood. "Do you wish to buy any baskets?" he asked. "No, we do not want any," was the reply. "What!" exclaimed the Indian as he went out the gate, "do you mean to starve us?" Having seen his industrious white neighbors so well off—that the lawyer had only to weave arguments, and, by some magic, wealth and standing followed—he had said to himself: I will go into business; I will weave baskets; it is a thing which I can do. Thinking that when he had made the baskets he would have done his part, and then it would be the white man's to buy them. He had not discovered that it was necessary for him to make it worth the other's while to buy them, or at least make him think that it was so, or to make something else which it would be worth his while to buy. I too had woven a kind of basket of a delicate texture, but I had not made it worth any one's while to buy them. Yet not the less, in my case, did I think it worth my while to weave them, and instead of studying how to make it worth men's while to buy my baskets, I studied rather how to avoid the necessity of selling them. The life which men praise and regard as successful is but one kind. Why should we exaggerate any one kind at the expense of the others?

Finding that my fellow-citizens were not likely to offer me any room in the court house, or any curacy or living anywhere else, but I must shift for myself, I turned my face more exclusively than ever to the woods, where I was better known. I determined to go into business at once, and not wait to acquire the usual capital, using such slender means as I had already got. My purpose in going to Walden Pond was not to live cheaply nor to live dearly there, but to transact some private business with the fewest obstacles; to be hindered from accomplishing which for want of a little common sense, a little enterprise and business talent, appeared not so sad as foolish.

I have always endeavored to acquire strict business habits; they are indispensable to every man. If your trade is with the Celestial Empire, then some small counting house on the coast, in some Salem harbor, will be fixture enough. You will export such articles as the country affords, purely native products, much ice and pine timber and a little granite, always in native bottoms. These will be good ventures. To oversee all the details yourself in person; to be at once pilot and captain, and owner and underwriter; to buy and sell and keep the accounts; to read every letter received, and write or read every letter sent; to superintend the discharge of imports night and day; to be upon many parts of the coast almost at the same time—often the richest freight will be discharged upon a Jersey shore;—to be your own telegraph, unweariedly sweeping the horizon, speaking all passing vessels bound coastwise; to keep up a steady despatch of commodities, for the supply of such a distant and exorbitant market; to keep yourself informed of the state of the markets, prospects of war and peace everywhere, and anticipate the tendencies of trade and civilization—taking advantage of the results of all exploring expeditions, using new passages and all improvements in navigation;—charts to be studied, the position of reefs and new lights and buoys to be ascertained, and ever, and ever, the logarithmic tables to be corrected, for by the error of some calculator the vessel often splits upon a rock that should have reached a friendly pier—there is the untold fate of La Perouse;—universal science to be kept pace with, studying the lives of all great discoverers and navigators, great adventurers and merchants, from Hanno and the Phoenicians down to our day; in fine, account of stock to be taken from time to time, to know how you stand. It is a labor to task the faculties of a man—such problems of profit and loss, of interest, of tare and tret, and gauging of all kinds in it, as demand a universal knowledge.

I have thought that Walden Pond would be a good place for business, not solely on account of the railroad and the ice trade; it offers advantages which it may not be good policy to divulge; it is a good port and a good foundation. No Neva marshes to be filled; though you must everywhere build on piles of your own driving. It is said that a flood-tide, with a westerly wind, and ice in the Neva, would sweep St. Petersburg from the face of the earth.

[. . .]

Near the end of March, 1845, I borrowed an axe and went down to the woods by Walden Pond, nearest to where I intended to build my house, and began to cut down some tall, arrowy white pines, still in their youth, for timber. It is difficult to begin without borrowing, but perhaps it is the most generous course thus to permit your fellow-men to have an interest in your enterprise. The owner of the axe, as he released his hold on it, said that it was the apple of his eye; but I returned it sharper than I received it. It was a pleasant hillside where I worked, covered with pine woods, through which I looked out on the pond, and a small open field in the woods where pines and hickories were springing up. The ice in the pond was not yet dissolved, though there were some open spaces, and it was all dark-colored and saturated with water.

There were some slight flurries of snow during the days that I worked there; but for the most part when I came out on to the railroad, on my way home, its yellow sand heap stretched away gleaming in the hazy atmosphere, and the rails shone in the spring sun, and I heard the lark and pewee and other birds already come to commence another year with us. They were pleasant spring days, in which the winter of man's discontent was thawing as well as the earth, and the life that had lain torpid began to stretch itself. One day, when my axe had come off and I had cut a green hickory for a wedge, driving it with a stone, and had placed the whole to soak in a pond-hole in order to swell the wood, I saw a striped snake run into the water, and he lay on the bottom, apparently without inconvenience, as long as I stayed there, or more than a quarter of an hour; perhaps because he had not yet fairly come out of the torpid state. It appeared to me that for a like reason men remain in their present low and primitive condition; but if they should feel the influence of the spring of springs arousing them, they would of necessity rise to a higher and more ethereal life. I had previously seen the snakes in frosty mornings in my path with portions of their bodies still numb and inflexible, waiting for the sun to thaw them. On the 1st of April it rained and melted the ice, and in the early part of the day, which was very foggy, I heard a stray goose groping about over the pond and cackling as if lost, or like the spirit of the fog.

So I went on for some days cutting and hewing timber, and also studs and rafters, all with my narrow axe, not having many communicable or scholar-like thoughts, singing to myself,—

> Men say they know many things;
> But lo! they have taken wings—
> The arts and sciences,
> And a thousand appliances;
> The wind that blows
> Is all that any body knows.

I hewed the main timbers six inches square, most of the studs on two sides only, and the rafters and floor timbers on one side, leaving the rest of the bark on, so that they were just as straight and much stronger than sawed ones. Each stick was carefully mortised or tenoned by its stump, for I had borrowed other tools by this time. My days in the woods were not very long ones; yet I usually carried my dinner of bread and butter, and read the newspaper in which it was wrapped, at noon, sitting amid the green pine boughs which I had cut off, and to my bread was imparted some of their fragrance, for my hands were covered with a thick coat of pitch. Before I had done I was more the friend than the foe of the pine tree, though I had cut down some of them, having become better acquainted with it. Sometimes a rambler in the wood was attracted by the sound of my axe, and we chatted pleasantly over the chips which I had made.

By the middle of April, for I made no haste in my work, but rather made the most of it, my house was framed and ready for the raising. I had already bought the shanty of James Collins, an Irishman who worked on the Fitchburg Railroad, for boards. James Collins' shanty was considered an uncommonly fine one. When I called to see it he was not at home. I walked about the outside, at first unobserved from within, the window was so deep and high. It was of small dimensions, with a peaked cottage roof, and not much else to be seen, the dirt being raised five feet all around as if it were a compost heap. The roof was the soundest part, though a good deal warped and made brittle by the sun. Doorsill there was none, but a perennial passage for the hens under the door board. Mrs. C. came to the door and asked me to view it from the inside. The hens were driven in by my approach. It was dark, and had a dirt floor for the most part, dank, clammy, and aguish, only here a board and there a board which would not bear removal. She lighted a lamp to show me the inside of the roof and the walls, and also that the board floor extended under the bed, warning me not to step into the cellar, a sort of dust hole two feet deep. In her own words, they were "good boards overhead, good boards all around, and a good window"—of two whole squares originally, only the cat had passed out that way lately. There was a stove, a bed, and a place to sit, an infant in the house where it was born, a silk parasol, gilt-framed looking-glass, and a patent new coffee-mill nailed to an oak sapling, all told. The bargain was soon concluded, for James had in the meanwhile returned. I to pay four dollars and twenty-five cents tonight, he to vacate at five tomorrow morning, selling to nobody else meanwhile: I to take possession at six. It were well, he said, to be there early, and anticipate certain indistinct but wholly unjust claims on the score of ground rent and fuel. This he assured me was the only encumbrance. At six I passed him and his family on the road. One large bundle held their all—bed, coffee-mill, looking-glass, hens—all but the cat; she took to the woods and became a wild cat, and, as I learned afterward, trod in a trap set for woodchucks, and so became a dead cat at last.

I took down this dwelling the same morning, drawing the nails, and removed it to the pond-side by small cartloads, spreading the boards on the grass there to bleach and warp back again in the sun. One early thrush gave me a note or two as I drove along the woodland path. I was informed treacherously by a young Patrick that neighbor Seeley, an Irishman, in the intervals of the carting, transferred the still tolerable, straight, and drivable nails, staples, and spikes to his pocket, and then stood when I came back to pass the time of day, and look freshly up, unconcerned, with spring thoughts, at the devastation; there being a dearth of work, as he said. He was there to represent spectatordom, and help make this seemingly insignificant event one with the removal of the gods of Troy.

I dug my cellar in the side of a hill sloping to the south, where a woodchuck had formerly dug his burrow, down through sumach and blackberry roots, and the lowest stain of vegetation, six feet square by seven deep, to a fine sand where potatoes would not freeze in any winter. The sides were left shelving, and not stoned; but the sun having never shone on them, the sand still keeps its place. It was but two hours' work. I took particular pleasure in this breaking of ground, for in almost all latitudes men dig into the earth for an equable temperature. Under the most splendid house in the city is still to be found the cellar where they store their roots as of old, and long after the superstructure has disappeared posterity remark its dent in the earth. The house is still but a sort of porch at the entrance of a burrow.

At length, in the beginning of May, with the help of some of my acquaintances, rather to improve so good an occasion for neighborliness than from any necessity, I set up the frame of my house. No man was ever more honored in the character of his raisers than I. They are destined, I trust, to assist at the raising of loftier structures one day. I began to occupy my house on the 4th of July, as soon as it was boarded and roofed, for the boards were carefully feather-edged and lapped, so that it was perfectly impervious to rain, but before boarding I laid the foundation of a chimney at one end, bringing two cartloads of stones up the hill from the pond in my arms. I built the chimney after my hoeing in the fall, before a fire became necessary for warmth, doing my cooking in the meanwhile out of doors on the ground, early in the morning: which mode I still think is in some respects more convenient and agreeable than the usual one. When it stormed before my bread was baked, I fixed a few boards over the fire, and sat under them to watch my loaf, and passed some pleasant hours in that way. In those days, when my hands were much employed, I read but little, but the least scraps of paper which lay on the ground, my holder, or tablecloth, afforded me as much entertainment, in fact answered the same purpose as the Iliad.

It would be worth the while to build still more deliberately than I did, considering, for instance, what foundation a door, a window, a cellar, a garret, have in the nature of man, and perchance never raising any superstructure until we found a better reason for it than our temporal necessities even. There is some of the same fitness in a man's building his own house that there is in a bird's building its own nest. Who knows but if men constructed their dwellings with their own hands, and provided food for themselves and families simply and honestly enough, the poetic faculty would be universally developed, as birds universally sing when they are so engaged? But alas! we do like cowbirds and cuckoos, which lay their eggs in nests which other birds have built, and cheer no traveller with their chattering and unmusical notes. Shall we forever resign the pleasure of construction to the carpenter? What does architecture amount to in the experience of the mass of men? I never in all my walks came across a man engaged in so simple and natural an occupation as building his house. We belong to the community. It is not the tailor alone who is the ninth part of a man; it is as much the preacher, and the merchant, and the farmer. Where is this division of labor to end? and what object does it finally serve? No doubt another *may* also think for me; but it is not therefore desirable that he should do so to the exclusion of my thinking for myself.

True, there are architects so called in this country, and I have heard of one at least possessed with the idea of making architectural ornaments have a core of truth, a necessity, and hence a beauty, as if it were a revelation to him. All very well perhaps from his point of view, but only a little better than the common dilettantism. A sentimental reformer in architecture, he began at the cornice, not at the foundation. It was only how to put a core of truth within the ornaments, that every sugarplum, in fact, might have an almond or caraway seed in it—though I hold that almonds are most wholesome without the sugar—and not how the inhabitant, the indweller, might build truly within and without, and let the ornaments take care of themselves. What reasonable man ever supposed that ornaments were something outward and in the skin merely—that the tortoise got his spotted shell, or the shell-fish its mother-o'-pearl tints, by such a contract as the inhabitants of Broadway their Trinity Church? But a man has no more to do with the style of architecture of his house than a tortoise with that of its shell: nor need the soldier be so idle as to try to paint the precise *color* of his virtue on his standard. The enemy will find it out. He may turn pale when the trial comes. This man seemed to me to lean over the cornice, and timidly whisper his half truth to the rude occupants who really knew it better than he. What of architectural beauty I now see, I know has gradually grown from within outward, out of the necessities and character of the indweller, who is the only builder—out of some unconscious truthfulness, and nobleness, without ever a thought for the appearance; and whatever additional beauty of this kind is destined to be produced will be preceded by a like unconscious beauty of life. The most interesting dwellings in this country, as the painter knows, are the most unpretending, humble log huts and cottages of the poor commonly; it is the life of the inhabitants whose shells they are, and not any peculiarity in their surfaces merely, which makes them *picturesque*; and equally interesting will be the citizen's suburban box, when his life shall be as simple and as agreeable to the imagination, and there is as little straining after effect in the style of his dwelling. A great proportion of architectural ornaments are literally hollow, and a September gale would strip them off, like borrowed plumes, without injury to the substantials. They can do without architecture who have no olives nor wines in the cellar. What if an equal ado were made about the ornaments of style in literature, and the architects of our bibles spent as much time about their cornices as the architects of our churches do? So are made the *belles-lettres* and the *beaux-arts* and their professors. Much it concerns a man, forsooth, how a few sticks are slanted over him or under him, and what colors are daubed upon his box. It would signify somewhat, if, in any earnest sense, he slanted them and daubed it; but the spirit having departed out of the tenant, it is of a piece with constructing his own coffin—the architecture of the grave—and "carpenter" is but another name for "coffin-maker." One man says, in his despair or indifference to life, take up a handful of the earth at your feet, and paint your house that color. Is he thinking of his last and narrow house? Toss up a copper for it as well. What an abundance of leisure he must have! Why do you take up a handful of dirt? Better paint your house your own complexion; let it turn pale or blush for you. An enterprise to improve the style of cottage architecture! When you have got my ornaments ready, I will wear them.

Before winter I built a chimney, and shingled the sides of my house, which were already impervious to rain, with imperfect and sappy shingles made of the first slice of the log, whose edges I was obliged to straighten with a plane.

I have thus a tight shingled and plastered house, ten feet wide by fifteen long, and eight-feet posts, with a garret and a closet, a large window on each side, two trap doors, one door at the end, and a brick fireplace opposite. The exact cost of my house, paying the usual price for such materials as I used, but not counting the work, all of which was done by myself, was as follows; and I give the details because very few are able to tell exactly what their houses cost, and fewer still, if any, the separate cost of the various materials which compose them:—

Boards	\$8.03½,	mostly shanty boards.
Refuse shingles for roof sides	4.00	
Laths	1.25	
Two second-hand windows with glass	2.43	
One thousand old brick	4.00	
Two casks of lime	2.40	That was high.
Hair	0.31	More than I needed.
Mantle-tree iron	0.15	
Nails	3.90	
Hinges and screws	0.14	
Latch	0.10	
Chalk	0.01	
Transportation	1.40	I carried a good part on my back.
In all	\$28.12½	

These are all the materials, excepting the timber, stones, and sand, which I claimed by squatter's right. I have also a small woodshed adjoining, made chiefly of the stuff which was left after building the house.

I intend to build me a house which will surpass any on the main street in Concord in grandeur and luxury, as soon as it pleases me as much and will cost me no more than my present one.

I thus found that the student who wishes for a shelter can obtain one for a lifetime at an expense not greater than the rent which he now pays annually. If I seem to boast more than is becoming, my excuse is that I brag for humanity rather than for myself; and my shortcomings and inconsistencies do not affect the truth of my statement. Notwithstanding much cant and hypocrisy—chaff which I find it difficult to separate from my wheat, but for which I am as sorry as any man—I will breathe freely and stretch myself in this respect, it is such a relief to both the moral and physical system; and I am resolved that I will not through humility become the devil's attorney. I will endeavor to speak a good word for the truth. At Cambridge College the mere rent of a student's room, which is only a little larger than my own, is thirty dollars each year, though the corporation had the advantage of building thirty-two side by side and under one roof, and the occupant suffers the inconvenience of many and noisy neighbors, and perhaps a residence in the fourth story. I cannot but think that if we had more true wisdom in these respects, not only less education would be needed, because, forsooth, more would already have been acquired, but the pecuniary expense of getting an education would in a great measure vanish. Those conveniences which the student requires at Cambridge or elsewhere cost him or somebody else ten times as great a sacrifice of life as they would with proper management on both sides. Those things for which the most money is demanded are never the things which the student most wants. Tuition, for instance, is an important item in the term bill, while for the far more valuable education which he gets by associating with the most cultivated of his contemporaries no charge is made. The mode of founding a college is, commonly, to get up a subscription of dollars and cents, and then, following blindly the principles of a division of labor to its extreme—a principle which should never be followed but with circumspection—to call in a contractor who makes this a subject of speculation, and he employs Irishmen or other operatives actually to lay the foundations, while the students that are to be are said to be fitting themselves for it; and for these oversights successive generations have to pay. I think that it would be *better than this,* for the students, or those who desire to be benefited by it, even to lay the foundation themselves. The student who secures his coveted leisure and retirement by systematically shirking any labor necessary to man obtains but an ignoble and unprofitable leisure, defrauding himself of the experience which alone can make leisure fruitful. "But," says one, "you do not mean that the students should go to work with their hands instead of their heads?" I do not mean that exactly, but I mean something which he might think a good deal like that; I mean that they should not *play* life, or *study* it merely, while the community supports them at this expensive game, but earnestly *live* it from beginning to end. How could youths better learn to live than by at once trying the experiment of living? Methinks this would exercise their minds as much as mathematics. If I wished a boy to know something about the arts and sciences, for instance, I would not pursue the common course, which is merely to send him into the neighborhood of some professor, where anything is professed and practised but the art of life;—to survey the world through a telescope or a microscope, and never with his natural eye; to study chemistry, and not learn how his bread is made, or mechanics, and not learn how it is earned; to discover new satellites to Neptune, and not detect the motes in his eyes, or to what vagabond he is a satellite himself; or to be devoured by the monsters that swarm all around him, while contemplating the monsters in a drop of vinegar. Which would have advanced the most at the end of a month—the boy who had made his own jackknife from the ore which he had dug and smelted, reading as much as would be necessary for this—or the boy who had attended the lectures on metallurgy at the Institute in the meanwhile, and had received a Rogers' penknife from his father? Which would be most likely to cut his fingers? . . . To my astonishment I was informed on leaving college that I had studied navigation!—why, if I had taken one turn down the harbor I should have known more about it. Even the *poor* student studies and is taught only *political* economy, while that economy of living which is synonymous with philosophy is not even sincerely professed in our colleges. The consequence is, that while he is reading Adam Smith, Ricardo, and Say, he runs his father in debt irretrievably.

As with our colleges, so with a hundred "modern improvements;" there is an illusion about them; there is not always a positive advance. The devil goes on exacting compound interest to the last for his early share and numerous succeeding investments in them. Our inventions are wont to be pretty toys, which distract our attention from serious things. They are but improved means to an unimproved end, an end which it was already but too easy to arrive at; as railroads lead to Boston or New York. We are in great haste to construct a magnetic telegraph from Maine to Texas; but Maine and Texas, it may be, have nothing important to communicate. Either is in such a predicament as the man who was earnest to be introduced to a distinguished deaf woman, but when he was presented, and one end of her ear trumpet was put into his hand, had nothing to say. As if the main object were to talk fast and not to talk sensibly. We are eager to tunnel under the Atlantic and bring the Old World some weeks nearer to the New; but perchance the first news that will leak through into the broad, flapping American ear will be that the Princess Adelaide has the whooping cough. After all, the man whose horse trots a mile in a minute does not carry the most important messages; he is not an evangelist, nor does he come round eating locusts and wild honey. I doubt if Flying Childers ever carried a peck of corn to mill.

One says to me, "I wonder that you do not lay up money; you love to travel; you might take the cars and go to Fitchburg today and see the country." But I am wiser than that. I have learned that the swiftest traveller is he that goes afoot. I say to my friend, Suppose we try who will get there first. The distance is thirty miles; the fare ninety cents. That is almost a day's wages. I remember when wages were sixty cents a day for laborers on this very road. Well, I start now on foot, and get there before night; I have travelled at that rate by the week together. You will in the meanwhile have earned your fare, and arrive there some time tomorrow, or possibly this evening, if you are lucky enough to get a job in season. Instead of going to Fitchburg, you will be working here the greater part of the day. And so, if the railroad reached round the world, I think that I should keep ahead of you; and as for seeing the country and getting experience of that kind, I should have to cut your acquaintance altogether.

Such is the universal law, which no man can ever outwit, and with regard to the railroad even we may say it is as broad as it is long. To make a railroad round the world available to all mankind is equivalent to grading the whole surface of the planet. Men have an indistinct notion that if they keep up this activity of joint stocks and spades long enough all will at length ride somewhere, in next to no time, and for nothing; but though a crowd rushes to the depot, and the conductor shouts "All aboard!" when the smoke is blown away and the vapor condensed, it will be perceived that a few are riding, but the rest are run over—and it will be called, and will be, "A melancholy accident." No doubt they can ride at last who shall have earned their fare, that is, if they survive so long, but they will probably have lost their elasticity and desire to travel by that time. This spending of the best part of one's life earning money in order to enjoy a questionable liberty during the least valuable part of it reminds me of the Englishman who went to India to make a fortune first, in order that he might return to England and live the life of a poet. He should have gone up garret at once. "What!" exclaim a million Irishmen starting up from all the shanties in the land, "is not this railroad which we have built a good thing?" Yes, I answer, comparatively good, that is, you might have done worse; but I wish, as you are brothers of mine, that you could have spent your time better than digging in this dirt.

[. . .]

For more than five years I maintained myself thus solely by the labor of my hands, and I found that, by working about six weeks in a year, I could meet all the expenses of living. The whole of my winters, as well as most of my summers, I had free and clear for study. I have thoroughly tried school-keeping, and found that my expenses were in proportion, or rather out of proportion, to my income, for I was obliged to dress and train, not to say think and believe, accordingly, and I lost my time into the bargain. As I did not teach for the good of my fellow-men, but simply for a livelihood, this was a failure. I have tried trade but I found that it would take ten years to get under way in that, and that then I should probably be on my way to the devil. I was actually afraid that I might by that time be doing what is called a good business. When formerly I was looking about to see what I could do for a living, some sad experience in conforming to the wishes of friends being fresh in my mind to tax my ingenuity, I thought often and seriously of picking huckleberries; that surely I could do, and its small profits might suffice—for my greatest skill has been to want but little—so little capital it required, so little distraction from my wonted moods, I foolishly thought. While my acquaintances went unhesitatingly into trade or the professions, I contemplated this occupation as most like theirs; ranging the hills all summer to pick the berries which came in my way, and thereafter carelessly dispose of them; so, to keep the flocks of Admetus. I also dreamed that I might gather the wild herbs, or carry evergreens to such villagers as loved to be reminded of the woods, even to the city, by hay-cart loads. But I have since learned that trade curses everything it handles; and though you trade in messages from heaven, the whole curse of trade attaches to the business.

As I preferred some things to others, and especially valued my freedom, as I could fare hard and yet succeed well, I did not wish to spend my time in earning rich carpets or other fine furniture, or delicate cookery, or a house in the Grecian or the Gothic style just yet. If there are any to whom it is no interruption to acquire these things, and who know how to use them when acquired, I relinquish to them the pursuit. Some are "industrious," and appear to love labor for its own sake, or perhaps because it keeps them out of worse mischief; to such I have at present nothing to say. Those who would not know what to do with more leisure than they now enjoy, I might advise to work twice as hard as they do—work till they pay for themselves, and get their free papers. For myself I found that the occupation of a day-laborer was the most independent of any, especially as it required only thirty or forty days in a year to support one. The laborer's day ends with the going down of the sun, and he is then free to devote himself to his chosen pursuit, independent of his labor; but his employer, who speculates from month to month, has no respite from one end of the year to the other.

In short, I am convinced, both by faith and experience, that to maintain one's self on this earth is not a hardship but a pastime, if we will live simply and wisely; as the pursuits of the simpler nations are still the sports of the more artificial. It is not necessary that a man should earn his living by the sweat of his brow, unless he sweats easier than I do.

One young man of my acquaintance, who has inherited some acres, told me that he thought he should live as I did, *if he had the means*. I would not have any one adopt my mode of living on any account; for, beside that before he has fairly learned it I may have found out another for myself, I desire that there may be as many different persons in the world as possible; but I would have each one be very careful to find out and pursue *his own* way, and not his father's or his mother's or his neighbor's instead. The youth may build or plant or sail, only let him not be hindered from doing that which he tells me he would like to do. It is by a mathematical point only that we are wise, as the sailor or the fugitive slave keeps the polestar in his eye; but that is sufficient guidance for all our life. We may not arrive at our port within a calculable period, but we would preserve the true course.

Undoubtedly, in this case, what is true for one is truer still for a thousand, as a large house is not proportionally more expensive than a small one, since one roof may cover, one cellar underlie, and one wall separate several apartments. But for my part, I preferred the solitary dwelling. Moreover, it will commonly be cheaper to build the whole yourself than to convince another of the advantage of the common wall; and when you have done this, the common partition, to be much cheaper, must be a thin one, and that other may prove a bad neighbor, and also not keep his side in repair. The only cooperation which is commonly possible is exceedingly partial and superficial; and what little true cooperation there is, is as if it were not, being a harmony inaudible to men. If a man has faith, he will cooperate with equal faith everywhere; if he has not faith, he will continue to live like the rest of the world, whatever company he is joined to. To cooperate in the highest as well as the lowest sense, means *to get our living together.* I heard it proposed lately that two young men should travel together over the world, the one without money, earning his means as he went, before the mast and behind the plow, the other carrying a bill of exchange in his pocket. It was easy to see that they could not long be companions or cooperate, since one would not *operate* at all. They would part at the first interesting crisis in their adventures. Above all, as I have implied, the man who goes alone can start today; but he who travels with another must wait till that other is ready, and it may be a long time before they get off.

But all this is very selfish, I have heard some of my townsmen say. I confess that I have hitherto indulged very little in philanthropic enterprises. I have made some sacrifices to a sense of duty, and among others have sacrificed this pleasure also. There are those who have used all their arts to persuade me to undertake the support of some poor family in the town; and if I had nothing to do—for the devil finds employment for the idle—I might try my hand at some such pastime as that. However, when I have thought to indulge myself in this respect, and lay their Heaven under an obligation by maintaining certain poor persons in all respects as comfortably as I maintain myself, and have even ventured so far as to make them the offer, they have one and all unhesitatingly preferred to remain poor. While my townsmen and women are devoted in so many ways to the good of their fellows, I trust that one at least may be spared to other and less humane pursuits. You must have a genius for charity as well as for anything else. As for Doing-good, that is one of the professions which are full. Moreover, I have tried it fairly, and, strange as it may seem, am satisfied that it does not agree with my constitution. Probably I should not consciously and deliberately forsake my particular calling to do the good which society demands of me, to save the universe from annihilation; and I believe that a like but infinitely greater steadfastness elsewhere is all that now preserves it. But I would not stand between any man and his genius; and to him who does this work, which I decline, with his whole heart and soul and life, I would say, Persevere, even if the world call it doing evil, as it is most likely they will.

I am far from supposing that my case is a peculiar one; no doubt many of my readers would make a similar defence. At doing something—I will not engage that my neighbors shall pronounce it good—I do not hesitate to say that I should be a capital fellow to hire; but what that is, it is for my employer to find out. What *good* I do, in the common sense of that word, must be aside from my main path, and for the most part wholly unintended. Men say, practically, Begin where you are and such as you are, without aiming mainly to become of more worth, and with kindness aforethought go about doing good. If I were to preach at all in this strain, I should say rather, Set about being good. As if the sun should stop when he had kindled his fires up to the splendor of a moon or a star of the sixth magnitude, and go about like a Robin Goodfellow, peeping in at every cottage window, inspiring lunatics, and tainting meats, and making darkness visible, instead of steadily increasing his genial heat and beneficence till he is of such brightness that no mortal can look him in the face, and then, and in the meanwhile too, going about the world in his own orbit, doing it good, or rather, as a truer philosophy has discovered, the world going about him getting good. When Phaeton, wishing to prove his heavenly birth by his beneficence, had the sun's chariot but one day, and drove out of the beaten track, he burned several blocks of houses in the lower streets of heaven, and scorched the surface of the earth, and dried up every spring, and made the great desert of Sahara, till at length Jupiter hurled him headlong to the earth with a thunderbolt, and the sun, through grief at his death, did not shine for a year.

There is no odor so bad as that which arises from goodness tainted. It is human, it is divine, carrion. If I knew for a certainty that a man was coming to my house with the conscious design of doing me good, I should run for my life, as from that dry and parching wind of the African deserts called the simoom, which fills the mouth and nose and ears and eyes with dust till you are suffocated, for fear that I should get some of his good done to me—some of its virus mingled with my blood. No—in this case I would rather suffer evil the natural way. A man is not a good *man* to me because he will feed me if I should be starving, or warm me if I should be freezing, or pull me out of a ditch if I should ever fall into one. I can find you a Newfoundland dog that will do as much. Philanthropy is not love for one's fellow-man in the broadest sense. Howard was no doubt an exceedingly kind and worthy man in his way, and has his reward; but, comparatively speaking, what are a hundred Howards to *us*, if their philanthropy do not help us in our best estate, when we are most worthy to be helped? I never heard of a philanthropic meeting in which it was sincerely proposed to do any good to me, or the like of me.

The Jesuits were quite balked by those Indians who, being burned at the stake, suggested new modes of torture to their tormentors. Being superior to physical suffering, it sometimes chanced that they were superior to any consolation which the missionaries could offer; and the law to do as you would be done by fell with less persuasiveness on the ears of those who, for their part, did not care how they were done by, who loved their enemies after a new fashion, and came very near freely forgiving them all they did.

Be sure that you give the poor the aid they most need, though it be your example which leaves them far behind. If you give money, spend yourself with it, and do not merely abandon it to them. We make curious mistakes sometimes. Often the poor man is not so cold and hungry as he is dirty and ragged and gross. It is partly his taste, and not merely his misfortune. If you give him money, he will perhaps buy more rags with it. I was wont to pity the clumsy Irish laborers who cut ice on the pond, in such mean and ragged clothes, while I shivered in my more tidy and somewhat more fashionable garments, till, one bitter cold day, one who had slipped into the water came to my house to warm him, and I saw him strip off three pairs of pants and two pairs of stockings ere he got down to the skin, though they were dirty and ragged enough, it is true, and that he could afford to refuse the extra garments which I offered him, he had so many *intra* ones. This ducking was the very thing he needed. Then I began to pity myself, and I saw that it would be a greater charity to bestow on me a flannel shirt than a whole slop-shop on him. There are a thousand hacking at the branches of evil to one who is striking at the root, and it may be that he who bestows the largest amount of time and money on the needy is doing the most by his mode of life to produce that misery which he strives in vain to relieve. It is the pious slave-breeder devoting the proceeds of every tenth slave to buy a Sunday's liberty for the rest. Some show their kindness to the poor by employing them in their kitchens. Would they not be kinder if they employed themselves there? You boast of spending a tenth part of your income in charity; may be you should spend the nine tenths so, and done with it. Society recovers only a tenth part of the property then. Is this owing to the generosity of him in whose possession it is found, or to the remissness of the officers of justice?

Philanthropy is almost the only virtue which is sufficiently appreciated by mankind. Nay, it is greatly overrated; and it is our selfishness which overrates it. A robust poor man, one sunny day here in Concord, praised a fellow-townsman to me, because, as he said, he was kind to the poor; meaning himself. The kind uncles and aunts of the race are more esteemed than its true spiritual fathers and mothers. I once heard a reverend lecturer on England, a man of learning and intelligence, after enumerating her scientific, literary, and political worthies, Shakespeare, Bacon, Cromwell, Milton, Newton, and others, speak next of her Christian heroes, whom, as if his profession required it of him, he elevated to a place far above all the rest, as the greatest of the great. They were Penn, Howard, and Mrs. Fry. Every one must feel the falsehood and cant of this. The last were not England's best men and women; only, perhaps, her best philanthropists.

I would not subtract anything from the praise that is due to philanthropy, but merely demand justice for all who by their lives and works are a blessing to mankind. I do not value chiefly a man's uprightness and benevolence, which are, as it were, his stem and leaves. Those plants of whose greenness withered we make herb tea for the sick serve but a humble use, and are most employed by quacks. I want the flower and fruit of a man; that some fragrance be wafted over from him to me, and some ripeness flavor our intercourse. His goodness must not be a partial and transitory act, but a constant superfluity, which costs him nothing and of which he is unconscious. This is a charity that hides a multitude of sins. The philanthropist too often surrounds mankind with the remembrance of his own castoff griefs as an atmosphere, and calls it sympathy. We should impart our courage, and not our despair, our health and ease, and not our disease, and take care that this does not spread by contagion. From what southern plains comes up the voice of wailing? Under what latitudes reside the heathen to whom we would send light? Who is that intemperate and brutal man whom we would redeem? If anything ail a man, so that he does not perform his functions, if he have a pain in his bowels even—for that is the seat of sympathy—he forthwith sets about reforming—the world. Being a microcosm himself, he discovers—and it is a true discovery, and he is the man to make it—that the world has been eating green apples; to his eyes, in fact, the globe itself is a great green apple, which there is danger awful to think of that the children of men will nibble before it is ripe; and straightway his drastic philanthropy seeks out the Esquimaux and the Patagonian, and embraces the populous Indian and Chinese villages; and thus, by a few years of philanthropic activity, the powers in the meanwhile using him for their own ends, no doubt, he cures himself of his dyspepsia, the globe acquires a faint blush on one or both of its cheeks, as if it were beginning to be ripe, and life loses its crudity and is once more sweet and wholesome to live. I never dreamed of any enormity greater than I have committed. I never knew, and never shall know, a worse man than myself.

I believe that what so saddens the reformer is not his sympathy with his fellows in distress, but, though he be the holiest son of God, is his private ail. Let this be righted, let the spring come to him, the morning rise over his couch, and he will forsake his generous companions without apology. My excuse for not lecturing against the use of tobacco is, that I never chewed it, that is a penalty which reformed tobacco-chewers have to pay; though there are things enough I have chewed which I could lecture against. If you should ever be betrayed into any of these philanthropies, do not let your left hand know what your right hand does, for it is not worth knowing. Rescue the drowning and tie your shoestrings. Take your time, and set about some free labor.

Our manners have been corrupted by communication with the saints. Our hymn-books resound with a melodious cursing of God and enduring Him forever. One would say that even the prophets and redeemers had rather consoled the fears than confirmed the hopes of man. There is nowhere recorded a simple and irrepressible satisfaction with the gift of life, any memorable praise of God. All health and success does me good, however far off and withdrawn it may appear; all disease and failure helps to make me sad and does me evil, however much sympathy it may have with me or I with it. If, then, we would indeed restore mankind by truly Indian, botanic, magnetic, or natural means, let us first be as simple and well as Nature ourselves, dispel the clouds which hang over our own brows, and take up a little life into our pores. Do not stay to be an overseer of the poor, but endeavor to become one of the worthies of the world.

I read in the Gulistan, or Flower Garden, of Sheik Sadi of Shiraz, that "they asked a wise man, saying: Of the many celebrated trees which the Most High God has created lofty and umbrageous, they call none azad, or free, excepting the cypress, which bears no fruit; what mystery is there in this? He replied, Each has its appropriate produce, and appointed season, during the continuance of which it is fresh and blooming, and during their absence dry and withered; to neither of which states is the cypress exposed, being always flourishing; and of this nature are the azads, or religious independents.—Fix not thy heart on that which is transitory; for the Dijlah, or Tigris, will continue to flow through Bagdad after the race of caliphs is extinct: if thy hand has plenty, be liberal as the date tree; but if it affords nothing to give away, be an azad, or free man, like the cypress."

SOURCE: Henry David Thoreau. *Walden; or, Life in the Woods*. Boston: Ticknor and Fields, 1854.

HERMAN MELVILLE

The immediate lack of success for Moby-Dick, *which has since become one of the three or four most famous American novels, did not surprise Herman Melville (1819–1891). Born in New York City, Melville is arguably the first American novelist who wrote with the grandeur of Europe's nineteenth-century masters while remaining distinctly American; his peculiar sensitivities and humor are ever surprising. This great novel must be experienced. "Melville manages to keep it a real whaling ship, on a real cruise, in spite of all the fanatics," observed the British novelist and critic D. H. Lawrence.*[1]

We present fifteen of the marvelous 135 chapters of this ambitious and unusual work that has long excited and delighted its readers. The narrator of Chapter 1, Ishmael, tries to explain his motives for joining the whaling crew, among them: ". . . the overwhelming idea of the great whale himself. Such a portentous and mysterious monster roused all my curiosity. Then the wild and distant seas where he rolled his island bulk; the undeliverable, nameless perils of the whale; these, with all the attending marvels of a thousand Patagonian sights and sounds, helped to sway me to my wish. With other men, perhaps, such things would not have been inducements; but as for me, I am tormented with an everlasting itch for things remote."

Chapters from *Moby-Dick* (1851)

Chapter 1: Loomings

CALL ME ISHMAEL. Some years ago—never mind how long precisely—having little or no money in my purse, and nothing particular to interest me on shore, I thought I would sail about a little and see the watery part of the world. It is a way I have of driving off the spleen, and regulating the circulation. Whenever I find myself growing grim about the mouth; whenever it is a damp,

1. D. H. Lawrence. "Herman Melville's *Moby Dick.*" *Studies in Classic American Literature.* Harmondsworth, England: Penguin, 1977. 159.

drizzly November in my soul; whenever I find myself involuntarily pausing before coffin warehouses, and bringing up the rear of every funeral I meet; and especially whenever my hypos get such an upper hand of me, that it requires a strong moral principle to prevent me from deliberately stepping into the street, and methodically knocking people's hats off—then, I account it high time to get to sea as soon as I can. This is my substitute for pistol and ball. With a philosophical flourish Cato throws himself upon his sword; I quietly take to the ship. There is nothing surprising in this. If they but knew it, almost all men in their degree, some time or other, cherish very nearly the same feelings towards the ocean with me.

There now is your insular city of the Manhattoes, belted round by wharves as Indian isles by coral reefs—commerce surrounds it with her surf. Right and left, the streets take you waterward. Its extreme down-town is the battery, where that noble mole is washed by waves, and cooled by breezes, which a few hours previous were out of sight of land. Look at the crowds of water-gazers there.

Circumambulate the city of a dreamy Sabbath afternoon. Go from Corlears Hook to Coenties Slip, and from thence, by Whitehall, northward. What do you see?—Posted like silent sentinels all around the town, stand thousands upon thousands of mortal men fixed in ocean reveries. Some leaning against the spiles; some seated upon the pier-heads; some looking over the bulwarks of ships from China; some high aloft in the rigging, as if striving to get a still better seaward peep. But these are all landsmen; of week days pent up in lath and plaster—tied to counters, nailed to benches, clinched to desks. How then is this? Are the green fields gone? What do they here?

But look! here come more crowds, pacing straight for the water, and seemingly bound for a dive. Strange! Nothing will content them but the extremest limit of the land; loitering under the shady lee of yonder warehouses will not suffice. No. They must get just as nigh the water as they possibly can without falling in. And there they stand—miles of them—leagues. Inlanders all, they come from lanes and alleys, streets and avenues,—north, east, south, and west. Yet here they all unite. Tell me, does the magnetic virtue of the needles of the compasses of all those ships attract them thither?

Once more. Say, you are in the country; in some high land of lakes. Take almost any path you please, and ten to one it carries you down in a dale, and leaves you there by a pool in the stream.

There is magic in it. Let the most absent-minded of men be plunged in his deepest reveries—stand that man on his legs, set his feet a-going, and he will infallibly lead you to water, if water there be in all that region. Should you ever be athirst in the great American desert, try this experiment, if your caravan happen to be supplied with a metaphysical professor. Yes, as every one knows, meditation and water are wedded for ever.

But here is an artist. He desires to paint you the dreamiest, shadiest, quietest, most enchanting bit of romantic landscape in all the valley of the Saco. What is the chief element he employs? There stand his trees, each with a hollow trunk, as if a hermit and a crucifix were within; and here sleeps his meadow, and there sleep his cattle; and up from yonder cottage goes a sleepy smoke. Deep into distant woodlands winds a mazy way, reaching to overlapping spurs of mountains bathed in their hill-side blue. But though the picture lies thus tranced, and though this pine-tree shakes down its sighs like leaves upon this shepherd's head, yet all were vain, unless the shepherd's eye were fixed upon the magic stream before him. Go visit the Prairies in June, when for scores on scores of miles you wade knee-deep among Tiger-lilies—what is the one charm wanting?—Water—there is not a drop of water there! Were Niagara but a cataract of sand, would you travel your thousand miles to see it? Why did the poor poet of Tennessee, upon suddenly receiving two handfuls of silver, deliberate whether to buy him a coat, which he sadly needed, or invest his money in a pedestrian trip to Rockaway Beach? Why is almost every robust healthy boy with a robust healthy soul in him, at some time or other crazy to go to sea? Why upon your first voyage as a passenger, did you yourself feel such a mystical vibration, when first told that you and your ship were now out of sight of land? Why did the old Persians hold the sea holy? Why did the Greeks give it a separate deity, and own brother of Jove? Surely all this is not without meaning. And still deeper the meaning of that story of Narcissus, who because he could not grasp the tormenting, mild image he saw in the fountain, plunged into it and was drowned. But that same image, we ourselves see in all rivers and oceans. It is the image of the ungraspable phantom of life; and this is the key to it all.

Now, when I say that I am in the habit of going to sea whenever I begin to grow hazy about the eyes, and begin to be over conscious of my lungs, I do not mean to have it inferred that I ever go to sea as a passenger. For to go as a passenger you must needs have a purse, and a purse is but a rag unless you have something in it. Besides, passengers get sea-sick—grow quarrelsome—don't sleep of nights—do not enjoy themselves much, as a general thing;—no, I never go as a passenger; nor, though I am something of a salt, do I ever go to sea as a Commodore, or a Captain, or a Cook. I abandon the glory and distinction of such offices to those who like them. For my part, I abominate all honorable respectable toils, trials, and tribulations of every kind whatsoever. It is quite as much as I can do to take care of myself, without taking care of ships, barques, brigs, schooners, and what not. And as for going as cook,—though I confess there is considerable glory in that, a cook being a sort of officer on ship-board—yet, somehow, I never fancied broiling fowls;—though once broiled, judiciously buttered, and judgmatically salted and peppered, there is no one who will speak more respectfully, not to say reverentially, of a broiled fowl than I will. It is out of the idolatrous dotings of the old Egyptians upon broiled ibis and roasted river horse, that you see the mummies of those creatures in their huge bake-houses the pyramids.

No, when I go to sea, I go as a simple sailor, right before the mast, plumb down into the forecastle, aloft there to the royal masthead. True, they rather order me about some, and make me jump from spar to spar, like a grasshopper in a May meadow. And at first, this sort of thing is unpleasant enough. It touches one's sense of honor, particularly if you come of an old established family in the land, the van Rensselaers, or Randolphs, or Hardicanutes. And more than all, if just previous to putting your hand into the tarpot, you have been lording it as a country schoolmaster, making the tallest boys stand in awe of you. The transition is a keen one, I assure you, from the schoolmaster to a sailor, and requires a strong decoction of Seneca and the Stoics to enable you to grin and bear it. But even this wears off in time.

What of it, if some old hunks of a sea-captain orders me to get a broom and sweep down the decks? What does that indignity amount to, weighed, I mean, in the scales of the New Testament? Do you think the archangel Gabriel thinks anything the less of me, because I promptly and respectfully obey that old hunks in that particular instance? Who ain't a slave? Tell me that. Well, then, however the old sea-captains may order me about—however they may thump and punch me about, I have the satisfaction of knowing that it is all right; that everybody else is one way or other served in much the same way—either in a physical or metaphysical point of view, that is; and so the universal thump is passed round, and all hands should rub each other's shoulder-blades, and be content.

Again, I always go to sea as a sailor, because they make a point of paying me for my trouble, whereas they never pay passengers a single penny that I ever heard of. On the contrary, passengers themselves must pay. And there is all the difference in the world between paying and being paid. The act of paying is perhaps the most uncomfortable infliction that the two orchard thieves entailed upon us. But *being paid,*—what will compare with it? The urbane activity with which a man receives money is really marvellous, considering that we so earnestly believe money to be the root of all earthly ills, and that on no account can a monied man enter heaven. Ah! how cheerfully we consign ourselves to perdition!

Finally, I always go to sea as a sailor, because of the wholesome exercise and pure air of the forecastle deck. For as in this world, head winds are far more prevalent than winds from astern (that is, if you never violate the Pythagorean maxim), so for the most part the Commodore on the quarter-deck gets his atmosphere at second hand from the sailors on the forecastle. He thinks he breathes it first; but not so. In much the same way do the commonalty lead their leaders in many other things, at the same time that the leaders little suspect it. But wherefore it was that after having repeatedly smelt the sea as a merchant sailor, I should now take it into my head to go on a whaling voyage; this the invisible police officer of the Fates, who has the constant surveillance of me, and secretly dogs me, and influences me in some unaccountable way—he can better answer than any one else. And, doubtless, my going on this whaling voyage, formed part of the grand programme of Providence that was drawn up a long time ago. It came in as a sort of brief interlude and solo between more extensive performances. I take it that this part of the bill must have run something like this:

"Grand Contested Election for the
Presidency of the United States.

"WHALING VOYAGE BY ONE ISHMAEL.

"BLOODY BATTLE IN AFFGHANISTAN."

Though I cannot tell why it was exactly that those stage managers, the Fates, put me down for this shabby part of a whaling voyage, when others were set down for magnificent parts in high tragedies, and short and easy parts in genteel comedies, and jolly parts in farces—though I cannot tell why this was exactly; yet, now that I recall all the circumstances, I think I can see a little into the springs and motives which being cunningly presented to me under various disguises, induced me to set about performing the part I did, besides cajoling me into the delusion that it was a choice resulting from my own unbiased freewill and discriminating judgment.

Chief among these motives was the overwhelming idea of the great whale himself. Such a portentous and mysterious monster roused all my curiosity. Then the wild and distant seas where he rolled his island bulk; the undeliverable, nameless perils of the whale; these, with all the attending marvels of a thousand Patagonian sights and sounds, helped to sway me to my wish. With other men, perhaps, such things would not have been inducements; but as for me, I am tormented with an everlasting itch for things remote. I love to sail forbidden seas, and land on barbarous coasts. Not ignoring what is good, I am quick to perceive a horror, and could still be social with it—would they let me—since it is but well to be on friendly terms with all the inmates of the place one lodges in.

By reason of these things, then, the whaling voyage was welcome; the great flood-gates of the wonder-world swung open, and in the wild conceits that swayed me to my purpose, two and two there floated into my inmost soul, endless processions of the whale, and, mid most of them all, one grand hooded phantom, like a snow hill in the air.

Chapter 10: A Bosom Friend

Ishmael improves his acquaintanceship with Queequeg, one of Melville's comic and irreducible characters: "Queequeg was George Washington cannibalistically developed." And yet, "Here was a man some twenty thousand miles from home, by the way of Cape Horn, that is—which was the only way he could get there—thrown among people as strange to him as though he were in the planet Jupiter; and yet he seemed entirely at his ease; preserving the utmost serenity; content with his own companionship; always equal to himself." In these next three (consecutive) chapters, Ishmael and Queequeg share friendship, worship, confidences and a bed.

Returning to the Spouter-Inn from the Chapel, I found Queequeg there quite alone; he having left the Chapel before the benediction some time. He was sitting on a bench before the fire, with his feet on the stove hearth, and in one hand was holding close up to his face that little negro idol of his; peering hard into its face, and with a jack-knife gently whittling away at its nose, meanwhile humming to himself in his heathenish way.

But being now interrupted, he put up the image; and pretty soon, going to the table, took up a large book there, and placing it on his lap began counting the pages with deliberate regularity; at every fiftieth page—as I fancied—stopping a moment, looking vacantly around him, and giving utterance to a long-drawn gurgling whistle of astonishment. He would then begin again at the next fifty; seeming to commence at number one each time, as though he could not count more than fifty, and it was only by such a large number of fifties being found together, that his astonishment at the multitude of pages was excited.

With much interest I sat watching him. Savage though he was, and hideously marred about the face—at least to my taste—his countenance yet had a something in it which was by no means disagreeable. You cannot hide the soul. Through all his unearthly tattooings, I thought I saw the traces of a simple honest heart; and in his large, deep eyes, fiery black and bold, there seemed tokens of a spirit that would dare a thousand devils. And besides all this, there was a certain lofty bearing about the Pagan, which even his uncouthness could not altogether maim. He looked like a man who had never cringed and never had had a creditor. Whether it was, too, that his head being shaved, his forehead was drawn out in freer and brighter relief, and looked more expansive than it otherwise would, this I will not venture to decide; but certain it was his head was phrenologically an excellent one. It may seem ridiculous, but it reminded me of General Washington's head, as seen in the popular busts of him. It had the same long regularly graded retreating slope from above the brows, which were likewise very projecting, like two long promontories thickly wooded on top. Queequeg was George Washington cannibalistically developed.

Whilst I was thus closely scanning him, half-pretending meanwhile to be looking out at the storm from the casement, he never heeded my presence, never troubled himself with so much as a single glance; but appeared wholly occupied with counting the pages of the marvellous book. Considering how sociably we had been sleeping together the night previous, and especially considering the affectionate arm I had found thrown over me upon waking in the morning, I thought this indifference of his very strange. But savages are strange beings; at times you do not know exactly how to take them. At first they are overawing; their calm self-collectedness of simplicity seems a Socratic wisdom. I had noticed also that Queequeg never consorted at all, or but very little, with the other seamen in the inn. He made no advances whatever; appeared to have no desire to enlarge the circle of his acquaintances. All this struck me as mighty singular; yet, upon second thoughts, there was something almost sublime in it. Here was a man some twenty thousand miles from home, by the way of Cape Horn, that is—which was the only way he could get there—thrown among people as strange to him as though he were in the planet Jupiter; and yet he seemed entirely at his ease; preserving the utmost serenity; content with his own companionship; always equal to himself. Surely this was a touch of fine philosophy; though no doubt he had never heard there was such a thing as that. But, perhaps, to be true philosophers, we mortals should not be conscious of so living or so striving. So soon as I hear that such or such a man gives himself out for a philosopher, I conclude that, like the dyspeptic old woman, he must have "broken his digester."

As I sat there in that now lonely room; the fire burning low, in that mild stage when, after its first intensity has warmed the air, it then only glows to be looked at; the evening shades and phantoms gathering round the casements, and peering in upon us silent, solitary twain; the storm booming without in solemn swells; I began to be sensible of strange feelings. I felt a melting in me. No more my splintered heart and maddened hand were turned against the wolfish world. This soothing savage had redeemed it. There he sat, his very indifference speaking a nature in which there lurked no civilized hypocrisies and bland deceits. Wild he was; a very sight of sights to see; yet I began to feel myself mysteriously drawn towards him. And those same things that would have repelled most others, they were the very magnets that thus drew me. I'll try a pagan friend, thought I, since Christian kindness has proved but hollow courtesy. I drew my bench near him, and made some friendly signs and hints, doing my best to talk with him meanwhile. At first he little noticed these advances; but presently, upon my referring to his last night's hospitalities, he made out to ask me whether we were again to be bedfellows. I told him yes; whereat I thought he looked pleased, perhaps a little complimented.

We then turned over the book together, and I endeavored to explain to him the purpose of the printing, and the meaning of the few pictures that were in it. Thus I soon engaged his interest; and from that we went to jabbering the best we could about the various outer sights to be seen in this famous town. Soon I proposed a social smoke; and, producing his pouch and tomahawk, he quietly offered me a puff. And then we sat exchanging puffs from that wild pipe of his, and keeping it regularly passing between us.

If there yet lurked any ice of indifference towards me in the Pagan's breast, this pleasant, genial smoke we had, soon thawed it out, and left us cronies. He seemed to take to me quite as naturally and unbiddenly as I to him; and when our smoke was over, he pressed his forehead against mine, clasped me round the waist, and said that henceforth we were married; meaning, in his country's phrase, that we were bosom friends; he would gladly die for me, if need should be. In a countryman, this sudden flame of friendship would have seemed far too premature, a thing to be much distrusted; but in this simple savage those old rules would not apply.

After supper, and another social chat and smoke, we went to our room together. He made me a present of his embalmed head; took out his enormous tobacco wallet, and groping under the tobacco, drew out some thirty dollars in silver; then spreading them on the table, and mechanically dividing them into two equal portions, pushed one of them towards me, and said it was mine. I was going to remonstrate; but he silenced me by pouring them into my trowsers' pockets. I let them stay. He then went about his evening prayers, took out his idol, and removed the paper fireboard. By certain signs and symptoms, I thought he seemed anxious for me to join him; but well knowing what was to follow, I deliberated a moment whether, in case he invited me, I would comply or otherwise.

I was a good Christian; born and bred in the bosom of the infallible Presbyterian Church. How then could I unite with this wild idolator in worshipping his piece of wood? But what is worship? thought I. Do you suppose now, Ishmael, that the magnanimous God of heaven and earth—pagans and all included—can possibly be jealous of an insignificant bit of black wood? Impossible! But what is worship?—to do the will of God—that is worship. And what is the will of God?—to do to my fellow man what I would have my fellow man to do to me—that is the will of God. Now,

Queequeg is my fellow man. And what do I wish that this Queequeg would do to me? Why, unite with me in my particular Presbyterian form of worship. Consequently, I must then unite with him in his; ergo, I must turn idolator. So I kindled the shavings; helped prop up the innocent little idol; offered him burnt biscuit with Queequeg; salaamed before him twice or thrice; kissed his nose; and that done, we undressed and went to bed, at peace with our own consciences and all the world. But we did not go to sleep without some little chat.

How it is I know not; but there is no place like a bed for confidential disclosures between friends. Man and wife, they say, there open the very bottom of their souls to each other; and some old couples often lie and chat over old times till nearly morning. Thus, then, in our hearts' honeymoon, lay I and Queequeg—a cosy, loving pair.

Chapter 11: Nightgown

We had lain thus in bed, chatting and napping at short intervals, and Queequeg now and then affectionately throwing his brown tattooed legs over mine, and then drawing them back; so entirely sociable and free and easy were we; when, at last, by reason of our confabulations, what little nappishness remained in us altogether departed, and we felt like getting up again, though day-break was yet some way down the future.

Yes, we became very wakeful; so much so that our recumbent position began to grow wearisome, and by little and little we found ourselves sitting up; the clothes well tucked around us, leaning against the head-board with our four knees drawn up close together, and our two noses bending over them, as if our kneepans were warming-pans. We felt very nice and snug, the more so since it was so chilly out of doors; indeed out of bed-clothes too, seeing that there was no fire in the room. The more so, I say, because truly to enjoy bodily warmth, some small part of you must be cold, for there is no quality in this world that is not what it is merely by contrast. Nothing exists in itself. If you flatter yourself that you are all over comfortable, and have been so a long time, then you cannot be said to be comfortable any more. But if, like Queequeg and me in the bed, the tip of your nose or the crown of your head be slightly chilled, why then, indeed, in the general consciousness you feel most delightfully and unmistakably warm. For this reason a sleeping apartment should never be furnished with a fire, which is one of the luxurious discomforts of the rich. For the height of this sort of deliciousness is to have nothing but the blanket between you and your snugness and the cold of the outer air. Then there you lie like the one warm spark in the heart of an arctic crystal.

We had been sitting in this crouching manner for some time, when all at once I thought I would open my eyes; for when between sheets, whether by day or by night, and whether asleep or awake, I have a way of always keeping my eyes shut, in order the more to concentrate the snugness of being in bed. Because no man can ever feel his own identity aright except his eyes be closed; as if darkness were indeed the proper element of our essences, though light be more congenial to our clayey part. Upon opening my eyes then, and coming out of my own pleasant and self-created darkness into the imposed and coarse outer gloom of the unilluminated twelve-o'clock-at-night, I experienced a disagreeable revulsion. Nor did I at all object to the hint from Queequeg that perhaps it were best to strike a light, seeing that we were so wide awake; and besides he felt a strong desire to have a few quiet puffs from his Tomahawk. Be it said, that though I had felt such a strong repugnance to his smoking in the bed the night before, yet see how elastic our stiff prejudices grow when love once comes to bend them. For now I liked nothing better than to have Queequeg smoking by me, even in bed, because he seemed to be full of such serene household joy then. I no more felt unduly concerned for the landlord's policy of insurance. I was only alive to the condensed confidential comfortableness of sharing a pipe and a blanket with a real friend. With our shaggy jackets drawn about our shoulders, we now passed the Tomahawk from one to the other, till slowly there grew over us a blue hanging tester of smoke, illuminated by the flame of the new-lit lamp.

Whether it was that this undulating tester rolled the savage away to far distant scenes, I know not, but he now spoke of his native island; and, eager to hear his history, I begged him to go on and tell it. He gladly complied. Though at the time I but ill comprehended not a few of his words, yet subsequent disclosures, when I had become more familiar with his broken phraseology, now enable me to present the whole story such as it may prove in the mere skeleton I give.

Chapter 12: Biographical

Queequeg was a native of Kokovoko, an island far away to the West and South. It is not down in any map; true places never are.

When a new-hatched savage running wild about his native woodlands in a grass clout, followed by the nibbling goats, as if he were a green sapling; even then, in Queequeg's ambitious soul, lurked a strong desire to see something more of Christendom than a specimen whaler or two. His father was a High Chief, a King; his uncle a High Priest; and on the maternal side he boasted aunts who were the wives of unconquerable warriors. There was excellent blood in his veins—royal stuff; though sadly vitiated, I fear, by the cannibal propensity he nourished in his untutored youth.

A Sag Harbor ship visited his father's bay, and Queequeg sought a passage to Christian lands. But the ship, having her full complement of seamen, spurned his suit; and not all the King his father's influence could prevail. But Queequeg vowed a vow. Alone in his canoe, he paddled off to a distant strait, which he knew the ship must pass through when she quitted the island. On one side was a coral reef; on the other a low tongue of land, covered with mangrove thickets that grew out into the water. Hiding his canoe, still afloat, among these thickets, with its prow seaward, he sat down in the stern, paddle low in hand; and when the ship was gliding by, like a flash he darted out; gained her side; with one backward dash of his foot capsized and sank his canoe; climbed up the chains; and throwing himself at full length upon the deck, grappled a ring-bolt there, and swore not to let it go, though hacked in pieces.

In vain the captain threatened to throw him overboard; suspended a cutlass over his naked wrists; Queequeg was the son of a King, and Queequeg budged not. Struck by his desperate dauntlessness, and his wild desire to visit Christendom, the captain at last relented, and told him he might make himself at home. But this fine young savage—this sea Prince of Wales, never saw the captain's cabin. They put him down among the sailors, and made a whaleman of him. But like Czar Peter content to toil in the shipyards of foreign cities, Queequeg disdained no seeming ignominy, if thereby he might happily gain the power of enlightening his untutored countrymen. For at bottom—so he told me—he was actuated by a profound desire to learn among the Christians, the arts whereby to make his people still happier than they were; and more than that, still better than they were. But, alas! the practices of whalemen soon convinced him that even Christians could be both miserable and wicked; infinitely more so, than all his father's heathens. Arrived at last in old Sag Harbor; and seeing what the sailors did there; and then going on to Nantucket, and seeing how they spent their wages in that place also, poor Queequeg gave it up for lost. Thought he, it's a wicked world in all meridians; I'll die a pagan.

And thus an old idolator at heart, he yet lived among these Christians, wore their clothes, and tried to talk their gibberish. Hence the queer ways about him, though now some time from home.

By hints, I asked him whether he did not propose going back, and having a coronation; since he might now consider his father dead and gone, he being very old and feeble at the last accounts. He answered no, not yet; and added that he was fearful Christianity, or rather Christians, had unfitted him for ascending the pure and undefiled throne of thirty pagan Kings before him. But by and by, he said, he would return,—as soon as he felt himself baptized again. For the nonce, however, he proposed to sail about, and sow his wild oats in all four oceans. They had made a harpooneer of him, and that barbed iron was in lieu of a sceptre now.

I asked him what might be his immediate purpose, touching his future movements. He answered, to go to sea again, in his old vocation. Upon this, I told him that whaling was my own design, and informed him of my intention to sail out of Nantucket, as being the most promising port for an adventurous whaleman to embark from. He at once resolved to accompany me to that island, ship aboard the same vessel, get into the same watch, the same boat, the same mess with me, in short to share my every hap; with both my hands in his, boldly dip into the Potluck of both worlds. To all this I joyously assented; for besides the affection I now felt for Queequeg, he was an experienced harpooneer, and as such, could not fail to be of great usefulness to one, who, like me, was wholly ignorant of the mysteries of whaling, though well acquainted with the sea, as known to merchant seamen.

His story being ended with his pipe's last dying puff, Queequeg embraced me, pressed his forehead against mine, and blowing out the light, we rolled over from each other, this way and that, and very soon were sleeping.

Chapter 28: Ahab

Ishmael is awed by the long anticipated first sighting of Ahab, the captain of the Pequod, *who "looked like a man cut away from the stake, when the fire has overrunningly wasted all the limbs without consuming them, or taking away one particle from their compacted aged robustness. His whole high, broad form, seemed made of solid bronze, and shaped in an unalterable mould." That is not to mention his peg leg: "So powerfully did the whole grim aspect of Ahab affect me, and the livid brand which streaked it, that for the first few moments I hardly noted that not a little of this overbearing grimness was owing to the barbaric white leg upon which he partly stood. It had previously come to me that this ivory leg had at sea been fashioned from the polished bone of the sperm whale's jaw."*

For several days after leaving Nantucket, nothing above hatches was seen of Captain Ahab. The mates regularly relieved each other at the watches, and for aught that could be seen to the contrary, they seemed to be the only commanders of the ship; only they sometimes issued from the cabin with orders so sudden and peremptory, that after all it was plain they but commanded vicariously. Yes, their supreme lord and dictator was there, though hitherto unseen by any eyes not permitted to penetrate into the now sacred retreat of the cabin.

Every time I ascended to the deck from my watches below, I instantly gazed aft to mark if any strange face were visible; for my first vague disquietude touching the unknown captain, now in the seclusion of the sea, became almost a perturbation. This was strangely heightened at times by the ragged Elijah's diabolical incoherences uninvitedly recurring to me, with a subtle energy I could not have before conceived of. But poorly could I withstand them, much as in other moods I was almost ready to smile at the solemn whimsicalities of that outlandish prophet of the wharves. But whatever it was of apprehensiveness or uneasiness—to call it so—which I felt, yet whenever I came to look about me in the ship, it seemed against all warrantry to cherish such emotions. For though the harpooneers, with the great body of the crew, were a far more barbaric, heathenish, and motley set than any of the tame merchant-ship companies which my previous experiences had made me acquainted with, still I ascribed this—and rightly ascribed it—to the fierce uniqueness of the very nature of that wild Scandinavian vocation in which I had so abandonedly embarked. But it was especially the aspect of the three chief officers of the ship, the mates, which was most forcibly calculated to allay these colorless misgivings, and induce confidence and cheerfulness in every presentment of the voyage. Three better, more likely sea-officers and men, each in his own different way, could not readily be found, and they were every one of them Americans; a Nantucketer, a Vineyarder, a Cape man. Now, it being Christmas when the ship shot from out her harbor, for a space we had biting Polar weather, though all the time running away from it to the southward; and by every degree and minute of latitude which we sailed, gradually leaving that merciless winter, and all its intolerable weather behind us. It was one of those less lowering, but still grey and gloomy enough mornings of the transition, when with a fair wind the ship was rushing through the water with a vindictive sort of leaping and melancholy rapidity, that as I mounted to the deck at the call of the forenoon watch, so soon as I levelled my glance towards the taffrail, foreboding shivers ran over me. Reality outran apprehension; Captain Ahab stood upon his quarter-deck.

There seemed no sign of common bodily illness about him, nor of the recovery from any. He looked like a man cut away from the stake, when the fire has overrunningly wasted all the limbs without consuming them, or taking away one particle from their compacted aged robustness. His whole high, broad form, seemed made of solid bronze, and shaped in an unalterable mould, like Cellini's cast Perseus. Threading its way out from among his grey hairs, and continuing right down one side of his tawny scorched face and neck, till it disappeared in his clothing, you saw a slender rod-like mark, lividly whitish. It resembled that perpendicular seam sometimes made in the straight, lofty trunk of a great tree, when the upper lightning tearingly darts down it, and without wrenching a single twig, peels and grooves out the bark from top to bottom, ere running off into the soil, leaving the tree still greenly alive, but branded. Whether that mark was born with him, or whether it was the scar left by some desperate wound, no one could certainly say. By some tacit consent, throughout the voyage little or no allusion was made to it, especially by the mates. But once Tashtego's senior, an old Gay-Head Indian among the crew, superstitiously asserted that not till he was full forty years old did Ahab become that way branded, and then it came upon him, not in the fury of any mortal fray, but in an elemental strife at sea. Yet, this wild hint seemed inferentially negatived, by what a grey Manxman insinuated, an old sepulchral man, who, having never before sailed out of Nantucket, had never ere this laid eye upon wild Ahab. Nevertheless, the old sea-traditions, the immemorial credulities, popularly invested this old Manxman with preternatural powers of discernment. So that no white sailor seriously contradicted him when he said that if ever Captain Ahab should be tranquilly laid out—which might hardly come to pass, so he muttered—then, whoever should do that last office for the dead, would find a birthmark on him from crown to sole.

So powerfully did the whole grim aspect of Ahab affect me, and the livid brand which streaked it, that for the first few moments I hardly noted that not a little of this overbearing grimness was owing to the barbaric white leg upon which he partly stood. It had previously come to me that this ivory leg had at sea been fashioned from the polished bone of the sperm whale's jaw. "Aye, he was dismasted off Japan," said the old Gay-Head Indian once; "but like his dismasted craft, he shipped another mast without coming home for it. He has a quiver of 'em."

I was struck with the singular posture he maintained. Upon each side of the *Pequod*'s quarter deck, and pretty close to the mizen shrouds, there was an auger hole, bored about half an inch or so, into the plank. His bone leg steadied in that hole; one arm elevated, and holding by a shroud; Captain Ahab stood erect, looking straight out beyond the ship's ever-pitching prow. There was an infinity of firmest fortitude, a determinate, unsurrenderable wilfulness, in the fixed and fearless, forward dedication of that glance. Not a word he spoke; nor did his officers say aught to him; though by all their minutest gestures and expressions, they plainly showed the uneasy, if not painful, consciousness of being under a troubled master-eye. And not only that, but moody stricken Ahab stood before them with a crucifixion in his face; in all the nameless regal overbearing dignity of some mighty woe.

Ere long, from his first visit in the air, he withdrew into his cabin. But after that morning, he was every day visible to the crew; either standing in his pivot-hole, or seated upon an ivory stool he had; or heavily walking the deck. As the sky grew less gloomy; indeed, began to grow a little genial, he became still less and less a recluse; as if, when the ship had sailed from home, nothing but the dead wintry bleakness of the sea had then kept him so secluded. And, by and by, it came to pass, that he was almost continually in the air; but, as yet, for all that he said, or perceptibly did, on the at last sunny deck, he seemed as unnecessary there as another mast. But the *Pequod* was only making a passage now; not regularly cruising; nearly all whaling preparatives needing supervision the mates were fully competent to, so that there was little or nothing, out of himself, to employ or excite Ahab, now; and thus chase away, for that one interval, the clouds that layer upon layer were piled upon his brow, as ever all clouds choose the loftiest peaks to pile themselves upon.

Nevertheless, ere long, the warm, warbling persuasiveness of the pleasant, holiday weather we came to, seemed gradually to charm him from his mood. For, as when the red-cheeked, dancing girls, April and May, trip home to the wintry, misanthropic woods; even the barest, ruggedest, most thunder-cloven old oak will at least send forth some few green sprouts, to welcome such glad-hearted visitants; so Ahab did, in the end, a little respond to the playful allurings of that girlish air. More than once did he put forth the faint blossom of a look, which, in any other man, would have soon flowered out in a smile.

Chapter 36: The Quarter-Deck

Melville renders this chapter (one among several) dramatically, as if by Shakespeare. Ahab reveals his mysterious quest to the men, rallies their support through a vigorous speech to chase Moby-Dick, and seals the deal with liquor. His only verbal opposition is from Starbuck, who wonders: "'Vengeance on a dumb brute! . . . that simply smote thee from blindest instinct! Madness! To be enraged with a dumb thing, Captain Ahab, seems blasphemous.'"

(Enter Ahab: Then, all)

It was not a great while after the affair of the pipe, that one morning shortly after breakfast, Ahab, as was his wont, ascended the cabin-gangway to the deck. There most sea-captains usually walk at that hour, as country gentlemen, after the same meal, take a few turns in the garden.

Soon his steady, ivory stride was heard, as to and fro he paced his old rounds, upon planks so familiar to his tread, that they were all over dented, like geological stones, with the peculiar mark of his walk. Did you fixedly gaze, too, upon that ribbed and dented brow; there also, you would see still stranger foot-prints—the foot-prints of his one unsleeping, ever-pacing thought.

But on the occasion in question, those dents looked deeper, even as his nervous step that morning left a deeper mark. And, so full of his thought was Ahab, that at every uniform turn that he made, now at the main-mast and now at the binnacle, you could almost see that thought turn in him as he turned, and pace in him as he paced; so completely possessing him, indeed, that it all but seemed the inward mould of every outer movement.

"D'ye mark him, Flask?" whispered Stubb; "the chick that's in him pecks the shell. T'will soon be out."

The hours wore on;—Ahab now shut up within his cabin; anon, pacing the deck, with the same intense bigotry of purpose in his aspect.

It drew near the close of day. Suddenly he came to a halt by the bulwarks, and inserting his bone leg into the auger-hole there, and with one hand grasping a shroud, he ordered Starbuck to send everybody aft.

"Sir!" said the mate, astonished at an order seldom or never given on ship-board except in some extraordinary case.

"Send everybody aft," repeated Ahab. "Mast-heads, there! come down!"

When the entire ship's company were assembled, and with curious and not wholly unapprehensive faces, were eyeing him, for he looked not unlike the weather horizon when a storm is coming up, Ahab, after rapidly glancing over the bulwarks, and then darting his eyes among the crew, started from his standpoint; and as though not a soul were nigh him resumed his heavy turns upon the deck. With bent head and half-slouched hat he continued to pace, unmindful of the wondering whispering among the men; till Stubb cautiously whispered to Flask, that Ahab must have summoned them there for the purpose of witnessing a pedestrian feat. But this did not last long. Vehemently pausing, he cried:—"What do ye do when ye see a whale, men?"

"Sing out for him!" was the impulsive rejoinder from a score of clubbed voices.

"Good!" cried Ahab, with a wild approval in his tones; observing the hearty animation into which his unexpected question had so magnetically thrown them.

"And what do ye next, men?"

"Lower away, and after him!"

"And what tune is it ye pull to, men?"

"A dead whale or a stove boat!"

More and more strangely and fiercely glad and approving, grew the countenance of the old man at every shout; while the mariners began to gaze curiously at each other, as if marvelling how it was that they themselves became so excited at such seemingly purposeless questions.

But, they were all eagerness again, as Ahab, now half-revolving in his pivot-hole, with one hand reaching high up a shroud, and tightly, almost convulsively grasping it, addressed them thus:—

"All ye mast-headers have before now heard me give orders about a White Whale. Look ye! d'ye see this Spanish ounce of gold?"—holding up a broad bright coin to the sun—"it is a sixteen dollar piece, men. D'ye see it? Mr. Starbuck, hand me yon top-maul."

While the mate was getting the hammer, Ahab, without speaking, was slowly rubbing the gold piece against the skirts of his jacket, as if to heighten its lustre, and without using any words was meanwhile lowly humming to himself, producing a sound so strangely muffled and inarticulate that it seemed the mechanical humming of the wheels of his vitality in him.

Receiving the top-maul from Starbuck, he advanced towards the main-mast with the hammer uplifted in one hand, exhibiting the gold with the other, and with a high raised voice exclaiming: "Whosoever of ye raises me a white-headed whale with a wrinkled brow and a crooked jaw; whosoever of ye raises me that white-headed whale, with three holes punctured in his starboard fluke—look ye, whosoever of ye raises me that same white whale, he shall have this gold ounce, my boys!"

"Huzza! huzza!" cried the seamen, as with swinging tarpaulins they hailed the act of nailing the gold to the mast.

"It's a white whale, I say," resumed Ahab, as he threw down the top-maul; "a white whale. Skin your eyes for him, men; look sharp for white water; if ye see but a bubble, sing out."

All this while Tashtego, Daggoo, and Queequeg had looked on with even more intense interest and surprise than the rest, and at the mention of the wrinkled brow and crooked jaw they had started as if each was separately touched by some specific recollection.

"Captain Ahab," said Tashtego, "that white whale must be the same that some call Moby-Dick."

"Moby-Dick?" shouted Ahab. "Do ye know the white whale then, Tash?"

"Does he fan-tail a little curious, sir, before he goes down?" said the Gay-Header deliberately.

"And has he a curious spout, too," said Daggoo, "very bushy, even for a parmacetty, and mighty quick, Captain Ahab?"

"And he have one, two, tree—oh! good many iron in him hide, too, Captain," cried Queequeg disjointedly, "all twiske-tee be-twisk, like him—him—" faltering hard for a word, and screwing his hand round and round as though uncorking a bottle—"like him—him—"

"Corkscrew!" cried Ahab, "aye, Queequeg, the harpoons lie all twisted and wrenched in him; aye, Daggoo, his spout is a big one, like a whole shock of wheat, and white as a pile of our Nantucket wool after the great annual sheep-shearing; aye, Tashtego, and he fan-tails like a split jib in a squall. Death and devils! men, it is Moby-Dick ye have seen—Moby-Dick—Moby-Dick!"

"Captain Ahab," said Starbuck, who, with Stubb and Flask, had thus far been eyeing his superior with increasing surprise, but at last seemed struck with a thought which somewhat explained all the wonder. "Captain Ahab, I have heard of Moby-Dick—but it was not Moby-Dick that took off thy leg?"

"Who told thee that?" cried Ahab; then pausing, "Aye, Starbuck; aye, my hearties all round; it was Moby-Dick that dismasted me; Moby-Dick that brought me to this dead stump I stand on now. Aye, aye," he shouted with a terrific, loud, animal sob, like that of a heart-stricken moose; "Aye, aye! it was that accursed white whale that razeed me; made a poor pegging lubber of me for ever and a day!" Then tossing both arms, with measureless imprecations he shouted out: "Aye, aye! and I'll chase him round Good Hope, and round the horn, and round the Norway Maelstrom, and round perdition's flames before I give him up. And this is what ye have shipped for, men! to chase that white whale on both sides of land, and over all sides of earth, till he spouts black blood and rolls fin out. What say ye, men, will ye splice hands on it, now? I think ye do look brave."

"Aye, aye!" shouted the harpooneers and seamen, running closer to the excited old man: "A sharp eye for the White Whale; a sharp lance for Moby-Dick!"

"God bless ye," he seemed to half sob and half shout. "God bless ye, men. Steward! go draw the great measure of grog. But what's this long face about, Mr. Starbuck; wilt thou not chase the white whale? art not game for Moby-Dick?"

"I am game for his crooked jaw, and for the jaws of Death too, Captain Ahab, if it fairly comes in the way of the business we follow; but I came here to hunt whales, not my commander's vengeance. How many barrels will thy vengeance yield thee even if thou gettest it, Captain Ahab? it will not fetch thee much in our Nantucket market."

"Nantucket market! Hoot! But come closer, Starbuck; thou requirest a little lower layer. If money's to be the measurer, man, and the accountants have computed their great counting-house the globe, by girdling it with guineas, one to every three parts of an inch; then, let me tell thee, that my vengeance will fetch a great premium *here*!"

"He smites his chest," whispered Stubb, "what's that for? methinks it rings most vast, but hollow."

"Vengeance on a dumb brute!" cried Starbuck, "that simply smote thee from blindest instinct! Madness! To be enraged with a dumb thing, Captain Ahab, seems blasphemous."

"Hark ye yet again,—the little lower layer. All visible objects, man, are but as pasteboard masks. But in each event—in the living act, the undoubted deed—there, some unknown but still reasoning thing puts forth the mouldings of its features from behind the unreasoning mask. If man will strike, strike through the mask! How can the prisoner reach outside except by thrusting through the wall? To me, the white whale is that wall, shoved near to me. Sometimes I think there's naught beyond. But 'tis enough. He tasks me; he heaps me; I see in him outrageous strength, with an inscrutable malice sinewing it. That inscrutable thing is chiefly what I hate; and be the white whale agent, or be the white whale principal, I will wreak that hate upon him. Talk not to me of blasphemy, man; I'd strike the sun if it insulted me. For could the sun do that, then could I do the other; since there is ever a sort of fair play herein, jealousy presiding over all creations. But not my master, man, is even that fair play. Who's over me? Truth hath no confines. Take off thine eye! more intolerable than fiends' glarings is a doltish stare! So, so; thou reddenest and palest; my heat has melted thee to anger-glow. But look ye, Starbuck, what is said in heat, that thing unsays itself. There are men from whom warm words are small indignity. I meant not to incense thee. Let it go. Look! see yonder Turkish cheeks of spotted tawn—living, breathing pictures painted by the sun. The Pagan leopards—the unrecking and unworshipping things, that live; and seek, and give no reasons for the torrid life they feel! The crew, man, the crew! Are they not one and all with Ahab, in this matter of the whale? See Stubb! he laughs! See yonder Chilian! he snorts to think of it. Stand up amid the general hurricane, thy one tost sapling cannot, Starbuck! And what is it? Reckon it. 'Tis but to help strike a fin; no wondrous feat for Starbuck. What is it more? From this one poor hunt, then, the best lance out of all Nantucket, surely he will not hang back, when every foremast-hand has clutched a whetstone? Ah! constrainings seize thee; I see! the billow lifts thee! Speak, but speak!—Aye, aye! thy silence, then, *that* voices thee. (*Aside*) Something shot from my dilated nostrils, he has inhaled it in his lungs. Starbuck now is mine; cannot oppose me now, without rebellion."

"God keep me!—keep us all!" murmured Starbuck, lowly.

But in his joy at the enchanted, tacit acquiescence of the mate, Ahab did not hear his foreboding invocation; nor yet the low laugh from the hold; nor yet the presaging vibrations of the winds in the cordage; nor yet the hollow flap of the sails against the masts, as for a moment their hearts sank in. For again Starbuck's downcast eyes lighted up with the stubbornness of life; the subterranean laugh died away; the winds blew on; the sails filled out; the ship heaved and rolled as before. Ah, ye admonitions and warnings! why stay ye not when ye come? But rather are ye predictions than warnings, ye shadows! Yet not so much predictions from without, as verifications of the foregoing things within. For with little external to constrain us, the innermost necessities in our being, these still drive us on.

"The measure! the measure!" cried Ahab.

Receiving the brimming pewter, and turning to the harpooneers, he ordered them to produce their weapons. Then ranging them before him near the capstan, with their harpoons in their hands, while his three mates stood at his side with their lances, and the rest of the ship's company formed a circle round the group; he stood for an instant searchingly eyeing every man of his crew. But those wild eyes met his, as the bloodshot eyes of the prairie wolves meet the eye of their leader, ere he rushes on at their head in the trail of the bison; but, alas! only to fall into the hidden snare of the Indian.

"Drink and pass!" he cried, handing the heavy charged flagon to the nearest seaman. "The crew alone now drink. Round with it, round! Short draughts—long swallows, men; 'tis hot as Satan's hoof. So, so; it goes round excellently. It spiralizes in ye; forks out at the serpent-snapping eye. Well done; almost drained. That way it went, this way it comes. Hand it me—here's a hollow! Men, ye seem the years; so brimming life is gulped and gone. Steward, refill!

"Attend now, my braves. I have mustered ye all round this capstan; and ye mates, flank me with your lances; and ye harpooneers, stand there with your irons; and ye, stout mariners, ring me in, that I may in some sort revive a noble custom of my fisherman fathers before me. O men, you will yet see that—Ha! boy, come back? bad pennies come not sooner. Hand it me. Why, now, this pewter had run brimming again, wer't not thou St. Vitus' imp—away, thou ague!

"Advance, ye mates! Cross your lances full before me. Well done! Let me touch the axis." So saying, with extended arm, he grasped the three level, radiating lances at their crossed centre; while so doing, suddenly and nervously twitched them; meanwhile, glancing intently from Starbuck to Stubb; from Stubb to Flask. It seemed as though, by some nameless, interior volition, he would fain have shocked into them the same fiery emotion accumulated within the Leyden jar of his own magnetic life. The three mates quailed before his strong, sustained, and mystic aspect. Stubb and Flask looked sideways from him; the honest eye of Starbuck fell downright.

"In vain!" cried Ahab; "but, maybe, 'tis well. For did ye three but once take the full-forced shock, then mine own electric thing, that had perhaps expired from out me. Perchance, too, it would have dropped ye dead. Perchance ye need it not. Down lances! And now, ye mates, I do appoint ye three cup-bearers to my three pagan kinsmen there—yon three most honorable gentlemen and noblemen, my valiant harpooneers. Disdain the task? What, when the great Pope washes the feet of beggars, using his tiara for ewer? Oh, my sweet cardinals! your own condescension, *that* shall bend ye to it. I do not order ye; ye will it. Cut your seizings and draw the poles, ye harpooneers!"

Silently obeying the order, the three harpooneers now stood with the detached iron part of their harpoons, some three feet long, held, barbs up, before him.

"Stab me not with that keen steel! Cant them; cant them over! know ye not the goblet end? Turn up the socket! So, so; now, ye cup-bearers, advance. The irons! take them; hold them while I fill!" Forthwith, slowly going from one officer to the other, he brimmed the harpoon sockets with the fiery waters from the pewter.

"Now, three to three, ye stand. Commend the murderous chalices! Bestow them, ye who are now made parties to this indissoluble league. Ha! Starbuck! but the deed is done! Yon ratifying sun now waits to sit upon it. Drink, ye harpooneers! drink and swear, ye men that man the deathful whaleboat's bow—Death to Moby-Dick! God hunt us all, if we do not hunt Moby-Dick to his death!" The long, barbed steel goblets were lifted; and to cries and maledictions against the white whale, the spirits were simultaneously quaffed down with a hiss. Starbuck paled, and turned, and shivered. Once more, and finally, the replenished pewter went the rounds among the frantic crew; when, waving his free hand to them, they all dispersed; and Ahab retired within his cabin.

Chapter 41: Moby-Dick

Here Ishmael narrates his experience of learning "the history of that murderous monster against whom I and all the others had taken our oaths of violence and revenge." Also, there are two sentences from the chapter below that sum up the plot, which, it must be noted, while establishing the framework of the novel, is probably not Melville's art's most important component: "The White Whale swam before him as the monomaniac incarnation of all those malicious agencies which some deep men feel eating in them, till they are left living on with half a heart and half a lung." And, "Here, then, was this grey-headed, ungodly old man [i.e., Captain Ahab], chasing with curses a Job's whale round the world, at the head of a crew, too, chiefly made up of mongrel renegades, and castaways, and cannibals . . ."

I, Ishmael, was one of that crew; my shouts had gone up with the rest; my oath had been welded with theirs; and stronger I shouted, and more did I hammer and clinch my oath, because of the dread in my soul. A wild, mystical, sympathetical feeling was in me; Ahab's quenchless feud seemed mine. With greedy ears I learned the history of that murderous monster against whom I and all the others had taken our oaths of violence and revenge.

For some time past, though at intervals only, the unaccompanied, secluded White Whale had haunted those uncivilized seas mostly frequented by the Sperm Whale fishermen. But not all of them knew of his existence; only a few of them, comparatively, had knowingly seen him; while the number who as yet had actually and knowingly given battle to him, was small indeed. For, owing to the large number of whale-cruisers; the disorderly way they were sprinkled over the entire watery circumference, many of them adventurously pushing their quest along solitary latitudes, so as seldom or never for a whole twelvemonth or more on a stretch, to encounter a single news-telling sail of any sort; the inordinate length of each separate voyage; the irregularity of the times of sailing from home; all these, with other circumstances, direct and indirect, long obstructed the spread through the whole world-wide whaling-fleet of the special individualizing tidings concerning Moby-Dick. It was hardly to be doubted, that several vessels reported to have encountered, at such or such a time, or on such or such a meridian, a Sperm Whale of uncommon magnitude and malignity, which whale, after doing great mischief to his assailants, had completely escaped them; to some minds it was not an unfair presumption, I say, that the whale in question must have been no other than Moby-Dick. Yet as of late the Sperm Whale fishery had been marked by various and not unfrequent instances of great ferocity, cunning, and malice in the monster attacked; therefore it was, that those who by accident ignorantly gave battle to Moby-Dick; such hunters, perhaps, for the most part, were content to ascribe the peculiar terror he bred, more, as it were, to the perils of the Sperm Whale fishery at large, than to the individual cause. In that way, mostly, the disastrous encounter between Ahab and the whale had hitherto been popularly regarded.

And as for those who, previously hearing of the White Whale, by chance caught sight of him; in the beginning of the thing they had every one of them, almost, as boldly and fearlessly lowered for him, as for any other whale of that species. But at length, such calamities did ensue in these assaults—not restricted to sprained wrists and ankles, broken limbs, or devouring amputations—but fatal to the last degree of fatality; those repeated disastrous repulses, all accumulating and piling their terrors upon Moby-Dick; those things had gone far to shake the fortitude of many brave hunters, to whom the story of the White Whale had eventually come.

Nor did wild rumors of all sorts fail to exaggerate, and still the more horrify the true histories of these deadly encounters. For not only do fabulous rumors naturally grow out of the very body of all surprising terrible events,—as the smitten tree gives birth to its fungi; but, in maritime life, far more than in that of terra firma, wild rumors abound, wherever there is any adequate reality for them to cling to. And as the sea surpasses the land in this matter, so the whale fishery surpasses every other sort of maritime life, in the wonderfulness and fearfulness of the rumors which sometimes circulate there. For not only are whalemen as a body unexempt from that ignorance and superstitiousness hereditary to all sailors; but of all sailors, they are by all odds the most directly brought into contact with whatever is appallingly astonishing in the sea; face to face they not only eye its greatest marvels, but, hand to jaw, give battle to them. Alone, in such remotest waters, that though you sailed a thousand miles, and passed a thousand shores, you would not come to any chiselled hearthstone, or aught hospitable beneath that part of the sun; in such latitudes and longitudes, pursuing too such a calling as he does, the whaleman is wrapped by influences all tending to make his fancy pregnant with many a mighty birth.

No wonder, then, that ever gathering volume from the mere transit over the widest watery spaces, the outblown rumors of the White Whale did in the end incorporate with themselves all manner of morbid hints, and half-formed foetal suggestions of supernatural agencies, which eventually invested Moby-Dick with new terrors unborrowed from anything that visibly appears. So that in many cases such a panic did he finally strike, that few who by those rumors, at least, had heard of the White Whale, few of those hunters were willing to encounter the perils of his jaw.

But there were still other and more vital practical influences at work. Not even at the present day has the original prestige of the Sperm Whale, as fearfully distinguished from all other species of the leviathan, died out of the minds of the whalemen as a body. There are those this day among them, who, though intelligent and courageous enough in offering battle to the Greenland or Right Whale, would perhaps—either from professional inexperience, or incompetency, or timidity, decline a contest with the Sperm Whale; at any rate, there are plenty of whalemen, especially among those whaling nations not sailing under the American flag, who have never hostilely encountered the Sperm Whale, but whose sole knowledge of the leviathan is restricted to the ignoble monster primitively pursued in the North; seated on their hatches, these men will hearken with a childish fire-side interest and awe, to the wild, strange tales of Southern whaling. Nor is the pre-eminent tremendousness of the great Sperm Whale anywhere more feelingly comprehended, than on board of those prows which stem him.

And as if the now tested reality of his might had in former legendary times thrown its shadow before it; we find some book naturalists—Olassen and Povelson—declaring the Sperm Whale not only to be a consternation to every other creature in the sea, but also to be so incredibly ferocious as continually to be athirst for human blood. Nor even down to so late a time as Cuvier's, were these or almost similar impressions effaced. For in his Natural History, the Baron himself affirms that at sight of the Sperm Whale, all fish (sharks included) are "struck with the most lively terrors," and "often in the precipitancy of their flight dash themselves against the rocks with such violence as to cause instantaneous death." And however the general experiences in the fishery may amend such reports as these; yet in their full terribleness, even to the bloodthirsty item of Povelson, the superstitious belief in them is, in some vicissitudes of their vocation, revived in the minds of the hunters.

So that overawed by the rumors and portents concerning him, not a few of the fishermen recalled, in reference to Moby-Dick, the earlier days of the Sperm Whale fishery, when it was oftentimes hard to induce long practised Right whalemen to embark in the perils of this new and daring warfare; such men protesting that although other leviathans might be hopefully pursued, yet to chase and point lance at such an apparition as the Sperm Whale was not for mortal man. That to attempt it, would be inevitably to be torn into a quick eternity. On this head, there are some remarkable documents that may be consulted.

Nevertheless, some there were, who even in the face of these things were ready to give chase to Moby-Dick; and a still greater number who, chancing only to hear of him distantly and vaguely, without the specific details of any certain calamity, and without superstitious accompaniments, were sufficiently hardy not to flee from the battle if offered.

One of the wild suggestings referred to, as at last coming to be linked with the White Whale in the minds of the superstitiously inclined, was the unearthly conceit that Moby-Dick was ubiquitous; that he had actually been encountered in opposite latitudes at one and the same instant of time.

Nor, credulous as such minds must have been, was this conceit altogether without some faint show of superstitious probability. For as the secrets of the currents in the seas have never yet been divulged, even to the most erudite research; so the hidden ways of the Sperm Whale when beneath the surface remain, in great part, unaccountable to his pursuers; and from time to time have originated the most curious and contradictory speculations regarding them, especially concerning the mystic modes whereby, after sounding to a great depth, he transports himself with such vast swiftness to the most widely distant points.

It is a thing well known to both American and English whale-ships, and as well a thing placed upon authoritative record years ago by Scoresby, that some whales have been captured far north in the Pacific, in whose bodies have been found the barbs of harpoons darted in the Greenland seas. Nor is it to be gainsaid, that in some of these instances it has been declared that the interval of time between the two assaults could not have exceeded very many days. Hence, by inference, it has been believed by some whalemen, that the Nor' West Passage, so long a problem to man, was never a problem to the whale. So that here, in the real living experience of living men, the prodigies related in old times of the inland Strello mountain in Portugal (near whose top there was said to be a lake in which the wrecks of ships floated up to the surface); and that still more wonderful story of the Arethusa fountain near Syracuse (whose waters were believed to have come from the Holy Land by an underground passage); these fabulous narrations are almost fully equalled by the realities of the whaleman.

Forced into familiarity, then, with such prodigies as these; and knowing that after repeated, intrepid assaults, the White Whale had escaped alive; it cannot be much matter of surprise that some whalemen should go still further in their superstitions; declaring Moby-Dick not only ubiquitous, but immortal (for immortality is but ubiquity in time); that though groves of spears should be planted in his flanks, he would still swim away unharmed; or if indeed he should ever be made to spout thick blood, such a sight would be but a ghastly deception; for again in unensanguined billows hundreds of leagues away, his unsullied jet would once more be seen.

But even stripped of these supernatural surmisings, there was enough in the earthly make and incontestable character of the monster to strike the imagination with unwonted power. For, it was not so much his uncommon bulk that so much distinguished him from other Sperm Whales, but, as was elsewhere thrown out—a peculiar snow-white wrinkled forehead, and a high, pyramidical white hump. These were his prominent features; the tokens whereby, even in the limitless, uncharted seas, he revealed his identity, at a long distance, to those who knew him.

The rest of his body was so streaked, and spotted, and marbled with the same shrouded hue, that, in the end, he had gained his distinctive appellation of the White Whale; a name, indeed, literally justified by his vivid aspect, when seen gliding at high noon through a dark blue sea, leaving a milky-way wake of creamy foam, all spangled with golden gleamings.

Nor was it his unwonted magnitude, nor his remarkable hue, nor yet his deformed lower jaw, that so much invested the whale with natural terror, as that unexampled, intelligent malignity which, according to specific accounts, he had over and over again evinced in his assaults. More than all, his treacherous retreats struck more of dismay than perhaps aught else. For, when swimming before his exulting pursuers, with every apparent symptom of alarm, he had several times been known to turn around suddenly, and, bearing down upon them, either stave their boats to splinters, or drive them back in consternation to their ship.

Already several fatalities had attended his chase. But though similar disasters, however little bruited ashore, were by no means unusual in the fishery; yet, in most instances, such seemed the White Whale's infernal aforethought of ferocity, that every dismembering or death that he caused, was not wholly regarded as having been inflicted by an unintelligent agent.

Judge, then, to what pitches of inflamed, distracted fury the minds of his more desperate hunters were impelled, when amid the chips of chewed boats, and the sinking limbs of torn comrades, they swam out of the white curds of the whale's direful wrath into the serene, exasperating sunlight, that smiled on, as if at a birth or a bridal.

His three boats stove around him, and oars and men both whirling in the eddies; one captain, seizing the line-knife from his broken prow, had dashed at the whale, as an Arkansas duellist at his foe, blindly seeking with a six-inch blade to reach the fathom-deep life of the whale. That captain was Ahab. And then it was, that suddenly sweeping his sickle-shaped lower jaw beneath him, Moby-Dick had reaped away Ahab's leg, as a mower a blade of grass in the field. No turbaned Turk, no hired Venetian or Malay, could have smote him with more seeming malice. Small reason was there to doubt, then, that ever since that almost fatal encounter, Ahab had cherished a wild vindictiveness against the whale, all the more fell for that in his frantic morbidness he at last came to identify with him, not only all his bodily woes, but all his intellectual and spiritual exasperations. The White Whale swam before him as the monomaniac incarnation of all those malicious agencies which some deep men feel eating in them, till they are left living on with half a heart and half a lung. That intangible malignity which has been from the beginning; to whose dominion even the modern Christians ascribe one-half of the worlds; which the ancient Ophites of the east reverenced in their statue devil;—Ahab did not fall down and worship it like them; but deliriously transferring its idea to the abhorred White Whale, he pitted himself, all mutilated, against it. All that most maddens and torments; all that stirs up the lees of things; all truth with malice in it; all that cracks the sinews and cakes the brain; all the subtle demonisms of life and thought; all evil, to crazy Ahab, were visibly personified, and made practically assailable in Moby-Dick. He piled upon the whale's white hump the sum of all the general rage and hate felt by his whole race from Adam down; and then, as if his chest had been a mortar, he burst his hot heart's shell upon it.

It is not probable that this monomania in him took its instant rise at the precise time of his bodily dismemberment. Then, in darting at the monster, knife in hand, he had but given loose to a sudden, passionate, corporal animosity; and when he received the stroke that tore him, he probably but felt the agonizing bodily laceration, but nothing more. Yet, when by this collision forced to turn towards home, and for long months of days and weeks, Ahab and anguish lay stretched together in one hammock, rounding in mid winter that dreary, howling Patagonian Cape; then it was, that his torn body and gashed soul bled into one another; and so interfusing, made him mad. That it was only then, on the homeward voyage, after the encounter, that the final monomania seized him, seems all but certain from the fact that, at intervals during the passage, he was a raving lunatic; and, though unlimbed of a leg, yet such vital strength yet lurked in his Egyptian chest, and was moreover intensified by his delirium, that his mates were forced to lace him fast, even there, as he sailed, raving in his hammock. In a strait-jacket, he swung to the mad rockings of the gales. And, when running into more sufferable latitudes, the ship, with mild stun'sails spread, floated across the tranquil tropics, and, to all appearances, the old man's delirium seemed left behind him with the Cape Horn swells, and he came forth from his dark den into the blessed light and air; even then, when he bore that firm, collected front, however pale, and issued his calm orders once again; and his mates thanked God the direful madness was now gone; even then, Ahab, in his hidden self, raved on. Human madness is oftentimes a cunning and most feline thing. When you think it fled, it may have but become transfigured into some still subtler form. Ahab's full lunacy subsided not, but deepeningly contracted; like the unabated Hudson, when that noble Northman flows narrowly, but unfathomably through the Highland gorge. But, as in his narrow-flowing monomania, not one jot of Ahab's broad madness had been left behind; so in that broad madness, not one jot of his great natural intellect had perished. That before living agent, now became the living instrument. If such a furious trope may stand, his special lunacy stormed his general sanity, and carried it, and turned all its concentred cannon upon its own mad mark; so that far from having lost his strength, Ahab, to that one end, did now possess a thousand fold more potency than ever he had sanely brought to bear upon any one reasonable object.

This is much; yet Ahab's larger, darker, deeper part remains unhinted. But vain to popularize profundities, and all truth is profound. Winding far down from within the very heart of this spiked Hotel de Cluny where we here stand—however grand and wonderful, now quit it;—and take your way, ye nobler, sadder souls, to those vast Roman halls of Thermes; where far beneath the fantastic towers of man's upper earth, his root of grandeur, his whole awful essence sits in bearded state; an antique buried beneath antiquities, and throned on torsoes! So with a broken throne, the great gods mock that captive king; so like a Caryatid, he patient sits, upholding on his frozen brow the piled entablatures of ages. Wind ye down there, ye prouder, sadder souls! question that proud, sad king! A family likeness! aye, he did beget ye, ye young exiled royalties; and from your grim sire only will the old State-secret come.

Now, in his heart, Ahab had some glimpse of this, namely: all my means are sane, my motive and my object mad. Yet without power to kill, or change, or shun the fact; he likewise knew that to mankind he did now long dissemble; in some sort, did still. But that thing of his dissembling was only subject to his perceptibility, not to his will determinate. Nevertheless, so well did he succeed in that dissembling, that when with ivory leg he stepped ashore at last, no Nantucketer thought him otherwise than but naturally grieved, and that to the quick, with the terrible casualty which had overtaken him.

The report of his undeniable delirium at sea was likewise popularly ascribed to a kindred cause. And so too, all the added moodiness which always afterwards, to the very day of sailing in the *Pequod* on the present voyage, sat brooding on his brow. Nor is it so very unlikely, that far from distrusting his fitness for another whaling voyage, on account of such dark symptoms, the calculating people of that prudent isle were inclined to harbor the conceit, that for those very reasons he was all the better qualified and set on edge, for a pursuit so full of rage and wildness as the bloody hunt of whales. Gnawed within and scorched without, with the infixed, unrelenting fangs of some incurable idea; such an one, could he be found, would seem the very man to dart his iron and lift his lance against the most appalling of all brutes. Or, if for any reason thought to be corporeally incapacitated for that, yet such an one would seem superlatively competent to cheer and howl on his underlings to the attack. But be all this as it may, certain it is, that with the mad secret of his unabated rage bolted up and keyed in him, Ahab had purposely sailed upon the present voyage with the one only and all-engrossing object of hunting the White Whale. Had any one of his old acquaintances on shore but half dreamed of what was lurking in him then, how soon would their aghast and righteous souls have wrenched the ship from such a fiendish man! They were bent on profitable cruises, the profit to be counted down in dollars from the mint. He was intent on an audacious, immitigable, and supernatural revenge.

Here, then, was this grey-headed, ungodly old man, chasing with curses a Job's whale round the world, at the head of a crew, too, chiefly made up of mongrel renegades, and castaways, and cannibals—morally enfeebled also, by the incompetence of mere unaided virtue or right-mindedness in Starbuck, the invulnerable jollity of indifference and recklessness in Stubb, and the pervading mediocrity in Flask. Such a crew, so officered, seemed specially picked and packed by some infernal fatality to help him to his monomaniac revenge. How it was that they so aboundingly responded to the old man's ire—by what evil magic their souls were possessed, that at times his hate seemed almost theirs; the White Whale as much their insufferable foe as his; how all this came to be—what the White Whale was to them, or how to their unconscious understandings, also, in some dim, unsuspected way, he might have seemed the gliding great demon of the seas of life,—all this to explain, would be to dive deeper than Ishmael can go. The subterranean miner that works in us all, how can one tell whither leads his shaft by the ever shifting, muffled sound of his pick? Who does not feel the irresistible arm drag? What skiff in tow of a seventy-four can stand still? For one, I gave myself up to the abandonment of the time and the place; but while yet all a-rush to encounter the whale, could see naught in that brute but the deadliest ill.

Chapter 65: The Whale as a Dish

There is no end to the unexpected turns and depths Melville's thoughts take.

That mortal man should feed upon the creature that feeds his lamp, and, like Stubb, eat him by his own light, as you may say; this seems so outlandish a thing that one must needs go a little into the history and philosophy of it.

It is upon record, that three centuries ago the tongue of the Right Whale was esteemed a great delicacy in France, and commanded large prices there. Also, that in Henry VIIIth's time, a certain cook of the court obtained a handsome reward for inventing an admirable sauce to be eaten with barbecued porpoises, which, you remember, are a species of whale. Porpoises, indeed, are to this day considered fine eating. The meat is made into balls about the size of billiard balls, and being well seasoned and spiced might be taken for turtle-balls or veal balls. The old monks of Dunfermline were very fond of them. They had a great porpoise grant from the crown.

The fact is, that among his hunters at least, the whale would by all hands be considered a noble dish, were there not so much of him; but when you come to sit down before a meat-pie nearly one hundred feet long, it takes away your appetite. Only the most unprejudiced of men like Stubb, nowadays partake of cooked whales; but the Esquimaux are not so fastidious. We all know how they live upon whales, and have rare old vintages of prime old train oil. Zogranda, one of their most famous doctors, recommends strips of blubber for infants, as being exceedingly juicy and nourishing. And this reminds me that certain Englishmen, who long ago were accidentally left in Greenland by a whaling vessel—that these men actually lived for several months on the mouldy scraps of whales which had been left ashore after trying out the blubber. Among the Dutch whalemen these scraps are called "fritters;" which, indeed, they greatly resemble, being brown and crisp, and smelling something like old Amsterdam housewives' dough-nuts or oly-cooks, when fresh. They have such an eatable look that the most self-denying stranger can hardly keep his hands off.

But what further depreciates the whale as a civilized dish, is his exceeding richness. He is the great prize ox of the sea, too fat to be delicately good. Look at his hump, which would be as fine eating as the buffalo's (which is esteemed a rare dish), were it not such a solid pyramid of fat. But the spermaceti itself, how bland and creamy that is; like the transparent, half-jellied, white meat of a cocoanut in the third month of its growth, yet far too rich to supply a substitute for butter. Nevertheless, many whalemen have a method of absorbing it into some other substance, and then partaking of it. In the long try watches of the night it is a common thing for the seamen to dip their ship-biscuit into the huge oil-pots and let them fry there awhile. Many a good supper have I thus made.

In the case of a small Sperm Whale the brains are accounted a fine dish. The casket of the skull is broken into with an axe, and the two plump, whitish lobes being withdrawn (precisely resembling two large puddings), they are then mixed with flour, and cooked into a most delectable mess, in flavor somewhat resembling calves' head, which is quite a dish among some epicures; and every one knows that some young bucks among the epicures, by continually dining upon calves' brains, by and by get to have a little brains of their own, so as to be able to tell a calf's head from their own heads; which, indeed, requires uncommon discrimination. And that is the reason why a young buck with an intelligent looking calf's head before him, is somehow one of the saddest sights you can see. The head looks a sort of reproachfully at him, with an "Et tu Brute!" expression.

It is not, perhaps, entirely because the whale is so excessively unctuous that landsmen seem to regard the eating of him with abhorrence; that appears to result, in some way, from the consideration before mentioned: i. e. that a man should eat a newly murdered thing of the sea, and eat it too by its own light. But no doubt the first man that ever murdered an ox was regarded as a murderer; perhaps he was hung; and if he had been put on his trial by oxen, he certainly would have been; and he certainly deserved it if any murderer does. Go to the meat-market of a Saturday night and see the crowds of live bipeds staring up at the long rows of dead quadrupeds. Does not that sight take a tooth out of the cannibal's jaw? Cannibals? who is not a cannibal? I tell you it will be more tolerable for the Fejee that salted down a lean missionary in his cellar against a coming famine; it will be more tolerable for that provident Fejee, I say, in the day of judgment, than for thee, civilized and enlightened gourmand, who nailest geese to the ground and feastest on their bloated livers in thy paté-de-foie-gras.

But Stubb, he eats the whale by its own light, does he? and that is adding insult to injury, is it? Look at your knife-handle, there, my civilized and enlightened gourmand dining off that roast beef, what is that handle made of?—what but the bones of the brother of the very ox you are eating? And what do you pick your teeth with, after devouring that fat goose? With a feather of the same fowl. And with what quill did the Secretary of the Society for the Suppression of Cruelty to Ganders formally indite his circulars? It is only within the last month or two that that society passed a resolution to patronize nothing but steel pens.

Chapter 66: The Shark Massacre

There are shocking details in Melville's brief description of a shark frenzy.

When in the Southern Fishery, a captured Sperm Whale, after long and weary toil, is brought alongside late at night, it is not, as a general thing at least, customary to proceed at once to the business of cutting him in. For that business is an exceedingly laborious one; is not very soon completed; and requires all hands to set about it. Therefore, the common usage is to take in all sail; lash the helm a'lee; and then send every one below to his hammock till daylight, with the reservation that, until that time, anchor-watches shall be kept; that is, two and two for an hour, each couple, the crew in rotation shall mount the deck to see that all goes well.

But sometimes, especially upon the Line in the Pacific, this plan will not answer at all; because such incalculable hosts of sharks gather round the moored carcase, that were he left so for six hours, say, on a stretch, little more than the skeleton would be visible by morning. In most other parts of the ocean, however, where these fish do not so largely abound, their wondrous voracity can be at times considerably diminished, by vigorously stirring them up with sharp whaling-spades, a procedure notwithstanding, which, in some instances, only seems to tickle them into still greater activity. But it was not thus in the present case with the *Pequod*'s sharks; though, to be sure, any man unaccustomed to such sights, to have looked over her side that night, would have almost thought the whole round sea was one huge cheese, and those sharks the maggots in it.

Nevertheless, upon Stubb setting the anchor-watch after his supper was concluded; and when, accordingly, Queequeg and a forecastle seaman came on deck, no small excitement was created among the sharks; for immediately suspending the cutting stages over the side, and lowering three lanterns, so that they cast long gleams of light over the turbid sea, these two mariners, darting their long whaling-spades, kept up an incessant murdering of the sharks,[2] by striking the keen steel deep into their skulls, seemingly their only vital part. But in the foamy confusion of their mixed and struggling hosts, the marksmen could not always hit their mark; and this brought about new revelations of the incredible ferocity of the foe. They viciously snapped, not only at each other's disembowelments, but like flexible bows, bent round, and bit their own; till those entrails seemed swallowed over and over again by the same mouth, to be oppositely voided by the gaping wound. Nor was this all. It was unsafe to meddle with the corpses and ghosts of these creatures. A sort of generic or Pantheistic vitality seemed to lurk in their very joints and bones, after what might be called the individual life had departed. Killed and hoisted on deck for the sake of his skin, one of these sharks almost took poor Queequeg's hand off, when he tried to shut down the dead lid of his murderous jaw.

"Queequeg no care what god made him shark," said the savage, agonizingly lifting his hand up and down; "wedder Fejee god or Nantucket god; but de god wat made shark must be one dam Ingin."

Chapter 87: The Grand Armada

"Perhaps the most stupendous chapter," remarked D. H. Lawrence.[3]

The long and narrow peninsula of Malacca, extending southeastward from the territories of Birmah, forms the most southerly point of all Asia. In a continuous line from that peninsula stretch

2. Melville's note: The whaling-spade used for cutting-in is made of the very best steel; is about the bigness of a man's spread hand; and in general shape, corresponds to the garden implement after which it is named; only its sides are perfectly flat, and its upper end considerably narrower than the lower. This weapon is always kept as sharp as possible; and when being used is occasionally honed, just like a razor. In its socket, a stiff pole, from twenty to thirty feet long, is inserted for a handle.

3. D. H. Lawrence. "Herman Melville's *Moby Dick*." *Studies in Classic American Literature*. Harmondsworth, England: Penguin, 1977. 163.

the long islands of Sumatra, Java, Bally, and Timor; which, with many others, form a vast mole, or rampart, lengthwise connecting Asia with Australia, and dividing the long unbroken Indian ocean from the thickly studded oriental archipelagoes. This rampart is pierced by several sally-ports for the convenience of ships and whales; conspicuous among which are the straits of Sunda and Malacca. By the straits of Sunda, chiefly, vessels bound to China from the west, emerge into the China seas.

Those narrow straits of Sunda divide Sumatra from Java; and standing midway in that vast rampart of islands, buttressed by that bold green promontory, known to seamen as Java Head; they not a little correspond to the central gateway opening into some vast walled empire: and considering the inexhaustible wealth of spices, and silks, and jewels, and gold, and ivory, with which the thousand islands of that oriental sea are enriched, it seems a significant provision of nature, that such treasures, by the very formation of the land, should at least bear the appearance, however ineffectual, of being guarded from the all-grasping western world. The shores of the Straits of Sunda are unsupplied with those domineering fortresses which guard the entrances to the Mediterranean, the Baltic, and the Propontis. Unlike the Danes, these Orientals do not demand the obsequious homage of lowered top-sails from the endless procession of ships before the wind, which for centuries past, by night and by day, have passed between the islands of Sumatra and Java, freighted with the costliest cargoes of the east. But while they freely waive a ceremonial like this, they do by no means renounce their claim to more solid tribute.

Time out of mind the piratical proas of the Malays, lurking among the low shaded coves and islets of Sumatra, have sallied out upon the vessels sailing through the straits, fiercely demanding tribute at the point of their spears. Though by the repeated bloody chastisements they have received at the hands of European cruisers, the audacity of these corsairs has of late been somewhat repressed; yet, even at the present day, we occasionally hear of English and American vessels, which, in those waters, have been remorselessly boarded and pillaged.

With a fair, fresh wind, the *Pequod* was now drawing nigh to these straits; Ahab purposing to pass through them into the Javan sea, and thence, cruising northwards, over waters known to be frequented here and there by the Sperm Whale, sweep inshore by the Philippine Islands, and gain the far coast of Japan, in time for the great whaling season there. By these means, the circumnavigating *Pequod* would sweep almost all the known Sperm Whale cruising grounds of the world, previous to descending upon the Line in the Pacific; where Ahab, though everywhere else foiled in his pursuit, firmly counted upon giving battle to Moby-Dick, in the sea he was most known to frequent; and at a season when he might most reasonably be presumed to be haunting it.

But how now? in this zoned quest, does Ahab touch no land? does his crew drink air? Surely, he will stop for water. Nay. For a long time, now, the circus-running sun has raced within his fiery ring, and needs no sustenance but what's in himself. So Ahab. Mark this, too, in the whaler. While other hulls are loaded down with alien stuff, to be transferred to foreign wharves; the world-wandering whale-ship carries no cargo but herself and crew, their weapons and their wants. She has a whole lake's contents bottled in her ample hold. She is ballasted with utilities; not altogether with unusable pig-lead and kentledge. She carries years' water in her. Clear old prime Nantucket water; which, when three years afloat, the Nantucketer, in the Pacific, prefers to drink before the brackish fluid, but yesterday rafted off in casks, from the Peruvian or Indian streams. Hence it is, that, while other ships may have gone to China from New York, and back again, touching at a score of ports, the whale-ship, in all that interval, may not have sighted one grain of soil; her crew having seen no man but floating seamen like themselves. So that did you carry them the news that another flood had come; they would only answer—"Well, boys, here's the ark!"

Now, as many Sperm Whales had been captured off the western coast of Java, in the near vicinity of the straits of Sunda; indeed, as most of the ground, roundabout, was generally recognised by the fishermen as an excellent spot for cruising; therefore, as the *Pequod* gained more and more upon Java Head, the look-outs were repeatedly hailed, and admonished to keep wide awake. But though the green palmy cliffs of the land soon loomed on the starboard bow, and with delighted nostrils the fresh cinnamon was snuffed in the air, yet not a single jet was descried. Almost renouncing all thought of falling in with any game hereabouts, the ship had well nigh entered the straits, when the customary cheering cry was heard from aloft, and ere long a spectacle of singular magnificence saluted us.

But here be it premised, that owing to the unwearied activity with which of late they have been hunted over all four oceans, the

Sperm Whales, instead of almost invariably sailing in small detached companies, as in former times, are now frequently met with in extensive herds, sometimes embracing so great a multitude, that it would almost seem as if numerous nations of them had sworn solemn league and covenant for mutual assistance and protection. To this aggregation of the Sperm Whale into such immense caravans, may be imputed the circumstance that even in the best cruising grounds, you may now sometimes sail for weeks and months together, without being greeted by a single spout; and then be suddenly saluted by what sometimes seems thousands on thousands.

Broad on both bows, at the distance of some two or three miles, and forming a great semicircle, embracing one half of the level horizon, a continuous chain of whale-jets were up-playing and sparkling in the noon-day air. Unlike the straight perpendicular twin-jets of the Right Whale, which, dividing at top, falls over in two branches, like the cleft drooping boughs of a willow, the single forward-slanting spout of the Sperm Whale presents a thick curled bush of white mist, continually rising and falling away to leeward.

Seen from the *Pequod*'s deck, then, as she would rise on a high hill of the sea, this host of vapory spouts, individually curling up into the air, and beheld through a blending atmosphere of bluish haze, showed like the thousand cheerful chimneys of some dense metropolis, descried of a balmy autumnal morning, by some horseman on a height.

As marching armies approaching an unfriendly defile in the mountains, accelerate their march, all eagerness to place that perilous passage in their rear, and once more expand in comparative security upon the plain; even so did this vast fleet of whales now seem hurrying forward through the straits; gradually contracting the wings of their semicircle, and swimming on, in one solid, but still crescentic centre.

Crowding all sail the *Pequod* pressed after them; the harpooneers handling their weapons, and loudly cheering from the heads of their yet suspended boats. If the wind only held, little doubt had they, that chased through these Straits of Sunda, the vast host would only deploy into the Oriental seas to witness the capture of not a few of their number. And who could tell whether, in that congregated caravan, Moby-Dick himself might not temporarily be swimming, like the worshipped white-elephant in the coronation procession of the Siamese! So with stun-sail piled on stun-sail, we sailed along, driving these Leviathans before us; when, of a sudden, the voice of Tashtego was heard, loudly directing attention to something in our wake.

Corresponding to the crescent in our van, we beheld another in our rear. It seemed formed of detached white vapors, rising and falling something like the spouts of the whales; only they did not so completely come and go; for they constantly hovered, without finally disappearing. Levelling his glass at this sight, Ahab quickly revolved in his pivot-hole, crying, "Aloft there, and rig whips and buckets to wet the sails;—Malays, sir, and after us!"

As if too long lurking behind the headlands, till the *Pequod* should fairly have entered the straits, these rascally Asiatics were now in hot pursuit, to make up for their over-cautious delay. But when the swift *Pequod*, with a fresh leading wind, was herself in hot chase; how very kind of these tawny philanthropists to assist in speeding her on to her own chosen pursuit,—mere riding-whips and rowels to her, that they were. As with glass under arm, Ahab to-and-fro paced the deck; in his forward turn beholding the monsters he chased, and in the after one the bloodthirsty pirates chasing him; some such fancy as the above seemed his. And when he glanced upon the green walls of the watery defile in which the ship was then sailing, and bethought him that through that gate lay the route to his vengeance, and beheld, how that through that same gate he was now both chasing and being chased to his deadly end; and not only that, but a herd of remorseless wild pirates and inhuman atheistical devils were infernally cheering him on with their curses;—when all these conceits had passed through his brain, Ahab's brow was left gaunt and ribbed, like the black sand beach after some stormy tide has been gnawing it, without being able to drag the firm thing from its place.

But thoughts like these troubled very few of the reckless crew; and when, after steadily dropping and dropping the pirates astern, the *Pequod* at last shot by the vivid green Cockatoo Point on the Sumatra side, emerging at last upon the broad waters beyond; then, the harpooneers seemed more to grieve that the swift whales had been gaining upon the ship, than to rejoice that the ship had so victoriously gained upon the Malays. But still driving on in the wake of the whales, at length they seemed abating their speed; gradually the ship neared them; and the wind now dying away, word was passed to spring to the boats. But no sooner did the herd, by some presumed wonderful instinct of the Sperm Whale, become notified of the three keels that were after them,—though as yet a mile in their rear,—than they rallied again, and forming in close ranks and battalions, so that their spouts all looked like flashing lines of stacked bayonets, moved on with redoubled velocity.

Stripped to our shirts and drawers, we sprang to the white-ash, and after several hours' pulling were almost disposed to renounce the chase, when a general pausing commotion among the whales gave animating token that they were now at last under the influence of that strange perplexity of inert irresolution, which, when the fishermen perceive it in the whale, they say he is gallied. The compact martial columns in which they had been hitherto rapidly and steadily swimming, were now broken up in one measureless rout; and like King Porus' elephants in the Indian battle with Alexander, they seemed going mad with consternation. In all directions expanding in vast irregular circles, and aimlessly swimming hither and thither, by their short thick spoutings, they plainly betrayed their distraction of panic. This was still more strangely evinced by those of their number, who, completely paralysed as it were, helplessly floated like water-logged dismantled ships on the sea. Had these Leviathans been but a flock of simple sheep, pursued over the pasture by three fierce wolves, they could not possibly have evinced such excessive dismay. But this occasional timidity is characteristic of almost all herding creatures. Though banding together in tens of thousands, the lion-maned buffaloes of the West have fled before a solitary horseman. Witness, too, all human beings, how when herded together in the sheepfold of a theatre's pit, they will, at the slightest alarm of fire, rush helter-skelter for the outlets, crowding, trampling, jamming, and remorselessly dashing each other to death. Best, therefore, withhold any amazement at the strangely gallied whales before us, for there is no folly of the beasts of the earth which is not infinitely outdone by the madness of men.

Though many of the whales, as has been said, were in violent motion, yet it is to be observed that as a whole the herd neither advanced nor retreated, but collectively remained in one place. As is customary in those cases, the boats at once separated, each making for some one lone whale on the outskirts of the shoal. In about three minutes' time, Queequeg's harpoon was flung; the stricken fish darted blinding spray in our faces, and then running away with us like light, steered straight for the heart of the herd. Though such a movement on the part of the whale struck under such circumstances, is in no wise unprecedented; and indeed is almost always more or less anticipated; yet does it present one of the more perilous vicissitudes of the fishery. For as the swift monster drags you deeper and deeper into the frantic shoal, you bid adieu to circumspect life and only exist in a delirious throb.

As, blind and deaf, the whale plunged forward, as if by sheer power of speed to rid himself of the iron leech that had fastened to him; as we thus tore a white gash in the sea, on all sides menaced as we flew, by the crazed creatures to and fro rushing about us; our beset boat was like a ship mobbed by ice-isles in a tempest, and striving to steer through their complicated channels and straits, knowing not at what moment it may be locked in and crushed.

But not a bit daunted, Queequeg steered us manfully; now sheering off from this monster directly across our route in advance; now edging away from that, whose colossal flukes were suspended overhead, while all the time, Starbuck stood up in the bows, lance in hand, pricking out of our way whatever whales he could reach by short darts, for there was no time to make long ones. Nor were the oarsmen quite idle, though their wonted duty was now altogether dispensed with. They chiefly attended to the shouting part of the business. "Out of the way, Commodore!" cried one, to a great dromedary that of a sudden rose bodily to the surface, and for an instant threatened to swamp us. "Hard down with your tail, there!" cried a second to another, which, close to our gunwale, seemed calmly cooling himself with his own fan-like extremity.

All whaleboats carry certain curious contrivances, originally invented by the Nantucket Indians, called druggs. Two thick squares of wood of equal size are stoutly clenched together, so that they cross each other's grain at right angles; a line of considerable length is then attached to the middle of this block, and the other end of the line being looped, it can in a moment be fastened to a harpoon. It is chiefly among gallied whales that this drugg is used. For then, more whales are close round you than you can possibly chase at one time. But Sperm Whales are not every day encountered; while you may, then, you must kill all you can. And if you cannot kill them all at once, you must wing them, so that they can be afterwards killed at your leisure. Hence it is, that at times like these the drugg comes into requisition. Our boat was furnished with three of them. The first and second were successfully darted, and we saw the whales staggeringly running off, fettered by the enormous sidelong resistance of the towing drugg. They were cramped like malefactors with the chain and ball. But upon flinging the third, in the act of tossing overboard the clumsy wooden block, it caught under one of the seats of the boat, and in an instant tore it out and carried it away, dropping the oarsman in the boat's bottom as the seat slid from under him. On both sides the sea came in at the wounded planks, but we stuffed two or three drawers and shirts in, and so stopped the leaks for the time.

It had been next to impossible to dart these drugged-harpoons, were it not that as we advanced into the herd, our whale's way greatly diminished; moreover, that as we went still further and further from the circumference of commotion, the direful disorders seemed waning. So that when at last the jerking harpoon drew out, and the towing whale sideways vanished; then, with the tapering force of his parting momentum, we glided between two whales into the innermost heart of the shoal, as if from some mountain torrent we had slid into a serene valley lake. Here the storms in the roaring glens between the outermost whales, were heard but not felt. In this central expanse the sea presented that smooth satin-like surface, called a sleek, produced by the subtle moisture thrown off by the whale in his more quiet moods. Yes, we were now in that enchanted calm which they say lurks at the heart of every commotion. And still in the distracted distance we beheld the tumults of the outer concentric circles, and saw successive pods of whales, eight or ten in each, swiftly going round and round, like multiplied spans of horses in a ring; and so closely shoulder to shoulder, that a Titanic circus-rider might easily have over-arched the middle ones, and so have gone round on their backs. Owing to the density of the crowd of reposing whales, more immediately surrounding the embayed axis of the herd, no possible chance of escape was at present afforded us. We must watch for a breach in the living wall that hemmed us in; the wall that had only admitted us in order to shut us up. Keeping at the centre of the lake, we were occasionally visited by small tame cows and calves; the women and children of this routed host.

Now, inclusive of the occasional wide intervals between the revolving outer circles, and inclusive of the spaces between the various pods in any one of those circles, the entire area at this juncture, embraced by the whole multitude, must have contained at least two or three square miles. At any rate—though indeed such a test at such a time might be deceptive—spoutings might be discovered from our low boat that seemed playing up almost from the rim of the horizon. I mention this circumstance, because, as if the cows and calves had been purposely locked up in this innermost fold; and as if the wide extent of the herd had hitherto prevented them from learning the precise cause of its stopping; or, possibly, being so young, unsophisticated, and every way innocent and inexperienced; however it may have been, these smaller whales—now and then visiting our becalmed boat from the margin of the lake—evinced a wondrous fearlessness and confidence, or else a still becharmed panic which it was impossible not to marvel at. Like household dogs they came snuffling round us, right up to our gunwales, and touching them; till it almost seemed that some spell had suddenly domesticated them. Queequeg patted their foreheads; Starbuck scratched their backs with his lance; but fearful of the consequences, for the time refrained from darting it.

But far beneath this wondrous world upon the surface, another and still stranger world met our eyes as we gazed over the side. For, suspended in those watery vaults, floated the forms of the nursing mothers of the whales, and those that by their enormous girth seemed shortly to become mothers. The lake, as I have hinted, was to a considerable depth exceedingly transparent; and as human infants while suckling will calmly and fixedly gaze away from the breast, as if leading two different lives at the time; and while yet drawing mortal nourishment, be still spiritually feasting upon some unearthly reminiscence;—even so did the young of these whales seem looking up towards us, but not at us, as if we were but a bit of Gulf-weed in their new-born sight. Floating on their sides, the mothers also seemed quietly eyeing us. One of these little infants, that from certain queer tokens seemed hardly a day old, might have measured some fourteen feet in length, and some six feet in girth. He was a little frisky; though as yet his body seemed scarce yet recovered from that irksome position it had so lately occupied in the maternal reticule; where, tail to head, and all ready for the final spring, the unborn whale lies bent like a Tartar's bow. The delicate side-fins, and the palms of his flukes, still freshly retained the plaited crumpled appearance of a baby's ears newly arrived from foreign parts.

"Line! line!" cried Queequeg, looking over the gunwale; "him fast! him fast!—Who line him! Who struck?—Two whale; one big, one little!"

"What ails ye, man?" cried Starbuck.

"Look-e here," said Queequeg pointing down.

As when the stricken whale, that from the tub has reeled out hundreds of fathoms of rope; as, after deep sounding, he floats up again, and shows the slackened curling line buoyantly rising and spiralling towards the air; so now, Starbuck saw long coils of the umbilical cord of Madame Leviathan, by which the young cub seemed still tethered to its dam. Not seldom in the rapid vicissitudes of the chase, this natural line, with the maternal end loose, becomes entangled with the hempen one, so that the cub is thereby trapped. Some of the subtlest secrets of the seas seemed divulged to us in this enchanted pond. We saw young Leviathan amours in the deep.[4]

And thus, though surrounded by circle upon circle of consternations and affrights, did these inscrutable creatures at the centre freely and fearlessly indulge in all peaceful concernments; yea, serenely revelled in dalliance and delight. But even so, amid the tornadoed Atlantic of my being, do I myself still for ever centrally disport in mute calm; and while ponderous planets of unwaning woe revolve round me, deep down and deep inland there I still bathe me in eternal mildness of joy.

Meanwhile, as we thus lay entranced, the occasional sudden frantic spectacles in the distance evinced the activity of the other boats, still engaged in drugging the whales on the frontier of the host; or possibly carrying on the war within the first circle, where abundance of room and some convenient retreats were afforded them. But the sight of the enraged drugged whales now and then blindly darting to and fro across the circles, was nothing to what at last met our eyes. It is sometimes the custom when fast to a whale more than commonly powerful and alert, to seek to hamstring him, as it were, by sundering or maiming his gigantic tail-tendon. It is done by darting a short-handled cutting-spade, to which is attached a rope for hauling it back again. A whale wounded (as we

---

4. Melville's note: The Sperm Whale, as with all other species of the Leviathan, but unlike most other fish, breeds indifferently at all seasons; after a gestation which may probably be set down at nine months, producing but one at a time; though in some few known instances giving birth to an Esau and Jacob:—a contingency provided for in suckling by two teats, curiously situated, one on each side of the anus; but the breasts themselves extend upwards from that. When by chance these precious parts in a nursing whale are cut by the hunter's lance, the mother's pouring milk and blood rivallingly discolor the sea for rods. The milk is very sweet and rich; it has been tasted by man; it might do well with strawberries. When overflowing with mutual esteem, the whales salute *more hominum*.

afterwards learned) in this part, but not effectually, as it seemed, had broken away from the boat, carrying along with him half of the harpoon line; and in the extraordinary agony of the wound, he was now dashing among the revolving circles like the lone mounted desperado Arnold, at the battle of Saratoga, carrying dismay wherever he went.

But agonizing as was the wound of this whale, and an appalling spectacle enough, any way; yet the peculiar horror with which he seemed to inspire the rest of the herd, was owing to a cause which at first the intervening distance obscured from us. But at length we perceived that by one of the unimaginable accidents of the fishery, this whale had become entangled in the harpoon-line that he towed; he had also run away with the cutting-spade in him; and while the free end of the rope attached to that weapon, had permanently caught in the coils of the harpoon-line round his tail, the cutting-spade itself had worked loose from his flesh. So that tormented to madness, he was now churning through the water, violently flailing with his flexible tail, and tossing the keen spade about him, wounding and murdering his own comrades.

This terrific object seemed to recall the whole herd from their stationary fright. First, the whales forming the margin of our lake began to crowd a little, and tumble against each other, as if lifted by half spent billows from afar; then the lake itself began faintly to heave and swell; the submarine bridal-chambers and nurseries vanished; in more and more contracting orbits the whales in the more central circles began to swim in thickening clusters. Yes, the long calm was departing. A low advancing hum was soon heard; and then like to the tumultuous masses of block-ice when the great river Hudson breaks up in Spring, the entire host of whales came tumbling upon their inner centre, as if to pile themselves up in one common mountain. Instantly Starbuck and Queequeg changed places; Starbuck taking the stern.

"Oars! Oars!" he intensely whispered, seizing the helm—"gripe your oars, and clutch your souls, now! My God, men, stand by! Shove him off, you Queequeg—the whale there!—prick him!—hit him! Stand up—stand up, and stay so! Spring, men—pull, men; never mind their backs—scrape them!—scrape away!"

The boat was now all but jammed between two vast black bulks, leaving a narrow Dardanelles between their long lengths. But by desperate endeavor we at last shot into a temporary opening; then giving way rapidly, and at the same time earnestly watching for another outlet. After many similar hair-breadth escapes, we at last swiftly glided into what had just been one of the outer circles, but now crossed by random whales, all violently making for one centre. This lucky salvation was cheaply purchased by the loss of Queequeg's hat, who, while standing in the bows to prick the fugitive whales, had his hat taken clean from his head by the air-eddy made by the sudden tossing of a pair of broad flukes close by.

Riotous and disordered as the universal commotion now was, it soon resolved itself into what seemed a systematic movement; for having clumped together at last in one dense body, they then renewed their onward flight with augmented fleetness. Further pursuit was useless; but the boats still lingered in their wake to pick up what drugged whales might be dropped astern, and likewise to secure one which Flask had killed and waifed. The waif is a pennoned pole, two or three of which are carried by every boat; and which, when additional game is at hand, are inserted upright into the floating body of a dead whale, both to mark its place on the sea, and also as token of prior possession, should the boats of any other ship draw near.

The result of this lowering was somewhat illustrative of that sagacious saying in the Fishery,—the more whales the less fish. Of all the drugged whales only one was captured. The rest contrived to escape for the time, but only to be taken, as will hereafter be seen, by some other craft than the *Pequod*.

Chapter 110: Queequeg in His Coffin

There are odder chapters but none so touching as this, wherein Ishmael's dear friend Queequeg, believing in his imminent death, is allowed to request a coffin of the ship's carpenter.

Upon searching, it was found that the casks last struck into the hold were perfectly sound, and that the leak must be further off. So, it being calm weather, they broke out deeper and deeper, disturbing the slumbers of the huge ground-tier butts; and from that black midnight sending those gigantic moles into the daylight above. So deep did they go; and so ancient, and corroded, and weedy the aspect of the lowermost puncheons, that you almost looked next for some mouldy corner-stone cask containing coins of Captain Noah, with copies of the posted placards, vainly warning the infatuated old world from the flood. Tierce after tierce, too, of water, and bread, and beef, and shooks of staves, and iron bundles of hoops, were hoisted out, till at last the piled decks were hard to get about; and the hollow hull echoed under foot, as if you were treading over empty catacombs, and reeled and rolled in the sea like an air-freighted demijohn. Top-heavy was the ship as a dinnerless student with all Aristotle in his head. Well was it that the Typhoons did not visit them then.

Now, at this time it was that my poor pagan companion, and fast bosom-friend, Queequeg, was seized with a fever, which brought him nigh to his endless end.

Be it said, that in this vocation of whaling, sinecures are unknown; dignity and danger go hand in hand; till you get to be Captain, the higher you rise the harder you toil. So with poor Queequeg, who, as harpooneer, must not only face all the rage of the living whale, but—as we have elsewhere seen—mount his dead back in a rolling sea; and finally descend into the gloom of the hold, and bitterly sweating all day in that subterraneous confinement, resolutely manhandle the clumsiest casks and see to their stowage. To be short, among whalemen, the harpooneers are the holders, so called.

Poor Queequeg! when the ship was about half disembowelled, you should have stooped over the hatchway, and peered down upon him there; where, stripped to his woollen drawers, the tattooed savage was crawling about amid that dampness and slime, like a green spotted lizard at the bottom of a well. And a well, or an ice-house, it somehow proved to him, poor pagan; where, strange to say, for all the heat of his sweatings, he caught a terrible chill which lapsed into a fever; and at last, after some days' suffering, laid him in his hammock, close to the very sill of the door of death. How he wasted and wasted away in those few long-lingering days, till there seemed but little left of him but his frame and tattooing. But as all else in him thinned, and his cheek-bones grew sharper, his eyes, nevertheless, seemed growing fuller and fuller; they became of a strange softness of lustre; and mildly but deeply looked out at you there from his sickness, a wondrous testimony to that immortal health in him which could not die, or be weakened. And like circles on the water, which, as they grow fainter, expand; so his eyes seemed rounding and rounding, like the rings of Eternity. An awe that cannot be named would steal over you as you sat by the side of this waning savage, and saw as strange things in his face, as any beheld who were bystanders when Zoroaster died. For whatever is truly wondrous and fearful in man, never yet was put into words or books. And the drawing near of Death, which alike levels all, alike impresses all with a last revelation, which only an author from the dead could adequately tell. So that—let us say it again—no dying Chaldee or Greek had higher and holier thoughts than those, whose mysterious shades you saw creeping over the face of poor Queequeg, as he quietly lay in his swaying hammock, and the rolling sea seemed gently rocking him to his final rest, and the ocean's invisible flood-tide lifted him higher and higher towards his destined heaven.

Not a man of the crew but gave him up; and, as for Queequeg himself, what he thought of his case was forcibly shown by a curious favor he asked. He called one to him in the grey morning watch, when the day was just breaking, and taking his hand, said that while in Nantucket he had chanced to see certain little canoes of dark wood, like the rich war-wood of his native isle; and upon inquiry, he had learned that all whalemen who died in Nantucket, were laid in those same dark canoes, and that the fancy of being so laid had much pleased him; for it was not unlike the custom of his own race, who, after embalming a dead warrior, stretched him out in his canoe, and so left him to be floated away to the starry archipelagoes; for not only do they believe that the stars are isles, but that far beyond all visible horizons, their own mild, uncontinented seas, interflow with the blue heavens; and so form the white breakers of the milky way. He added, that he shuddered at the thought of being buried in his hammock, according to the usual sea-custom, tossed like something vile to the death-devouring sharks. No: he desired a canoe like those of Nantucket, all the more congenial to him, being a whaleman, that like a whale-boat these coffin-canoes were without a keel; though that involved but uncertain steering, and much lee-way adown the dim ages.

Now, when this strange circumstance was made known aft, the carpenter was at once commanded to do Queequeg's bidding, whatever it might include. There was some heathenish, coffin-colored old lumber aboard, which, upon a long previous voyage, had been cut from the aboriginal groves of the Lackaday islands, and from these dark planks the coffin was recommended to be made. No sooner was the carpenter apprised of the order, than taking his rule, he forthwith with all the indifferent promptitude of his character, proceeded into the forecastle and took Queequeg's measure with great accuracy, regularly chalking Queequeg's person as he shifted the rule.

"Ah! poor fellow! he'll have to die now," ejaculated the Long Island sailor.

Going to his vice-bench, the carpenter for convenience' sake and general reference, now transferringly measured on it the exact length the coffin was to be, and then made the transfer permanent by cutting two notches at its extremities. This done, he marshalled the planks and his tools, and to work.

When the last nail was driven, and the lid duly planed and fitted, he lightly shouldered the coffin and went forward with it, inquiring whether they were ready for it yet in that direction.

Overhearing the indignant but half-humorous cries with which the people on deck began to drive the coffin away, Queequeg, to every one's consternation, commanded that the thing should be instantly brought to him, nor was there any denying him; seeing that, of all mortals, some dying men are the most tyrannical; and certainly, since they will shortly trouble us so little for evermore, the poor fellows ought to be indulged.

Leaning over in his hammock, Queequeg long regarded the coffin with an attentive eye. He then called for his harpoon, had the wooden stock drawn from it, and then had the iron part placed in the coffin along with one of the paddles of his boat. All by his own request, also, biscuits were then ranged round the sides within: a flask of fresh water was placed at the head, and a small bag of woody earth scraped up in the hold at the foot; and a piece of sail-cloth being rolled up for a pillow, Queequeg now entreated to be lifted into his final bed, that he might make trial of its comforts, if any it had. He lay without moving a few minutes, then told one to go to his bag and bring out his little god, Yojo. Then crossing his arms on his breast with Yojo between, he called for the coffin lid (hatch he called it) to be placed over him. The head part turned over with a leather hinge, and there lay Queequeg in his coffin with little but his composed countenance in view. "Rarmai" (it will do; it is easy), he murmured at last, and signed to be replaced in his hammock.

But ere this was done, Pip, who had been slily hovering near by all this while, drew nigh to him where he lay, and with soft sobbings, took him by the hand; in the other, holding his tambourine.

"Poor rover! will ye never have done with all this weary roving? Where go ye now? But if the currents carry ye to those sweet

Antilles where the beaches are only beat with water-lilies, will ye do one little errand for me? Seek out one Pip, who's now been missing long: I think he's in those far Antilles. If ye find him, then comfort him; for he must be very sad; for look! he's left his tambourine behind;—I found it. Rig-a-dig, dig, dig! Now, Queequeg, die; and I'll beat ye your dying march."

"I have heard," murmured Starbuck, gazing down the scuttle, "that in violent fevers, men, all ignorance, have talked in ancient tongues; and that when the mystery is probed, it turns out always that in their wholly forgotten childhood those ancient tongues had been really spoken in their hearing by some lofty scholars. So, to my fond faith, poor Pip, in this strange sweetness of his lunacy, brings heavenly vouchers of all our heavenly homes. Where learned he that, but there?—Hark! he speaks again: but more wildly now."

"From two and two! Let's make a General of him! Ho, where's his harpoon? Lay it across here.—Rig-a-dig, dig, dig! huzza! Oh for a game cock now to sit upon his head and crow! Queequeg dies game!—mind ye that; Queequeg dies game!—take ye good heed of that; Queequeg dies game! I say; game, game, game! but base little Pip, he died a coward; died all a'shiver;—out upon Pip! Hark ye; if ye find Pip, tell all the Antilles he's a runaway; a coward, a coward, a coward! Tell them he jumped from a whale-boat! I'd never beat my tambourine over base Pip, and hail him General, if he were once more dying here. No, no! shame upon all cowards—shame upon them! Let 'em go drown like Pip, that jumped from a whale-boat. Shame! shame!"

During all this, Queequeg lay with closed eyes, as if in a dream. Pip was led away, and the sick man was replaced in his hammock.

But now that he had apparently made every preparation for death; now that his coffin was proved a good fit, Queequeg suddenly rallied; soon there seemed no need of the carpenter's box: and thereupon, when some expressed their delighted surprise, he, in substance, said, that the cause of his sudden convalescence was this;—at a critical moment, he had just recalled a little duty ashore, which he was leaving undone; and therefore had changed his mind about dying: he could not die yet, he averred. They asked him, then, whether to live or die was a matter of his own sovereign will and pleasure. He answered, certainly. In a word, it was Queequeg's conceit, that if a man made up his mind to live, mere sickness could not kill him: nothing but a whale, or a gale, or some violent, ungovernable, unintelligent destroyer of that sort.

Now, there is this noteworthy difference between savage and civilized; that while a sick, civilized man may be six months convalescing, generally speaking, a sick savage is almost half-well again in a day. So, in good time my Queequeg gained strength; and at length after sitting on the windlass for a few indolent days (but eating with a vigorous appetite) he suddenly leaped to his feet, threw out arms and legs, gave himself a good stretching, yawned a little bit, and then springing into the head of his hoisted boat, and poising a harpoon, pronounced himself fit for a fight.

With a wild whimsiness, he now used his coffin for a sea-chest; and emptying into it his canvas bag of clothes, set them in order there. Many spare hours he spent, in carving the lid with all manner of grotesque figures and drawings; and it seemed that hereby he was striving, in his rude way, to copy parts of the twisted tattooing on his body. And this tattooing, had been the work of a departed prophet and seer of his island, who, by those hieroglyphic marks, had written out on his body a complete theory of the heavens and the earth, and a mystical treatise on the art of attaining truth; so that Queequeg in his own proper person was a riddle to unfold; a wondrous work in one volume; but whose mysteries not even himself could read, though his own live heart beat against them; and these mysteries were therefore destined in the end to moulder away with the living parchment whereon they were inscribed, and so be unsolved to the last. And this thought it must have been which suggested to Ahab that wild exclamation of his, when one morning turning away from surveying poor Queequeg—"Oh, devilish tantalization of the gods!"

Chapter 128: The *Pequod* Meets the *Rachel*

While the intervening chapters have been full of remarkable details about whaling ships and tools, the characterization of Ahab has continued through soliloquies that Melville infused with Shakespearean rhetoric. Finally, more poignantly than in any chapter preceding it, Melville contrasts Ahab's madness with the grief of the captain of a sister whaling ship.

Next day, a large ship, the *Rachel*, was descried, bearing directly down upon the *Pequod*, all her spars thickly clustering with men. At the time the *Pequod* was making good speed through the water; but as the broad-winged windward stranger shot nigh to her, the boastful sails all fell together as blank bladders that are burst, and all life fled from the smitten hull.

"Bad news; she brings bad news," muttered the old Manxman. But ere her commander, who, with trumpet to mouth, stood up in his boat; ere he could hopefully hail, Ahab's voice was heard.

"Hast seen the White Whale?"

"Aye, yesterday. Have ye seen a whale-boat adrift?"

Throttling his joy, Ahab negatively answered this unexpected question; and would then have fain boarded the stranger, when the stranger Captain himself, having stopped his vessel's way, was seen descending her side. A few keen pulls, and his boat-hook soon clinched the *Pequod*'s main-chains, and he sprang to the deck. Immediately he was recognised by Ahab for a Nantucketer he knew. But no formal salutation was exchanged.

"Where was he?—not killed!—not killed!" cried Ahab, closely advancing. "How was it?"

It seemed that somewhat late on the afternoon of the day previous, while three of the stranger's boats were engaged with a shoal of whales, which had led them some four or five miles from the ship; and while they were yet in swift chase to windward, the white hump and head of Moby-Dick had suddenly loomed up out of the water, not very far to leeward; whereupon, the fourth rigged boat—a reserved one—had been instantly lowered in chase. After a keen sail before the wind, this fourth boat—the swiftest keeled of all—seemed to have succeeded in fastening—at least, as well as the man at the mast-head could tell anything about it. In the distance he saw the diminished dotted boat; and then a swift gleam of bubbling white water; and after that nothing more; whence it was concluded that the stricken whale must have indefinitely run away with his pursuers, as often happens. There was some apprehension, but no positive alarm, as yet. The recall signals were placed in the rigging; darkness came on; and forced to pick up her three far to windward boats—ere going in quest of the fourth one in the precisely opposite direction—the ship had not only been necessitated to leave that boat to its fate till near midnight, but, for the time, to increase her distance from it. But the rest of her crew being at last safe aboard, she crowded all sail—stunsail on stunsail—after the missing boat; kindling a fire in her try-pots for a beacon; and every other man aloft on the look-out. But though when she had thus sailed a sufficient distance to gain the presumed place of the absent ones when last seen; though she then paused to lower her spare boats to pull all around her; and not finding anything, had again dashed on; again paused, and lowered her boats; and though she had thus continued doing till daylight; yet not the least glimpse of the missing keel had been seen.

The story told, the stranger Captain immediately went on to reveal his object in boarding the *Pequod*. He desired that ship to unite with his own in the search; by sailing over the sea some four or five miles apart, on parallel lines, and so sweeping a double horizon, as it were.

"I will wager something now," whispered Stubb to Flask, "that some one in that missing boat wore off that Captain's best coat; mayhap, his watch—he's so cursed anxious to get it back. Who ever heard of two pious whale-ships cruising after one missing whale-boat in the height of the whaling season? See, Flask, only see how pale he looks—pale in the very buttons of his eyes—look—it wasn't the coat—it must have been the—"

"My boy, my own boy is among them. For God's sake—I beg, I conjure"—here exclaimed the stranger Captain to Ahab, who thus far had but icily received his petition. "For eight-and-forty hours let me charter your ship—I will gladly pay for it, and roundly pay for it—if there be no other way—for eight-and-forty hours only—only that—you must, oh, you must, and you *shall* do this thing."

"His son!" cried Stubb, "oh, it's his son he's lost! I take back the coat and watch—what says Ahab? We must save that boy."

"He's drowned with the rest on 'em, last night," said the old Manx sailor standing behind them; "I heard; all of ye heard their spirits."

Now, as it shortly turned out, what made this incident of the *Rachel*'s the more melancholy, was the circumstance, that not only was one of the Captain's sons among the number of the missing boat's crew; but among the number of the other boat's crews, at the same time, but on the other hand, separated from the ship during the dark vicissitudes of the chase, there had been still another son; as that for a time, the wretched father was plunged to the bottom of the cruellest perplexity; which was only solved for him by his chief mate's instinctively adopting the ordinary procedure of a whale-ship in such emergencies, that is, when placed between jeopardized but divided boats, always to pick up the majority first. But the captain, for some unknown constitutional reason, had refrained from mentioning all this, and not till forced to it by Ahab's iciness did he allude to his one yet missing boy; a little lad, but twelve years old, whose father with the earnest but unmisgiving hardihood of a Nantucketer's paternal love, had thus early sought to initiate him in the perils and wonders of a vocation almost immemorially the destiny of all his race. Nor does it unfrequently occur, that Nantucket captains will send a son of such tender age away from them, for a protracted three or four years' voyage in some other ship than their own; so that their first knowledge of a whaleman's career shall be unenervated by any chance display of a father's natural but untimely partiality, or undue apprehensiveness and concern.

Meantime, now the stranger was still beseeching his poor boon of Ahab; and Ahab still stood like an anvil, receiving every shock, but without the least quivering of his own.

"I will not go," said the stranger, "till you say *aye* to me. Do to me as you would have me do to you in the like case. For *you* too have a boy, Captain Ahab—though but a child, and nestling safely at home now—a child of your old age too—Yes, yes, you relent; I see it—run, run, men, now, and stand by to square in the yards."

"Avast," cried Ahab—"touch not a rope-yarn"; then in a voice that prolongingly moulded every word—"Captain Gardiner, I will not do it. Even now I lose time. Good-bye, good-bye. God bless ye, man, and may I forgive myself, but I must go. Mr. Starbuck, look at the binnacle watch, and in three minutes from this present instant warn off all strangers: then brace forward again, and let the ship sail as before."

Hurriedly turning, with averted face, he descended into his cabin, leaving the strange captain transfixed at this unconditional and utter rejection of his so earnest suit. But starting from his enchantment, Gardiner silently hurried to the side; more fell than stepped into his boat, and returned to his ship.

Soon the two ships diverged their wakes; and long as the strange vessel was in view, she was seen to yaw hither and thither at every dark spot, however small, on the sea. This way and that her yards were swung round; starboard and larboard, she continued to tack; now she beat against a head sea; and again it pushed her before it; while all the while, her masts and yards were thickly clustered with men, as three tall cherry trees, when the boys are cherrying among the boughs. But by her still halting course and winding, woeful way, you plainly saw that this ship that so wept with spray, still remained without comfort. She was Rachel, weeping for her children, because they were not.

Chapter 133: The Chase—First Day

The most famous scenes, comprising the novel's last three chapters, finally bring Ahab and Moby-Dick together.

That night, in the mid-watch, when the old man—as his wont at intervals—stepped forth from the scuttle in which he leaned, and went to his pivot-hole, he suddenly thrust out his face fiercely, snuffing up the sea air as a sagacious ship's dog will, in drawing nigh to some barbarous isle. He declared that a whale must be near. Soon that peculiar odor, sometimes to a great distance given forth by the living sperm whale, was palpable to all the watch; nor was any mariner surprised when, after inspecting the compass, and then the dog-vane, and then ascertaining the precise bearing of the odor as nearly as possible, Ahab rapidly ordered the ship's course to be slightly altered, and the sail to be shortened.

The acute policy dictating these movements was sufficiently vindicated at daybreak, by the sight of a long sleek on the sea directly and lengthwise ahead, smooth as oil, and resembling in the pleated watery wrinkles bordering it, the polished metallic-like marks of some swift tide-rip, at the mouth of a deep, rapid stream.

"Man the mast-heads! Call all hands!"

Thundering with the butts of three clubbed handspikes on the forecastle deck, Daggoo roused the sleepers with such judgment claps that they seemed to exhale from the scuttle, so instantaneously did they appear with their clothes in their hands.

"What d'ye see?" cried Ahab, flattening his face to the sky.

"Nothing, nothing, sir!" was the sound hailing down in reply.

"T'gallant sails!—stunsails! alow and aloft, and on both sides!"

All sail being set, he now cast loose the life-line, reserved for swaying him to the main royal-mast head; and in a few moments they were hoisting him thither, when, while but two thirds of the way aloft, and while peering ahead through the horizontal vacancy between the main-top-sail and top-gallant-sail, he raised a gull-like cry in the air, "There she blows!—there she blows! A hump like a snow-hill! It is Moby-Dick!"

Fired by the cry which seemed simultaneously taken up by the three look-outs, the men on deck rushed to the rigging to behold the famous whale they had so long been pursuing. Ahab had now gained his final perch, some feet above the other look-outs, Tashtego standing just beneath him on the cap of the top-gallant mast, so that the Indian's head was almost on a level with Ahab's heel. From this height the whale was now seen some mile or so ahead, at every roll of the sea revealing his high sparkling hump, and regularly jetting his silent spout into the air. To the credulous mariners it seemed the same silent spout they had so long ago beheld in the moonlit Atlantic and Indian Oceans.

"And did none of ye see it before?" cried Ahab, hailing the perched men all around him.

"I saw him almost that same instant, sir, that Captain Ahab did, and I cried out," said Tashtego.

"Not the same instant; not the same—no, the doubloon is mine, Fate reserved the doubloon for me. *I* only; none of ye could have raised the White Whale first. There she blows! there she blows!—there she blows! There again!—there again!" he cried, in long-drawn, lingering, methodic tones, attuned to the gradual prolongings of the whale's visible jets. "He's going to sound! In stunsails! Down top-gallant-sails! Stand by three boats. Mr. Starbuck, remember, stay on board, and keep the ship. Helm there! Luff, luff a point! So; steady, man, steady! There go flukes! No, no; only black water! All ready the boats there? Stand by, stand by! Lower me, Mr. Starbuck; lower, lower,—quick, quicker!" and he slid through the air to the deck.

"He is heading straight to leeward, sir," cried Stubb, "right away from us; cannot have seen the ship yet."

"Be dumb, man! Stand by the braces! Hard down the helm!—brace up! Shiver her!—shiver her! So; well that! Boats, boats!"

Soon all the boats but Starbuck's were dropped; all the boat-sails set—all the paddles plying; with rippling swiftness, shooting to leeward; and Ahab heading the onset. A pale, death-glimmer lit up Fedallah's sunken eyes; a hideous motion gnawed his mouth.

Like noiseless nautilus shells, their light prows sped through the sea; but only slowly they neared the foe. As they neared him, the ocean grew still more smooth; seemed drawing a carpet over its waves; seemed a noon-meadow, so serenely it spread. At length the breathless hunter came so nigh his seemingly unsuspecting prey, that his entire dazzling hump was distinctly visible, sliding along the sea as if an isolated thing, and continually set in a revolving ring of finest, fleecy, greenish foam. He saw the vast, involved wrinkles of the slightly projecting head beyond. Before it, far out on the soft Turkish-rugged waters, went the glistening white shadow from his broad, milky forehead, a musical rippling playfully accompanying the shade; and behind, the blue waters interchangeably flowed over into the moving valley of his steady wake; and on either hand bright bubbles arose and danced by his side. But these were broken again by the light toes of hundreds of gay fowl softly feathering the sea, alternate with their fitful flight; and like to some flag-staff rising from the painted hull of an argosy, the tall but shattered pole of a recent lance projected from the white whale's back; and at intervals one of the cloud of soft-toed fowls hovering, and to and fro skimming like a canopy over the fish, silently perched and rocked on this pole, the long tail feathers streaming like pennons.

A gentle joyousness—a mighty mildness of repose in swiftness, invested the gliding whale. Not the white bull Jupiter swimming away with ravished Europa clinging to his graceful horns; his lovely, leering eyes sideways intent upon the maid; with smooth bewitching fleetness, rippling straight for the nuptial bower in Crete; not Jove, not that great majesty Supreme! did surpass the glorified White Whale as he so divinely swam.

On each soft side—coincident with the parted swell, that but once leaving him, then flowed so wide away—on each bright side, the whale shed off enticings. No wonder there had been some among the hunters who namelessly transported and allured by all this serenity, had ventured to assail it; but had fatally found that quietude but the vesture of tornadoes. Yet calm, enticing calm, oh, whale! thou glidest on, to all who for the first time eye thee, no matter how many in that same way thou may'st have bejuggled and destroyed before.

And thus, through the serene tranquillities of the tropical sea, among waves whose hand-clappings were suspended by exceeding rapture, Moby-Dick moved on, still withholding from sight the full terrors of his submerged trunk, entirely hiding the wrenched hideousness of his jaw. But soon the fore part of him slowly rose from the water; for an instant his whole marbleized body formed a high arch, like Virginia's Natural Bridge, and warningly waving his bannered flukes in the air, the grand god revealed himself, sounded, and went out of sight. Hoveringly halting, and dipping on the wing, the white sea-fowls longingly lingered over the agitated pool that he left.

With oars apeak, and paddles down, the sheets of their sails adrift, the three boats now stilly floated, awaiting Moby-Dick's reappearance.

"An hour," said Ahab, standing rooted in his boat's stern; and he gazed beyond the whale's place, towards the dim blue spaces and wide wooing vacancies to leeward. It was only an instant; for again his eyes seemed whirling round in his head as he swept the watery circle. The breeze now freshened; the sea began to swell.

"The birds!—the birds!" cried Tashtego.

In long Indian file, as when herons take wing, the white birds were now all flying towards Ahab's boat; and when within a few yards began fluttering over the water there, wheeling round and round, with joyous, expectant cries. Their vision was keener than man's; Ahab could discover no sign in the sea. But suddenly as he peered down and down into its depths, he profoundly saw a white living spot no bigger than a white weasel, with wonderful celerity uprising, and magnifying as it rose, till it turned, and then there were plainly revealed two long crooked rows of white, glistening teeth, floating up from the undiscoverable bottom. It was Moby-Dick's open mouth and scrolled jaw; his vast, shadowed bulk still half blending with the blue of the sea. The glittering mouth yawned beneath the boat like an open-doored marble tomb; and giving one side-long sweep with his steering oar, Ahab whirled the craft aside from this tremendous apparition. Then, calling upon Fedallah to change places with him, went forward to the bows, and seizing Perth's harpoon, commanded his crew to grasp their oars and stand by to stern.

Now, by reason of this timely spinning round the boat upon its axis, its bow, by anticipation, was made to face the whale's head while yet under water. But as if perceiving this strategem, Moby-Dick, with that malicious intelligence ascribed to him, sidelingly transplanted himself, as it were, in an instant, shooting his pleated head lengthwise beneath the boat.

Through and through; through every plank and each rib, it thrilled for an instant, the whale obliquely lying on his back, in the manner of a biting shark, slowly and feelingly taking its bows full within his mouth, so that the long, narrow, scrolled lower jaw curled high up into the open air, and one of the teeth caught in a row-lock. The bluish pearl-white of the inside of the jaw was within six inches of Ahab's head, and reached higher than that. In this attitude the White Whale now shook the slight cedar as a mildly cruel cat her mouse. With unastonished eyes Fedallah gazed, and crossed his arms; but the tiger-yellow crew were tumbling over each other's heads to gain the uttermost stern.

And now, while both elastic gunwales were springing in and out, as the whale dallied with the doomed craft in this devilish way; and from his body being submerged beneath the boat, he could not be darted at from the bows, for the bows were almost inside of him, as it were; and while the other boats involuntarily paused, as before a quick crisis impossible to withstand, then it was that monomaniac Ahab, furious with this tantalizing vicinity of his foe, which placed him all alive and helpless in the very jaws he hated; frenzied with all this, he seized the long bone with his naked hands, and wildly strove to wrench it from its gripe. As now he thus vainly strove, the jaw slipped from him; the frail gunwales bent in, collapsed, and snapped, as both jaws, like an enormous shears, sliding further aft, bit the craft completely in twain, and locked themselves fast again in the sea, midway between the two floating wrecks. These floated aside, the broken ends drooping, the crew at the stern-wreck clinging to the gunwales, and striving to hold fast to the oars to lash them across.

At that preluding moment, ere the boat was yet snapped, Ahab, the first to perceive the whale's intent, by the crafty upraising of his head, a movement that loosed his hold for the time; at that moment his hand had made one final effort to push the boat out of the bite. But only slipping further into the whale's mouth, and tilting over sideways as it slipped, the boat had shaken off his hold on the jaw; spilled him out of it, as he leaned to the push; and so he fell flat-faced upon the sea.

Ripplingly withdrawing from his prey, Moby-Dick now lay at a little distance, vertically thrusting his oblong white head up and down in the billows; and at the same time slowly revolving his whole spindled body; so that when his vast wrinkled forehead rose—some twenty or more feet out of the water—the now rising swells, with all their confluent waves, dazzlingly broke against it; vindictively tossing their shivered spray still higher into the air.[5] So, in a gale, the but half-baffled Channel billows only recoil from the base of the Eddystone, triumphantly to overleap its summit with their scud.

---

5. Melville's note: This motion is peculiar to the sperm whale. It receives its designation (pitchpoling) from its being likened to that preliminary up-and-down poise of the whale-lance, in the exercise called pitchpoling. By this motion the whale must best and most comprehensively view whatever objects may be encircling him.

But soon resuming his horizontal attitude, Moby-Dick swam swiftly round and round the wrecked crew; sideways churning the water in his vengeful wake, as if lashing himself up to still another and more deadly assault. The sight of the splintered boat seemed to madden him, as the blood of grapes and mulberries cast before Antiochus's elephants in the book of Maccabees. Meanwhile Ahab half smothered in the foam of the whale's insolent tail, and too much of a cripple to swim,—though he could still keep afloat, even in the heart of such a whirlpool as that; helpless Ahab's head was seen, like a tossed bubble which the least chance shock might burst. From the boat's fragmentary stern, Fedallah incuriously and mildly eyed him; the clinging crew, at the other drifting end, could not succor him; more than enough was it for them to look to themselves. For so revolvingly appalling was the White Whale's aspect, and so planetarily swift the ever-contracting circles he made, that he seemed horizontally swooping upon them. And though the other boats, unharmed, still hovered hard by; still they dared not pull into the eddy to strike, lest that should be the signal for the instant destruction of the jeopardized castaways, Ahab and all; nor in that case could they themselves hope to escape. With straining eyes, then, they remained on the outer edge of the direful zone, whose centre had now become the old man's head.

Meantime, from the beginning all this had been descried from the ship's mast heads; and squaring her yards, she had borne down upon the scene; and was now so nigh, that Ahab in the water hailed her;—"Sail on the"—but that moment a breaking sea dashed on him from Moby-Dick, and whelmed him for the time. But struggling out of it again, and chancing to rise on a towering crest, he shouted,—"Sail on the whale!—Drive him off!"

The *Pequod*'s prows were pointed; and breaking up the charmed circle, she effectually parted the white whale from his victim. As he sullenly swam off, the boats flew to the rescue.

Dragged into Stubb's boat with blood-shot, blinded eyes, the white brine caking in his wrinkles; the long tension of Ahab's bodily strength did crack, and helplessly he yielded to his body's doom: for a time, lying all crushed in the bottom of Stubb's boat, like one trodden under foot of herds of elephants. Far inland, nameless wails came from him, as desolate sounds from out ravines.

But this intensity of his physical prostration did but so much the more abbreviate it. In an instant's compass, great hearts sometimes condense to one deep pang, the sum total of those shallow pains kindly diffused through feebler men's whole lives. And so, such hearts, though summary in each one suffering; still, if the gods decree it, in their life-time aggregate a whole age of woe, wholly made up of instantaneous intensities; for even in their pointless centres, those noble natures contain the entire circumferences of inferior souls.

"The harpoon," said Ahab, half way rising, and draggingly leaning on one bended arm—"is it safe?"

"Aye, sir, for it was not darted; this is it," said Stubb, showing it.

"Lay it before me;—any missing men?"

"One, two, three, four, five;—there were five oars, sir, and here are five men."

"That's good.—Help me, man; I wish to stand. So, so, I see him! there! there! going to leeward still; what a leaping spout!—Hands off from me! The eternal sap runs up in Ahab's bones again! Set the sail; out oars; the helm!"

It is often the case that when a boat is stove, its crew, being picked up by another boat, help to work that second boat; and the chase is thus continued with what is called double-banked oars. It was thus now. But the added power of the boat did not equal the added power of the whale, for he seemed to have treble-banked his every fin; swimming with a velocity which plainly showed, that if now, under these circumstances, pushed on, the chase would prove an indefinitely prolonged, if not a hopeless one; nor could any crew endure for so long a period, such an unintermitted, intense straining at the oar; a thing barely tolerable only in some one brief vicissitude. The ship itself, then, as it sometimes happens, offered the most promising intermediate means of overtaking the chase. Accordingly, the boats now made for her, and were soon swayed up to their cranes—the two parts of the wrecked boat having been previously secured by her—and then hoisting everything to her side, and stacking her canvas high up, and sideways outstretching it with stun-sails, like the double-jointed wings of an albatross; the *Pequod* bore down in the leeward wake of Moby-Dick. At the well known, methodic intervals, the whale's glittering spout was regularly announced from the manned mast-heads; and when he would be reported as just gone down, Ahab would take the time, and then pacing the deck, binnacle-watch in hand, so soon as the last second of the allotted hour expired, his voice was heard.—"Whose is the doubloon now? D'ye see him?" and if the reply was, No, sir! straightway he commanded them to lift him to his perch. In this way the day wore on; Ahab, now aloft and motionless; anon, unrestingly pacing the planks.

As he was thus walking, uttering no sound, except to hail the men aloft, or to bid them hoist a sail still higher, or to spread one to a still greater breadth—thus to and fro pacing, beneath his slouched hat, at every turn he passed his own wrecked boat, which had been dropped upon the quarter-deck, and lay there reversed; broken bow to shattered stern. At last he paused before it; and as in an already over-clouded sky fresh troops of clouds will sometimes sail across, so over the old man's face there now stole some such added gloom as this.

Stubb saw him pause; and perhaps intending, not vainly, though, to evince his own unabated fortitude, and thus keep up a valiant place in his Captain's mind, he advanced, and eyeing the wreck exclaimed—"The thistle the ass refused; it pricked his mouth too keenly, sir; ha! ha!"

"What soulless thing is this that laughs before a wreck? Man, man! did I not know thee brave as fearless fire (and as mechanical) I could swear thou wert a poltroon. Groan nor laugh should be heard before a wreck."

"Aye, sir," said Starbuck drawing near, "'tis a solemn sight; an omen, and an ill one."

"Omen? omen?—the dictionary! If the gods think to speak outright to man, they will honorably speak outright; not shake their heads, and give an old wives' darkling hint.—Begone! Ye two are the opposite poles of one thing; Starbuck is Stubb reversed, and Stubb is Starbuck; and ye two are all mankind; and Ahab stands alone among the millions of the peopled earth, nor gods nor men his neighbors! Cold, cold—I shiver!—How now? Aloft there! D'ye see him? Sing out for every spout, though he spout ten times a second!"

The day was nearly done; only the hem of his golden robe was rustling. Soon, it was almost dark, but the look-out men still remained unset.

"Can't see the spout now, sir;—too dark"—cried a voice from the air.

"How heading when last seen?"

"As before, sir,—straight to leeward."

"Good! he will travel slower now 'tis night. Down royals and top-gallant stun-sails, Mr. Starbuck. We must not run over him before morning; he's making a passage now, and may heave-to a while. Helm there! keep her full before the wind!—Aloft! come down!—Mr. Stubb, send a fresh hand to the fore-mast head, and see it manned till morning."—Then advancing towards the doubloon in the main-mast—"Men, this gold is mine, for I earned it; but I shall let it abide here till the White Whale is dead; and then, whosoever of ye first raises him, upon the day he shall be killed, this gold is that man's; and if on that day I shall again raise him, then, ten times its sum shall be divided among all of ye! Away now!—the deck is thine, sir."

And so saying, he placed himself half way within the scuttle, and slouching his hat, stood there till dawn, except when at intervals rousing himself to see how the night wore on.

Chapter 134: The Chase—Second Day

At day-break, the three mast-heads were punctually manned afresh.

"D'ye see him?" cried Ahab, after allowing a little space for the light to spread.

"See nothing, sir."

"Turn up all hands and make sail! he travels faster than I thought for;—the top-gallant sails!—aye, they should have been kept on her all night. But no matter—'tis but resting for the rush."

Here be it said, that this pertinacious pursuit of one particular whale, continued through day into night, and through night into day, is a thing by no means unprecedented in the South sea fishery. For such is the wonderful skill, prescience of experience, and invincible confidence acquired by some great natural geniuses among the Nantucket commanders; that from the simple observation of a whale when last descried, they will, under certain given circumstances, pretty accurately foretell both the direction in which he will continue to swim for a time, while out of sight, as well as his probable rate of progression during that period. And, in these cases, somewhat as a pilot, when about losing sight of a coast, whose general trending he well knows, and which he desires shortly to return to again, but at some further point; like as this pilot stands by his compass, and takes the precise bearing of the cape at present visible, in order the more certainly to hit aright the remote, unseen headland, eventually to be visited: so does the fisherman, at his compass, with the whale; for after being chased, and diligently marked, through several hours of daylight, then, when night obscures the fish, the creature's future wake through the darkness is almost as established to the sagacious mind of the hunter, as the pilot's coast is to him. So that to this hunter's wondrous skill, the proverbial evanescence of a thing writ in water, a wake, is to all desired purposes well nigh as reliable as the steadfast land. And as the mighty iron Leviathan of the modern railway is so familiarly known in its every pace, that, with watches in their hands, men time his rate as doctors that of a baby's pulse; and lightly say of it, the up train or the down train will reach such or such a spot, at such or such an hour; even so, almost, there are occasions when these Nantucketers time that other Leviathan of the deep, according to the observed humor of his speed; and say to themselves, so many hours hence this whale will have gone two hundred miles, will have about reached this or that degree of latitude or longitude. But to render this acuteness at all successful in the end, the wind and the sea must be the whaleman's allies; for of what present avail to the becalmed or windbound mariner is the skill that assures him he is exactly ninety-three leagues and a quarter from his port? Inferable from these statements, are many collateral subtile matters touching the chase of whales.

The ship tore on; leaving such a furrow in the sea as when a cannon-ball, missent, becomes a plough-share and turns up the level field.

"By salt and hemp!" cried Stubb, "but this swift motion of the deck creeps up one's legs and tingles at the heart. This ship and I are two brave fellows!—Ha! ha! Some one take me up, and launch me, spine-wise, on the sea,—for by live-oaks! my spine's a keel. Ha, ha! we go the gait that leaves no dust behind!"

"There she blows—she blows!—she blows!—right ahead!" was now the mast-head cry.

"Aye, aye!" cried Stubb. "I knew it—ye can't escape—blow on and split your spout, O whale! the mad fiend himself is after ye! blow your trump—blister your lungs!—Ahab will dam off your blood, as a miller shuts his water-gate upon the stream!"

And Stubb did but speak out for well nigh all that crew. The frenzies of the chase had by this time worked them bubblingly up, like old wine worked anew. Whatever pale fears and forebodings some of them might have felt before; these were not only now kept out of sight through the growing awe of Ahab, but they were broken up, and on all sides routed, as timid prairie hares that scatter before the bounding bison. The hand of Fate had snatched all their souls; and by the stirring perils of the previous day; the rack of the past night's suspense; the fixed, unfearing, blind, reckless way in which their wild craft went plunging towards its flying mark; by all these things, their hearts were bowled along. The wind that made great bellies of their sails, and rushed the vessel on by arms invisible as irresistible; this seemed the symbol of that unseen agency which so enslaved them to the race.

They were one man, not thirty. For as the one ship that held them all; though it was put together of all contrasting things—oak, and maple, and pine wood; iron, and pitch, and hemp—yet all these ran into each other in the one concrete hull, which shot on its way, both balanced and directed by the long central keel; even so, all the individualities of the crew, this man's valor, that man's fear; guilt and guiltiness, all varieties were welded into oneness, and were all directed to that fatal goal which Ahab their one lord and keel did point to.

The rigging lived. The mast-heads, like the tops of tall palms, were outspreadingly tufted with arms and legs. Clinging to a spar with one hand, some reached forth the other with impatient wavings; others, shading their eyes from the vivid sunlight, sat far out on the rocking yards; all the spars in full bearing of mortals, ready and ripe for their fate. Ah! how they still strove through that infinite blueness to seek out the thing that might destroy them!

"Why sing ye not out for him, if ye see him?" cried Ahab, when, after the lapse of some minutes since the first cry, no more had been heard. "Sway me up, men; ye have been deceived; not Moby-Dick casts one odd jet that way, and then disappears."

It was even so; in their headlong eagerness, the men had mistaken some other thing for the whale-spout, as the event itself soon proved; for hardly had Ahab reached his perch; hardly was the rope belayed to its pin on deck, when he struck the key-note to an orchestra, that made the air vibrate as with the combined discharges of rifles. The triumphant halloo of thirty buckskin lungs was heard, as—much nearer to the ship than the place of the imaginary jet, less than a mile ahead—Moby-Dick bodily burst into view! For not by any calm and indolent spoutings; not by the peaceable gush of that mystic fountain in his head, did the White Whale now reveal his vicinity; but by the far more wondrous phenomenon of breaching. Rising with his utmost velocity from the furthest depths, the Sperm Whale thus booms his entire bulk into the pure element of air, and piling up a mountain of dazzling foam, shows his place to the distance of seven miles and more. In those moments, the torn, enraged waves he shakes off, seem his mane; in some cases, this breaching is his act of defiance.

"There she breaches! there she breaches!" was the cry, as in his immeasureable bravadoes the White Whale tossed himself salmon-like to Heaven. So suddenly seen in the blue plain of the sea, and relieved against the still bluer margin of the sky, the spray that he raised, for the moment, intolerably glittered and glared like a glacier; and stood there gradually fading and fading away from its first sparkling intensity, to the dim mistiness of an advancing shower in a vale.

"Aye, breach your last to the sun, Moby-Dick!" cried Ahab, "thy hour and thy harpoon are at hand!—Down! down all of ye, but one man at the fore. The boats!—stand by!"

Unmindful of the tedious rope-ladders of the shrouds, the men, like shooting stars, slid to the deck, by the isolated back-stays and halyards; while Ahab, less dartingly, but still rapidly was dropped from his perch.

"Lower away," he cried, so soon as he had reached his boat—a spare one, rigged the afternoon previous. "Mr. Starbuck, the ship is thine—keep away from the boats, but keep near them. Lower, all!"

As if to strike a quick terror into them, by this time being the first assailant himself, Moby-Dick had turned, and was now coming for the three crews. Ahab's boat was central; and cheering his men, he told them he would take the whale head-and-head,—that is, pull straight up to his forehead,—a not uncommon thing; for when within a certain limit, such a course excludes the coming onset from the whale's sidelong vision. But ere that close limit was gained, and while yet all three boats were plain as the ship's three masts to his eye; the White Whale churning himself into furious speed, almost in an instant as it were, rushing among the boats with open jaws, and a lashing tail, offered appalling battle on every side; and heedless of the irons darted at him from every boat, seemed only intent on annihilating each separate plank of which those boats were made. But skilfully manoeuvred, incessantly wheeling like trained chargers in the field; the boats for a while eluded him; though, at times, but by a plank's breadth; while all the time, Ahab's unearthly slogan tore every other cry but his to shreds.

But at last in his untraceable evolutions, the White Whale so crossed and recrossed, and in a thousand ways entangled the slack of the three lines now fast to him, that they foreshortened, and, of themselves, warped the devoted boats towards the planted irons in him; though now for a moment the whale drew aside a little, as if to rally for a more tremendous charge. Seizing that opportunity, Ahab first paid out more line: and then was rapidly hauling and jerking in upon it again—hoping that way to disencumber it of some snarls—when lo!—a sight more savage than the embattled teeth of sharks!

Caught and twisted— corkscrewed in the mazes of the line, loose harpoons and lances, with all their bristling barbs and points, came flashing and dripping up to the chocks in the bows of Ahab's boat. Only one thing could be done. Seizing the boat-knife, he critically reached within—through—and then, without—the rays of steel; dragged in the line beyond, passed it, inboard, to the bowsman, and then, twice sundering the rope near the chocks—dropped the intercepted fagot of steel into the sea; and was all fast again. That instant, the White Whale made a sudden rush among the remaining tangles of the other lines; by so doing, irresistibly dragged the more involved boats of Stubb and Flask towards his flukes; dashed them together like two rolling husks on a surf-beaten beach, and then, diving down into the sea, disappeared in a boiling maelstrom, in which, for a space, the odorous cedar chips of the wrecks danced round and round, like the grated nutmeg in a swiftly stirred bowl of punch.

While the two crews were yet circling in the waters, reaching out after the revolving line-tubs, oars, and other floating furniture, while aslope little Flask bobbed up and down like an empty vial, twitching his legs upwards to escape the dreaded jaws of sharks; and Stubb was lustily singing out for some one to ladle him up; and while the old man's line—now parting—admitted of his pulling into the creamy pool to rescue whom he could;—in that wild simultaneousness of a thousand concreted perils,—Ahab's yet unstricken boat seemed drawn up towards Heaven by invisible wires,—as, arrow-like, shooting perpendicularly from the sea, the White Whale dashed his broad forehead against its bottom, and sent it, turning over and over, into the air; till it fell again—gunwale downwards—and Ahab and his men struggled out from under it, like seals from a seaside cave.

The first uprising momentum of the whale—modifying its direction as he struck the surface—involuntarily launched him along it, to a little distance from the centre of the destruction he had made; and with his back to it, he now lay for a moment slowly feeling with his flukes from side to side; and whenever a stray oar, bit of plank, the least chip or crumb of the boats touched his skin, his tail swiftly drew back, and came sideways smiting the sea. But soon, as if satisfied that his work for that time was done, he pushed his pleated forehead through the ocean, and trailing after him the intertangled lines, continued his leeward way at a traveller's methodic pace.

As before, the attentive ship having descried the whole fight, again came bearing down to the rescue, and dropping a boat, picked up the floating mariners, tubs, oars and whatever else could be caught at, and safely landed them on her decks. Some sprained shoulders, wrists, and ankles; livid contusions; wrenched harpoons and lances; inextricable intricacies of rope; shattered oars and planks; all these were there; but no fatal or even serious ill seemed to have befallen any one. As with Fedallah the day before, so Ahab was now found grimly clinging to his boat's broken half, which afforded a comparatively easy float; nor did it so exhaust him as the previous day's mishap.

But when he was helped to the deck, all eyes were fastened upon him; as instead of standing by himself he still half-hung upon the shoulder of Starbuck, who had thus far been the foremost to assist him. His ivory leg had been snapped off, leaving but one short sharp splinter.

"Aye, aye, Starbuck, 'tis sweet to lean sometimes, be the leaner who he will; and would old Ahab had leaned oftener than he has."

"The ferrule has not stood, sir," said the carpenter, now coming up; "I put good work into that leg."

"But no bones broken, sir, I hope," said Stubb with true concern.

"Aye! and all splintered to pieces, Stubb!—d'ye see it.—But even with a broken bone, old Ahab is untouched; and I account no living bone of mine one jot more me, than this dead one that's lost. Nor white whale, nor man, nor fiend, can so much as graze old Ahab in his own proper and inaccessible being. Can any lead touch yonder floor, any mast scrape yonder roof?—Aloft there! which way?"

"Dead to leeward, sir."

"Up helm, then; pile on the sail again, ship keepers! down the rest of the spare boats and rig them—Mr. Starbuck away, and muster the boat's crews."

"Let me first help thee towards the bulwarks, sir."

"Oh, oh, oh! how this splinter gores me now! Accursed fate! that the unconquerable captain in the soul should have such a craven mate!"

"Sir?"

"My body, man, not thee. Give me something for a cane—there, that shivered lance will do. Muster the men. Surely I have not seen him yet. By heaven it cannot be!—missing?—quick! call them all."

The old man's hinted thought was true. Upon mustering the company, the Parsee was not there.

"The Parsee!" cried Stubb—"he must have been caught in—"

"The black vomit wrench thee!—run all of ye above, alow, cabin, forecastle—find him—not gone—not gone!"

But quickly they returned to him with the tidings that the Parsee was nowhere to be found.

"Aye, sir," said Stubb—"caught among the tangles of your line—I thought I saw him dragging under."

"*My* line! *my* line? Gone?—gone? What means that little word?—What death-knell rings in it, that old Ahab shakes as if he were the belfry. The harpoon, too!—toss over the litter there,—d'ye see it?—the forged iron, men, the white whale's—no, no, no,—blistered fool; this hand did dart it!—'tis in the fish!—Aloft there! Keep him nailed—quick!—all hands to the rigging of the boats—collect the oars—harpooneers! the irons, the irons!—hoist the royals higher—a pull on all the sheets!—helm there! steady, steady for your life! I'll ten times girdle the unmeasured globe; yea and dive straight through it, but I'll slay him yet!"

"Great God! but for one single instant show thyself," cried Starbuck; "never, never wilt thou capture him, old man—In Jesus' name no more of this, that's worse than devil's madness. Two days chased; twice stove to splinters; thy very leg once more snatched from under thee; thy evil shadow gone—all good angels mobbing thee with warnings:—what more wouldst thou have?—Shall we keep chasing this murderous fish till he swamps the last man? Shall we be dragged by him to the bottom of the sea? Shall we be towed by him to the infernal world? Oh, oh,—Impiety and blasphemy to hunt him more!"

"Starbuck, of late I've felt strangely moved to thee; ever since that hour we both saw—thou know'st what, in one another's eyes. But in this matter of the whale, be the front of thy face to me as the palm of this hand—a lipless, unfeatured blank. Ahab is for ever Ahab, man. This whole act's immutably decreed. 'Twas rehearsed by thee and me a billion years before this ocean rolled. Fool! I am the Fates' lieutenant; I act under orders. Look thou, underling! that thou obeyest mine.—Stand round me, men. Ye see an old man cut down to the stump; leaning on a shivered lance; propped up on a lonely foot. 'Tis Ahab—his body's part; but Ahab's soul's a centipede, that moves upon a hundred legs. I feel strained, half stranded, as ropes that tow dismasted frigates in a gale; and I may look so. But ere I break, ye'll hear me crack; and till ye hear *that*, know that Ahab's hawser tows his purpose yet. Believe ye, men, in the things called omens? Then laugh aloud, and cry encore! For ere they drown, drowning things will twice rise to the surface; then rise again, to sink for evermore. So with Moby-Dick—two days he's floated—to-morrow will be the third. Aye, men, he'll rise once more,—but only to spout his last! D'ye feel brave men, brave?"

"As fearless fire," cried Stubb.

"And as mechanical," muttered Ahab. Then as the men went forward, he muttered on:—"The things called omens! And yesterday I talked the same to Starbuck there, concerning my broken boat. Oh! how valiantly I seek to drive out of others' hearts what's clinched so fast in mine!—The Parsee—the Parsee!—gone, gone? and he was to go before:—but still was to be seen again ere I could perish—How's that?—There's a riddle now might baffle all the lawyers backed by the ghosts of the whole line of judges:—like a hawk's beak it pecks my brain. *I'll, I'll* solve it, though!"

When dusk descended, the whale was still in sight to leeward.

So once more the sail was shortened, and everything passed nearly as on the previous night; only, the sound of hammers, and the hum of the grindstone was heard till nearly daylight, as the men toiled by lanterns in the complete and careful rigging of the spare boats and sharpening their fresh weapons for the morrow. Meantime, of the broken keel of Ahab's wrecked craft the carpenter made him another leg; while still as on the night before, slouched Ahab stood fixed within his scuttle; his hid, heliotrope glance anticipatingly gone backward on its dial; sat due eastward for the earliest sun.

Chapter 135: The Chase—Third Day

The morning of the third day dawned fair and fresh, and once more the solitary night-man at the fore-mast-head was relieved by crowds of the daylight look-outs, who dotted every mast and almost every spar.

"D'ye see him?" cried Ahab; but the whale was not yet in sight.

"In his infallible wake, though; but follow that wake, that's all. Helm there; steady, as thou goest, and hast been going. What a lovely day again; were it a new-made world, and made for a summer-house to the angels, and this morning the first of its throwing open to them, a fairer day could not dawn upon that world. Here's food for thought, had Ahab time to think; but Ahab never thinks; he only feels, feels, feels; *that's* tingling enough for mortal man! to think's audacity. God only has that right and privilege. Thinking is, or ought to be, a coolness and a calmness; and our poor hearts throb, and our poor brains beat too much for that. And yet, I've sometimes thought my brain was very calm—frozen calm, this old skull cracks so, like a glass in which the contents turned to ice, and shiver it. And still this hair is growing now; this moment growing, and heat must breed it; but no, it's like that sort of common grass that will grow anywhere, between the earthy clefts of Greenland ice or in Vesuvius lava. How the wild winds blow it; they whip it about me as the torn shreds of split sails lash the tossed ship they cling to. A vile wind that has no doubt blown ere this through prison corridors and cells, and wards of hospitals, and ventilated them, and now comes blowing hither as innocent as fleeces. Out upon it!—it's tainted. Were I the wind, I'd blow no more on such a wicked, miserable world. I'd crawl somewhere to a cave, and slink there. And yet, 'tis a noble and heroic thing, the wind! who ever conquered it? In every fight it has the last and bitterest blow. Run tilting at it, and you but run through it. Ha! a coward wind that strikes stark naked men, but will not stand to receive a single blow. Even Ahab is a braver thing—a nobler thing that that. Would now the wind but had a body; but all the things that most exasperate and outrage mortal man, all these things are bodiless, but only bodiless as objects, not as agents. There's a most special, a most cunning, oh, a most malicious difference! And yet, I say again, and swear it now, that there's something all glorious and gracious in the wind. These warm Trade Winds, at least, that in the clear heavens blow straight on, in strong and steadfast, vigorous mildness; and veer not from their mark, however the baser currents of the sea may turn and tack, and mightiest Mississippies of the land swift and swerve about, uncertain where to go at last. And by the eternal Poles! these same Trades that so directly blow my good ship on; these Trades, or something like them—something so unchangeable, and full as strong, blow my keeled soul along! To it! Aloft there! What d'ye see?"

"Nothing, sir."

"Nothing! and noon at hand! The doubloon goes a-begging! See the sun! Aye, aye, it must be so. I've oversailed him. How, got the start? Aye, he's chasing me now; not I, him—that's bad; I might have known it, too. Fool! the lines—the harpoons he's towing. Aye, aye, I have run him by last night. About! about! Come down, all of ye, but the regular look outs! Man the braces!"

Steering as she had done, the wind had been somewhat on the *Pequod*'s quarter, so that now being pointed in the reverse direction, the braced ship sailed hard upon the breeze as she rechurned the cream in her own white wake.

"Against the wind he now steers for the open jaw," murmured Starbuck to himself, as he coiled the new-hauled main-brace upon the rail. "God keep us, but already my bones feel damp within me, and from the inside wet my flesh. I misdoubt me that I disobey my God in obeying him!"

"Stand by to sway me up!" cried Ahab, advancing to the hempen basket. "We should meet him soon."

"Aye, aye, sir," and straightway Starbuck did Ahab's bidding, and once more Ahab swung on high.

A whole hour now passed; gold-beaten out to ages. Time itself now held long breaths with keen suspense. But at last, some three points off the weather bow, Ahab descried the spout again, and instantly from the three mast-heads three shrieks went up as if the tongues of fire had voiced it.

"Forehead to forehead I meet thee, this third time, Moby-Dick! On deck there!—brace sharper up; crowd her into the wind's eye. He's too far off to lower yet, Mr. Starbuck. The sails shake! Stand over that helmsman with a top-maul! So, so; he travels fast, and I must down. But let me have one more good round look aloft here at the sea; there's time for that. An old, old sight, and yet somehow so young; aye, and not changed a wink since I first saw it, a boy, from the sand-hills of Nantucket! The same!—the same!—the same to Noah as to me. There's a soft shower to leeward. Such lovely leewardings! They must lead somewhere—to something else than common land, more palmy than the palms. Leeward! the white whale goes that way; look to windward, then; the better if the bitterer quarter. But good bye, good bye, old mast-head! What's this?—green? aye, tiny mosses in these warped cracks. No such green weather stains on Ahab's head! There's the difference now between man's old age and matter's. But aye, old mast, we both grow old together; sound in our hulls, though, are we not, my ship? Aye, minus a leg, that's all. By heaven this dead wood has the better of my live flesh every way. I can't compare with it; and I've known some ships made of dead trees outlast the lives of men made of the most vital stuff of vital fathers. What's that he said? he should still go before me, my pilot; and yet to be seen again? But where? Will I have eyes at the bottom of the sea, supposing I descend those endless stairs? and all night I've been sailing from him, wherever he did sink to. Aye, aye, like many more thou told'st direful truth as touching thyself, O Parsee; but, Ahab, there thy shot fell short. Good by, mast-head—keep a good eye upon the whale, the while I'm gone. We'll talk to-morrow, nay, to-night, when the white whale lies down there, tied by head and tail."

He gave the word; and still gazing round him, was steadily lowered through the cloven blue air to the deck.

In due time the boats were lowered, but as standing in his shallop's stern, Ahab just hovered upon the point of the descent, he waved to the mate,—who held one of the tackle-ropes on deck—and bade him pause.

"Starbuck!"

"Sir?"

"For the third time my soul's ship starts upon this voyage, Starbuck."

"Aye, sir, thou wilt have it so."

"Some ships sail from their ports, and ever afterwards are missing, Starbuck!"

"Truth, sir: saddest truth."

"Some men die at ebb tide; some at low water; some at the full of the flood;—and I feel now like a billow that's all one crested comb, Starbuck. I am old;—shake hands with me, man."

Their hands met; their eyes fastened; Starbuck's tears the glue.

"Oh, my captain, my captain!—noble heart—go not—go not!—see, it's a brave man that weeps; how great the agony of the persuasion then!"

"Lower away!"—cried Ahab, tossing the mate's arm from him. "Stand by the crew!"

In an instant the boat was pulling round close under the stern.

"The sharks! the sharks!" cried a voice from the low cabin-window there; "O master, my master, come back!"

But Ahab heard nothing; for his own voice was high-lifted then; and the boat leaped on.

Yet the voice spake true; for scarce had he pushed from the ship, when numbers of sharks, seemingly rising from out the dark waters beneath the hull, maliciously snapped at the blades of the oars, every time they dipped in the water; and in this way accompanied the boat with their bites. It is a thing not uncommonly happening to the whale-boats in those swarming seas; the sharks at times apparently following them in the same prescient way that vultures hover over the banners of marching regiments in the east. But these were the first sharks that had been observed by the *Pequod* since the White Whale had been first descried; and whether it was that Ahab's crew were all such tiger-yellow barbarians, and therefore their flesh more musky to the senses of the sharks—a matter sometimes well known to affect them,—however it was, they seemed to follow that one boat without molesting the others.

"Heart of wrought steel!" murmured Starbuck gazing over the side, and following with his eyes the receding boat—"canst thou yet ring boldly to that sight?"—lowering thy keel among ravening sharks, and followed by them, open-mouthed to the chase; and this the critical third day?—For when three days flow together in one continuous intense pursuit; be sure the first is the morning, the second the noon, and the third the evening and the end of that thing—be that end what it may. Oh! my God! what is this that shoots through me, and leaves me so deadly calm, yet expectant,—fixed at the top of a shudder! Future things swim before me, as in empty outlines and skeletons; all the past is somehow grown dim. Mary, girl! thou fadest in pale glories behind me; boy! I seem to see but thy eyes grown wondrous blue. Strangest problems of life seem clearing; but clouds sweep between—Is my journey's end coming? My legs feel faint; like his who has footed it all day. Feel thy heart,—beats it yet?—Stir thyself, Starbuck!—stave it off—move, move! speak aloud!—Mast-head there! See ye my boy's hand on the hill?—Crazed;—aloft there!—keep thy keenest eye upon the boats:—mark well the whale!—Ho! again!—drive off that hawk! see! he pecks—he tears the vane—pointing to the red flag flying at the main-truck—"Ha! he soars away with it!—Where's the old man now? sees't thou that sight, oh Ahab!—shudder, shudder!"

The boats had not gone very far, when by a signal from the mast-heads—a downward pointed arm, Ahab knew that the whale had sounded; but intending to be near him at the next rising, he held on his way a little sideways from the vessel; the becharmed crew maintaining the profoundest silence, as the head-beat waves hammered and hammered against the opposing bow.

"Drive, drive in your nails, oh ye waves! to their uttermost heads, drive them in! ye but strike a thing without a lid; and no coffin and no hearse can be mine:—and hemp only can kill me! Ha! ha!"

Suddenly the waters around them slowly swelled in broad circles; then quickly upheaved, as if sideways sliding from a submerged berg of ice, swiftly rising to the surface. A low rumbling sound was heard; a subterraneous hum; and then all held their breaths; as bedraggled with trailing ropes, and harpoons, and lances, a vast form shot lengthwise, but obliquely from the sea. Shrouded in a thin drooping veil of mist, it hovered for a moment in the rainbowed air; and then fell swamping back into the deep. Crushed thirty feet upwards, the waters flashed for an instant like heaps of fountains, then brokenly sank in a shower of flakes, leaving the circling surface creamed like new milk round the marble trunk of the whale.

"Give way!" cried Ahab to the oarsmen, and the boats darted forward to the attack; but maddened by yesterday's fresh irons that corroded in him, Moby-Dick seemed combinedly possessed by all the angels that fell from heaven. The wide tiers of welded tendons overspreading his broad white forehead, beneath the transparent skin, looked knitted together; as head on, he came churning his tail among the boats; and once more flailed them apart; spilling out the irons and lances from the two mates' boats, and dashing in one side of the upper part of their bows, but leaving Ahab's almost without a scar.

While Daggoo and Queequeg were stopping the strained planks; and as the whale swimming out from them, turned, and showed one entire flank as he shot by them again; at that moment a quick cry went up. Lashed round and round to the fish's back; pinioned in the turns upon turns in which, during the past night, the whale had reeled the involutions of the lines around him, the half torn body of the Parsee was seen; his sable raiment frayed to shreds; his distended eyes turned full upon old Ahab.

The harpoon dropped from his hand.

"Befooled, befooled!"—drawing in a long lean breath—"Aye, Parsee! I see thee again.—Aye, and thou goest before; and this, this then is the hearse that thou didst promise. But I hold thee to the last letter of thy word. Where is the second hearse? Away, mates, to the ship! those boats are useless now; repair them if ye can in time, and return to me; if not, Ahab is enough to die—Down, men! the first thing that but offers to jump from this boat I stand in, that thing I harpoon. Ye are not other men, but my arms and my legs; and so obey me.—Where's the whale? gone down again?"

But he looked too nigh the boat; for as if bent upon escaping with the corpse he bore, and as if the particular place of the last encounter had been but a stage in his leeward voyage, Moby-Dick was now again steadily swimming forward; and had almost passed the ship,—which thus far had been sailing in the contrary direction to him, though for the present her headway had been stopped. He seemed swimming with his utmost velocity, and now only intent upon pursuing his own straight path in the sea.

"Oh! Ahab," cried Starbuck, "not too late is it, even now, the third day, to desist. See! Moby-Dick seeks thee not. It is thou, thou, that madly seekest him!"

Setting sail to the rising wind, the lonely boat was swiftly impelled to leeward, by both oars and canvas. And at last when Ahab was sliding by the vessel, so near as plainly to distinguish Starbuck's face as he leaned over the rail, he hailed him to turn the vessel about, and follow him, not too swiftly, at a judicious interval. Glancing upwards, he saw Tashtego, Queequeg, and Daggoo, eagerly mounting to the three mast-heads; while the oarsmen were rocking in the two staved boats which had but just been hoisted to the side, and were busily at work in repairing them. One after the other, through the portholes, as he sped, he also caught flying glimpses of Stubb and Flask, busying themselves on deck among bundles of new irons and lances. As he saw all this; as he heard the hammers in the broken boats; far other hammers seemed driving a nail into his heart. But he rallied. And now marking that the vane or flag was gone from the main-mast-head, he shouted to Tashtego, who had just gained that perch, to descend again for another flag, and a hammer and nails, and so nail it to the mast.

Whether fagged by the three days' running chase, and the resistance to his swimming in the knotted hamper he bore; or whether it was some latent deceitfulness and malice in him: whichever was true, the White Whale's way now began to abate, as it seemed, from the boat so rapidly nearing him once more; though indeed the whale's last start had not been so long a one as before. And still as Ahab glided over the waves the unpitying sharks accompanied him; and so pertinaciously stuck to the boat; and so continually bit at the plying oars, that the blades became jagged and crunched, and left small splinters in the sea, at almost every dip.

"Heed them not! those teeth but give new rowlocks to your oars. Pull on! 'tis the better rest, the shark's jaw than the yielding water."

"But at every bite, sir, the thin blades grow smaller and smaller!"

"They will last long enough! pull on!—But who can tell"—he muttered—"whether these sharks swim to feast on the whale or on Ahab?—But pull on! Aye, all alive, now—we near him. The helm! take the helm; let me pass,"—and so saying, two of the oarsmen helped him forward to the bows of the still flying boat.

At length as the craft was cast to one side, and ran ranging along with the White Whale's flank, he seemed strangely oblivious of its advance—as the whale sometimes will—and Ahab was fairly within the smoky mountain mist, which, thrown off from the whale's spout, curled round his great, Monadnock hump; he was even thus close to him; when, with body arched back, and both arms lengthwise high-lifted to the poise, he darted his fierce iron, and his far fiercer curse into the hated whale. As both steel and curse sank to the socket, as if sucked into a morass, Moby-Dick sideways writhed; spasmodically rolled his nigh flank against the bow, and, without staving a hole in it, so suddenly canted the boat over, that had it not been for the elevated part of the gunwale to which he then clung, Ahab would once more have been tossed into the sea. As it was, three of the oarsmen—who foreknew not the precise instant of the dart, and were therefore unprepared for its effects—these were flung out; but so fell, that, in an instant two of them clutched the gunwale again, and rising to its level on a combing wave, hurled themselves bodily inboard again; the third man helplessly dropping astern, but still afloat and swimming.

Almost simultaneously, with a mighty volition of ungraduated, instantaneous swiftness, the White Whale darted through the weltering sea. But when Ahab cried out to the steersman to take new turns with the line, and hold it so; and commanded the crew to turn round on their seats, and tow the boat up to the mark; the moment the treacherous line felt that double strain and tug, it snapped in the empty air!

"What breaks in me? Some sinew cracks!—'tis whole again; oars! oars! Burst in upon him!"

Hearing the tremendous rush of the sea-crashing boat, the whale wheeled round to present his blank forehead at bay; but in that evolution, catching sight of the nearing black hull of the ship; seemingly seeing in it the source of all his persecutions; bethinking it—it may be—a larger and nobler foe; of a sudden, he bore down upon its advancing prow, smiting his jaws amid fiery showers of foam.

Ahab staggered; his hand smote his forehead. "I grow blind; hands! stretch out before me that I may yet grope my way. Is't night?"

"The whale! The ship!" cried the cringing oarsmen.

"Oars! oars! Slope downwards to thy depths, O sea, that ere it be for ever too late, Ahab may slide this last, last time upon his mark! I see: the ship! the ship! Dash on, my men! Will ye not save my ship?"

But as the oarsmen violently forced their boat through the sledge-hammering seas, the before whale-smitten bow-ends of two planks burst through, and in an instant almost, the temporarily disabled boat lay nearly level with the waves; its half-wading, splashing crew, trying hard to stop the gap and bale out the pouring water.

Meantime, for that one beholding instant, Tashtego's mast-head hammer remained suspended in his hand; and the red flag, half-wrapping him as with a plaid, then streamed itself straight out from him, as his own forward-flowing heart; while Starbuck and Stubb, standing upon the bowsprit beneath, caught sight of the down-coming monster just as soon as he.

"The whale, the whale! Up helm, up helm! Oh, all ye sweet powers of air, now hug me close! Let not Starbuck die, if die he must, in a woman's fainting fit. Up helm, I say—ye fools, the jaw! the jaw! Is this the end of all my bursting prayers? all my life-long fidelities? Oh, Ahab, Ahab, lo, thy work. Steady! helmsman, steady. Nay, nay! Up helm again! He turns to meet us! Oh, his unappeasable brow drives on towards one, whose duty tells him he cannot depart. My God, stand by me now!"

"Stand not by me, but stand under me, whoever you are that will now help Stubb; for Stubb, too, sticks here. I grin at thee, thou grinning whale! Who ever helped Stubb, or kept Stubb awake, but Stubb's own unwinking eye? And now poor Stubb goes to bed upon a mattrass that is all too soft; would it were stuffed with brushwood! I grin at thee, thou grinning whale! Look ye, sun, moon, and stars! I call ye assassins of as good a fellow as ever spouted up his ghost. For all that, I would yet ring glasses with ye, would ye but hand the cup! Oh, oh! oh, oh! thou grinning whale, but there'll be plenty of gulping soon! Why fly ye not, O Ahab! For me, off shoes and jacket to it; let Stubb die in his drawers! A most mouldy and over salted death, though;—cherries! cherries! cherries! Oh, Flask, for one red cherry ere we die!"

"Cherries? I only wish that we were where they grow. Oh, Stubb, I hope my poor mother's drawn my part-pay ere this; if not, few coppers will now come to her, for the voyage is up."

From the ship's bows, nearly all the seamen now hung inactive; hammers, bits of plank, lances, and harpoons, mechanically retained in their hands, just as they had darted from their various employments; all their enchanted eyes intent upon the whale, which from side to side strangely vibrating his predestinating head, sent a broad band of overspreading semicircular foam before him as he rushed. Retribution, swift vengeance, eternal malice were in his whole aspect, and spite of all that mortal man could do, the solid white buttress of his forehead smote the ship's starboard bow, till men and timbers reeled. Some fell flat upon their faces. Like dislodged trucks, the heads of the harpooneers aloft shook on their bull-like necks. Through the breach, they heard the waters pour, as mountain torrents down a flume.

"The ship! The hearse!—the second hearse!" cried Ahab from the boat; "its wood could only be American!"

Diving beneath the settling ship, the whale ran quivering along its keel; but turning under water, swiftly shot to the surface again, far off the other bow, but within a few yards of Ahab's boat, where, for a time, he lay quiescent.

"I turn my body from the sun. What ho, Tashtego! let me hear thy hammer. Oh! ye three unsurrendered spires of mine; thou uncracked keel; and only god-bullied hull; thou firm deck, and haughty helm, and Pole-pointed prow,—death-glorious ship! must ye then perish, and without me? Am I cut off from the last fond pride of meanest shipwrecked captains? Oh, lonely death on lonely life! Oh, now I feel my topmost greatness lies in my topmost grief. Ho, ho! from all your furthest bounds, pour ye now in, ye bold billows of my whole foregone life, and top this one piled comber of my death! Towards thee I roll, thou all-destroying but unconquering whale; to the last I grapple with thee; from hell's heart I stab at thee; for hate's sake I spit my last breath at thee. Sink all coffins and all hearses to one common pool! and since neither can be mine, let me then tow to pieces, while still chasing thee, though tied to thee, thou damned whale! *Thus*, I give up the spear!"

The harpoon was darted; the stricken whale flew forward; with igniting velocity the line ran through the groove;—ran foul. Ahab stooped to clear it; he did clear it; but the flying turn caught him round the neck, and voicelessly as Turkish mutes bowstring their victim, he was shot out of the boat, ere the crew knew he was gone. Next instant, the heavy eye-splice in the rope's final end flew out of the stark-empty tub, knocked down an oarsman, and smiting the sea, disappeared in its depths.

For an instant, the tranced boat's crew stood still; then turned. "The ship? Great God, where is the ship?" Soon they through dim, bewildering mediums saw her sidelong fading phantom, as in the gaseous Fata Morgana; only the uppermost masts out of water; while fixed by infatuation, or fidelity, or fate, to their once lofty perches, the pagan harpooneers still maintained their sinking lookouts on the sea. And now, concentric circles seized the lone boat itself, and all its crew, and each floating oar, and every lance-pole, and spinning, animate and inanimate, all round and round in one vortex, carried the smallest chip of the *Pequod* out of sight.

But as the last whelmings intermixingly poured themselves over the sunken head of the Indian at the mainmast, leaving a few inches of the erect spar yet visible, together with long streaming yards of the flag, which calmly undulated, with ironical coincidings, over the destroying billows they almost touched;—at that instant, a red arm and a hammer hovered backwardly uplifted in the open air, in the act of nailing the flag faster and yet faster to the subsiding spar. A sky-hawk that tauntingly had followed the maintruck downwards from its natural home among the stars, pecking at the flag, and incommoding Tashtego there; this bird now chanced to intercept its broad fluttering wing between the hammer and the wood; and simultaneously feeling that ethereal thrill, the submerged savage beneath, in his death-gasp, kept his hammer frozen there; and so the bird of heaven, with archangelic shrieks, and his imperial beak thrust upwards, and his whole captive form folded in the flag of Ahab, went down with his ship, which, like

Satan, would not sink to hell till she had dragged a living part of heaven along with her, and helmeted herself with it.

Now small fowls flew screaming over the yet yawning gulf; a sullen white surf beat against its steep sides; then all collapsed, and the great shroud of the sea rolled on as it rolled five thousand years ago.

Ishmael, atop Queequeg's coffin, is the Pequod*'s lone survivor; he is rescued by the* Rachel, *whose captain was so cruelly refused help by Ahab.*

SOURCE: Herman Melville. *Moby-Dick.* New York: Harper & Brothers, 1851.

HARRIET BEECHER STOWE

The novel is more famous than it is read, perhaps due to unfortunate stereotypes that the novel itself helped create. Harriet Beecher Stowe (1811–1896) was a sophisticated and experienced novelist when she set to work on this novel, one of the most socially and politically influential creative works in world history. Yet the novel is not a political tract; it is, rather, comparable in its range of feeling to novels by her British contemporary Charles Dickens. She charged it with sympathy, humor and unashamed pathos, which, admittedly, occasionally veers into the broadest sentimentality. Stowe presents the novel from various points of view, from slaves to slave-owners to slave-catchers, to ordinary citizens, extraordinary Quakers, clowns, heroes and villains. Stowe's ambitious and moving novel helped awaken America's and the world's conscience in regard to slavery. As President Abraham Lincoln was reputed to have said to the author ten years later, in the midst of the Civil War, "So this is the little lady who made this big war?"

Chapters from *Uncle Tom's Cabin* (1852)

Chapter 7: The Mother's Struggle

These two early chapters display something of Stowe's customary style, describing the slave Eliza's desperate escape with her four-year-old son, an escape abetted by the sympathy of her former mistress, a white Kentucky woman who is stirred to consciousness about the immorality of slavery when her husband must sell Eliza's son and Uncle Tom to maintain ownership of the farm. Stowe based "Eliza's Escape," perhaps the most famous dramatized scene in American literature, on a real incident—but its actual description in the novel is remarkably brief (though it is almost immediately turned into a legend by a character who has witnessed it).[1]

---

1. See Levi Coffin's account of the escape, "The Slave Woman Who Crossed the Ohio River on the Drifting Ice with Her Child in Her Arms," in *Slave Narratives of the Underground Railroad*, edited by Christine Rudisel and Bob Blaisdell. Mineola, New York: Dover Publications, 2014.

IT IS IMPOSSIBLE to conceive of a human creature more wholly desolate and forlorn than Eliza, when she turned her footsteps from Uncle Tom's cabin.

Her husband's suffering and dangers, and the danger of her child, all blended in her mind, with a confused and stunning sense of the risk she was running, in leaving the only home she had ever known, and cutting loose from the protection of a friend whom she loved and revered. Then there was the parting from every familiar object,—the place where she had grown up, the trees under which she had played, the groves where she had walked many an evening in happier days, by the side of her young husband,—everything, as it lay in the clear, frosty starlight, seemed to speak reproachfully to her, and ask her whither could she go from a home like that?

But stronger than all was maternal love, wrought into a paroxysm of frenzy by the near approach of a fearful danger. Her boy was old enough to have walked by her side, and, in an indifferent case, she would only have led him by the hand; but now the bare thought of putting him out of her arms made her shudder, and she strained him to her bosom with a convulsive grasp, as she went rapidly forward.

The frosty ground creaked beneath her feet, and she trembled at the sound; every quaking leaf and fluttering shadow sent the blood backward to her heart, and quickened her footsteps. She wondered within herself at the strength that seemed to be come upon her; for she felt the weight of her boy as if it had been a feather, and every flutter of fear seemed to increase the supernatural power that bore her on, while from her pale lips burst forth, in frequent ejaculations, the prayer to a Friend above—"Lord, help! Lord, save me!"

If it were *your* Harry, mother, or your Willie, that were going to be torn from you by a brutal trader, tomorrow morning,—if you had seen the man, and heard that the papers were signed and delivered, and you had only from twelve o'clock till morning to make good your escape,—how fast could *you* walk? How many miles could you make in those few brief hours, with the darling at your bosom,—the little sleepy head on your shoulder,—the small, soft arms trustingly holding on to your neck?

For the child slept. At first, the novelty and alarm kept him waking; but his mother so hurriedly repressed every breath or sound, and so assured him that if he were only still she would certainly save him, that he clung quietly round her neck, only asking, as he found himself sinking to sleep,

"Mother, I don't need to keep awake, do I?"

"No, my darling; sleep, if you want to."

"But, mother, if I do get asleep, you won't let him get me?"

"No! so may God help me!" said his mother, with a paler cheek, and a brighter light in her large dark eyes.

"You're *sure*, an't you, mother?"

"Yes, *sure*!" said the mother, in a voice that startled herself; for it seemed to her to come from a spirit within, that was no part of her; and the boy dropped his little weary head on her shoulder, and was soon asleep. How the touch of those warm arms, the gentle breathings that came in her neck, seemed to add fire and spirit to her movements! It seemed to her as if strength poured into her in electric streams, from every gentle touch and movement of the sleeping, confiding child. Sublime is the dominion of the mind over the body, that, for a time, can make flesh and nerve impregnable, and string the sinews like steel, so that the weak become so mighty.

The boundaries of the farm, the grove, the woodlot, passed by her dizzily, as she walked on; and still she went, leaving one familiar object after another, slacking not, pausing not, till reddening daylight found her many a long mile from all traces of any familiar objects upon the open highway.

She had often been, with her mistress, to visit some connections, in the little village of T——, not far from the Ohio river, and knew the road well. To go thither, to escape across the Ohio river, were the first hurried outlines of her plan of escape; beyond that, she could only hope in God.

When horses and vehicles began to move along the highway, with that alert perception peculiar to a state of excitement, and which seems to be a sort of inspiration, she became aware that her headlong pace and distracted air might bring on her remark and suspicion. She therefore put the boy on the ground, and, adjusting her dress and bonnet, she walked on at as rapid a pace as she thought consistent with the preservation of appearances. In her little bundle she had provided a store of cakes and apples, which she used as expedients for quickening the speed of the child, rolling the apple some yards before them, when the boy would run with all his might after it; and this ruse, often repeated, carried them over many a half-mile.

After a while, they came to a thick patch of woodland, through which murmured a clear brook. As the child complained of hunger and thirst, she climbed over the fence with him; and, sitting down behind a large rock which concealed them from the road, she gave him a breakfast out of her little package. The boy wondered and grieved that she could not eat; and when, putting his arms round her neck, he tried to wedge some of his cake into her mouth, it seemed to her that the rising in her throat would choke her.

"No, no, Harry darling! mother can't eat till you are safe! We must go on—on—till we come to the river!" And she hurried again into the road, and again constrained herself to walk regularly and composedly forward.

She was many miles past any neighborhood where she was personally known. If she should chance to meet any who knew her, she reflected that the well-known kindness of the family would be of itself a blind to suspicion, as making it an unlikely supposition that she could be a fugitive. As she was also so white as not to be known as of colored lineage, without a critical survey, and her child was white also, it was much easier for her to pass on unsuspected.

On this presumption, she stopped at noon at a neat farmhouse, to rest herself, and buy some dinner for her child and self; for, as the danger decreased with the distance, the supernatural tension of the nervous system lessened, and she found herself both weary and hungry.

The good woman, kindly and gossipping, seemed rather pleased than otherwise with having somebody come in to talk with; and accepted, without examination, Eliza's statement, that she "was going on a little piece, to spend a week with her friends,"—all which she hoped in her heart might prove strictly true.

An hour before sunset, she entered the village of T——, by the Ohio river, weary and foot-sore, but still strong in heart. Her first glance was at the river, which lay, like Jordan, between her and the Canaan of liberty on the other side.

It was now early spring, and the river was swollen and turbulent; great cakes of floating ice were swinging heavily to and fro in the turbid waters. Owing to the peculiar form of the shore on the Kentucky side, the land bending far out into the water, the ice had been lodged and detained in great quantities, and the narrow channel which swept round the bend was full of ice, piled one cake over another, thus forming a temporary barrier to the descending ice, which lodged, and formed a great, undulating raft, filling up the whole river, and extending almost to the Kentucky shore.

Eliza stood, for a moment, contemplating this unfavorable aspect of things, which she saw at once must prevent the usual ferry-boat from running, and then turned into a small public house on the bank, to make a few inquiries.

The hostess, who was busy in various fizzing and stewing operations over the fire, preparatory to the evening meal, stopped, with a fork in her hand, as Eliza's sweet and plaintive voice arrested her.

"What is it?" she said.

"Isn't there any ferry or boat, that takes people over to B——, now?" she said.

"No, indeed!" said the woman; "the boats has stopped running."

Eliza's look of dismay and disappointment struck the woman, and she said, inquiringly,

"May be you're wanting to get over?—anybody sick? Ye seem mighty anxious?"

"I've got a child that's very dangerous," said Eliza. "I never heard of it till last night, and I've walked quite a piece to-day, in hopes to get to the ferry."

"Well, now, that's onlucky," said the woman, whose motherly sympathies were much aroused; "I'm re'lly consarned for ye. Solomon!" she called, from the window, towards a small back building. A man, in leather apron and very dirty hands, appeared at the door.

"I say, Sol," said the woman, "is that ar man going to tote them bar'ls over to-night?"

"He said he should try, if 't was any way prudent," said the man.

"There's a man a piece down here, that's going over with some truck this evening, if he durs' to; he'll be in here to supper to-night, so you'd better set down and wait. That's a sweet little fellow," added the woman, offering him a cake.

But the child, wholly exhausted, cried with weariness.

"Poor fellow! he isn't used to walking, and I've hurried him on so," said Eliza.

"Well, take him into this room," said the woman, opening into a small bed-room, where stood a comfortable bed. Eliza laid the weary boy upon it, and held his hands in hers till he was fast asleep. For her there was no rest. As a fire in her bones, the thought of the pursuer urged her on; and she gazed with longing eyes on the sullen, surging waters that lay between her and liberty.

Here we must take our leave of her for the present, to follow the course of her pursuers.

Though Mrs. Shelby had promised that the dinner should be hurried on table, yet it was soon seen, as the thing has often been seen before, that it required more than one to make a bargain. So, although the order was fairly given out in Haley's hearing, and carried to Aunt Chloe by at least half a dozen juvenile messengers, that dignitary only gave certain very gruff snorts, and tosses of her head, and went on with every operation in an unusually leisurely and circumstantial manner.

For some singular reason, an impression seemed to reign among the servants generally that Missis would not be particularly disobliged by delay; and it was wonderful what a number of counter accidents occurred constantly, to retard the course of things. One luckless wight contrived to upset the gravy; and then gravy had to be got up *de novo*, with due care and formality, Aunt Chloe watching and stirring with dogged precision, answering shortly, to all suggestions of haste, that she "warn't a going to have raw gravy on the table, to help nobody's catchings." One tumbled down with the water, and had to go to the spring for more; and another precipitated the butter into the path of events; and there was from time to time giggling news brought into the kitchen that "Mas'r Haley was mighty oneasy, and that he couldn't sit in his cheer no ways, but was a walkin' and stalkin' to the winders and through the porch."

"Sarves him right!" said Aunt Chloe, indignantly. He'll get wus nor oneasy, one of these days, if he don't mend his ways. *His* master'll be sending for him, and then see how he'll look!"

"He'll go to torment, and no mistake," said little Jake.

"He desarves it!" said Aunt Chloe, grimly; "he's broke a many, many, many hearts,—I tell ye all!" she said, stopping, with a fork uplifted in her hands; "it's like what Mas'r George reads in Ravelations,—souls a callin' under the altar! and a callin' on the Lord for vengeance on sich!—and by and by the Lord he'll hear 'em—so he will!"

Aunt Chloe, who was much revered in the kitchen, was listened to with open mouth; and, the dinner being now fairly sent in, the whole kitchen was at leisure to gossip with her, and to listen to her remarks.

"Sich'll be burnt up forever, and no mistake; won't ther?" said Andy.

"I'd be glad to see it, I'll be boun'," said little Jake.

"Chil'en!" said a voice, that made them all start. It was Uncle Tom, who had come in, and stood listening to the conversation at the door.

"Chil'en!" he said, "I'm afeard you don't know what ye're sayin'. Forever is a *dre'ful* word, chil'en; it's awful to think on 't. You oughtenter wish that ar to any human crittur."

"We wouldn't to anybody but the soul-drivers," said Andy; "nobody can help wishing it to them, they's so awful wicked."

"Don't natur herself kinder cry out on 'em?" said Aunt Chloe. "Don't dey tear der suckin' baby right off his mother's breast, and sell him, and der little children as is crying and holding on by her clothes,—don't dey pull 'em off and sells 'em? Don't dey tear wife and husband apart?" said Aunt Chloe, beginning to cry, "when it's jest takin' the very life on 'em?—and all the while does they feel one bit, don't dey drink and smoke, and take it oncommon easy? Lor, if the devil don't get them, what's he good for?" And Aunt Chloe covered her face with her checked apron, and began to sob in good earnest.

"Pray for them that spitefully use you, the good book says," says Tom.

"Pray for 'em!" said Aunt Chloe; "Lor, it's too tough! I can't pray for 'em."

"It's natur, Chloe, and natur's strong," said Tom, "but the Lord's grace is stronger; besides, you oughter think what an awful state a poor crittur's soul's in that'll do them ar things,—you oughter thank God that you an't *like* him, Chloe. I'm sure I'd rather be sold, ten thousand times over, than to have all that ar poor crittur's got to answer for."

"So 'd I, a heap," said Jake. "Lor, *shouldn't* we cotch it, Andy?"

Andy shrugged his shoulders, and gave an acquiescent whistle.

"I'm glad Mas'r didn't go off this morning, as he looked to," said Tom; "that ar hurt me more than sellin', it did. Mebbe it might have been natural for him, but 't would have come desp't hard on me, as has known him from a baby; but I've seen Mas'r, and I begin ter feel sort o' reconciled to the Lord's will now. Mas'r couldn't help hisself; he did right, but I'm feared things will be kinder goin' to rack, when I'm gone Mas'r can't be spected to be a pryin' round everywhar, as I've done, a keepin' up all the ends. The boys all means well, but they 's powerful car'less. That ar troubles me."

The bell here rang, and Tom was summoned to the parlor.

"Tom," said his master, kindly, "I want you to notice that I give this gentleman bonds to forfeit a thousand dollars if you are not on the spot when he wants you; he's going to-day to look after his other business, and you can have the day to yourself. Go anywhere you like, boy."

"Thank you, Mas'r," said Tom.

"And mind yourself," said the trader, "and don't come it over your master with any o' yer nigger tricks; for I'll take every cent out of him, if you an't thar. If he'd hear to me, he wouldn't trust any on ye—slippery as eels!"

"Mas'r," said Tom,—and he stood very straight,—"I was jist eight years old when ole Missis put you into my arms, and you wasn't a year old. 'Thar,' says she, 'Tom, that's to be *your* young Mas'r; take good care on him,' says she. And now I jist ask you, Mas'r, have I ever broke word to you, or gone contrary to you, 'specially since I was a Christian?"

Mr. Shelby was fairly overcome, and the tears rose to his eyes.

"My good boy," said he, "the Lord knows you say but the truth; and if I was able to help it, all the world shouldn't buy you."

"And sure as I am a Christian woman," said Mrs. Shelby, "you shall be redeemed as soon as I can any way bring together means. Sir," she said to Haley, "take good account of who you sell him to, and let me know."

"Lor, yes, for that matter," said the trader, "I may bring him up in a year, not much the wuss for wear, and trade him back."

"I'll trade with you then, and make it for your advantage," said Mrs. Shelby.

"Of course," said the trader, "all's equal with me; li'ves trade 'em up as down, so I does a good business. All I want is a livin', you know, ma'am; that's all any on us wants, I, s'pose."

Mr. and Mrs. Shelby both felt annoyed and degraded by the familiar impudence of the trader, and yet both saw the absolute necessity of putting a constraint on their feelings. The more hopelessly sordid and insensible he appeared, the greater became Mrs. Shelby's dread of his succeeding in recapturing Eliza and her child, and of course the greater her motive for detaining him by every female artifice. She therefore graciously smiled, assented, chatted familiarly, and did all she could to make time pass imperceptibly.

At two o'clock Sam and Andy brought the horses up to the posts, apparently greatly refreshed and invigorated by the scamper of the morning.

Sam was there new oiled from dinner, with an abundance of zealous and ready officiousness. As Haley approached, he was boasting, in flourishing style, to Andy, of the evident and eminent success of the operation, now that he had "farly come to it."

"Your master, I s'pose, don't keep no dogs," said Haley, thoughtfully, as he prepared to mount.

"Heaps on 'em," said Sam, triumphantly; "thar's Bruno—he's a roarer! and, besides that, 'bout every nigger of us keeps a pup of some natur or uther."

"Poh!" said Haley—and he said something else, too, with regard to the said dogs, at which Sam muttered:

"I don't see no use cussin' on 'em, no way."

"But your master don't keep no dogs (I pretty much know he don't) for trackin' out niggers."

Sam knew exactly what he meant, but he kept on a look of earnest and desperate simplicity.

"Our dogs all smells round considable sharp. I spect they's the kind, though they han't never had no practice. They's *far* dogs, though, at most anything, if you'd get 'em started. Here, Bruno," he called, whistling to the lumbering Newfoundland, who came pitching tumultuously toward them.

"You go hang!" said Haley, getting up. "Come, tumble up now."

Sam tumbled up accordingly, dexterously contriving to tickle Andy as he did so, which occasioned Andy to split out into a laugh, greatly to Haley's indignation, who made a cut at him with his riding-whip.

"I's 'stonished at yer, Andy," said Sam, with awful gravity. "This yer's a seris bisness, Andy. Yer mustn't be a makin' game. This yer an't no way to help Mas'r."

"I shall take the straight road to the river," said Haley, decidedly, after they had come to the boundaries of the estate. "I know the way of all of 'em,—they makes tracks for the underground."

"Sartin," said Sam, "dat's de idee. Mas'r Haley hits de thing right in de middle. Now, der's two roads to de river,—de dirt road and der pike,—which Mas'r mean to take?"

Andy looked up innocently at Sam, surprised at hearing this new geographical fact, but instantly confirmed what he said, by a vehement reiteration.

"Cause," said Sam, "I'd rather be 'clined to 'magine that Lizy 'd take de dirt road, bein' it's the least travelled."

Haley, notwithstanding that he was a very old bird, and naturally inclined to be suspicious of chaff, was rather brought up by this view of the case.

"If yer warn't both on yer such cussed liars, now!" he said, contemplatively as he pondered a moment.

The pensive, reflective tone in which this was spoken appeared to amuse Andy prodigiously, and he drew a little behind, and shook so as apparently to run a great risk of falling off his horse, while Sam's face was immovably composed into the most doleful gravity.

"Course," said Sam, "Mas'r can do as he'd ruther; go de straight road, if Mas'r thinks best,—it's all one to us. Now, when I study 'pon it, I think de straight road de best, *deridedly*."

"She would naturally go a lonesome way," said Haley, thinking aloud, and not minding Sam's remark.

"Dar an't no sayin'," said Sam; "gals is pecular; they never does nothin' ye thinks they will; mose gen'lly the contrary. Gals is nat'lly made contrary; and so, if you thinks they've gone one road, it is sartin you'd better go t' other, and then you'll be sure to find 'em. Now, my private 'pinion is, Lizy took der dirt road; so I think we'd better take de straight one."

This profound generic view of the female sex did not seem to dispose Haley particularly to the straight road, and he announced decidedly that he should go the other, and asked Sam when they should come to it.

"A little piece ahead," said Sam, giving a wink to Andy with the eye which was on Andy's side of the head; and he added, gravely, "but I've studded on de matter, and I'm quite clar we ought not to go dat ar way. I nebber been over it no way. It's despit lonesome, and we might lose our way,—whar we'd come to, de Lord only knows."

"Nevertheless," said Haley, "I shall go that way."

"Now I think on 't, I think I hearn 'em tell that dat ar road was all fenced up and down by der creek, and thar, an't it, Andy?"

Andy wasn't certain; he'd only "hearn tell" about that road, but never been over it. In short, he was strictly noncommittal.

Haley, accustomed to strike the balance of probabilities between lies of greater or lesser magnitude, thought that it lay in favor of the dirt road aforesaid. The mention of the thing he thought he perceived was involuntary on Sam's part at first, and his confused attempts to dissuade him he set down to a desperate lying on second thoughts, as being unwilling to implicate Liza.

When, therefore, Sam indicated the road, Haley plunged briskly into it, followed by Sam and Andy.

Now, the road, in fact, was an old one, that had formerly been a thoroughfare to the river, but abandoned for many years after the laying of the new pike. It was open for about an hour's ride, and after that it was cut across by various farms and fences. Sam knew this fact perfectly well,—indeed, the road had been so long closed up, that Andy had never heard of it. He therefore rode along with an air of dutiful submission, only groaning and vociferating occasionally that 't was "desp't rough, and bad for Jerry's foot."

"Now, I jest give yer warning," said Haley, "I know yer; yer won't get me to turn off this road, with all yer fussin'—so you shet up!"

"Mas'r will go his own way!" said Sam, with rueful submission, at the same time winking most portentously to Andy, whose delight was now very near the explosive point.

Sam was in wonderful spirits,—professed to keep a very brisk look-out,—at one time exclaiming that he saw "a gal's bonnet" on the top of some distant eminence, or calling to Andy "if that thar wasn't 'Lizy' down in the hollow;" always making these exclamations in some rough or craggy part of the road, where the sudden quickening of speed was a special inconvenience to all parties concerned, and thus keeping Haley in a state of constant commotion.

After riding about an hour in this way, the whole party made a precipitate and tumultuous descent into a barn-yard belonging to a large farming establishment. Not a soul was in sight, all the hands being employed in the fields; but, as the barn stood conspicuously and plainly square across the road, it was evident that their journey in that direction had reached a decided finale.

"Wan't dat ar what I telled Mas'r?" said Sam, with an air of injured innocence. "How does strange gentleman spect to know more about a country dan de natives born and raised?"

"You rascal!" said Haley, "you knew all about this."

"Didn't I tell yer I *know'd*, and yer wouldn't believe me? I telled Mas'r 't was all shet up, and fenced up, and I didn't spect we could get through,—Andy heard me."

It was all too true to be disputed, and the unlucky man had to pocket his wrath with the best grace he was able, and all three faced to the right about, and took up their line of march for the highway.

In consequence of all the various delays, it was about three-quarters of an hour after Eliza had laid her child to sleep in the village tavern that the party came riding into the same place. Eliza was standing by the window, looking out in another direction, when Sam's quick eye caught a glimpse of her. Haley and Andy were two yards behind. At this crisis, Sam contrived to have his hat blown off, and uttered a loud and characteristic ejaculation, which startled her at once; she drew suddenly back; the whole train swept by the window, round to the front door.

A thousand lives seemed to be concentrated in that one moment to Eliza. Her room opened by a side door to the river. She caught her child, and sprang down the steps towards it. The trader caught a full glimpse of her just as she was disappearing down the bank; and throwing himself from his horse, and calling loudly on Sam and Andy, he was after her like a hound after a deer. In that dizzy moment her feet to her scarce seemed to touch the ground, and a moment brought her to the water's edge. Right on behind they came; and, nerved with strength such as God gives only to the desperate, with one wild cry and flying leap, she vaulted sheer over the turbid current by the shore, on to the raft of ice beyond. It was a desperate leap—impossible to anything but madness and despair; and Haley, Sam, and Andy, instinctively cried out, and lifted up their hands, as she did it.

The huge green fragment of ice on which she alighted pitched and creaked as her weight came on it, but she staid there not a moment. With wild cries and desperate energy she leaped to another and still another cake;—stumbling—leaping—slipping—springing upwards again! Her shoes are gone—her stockings cut from her feet—while blood marked every step; but she saw nothing, felt nothing, till dimly, as in a dream, she saw the Ohio side, and a man helping her up the bank.

"Yer a brave gal, now, whoever ye ar!" said the man, with an oath.

Eliza recognized the voice and face for a man who owned a farm not far from her old home.

"O, Mr. Symmes!—save me—do save me—do hide me!" said Eliza.

"Why, what's this?" said the man. "Why, if 'tan't Shelby's gal!"

"My child!—this boy!—he'd sold him! There is his Mas'r," said she, pointing to the Kentucky shore. "O, Mr. Symmes, you've got a little boy!"

"So I have," said the man, as he roughly, but kindly, drew her up the steep bank. "Besides, you're a right brave gal. I like grit, wherever I see it."

When they had gained the top of the bank, the man paused.

"I'd be glad to do something for ye," said he; "but then there's nowhar I could take ye. The best I can do is to tell ye to go *thar,*" said he, pointing to a large white house which stood by itself, off the main street of the village. "Go thar; they're kind folks. Thar's no kind o' danger but they'll help you,—they're up to all that sort o' thing."

"The Lord bless you!" said Eliza, earnestly.

"No 'casion, no 'casion in the world," said the man. "What I've done's of no 'count."

"And, oh, surely, sir, you won't tell any one!"

"Go to thunder, gal! What do you take a feller for? In course not," said the man. "Come, now, go along like a likely, sensible gal, as you are. You've arnt your liberty, and you shall have it, for all me."

The woman folded her child to her bosom, and walked firmly and swiftly away. The man stood and looked after her.

"Shelby, now, mebbe won't think this yer the most neighborly thing in the world; but what's a feller to do? If he catches one of my gals in the same fix, he's welcome to pay back. Somehow I never could see no kind o' critter a strivin' and pantin', and trying to clar theirselves, with the dogs arter 'em and go agin 'em. Besides, I don't see no kind of 'casion for me to be hunter and catcher for other folks, neither."

So spoke this poor, heathenish Kentuckian, who had not been instructed in his constitutional relations, and consequently was betrayed into acting in a sort of Christianized manner, which, if he had been better situated and more enlightened, he would not have been left to do.

Haley had stood a perfectly amazed spectator of the scene, till Eliza had disappeared up the bank, when he turned a blank, inquiring look on Sam and Andy.

"That ar was a tolable fair stroke of business," said Sam.

"The gal 's got seven devils in her, I believe!" said Haley. "How like a wildcat she jumped!"

"Wal, now," said Sam, scratching his head, "I hope Mas'r'll 'scuse us trying dat ar road. Don't think I feel spry enough for dat ar, no way!" and Sam gave a hoarse chuckle.

"*You* laugh!" said the trader, with a growl.

"Lord bless you, Mas'r, I couldn't help it now," said Sam, giving way to the long pent-up delight of his soul. "She looked so curi's, a leapin' and springin'—ice a crackin'—and only to hear her,—plump! ker chunk! ker splash! Spring! Lord! how she goes it!" and Sam and Andy laughed till the tears rolled down their cheeks.

"I'll make ye laugh t' other side yer mouths!" said the trader, laying about their heads with his riding-whip.

Both ducked, and ran shouting up the bank, and were on their horses before he was up.

"Good-evening, Mas'r!" said Sam, with much gravity. "I berry much spect Missis be anxious 'bout Jerry. Mas'r Haley won't want us no longer. Missis wouldn't hear of our ridin' the critters over Lizy's bridge tonight;" and, with a facetious poke into Andy's ribs, he started off, followed by the latter, at full speed,—their shouts of laughter coming faintly on the wind.

Chapter 8: Eliza's Escape

Eliza made her desperate retreat across the river just in the dusk of twilight. The gray mist of evening, rising slowly from the river, enveloped her as she disappeared up the bank, and the swollen current and floundering masses of ice presented a hopeless barrier between her and her pursuer. Haley therefore slowly and discontentedly returned to the little tavern, to ponder further what was to be done. The woman opened to him the door of a little parlor, covered with a rag carpet, where stood a table with a very shining black oil-cloth, sundry lank, high-backed wood chairs, with some plaster images in resplendent colors on the mantel-shelf, above a very dimly-smoking grate; a long hard-wood settle extended its uneasy length by the chimney, and here Haley sat him down to meditate on the instability of human hopes and happiness in general.

"What did I want with the little cuss, now," he said to himself, "that I should have got myself treed like a coon, as I am, this yer way?" and Haley relieved himself by repeating over a not very select litany of imprecations on himself, which, though there was the best possible reason to consider them as true, we shall, as a matter of taste, omit.

He was startled by the loud and dissonant voice of a man who was apparently dismounting at the door. He hurried to the window.

"By the land! if this yer an't the nearest, now, to what I've heard folks call Providence," said Haley. "I do b'lieve that ar's Tom Loker."

Haley hastened out. Standing by the bar, in the corner of the room, was a brawny, muscular man, full six feet in height, and broad in proportion. He was dressed in a coat of buffalo-skin, made with the hair outward, which gave him a shaggy and fierce appearance, perfectly in keeping with the whole air of his physiognomy. In the head and face every organ and lineament expressive of brutal and unhesitating violence was in a state of the highest possible development. Indeed, could our readers fancy a bull-dog come unto man's estate, and walking about in a hat and coat, they would have no unapt idea of the general style and effect of his physique. He was accompanied by a travelling companion, in many respects an exact contrast to himself. He was short and slender, lithe and catlike in his motions, and had a peering, mousing expression about his keen black eyes, with which every feature of his face seemed sharpened into sympathy; his thin, long nose, ran out as if it was eager to bore into the nature of things in general; his sleek, thin, black hair was stuck eagerly forward, and all his motions and evolutions expressed a dry, cautious acuteness. The great man poured out a big tumbler half full of raw spirits, and gulped it down without a word. The little man stood tip-toe, and putting his head first to one side and then the other, and snuffing considerately in the directions of the various bottles, ordered at last a mint julep, in a thin and quivering voice, and with an air of great circumspection. When poured out, he took it and looked at it with a sharp, complacent air, like a man who thinks he has done about the right thing, and hit the nail on the head, and proceeded to dispose of it in short and well-advised sips.

"Wal, now, who'd a thought this yer luck 'ad come to me? Why, Loker, how are ye?" said Haley, coming forward, and extending his hand to the big man.

"The devil!" was the civil reply. "What brought you here, Haley?"

The mousing man, who bore the name of Marks, instantly stopped his sipping, and, poking his head forward, looked shrewdly on the new acquaintance, as a cat sometimes looks at a moving dry leaf, or some other possible object of pursuit.

"I say, Tom, this yer's the luckiest thing in the world. I'm in a devil of a hobble, and you must help me out."

"Ugh? aw! like enough!" grunted his complacent acquaintance. "A body may be pretty sure of that, when *you're* glad to see 'em; something to be made off of 'em. What's the blow now?"

"You've got a friend here?" said Haley, looking doubtfully at Marks; "partner, perhaps?"

"Yes, I have. Here, Marks! here's that ar feller that I was in with in Natchez."

"Shall be pleased with his acquaintance," said Marks, thrusting out a long, thin hand, like a raven's claw. "Mr. Haley, I believe?"

"The same, sir," said Haley. "And now, gentlemen, seein' as we've met so happily, I think I'll stand up to a small matter of a treat in this here parlor. So, now, old coon," said he to the man at the bar, "get us hot water, and sugar, and cigars, and plenty of the *real stuff* and we'll have a blow-out."

Behold, then, the candles lighted, the fire stimulated to the burning point in the grate, and our three worthies seated round a table, well spread with all the accessories to good fellowship enumerated before.

Haley began a pathetic recital of his peculiar troubles. Loker shut up his mouth, and listened to him with gruff and surly attention. Marks, who was anxiously and with much fidgeting compounding a tumbler of punch to his own peculiar taste, occasionally looked up from his employment, and, poking his sharp nose and chin almost into Haley's face, gave the most earnest heed to the whole narrative. The conclusion of it appeared to amuse him extremely, for he shook his shoulders and sides in silence, and perked up his thin lips with an air of great internal enjoyment.

"So, then, ye'r fairly sewed up, an't ye?" he said; "he! he! he! It's neatly done, too."

"This yer young-un business makes lots of trouble in the trade," said Haley, dolefully.

"If we could get a breed of gals that didn't care, now, for their young uns," said Marks; "tell ye, I think 't would be 'bout the greatest mod'rn improvement I knows on,"—and Marks patronized his joke by a quiet introductory sniggle.

"Jes so," said Haley; "I never couldn't see into it; young uns is heaps of trouble to 'em; one would think, now, they'd be glad to get clar on 'em; but they arn't. And the more trouble a young un is, and the more good for nothing, as a gen'l thing, the tighter they sticks to 'em."

"Wal, Mr. Haley," said Marks, " 'est pass the hot water. Yes, sir, you say 'est what I feel and all'us have. Now, I bought a gal once, when I was in the trade,—a tight, likely wench she was, too, and quite considerable smart,—and she had a young un that was mis'able sickly; it had a crooked back, or something or other; and I jest gin 't away to a man that thought he'd take his chance raising on 't, being it didn't cost nothin';—never thought, yer know, of the gal's takin' on about it,—but, Lord, yer oughter seen how she went on. Why, re'lly, she did seem to me to valley the child more 'cause *'t was sickly* and cross, and plagued her; and she warn't making b'lieve, neither,—cried about it, she did, and lopped round, as if she'd lost every friend she had. It re'lly was droll to think on 't. Lord, there ain't no end to women's notions."

"Wal, jest so with me," said Haley. "Last summer, down on Red river, I got a gal traded off on me, with a likely lookin' child enough, and his eyes looked as bright as yourn; but, come to look, I found him stone blind. Fact—he was stone blind. Wal, ye see, I thought there warn't no harm in my jest passing him along, and not sayin' nothin'; and I'd got him nicely swapped off for a keg o' whiskey; but come to get him away from the gal, she was jest like a tiger. So 't was before we started, and I hadn't got my gang chained up; so what should she do but ups on a cotton-bale, like a cat, ketches a knife from one of the deck hands, and, I tell ye, she made all fly for a minit, till she saw 'twan't no use; and she jest turns round, and pitches head first, young un and all, into the river,—went down plump, and never ris."

"Bah!" said Tom Loker, who had listened to these stories with ill-repressed disgust,—"shif'less, both on ye! *my* gals don't cut up no such shines, I tell ye!"

"Indeed! how do you help it?" said Marks, briskly.

"Help it? why, I buys a gal, and if she's got a young un to be sold, I jest walks up and puts my fist to her face, and says, 'Look here, now, if you give me one word out of your head, I'll smash yer face in. I won't hear one word—not the beginning of a word.' I says to 'em, 'This yer young un's mine, and not yourn, and you've no kind o' business with it. I'm going to sell it, first chance; mind, you don't cut up none o' yer shines about it, or I'll make ye wish ye'd never been born.' I tell ye, they sees it an't no play, when I gets hold. I makes 'em as whist as fishes; and if one on 'em begins and gives a yelp, why,—" and Mr. Loker brought down his fist with a thump that fully explained the hiatus.

"That ar's what ye may call *emphasis*," said Marks, poking Haley in the side, and going into another small giggle. "An't Tom peculiar? he! he! I say, Tom, I s'pect you make 'em *understand*, for all niggers' heads is woolly. They don't never have no doubt o' your meaning, Tom. If you an't the devil, Tom, you 's his twin brother, I'll say that for ye!"

Tom received the compliment with becoming modesty, and began to look as affable as was consistent, as John Bunyan says, "with his doggish nature."

Haley, who had been imbibing very freely of the staple of the evening, began to feel a sensible elevation and enlargement of his moral faculties,—a phenomenon not unusual with gentlemen of a serious and reflective turn, under similar circumstances.

"Wal, now, Tom," he said, "ye re'lly is too bad, as I al'ays have told ye; ye know, Tom, you and I used to talk over these yer matters down in Natchez, and I used to prove to ye that we made full as much, and was as well off for this yer world, by treatin' on 'em well, besides keepin' a better chance for comin' in the kingdom at last, when wust comes to wust, and thar an't nothing else left to get, ye know."

"Boh!" said Tom, "*don't* I know?—don't make me too sick with any yer stuff,—my stomach is a leetle riled now;" and Tom drank half a glass of raw brandy.

"I say," said Haley, and leaning back in his chair and gesturing impressively, "I'll say this now, I al'ays meant to drive my trade so as to make money on 't *fust and foremost*, as much as any man; but, then, trade an't everything, and money an't everything, 'cause we 's all got souls. I don't care, now, who hears me say it,—and I think a cussed sight on it,—so I may as well come out with it. I b'lieve in religion, and one of these days, when I've got matters tight and snug, I calculates to tend to my soul and them ar matters; and so what's the use of doin' any more wickedness than's re'lly necessary?—it don't seem to me it's 't all prudent."

"Tend to yer soul!" repeated Tom, contemptuously; "take a bright look-out to find a soul in you,—save yourself any care on that score. If the devil sifts you through a hair sieve, he won't find one."

"Why, Tom, you're cross," said Haley; "why can't ye take it pleasant, now, when a feller's talking for your good?"

"Stop that ar jaw o' yourn, there," said Tom, gruffly. "I can stand most any talk o' yourn but your pious talk,—that kills me right up. After all, what's the odds between me and you? 'Tan't that you care one bit more, or have a bit more feelin'—it's clean, sheer, dog meanness, wanting to cheat the devil and save your own skin; don't I see through it? And your 'gettin' religion,' as you call it, arter all, is too p'isin mean for any crittur;—run up a bill with the devil all your life, and then sneak out when pay time comes! Boh!"

"Come, come, gentlemen, I say; this isn't business," said Marks. "There's different ways, you know, of looking at all subjects. Mr. Haley is a very nice man, no doubt, and has his own conscience; and, Tom, you have your ways, and very good ones, too, Tom; but quarrelling, you know, won't answer no kind of purpose. Let's go to business. Now, Mr. Haley, what is it?—you want us to undertake to catch this yer gal?"

"The gal's no matter of mine,—she's Shelby's; it's only the boy. I was a fool for buying the monkey!"

"You're generally a fool!" said Tom, gruffly.

"Come, now, Loker, none of your huffs," said Marks, licking his lips; "you see, Mr. Haley's a puttin' us in a way of a good job, I reckon; just hold still—these yer arrangements is my forte. This yer gal, Mr. Haley, how is she? what is she?"

"Wal! white and handsome—well brought up. I'd a gin Shelby eight hundred or a thousand, and then made well on her."

"White and handsome—well brought up!" said Marks, his sharp eyes, nose and mouth, all alive with enterprise. "Look here, now, Loker, a beautiful opening. We'll do a business here on our own account;—we does the catchin'; the boy, of course, goes to Mr. Haley,—we takes the gal to Orleans to speculate on. An't it beautiful?"

Tom, whose great heavy mouth had stood ajar during this communication, now suddenly snapped it together, as a big dog closes on a piece of meat, and seemed to be digesting the idea at his leisure.

"Ye see," said Marks to Haley, stirring his punch as he did so, "ye see, we has justices convenient at all p'ints along shore, that does up any little jobs in our line quite reasonable. Tom, he does the knockin' down and that ar; and I come in all dressed up—shining boots—everything first chop, when the swearin' 's to be done. You oughter see, now," said Marks, in a glow of professional pride, "how I can tone it off. One day, I'm Mr. Twickem, from New Orleans; 'nother day, I'm just come from my plantation on Pearl river, where I works seven hundred niggers; then, again, I come out a distant relation of Henry Clay, or some old cock in Kentuck. Talents is different, you know. Now, Tom's roarer when there's any thumping or fighting to be done; but at lying he an't good, Tom an't,—ye see it don't come natural to him; but, Lord, if thar's a feller in the country that can swear to anything and everything, and put in all the circumstances and flourishes with a long face, and carry 't through better 'n I can, why, I'd like to see him, that's all! I b'lieve my heart, I could get along and snake through, even if justices were more particular than they is. Sometimes I rather wish they was more particular; 't would be a heap more relishin' if they was,—more fun, yer know."

Tom Loker, who, as we have made it appear, was a man of slow thoughts and movements, here interrupted Marks by bringing his heavy fist down on the table, so as to make all ring again, *"It'll do!"* he said.

"Lord bless ye, Tom, ye needn't break all the glasses!" said Marks; "save your fist for time o' need."

"But, gentlemen, an't I to come in for a share of the profits?" said Haley.

"An't it enough we catch the boy for ye?" said Loker. "What do ye want?"

"Wal," said Haley, "if I gives you the job, it's worth something,—say ten per cent. on the profits, expenses paid."

"Now," said Loker, with a tremendous oath, and striking the table with his heavy fist, "don't I know *you*, Dan Haley? Don't you think to come it over me! Suppose Marks and I have taken up the catchin' trade, jest to 'commodate gentlemen like you, and get nothin' for ourselves?—Not by a long chalk! we'll have the gal out and out, and you keep quiet, or, ye see, we'll have both,—what's to hinder? Han't you show'd us the game? It's as free to us as you, I hope. If you or Shelby wants to chase us, look where the partridges was last year; if you find them or us, you're quite welcome."

"O, wal, certainly, jest let it go at that," said Haley, alarmed; "you catch the boy for the job;—you allers did trade *far* with me, Tom, and was up to yer word."

"Ye know that," said Tom; "I don't pretend none of your snivelling ways, but I won't lie in my 'counts with the devil himself. What I ses I'll do, I will do,—you know *that*, Dan Haley."

"Jes so, jes so,—I said so, Tom," said Haley; "and if you'd only promise to have the boy for me in a week, at any point you'll name, that's all I want."

"But it an't all I want, by a long jump," said Tom. "Ye don't think I did business with you, down in Natchez, for nothing, Haley; I've learned to hold an eel, when I catch him. You've got to fork over fifty dollars, flat down, or this child don't start a peg. I know yer."

"Why, when you have a job in hand that may bring a clean profit of somewhere about a thousand or sixteen hundred, why, Tom, you're onreasonable," said Haley.

"Yes, and hasn't we business booked for five weeks to come,—all we can do? And suppose we leaves all, and goes to bushwhacking round arter yer young uns, and finally doesn't catch the gal,—and gals allers is the devil *to* catch,—what's then? would you pay us a cent—would you? I think I see you a doin' it—ugh! No, no; flap down your fifty. If we get the job, and it pays, I'll hand it back; if we don't, it's for our trouble,—that's *far*, an't it, Marks?"

"Certainly, certainly," said Marks, with a conciliatory tone; "it's only a retaining fee, you see,—he! he! he!—we lawyers, you know. Wal, we must all keep good-natured,—keep easy, yer know. Tom'll have the boy for yer, anywhere ye'll name; won't ye, Tom?"

"If I find the young un, I'll bring him on to Cincinnati, and leave him at Granny Belcher's, on the landing," said Loker.

Marks had got from his pocket a greasy pocket-book, and taking a long paper from thence, he sat down, and fixing his keen black eyes on it, began mumbling over its contents: "Barnes—Shelby County—boy Jim, three hundred dollars for him, dead or alive.

"Edwards—Dick and Lucy—man and wife, six hundred dollars; wench Polly and two children—six hundred for her or her head.

"I'm jest a runnin' over our business, to see if we can take up this yer handily. Loker," he said, after a pause, "we must set Adams and Springer on the track of these yer; they've been booked some time."

"They'll charge too much," said Tom.

"I'll manage that ar; they 's young in the business, and must spect to work cheap," said Marks, as he continued to read. "Ther's three on 'em easy cases, 'cause all you've got to do is to shoot 'em, or swear they is shot; they couldn't, of course, charge much for that. Them other cases," he said, folding the paper, "will bear puttin' off a spell. So now let's come to the particulars. Now, Mr. Haley, you saw this yer gal when she landed?"

"To be sure,—plain as I see you."

"And a man helpin' on her up the bank?" said Loker.

"To be sure, I did."

"Most likely," said Marks, "she's took in somewhere; but where, 's a question. Tom, what do you say?"

"We must cross the river to-night, no mistake," said Tom.

"But there's no boat about," said Marks. "The ice is running awfully, Tom; an't it dangerous?"

"Don'no nothing 'bout that,—only it's got to be done," said Tom, decidedly.

"Dear me," said Marks, fidgeting, "it'll be—I say," he said, walking to the window, "it's dark as a wolf's mouth, and, Tom—"

"The long and short is, you're scared, Marks; but I can't help that,—you've got to go. Suppose you want to lie by a day or two, till the gal 's been carried on the underground line up to Sandusky or so, before you start."

"O, no; I an't a grain afraid," said Marks, "only—"

"Only what?" said Tom.

"Well, about the boat. Yer see there an't any boat."

"I heard the woman say there was one coming along this evening, and that a man was going to cross over in it. Neck or nothing, we must go with him," said Tom.

"I s'pose you've got good dogs," said Haley.

"First rate," said Marks. "But what's the use? you han't got nothin' o' hers to smell on."

"Yes, I have," said Haley, triumphantly. "Here's her shawl she left on the bed in her hurry; she left her bonnet, too."

"That ar's lucky," said Loker; "fork over."

"Though the dogs might damage the gal, if they come on her unawars," said Haley.

"That ar's a consideration," said Marks. "Our dogs tore a feller half to pieces, once, down in Mobile, 'fore we could get 'em off."

"Well, ye see, for this sort that's to be sold for their looks, that ar won't answer, ye see," said Haley.

"I do see," said Marks. "Besides, if she's got took in, 'tan't no go, neither. Dogs is no 'count in these yer up states where these critters gets carried; of course, ye can't get on their track. They only does down in plantations, where niggers, when they runs, has to do their own running, and don't get no help."

"Well," said Loker, who had just stepped out to the bar to make some inquiries, "they say the man's come with the boat; so, Marks—"

That worthy cast a rueful look at the comfortable quarters he was leaving, but slowly rose to obey. After exchanging a few words of further arrangement, Haley, with visible reluctance, handed over the fifty dollars to Tom, and the worthy trio separated for the night.

If any of our refined and Christian readers object to the society into which this scene introduces them, let us beg them to begin and conquer their prejudices in time. The catching business, we beg to remind them, is rising to the dignity of a lawful and patriotic profession. If all the broad land between the Mississippi and the Pacific becomes one great market for bodies and souls, and human property retains the locomotive tendencies of this nineteenth century, the trader and catcher may yet be among our aristocracy.

While this scene was going on at the tavern, Sam and Andy, in a state of high felicitation, pursued their way home.

Sam was in the highest possible feather, and expressed his exultation by all sorts of supernatural howls and ejaculations, by divers odd motions and contortions of his whole system. Sometimes he would sit backward, with his face to the horse's tail and sides, and then, with a whoop and a somerset, come right side up in his place again, and, drawing on a grave face, begin to lecture Andy in high-sounding tones for laughing and playing the fool. Anon, slapping his sides with his arms, he would burst forth in peals of laughter, that made the old woods ring as they passed. With all these evolutions, he contrived to keep the horses up to the top of their speed, until, between ten and eleven, their heels resounded on the gravel at the end of the balcony. Mrs. Shelby flew to the railings.

"Is that you, Sam? Where are they?"

"Mas'r Haley 's a-restin' at the tavern; he's drefful fatigued, Missis."

"And Eliza, Sam?"

"Wal, she's clar 'cross Jordan. As a body may say, in the land o' Canaan."

"Why, Sam, what *do* you mean?" said Mrs. Shelby, breathless, and almost faint, as the possible meaning of these words came over her.

"Wal, Missis, de Lord he persarves his own. Lizy's done gone over the river into 'Hio, as 'markably as if de Lord took her over in a charrit of fire and two hosses."

Sam's vein of piety was always uncommonly fervent in his mistress' presence; and he made great capital of scriptural figures and images.

"Come up here, Sam," said Mr. Shelby, who had followed on to the verandah, "and tell your mistress what she wants. Come, come, Emily," said he, passing his arm round her, "you are cold and all in a shiver; you allow yourself to feel too much."

"Feel too much! Am not I a woman,—a mother? Are we not both responsible to God for this poor girl? My God! lay not this sin to our charge."

"What sin, Emily? You see yourself that we have only done what we were obliged to."

"There's an awful feeling of guilt about it, though," said Mrs. Shelby. "I can't reason it away."

"Here, Andy, you nigger, be alive!" called Sam, under the verandah; "take these yer hosses to der barn; don't ye hear Mas'r a callin'?" and Sam soon appeared, palm-leaf in hand, at the parlor door.

"Now, Sam, tell us distinctly how the matter was," said Mr. Shelby. "Where is Eliza, if you know?"

"Wal, Mas'r, I saw her, with my own eyes, a crossin' on the floatin' ice. She crossed most 'markably; it wasn't no less nor a miracle; and I saw a man help her up the 'Hio side, and then she was lost in the dusk."

"Sam, I think this rather apocryphal,—this miracle. Crossing on floating ice isn't so easily done," said Mr. Shelby.

"Easy! couldn't nobody a done it, without de Lord. Why, now," said Sam, " 't was jist dis yer way. Mas'r Haley, and me, and Andy, we comes up to de little tavern by the river, and I rides a leetle ahead,—(I's so zealous to be a cotchin' Lizy, that I couldn't hold in, no way),—and when I comes by the tavern winder, sure enough there she was, right in plain sight, and dey diggin' on behind. Wal, I loses off my hat, and sings out nuff to raise the dead. Course Lizy she hars, and she dodges back, when Mas'r Haley he goes past the door; and then, I tell ye, she clared out de side door; she went down de river bank;—Mas'r Haley he seed her, and yelled out, and him, and me, and Andy, we took arter. Down she come to the river, and thar was the current running ten feet wide by the shore, and over t' other side ice a sawin' and a jiggling up and down, kinder as 't were a great island. We come right behind her, and I thought my soul he'd got her sure enough,—when she gin sich a screech as I never hearn, and thar she was, clar over t' other side of the current, on the ice, and then on she went, a screeching and a jumpin',—the ice went crack! c'wallop! cracking!

chunk! and she a boundin' like a buck! Lord, the spring that ar gal's got in her an't common, I'm o' 'pinion."

Mrs. Shelby sat perfectly silent, pale with excitement, while Sam told his story.

"God be praised, she isn't dead!" she said; "but where is the poor child now?"

"De Lord will pervide," said Sam, rolling up his eyes piously. "As I've been a sayin', dis yer 's a providence and no mistake, as Missis has allers been a instructin' on us. Thar's allers instruments ris up to do de Lord's will. Now, if 't hadn't been for me to-day, she'd a been took a dozen times. Warn't it I started off de hosses, dis yer mornin', and kept 'em chasin' till nigh dinner time? And didn't I car Mas'r Haley nigh five miles out of de road, dis evening, or else he'd a come up with Lizy as easy as a dog arter a coon. These yer 's all providences."

"They are a kind of providences that you'll have to be pretty sparing of, Master Sam. I allow no such practices with gentlemen on my place," said Mr. Shelby, with as much sternness as he could command, under the circumstances.

Now, there is no more use in making believe to be angry with a negro than with a child; both instinctively see the true state of the case, through all attempts to affect the contrary; and Sam was in no wise disheartened by this rebuke, though he assumed an air of doleful gravity, and stood with the corners of his mouth lowered in most penitential style.

"Mas'r's quite right,—quite; it was ugly on me,—there's no disputin' that ar; and of course Mas'r and Missis wouldn't encourage no such works. I'm sensible of dat ar; but a poor nigger like me 's 'mazin' tempted to act ugly sometimes, when fellers will cut up such shines as dat ar Mas'r Haley; he an't no gen'l'man no way; anybody's been raised as I've been can't help a seein' dat ar."

"Well, Sam," said Mrs. Shelby, "as you appear to have a proper sense of your errors, you may go now and tell Aunt Chloe she may get you some of that cold ham that was left of dinner to-day. You and Andy must be hungry."

"Missis is a heap too good for us," said Sam, making his bow with alacrity, and departing.

It will be perceived, as has been before intimated, that Master Sam had a native talent that might, undoubtedly, have raised him to eminence in political life,—a talent of making capital out of everything that turned up, to be invested for his own especial praise and glory; and having done up his piety and humility, as he trusted, to the satisfaction of the parlor, he clapped his palm-leaf on his head, with a sort of rakish, free-and-easy air, and proceeded to the dominions of Aunt Chloe, with the intention of flourishing largely in the kitchen.

"I'll speechify these yer niggers," said Sam to himself, "now I've got a chance. Lord, I'll reel it off to make 'em stare!"

It must be observed that one of Sam's especial delights had been to ride in attendance on his master to all kinds of political gatherings, where, roosted on some rail fence, or perched aloft in some tree, he would sit watching the orators, with the greatest apparent gusto, and then, descending among the various brethren of his own color, assembled on the same errand, he would edify and delight them with the most ludicrous burlesques and imitations, all delivered with the most imperturbable earnestness and solemnity; and though the auditors immediately about him were generally of his own color, it not unfrequently happened that they were fringed pretty deeply with those of a fairer complexion, who listened, laughing and winking, to Sam's great self-congratulation. In fact, Sam considered oratory as his vocation, and never let slip an opportunity of magnifying his office.

Now, between Sam and Aunt Chloe there had existed, from ancient times, a sort of chronic feud, or rather a decided coolness; but, as Sam was meditating something in the provision department, as the necessary and obvious foundation of his operations, he determined, on the present occasion, to be eminently conciliatory; for he well knew that although "Missis' orders" would undoubtedly be followed to the letter, yet he should gain a considerable deal by enlisting the spirit also. He therefore appeared before Aunt Chloe with a touchingly subdued, resigned expression, like one who has suffered immeasurable hardships in behalf of a persecuted fellow-creature,—enlarged upon the fact that Missis had directed him to come to Aunt Chloe for whatever might be wanting to make up the balance in his solids and fluids,—and thus unequivocally acknowledged her right and supremacy in the cooking department, and all thereto pertaining.

The thing took accordingly. No poor, simple, virtuous body was ever cajoled by the attentions of an electioneering politician with more ease than Aunt Chloe was won over by Master Sam's suavities; and if he had been the prodigal son himself, he could not have been overwhelmed with more maternal bountifulness; and he soon found himself seated, happy and glorious, over a large tin pan, containing a sort of *olla podrida* of all that had appeared on the table for two or three days past. Savory morsels of ham, golden blocks of corn-cake, fragments of pie of every conceivable mathematical figure, chicken wings, gizzards, and drumsticks, all appeared in picturesque confusion; and Sam, as monarch of all he surveyed, sat with his palm-leaf cocked rejoicingly to one side, and patronizing Andy at his right hand.

The kitchen was full of all his compeers, who had hurried and crowded in, from the various cabins, to hear the termination of the day's exploits. Now was Sam's hour of glory. The story of the day was rehearsed, with all kinds of ornament and varnishing which might be necessary to heighten its effect; for Sam, like some of our fashionable dilettanti, never allowed a story to lose any of its gilding by passing through his hands. Roars of laughter attended the narration, and were taken up and prolonged by all the smaller fry, who were lying, in any quantity, about on the floor, or perched in every corner. In the height of the uproar and laughter, Sam, however, preserved an immovable gravity, only from time to time rolling his eyes up, and giving his auditors divers inexpressibly droll glances, without departing from the sententious elevation of his oratory.

"Yer see, fellow-countrymen," said Sam, elevating a turkey's leg, with energy, "yer see, now what dis yer chile 's up ter, for fendin' yer all,—yes, all on yer. For him as tries to get one o' our people is as good as tryin' to get all; yer see the principle 's de same,—dat ar's clar. And any one o' these yer drivers that comes smelling round arter any our people, why, he's got *me* in his way; *I'm* the feller he's got to set in with,—I'm the feller for yer all to come to, bredren,—I'll stand up for yer rights,—I'll fend 'em to the last breath!"

"Why, but Sam, yer telled me, only this mornin', that you'd help this yer Mas'r to cotch Lizy; seems to me yer talk don't hang together," said Andy.

"I tell you now, Andy," said Sam, with awful superiority, "don't yer be a talkin' 'bout what yer don't know nothin' on; boys like you, Andy, means well, but they can't be spected to collusitate the great principles of action."

Andy looked rebuked, particularly by the hard word collusitate, which most of the youngerly members of the company seemed to consider as a settler in the case, while Sam proceeded.

"Dat ar was *conscience*, Andy; when I thought of gwine arter Lizy, I railly spected Mas'r was sot dat way. When I found Missis was sot the contrar, dat ar was conscience *more yet*,—cause fellers allers gets more by stickin' to Missis' side,—so yer see I's persistent either way, and sticks up to conscience, and holds on to principles. Yes, *principles*," said Sam, giving an enthusiastic toss to a chicken's neck,—"what's principles good for, if we isn't persistent, I wanter know? Thar, Andy, you may have dat ar bone,—'tan't picked quite clean."

Sam's audience hanging on his words with open mouth, he could not but proceed.

"Dis yer matter 'bout persistence, feller-niggers," said Sam, with the air of one entering into an abstruse subject, "dis yer 'sistency 's a thing what an't seed into very clar, by most anybody. Now, yer see, when a feller stands up for a thing one day and night, de contrar de next, folks ses (and nat'rally enough dey ses), why he an't persistent,—hand me dat ar bit o' corn-cake, Andy. But let's look inter it. I hope the gen'lmen and der fair sex will scuse my usin' an or'nary sort o' 'parison. Here! I'm a trying to get top o' der hay. Wal, I puts up my larder dis yer side; 'tan't no go;—den, cause I don't try dere no more, but puts my larder right de contrar side, an't I persistent? I'm persistent in wantin' to get up which ary side my larder is; don't you see, all on yer?"

"It's the only thing ye ever was persistent in, Lord knows!" muttered Aunt Chloe, who was getting rather restive; the merriment of the evening being to her somewhat after the Scripture comparison,—like "vinegar upon nitre."

"Yes, indeed!" said Sam, rising, full of supper and glory, for a closing effort. "Yes, my feller-citizens and ladies of de other sex in general, I has principles,—I'm proud to 'oon 'em,—they 's perquisite to dese yer times, and ter *all* times. I has principles, and I sticks to 'em like forty,—jest anything that I thinks is principle, I goes in to 't;—I wouldn't mind if dey burnt me 'live,—I'd walk right up to de stake, I would, and say, here I comes to shed my last blood fur my principles, fur my country, fur de gen'l interests of society."

"Well," said Aunt Chloe, "one o' yer principles will have to be to get to bed some time to-night, and not be a keepin' everybody up till mornin'; now, every one of you young uns that don't want to be cracked, had better be scase, mighty sudden."

"Niggers! all on yer," said Sam, waving his palm-leaf with benignity, "I give yer my blessin'; go to bed now, and be good boys."

And, with this pathetic benediction, the assembly dispersed.

SOURCE: Harriet Beecher Stowe. *Uncle Tom's Cabin; or, Life among the Lowly*. Boston: John P. Jewett & Company and Cleveland: Jewett, Proctor & Worthington, 1852.

WALT WHITMAN

Walt Whitman (1819–1892) is America's most famous poet. He celebrated and promoted his own vision while simultaneously celebrating America's. He delighted in his sensations; he cultivated his perceptions and trusted his intuitions to make declarations about the nature of America and Americans. He was a journalist and, during the Civil War, was a comfort to many wounded soldiers in Washington, D.C. Whitman had originally gone there to find his brother, a wounded Union soldier, in a hospital. Whitman never married but admired and worshiped many men, among them President Lincoln, whom he met once or twice and for whom he mourned with a rawness that we see in "O Captain! My Captain!" In Whitman's original Leaves of Grass *(1855), an edition he continued adding to and editing for the rest of his life, there were no individual poem titles; all the pages of his book were his "leaves of grass." We have included a fair portion of the first section of the original volume as well as the final section. Whitman concludes his celebration of himself, America and poetry, declaring that "Great is language . . . it is the mightiest of the sciences, / It is the fulness and color and form and diversity of the earth . . . and of men and women . . . and of all qualities and processes; / It is greater than wealth . . . it is greater than buildings or ships or religions or paintings or music." We agree.*

From *Leaves of Grass* (1855)

I celebrate myself,
And what I assume you shall assume,
For every atom belonging to me as good belongs to you.

I loafe and invite my soul,
I lean and loafe at my ease . . . observing a spear of summer
grass.

Houses and rooms are full of perfumes . . . the shelves are crowded with perfumes,
I breathe the fragrance myself, and know it and like it,
The distillation would intoxicate me also, but I shall not let it.

The atmosphere is not a perfume . . . it has no taste of the distillation . . . it is odorless,
It is for my mouth forever . . . I am in love with it,
I will go to the bank by the wood and become undisguised and naked,
I am mad for it to be in contact with me.

The smoke of my own breath,
Echos, ripples, and buzzed whispers . . . loveroot, silkthread, crotch and vine,
My respiration and inspiration . . . the beating of my heart . . . the passing of blood and air through my lungs,
The sniff of green leaves and dry leaves, and of the shore and dark-colored sea-rocks, and of hay in the barn,
The sound of the belched words of my voice . . . words loosed to the eddies of the wind,
A few light kisses . . . a few embraces . . . a reaching around of arms,
The play of shine and shade on the trees as the supple boughs wag,
The delight alone or in the rush of the streets, or along the fields and hillsides,
The feeling of health . . . the full-noon trill . . . the song of me rising from bed and meeting the sun.
Have you reckoned a thousand acres much? Have you reckoned the earth much?
Have you practiced so long to learn to read?
Have you felt so proud to get at the meaning of poems?

Stop this day and night with me and you shall possess the origin of all poems,
You shall possess the good of the earth and sun . . . there are millions of suns left,
You shall no longer take things at second or third hand . . . nor look through the eyes of the dead . . . nor feed on the spectres in books,

You shall not look through my eyes either, nor take things from me,
You shall listen to all sides and filter them from yourself.

I have heard what the talkers were talking . . . the talk of the beginning and the end,
But I do not talk of the beginning or the end.

There was never any more inception than there is now,
Nor any more youth or age than there is now;
And will never be any more perfection than there is now,
Nor any more heaven or hell than there is now.

Urge and urge and urge,
Always the procreant urge of the world.

Out of the dimness opposite equals advance . . . Always substance and increase,
Always a knit of identity . . . always distinction . . . always a breed of life.

To elaborate is no avail . . . Learned and unlearned feel that it is so.

Sure as the most certain sure . . . plumb in the uprights, well entretied, braced in the beams,
Stout as a horse, affectionate, haughty, electrical,
I and this mystery here we stand.

Clear and sweet is my soul . . . and clear and sweet is all that is not my soul.

Lack one lacks both . . . and the unseen is proved by the seen,
Till that becomes unseen and receives proof in its turn.

Showing the best and dividing it from the worst, age vexes age,
Knowing the perfect fitness and equanimity of things, while they discuss I am silent, and go bathe and admire myself.

Welcome is every organ and attribute of me, and of any man hearty and clean,

Not an inch nor a particle of an inch is vile, and none shall be less familiar than the rest.

I am satisfied . . . I see, dance, laugh, sing;
As God comes a loving bedfellow and sleeps at my side all night and close on the peep of the day,
And leaves for me baskets covered with white towels bulging the house with their plenty,
Shall I postpone my acceptation and realization and scream at my eyes,
That they turn from gazing after and down the road,
And forthwith cipher and show me to a cent,
Exactly the contents of one, and exactly the contents of two, and which is ahead?

Trippers and askers surround me,
People I meet . . . the effect upon me of my early life . . . of the ward and city I live in . . . of the nation,
The latest news . . . discoveries, inventions, societies . . . authors old and new,
My dinner, dress, associates, looks, business, compliments, dues,
The real or fancied indifference of some man or woman I love,
The sickness of one of my folks—or of myself . . . or ill-doing . . . or loss or lack of money . . . or depressions or exaltations,
They come to me days and nights and go from me again,
But they are not the Me myself.

Apart from the pulling and hauling stands what I am,
Stands amused, complacent, compassionating, idle, unitary,
Looks down, is erect, bends an arm on an impalpable certain rest,
Looks with its sidecurved head curious what will come next,
Both in and out of the game, and watching and wondering at it.

Backward I see in my own days where I sweated through fog with linguists and contenders,
I have no mockings or arguments . . . I witness and wait.

I believe in you my soul . . . the other I am must not abase itself to you,
And you must not be abased to the other.

Loafe with me on the grass . . . loose the stop from your throat,
Not words, not music or rhyme I want . . . not custom or lecture, not even the best,
Only the lull I like, the hum of your valved voice.

I mind how we lay in June, such a transparent summer morning;
You settled your head athwart my hips and gently turned over upon me,
And parted the shirt from my bosom-bone, and plunged your tongue to my barestript heart,
And reached till you felt my beard, and reached till you held my feet.

Swiftly arose and spread around me the peace and joy and knowledge that pass all the art and argument of the earth;
And I know that the hand of God is the elderhand of my own,
And I know that the spirit of God is the eldest brother of my own,
And that all the men ever born are also my brothers . . . and the women my sisters and lovers,
And that a kelson of the creation is love;
And limitless are leaves stiff or drooping in the fields,
And brown ants in the little wells beneath them,
And mossy scabs of the wormfence, and heaped stones, and elder and mullen and pokeweed.

A child said, What is the grass? fetching it to me with full hands;
How could I answer the child? . . . I do not know what it is any more than he.

I guess it must be the flag of my disposition, out of hopeful green stuff woven.

Or I guess it is the handkerchief of the Lord,
A scented gift and remembrancer designedly dropped,
Bearing the owner's name someway in the corners, that we may see and remark, and say Whose?

Or I guess the grass is itself a child . . . the produced babe of the vegetation.

Or I guess it is a uniform hieroglyphic,
And it means, Sprouting alike in broad zones and narrow zones,
Growing among black folks as among white,
Kanuck, Tuckahoe, Congressman, Cuff, I give them the same, I
receive them the same.

And now it seems to me the beautiful uncut hair of graves.

Tenderly will I use you curling grass,
It may be you transpire from the breasts of young men,
It may be if I had known them I would have loved them;
It may be you are from old people and from women, and from
offspring taken soon out of their mothers' laps,
And here you are the mothers' laps.

This grass is very dark to be from the white heads of old
mothers,
Darker than the colorless beards of old men,
Dark to come from under the faint red roofs of mouths.

O I perceive after all so many uttering tongues!
And I perceive they do not come from the roofs of mouths for
nothing.

I wish I could translate the hints about the dead young men and
women,
And the hints about old men and mothers, and the offspring
taken soon out of their laps.

What do you think has become of the young and old men?
And what do you think has become of the women and children?

They are alive and well somewhere;
The smallest sprout shows there is really no death,
And if ever there was it led forward life, and does not wait at the
end to arrest it,
And ceased the moment life appeared.

All goes onward and outward . . . and nothing collapses,
And to die is different from what any one supposed, and luckier.

Has any one supposed it lucky to be born?
I hasten to inform him or her it is just as lucky to die, and I know it.

I pass death with the dying, and birth with the new-washed babe . . . and am not contained between my hat and boots,
And peruse manifold objects, no two alike, and every one good,
The earth good, and the stars good, and their adjuncts all good.

I am not an earth nor an adjunct of an earth,
I am the mate and companion of people, all just as immortal and fathomless as myself;
They do not know how immortal, but I know.

Every kind for itself and its own . . . for me mine male and female,
For me all that have been boys and that love women,
For me the man that is proud and feels how it stings to be slighted,
For me the sweetheart and the old maid . . . for me mothers and the mothers of mothers,
For me lips that have smiled, eyes that have shed tears,
For me children and the begetters of children.

Who need be afraid of the merge?
Undrape . . . you are not guilty to me, nor stale nor discarded,
I see through the broadcloth and gingham whether or no,
And am around, tenacious, acquisitive, tireless . . . and can never be shaken away.

The little one sleeps in its cradle,
I lift the gauze and look a long time, and silently brush away flies with my hand.

The youngster and the redfaced girl turn aside up the bushy hill,
I peeringly view them from the top.

The suicide sprawls on the bloody floor of the bedroom.
It is so . . . I witnessed the corpse . . . there the pistol had fallen.

The blab of the pave . . . the tires of carts and sluff of bootsoles and talk of the promenaders,
The heavy omnibus, the driver with his interrogating thumb, the clank of the shod horses on the granite floor,
The carnival of sleighs, the clinking and shouted jokes and pelts of snowballs;
The hurrahs for popular favorites . . . the fury of roused mobs,
The flap of the curtained litter—the sick man inside, borne to the hospital,
The meeting of enemies, the sudden oath, the blows and fall,
The excited crowd—the policeman with his star quickly working his passage to the centre of the crowd;
The impassive stones that receive and return so many echoes,
The souls moving along . . . are they invisible while the least atom of the stones is visible?
What groans of overfed or half-starved who fall on the flags sunstruck or in fits,
What exclamations of women taken suddenly, who hurry home and give birth to babes,
What living and buried speech is always vibrating here . . . what howls restrained by decorum,
Arrests of criminals, slights, adulterous offers made, acceptances, rejections with convex lips,
I mind them or the resonance of them . . . I come again and again.

The big doors of the country-barn stand open and ready
The dried grass of the harvest-time loads the slow-drawn wagon,
The clear light plays on the brown gray and green intertinged,
The armfuls are packed to the sagging mow:
I am there . . . I help . . . I came stretched atop of the load,
I felt its soft jolts . . . one leg reclined on the other,
I jump from the crossbeams, and seize the clover and timothy,
And roll head over heels, and tangle my hair full of wisps.

Alone far in the wilds and mountains I hunt,
Wandering amazed at my own lightness and glee,
In the late afternoon choosing a safe spot to pass the night,
Kindling a fire and broiling the freshkilled game,
Soundly falling asleep on the gathered leaves, my dog and gun by my side.

The Yankee clipper is under her three skysails . . . she cuts the sparkle and scud,
My eyes settle the land . . . I bend at her prow or shout joyously from the deck.

The boatmen and clamdiggers arose early and stopped for me,
I tucked my trowser-ends in my boots and went and had a good time,
You should have been with us that day round the chowder-kettle.

I saw the marriage of the trapper in the open air in the far-west . . . the bride was a red girl,
Her father and his friends sat nearby crosslegged and dumbly smoking . . . they had moccasins to their feet and large thick blankets hanging from their shoulders;
On a bank lounged the trapper . . . he was dressed mostly in skins . . . his luxuriant beard and curls protected his neck,
One hand rested on his rifle . . . the other hand held firmly the wrist of the red girl,
She had long eyelashes . . . her head was bare . . . her coarse straight locks descended upon her voluptuous limbs and reached to her feet.

The runaway slave came to my house and stopped outside,
I heard his motions crackling the twigs of the woodpile,
Through the swung half-door of the kitchen I saw him limpsey and weak,
And went where he sat on a log, and led him in and assured him,
And brought water and filled a tub for his sweated body and bruised feet,
And gave him a room that entered from my own, and gave him some coarse clean clothes,
And remember perfectly well his revolving eyes and his awkwardness,
And remember putting plasters on the galls of his neck and ankles;
He staid with me a week before he was recuperated and passed north,
I had him sit next me at table . . . my firelock leaned in the corner.

Twenty-eight young men bathe by the shore,
Twenty-eight young men, and all so friendly,
Twenty-eight years of womanly life, and all so lonesome.

She owns the fine house by the rise of the bank,
She hides handsome and richly drest aft the blinds of the window.

Which of the young men does she like the best?
Ah the homeliest of them is beautiful to her.

Where are you off to, lady? for I see you,
You splash in the water there, yet stay stock still in your room.

Dancing and laughing along the beach came the twenty-ninth bather,
The rest did not see her, but she saw them and loved them.

The beards of the young men glistened with wet, it ran from their long hair,
Little streams passed all over their bodies.

An unseen hand also passed over their bodies,
It descended tremblingly from their temples and ribs.

The young men float on their backs, their white bellies swell to the sun . . . they do not ask who seizes fast to them,
They do not know who puffs and declines with pendant and bending arch,
They do not think whom they souse with spray.

The butcher-boy puts off his killing-clothes, or sharpens his knife at the stall in the market,
I loiter enjoying his repartee and his shuffle and breakdown.

Blacksmiths with grimed and hairy chests environ the anvil,
Each has his main-sledge . . . they are all out . . . there is a great heat in the fire.

From the cinder-strewed threshold I follow their movements,
The lithe sheer of their waists plays even with their massive arms,

Overhand the hammers roll—overhand so slow—overhand so sure,
They do not hasten, each man hits in his place.

The negro holds firmly the reins of his four horses . . . the block swags underneath on its tied-over chain,
The negro that drives the huge dray of the stoneyard . . . steady and tall he stands poised on one leg on the stringpiece,
His blue shirt exposes his ample neck and breast and loosens over his hipband,
His glance is calm and commanding . . . he tosses the slouch of his hat away from his forehead,
The sun falls on his crispy hair and moustache . . . falls on the black of his polish'd and perfect limbs.

I behold the picturesque giant and love him . . . and I do not stop there,
I go with the team also.

In me the caresser of life wherever moving . . . backward as well as forward slueing,
To niches aside and junior bending.

Oxen that rattle the yoke or halt in the shade, what is that you express in your eyes?
It seems to me more than all the print I have read in my life.

My tread scares the wood-drake and wood-duck on my distant and daylong ramble,
They rise together, they slowly circle around.
. . . I believe in those winged purposes,
And acknowledge the red yellow and white playing within me,
And consider the green and violet and the tufted crown intentional;
And do not call the tortoise unworthy because she is not something else,
And the mockingbird in the swamp never studied the gamut, yet trills pretty well to me,
And the look of the bay mare shames silliness out of me.

The wild gander leads his flock through the cool night,
Ya-honk! he says, and sounds it down to me like an invitation;
The pert may suppose it meaningless, but I listen closer,
I find its purpose and place up there toward the November sky.

The sharphoofed moose of the north, the cat on the housesill,
the chickadee, the prairie-dog,
The litter of the grunting sow as they tug at her teats,
The brood of the turkeyhen, and she with her halfspread wings,
I see in them and myself the same old law.

The press of my foot to the earth springs a hundred affections,
They scorn the best I can do to relate them.

I am enamoured of growing outdoors,
Of men that live among cattle or taste of the ocean or woods,
Of the builders and steerers of ships, of the wielders of axes and
mauls, of the drivers of horses,
I can eat and sleep with them week in and week out.

What is commonest and cheapest and nearest and easiest is Me,
Me going in for my chances, spending for vast returns,
Adorning myself to bestow myself on the first that will take me,
Not asking the sky to come down to my goodwill,
Scattering it freely forever.

[. . .]

The city sleeps and the country sleeps,
The living sleep for their time . . . the dead sleep for their time,
The old husband sleeps by his wife and the young husband sleeps
by his wife;
And these one and all tend inward to me, and I tend outward to
them,
And such as it is to be of these more or less I am.

I am of old and young, of the foolish as much as the wise,
Regardless of others, ever regardful of others,
Maternal as well as paternal, a child as well as a man,
Stuffed with the stuff that is coarse, and stuffed with the stuff that
is fine,

One of the great nation, the nation of many nations—the smallest the same and the largest the same,
A southerner soon as a northerner, a planter nonchalant and hospitable,
A Yankee bound my own way . . . ready for trade . . . my joints the limberest joints on earth and the sternest joints on earth,
A Kentuckian walking the vale of the Elkhorn in my deerskin leggings,
A boatman over the lakes or bays or along coasts . . . a Hoosier, a Badger, a Buckeye,
A Louisianian or Georgian, a poke-easy from sandhills and pines,
At home on Canadian snowshoes or up in the bush, or with fishermen off Newfoundland,
At home in the fleet of iceboats, sailing with the rest and tacking,
At home on the hills of Vermont or in the woods of Maine or the Texan ranch,
Comrade of Californians . . . comrade of free northwesterners, loving their big proportions,
Comrade of raftsmen and coalmen—comrade of all who shake hands and welcome to drink and meat;
A learner with the simplest, a teacher of the thoughtfulest,
A novice beginning experient of myriads of seasons,
Of every hue and trade and rank, of every caste and religion,
Not merely of the New World but of Africa Europe or Asia . . . a wandering savage,
A farmer, mechanic, or artist . . . a gentleman, sailor, lover or quaker,
A prisoner, fancy-man, rowdy, lawyer, physician or priest.

I resist anything better than my own diversity,
And breathe the air and leave plenty after me,
And am not stuck up, and am in my place.

[. . .]

This is the meal pleasantly set . . . this is the meat and drink for natural hunger,
It is for the wicked just the same as the righteous . . . I make appointments with all,
I will not have a single person slighted or left away,

The keptwoman and sponger and thief are hereby invited . . . the heavy-lipped slave is invited . . . the venerealee is invited,
There shall be no difference between them and the rest.

This is the press of a bashful hand . . . this is the float and odor of hair,
This is the touch of my lips to yours . . . this is the murmur of yearning,
This is the far-off depth and height reflecting my own face,
This is the thoughtful merge of myself and the outlet again.

Do you guess I have some intricate purpose?
Well I have . . . for the April rain has, and the mica on the side of a rock has.

Do you take it I would astonish?
Does the daylight astonish? or the early redstart twittering through the woods?
Do I astonish more than they?

This hour I tell things in confidence,
I might not tell everybody but I will tell you.

Who goes there! hankering, gross, mystical, nude?
How is it I extract strength from the beef I eat?

What is a man anyhow? What am I? and what are you?
All I mark as my own you shall offset it with your own,
Else it were time lost listening to me.

I do not snivel that snivel the world over,
That months are vacuums and the ground but wallow and filth,
That life is a suck and a sell, and nothing remains at the end but threadbare crape and tears.

Whimpering and truckling fold with powders for invalids . . . conformity goes to the fourth-removed,
I cock my hat as I please indoors or out.

Shall I pray? Shall I venerate and be ceremonious?

I have pried through the strata and analyzed to a hair,
And counselled with doctors and calculated close and found no sweeter fat than sticks to my own bones.

In all people I see myself, none more and not one a barleycorn less,
And the good or bad I say of myself I say of them.

And I know I am solid and sound,
To me the converging objects of the universe perpetually flow,
All are written to me, and I must get what the writing means.

And I know I am deathless,
I know this orbit of mine cannot be swept by a carpenter's compass,
I know I shall not pass like a child's carlacue cut with a burnt stick at night.

I know I am august,
I do not trouble my spirit to vindicate itself or be understood,
I see that the elementary laws never apologize,
I reckon I behave no prouder than the level I plant my house by after all.

I exist as I am, that is enough,
If no other in the world be aware I sit content,
And if each and all be aware I sit content.

One world is aware, and by far the largest to me, and that is myself,
And whether I come to my own today or in ten thousand or ten million years,
I can cheerfully take it now, or with equal cheerfulness I can wait.

My foothold is tenoned and mortised in granite,
I laugh at what you call dissolution,
And I know the amplitude of time.

I am the poet of the body,
And I am the poet of the soul.

The pleasures of heaven are with me, and the pains of hell are with me,
The first I graft and increase upon myself . . . the latter I translate into a new tongue.

I am the poet of the woman the same as the man,
And I say it is as great to be a woman as to be a man,
And I say there is nothing greater than the mother of men.

I chant a new chant of dilation or pride,
We have had ducking and deprecating about enough,
I show that size is only developement.

Have you outstript the rest? Are you the President?
It is a trifle . . . they will more than arrive there every one, and still pass on.

I am he that walks with the tender and growing night;
I call to the earth and sea half-held by the night.

Press close barebosomed night! Press close magnetic nourishing night!
Night of south winds! Night of the large few stars!
Still nodding night! Mad naked summer night!

Smile O voluptuous coolbreathed earth!
Earth of the slumbering and liquid trees!
Earth of departed sunset! Earth of the mountains misty-topt!
Earth of the vitreous pour of the full moon just tinged with blue!
Earth of shine and dark mottling the tide of the river!
Earth of the limpid gray of clouds brighter and clearer for my sake!
Far-swooping elbowed earth! Rich apple-blossomed earth!
Smile, for your lover comes!

Prodigal! you have given me love! . . . therefore I to you give love!
O unspeakable passionate love!

Thruster holding me tight and that I hold tight!
We hurt each other as the bridegroom and the bride hurt each other.

You sea! I resign myself to you also . . . I guess what you mean,
I behold from the beach your crooked inviting fingers,
I believe you refuse to go back without feeling of me;
We must have a turn together . . . I undress . . . hurry me out of sight of the land,
Cushion me soft . . . rock me in billowy drowse,
Dash me with amorous wet . . . I can repay you.

Sea of stretched ground-swells!
Sea breathing broad and convulsive breaths!
Sea of the brine of life! Sea of unshovelled and always-ready graves!
Howler and scooper of storms! Capricious and dainty sea!
I am integral with you . . . I too am of one phase and of all phases.

Partaker of influx and efflux . . . extoler of hate and conciliation,
Extoler of amies and those that sleep in each others' arms.

I am he attesting sympathy;
Shall I make my list of things in the house and skip the house that supports them?

I am the poet of commonsense and of the demonstrable and of immortality;
And am not the poet of goodness only . . . I do not decline to be the poet of wickedness also.

Washes and razors for foofoos . . . for me freckles and a bristling beard.

What blurt is it about virtue and about vice?
Evil propels me, and reform of evil propels me . . . I stand indifferent,
My gait is no faultfinder's or rejecter's gait,
I moisten the roots of all that has grown.

[. . .]

[Final section]

Great are the myths . . . I too delight in them,
Great are Adam and Eve . . . I too look back and accept them;
Great the risen and fallen nations, and their poets, women, sages, inventors, rulers, warriors and priests.

Great is liberty! Great is equality! I am their follower,
Helmsmen of nations, choose your craft . . . where you sail I sail,
Yours is the muscle of life or death . . . yours is the perfect science . . . in you I have absolute faith.

Great is today, and beautiful,
It is good to live in this age . . . there never was any better.

Great are the plunges and throes and triumphs and falls of democracy,
Great the reformers with their lapses and screams,
Great the daring and venture of sailors on new explorations.

Great are yourself and myself,
We are just as good and bad as the oldest and youngest or any,
What the best and worst did we could do,
What they felt . . . do not we feel it in ourselves?
What they wished . . . do we not wish the same?

Great is youth, and equally great is old age . . . great are the day and night;
Great is wealth and great is poverty . . . great is expression and great is silence.

Youth large lusty and loving . . . youth full of grace and force and fascination,
Do you know that old age may come after you with equal grace and force and fascination?

Day fullblown and splendid . . . day of the immense sun, and action and ambition and laughter,
The night follows close, with millions of suns, and sleep and restoring darkness.

Wealth with the flush hand and fine clothes and hospitality:
But then the soul's wealth—which is candor and knowledge and pride and enfolding love:
Who goes for men and women showing poverty richer than wealth?

Expression of speech . . . in what is written or said forget not that silence is also expressive,
That anguish as hot as the hottest and contempt as cold as the coldest may be without words,
That the true adoration is likewise without words and without kneeling.

Great is the greatest nation . . . the nation of clusters of equal nations.

Great is the earth, and the way it became what it is,
Do you imagine it is stopped at this? . . . and the increase abandoned?
Understand then that it goes as far onward from this as this is from the times when it lay in covering waters and gases.

Great is the quality of truth in man,
The quality of truth in man supports itself through all changes,
It is inevitably in the man . . . He and it are in love, and never leave each other.

The truth in man is no dictum . . . it is vital as eyesight,
If there be any soul there is truth . . . if there be man or woman there is truth . . . If there be physical or moral there is truth,
If there be equilibrium or volition there is truth . . . if there be things at all upon the earth there is truth.

O truth of the earth! O truth of things! I am determined to press the whole way toward you,
Sound your voice! I scale mountains or dive in the sea after you.

Great is language . . . it is the mightiest of the sciences,
It is the fulness and color and form and diversity of the earth . . . and of men and women . . . and of all qualities and processes;

It is greater than wealth . . . it is greater than buildings or ships
or religions or paintings or music.

Great is the English speech . . . What speech is so great as the
English?
Great is the English brood . . . What brood has so vast a destiny
as the English?
It is the mother of the brood that must rule the earth with the
new rule,
The new rule shall rule as the soul rules, and as the love and justice and equality that are in the soul rule.

Great is the law . . . Great are the old few landmarks of the law
. . . they are the same in all times and shall not be disturbed.

Great are marriage, commerce, newspapers, books, freetrade, railroads, steamers, international mails and telegraphs and
exchanges.

Great is Justice;
Justice is not settled by legislators and laws . . . it is in the soul,
It cannot be varied by statutes any more than love or pride or the
attraction of gravity can,
It is immutable . . . it does not depend on majorities . . . majorities or what not come at last before the same passionless and
exact tribunal.

For justice are the grand natural lawyers and perfect judges . . . it
is in their souls,
It is well assorted . . . they have not studied for nothing . . . the
great includes the less,
They rule on the highest grounds . . . they oversee all eras and
states and administrations.

The perfect judge fears nothing . . . he could go front to front
before God,
Before the perfect judge all shall stand back . . . life and death
shall stand back . . . heaven and hell shall stand back.

Great is goodness;

I do not know what it is any more than I know what health is
 . . . but I know it is great.

Great is wickedness . . . I find I often admire it just as much as I
 admire goodness:
Do you call that a paradox? It certainly is a paradox.

The eternal equilibrium of things is great, and the eternal over-
 throw of things is great,
And there is another paradox.

Great is life . . . and real and mystical . . . wherever and
 whoever,
Great is death . . . Sure as life holds all parts together, death holds
 all parts together;
Sure as the stars return again after they merge in the light, death
 is great as life.

SOURCE: Walt Whitman. *Leaves of Grass: The Original 1855 Edition.* Originally published by the author, Brooklyn, New York, 1855.

The Wound-Dresser (1865)

Whitman seems to have been able to catch more feeling and detail about the Civil War in his long tumbling lines than any other war-era poet. He not only described his experiences as a nurse in various Washington, D.C., hospitals, but traveled in his imagination to the soldiers on the battlegrounds and on the march. The next six poems come from his 1865 collection, Drum-Taps. *One of his greatest poems describes the activities of a wound-dresser, a job in which he continually had to explain he did not actually have himself. (The original title was simply "The Dresser." We have used the title he later gave it.) Whitman did, however, spend much time in the hospitals "among new faces," ministering to the wounded soldiers' hearts and souls during the Civil War.*

An old man bending, I come, among new faces,
Years looking backward, resuming, in answer to children,
Come tell us, old man, as from young men and maidens that love
 me;
Years hence of these scenes, of these furious passions, these
 chances,

Of unsurpass'd heroes, (was one side so brave? the other was
equally brave;)
Now be witness again—paint the mightiest armies of earth;
Of those armies so rapid, so wondrous, what saw you to tell us?
What stays with you latest and deepest? of curious panics,
Of hard-fought engagements, or sieges tremendous, what deepest
remains?

O maidens and young men I love, and that love me,
What you ask of my days, those the strangest and sudden your
talking recalls;
Soldier alert I arrive, after a long march, cover'd with sweat and
dust;
In the nick of time I come, plunge in the fight, loudly shout in
the rush of successful charge;
Enter the captur'd works . . . yet lo! like a swift-running river,
they fade;
Pass and are gone, they fade—I dwell not on soldiers' perils or
soldiers' joys;
(Both I remember well—many the hardships, few the joys, yet I
was content.)

But in silence, in dreams' projections,
While the world of gain and appearance and mirth goes on,
So soon what is over forgotten, and waves wash the imprints off
the sand,
In nature's reverie sad, with hinged knees returning, I enter the
doors—(while for you up there,
Whoever you are, follow me without noise, and be of strong heart.)

Bearing the bandages, water and sponge,
Straight and swift to my wounded I go,
Where they lie on the ground, after the battle brought in;
Where their priceless blood reddens the grass, the ground;
Or to the rows of the hospital tent, or under the roof'd hospital;
To the long rows of cots, up and down, each side, I return;
To each and all, one after another, I draw near—not one do I miss;
An attendant follows, holding a tray—he carries a refuse pail,
Soon to be fill'd with clotted rags and blood, emptied and fill'd
again.

I onward go, I stop,
With hinged knees and steady hand, to dress wounds;
I am firm with each—the pangs are sharp, yet unavoidable;
One turns to me his appealing eyes—(poor boy! I never knew
you,
Yet I think I could not refuse this moment to die for you, if that
would save you.)

On, on I go—(open doors of time! open, hospital doors!)
The crush'd head I dress, (poor crazed hand, tear not the ban-
dage away;)
The neck of the cavalry-man, with the bullet through and
through, I examine;
Hard the breathing rattles, quite glazed already the eye, yet life
struggles hard;
(Come, sweet death! be persuaded, O beautiful death!
In mercy come quickly.)

From the stump of the arm, the amputated hand,
I undo the clotted lint, remove the slough, wash off the matter
and blood;
Back on his pillow the soldier bends, with curv'd neck, and side-
falling head;
His eyes are closed, his face is pale, he dares not look on the
bloody stump,
And has not yet look'd on it.

I dress a wound in the side, deep, deep;
But a day or two more—for see, the frame all wasted already,
and sinking,
And the yellow-blue countenance see.

I dress the perforated shoulder, the foot with the bullet wound,
Cleanse the one with a gnawing and putrid gangrene, so
sickening, so offensive,
While the attendant stands behind aside me, holding the tray and
pail.

I am faithful, I do not give out;
The fractur'd thigh, the knee, the wound in the abdomen,

These and more I dress with impassive hand—(yet deep in my
breast a fire, a burning flame.)

Thus in silence, in dream's projections,
Returning, resuming, I thread my way through the hospitals;
The hurt and wounded I pacify with soothing hand,
I sit by the restless all the dark night—some are so young;
Some suffer so much—I recall the experience sweet and sad;
(Many a soldier's loving arms about this neck have cross'd and
rested,
Many a soldier's kiss dwells on these bearded lips.)

Cavalry Crossing a Ford (1865)

A line in long array, where they wind betwixt green islands;
They take a serpentine course—their arms flash in the sun—Hark
to the musical clank;
Behold the silvery river—in it the splashing horses, loitering, stop
to drink;
Behold the brown-faced men—each group, each person, a pic-
ture—the negligent rest on the saddles;
Some emerge on the opposite bank—others are just entering the
ford;
The guidon flags flutter gaily in the wind.

A March in the Ranks Hard-Prest, and the Road Unknown (1865)

A march in the ranks hard-prest, and the road unknown;
A route through a heavy wood, with muffled steps in the
darkness;
Our army foil'd with loss severe, and the sullen remnant
retreating;
Till after midnight glimmer upon us, the lights of a dim-lighted
building;
We come to an open space in the woods, and halt by the dim-
lighted building;
'Tis a large old church at the crossing roads—'tis now an
impromptu hospital;

—Entering but for a minute, I see a sight beyond all the pictures and poems ever made:
Shadows of deepest, deepest black, just lit by moving candles and lamps,
And by one great pitchy torch, stationary, with wild red flame and clouds of smoke;
By these, crowds, groups of forms, vaguely I see, on the floor, some in the pews laid down;
At my feet more distinctly, a soldier, a mere lad, in danger of bleeding to death, (he is shot in the abdomen;)
I staunch the blood temporarily, (the youngster's face is white as a lily;)
Then before I depart I sweep my eyes o'er the scene, fain to absorb it all;
Faces, varieties, postures beyond description, most in obscurity, some of them dead;
Surgeons operating, attendants holding lights, the smell of ether, the odor of blood;
The crowd, O the crowd of the bloody forms of soldiers—the yard outside also fill'd;
Some on the bare ground, some on planks or stretchers, some in the death-spasm sweating;
An occasional scream or cry, the doctor's shouted orders or calls;
The glisten of the little steel instruments catching the glint of the torches;
These I resume as I chant—I see again the forms, I smell the odor;
Then hear outside the orders given, *Fall in, my men, Fall in;*
But first I bend to the dying lad—his eyes open—a half-smile gives he me;
Then the eyes close, calmly close, and I speed forth to the darkness,
Resuming, marching, ever in darkness marching, on in the ranks,
The unknown road still marching.

A Sight in Camp in the Day-Break Grey and Dim (1865)

A sight in camp in the day-break grey and dim,
As from my tent I emerge so early, sleepless,

As slow I walk in the cool fresh air, the path near by the
hospital-tent,
Three forms I see on stretchers lying, brought out there,
untended lying,
Over each the blanket spread, ample brownish woollen blanket,
Grey and heavy blanket, folding, covering all.

Curious, I halt, and silent stand;
Then with light fingers I from the face of the nearest, the first,
just lift the blanket:
Who are you, elderly man so gaunt and grim, with well-grey'd
hair, and flesh all sunken about the eyes?
Who are you, my dear comrade?

Then to the second I step—And who are you, my child and
darling?
Who are you, sweet boy, with cheeks yet blooming?

Then to the third—a face nor child, nor old, very calm, as of
beautiful yellow-white ivory;
Young man, I think I know you—I think this face of yours is
the face of the Christ himself;
Dead and divine, and brother of all, and here again he lies.

Not Youth Pertains to Me (1865)

Not youth pertains to me,
Nor delicatesse—I cannot beguile the time with talk;
Awkward in the parlor, neither a dancer nor elegant;
In the learn'd coterie sitting constrain'd and still—for learning
inures not to me;
Beauty, knowledge, fortune, inure not to me—yet there are two
things inure to me;
I have nourish'd the wounded, and sooth'd many a dying
soldier;
And at intervals I have strung together a few songs,
Fit for war, and life of the camp.

SOURCE: Walt Whitman. *Drum-Taps*. New York. 1865.

O Captain! My Captain! (1865)

The last poem commemorates the life and death of President Abraham Lincoln, who was shot on April 14, 1865, and died the next morning.

1

O captain! my captain! our fearful trip is done;
The ship has weather'd every rack, the prize we sought is won;
The port is near, the bells I hear, the people all exulting,
While follow eyes the steady keel, the vessel grim and daring:
  But O heart! heart! heart!
    Leave you not the little spot,
      Where on the deck my captain lies,
        Fallen cold and dead.

2

O captain! my captain! rise up and hear the bells;
Rise up—for you the flag is flung—for you the bugle trills;
For you bouquets and ribbon'd wreaths—for you the shores
  a-crowding;
For you they call, the swaying mass, their eager faces turning;
  O captain! dear father!
    This arm I push beneath you;
      It is some dream that on the deck,
        You've fallen cold and dead.

3

My captain does not answer, his lips are pale and still;
My father does not feel my arm, he has no pulse nor will;
But the ship, the ship is anchor'd safe, its voyage closed and done;
From fearful trip, the victor ship, comes in with object won:
  Exult, O shores, and ring, O bells!
    But I, with silent tread,
      Walk the spot my captain lies,
        Fallen cold and dead.

SOURCE: Walt Whitman. *Sequel to Drum-Taps: When Lilacs Last in the Door-Yard Bloom'd. And Other Pieces.* Washington, D.C.: Gibson Brothers, 1865–1866.

P. T. BARNUM

Phineas Taylor Barnum (1810–1891) was nineteenth-century America's best known showman. He tells the story here of how and why he started a museum of curiosities in New York City, and of some of his adventures and follies with newspapermen and performers, among them the "Fejee Mermaid" and "General Tom Thumb."

The American Museum (Chapter 9) from *The Life of P. T. Barnum Written by Himself* (1855)

APRIL 26, 1841, I called on Robert Sears, the publisher of "Sears' Pictorial Illustrations of the Bible," and contracted for five hundred copies of the work for $500, accepted the United States agency, opened an office, May 10, at the corner of Beekman and Nassau streets, which was subsequently taken by Mr. Redfield as a bookstore, and is the present site of the Nassau Bank. I had thus made another effort to quit the life of a showman for ever, and settle down into a respectable calling. I advertised largely, appointed agents and sub-agents, and managed in the course of six months to sell thousands of books, and at the same time to place a sufficient number in the hands of irresponsible agents to use up all my profits and all my capital!

In the mean time I again leased Vauxhall saloon, and opened it June 14, 1841. I thought it would be compromising my dignity as a "Bible man" to be known as the lessee of a theatre, and the concern was managed, under my directions, by Mr. John Hallett, my brother-in-law. We closed the season, Sept. 25, having cleared about two hundred dollars above expenses.

Living in the city of New-York with nothing to do and a family to support, in a very short time exhausted my funds, and I became about as poor as I should ever wish to be. I looked around in vain for employment congenial to my feelings, that would serve to keep my head above water. I finally obtained the post of writing advertisements and notices for the Bowery Amphitheatre, my duties including daily visits to the upper stories of many newspaper offices to deliver what I had prepared, and see that they were inserted. For this I received $4.00 per week! and was thankful for even that.

I also wrote articles for the Sunday press, for the purpose of enabling me to "keep the pot boiling" at home.

These productions afforded me a fair remuneration, but it was at best a precarious way of living, and I began to realize, seriously, that I was at the very bottom round of fortune's ladder, and that I had now arrived at an age when it was necessary to make one grand effort to raise myself above want, and to think soberly of laying up something for "a rainy day." I had hitherto been careless upon that point. I had engaged in divers enterprises, caring little what the result was, so that I made a present living for my family. I now saw that it was time to provide for the future.

About this period, I received a letter from my esteemed friend, Hon. Thomas T. Whittlesey, of Danbury. He had long held a mortgage of $500 on a piece of property which I owned in that town. He wrote to say that he was satisfied I never would lay up any thing until I could "invent a riddle that would hold water," and as that was not very likely to occur, I might as well pay him now as ever. That letter strengthened the resolutions I had made, and laying it aside unanswered, I said to myself, "Now, Mr. B., no more nonsense, no more living from hand to mouth, but from this moment please to concentrate your energies upon providing permanently for *the future*."

While engaged as outside clerk for the Bowery Amphitheatre, I casually learned that the collection of curiosities comprising Scudder's American Museum, at the corner of Broadway and Ann street, was for sale. It belonged to the daughters of Mr. Scudder, and was conducted for their benefit by John Furzman, under the authority of Mr. John Heath, administrator. The price asked for the entire collection was $15,000. It had cost its founder, Mr. Scudder, probably $50,000, and from the profits of the establishment he had been able to leave a large competency to his children. The Museum, however, had been for several years a losing concern, and the heirs were anxious to sell it.

It will not be considered surprising, under all the circumstances, that my speculative spirit should look in that direction for a permanent investment. My recent enterprises had not indeed been productive, and my funds were decidedly low; but my family was in poor health, I desired to enjoy the blessing of a fixed home—and so I repeatedly visited that Museum as a thoughtful looker-on. I saw, or believed I saw, that only energy, tact and liberality were needed, to give it life and to put it on a profitable footing; and although it might have appeared presumptuous, on my part, to dream of buying so valuable a property without having any money to do it with, I seriously determined to make the purchase, if possible.

I met a friend one day in the street, and told him my intentions. "*You* buy the American Museum?" said he with surprise, for he knew that my funds were at ebb-tide; "what do you intend buying it with?"

"*Brass,*" I replied, "for silver and gold I have none."

It was even so.

The Museum building, I learned, belonged to Mr. Francis W. Olmsted, a retired merchant, who had a suite of rooms in Park Place. How to approach this great man was a question. I was acquainted with no one who knew him, and to enter his presence without an introduction, I considered equivalent to being kicked out of his house. I therefore wrote him a letter, informing him that I desired to purchase the Museum collection, and that although I had no ready means, if it could be purchased upon a reasonable credit I was entirely confident that my tact and experience, added to a most determined devotion to business, would enable me to make the payments when due. On this basis I asked him to purchase the collection in his own name—give me a writing securing it to me provided I made the payments punctually, including the rent of his building—allow me twelve dollars and a half a week on which to support my family—and if at any time I failed to meet the instalment due, I would vacate the premises and forfeit all that might have been paid to that date. "In fact, Mr. Olmsted," I continued in my earnestness, "you may bind me in any way, and as tightly as you please—only give me a chance to dig out, or scratch out, and I will either do so or forfeit all the labor and trouble which I may have incurred."

I also endeavored to show Mr. Olmsted, that by making this arrangement he would secure a permanent tenant, whereas if I did not make the purchase the Museum would probably soon be closed. I added, that if he would have the goodness to grant me an interview, I should be happy to give him satisfactory references, and would also submit to any reasonable conditions which he might propose.

I took the letter myself, handed it to his servant, and in two days afterwards I received a reply, naming an hour for me to call on him. I was there at the exact moment, and Mr. Olmsted expressed himself pleased with my punctuality. He eyed me closely, and put several home questions regarding my habits and antecedents. I told him frankly my experience in the way of a caterer for public amusements—mentioned Vauxhall Garden, the circus, and several exhibitions that I had managed in the South. I was favorably impressed with Mr. Olmsted's appearance and manner. He indeed tried to assume an austere look, and to affect the aristocrat; but I thought I could see the good, open-hearted, noble *man* peering through his eyes, and a subsequent intimate acquaintance proved the correctness of my impressions respecting him.

"Who are your references?" he inquired.

"Any man in my line," I replied; "from Edmund Simpson, manager of the Park Theatre, or William Niblo, to Messrs. Welch, June, Titus, Turner, Angevine, or other circus or menagerie proprietors; also Moses Y. Beach of the New-York Sun."

"Can you get any of them to call on me?" he continued.

I informed him that I could, and it was arranged that they should call on him the next day, and myself the day afterwards. My friend Niblo willingly rode down in his carriage, and had an interview with Mr. Olmsted. Mr. Beach and several others among the gentlemen named also called, and on the following morning I waited upon the arbiter of my fate.

"I don't like your references, Mr. Barnum," said Mr. Olmsted abruptly, as soon as I entered the room.

I was confused, and said "I regretted to hear it."

"They all speak too well of you," he added, laughing; "in fact they talk as if they were all partners of yours, and intended to share the profits."

This intelligence, of course, pleased me. Mr. Olmsted then inquired if I could not induce some friend to give bonds as security that I should meet the instalments as they became due. I thought it was doubtful.

"Can you offer me any security in case I should make the purchase for you?" was his still more direct question.

I thought of several small pieces of land which I owned in Connecticut, but they were severely afflicted with mortgages. "I have some land and buildings in Connecticut, but there are encumbrances on them," I replied.

"Yes, yes; I don't want mortgaged property," said Mr. O.; "I should probably have to redeem it."

During further conversation, it was agreed that if he concluded to make the purchase for me, he should retain the property until it was all paid for; and should also appoint (at my expense) a ticket-receiver and accountant, who should render him a weekly statement. It was further stipulated that I should take in an apartment in the adjoining building, hitherto used as a billiard-room, and allow therefore five hundred dollars per year, making the entire rent three thousand dollars per annum, on a lease of ten years. I felt that in all this I had been liberal in my propositions and agreements, and hoped that the wealthy landlord would demand no more concessions. But he wanted something more.

"Now," said he, "if you only had a piece of unencumbered real estate that you could offer as additional security, I think I might venture to negotiate with you."

This seemed the turning-point of my fortune. Thinks I to myself, "It is now or never," and memory rapidly ran over my small possessions in search of the coveted bit of land. *Ivy Island,* in all the beauty in which my youthful imagination had pictured it, came dancing to my relief. I hesitated an instant. He is amply secured already—so I thought within myself—and without *some* piece of land, I may lose the Museum altogether. I saw no particular harm in it, and after a moment's hesitation I replied:

"I have five acres of land in Connecticut which is free from all lien or encumbrance."

"Indeed! what did you pay for it?"

"It was a present from my late grandfather, Phineas Taylor, given me on account of my name."

"Was he rich?" inquired Mr. Olmsted.

"He was considered well off in those parts," I answered.

"Very kind in him to give you the land. It is doubtless valuable. But I suppose you would not like to part with it, considering it was a present."

"I shall not have to part with it, if I make my payments punctually," I replied, "and I am sure I shall do that."

"Well," said Mr. Olmsted, "I think I will make the purchase for you. At all events, I'll think it over, and in the mean time you must see the administrator and heirs of the estate—get their best terms, and meet me here on my return to town a week hence."

I withdrew, and proceeded at once to the house of Mr. John Heath, the administrator. His price was $15,000. I offered him $10,000, payable in seven equal annual instalments, with good security. He could not think of selling at that price, and I agreed to call again.

During the week I had several interviews with Mr. Heath, and it was finally agreed that I should have it for $12,000, payable as above—possession to be given on the 15th November. Mr. Olmsted assented to this, and a morning was appointed to draw and sign the writings. Mr. Heath appeared, but said he must decline proceeding any farther in my case, as he had sold the collection to the directors of Peale's Museum (an incorporated institution) for $15,000, and had received $1000 in advance.

I was thunderstruck. I appealed to his honor. He replied that he had signed no writing with me, was not therefore legally bound, and he felt it his duty to do the best he could for the orphan girls. Mr. Olmsted said he was sorry for me, but could not help me. He would now have permanent tenants who would not require him to incur any risk, and I must necessarily be thrown overboard.

I withdrew, with feelings which I need not attempt to describe. I immediately informed myself as to the character of this Peale's Museum Company. It proved to consist of a company of speculators, headed by an unsuccessful ex-president of a bank, who had bought Peale's collection for a few thousand dollars, were now to join the American Museum with it, issue and sell stock to the amount of $50,000, pocket $30,000 profits, and permit the stockholders to look out for themselves.

I went immediately to several of the editors, including Major M. M. Noah, M. Y. Beach, my good friends, West, Herrick and Ropes, of the Atlas, and others, and stated my grievances. "Now," said I, "if you will grant me the use of your columns, I'll blow that speculation sky-high." They all consented, and I wrote a large number of squibs, cautioning the public against buying the Museum stock, ridiculed the idea of a board of broken-down bank directors engaging in the exhibition of stuffed monkey and gander skins, appealed to the case of the Zoological Institute, which had failed by adopting such a plan as the one now proposed, and finally told the public that such a speculation would be infinitely more unwise than Dickens's "Grand United Metropolitan Hot Muffin and Crumpet-baking and Punctual Delivery Company."

The stock was as dead as a herring! I then went to Mr. Heath and solicited a confidential conversation. He granted it. I asked him when the directors were to pay the other $14,000. "On the 26th day of December, or forfeit the $1000 already paid," was the reply. I assured him that they would never pay it, that they could not raise it, and that he would ultimately find himself with the Museum collection on his hands, and if once I started off with an exhibition for the South, I would not touch the Museum at *any* price. "Now," said I, " if you will agree with me confidentially, that in case these gentlemen do not pay you on the 26th December, I may have it on the 27th for $12,000, I will run the risk, and wait in this city until that date." He readily agreed to the proposition, but said he was sure they would not forfeit their $1000.

"Very well," said I; "all I ask of you is, that this arrangement shall not be mentioned." He assented. "On the 27th day of December, at ten o'clock A. M., I wish you to meet me in Mr. Olmsted's apartments, prepared to sign the writings, provided this incorporated company do not pay you $14,000 on the 26th." He agreed to this, and by my request put it in writing.

From that moment I felt that the Museum was mine. I saw Mr. Olmsted, and told him so. He promised secrecy, and agreed to sign the documents if the other parties did not meet their engagement.

This was about the 15th November. To all who spoke to me about the Museum, I simply remarked, that I had lost it. In the mean time the new company could not sell a dollar's worth of stock, for I kept up a perfect shower of squibs through the papers.

About the 1st of December, I received a letter from the Secretary of the Peale's Museum Company, or rather the " New-York Museum Company," as it was called, desiring me to meet the directors on the following Monday morning at the Museum, when and where I should probably hear something to my advantage. I saw that the newspaper medicine was doing its office. It was evident that those gentlemen wished to purchase my silence.

I was punctual at the meeting. The "honorable board of directors" was in session. The venerable President, a gray-haired, hawk-eyed old man, who had recently been President of a broken bank, accosted me with his blandest smile and smoothest tone of language. The upshot of the matter was, they proposed to hire me to manage the united museums. I professed to take it all in earnest, and when asked to mention the salary I should expect, I specified $3000 per annum. They complimented me on my character for ability in that department, and engaged me at the sum I demanded, my salary to commence on the 1st day of January, 1842. As I was leaving the "august presence," the amiable President pleasantly remarked, "Of course, Mr. Barnum, we shall have no more of your squibs through the newspapers."

"I ever try to serve the interests of my employers," I replied.

The jolly directors probably had a hearty laugh so soon as I was beyond hearing their unseemly mirth. They probably meant by thus keeping me quiet to sell their stock, and permit the stockholders to throw me overboard as soon as they pleased. They thought they had caught me securely. I *knew* that I had caught *them*.

Finding that I was now removed out of the way, those directors did not fear that any other person would attempt to buy the American Museum, and they concluded not to advertise their stock until the first of January, as that would give the people longer time to forget the attacks which I had made on it. As for their promised payment on the 26th December, unaware that Mr. Heath had contracted to me for $12,000, they thought he would cheerfully wait on them until it suited their pleasure to pay him. In fact, so unconcerned were they upon this point, that they did not even call on the administrator on the 26th inst., nor send him the slightest apology for not doing so!

On the morning of the 27th, I was at Mr. Olmsted's apartment, with my legal counsellor, CHAS. T. CROMWELL, Esq., at half-past nine o'clock. Mr. Heath came with his lawyer punctually at ten, and before two o'clock that day I was put in formal possession of the American Museum. The first act which I performed, after being thus installed, was to write and dispatch the following note:

AMERICAN MUSEUM, NEW-YORK, Dec. 27, 1841.

To the President and Directors of the New-York Museum:

GENTLEMEN:—It gives me great pleasure to inform you that you are placed upon the Free List of this establishment until further notice.

P. T. BARNUM, Proprietor.

The President was astonished beyond measure, and could scarcely believe his eyes. He called upon Mr. Heath, and learned that I had indeed bought and was in possession of the American Museum. His indignation knew no bounds. He threatened him with a prosecution, but finding that this availed him nothing, he demanded the return of the thousand dollars which had been paid on the agreement. It was refused because forfeited, and the company lost it.

No one will doubt that I now put forth all my energy. It was strictly "neck or nothing." I must either pay for the establishment within a stipulated period, or forfeit it, including all I might have paid on account, provided Mr. Olmsted should insist on the letter of the contract. Let "come what would," I was determined to *deserve* success, and brain and hands and feet were alike busy in forwarding the interests of the Museum.

The system of economy necessary to support my family in the city of New-York upon $600 a year, was not only assented to by my treasure of a wife, but she expressed her willingness to reduce the expenses to four hundred dollars per year, if necessary.

One day, about six months after I had purchased the Museum, my friend Mr. Olmsted happened in at my ticket office about twelve o'clock, and found me alone eating my dinner, which consisted of a few slices of corned beef and bread that I had brought from home in the morning. "Is this the way you eat your dinner?" he inquired.

"I have not eaten a warm dinner since I bought the Museum, except on the Sabbath," I replied, "and I intend never to eat another on a week-day until I am out of debt."

"Ah! you are safe, and will pay for the Museum before the year is out," he replied, clapping me familiarly on the shoulder. And he was right, for in less than a year from that period, I was in full possession of the Museum as my own property, every cent having been paid out of the profits of the establishment.

The American Museum, at the date of my purchase, was little more than the nucleus of what it is now. During the thirteen years of my proprietorship, I have considerably more than doubled the value of the permanent attractions and curiosities of the establishment. The additions were derived, partly from Peale's Museum, (which I bought and transferred to my former collection in the fall of 1842;) partly from the large and rare collection known as the Chinese Museum, (which I removed to the American Museum in 1848;) and partly by purchases wherever I could find curiosities, in both America and Europe.

The space now occupied for my Museum purposes is more than double what it was in 1841. The Lecture Room, which was originally narrow, ill-contrived and uncomfortable, has been several times enlarged and improved, and at present may be pronounced one of the most commodious and beautiful halls of entertainment in New-York.

There have been enlargement and improvement in other respects. At first, the Museum was merely a collection of curiosities by day, and in the evening there was a performance, consisting of disjointed and disconnected amusements, such as are still to be found at many of the inferior shows. Saturday *afternoon* was soon appropriated to performances, and shortly afterwards the *afternoon* of Wednesday was added. The programme has for years included the afternoon and evening of every day in the week, (of course excepting the Sabbath,) and on great holidays, we have sometimes given as many as twelve performances.

There has been a gradual change in these, and the transient attractions of the Museum have been greatly diversified. Industrious fleas, educated dogs, jugglers, automatons, ventriloquists, living statuary, tableaux, gipsies, albinoes, fat boys, giants, dwarfs, rope-dancers, caricatures of phrenology, and "live Yankees," pantomime, instrumental music, singing and dancing in great variety, (including Ethiopians,) etc. Dioramas, panoramas, models of Dublin, Paris, Niagara, Jerusalem, etc., mechanical figures, fancy glassblowing, knitting machines and other triumphs in the mechanical arts, dissolving views, American Indians, including their warlike and religious ceremonies enacted on the stage, etc., etc.

I need not specify the order of time in which these varieties were presented to the public. In one respect there has been a thorough though gradual change in the general plan, for the *moral drama* is now, and has been for several years, the principal feature of the Lecture Room of the American Museum.

Apart from the merit and interest of these performances, and apart from every thing connected with the stage, my permanent collection of curiosities is, without doubt, abundantly worth the uniform charge of admission to all the entertainments of the establishment, and I can therefore afford to be accused of "humbug" when I add such transient novelties as increase its attractions. If I have exhibited a questionable dead mermaid in my Museum, it should not be overlooked that I have also exhibited cameleopards, a rhinoceros, grisly bears, orang-outangs, great serpents, etc., about which there could be no mistake because they were alive; and I should hope that a little "clap-trap" occasionally, in the way of transparencies, flags, exaggerated pictures, and puffing advertisements, might find an offset in a wilderness of wonderful, instructive, and amusing realities. Indeed I cannot doubt that the sort of "clap-trap" here referred to, is allowable, and that the public like a little of it mixed up with the great realities which I provide. The titles of "humbug," and the "prince of humbugs," were first applied to me by myself. I made these titles a part of my "stock in trade," and may here quote a passage from the "Fortunes of the Scattergood Family," a work by the popular English writer, Albert Smith:

> "'It's a great thing to be a humbug,' said Mr. Rossett. 'I've been called so often. It means hitting the public in reality. Anybody who can do so, is sure to be called a humbug by somebody who can't.'"

Among my first extra exhibitions produced at the American Museum, was a model of the Falls of Niagara, belonging to Grain the artist. It was undoubtedly a fine model, giving the mathematical proportions of that great cataract, and the trees, rocks, buildings, etc., in its vicinity. But the absurdity of the thing consisted in introducing water, thus pretending to present a *fac simile* of that great wonder of nature. The falls were about eighteen inches high, every thing else being in due proportion!

I confess I felt somewhat ashamed of this myself, yet it made a good line in the bill, and I bought the model for $200. My advertisements then announced among the attractions of the Museum,

THE GREAT MODEL OF NIAGARA FALLS,
WITH REAL WATER!

A single barrel of water answered the purpose of this model for an entire season; for the falls flowed into a reservoir behind the scenes, and the water was continually re-supplied to the cataract by means of a small pump.

Many visitors who could not afford to travel to Niagara, were doubtless induced to visit the "model with real water," and if they found it rather "small potatoes," they had the whole Museum to fall back upon for 25 cents, and no fault was found.

One day I was peremptorily summoned to appear before the Board of Croton Water Commissioners the next morning at ten o'clock. I was punctual.

"Sir," said the President, "you pay only $25 per annum for the Croton water at the Museum. That is simply intended to supply the ordinary purposes of your establishment. We cannot furnish water for your Niagara Falls without large extra compensation."

Begging "his honor" not to believe all he read in the papers, nor to be too literal in the interpretation of my large showbills, I explained the operation of the great cataract, and offered to pay a dollar a drop for all the water I used for Niagara Falls exceeding one barrel per month, provided my pump continued in good order! I was permitted to retire, amid a hearty burst of laughter from the Commissioners, in which his honor the President condescended to join.

On one occasion, Louis Gaylord Clark, Esq., the witty and popular editor of the "Knickerbocker," called to view my Museum. I had never had the pleasure of seeing him before, and he introduced himself. I was extremely anxious that my establishment should receive a "first-rate notice" in his popular magazine, and therefore accompanied him through the entire Museum, taking especial pains to point out all objects of interest. We passed the entrance of the hall containing Niagara Falls just as the visitors had entered it from the performances in the Lecture Room, and hearing the pump at work, I was aware that the great cataract was at that moment in full operation.

I desired to avoid that exhibition, feeling confident that if Mr. Clark should see the model Niagara, he would be so much disgusted with the entire show that he would "blow it up" in his "Knickerbocker," or (what I always consider much the worse for me) pass it by in *silent* contempt. Seeing him approach the entrance, I endeavored to call his attention to some object of interest in the other hall, but I was too late. He had noticed a concourse of visitors in the "Falls Room," and his curiosity to know what was going on was excited.

"Hold on, Barnum," said Clark; "let us see what you have here."

"It is only a model of Niagara Falls," I replied.

"Oh, ah, yes, yes, I remember now. I have noticed your advertisements and splendid posters announcing Niagara Falls with real water. I have some curiosity to see the cataract in operation," said

Clark, at the same time mounting upon a chair in order to obtain a full view over the heads of the visitors.

I felt considerably sheepish as I saw this movement, and listened to the working of the old pump, whose creakings seemed to me to be worse than ever. I held my breath, expecting to hear the sagacious editor pronounce this the silliest humbug that he ever saw. I was presently, however, as much surprised as delighted to hear him say:

"Well, Barnum, I declare that is quite a new idea. I never saw the like before."

I revived in a moment; and thinking that if Louis Gaylord Clark could see any thing attractive in the old model, he must be particularly green, I determined to do all in my power to assist his verdancy. "Yes," I replied, "it is quite a new idea."

"I declare I never saw any thing of the kind before in all my life," exclaimed Clark with much enthusiasm.

"I flatter myself it is, in point of originality and ingenuity, considerably ahead of any invention of modern times," I replied with a feeling of exultation, as I saw that I had caught the great critic, and was sure of a puff of the best sort.

"Original!" exclaimed the editor. "Yes, it is certainly original. I never dreamed of such a thing; I never saw any thing of the kind before since I was born—and I hope with all my heart I never shall again!"

It is needless to say that I was completely taken in, and felt that any ordinary keyhole was considerably larger than would be necessary for me to crawl through.

We then passed to the upper stories of the Museum, and finally to the roof, where I had advertised an "aerial garden," which consisted of two tubs, each containing a stunted and faded cedar, and ten or twelve pots of wilted flowers, backed up by a dozen small tables and a few chairs for the accommodation of such partakers of ice-cream as could appreciate the beauties of ever-verdant nature, as shown forth in the tubs and pots aforesaid.

The "Knickerbocker" appeared, and I felt happy to see that while it spoke of the assiduity in business manifested by the new proprietor of the Museum, and a prognostication that he would soon render his establishment highly popular, the editor had kindly refrained from making any allusion to "THE CATARACT OF NIAGARA WITH REAL WATER!"

Some months subsequent to this, Mr. Clark came rushing into the Museum almost out of breath, and with much earnestness saluted me thus: "Friend Barnum, I have come in to ask if you have got the club in the Museum that Captain Cook was killed with?"

Remembering that I had a large lot of Indian war-clubs among the collection of aboriginal curiosities, and feeling that I owed Clark a joke for his Niagara Falls catch, I instantly replied that I was the owner of the club in question.

"Well, I declare I am very glad to hear it," said he; "for do you know that I have for a long time had a singular and irrepressible desire to see that club?"

"Wait here a few minutes, and I will show it to you," I replied.

Passing up stairs, I commenced overhauling a lot of war-clubs, and finally selected a heavy one that looked as if it *might* have killed Captain Cook, or any body else whose head it came in contact with. Having affixed a small label on it, reading "The Capt. Cook Club," I took it down to Mr. Clark, assuring him that this was the instrument of death which he had inquired for.

"Is it possible!" said he, as he took it in his hand. Presently raising it above his head, he exclaimed, "Well, I declare, this is a terrible weapon with which to take a man's life."

"Yes," I replied seriously, but feeling an inward delight that I was now paying off Mr. Clark with interest; "I believe it killed the victim at the first blow!"

"Poor Captain Cook!" exclaimed Clark with a sigh; "I wonder if he was conscious after receiving the fatal blow."

"I don't think he could have been," I responded with a well-feigned look of sorrow.

"You are sure this is the identical club?" inquired Clark.

"We have documents which place its identity beyond all question," I replied.

"Poor Cook! poor Cook!" said Clark musingly. "Well, Mr. Barnum," he continued with great gravity, at the same time extending his hand and giving mine a hearty shake, "I am really very much obliged to you for your kindness. I had an irrepressible desire to see the club that killed Captain Cook, and I felt quite confident you could accommodate me. I have been in half a dozen smaller museums, and as *they all had it,* I was sure a large establishment like yours would not be without it!"

My laurels were fast withering, and I felt that unless I kept my wits about me and managed to pay Clark at least an instalment on what I owed him, I should be the laughing-stock of all his acquaintances. A few weeks afterwards, therefore, I wrote him a note, saying that I desired to consult him for a few moments at my office on a subject of serious importance to me. He came immediately.

"Now," said I, "I do not want any of your nonsense, but I want your sober advice."

"My dear Barnum," he replied in the fulness of his truly generous heart, "nothing will give me greater pleasure than to serve you in any way in my power."

I proceeded to inform him that a gentleman who had visited Egypt had brought from the river Nile a most remarkable living fish, which he offered to hire for exhibition. The fish, I told him, was of a peculiar formation, and that the owner of it would place $5000 in the hands of a responsible banker, to be forfeited if the fish did not within six weeks pass through a transformation by which its tail would disappear, and it would then have *legs*.

"Is it possible?" exclaimed Clark, in great astonishment.

I assured him that there was no mistake about it. "But," said I, "his price is high, and I want to ask your opinion in regard to its success. He asks $100 per week for the use of it."

"It is cheap enough, my dear fellow. It will draw you more than that sum extra per day. Why, the whole thing is incredible. It will startle the naturalists—wake up the whole scientific world—and draw in the masses."

"Do you really think so?" I asked.

"Upon my honor, I am sure of it," responded Clark with much enthusiasm. "Make an engagement for six months, or for a year if possible, then come out and state the facts regarding this wonderful transformation—announce that $5000 have been deposited in responsible hands which will be forfeited to the poor of this city if the change does not take place as described, and my word for it, your museum will not be large enough to contain your visitors. I declare I believe you will make $20,000 by the operation!"

I thanked Mr. Clark very warmly for his kind counsel, and assured him I should not fail to take his advice. "In fact," said I, "I thought well of the speculation, excepting that I did not like the name of the fish. I think *that* is an objection."

"Tush, tush, not at all; what's in a name? Nothing. That makes no difference whatever. What *is* the name of the fish?"

"Tadpole, but it is vulgarly called a pollywog," I replied, with becoming gravity.

"Sold, by thunder!" exclaimed Clark, springing to his feet and rushing down stairs.

The "Fejee Mermaid" was by many supposed to be a curiosity manufactured by myself, or made to my order. This is not the fact. I certainly had much to do in bringing it before the public, and as I am now in the confessional mood, I will "make a clean breast" of the ways and means I adopted for that purpose. I must first, however, relate how it came into my possession and its alleged history.

Early in the summer of 1842, Moses Kimball, Esq., the popular proprietor of the Boston Museum, came to New-York and exhibited to me what purported to be a mermaid. He stated that he had bought it of a sailor whose father, while in Calcutta in 1817 as captain of a Boston ship, (of which Captain John Ellery was principal owner,) had purchased it, believing it to be a preserved specimen of a veritable mermaid, obtained, as he was assured, from Japanese sailors. Not doubting that it would prove as surprising to others as it had been to himself, and hoping to make a rare speculation of it as an extraordinary curiosity, he appropriated $6000 of the ship's money to the purchase of it, left the ship in charge of the mate, and went to London.

He did not realize his expectations, and returned to Boston. Still believing that his curiosity was a genuine animal and therefore highly valuable, he preserved it with great care, not stinting himself in the expense of keeping it insured, though re-engaged as ship's captain under his former employers to reimburse the sum taken from their funds to pay for the mermaid. He died possessing no other property, and his only son and heir, who placed a low estimate on his father's purchase, sold it to Mr. Kimball, who brought it to New-York for my inspection.

Such was the story. Not trusting my own acuteness on such matters, I requested my naturalist's opinion of the *genuineness* of the animal. He replied that he could not conceive how it was manufactured; for he never knew a monkey with such peculiar teeth, arms, hands, etc., nor had he knowledge of a fish with such peculiar fins.

"Then why do you suppose it is manufactured?" I inquired.

"Because I don't believe in mermaids," replied the naturalist.

"That is no reason at all," said I, "and therefore I'll believe in the mermaid, and hire it."

This was the easiest part of the experiment. How to modify general incredulity in the existence of mermaids, so far as to awaken curiosity to see and examine the specimen, was now the all-important question. Some extraordinary means must be resorted to, and I saw no better method than to "start the ball a-rolling" at some distance from the centre of attraction.

In due time a communication appeared in the New-York Herald, dated and mailed in Montgomery, Ala., giving the news of the day, trade, the crops, political gossip, etc., and also an incidental paragraph about a certain Dr. Griffin, agent of the Lyceum of Natural History in London, recently from Pernambuco, who had in his possession a most remarkable curiosity, being nothing less than a veritable mermaid taken among the Fejee Islands, and preserved in China, where the Doctor had bought it at a high figure for the Lyceum of Natural History.

A week or ten days afterwards, a letter of similar tenor, dated and mailed in Charleston, S. C., varying of course in the items of local news, was published in another New-York paper.

This was followed by a third letter, dated and mailed in Washington city, published in still another New-York paper—there being in addition the expressed hope that the editors of the Empire City would beg a sight of the extraordinary curiosity before Dr. Griffin took ship for England.

A few days subsequently to the publication of this thrice-repeated announcement, Mr. Lyman (who was my employee in the case of Joice Heth) was duly registered at one of the principal hotels in Philadelphia as Dr. Griffin of Pernambuco for London. His gentlemanly, dignified, yet social manners and liberality gained him a fine reputation for a few days, and when he paid his bill one afternoon, preparatory to leaving for New-York the next day, he expressed his thanks to the landlord for special attention and courtesy. "If you will step to my room," said Lyman, alias Griffin, "I will permit you to see something that will surprise you." Whereupon the landlord was shown the most extraordinary curiosity in the world—a mermaid. He was so highly gratified and interested that he earnestly begged permission to introduce certain friends of his, including several editors, to view the wonderful specimen.

"Although it is no interest of mine," said the curiosity-hunter, "the Lyceum of Natural History, of which I am agent, will not be injured by granting the courtesy you request." And so an appointment was made for the evening.

The result might easily be gathered from the editorial columns of the Philadelphia papers a day or two subsequently to that interview with the mermaid. Suffice it to say, that the plan worked admirably, and the Philadelphia press aided the press of New-York in awakening a wide-reaching and increasing curiosity to see the mermaid.

I may as well confess that those three communications from the South were written by myself, and forwarded to friends of mine, with instructions respectively to mail them, each on the day of its date. This fact and the corresponding post-marks did much to prevent suspicion of a hoax, and the New-York editors thus unconsciously contributed to my arrangements for bringing the mermaid into public notice.

Lyman then returned to New-York with his precious treasure, and putting up at the Pacific Hotel in Greenwich street as Dr. Griffin, it soon reached the ears of the wide-awake reporters for the press that the mermaid was in town. They called at the Pacific Hotel, and the polite agent of the British Lyceum of Natural History kindly permitted them to gratify their curiosity. The New-York newspapers contained numerous reports of these examinations, all of which were quite satisfactory.

I am confident that the reporters and editors who examined this animal were honestly persuaded that it was what it purported to be—a veritable mermaid. Nor is this to be wondered at, since, if it was a work of art, the monkey and fish were so nicely conjoined that no human eye could detect the point where the junction was formed. The spine of the fish proceeded in a straight and apparently unbroken line to the base of the skull—the hair of the animal was found growing several inches down on the shoulders of the fish, and the application of a microscope absolutely revealed what seemed to be minute fish scales lying in myriads amidst the hair. The teeth and formation of the fingers and hands differed materially from those of any monkey or orang-outang ever discovered, while the location of the fins was different from those of any species of the fish tribe known to naturalists. The animal was an ugly, dried-up, black-looking, and diminutive specimen, about three feet long. Its mouth was open, its tail turned over, and its arms thrown up, giving it the appearance of having died in great agony.

Assuming, what is no doubt true, that the mermaid was manufactured, it was a most remarkable specimen of ingenuity and untiring patience. For my own part I really had scarcely cared at the time to form an opinion of the origin of this creature, but it was my impression that it was the work of some ingenious Japanese, Chinaman, or other eastern genius, and that it had probably been one among the many hideous objects of Buddhist or Hindoo worship.

Recently, however, in reading myself up on the history of Japan, I found the following article in a work entitled "Manners and Customs of the Japanese in the Nineteenth Century, from the accounts of recent Dutch residents in Japan, and from the German work of Dr. Ph. Fr. Von Siebold:"

> "Another Japanese fisherman displayed his ingenuity in a less honorable and useful form than Kiyemon, to make money out of his countrymen's passion for whatever is odd and strange. He contrived to unite the upper half of a monkey to the lower half of a fish, so neatly as to defy ordinary inspection. He then gave out that he had caught the creature alive in his net, but that it had died shortly after being taken out of the water; and he derived considerable pecuniary profit from his device in more ways than one. The exhibition of the sea monster to Japanese curiosity paid well; but yet more productive was the assertion that the half-human fish had spoken during the few minutes it existed out of its native element, predicting a certain number of years of wonderful fertility, to be followed by a fatal epidemic, the only remedy against which would be possession of the marine prophet's likeness. The sale of these pictured mermaids was immense. Either this composite animal, or another, the offspring of the success of the first, was sold to the Dutch factory and transmitted to Batavia, where it fell into the hands of a shrewd American, who brought it to Europe, and there, in the years 1822–3, exhibited his purchase as a real mermaid, at every capital, to the admiration of the ignorant, the perplexity of the learned, and the filling of his own purse."

Is it not a plausible conjecture that this account relates to the identical mermaid exhibited in the American Museum? Certainly the method adopted to induce people to buy the likeness, as related by Siebold, fairly entitles my Japanese *confrère* to the palm and title of "Prince of Humbugs."

Smaller specimens, purporting to be mermaids, but less elaborately gotten up, have been seen in various museums. I believe they are all made in Japan. I purchased one in the Peale collection in Philadelphia. It was burnt at the time the Museum opened by me in that city was destroyed by fire in 1851.

A small specimen, I have been informed, is also now lying on a shelf in the Royal Museum of Indian Antiquities at the Hague. I understand that it was purchased for the collection from an American sea captain, who procured it in China, probably an importation from Japan.

While Lyman was preparing public opinion on mermaids at the Pacific Hotel, I was industriously at work (though of course privately) in getting up wood-cuts and transparencies, as well as a pamphlet, proving the authenticity of mermaids, all in anticipation of the speedy exhibition of Dr. Griffin's specimen. I had three several and distinct pictures of mermaids engraved, and with a peculiar description written for each, had them inserted in 10,000 copies of the pamphlet which I had printed and quietly stored away in a back office until the time came to use them.

I then called respectively on the editors of the New-York Herald, and two of the Sunday papers, and tendered to each the free use of a mermaid cut, with a well-written description, for their papers of the ensuing Sunday. I informed each editor that I had hoped to use this cut in showing the Fejee Mermaid, but since Mr. Griffin had announced that as agent for the Lyceum of Natural History, he could not permit it to be exhibited in America, my chance seemed dubious, and therefore he was welcome to the use of the engraving and description. The three mermaids made their appearance in the three different papers on the morning of Sunday, July 17, 1842.

Each editor supposed he was giving his readers an exclusive treat in the mermaid line, but when they came to discover that I had played the same game with the three different papers, they pronounced it a *scaly* trick.

The mermaid fever was now getting pretty well up. Few city readers had missed seeing at least one of the illustrations, and as the several printed descriptions made direct allusion to *the* mermaid of Mr. Griffin now in town, a desire to see it was generally prevailing. My 10,000 mermaid pamphlets were then put into the hands of boys, and sold at a penny each, (half the cost,) in all the principal hotels, stores, etc., etc.

When I thought the public was thoroughly "posted up" on the subject of mermaids, I sent an agent to engage Concert Hall,

Broadway, for the exhibition, and the newspapers immediately contained the following advertisement:

> THE MERMAID, AND OTHER WONDERFUL SPECIMENS OF THE ANIMAL CREATION.—The public are respectfully informed that, in accordance with numerous and urgent solicitations from scientific gentlemen in this city, Mr. J. GRIFFIN, proprietor of the Mermaid, recently arrived from Pernambuco, S. A., has consented to exhibit it to the public, *positively for one week only!* For this purpose he has procured the spacious saloon known as Concert Hall, 404 Broadway, which will open on Monday, August 8, 1842, and will positively close on Saturday the 13th inst.
>
> This animal was taken near the Fejee Islands, and purchased for a large sum by the present proprietor, for the Lyceum of Natural History in London, and is exhibited for this short period more for the gratification of the public than for gain. The proprietor having been engaged for several years in various parts of the world in collecting wonderful specimens in Natural History, has in his possession, and will at the same time submit to public inspection, THE ORNITHORHINCHUS, from New-Holland, being the connecting link between the Seal and the Duck. THE FLYING FISH, two distinct species, one from the Gulf Stream, and the other from the West Indies. This animal evidently connects the Bird with the Fish. THE PADDLE-TAIL SNAKE from South-America. THE SIREN, or MUD IGUANA, an intermediate animal between the Reptile and the Fish. THE PROTEUS SANGUIHUS, a subterraneous animal from a grotto in Australia—with other animals forming connecting links in the great chain of Animated Nature.
>
> Tickets of admission 25 cents each.

A large number of visitors attended Concert Hall, and Lyman, alias Griffin, exhibited the mermaid with much dignity. I could not help fearing that some of the Joice Heth victims would discover in Professor Griffin the exhibitor of the "nurse of Washington," but happily no such catastrophe occurred. Lyman, surrounded by numerous connecting links in nature, as set forth in the advertisement, and with the hideous-looking mermaid firmly secured from the hands of visitors by a glass vase, enlightened his audiences by curious accounts of his travels and adventures, and by scientific harangues upon the works of nature in general, and mermaids in particular.

The public appeared to be satisfied, but as some persons always *will* take things literally, and make no allowance for poetic license even in mermaids, an occasional visitor, after having seen the large transparency in front of the hall, representing a beautiful creature half woman and half fish, about eight feet in length, would be slightly surprised in finding that the reality was a black-looking specimen of dried monkey and fish that a boy a few years old could easily run away with under his arm.

Several days subsequent to the opening of the exhibition at Concert Hall, an old Dutchman came to the Museum and said to me, in a drawling tone of voice, "Where is the *mare*-maid?"

"We have no mermaid here, sir," I replied.

"I've come over from Jarsey on purpose to see the mare-maid. I thought it was here."

I informed him that I had seen it advertised at Concert Hall, Broadway. He started off in pursuit of the object of his curiosity, remarking as he turned to go down stairs, "I have never seen a maremaid. It's alive I s'pose, ain't it?" But I did not profess ability to enlighten him on that point.

Immediately afterwards, I went up to Concert Hall to see how the exhibition was progressing, and just as I passed in, I saw the old Dutchman purchasing a ticket at the foot of the stairs. I found Lyman surrounded with twenty or thirty ladies and gentlemen, to whom he was learnedly descanting on the wonders of nature, as illustrated in the objects on the table before them. They were all attention. Presently the old Dutchman entered, and upon looking around, and being unable to discover the beautiful living lady-fish so elegantly displayed upon the transparency at the door, he approached Lyman, and, interrupting him in his learned discourse, said to him, "I want to see the *mare*-maid."

Lyman, somewhat disconcerted, but with as much dignity and deliberation as he could command, replied, "That is the mermaid, sir," at the same time pointing to the article in question.

The old Dutchman looked upon the diminutive, ugly creature, and exclaimed in great surprise, "Do you call *that* the *mare*-maid?"

"Yes, sir, that is the mermaid," said Lyman, evidently ill at ease. The Dutchman, with a look of scorn such as I have rarely seen equalled, turned to depart, exclaiming, "Well, that is the poorest show I ever *did* see."

On one occasion Lyman left the room for a few minutes. There were few visitors present, principally young students from the Medical College in Barclay street. Perceiving her fish-ship without protector, and being ripe for a joke, they removed the glass vase which covered the mermaid, and thrust into her mouth a cigar from which perhaps half an inch had been "whiffed." They replaced the vase and decamped.

Before Lyman returned, a score or more ladies and gentlemen had entered the room, and it is difficult to say what their feelings were when they saw the little, black, dried mermaid with a cigar in her mouth! They probably felt that the whole thing was an imposition, and that the exhibitor was purposely insulting his customers. Certainly it was the most ridiculous and ludicrous sight that can easily be conceived.

Lyman, wholly unconscious of the wicked trick which had been played upon him, and seeing the respectable number of visitors, approached the table with a dignity which no man could assume better than himself; and, without happening to cast his eyes upon the mermaid, commenced his usual harangue: "You see before you, ladies and gentlemen, the extraordinary mermaid captured at the Fejee Islands. The mermaid has long been deemed a fabulous animal by many persons, including naturalists, but the evidence I possess, as agent for the Lyceum of Natural History in London, places the fact beyond all reasonable doubt, that this identical animal was taken in a fisherman's net at the Fejee Islands. It lived upwards of three hours after its capture."

"Was her ladyship smoking the same cigar when she was captured that she is enjoying at present?" asked one of the gentlemen.

Poor Lyman now for the first time discovered the cigar, and this was probably the first and only time in his life that he was completely nonplussed, and could not utter a word in reply. In relating the incident, (which he afterwards did with great gusto in the private circles of his friends,) he declared that when he discovered that cigar, he began to perspire as if he had been mowing a heavy crop of grass, and that very soon he had not a dry thread upon his back.

The mermaid remained a single week at Concert Hall, and was then advertised to be seen at the American Museum, "without extra charge." Numerous transparencies had been prepared; show-bills were posted with a liberal hand; and on Monday morning a flag representing a mermaid eighteen feet in length was streaming directly in front of the Museum. Lyman saw it as he was slowly approaching to commence operations. He quickened his pace, entered my office, and demanded, "What in the name of all conscience is that immense flag out for?"

"In order that nobody shall enter Broadway without knowing where to find the mermaid," I replied.

"Well, that flag must come in. Nobody can satisfy the public with our dried-up specimen *eighteen inches* long, after exhibiting a picture representing it as *eighteen feet.* It is preposterous."

"Oh, nonsense," I replied; "that is only to catch the eye. They don't expect to see a mermaid of that size."

"I tell you it won't do," replied Lyman, "I think I ought to know something of the public 'swallow' by this tune, and I tell you the mermaid won't go down if that flag remains up."

"That flag cost me over seventy dollars, and it must remain up," I replied.

Lyman deliberately buttoned his coat, and said as he slowly walked towards the door, "Well, Mr. Barnum, if you like to fight under that flag, you can do so, but *I* won't."

"What! you are a deserter, then!" I replied, laughing.

"Yes, I desert false colors when they are too strong," said Lyman; "and *you* will desert them before night," he continued.

I could not spare "Professor Griffin," and was reluctantly compelled to take down the flag. It never saw the light again.[1]

The mermaid was afterwards exhibited in various parts of the country, and finally returned to its owner, Mr. KIMBALL, who has ever since given it a prominent niche in his truly beautiful and attractive "BOSTON MUSEUM." There it will remain until the 31st day of March, 1855. On the 1st of April next, (a most appropriate day,) it will again make its appearance in my AMERICAN MUSEUM, NEW-YORK, where it will remain until January 1st, 1856, to the admiration and astonishment, no doubt, of many thousand patrons. On the 2d day of January, 1856, the mysterious lady-fish will again take up her old quarters under the guardianship of her owner, the HON. MOSES KIMBALL, (he having recently been elected to the State Senate, and thus acquired the title,) and from that period the FEJEE MERMAID will be installed as a prominent and interesting *fixture* in the BOSTON MUSEUM.

That "her ladyship" was an attractive feature, may be inferred from these facts and figures:

---

1. Barnum's note: Lyman afterwards became a prominent Mormon, and removed to Nauvoo, where be died.

The receipts of the American Museum for the four weeks immediately preceding the exhibition of the mermaid, amounted to $1272. During the first four weeks of the mermaid's exhibition, the receipts amounted to $3341.93.

The New-York Museum Company, having failed in selling their stock, let their establishment, known as Peale's Museum, to Yankee Hill. After a management of a few months, he failed. Mr. Henry Bennett then took charge of it, reduced the price to one "York shilling," and endeavored to thrive by burlesquing whatever I produced. Thus, when I exhibited the Fejee Mermaid, he stuck a codfish and monkey together and advertised the *Fudg-ee* Mermaid. When I announced a company of talented vocalists, well known as the "Orphean Family," Bennett advertised the "*Orphan* Family." It was an invention creditable to his genius, and created some laughter at my expense, but it also served to draw attention to my Museum.

After the novelty of Bennett's opposition died away, he did a losing business, and on the 2d of January, 1843, he closed his Museum, having lost his last dollar. The entire collection fell into the hands of the proprietor of the building, on a claim of arrearages of rent amounting to six or eight thousand dollars. I purchased it privately for $7000, cash, hired the building, and secretly engaging Bennett as my agent, we run a spirited opposition. I found profit in the arrangement by attracting public attention, and at the end of six months, the whole establishment, including the splendid Gallery of American Portraits, was transferred to my American Museum.

I do not here intend to disparage Bennett's ability nor to glorify my own. Independently of any thing personal to either of us, I had superior advantages; and if the result of the real strife between us had at any time been doubtful, my lucky stars soon put me in possession of a means of overwhelming all opposition.

Being in Albany on business in November, 1842, the Hudson River was frozen tight, and I returned to New-York by way of the Housatonic Railroad. I stopped one night in Bridgeport, Ct., my brother, Philo F., keeping the Franklin Hotel at the time.

I had heard of a remarkably small child in Bridgeport; and by my request my brother brought him to the hotel. He was the smallest child I ever saw that could walk alone. He was not two feet in height, and weighed less than sixteen pounds. He was a bright-eyed little fellow, with light hair and ruddy cheeks, was perfectly healthy, and as symmetrical as an Apollo. He was exceedingly bashful, but after some coaxing he was induced to converse with me, and informed me that his name was CHARLES S. STRATTON, son of Sherwood E. Stratton.

He was only five years old, and to exhibit a dwarf of that age might provoke the question, How do you know that he *is* a dwarf? Some license might indeed be taken with the facts, but even with this advantage I really felt that the adventure was nothing more than an experiment, and I engaged him for the short term of *four weeks at three dollars per week*—all charges, including travelling and boarding of himself and mother, being at my expense.

They arrived in New-York on Thanksgiving Day, Dec. 8, 1842, and Mrs. Stratton was greatly astonished to find her son heralded in my Museum bills as Gen. TOM THUMB, a dwarf of eleven years of age, just arrived from England!

This announcement contained two deceptions. I shall not attempt to justify them, but may be allowed to plead the circumstances in extenuation. The boy was undoubtedly a dwarf, and I had the most reliable evidence that he had grown little, if any, since he was six months old; but had I announced him as only five years of age, it would have been impossible to excite the interest or awaken the curiosity of the public. The thing I aimed at was, to assure them that he was *really a dwarf*—and in *this,* at least, they were not deceived.

It was of no consequence, in reality, where he was born or where he came from, and if the announcement that he was *a foreigner* answered my purpose, the people had only themselves to blame if they did not get their money's worth when they visited the exhibition. I had observed (and sometimes, as in the case of Vivalla, had taken advantage of) the American fancy for European exotics; and if the deception, practiced for a season in my dwarf experiment, has done any thing towards checking our disgraceful preference for foreigners, I may readily be pardoned for the offence I here acknowledge.

I took great pains to train my diminutive prodigy, devoting many hours to that purpose, by day and by night, and succeeded, because he had native talent and an intense love of the ludicrous. He became very fond of me. I was, and yet am, sincerely attached to him, and I candidly believe him at this moment to be the most interesting and extraordinary natural curiosity of which the world has any knowledge.

Four weeks expired, and I re-engaged him for a year at seven dollars per week, (and a gratuity of fifty dollars at the end of the agreement,) with privilege of exhibition in any section of the United States. His parents were to accompany him, and I was to pay all travelling expenses. Long before the year was out, I voluntarily increased his weekly salary to $25—and he fairly earned it, for he speedily became a public favorite. I frequently exhibited him for successive weeks in my Museum, and when I wished to introduce fresh novelties there, I sent him to numerous cities and towns in many of the States, accompanied by my friend Fordyce Hitchcock.

In the mean time, I had entirely paid for the American Museum, and entered into an agreement with Gen. TOM THUMB for his services another year, at fifty dollars per week and all expenses, with the privilege of exhibition in Europe.

SOURCE: Phineas Taylor Barnum. *The Life of P. T. Barnum, Written by Himself.* London: Sampson Low, Son, and Co., 1855.

JOHN GREENLEAF WHITTIER

John Greenleaf Whittier (1807–1892) was a proud abolitionist and Quaker. In the first poem below he commemorates the death of the abolitionist-martyr John Brown. Whittier wrote many anti-slavery poems, among them "Ein Feste Burg Ist Unser Gott" ("A Mighty Fortress Is Our God"), in which he declares "What breaks the oath / Of the men o' the South? / What whets the knife / For the Union's life?—/ Hark to the answer: Slavery!"

Brown of Ossawatomie (1859)

John Brown of Ossawatomie spake on his dying day:
"I will not have, to shrive my soul a priest in Slavery's pay.
But let some poor slave-mother whom I have striven to free,
With her children, from the gallows stair put up a prayer for
me!"

John Brown of Ossawatomie, they led him out to die;
And lo! a poor slave-mother with her little child pressed nigh.
Then the bold, blue eye grew tender, and the old harsh face
grew mild,
As he stooped between the jeering ranks and kissed the negro's
child!

The shadows of his stormy life that moment fell apart;
And they who blamed the bloody hand forgave the loving heart.
That kiss from all its guilty means redeemed the good intent,
And round the grisly fighter's hair the martyr's aureole bent!

Perish with him the folly that seeks through evil good!
Long live the generous purpose unstained with human blood!
Not the raid of midnight terror, but the thought which underlies;
Not the borderer's pride of daring, but the Christian's sacrifice.

Nevermore may yon Blue Ridges the Northern rifle hear,
Nor see the light of blazing homes flash on the negro's spear.
But let the free winged angel Truth their guarded passes scale,
To teach that right is more than might, and justice more than mail!

So vainly shall Virginia set her battle in array;
In vain her trampling squadrons knead the winter snow with clay.
She may strike the pouncing eagle, but she dares not harm the dove;
And every gate she bars to Hate shall open wide to Love!

SOURCE: *New York Independent,* December 22, 1859.

Ein Feste Burg Ist Unser Gott (Luther's Hymn)
(1861)

We wait beneath the furnace-blast
The pangs of transformation;
Not painlessly doth God recast
And mould anew the nation.
Hot burns the fire
Where wrongs expire;
Nor spares the hand
That from the land
Uproots the ancient evil.

The hand-breadth cloud the sages feared
Its bloody rain is dropping;
The poison plant the fathers spared
All else is overtopping.

East, West, South, North,
It curses the earth;
All justice dies,
And fraud and lies
Live only in its shadow.

What gives the wheat-field blades of steel?
What points the rebel cannon?
What sets the roaring rabble's heel
On the old star-spangled pennon?
What breaks the oath
Of the men o' the South?
What whets the knife
For the Union's life?—
Hark to the answer: Slavery!

Then waste no blows on lesser foes
In strife unworthy freemen.
God lifts today the vail, and shows
The features of the demon!
O North and South,
Its victims both,
Can ye not cry,
"Let slavery die!"
And union find in freedom?

What though the cast-out spirit tear
The nation in his going?
We who have shared the guilt must share
The pang of his o'erthrowing!
Whate'er the loss,
Whate'er the cross,
Shall they complain
Of present pain
Who trust in God's hereafter?

For who that leans on His right arm
Was ever yet forsaken?
What righteous cause can suffer harm
If He its part has taken?

Though wild and loud
And dark the cloud
Behind its folds
His hand upholds
The calm sky of to-morrow!

Above the maddening cry for blood,
Above the wild war-drumming,
Let Freedom's voice be heard, with good
The evil overcoming.
Give prayer and purse
To stay the Curse
Whose wrong we share,
Whose shame we bear,
Whose end shall gladden Heaven!

In vain the bells of war shall ring
Of triumphs and revenges,
While still is spared the evil thing
That severs and estranges.
But blest the ear
That yet shall hear
The jubilant bell
That rings the knell
Of Slavery forever!

Then let the selfish lip be dumb,
And hushed the breath of sighing;
Before the joy of peace must come
The pains of purifying.
God give us grace
Each in his place
To bear his lot,
And, murmuring not,
Endure and wait and labor!

SOURCE: John Greenleaf Whittier. *In War Time: And Other Poems*. Boston: Ticknor and Fields, 1864.

Barbara Frietchie (1863)

Up from the meadows rich with corn,
Clear in the cool September morn,

The clustered spires of Frederick stand
Green-walled by the hills of Maryland.

Round about them orchards sweep,
Apple and peach tree fruited deep,

Fair as a garden of the Lord
To the eyes of the famished rebel horde,

On that pleasant morn of the early fall
When Lee marched over the mountain wall,—

Over the mountains winding down,
Horse and foot, into Frederick town.

Forty flags with their silver stars,
Forty flags with their crimson bars,

Flapped in the morning wind: the sun
Of noon looked down, and saw not one.

Up rose old Barbara Frietchie then,
Bowed with her fourscore years and ten;

Bravest of all in Frederick town,
She took up the flag the men hauled down;

In her attic window the staff she set,
To show that one heart was loyal yet.

Up the street came the rebel tread,
Stonewall Jackson riding ahead.

Under his slouched hat left and right
He glanced: the old flag met his sight.

"Halt!"—the dust-brown ranks stood fast.
"Fire!"—out blazed the rifle-blast.

It shivered the window, pane and sash;
It rent the banner with seam and gash.

Quick, as it fell, from the broken staff
Dame Barbara snatched the silken scarf;

She leaned far out on the window-sill,
And shook it forth with a royal will.

"Shoot, if you must, this old gray head,
But spare your country's flag," she said.

A shade of sadness, a blush of shame,
Over the face of the leader came;

The nobler nature within him stirred
To life at that woman's deed and word:

"Who touches a hair of yon gray head
Dies like a dog! March on!" he said.

All day long through Frederick street
Sounded the tread of marching feet:

All day long that free flag tost
Over the heads of the rebel host.

Ever its torn folds rose and fell
On the loyal winds that loved it well;

And through the hill-gaps sunset light
Shone over it with a warm good-night.

Barbara Frietchie's work is o'er,
And the Rebel rides on his raids no more.

Honor to her! and let a tear
Fall, for her sake, on Stonewall's bier.

Over Barbara Frietchie's grave
Flag of Freedom and Union, wave!

Peace and order and beauty draw
Round thy symbol of light and law;

And ever the stars above look down
On thy stars below in Frederick town!

SOURCE: John Greenleaf Whittier. *In War Time: And Other Poems.* Boston: Ticknor and Fields, 1864.

HARRIET A. JACOBS

Harriet A. Jacobs ("Linda Brent") (1813–1897) became a fugitive when she was twenty-one years old and could no longer endure enslavement or the sexual abuse that was the slave woman's particular torment. In her autobiography, written under the pseudonym Linda Brent, she recounts her experiences, hoping to further alert the men and women of the North to the awful truth about slavery. "I can testify," she writes, "from my own experiences and observations, that slavery is a curse to the whites as well as to the blacks. It makes the white fathers cruel and sensual; the sons violent and licentious; it contaminates the daughters, and makes the wives wretched. And as for the colored race, it needs an abler pen than mine to describe the extremity of their sufferings, the depth of their degradation." In the following excerpts, Jacobs discusses her escape, the help she received from family and friends, her interactions with a ship captain and members of the Anti-Slavery Society, her concern for her children, and her dread of the Fugitive Slave Act.[1]

Chapters from *Incidents in the Life of a Slave Girl* (1861)

Chapter 17: The Flight

MR. FLINT WAS hard pushed for house servants, and rather than lose me he had restrained his malice. I did my work faithfully, though not, of course, with a willing mind. They were evidently afraid I should leave them. Mr. Flint wished that I should sleep in the great house instead of the servants' quarters. His wife agreed to the proposition, but said I mustn't bring my bed into the house, because it would scatter feathers on her carpet. I knew when I went there that they would never think of such a thing as

1. This introductory note and the selections from Jacobs's work have been made by Professor Christine Rudisel.

furnishing a bed of any kind for me and my little one. I therefore carried my own bed, and now I was forbidden to use it. I did as I was ordered. But now that I was certain my children were to be put in their power, in order to give them a stronger hold on me, I resolved to leave them that night. I remembered the grief this step would bring upon my dear old grandmother; and nothing less than the freedom of my children would have induced me to disregard her advice. I went about my evening work with trembling steps. Mr. Flint twice called from his chamber door to inquire why the house was not locked up. I replied that I had not done my work. "You have had time enough to do it," said he. "Take care how you answer me!"

I shut all the windows, locked all the doors, and went up to the third story, to wait till midnight. How long those hours seemed, and how fervently I prayed that God would not forsake me in this hour of utmost need! I was about to risk every thing on the throw of a die; and if I failed, O what would become of me and my poor children? They would be made to suffer for my fault.

At half past twelve I stole softly down stairs. I stopped on the second floor, thinking I heard a noise. I felt my way down into the parlor, and looked out of the window. The night was so intensely dark that I could see nothing. I raised the window very softly and jumped out. Large drops of rain were falling, and the darkness bewildered me. I dropped on my knees, and breathed a short prayer to God for guidance and protection. I groped my way to the road, and rushed towards the town with almost lightning speed. I arrived at my grandmother's house, but dared not see her. She would say, "Linda, you are killing me;" and I knew that would unnerve me. I tapped softly at the window of a room, occupied by a woman, who had lived in the house several years. I knew she was a faithful friend, and could be trusted with my secret. I tapped several times before she heard me. At last she raised the window, and I whispered, "Sally, I have run away. Let me in, quick." She opened the door softly, and said in low tones, "For God's sake, don't. Your grandmother is trying to buy you and de chillern. Mr. Sands was here last week. He tole her he was going away on business, but he wanted her to go ahead about buying you and de chillern, and he would help her all he could. Don't run away, Linda. Your grandmother is all bowed down wid trouble now."

I replied, "Sally, they are going to carry my children to the plantation tomorrow; and they will never sell them to any body so long as they have me in their power. Now, would you advise me to go back?"

"No, chile, no," answered she. "When dey finds you is gone, dey won't want de plague ob de chillern; but where is you going to hide? Dey knows ebery inch ob dis house."

I told her I had a hiding-place, and that was all it was best for her to know. I asked her to go into my room as soon as it was light, and take all my clothes out of my trunk, and pack them in hers; for I knew Mr. Flint and the constable would be there early to search my room. I feared the sight of my children would be too much for my full heart; but I could not go out into the uncertain future without one last look. I bent over the bed where lay my little Benny and baby Ellen. Poor little ones! fatherless and motherless! Memories of their father came over me. He wanted to be kind to them; but they were not all to him, as they were to my womanly heart. I knelt and prayed for the innocent little sleepers. I kissed them lightly, and turned away.

As I was about to open the street door, Sally laid her hand on my shoulder, and said, "Linda, is you gwine all alone? Let me call your uncle."

"No, Sally," I replied, "I want no one to be brought into trouble on my account."

I went forth into the darkness and rain. I ran on till I came to the house of the friend who was to conceal me.

Early the next morning Mr. Flint was at my grandmother's inquiring for me. She told him she had not seen me, and supposed I was at the plantation. He watched her face narrowly, and said, "Don't you know any thing about her running off?" She assured him that she did not. He went on to say, "Last night she ran off without the least provocation. We had treated her very kindly. My wife liked her. She will soon be found and brought back. Are her children with you?" When told that they were, he said, "I am very glad to hear that. If they are here, she cannot be far off. If I find out that any of my niggers have had any thing to do with this damned business, I'll give 'em five hundred lashes." As he started to go to his father's, he turned round and added, persuasively, "Let her be brought back, and she shall have her children to live with her."

The tidings made the old doctor rave and storm at a furious rate. It was a busy day for them. My grandmother's house was searched from top to bottom. As my trunk was empty, they concluded I had taken my clothes with me. Before ten o'clock every vessel northward bound was thoroughly examined, and the law against harboring fugitives was read to all on board. At night a watch was set over the town. Knowing how distressed my grandmother would be, I wanted to send her a message; but it could not be done. Every one who went in or out of her house was closely watched. The doctor said he would take my children, unless she became responsible for them; which of course she willingly did. The next day was spent in searching. Before night, the following advertisement was posted at every corner, and in every public place for miles round:—

> $300 REWARD! Ran away from the subscriber, an intelligent, bright, mulatto girl, named Linda, 21 years of age. Five feet four inches high. Dark eyes, and black hair inclined to curl; but it can be made straight. Has a decayed spot on a front tooth. She can read and write, and in all probability will try to get to the Free States. All persons are forbidden, under penalty of the law, to harbor or employ said slave. $150 will be given to whoever takes her in the state, and $300 if taken out of the state and delivered to me, or lodged in jail.
>
> DR. FLINT.

Chapter 18: Months of Peril

The search for me was kept up with more perseverance than I had anticipated. I began to think that escape was impossible. I was in great anxiety lest I should implicate the friend who harbored me. I knew the consequences would be frightful; and much as I dreaded being caught, even that seemed better than causing an innocent person to suffer for kindness to me. A week had passed in terrible suspense, when my pursuers came into such close vicinity that I concluded they had tracked me to my hiding-place. I flew out of the house, and concealed myself in a thicket of bushes. There I remained in an agony of fear for two hours. Suddenly, a reptile of some kind seized my leg. In my fright, I struck a blow which loosened its hold, but I could not tell whether I had killed it; it was so dark, I could not see what it was; I only knew it was something cold and slimy. The pain I felt soon indicated that the bite was poisonous. I was compelled to leave my place of concealment, and I groped my way back into the house. The pain had become intense, and my friend was startled by my look of anguish. I asked her to prepare a poultice of warm ashes and vinegar, and I applied it to my leg, which was already much swollen. The application gave me some relief, but the swelling did not abate. The dread of being disabled was greater than the physical pain I endured. My friend asked an old woman, who doctored among the slaves, what was good for the bite of a snake or a lizard. She told her to steep a dozen coppers in vinegar, over night, and apply the cankered vinegar to the inflamed part.[2]

I had succeeded in cautiously conveying some messages to my relatives. They were harshly threatened, and despairing of my having a chance to escape, they advised me to return to my master, ask his forgiveness, and let him make an example of me. But such counsel had no influence on me. When I started upon this hazardous undertaking, I had resolved that, come what would, there should be no turning back. "Give me liberty, or give me death," was my motto. When my friend contrived to make known to my relatives the painful situation I had been in for twenty-four hours, they said no more about my going back to my master. Something must be done, and that speedily; but where to turn for help, they knew not. God in his mercy raised up "a friend in need."

Among the ladies who were acquainted with my grandmother, was one who had known her from childhood, and always been very friendly to her. She had also known my mother and her children, and felt interested for them. At this crisis of affairs she called to see my grandmother, as she not unfrequently did. She observed the sad and troubled expression of her face, and asked if she knew where Linda was, and whether she was safe. My grandmother shook her head, without answering. "Come, Aunt Martha," said the kind lady, "tell me all about it. Perhaps I can do something to help you." The husband of this lady held many slaves, and bought and sold slaves. She also held a number in her own name; but she treated them kindly, and would never allow any of them to be sold. She was unlike the majority of slaveholders' wives. My grandmother looked earnestly at her. Something in the expression of her face said "Trust me!" and she did trust her. She listened attentively to the details of my story, and sat thinking for a while. At last she

2. Note by Jacobs's original editor, L. Maria Child: The poison of a snake is a powerful acid, and is counteracted by powerful alkalies, such as potash, ammonia, &c. The Indians are accustomed to apply wet ashes, or plunge the limb into strong lie. White men, employed to lay out railroads in snaky places, often carry ammonia with them as an antidote.

said, "Aunt Martha, I pity you both. If you think there is any chance of Linda's getting to the Free States, I will conceal her for a time. But first you must solemnly promise that my name shall never be mentioned. If such a thing should become known, it would ruin me and my family. No one in my house must know of it, except the cook. She is so faithful that I would trust my own life with her; and I know she likes Linda. It is a great risk; but I trust no harm will come of it. Get word to Linda to be ready as soon as it is dark, before the patrols are out. I will send the housemaids on errands, and Betty shall go to meet Linda." The place where we were to meet was designated and agreed upon. My grandmother was unable to thank the lady for this noble deed; overcome by her emotions, she sank on her knees and sobbed like a child.

I received a message to leave my friend's house at such an hour, and go to a certain place where a friend would be waiting for me. As a matter of prudence no names were mentioned. I had no means of conjecturing who I was to meet, or where I was going. I did not like to move thus blindfolded, but I had no choice. It would not do for me to remain where I was. I disguised myself, summoned up courage to meet the worst, and went to the appointed place. My friend Betty was there; she was the last person I expected to see. We hurried along in silence. The pain in my leg was so intense that it seemed as if I should drop; but fear gave me strength. We reached the house and entered unobserved. Her first words were: "Honey, now you is safe. Dem devils ain't coming to search *dis* house. When I get you into missis' safe place, I will bring some nice hot supper. I specs you need it after all dis skeering." Betty's vocation led her to think eating the most important thing in life. She did not realize that my heart was too full for me to care much about supper.

The mistress came to meet us, and led me up stairs to a small room over her own sleeping apartment. "You will be safe here, Linda," said she; "I keep this room to store away things that are out of use. The girls are not accustomed to be sent to it, and they will not suspect anything unless they hear some noise. I always keep it locked, and Betty shall take care of the key. But you must be very careful, for my sake as well as your own; and you must never tell my secret; for it would ruin me and my family. I will keep the girls busy in the morning, that Betty may have a chance to bring your breakfast; but it will not do for her to come to you again till night. I will come to see you sometimes. Keep up your courage. I hope this state of things will not last long." Betty came with the "nice hot supper," and the mistress hastened down stairs to keep things straight till she returned. How my heart overflowed with gratitude! Words choked in my throat; but I could have kissed the feet of my benefactress. For that deed of Christian womanhood may God forever bless her!

I went to sleep that night with the feeling that I was for the present the most fortunate slave in town. Morning came and filled my little cell with light. I thanked the heavenly Father for this safe retreat. Opposite my window was a pile of feather beds. On the top of these I could lie perfectly concealed, and command a view of the street through which Dr. Flint passed to his office. Anxious as I was, I felt a gleam of satisfaction when I saw him. Thus far I had outwitted him, and I triumphed over it. Who can blame slaves for being cunning? They are constantly compelled to resort to it. It is the only weapon of the weak and oppressed against the strength of their tyrants. . . .

. . . As I sat very still in my retreat above stairs, cheerful visions floated through my mind. I thought Dr. Flint would soon get discouraged, and would be willing to sell my children, when he lost all hopes of making them the means of my discovery. I knew who was ready to buy them. Suddenly I heard a voice that chilled my blood. The sound was too familiar to me, it had been too dreadful, for me not to recognize at once my old master. He was in the house, and I at once concluded that he had come to seize me. I looked round in terror. There was no way of escape. The voice receded. I supposed the constable was with him, and they were searching the house. In my alarm I did not forget the trouble I was bringing on my generous benefactress. It seemed as if I were born to bring sorrow on all who befriended me, and that was the bitterest drop in the bitter cup of my life. After a while I heard approaching footsteps; the key was turned in my door. I braced myself against the wall to keep from falling. I ventured to look up, and there stood my kind benefactress. I was too much overcome to speak, and sunk down upon the floor.

"I thought you would hear your master's voice," she said; "and knowing you would be terrified, I came to tell you there is nothing to fear. You may even indulge in a laugh at the old gentleman's expense. He is so sure you are in New York, that he came to borrow five hundred dollars to go in pursuit of you. My sister had some money to loan on interest. He has obtained it, and proposes to start for New York to-night. So, for the present, you see you are safe. The doctor will merely lighten his pocket hunting after the bird he has left behind."

Chapter 20: New Perils

The doctor, more exasperated than ever, again tried to revenge himself on my relatives. He arrested uncle Phillip on the charge of having aided my flight. He was carried before a court, and swore truly that he knew nothing of my intention to escape, and that he had not seen me since I left my master's plantation. The doctor then demanded that he should give bail for five hundred dollars that he would have nothing to do with me. Several gentlemen offered to be security for him; but Mr. Sands told him he had better go back to jail, and he would see that he came out without giving bail.

The news of his arrest was carried to my grandmother, who conveyed it to Betty. In the kindness of her heart, she again stowed me away under the floor; and as she walked back and forth, in the performance of her culinary duties, she talked apparently to herself, but with the intention that I should hear what was going on. I hoped that my uncle's imprisonment would last but few days; still I was anxious. I thought it likely that Dr. Flint would do his utmost to taunt and insult him, and I was afraid my uncle might lose control of himself, and retort in some way that would be construed into a punishable offence; and I was well aware that in court his word would not be taken against any white man's. The search for me was renewed. Something had excited suspicions that I was in the vicinity. They searched the house I was in. I heard their steps and their voices. At night, when all were asleep, Betty came to release me from my place of confinement. The fright I had undergone, the constrained posture, and the dampness of the ground, made me ill for several days. My uncle was soon after taken out of prison; but the movements of all my relatives, and of all our friends, were very closely watched.

We all saw that I could not remain where I was much longer. I had already staid longer than was intended, and I knew my presence must be a source of perpetual anxiety to my kind benefactress. During this time, my friends had laid many plans for my escape, but the extreme vigilance of my persecutors made it impossible to carry them into effect. . . .

I had not the slightest idea where I was going. Betty brought me a suit of sailor's clothes,—jacket, trousers, and tarpaulin hat. She gave me a small bundle, saying I might need it where I was going. In cheery tones, she exclaimed, "I'se *so* glad you is gwine to free parts! Don't forget ole Betty. P'raps I'll come 'long by and by.

I tried to tell her how grateful I felt for all her kindness, but she interrupted me. "I don't want no tanks, honey. I'se glad I could help you, and I hope de good Lord vill open de path for you. I'se gwine wid you to de lower gate. Put your hands in your pockets, and walk ricketty, like de sailors."

I performed to her satisfaction. At the gate I found Peter, a young colored man, waiting for me. I had known him for years. He had been an apprentice to my father, and had always borne a good character. I was not afraid to trust to him. Betty bade me a hurried good by, and we walked off. "Take courage, Linda," said my friend Peter. "I've got a dagger, and no man shall take you from me, unless he passes over my dead body."

It was a long time since I had taken a walk out of doors, and the fresh air revived me. It was also pleasant to hear a human voice speaking to me above a whisper. I passed several people whom I knew, but they did not recognize me in my disguise. I prayed internally that, for Peter's sake, as well as my own, nothing might occur to bring out his dagger. We walked on till we came to the wharf. My aunt Nancy's husband was a seafaring man, and it had been deemed necessary to let him into our secret. He took me into his boat, rowed out to a vessel not far distant, and hoisted me on board. We three were the only occupants of the vessel. I now ventured to ask what they proposed to do with me. They said I was to remain on board till near dawn, and then they would hide me in Snaky Swamp, till my uncle Phillip had prepared a place of concealment for me. If the vessel had been bound north, it would have been of no avail to me, for it would certainly have been searched. About four o'clock, we were again seated in the boat, and rowed three miles to the swamp. My fear of snakes had been increased by the venomous bite I had received, and I dreaded to enter this hiding-place. But I was in no situation to choose, and I gratefully accepted the best that my poor, persecuted friends could do for me.

Peter landed first, and with a large knife cut a path through bamboos and briers of all descriptions. He came back, took me in his arms, and carried me to a seat made among the bamboos. Before we reached it, we were covered with hundreds of mosquitos. In an hour's time they had so poisoned my flesh that I was a pitiful sight to behold. As the light increased, I saw snake after snake crawling round us. I had been accustomed to the sight of snakes all my life, but these were larger than any I had ever seen. To this day I shudder when I remember that morning. As evening approached, the number of snakes increased so much that we were continually obliged to thrash them with sticks to keep them from crawling over us. The bamboos were so high and so thick that it was impossible to see beyond a very short distance. Just before it became dark we procured a seat nearer to the entrance of the swamp, being fearful of losing our way back to the boat. It was not long before we heard the paddle of oars, and the low whistle, which had been agreed upon as a signal. We made haste to enter the boat, and were rowed back to the vessel. I passed a wretched night; for the heat of the swamp, the mosquitos, and the constant terror of snakes, had brought on a burning fever. I had just dropped asleep, when they came and told me it was time to go back to that horrid swamp. I could scarcely summon courage to rise. But even those large, venomous snakes were less dreadful to my imagination than the white men in that community called civilized. This time Peter took a quantity of tobacco to burn, to keep off the mosquitos. It produced the desired effect on them, but gave me nausea and severe headache. At dark we returned to the vessel. I had been so sick during the day, that Peter declared I should go home that night, if the devil himself was on patrol. They told me a place of concealment had been provided for me at my grandmother's. I could not imagine how it was possible to hide me in her house, every nook and corner of which was known to the Flint family. They told me to wait and see. We were rowed ashore, and went boldly through the streets, to my grandmother's. I wore my sailor's clothes, and had blackened my face with charcoal. I passed several people whom I knew. The father of my children came so near that I brushed against his arm; but he had no idea who it was.

"You must make the most of this walk," said my friend Peter, "for you may not have another very soon."

I thought his voice sounded sad. It was kind of him to conceal from me what a dismal hole was to be my home for a long, long time.

Chapter 21: The Loophole of Retreat

A small shed had been added to my grandmother's house years ago. Some boards were laid across the joists at the top, and between these boards and the roof was a very small garret, never occupied by any thing but rats and mice. It was a pent roof, covered with nothing but shingles, according to the southern custom for such buildings. The garret was only nine feet long, and seven wide. The highest part was three feet high, and sloped down abruptly to the loose board floor. There was no admission for either light or air. My uncle Phillip, who was a carpenter, had very skillfully made a concealed trap door, which communicated with the storeroom. He had been doing this while I was waiting in the swamp. The storeroom opened upon a piazza. To this hole I was conveyed as soon as I entered the house. The air was stifling; the darkness total. A bed had been spread on the floor. I could sleep quite comfortably on one side; but the slope was so sudden that I could not turn on the other without hitting the roof. The rats and mice ran over my bed; but I was weary, and I slept such sleep as the wretched may, when a tempest has passed over them. Morning came. I knew it only by the noises I heard; for in my small den day and night were all the same. I suffered for air even more than for light. But I was not comfortless. I heard the voices of my children. There was joy and there was sadness in the sound. It made my tears flow. How I longed to speak to them! I was eager to look on their faces; but there was no hole, no crack, through which I could peep. This continued darkness was oppressive. It seemed horrible to sit or lie in a cramped position day after day, without one gleam of light. Yet I would have chosen this, rather than my lot as a slave, though white people considered it an easy one; and it was so compared with the fate of others. I was never cruelly over-worked; I was never lacerated with the whip from head to foot; I was never so beaten and bruised that I could not turn from one side to the other; I never had my heel-strings cut to prevent my running away; I was never chained to a log and forced to drag it about, while I toiled in the fields from morning till night; I was never branded with hot iron, or torn by bloodhounds. On the contrary, I had always been kindly treated, and tenderly cared for, until I came into the hands of Dr. Flint. I had never wished for freedom till then. But though my life in slavery was comparatively devoid of hardships, God pity the woman who is compelled to lead such a life!

My food was passed up to me through the trap-door my uncle had contrived; and my grandmother, my uncle Phillip, and aunt Nancy would seize such opportunities as they could, to mount up there and chat with me at the opening. But of course this was not safe in the daytime. It must all be done in darkness. It was impossible for me to move in an erect position, but I crawled about my den for exercise. One day I hit my head against something, and found it was a gimlet. My uncle had left it sticking there when he made the trap-door. I was as rejoiced as Robinson Crusoe could have been in finding such a treasure. It put a lucky thought into my head. I said to myself, "Now I will have some light. Now I will see my children." I did not dare to begin my work during the daytime, for fear of attracting attention. But I groped round; and having found the side next the street, where I could frequently see my children, I stuck the gimlet in and waited for evening. I bored three rows of holes, one above another; then I bored out the interstices between. I thus succeeded in making one hole about an inch long and an inch broad. I sat by it till late into the night, to enjoy the little whiff of air that floated in. In the morning I watched for my children. The first person I saw in the street was Dr. Flint. I had a shuddering, superstitious feeling that it was a bad omen. Several familiar faces passed by. At last I heard the merry laughing of children, and presently two sweet little faces were looking up at me, as though they knew I was there, and were conscious of the joy they imparted. How I longed to *tell* them I was there!

My condition was now a little improved. But for weeks I was tormented by hundreds of little red insects, fine as a needle's point, that pierced through my skin, and produced an intolerable burning. The good grandmother gave me herb teas and cooling medicines, and finally I got rid of them. The heat of my den was intense, for nothing but thin shingles protected me from the scorching summer's sun. But I had my consolations. Through my peeping-hole I could watch the children, and when they were near enough, I could hear their talk. Aunt Nancy brought me all the news she could hear at Dr. Flint's. From her I learned that the doctor had written to New York to a colored woman, who had been born and raised in our neighborhood, and had breathed his contaminating atmosphere. He offered her a reward if she could find out any thing about me. I know not what was the nature of her reply; but he soon after started for New York in haste, saying to his family that he had business of importance to transact. I peeped at him as he passed on his way to the steamboat. It was a satisfaction to have miles of land and water between us, even for a little while; and it was a still greater satisfaction to know that he believed me to be in the Free States. My little den seemed less dreary than it had done. He returned, as he did from his former journey to New York, without obtaining any satisfactory information. When he passed our house next morning, Benny was standing at the gate. He had heard them say that he had gone to find me, and he called out, "Dr. Flint, did you bring my mother home? I want to see her." The doctor stamped his foot at him in a rage, and exclaimed, "Get out of the way, you little damned rascal! If you don't, I'll cut off your head."

Benny ran terrified into the house, saying, "You can't put me in jail again. I don't belong to you now." It was well that the wind carried the words away from the doctor's ear. I told my grandmother of it, when we had our next conference at the trap-door; and begged of her not to allow the children to be impertinent to the irascible old man.

Autumn came, with a pleasant abatement of heat. My eyes had become accustomed to the dim light, and by holding my book or work in a certain position near the aperture I contrived to read and sew. That was a great relief to the tedious monotony of my life. But when winter came, the cold penetrated through the thin shingle roof, and I was dreadfully chilled. The winters there are not so long, or so severe, as in northern latitudes; but the houses are not built to shelter from cold, and my little den was peculiarly comfortless. The kind grandmother brought me bed-clothes and warm drinks. Often I was obliged to lie in bed all day to keep comfortable; but with all my precautions, my shoulders and feet were frostbitten. O, those long, gloomy days, with no object for my eye to rest upon, and no thoughts to occupy my mind, except the dreary past and the uncertain future! I was thankful when there came a day sufficiently mild for me to wrap myself up and sit at the loophole to watch the passers by. Southerners have the habit of stopping and talking in the streets, and I heard many conversations not intended to meet my ears. I heard slave-hunters planning how to catch some poor fugitive. Several times I heard allusions to Dr. Flint, myself, and the history of my children, who, perhaps, were playing near the gate. One would say, "I wouldn't move my little finger to catch her, as old Flint's property." Another would say, "I'll catch *any* nigger for the reward. A man ought to have what belongs to him, if he *is* a damned brute." The opinion was often expressed that I was in the Free States. Very rarely did any one suggest that I might be in the vicinity. Had the least suspicion rested on my grandmother's house, it would have been burned to the ground. But it was the last place they thought of. Yet there was no place, where slavery existed, that could have afforded me so good a place of concealment.

Dr. Flint and his family repeatedly tried to coax and bribe my children to tell something they had heard said about me. One day the doctor took them into a shop, and offered them some bright little silver pieces and gay handkerchiefs if they would tell where their mother was. Ellen shrank away from him, and would not speak; but Benny spoke up, and said, "Dr. Flint, I don't know where my mother is. I guess she's in New York; and when you go there again, I wish you'd ask her to come home, for I want to see her; but if you put her in jail, or tell her you'll cut her head off, I'll tell her to go right back."

Chapter 29: Preparations for Escape

I hardly expect that the reader will credit me, when I affirm that I lived in that little dismal hole, almost deprived of light and air, and with no space to move my limbs, for nearly seven years. But it is a fact; and to me a sad one, even now; for my body still suffers from the effects of that long imprisonment, to say nothing of my soul. Members of my family, now living in New York and Boston, can testify to the truth of what I say.

Countless were the nights that I sat late at the little loophole scarcely large enough to give me a glimpse of one twinkling star. There, I heard the patrols and slave-hunters conferring together about the capture of runaways, well knowing how rejoiced they would be to catch me.

Season after season, year after year, I peeped at my children's faces, and heard their sweet voices, with a heart yearning all the while to say, "Your mother is here." Sometimes it appeared to me as if ages had rolled away since I entered upon that gloomy, monotonous existence. At times, I was stupefied and listless; at other times I became very impatient to know when these dark years would end, and I should again be allowed to feel the sunshine, and breathe the pure air.

. . . I was likely to be drowned out of my den, if I remained much longer; for the slight roof was getting badly out of repair, and uncle Phillip was afraid to remove the shingles, lest some one should get a glimpse of me. When storms occurred in the night, they spread mats and bits of carpet, which in the morning appeared to have been laid out to dry; but to cover the roof in the daytime might have attracted attention. Consequently, my clothes and bedding were often drenched; a process by which the pains and aches in my cramped and stiffened limbs were greatly increased. I revolved various plans of escape in my mind, which I sometimes imparted to my grandmother, when she came to whisper with me at the trap-door. The kind-hearted old woman had an intense sympathy for runaways. She had known too much of the cruelties inflicted on those who were captured. Her memory always flew back at once to the sufferings of her bright and handsome son, Benjamin, the youngest and dearest of her flock. So, whenever I alluded to the subject, she would groan out, "O, don't think of it, child. You'll break my heart." I had no good old aunt Nancy now to encourage me; but my brother William and my children were continually beckoning me to the north. . . .

I was to escape in a vessel; but I forbear to mention any further particulars. . . .

I made all my arrangements to go on board as soon as it was dusk. The intervening time I resolved to spend with my son. I had not spoken to him for seven years, though I had been under the same roof, and seen him every day, when I was well enough to sit at the loophole. I did not dare to venture beyond the storeroom; so they brought him there, and locked us up together, in a place concealed from the piazza door. It was an agitating interview for both of us. After we had talked and wept together for a little while, he said, "Mother, I'm glad you're going away. I wish I could go with you. I knew you was here; and I have been *so* afraid they would come and catch you!"

I was greatly surprised, and asked him how he had found it out.

He replied, "I was standing under the eaves, one day, before Ellen went away, and I heard somebody cough up over the wood shed. I don't know what made me think it was you, but I did think so. I missed Ellen, the night before she went away; and grandmother brought her back into the room in the night; and I thought maybe she'd been to see *you*, before she went, for I heard grandmother whisper to her, 'Now go to sleep; and remember never to tell.' "

I asked him if he ever mentioned his suspicions to his sister. He said he never did; but after he heard the cough, if he saw her playing with other children on that side of the house, he always tried to coax her round to the other side, for fear they would hear me cough, too. He said he had kept a close lookout for Dr. Flint, and if he saw him speak to a constable, or a patrol, he always told grandmother. I now recollected that I had seen him manifest uneasiness, when people were on that side of the house, and I had at the time been puzzled to conjecture a motive for his actions. Such prudence may seem extraordinary in a boy of twelve years, but slaves, being surrounded by mysteries, deceptions, and dangers, early learn to be suspicious and watchful, and prematurely cautious and cunning. He had never asked a question of grandmother, or uncle Phillip, and I had often heard him chime in with other children, when they spoke of my being at the north.

I told him I was now really going to the Free States, and if he was a good, honest boy, and a loving child to his dear old grandmother, the Lord would bless him, and bring him to me, and we and Ellen would live together. He began to tell me that grandmother had not eaten any thing all day. While he was speaking, the door was unlocked, and she came in with a small bag of money, which she wanted me to take. I begged her to keep a part of it, at least, to pay for Benny's being sent to the north; but she insisted, while her tears were falling fast, that I should take the whole. "You may be sick among strangers," she said, "and they would send you to the poorhouse to die." Ah, that good grandmother!

For the last time I went up to my nook. Its desolate appearance no longer chilled me, for the light of hope had risen in my soul. Yet, even with the blessed prospect of freedom before me, I felt very sad at leaving forever that old homestead, where I had been sheltered so long by the dear old grandmother; where I had dreamed my first young dream of love; and where, after that had faded away, my children came to twine themselves so closely round my desolate heart. As the hour approached for me to leave, I again descended to the storeroom. My grandmother and Benny were there. She took me by the hand, and said, "Linda, let us pray." We knelt down together, with my child pressed to my heart, and my other arm round the faithful, loving old friend I was about to leave forever. On no other occasion has it ever been my lot to listen to so fervent a supplication for mercy and protection. It thrilled through my heart, and inspired me with trust in God.

Peter was waiting for me in the street. I was soon by his side, faint in body, but strong of purpose. I did not look back upon the old place, though I felt that I should never see it again.

Chapter 30: Northward Bound

I never could tell how we reached the wharf. My brain was all of a whirl, and my limbs tottered under me. At an appointed place we met my uncle Phillip, who had started before us on a different route, that he might reach the wharf first, and give us timely warning if there was any danger. A row-boat was in readiness. As I was about to step in, I felt something pull me gently, and turning round I saw Benny, looking pale and anxious. He whispered in my ear, "I've been peeping into the doctor's window, and he's at home. Don't cry; I'll come." He hastened away. I clasped the hand of my good uncle, to whom I owed so much, and of Peter, the brave, generous friend who had volunteered to run such terrible risks to secure my safety. To this day I remember how bright his face beamed with joy, when he told me he had discovered a safe method for me to escape. Yet that intelligent, enterprising, noble-hearted man was a chattel! liable, by the laws of a country that calls itself civilized, to be sold with horses and pigs! We parted in silence. Our hearts were all too full for words!

Swiftly the boat glided over the water. After a while, one of the sailors said, "Don't be down-hearted, madam. We will take you safely to your husband, in ——." At first I could not imagine what he meant; but I had presence of mind to think that it probably referred to something the captain had told him; so I thanked him, and said I hoped we should have pleasant weather.

When I entered the vessel the captain came forward to meet me. He was an elderly man, with a pleasant countenance. He showed me to a little box of a cabin, where sat my friend Fanny. She started as if she had seen a spectre. She gazed on me in utter astonishment, and exclaimed, "Linda, can this be *you*? or is it your ghost?" When we were locked in each other's arms, my overwrought feelings could no longer be restrained. My sobs reached the ears of the captain, who came and very kindly reminded us, that for his safety, as well as our own, it would be prudent for us not to attract any attention. He said that when there was a sail in sight he wished us to keep below; but at other times, he had no objection to our being on deck. He assured us that he would keep a good lookout, and if we acted prudently, he thought we should be in no danger. He had represented us as women going to meet our husbands in ——. We thanked him, and promised to observe carefully all the directions he gave us.

Fanny and I now talked by ourselves, low and quietly, in our little cabin. She told me of the sufferings she had gone through in making her escape, and of her terrors while she was concealed in her mother's house. Above all, she dwelt on the agony of separation from all her children on that dreadful auction day. She could scarcely credit me, when I told her of the place where I had passed nearly seven years. "We have the same sorrows," said I. "No," replied she, "you are going to see your children soon, and there is no hope that I shall ever even hear from mine."

The vessel was soon under way, but we made slow progress. The wind was against us. I should not have cared for this, if we had been out of sight of the town; but until there were miles of water between us and our enemies, we were filled with constant apprehension that the constables would come on board. Neither could I feel quite at ease with the captain and his men. I was an entire stranger to that class of people, and I had heard that sailors were rough, and sometimes cruel. We were so completely in their power, that if they were bad men, our situation would be dreadful. Now that the captain was paid for our passage, might he not be tempted to make more money by giving us up to those who claimed us as property? I was naturally of a confiding disposition, but slavery had made me suspicious of every body. Fanny did not share my distrust of the captain or his men. She said she was afraid at first, but she had been on board three days while the vessel lay in the dock, and nobody had betrayed her, or treated her otherwise than kindly.

The captain soon came to advise us to go on deck for fresh air. His friendly and respectful manner, combined with Fanny's testimony, reassured me, and we went with him. He placed us in a comfortable seat, and occasionally entered into conversation. He told us he was a Southerner by birth, and had spent the greater part of his life in the Slave States, and that he had recently lost a brother who traded in slaves. "But," said he, "it is a pitiable and degrading business, and I always felt ashamed to acknowledge my brother in connection with it." As we passed Snaky Swamp, he pointed to it, and said, "There is a slave territory that defies all the laws." I though of the terrible days I had spent there, and though it was not called Dismal Swamp, it made me feel very dismal as I looked at it.

I shall never forget that night. The balmy air of spring was so refreshing! And how shall I describe my sensations when we were fairly sailing on Chesapeake Bay? O, the beautiful sunshine! the exhilarating breeze! and I could enjoy them without fear or restraint. I had never realized what grand things air and sunlight are till I had been deprived of them.

Ten days after we left land we were approaching Philadelphia. The captain said we should arrive there in the night, but he thought we had better wait till morning, and go on shore in broad daylight, as the best way to avoid suspicion.

I replied, "You know best. But will you stay on board and protect us?"

He saw that I was suspicious, and he said he was sorry, now that he had brought us to the end of our voyage, to find I had so little confidence in him. Ah, if he had ever been a slave he would have known how difficult it was to trust a white man. He assured us that we might sleep through the night without fear; that he would take care we were not left unprotected. Be it said to the honor of this captain, Southerner as he was, that if Fanny and I had been white ladies, and our passage lawfully engaged, he could not have treated us more respectfully. My intelligent friend, Peter, had rightly estimated the character of the man to whose honor he had intrusted us.

The next morning I was on deck as soon as the day dawned. I called Fanny to see the sunrise, for the first time in our lives, on free soil; for such I *then* believed it to be. We watched the reddening sky, and saw the great orb come up slowly out of the water, as it seemed. Soon the waves began to sparkle, and every thing caught the beautiful glow. Before us lay the city of strangers. We looked at each other, and the eyes of both were moistened with tears. We had escaped from slavery, and we supposed ourselves to be safe from the hunters. But we were alone in the world, and we had left dear ties behind us; ties cruelly sundered by the demon Slavery.

Chapter 31: Incidents in Philadelphia

I had heard that the poor slave had many friends at the north. I trusted we should find some of them. Meantime, we would take it for granted that all were friends, till they proved to the contrary. I sought out the kind captain, thanked him for his attentions, and told him I should never cease to be grateful for the service he had rendered us. I gave him a message to the friends I had left at home, and he promised to deliver it. We were placed in a row-boat, and in about fifteen minutes were landed on a wood wharf in Philadelphia. As I stood looking round, the friendly captain touched me on the shoulder, and said, "There is a respectable-looking colored man behind you. I will speak to him about the New York trains, and tell him you wish to go directly on." I thanked him, and asked him to direct me to some shops where I could buy gloves and veils. He did so, and said he would talk with the colored man till I returned. I made what haste I could. Constant exercise on board the vessel, and frequent rubbing with salt water, had nearly restored the use of my limbs. The noise of the great city confused me, but I found the shops, and bought some double veils and gloves for Fanny and myself. The shopman told me they were so many levies. I had never heard the word before, but I did not tell him so. I thought if he knew I was a stranger he might ask me where I came from. I gave him a gold piece, and when he returned the change, I counted it, and found out how much a levy was. I made my way back to the wharf, where the captain introduced me to the colored man, as the Rev. Jeremiah Durham, minister of Bethel church. He took me by the hand, as if I had been an old friend. He told us we were too late for the morning cars to New York, and must wait until the evening, or the next morning. He invited me to go home with him, assuring me that his wife would give me a cordial welcome; and for my friend he would provide a home with one of his neighbors. I thanked him for so much kindness to strangers, and told him if I must be detained, I should like to hunt up some people who formerly went from our part of the country. Mr. Durham insisted that I should dine with him, and then he would assist me in finding my friends. The sailors came to bid us good by. I shook their hardy hands, with tears in my eyes. They had all been kind to us, and they had rendered us a greater service than they could possibly conceive of.

I had never seen so large a city, or been in contact with so many people in the streets. It seemed as if those who passed looked at us with an expression of curiosity. My face was so blistered and peeled by sitting on deck, in wind and sunshine, that I thought they could not easily decide to what nation I belonged.

Mrs. Durham met me with a kindly welcome, without asking any questions. I was tired, and her friendly manner was a sweet refreshment. God bless her! I was sure that she had comforted other weary hearts, before I received her sympathy. She was surrounded by her husband and children, in a home made sacred by protecting laws. I thought of my own children and sighed.

. . . I went to my room, glad to shut out the world for a while. . . . In the midst of my meditations I was startled by a knock at the door. Mrs. Durham entered, her face all beaming with kindness, to say that there was an anti-slavery friend down stairs, who would like to see me. I overcame my dread of encountering strangers, and went with her. Many questions were asked concerning my experiences, and my escape from slavery; but I observed how careful they all were not to say any thing that might wound my feelings. How gratifying this was, can be fully understood only by those who have been accustomed to be treated as if they were not included within the pale of human beings. The anti-slavery friend had come to inquire into my plans, and to offer assistance, if needed. Fanny was comfortably established, for the present, with a friend of Mr. Durham. The Anti-Slavery Society agreed to pay her expenses to New York. The same was offered to me but I declined to accept it; telling them that my grandmother had given me sufficient to pay my expenses to the end of my journey. We were urged to remain in Philadelphia a few days, until some suitable escort could be found for us. I gladly accepted the proposition, for I had a dread of meeting slaveholders, and some dread also of railroads. I had never entered a railroad car in my life, and it seemed to me quite an important event.

That night I sought my pillow with feelings I had never carried to it before. I verily believed myself to be a free woman. . . .

At the end of five days, one of Mrs. Durham's friends offered to accompany us to New York the following morning. . . .

When Mr. Durham handed us our tickets, he said, "I am afraid you will have a disagreeable ride, but I could not procure tickets for the first class cars."

Supposing I had not given him money enough, I offered more. "O, no," said he, "they could not be had for any money. They don't allow colored people to go in the first-class cars."

This was the first chill to my enthusiasm about the Free States. Colored people were allowed to ride in a filthy box, behind white people, at the south, but there they were not required to pay for the privilege. It made me sad to find how the north aped the customs of slavery.

We were stowed away in a large, rough car, with windows on each side, too high for us to look out without standing up. It was crowded with people, apparently of all nations. There were plenty of beds and cradles, containing screaming and kicking babies. Every other man had a cigar or pipe in his mouth, and jugs of whiskey were handed round freely. The fumes of the whiskey and the dense tobacco smoke were sickening to my senses, and my mind was equally nauseated by the coarse jokes and ribald songs around me. It was a very disagreeable ride. Since that time there has been some improvement in these matters.

Chapter 40: The Fugitive Slave Law

. . . About the time that I reentered the Bruce family, an event occurred of disastrous import to the colored people. The slave Hamlin, the first fugitive that came under the new law, was given up by the bloodhounds of the north to the bloodhounds of the south. It was the beginning of a reign of terror to the colored population. The great city rushed on in its whirl of excitement, taking no note of the "short and simple annals of the poor." But while fashionables were listening to the thrilling voice of Jenny Lind in Metropolitan Hall, the thrilling voices of poor hunted colored people went up, in an agony of supplication, to the Lord, from Zion's church. Many families, who had lived in the city for twenty years, fled from it now. Many a poor washerwoman, who, by hard labor, had made herself a comfortable home, was obliged to sacrifice her furniture, bid a hurried farewell to friends, and seek her fortune among strangers in Canada. Many a wife discovered a secret she had never known before—that her husband was a fugitive, and must leave her to insure his own safety. Worse still, many a husband discovered that his wife had fled from slavery years ago, and as "the child follows the condition of its mother," the children of his love were liable to be seized and carried into slavery. Every where, in those humble homes, there was consternation and anguish. But what cared the legislators of the "dominant race" for the blood they were crushing out of trampled hearts?

When my brother William spent his last evening with me, before he went to California, we talked nearly all the time of the distress brought on our oppressed people by the passage of this iniquitous law; and never had I seen him manifest such bitterness of spirit, such stern hostility to our oppressors. He was himself free from the operation of the law; for he did not run from any Slaveholding State, being brought into the Free States by his master. But I was subject to it; and so were hundreds of intelligent and industrious people all around us. I seldom ventured into the streets; and when it was necessary to do an errand for Mrs. Bruce, or any of the family, I went as much as possible through back streets and by-ways. What a disgrace to a city calling itself free, that inhabitants, guiltless of offence, and seeking to perform their duties conscientiously, should be condemned to live in such incessant fear, and have nowhere to turn for protection! This state of things, of course, gave rise to many impromptu vigilance committees. Every colored person, and every friend of their persecuted race, kept their eyes wide open. Every evening I examined the newspapers carefully, to see what Southerners had put up at the hotels. I did this for my own sake, thinking my young mistress and her husband might be among the list; I wished also to give information to others, if necessary; for if many were "running to and fro," I resolved that "knowledge should be increased."

. . . All that winter I lived in a state of anxiety. When I took the children out to breathe the air, I closely observed the countenances of all I met. I dreaded the approach of summer, when snakes and slaveholders make their appearance. I was, in fact, a slave in New York, as subject to slave laws as I had been in a Slave State. Strange incongruity in a State called free!

SOURCE: Harriet A. Jacobs. *Incidents in the Life of a Slave Girl.* Mineola, New York: Dover Publications, 2001. [Originally published in Boston in 1861.]

JULIA WARD HOWE

Julia Ward Howe (1819–1910) wrote the most famous marching poem in American history in 1861 and published it in The Atlantic Monthly *in February 1862. The "Hallelujah" chorus was subsequently added in April 1862 when the verses were accompanied by music.*

Battle Hymn of the Republic (1862)

Mine eyes have seen the glory of the coming of the Lord:
He is trampling out the vintage where the grapes of wrath are
stored;
He hath loosed the fateful lightning of his terrible swift sword:
His truth is marching on.

I have seen Him in the watch-fires of a hundred circling camps;
They have builded Him an altar in the evening dews and damps;
I can read His righteous sentence by the dim and flaring lamps.
His day is marching on.

I have read a fiery gospel, writ in burnished rows of steel:
"As ye deal with my contemners, so with you my grace shall
deal;
Let the Hero, born of woman, crush the serpent with his heel,
Since God is marching on."

He has sounded forth the trumpet that shall never call retreat;
He is sifting out the hearts of men before his judgment-seat:
Oh! be swift, my soul, to answer Him! be jubilant, my feet!
Our God is marching on.

In the beauty of the lilies Christ was born across the sea,
With a glory in his bosom that transfigures you and me:
As He died to make men holy, let us die to make men free,
While God is marching on.

SOURCE: *The Atlantic Monthly*. February 1862.

LOUISA MAY ALCOTT

These are two of the several short stories that Louisa May Alcott (1832–1888) wrote and published in Hospital Sketches, *which were closely based on her own personal experiences as a volunteer nurse in Washington, D.C., for six weeks during the Civil War. The first story dramatizes the narrator Tribulation Periwinkle's resolution to do some good, and the activities, bustle and obstacles in Boston surrounding her preparation to leave her family and home. "I'm a bashful individual, though I can't get any one to believe it," she remarks with a peculiar energy. Periwinkle's actions mirror those of the future author of* Little Women, *who arrived in the capital at the end of December 1862, in time to aid the wounded soldiers (there were several thousands) from the Battle of Fredericksburg.*

Obtaining Supplies (1863)

"I WANT SOMETHING to do."

This remark being addressed to the world in general, no one in particular felt it their duty to reply; so I repeated it to the smaller world about me, received the following suggestions, and settled the matter by answering my own inquiry, as people are apt to do when very much in earnest.

"Write a book," quoth the author of my being.

"Don't know enough, sir. First live, then write."

"Try teaching again," suggested my mother.

"No thank you, ma'am, ten years of that is enough."

"Take a husband like my Darby, and fulfill your mission," said sister Joan, home on a visit.

"Can't afford expensive luxuries, Mrs. Coobiddy."

"Turn actress, and immortalize your name," said sister Vashti, striking an attitude.

"I won't."

"Go nurse the soldiers," said my young neighbor, Tom, panting for "the tented field."

"I will!"

So far, very good. Here was the will, and plenty of it; now for the way. At first sight not a foot of it appeared; but that didn't matter, for the Periwinkles are a hopeful race. Their crest is an anchor, with three cock-a-doodles crowing atop. They all wear rose-colored spectacles, and are lineal descendants of the inventor of aerial architecture. An hour's conversation on the subject set the whole family in a blaze of enthusiasm. A model hospital was erected, and each member had accepted an honorable post therein. The paternal P. was chaplain, the maternal P. was matron, and all the youthful P.'s filled the pod of futurity with achievements whose brilliancy eclipsed the glories of the present and the past. Arriving at this satisfactory conclusion, the meeting adjourned; and the fact that Miss Tribulation was available as army nurse went abroad on the wings of the wind.

In a few days a townswoman heard of my desire, approved of it, and brought about an interview with one of the sisterhood which I wished to join, who was at home on a furlough, and able and willing to satisfy all inquiries. A morning chat with Miss General S.—we hear no end of Mrs. Generals, why not a Miss?—produced three results: I felt that I could do the work, was offered a place, and accepted it, promising not to desert, but stand ready to march on Washington at an hour's notice.

A few days were necessary for the letter containing my request and recommendation to reach headquarters, and another, containing my commission, to return; therefore no time was to be lost; and heartily thanking my pair of friends, I tore home through the December slush as if the rebels were after me, and like many another recruit, burst in upon my family with the announcement—

"I've enlisted!"

An impressive silence followed. Tom, the irrepressible, broke it with a slap on the shoulder and the graceful compliment—

"Old Trib, you're a trump!"

"Thank you; then I'll *take* something": which I did, in the shape of dinner, reeling off my news at the rate of three dozen words to a mouthful; and as every one else talked equally fast, and all together, the scene was most inspiring.

As boys going to sea immediately become nautical in speech, walk as if they already had their "sea legs" on, and shiver their timbers on all possible occasions, so I turned military at once, called my dinner my rations, saluted all new comers, and ordered a dress parade that very afternoon. Having reviewed every rag I possessed, I detailed some for picket duty while airing over the fence; some to the sanitary influences of the wash-tub; others to mount guard in the trunk; while the weak and wounded went to the Work-basket Hospital, to be made ready for active service again. To this squad I devoted myself for a week; but all was done, and I had time to get powerfully impatient before the letter came. It did arrive however, and brought a disappointment along with its good will and friendliness, for it told me that the place in the Armory Hospital that I supposed I was to take, was already filled, and a much less desirable one at Hurly-burly House was offered instead.

"That's just your luck, Trib. I'll take your trunk up garret for you again; for of course you won't go," Tom remarked, with the disdainful pity which small boys affect when they get into their teens. I was wavering in my secret soul, but that settled the matter, and I crushed him on the spot with martial brevity—

"It is now one; I shall march at six."

I have a confused recollection of spending the afternoon in pervading the house like an executive whirlwind, with my family swarming after me, all working, talking, prophesying and lamenting, while I packed my "go-abroady" possessions, tumbled the rest into two big boxes, danced on the lids till they shut, and gave them in charge, with the direction,—

"If I never come back, make a bonfire of them."

Then I choked down a cup of tea, generously salted instead of sugared, by some agitated relative, shouldered my knapsack—it was only a traveling bag, but do let me preserve the unities—hugged my family three times all round without a vestige of unmanly emotion, till a certain dear old lady broke down upon my neck, with a despairing sort of wail—

"Oh, my dear, my dear, how can I let you go?"

"I'll stay if you say so, mother."

"But I don't; go, and the Lord will take care of you."

Much of the Roman matron's courage had gone into the Yankee matron's composition, and, in spite of her tears, she would have sent ten sons to the war, had she possessed them, as freely as she sent one daughter, smiling and flapping on the door-step till I vanished, though the eyes that followed me were very dim, and the handkerchief she waved was very wet.

My transit from The Gables to the village depot was a funny mixture of good wishes and good byes, mud-puddles and shopping. A December twilight is not the most cheering time to enter upon a somewhat perilous enterprise, and, but for the presence of Vashti and neighbor Tom, I fear that I might have added a drop of the briny to the native moisture of—

"The town I left behind me";

though I'd no thought of giving out: oh, bless you, no! When the engine screeched "Here we are," I clutched my escort in a fervent embrace, and skipped into the car with as blithe a farewell as if going on a bridal tour—though I believe brides don't usually wear cavernous black bonnets and fuzzy brown coats, with a hair-brush, a pair of rubbers, two books, and a bag of ginger-bread distorting the pockets of the same. If I thought that any one would believe it, I'd boldly state that I slept from C. to B., which would simplify matters immensely; but as I know they wouldn't, I'll confess that the head under the funereal coal-hod fermented with all manner of high thoughts and heroio purposes "to do or die,"—perhaps both; and the heart under the fuzzy brown coat felt very tender with the memory of the dear old lady, probably sobbing over her army socks and the loss of her topsy-turvy Trib. At this juncture I took the veil, and what I did behind it is nobody's business; but I maintain that the soldier who cries when his mother says "Good bye," is the boy to fight best, and die bravest, when the time comes, or go back to her better than he went.

Till nine o'clock I trotted about the city streets, doing those last errands which no woman would even go to heaven with, out attempting, if she could. Then I went to my usual refuge, and, fully intending to keep awake, as a sort of vigil appropriate to the occasion, fell fast asleep and dreamed propitious dreams till my rosy-faced cousin waked me with a kiss.

A bright day smiled upon my enterprise, and at ten I reported myself to my General, received last instructions and no end of the sympathetic encouragement which women give, in look, touch, and tone more effectually than in words. The next step was to get a free pass to Washington, for I'd no desire to waste my substance on railroad companies when "the boys" needed even a spinster's mite. A friend of mine had procured such a pass, and I was bent on doing likewise, though I had to face the president of the railroad to accomplish it. I'm a bashful individual, though I can't get any one to believe it; so it cost me a great effort to poke about the Worcester depot till the right door appeared, then walk into a room containing several gentlemen, and blunder out my request in a high state of stammer and blush. Nothing could have been more courteous than this dreaded President, but it was evident that I had made as absurd a demand as if I had asked for the nose off his respectable face. He referred me to the Governor at the State House, and I backed out, leaving him no doubt to regret that such mild maniacs were left at large. Here was a Scylla and Charybdis business: as if a President wasn't trying enough, without the Governor of Massachusetts and the Hub of the Hub on top of that.

"I never can do it," thought I. "Tom will hoot at you if you don't," whispered the inconvenient little voice that is always goading people to the performance of disagreeable duties, and always appeals to the most effective agent to produce the proper result. The idea of allowing any boy that ever wore a felt basin and a shoddy jacket with a microscopic tail, to crow over me, was preposterous, so giving myself a mental slap for such faint-heartedness, I streamed away across the Common, wondering if I ought to say "your Honor," or simply "Sir," and decided upon the latter, fortifying myself with recollections of an evening in a charming green library, where I beheld the Governor placidly consuming oysters, and laughing as if Massachusetts was a myth, and he had no heavier burden on his shoulders than his host's handsome hands.

Like an energetic fly in a very large cobweb, I struggled through the State House, getting into all the wrong rooms and none of the right, till I turned desperate, and went into one, resolving not to come out till I'd made somebody hear and answer me. I suspect that of all the wrong places 1 had blundered into, this was the most so. But I didn't care; and, though the apartment was full of soldiers, surgeons, starers, and spittoons, I cornered a perfectly incapable person, and proceeded to pump for information with the following result:

"Was the Governor anywhere about?"

No, he wasn't.

"Could he tell me where to look?"

No, he couldn't.

"Did he know anything about free passes?"

No, he didn't.

"Was there any one there of whom I could inquire?"

Not a person.

"Did he know of any place where information could be obtained?"

Not a place.

"Could he throw the smallest gleam of light upon the matter, in any way?"

Not a ray.

I am naturally irascible, and if I could have shaken this negative gentleman vigorously, the relief would have been immense. The prejudices of society forbidding this mode of redress, I merely glowered at him; and, before my wrath found vent in words, my General appeared, having seen me from an opposite window, and come to know what I was about. At her command the languid gentleman woke up, and troubled himself to remember that Major or Sergeant or something Mc K. knew all about the tickets, and his office was in Milk Street. I perked up instanter, and then, as if the exertion was too much for him, what did this animated wet blanket do but add—

"I think Mc K. may have left Milk Street, now, and I don't know where he has gone."

"Never mind; the new comers will know where he has moved to, my dear, so don't be discouraged; and if you don't succeed, come to me, and we will see what to do next," said my General.

I blessed her in a fervent manner and a cool hall, fluttered round the corner, and bore down upon Milk street, bent on discovering Mc K. if such a being was to be found. He wasn't, and the ignorance of the neighborhood was really pitiable. Nobody knew anything, and after tumbling over bundles of leather, bumping against big boxes, being nearly annihilated by descending bales, and sworn at by aggravated truckmen, I finally elicited the advice to look for Mc K. in Haymarket Square. Who my informant was I've really forgotten; for, having hailed several busy gentlemen, some one of them fabricated this delusive quietus for the perturbed spirit, who instantly departed to the sequestered locality he named. If I had been in search of the Koh-i-noor diamond I should have been as likely to find it there as any vestige of Mc K. I stared at signs, inquired in shops, invaded an eating house, visited the recruiting tent in the middle of the Square, made myself a nuisance generally, and accumulated fine samples of mud from every gutter I fell into. All in vain; and I mournfully turned my face toward the

General's, feeling that I should be forced to enrich the railroad company after all, when, suddenly, I beheld that admirable young man, brother-in-law Darby Coobiddy, Esq. I arrested him with a burst of news, and wants, and woes, which caused his manly countenance to lose its usual repose.

"Oh, my dear boy, I'm going to Washington at five, and I can't find the free ticket man, and there won't be time to see Joan, and I'm so tired and cross I don't know what to do; and will you help me, like a cherub as you are?"

"Oh, yes, of course. I know a fellow who will set us right," responded Darby, mildly excited, and darting into some kind of an office, held counsel with an invisible angel, who sent him out radiant. "All serene. I've got him. I'll see you through the business, and then get Joan from the Dove Cote in time to see you off."

I'm a woman's rights woman, and if any man had offered help in the morning, I should have condescendingly refused it, sure that I could do everything as well, if not better, myself. My strong-mindedness had rather abated since then, and I was now quite ready to be a "timid trembler," if necessary. Dear me! how easily Darby did it all: he just asked one question, received an answer, tucked me under his arm, and in ten minutes I stood in the presence of Mc K., the Desired.

"Now my troubles are over," thought I, and as usual was direfully mistaken.

"You will have to get a pass from Dr. H., in Temple Place, before I can give you a pass, madam," answered Mc K., as blandly as if he wasn't carrying desolation to my soul. Oh, indeed! why didn't he send me to Dorchester Heights, India Wharf, or Bunker Hill Monument, and done with it? Here I was, after a morning's tramp, down in some place about Dock Square, and was told to step to Temple Place. Nor was that all; he might as well have asked me to catch a humming-bird, toast a salamander, or call on the man in the moon, as find a Doctor at home at the busiest hour of the day. It was a blow; but weariness had extinguished enthusiasm, and resignation clothed me as a garment. I sent Darby for Joan, and doggedly paddled off, feeling that mud was my native element, and quite sure that the evening papers would announce the appearance of the Wandering Jew, in feminine habiliments.

"Is Dr. H. in?"

"No, mum, he ain't."

Of course he wasn't; I knew that before I asked: and, considering it all in the light of a hollow mockery, added:

"When will he probably return?"

If the damsel had said, "ten to-night," I should have felt a grim satisfaction, in the fulfillment of my own dark prophecy; but she said, "At two, mum"; and I felt it a personal insult.

"I'll call, then. Tell him my business is important": with which mysteriously delivered message I departed, hoping that I left her consumed with curiosity; for mud rendered me an object of interest.

By way of resting myself, I crossed the Common, for the third time, bespoke the carriage, got some lunch, packed my purchases, smoothed my plumage, and was back again, as the clock struck two. The Doctor hadn't come yet; and I was morally certain that he would not, till, having waited till the last minute, I was driven to buy a ticket, and, five minutes after the irrevocable deed was done, he would be at my service, with all manner of helpful documents and directions. Everything goes by contraries with me; so, having made up my mind to be disappointed, of course I wasn't; for, presently, in walked Dr. H., and no sooner had he heard my errand, and glanced at my credentials, than he said, with the most engaging readiness:

"I will give you the order, with pleasure, madam."

Words connot express how soothing and delightful it was to find, at last, somebody who could do what I wanted, without sending me from Dan to Beersheba, for a dozen other bodies to do something else first. Peace descended, like oil, upon the ruffled waters of my being, as I sat listening to the busy scratch of his pen; and, when he turned about, giving me not only the order, but a paper of directions wherewith to smooth away all difficulties between Boston and Washington, I felt as did poor Christian when the Evangelist gave him the scroll, on the safe side of the Slough of Despond. I've no doubt many dismal nurses have inflicted themselves upon the worthy gentleman since then; but I am sure none have been more kindly helped, or are more grateful, than T. P.; for that short interview added another to the many pleasant associations that already surround his name.

Feeling myself no longer a "Martha Struggles," but a comfortable young woman, with plain sailing before her, and the worst of the voyage well over, I once more presented myself to the valuable

Mc K. The order was read, and certain printed papers, necessary to be filled out, were given a young gentleman—no, I prefer to say Boy, with a scornful emphasis upon the word, as the only means of revenge now left me. This Boy, instead of doing his duty with the diligence so charming in the young, loitered and lounged, in a manner which proved his education to have been sadly neglected in the—

"How doth the little busy bee,"

direction. He stared at me, gaped out of the window, ate peanuts, and gossiped with his neighbors—Boys, like himself, and all penned in a row, like colts at a Cattle Show. I don't imagine he knew the anguish he was inflicting; for it was nearly three, the train left at five, and I had my ticket to get, my dinner to eat, my blessed sister to see, and the depot to reach, if I didn't die of apoplexy. Meanwhile Patience certainly had her perfect work that day, and I hope she enjoyed the job more than I did. Having waited some twenty minutes, it pleased this reprehensible Boy to make various marks and blots on my documents, toss them to a venerable creature of sixteen, who delivered them to me with such paternal directions, that it only needed a pat on the head and an encouraging—"Now run home to your Ma, little girl, and mind the crossings, my dear," to make the illusion quite perfect.

Why I was sent to a steamboat office for car tickets, is not for me to say, though I went as meekly as I should have gone to the Probate Court, if sent. A fat, easy gentleman gave me several bits of paper, with coupons attached, with a warning not to separate them, which instantly inspired me with a yearning to pluck them apart, and see what came of it. But, remembering through what fear and tribulation I had obtained them, I curbed Satan's promptings, and, clutching my prize, as if it were my pass to the Elysian Fields, I hurried home. Dinner was rapidly consumed; Joan enlightened, comforted, and kissed; the dearest of apple-faced cousins hugged; the kindest of apple-faced cousins' fathers subjected to the same process; and I mounted the ambulance, baggage-wagon, or anything you please but hack, and drove away, too tired to feel excited, sorry, or glad.

A Day (1863)

In this story, we travel with Alcott's narrator Tribulation Periwinkle into a hospital for the wounded soldiers; again we are aware of Tribulation's archness, but we also encounter her frightfully clear reporting upon the suffering of the soldiers: "It is all very well to talk of the patience of woman; and far be it from me to pluck that feather from her cap, for, heaven knows, she isn't allowed to wear many; but the patient endurance of these men, under trials of the flesh, was truly wonderful." The eyewitness accounts of amputations by a surgeon are unsentimental and fascinating; on the other hand, the few instances of racial caricature herein are unfortunate.

"THEY'VE COME! THEY'VE come! hurry up, ladies—you're wanted."

"Who have come? the rebels?"

This sudden summons in the gray dawn was somewhat startling to a three days' nurse like myself, and, as the thundering knock came at our door, I sprang up in my bed, prepared

"To gird my woman's form,
And on the ramparts die,"

if necessary; but my room-mate took it more coolly, and, as she began a rapid toilet, answered my bewildered question,—

"Bless you, no child; it's the wounded from Fredericksburg; forty ambulances are at the door, and we shall have our hands full in fifteen minutes."

"What shall we have to do?"

"Wash, dress, feed, warm and nurse them for the next three months, I dare say. Eighty beds are ready, and we were getting impatient for the men to come. Now you will begin to see hospital life in earnest, for you won't probably find time to sit down all day, and may think yourself fortunate if you get to bed by midnight. Come to me in the ballroom when you are ready; the worst cases are always carried there, and I shall need your help."

So saying, the energetic little woman twirled her hair into a button at the back of her head, in a "cleared for action" sort of style, and vanished, wrestling her way into a feminine kind of pea-jacket as she went.

I am free to confess that I had a realizing sense of the fact that my hospital bed was not a bed of roses just then, or the prospect before me one of unmingled rapture. My three days' experiences had begun with a death, and, owing to the defalcation of another nurse, a somewhat abrupt plunge into the superintendence of a ward containing forty beds, where I spent my shining hours washing faces, serving rations, giving medicine, and sitting in a very hard chair, with pneumonia on one side, diptheria on the other, two typhoids opposite, and a dozen dilapidated patriots, hopping, lying, and lounging about, all staring more or less at the new "nuss," who suffered untold agonies, but concealed them under as matronly an aspect as a spinster could assume, and blundered through her trying labors with a Spartan firmness, which I hope they appreciated, but am afraid they didn't. Having a taste for "ghastliness," I had rather longed for the wounded to arrive, for rheumatism wasn't heroic, neither was liver complaint, or measles; even fever had lost its charms since "bathing burning brows" had been used up in romances, real and ideal. But when I peeped into the dusky street lined with what I at first had innocently called market carts, now unloading their sad freight at our door, I recalled sundry reminiscences I had heard from nurses of longer standing, my ardor experienced a sadden chill, and I indulged in a most unpatriotic wish that I was safe at home again, with a quiet day before me, and no necessity for being hustled up, as if I were a hen and had only to hop off my roost, give my plumage a peck, and be ready for action. A second bang at the door sent this recreant desire to the right about, as a little woolly head popped in, and Joey, (a six years' old contraband,[1]) announced—

"Miss Blank is jes' wild fer ye, and says fly round right away. They's comin' in, I tell yer, heaps on 'em—one was took out dead, and I see him,—hi! warn't he a goner!"

With which cheerful intelligence the imp scuttled away, singing like a blackbird, and I followed, feeling that Richard was *not* himself again, and wouldn't be for a long time to come.

The first thing I met was a regiment of the vilest odors that ever assaulted the human nose, and took it by storm. Cologne, with its seven and seventy evil savors, was a posy-bed to it; and the worst of this affliction was, everyone had assured me that it was a chronic weakness of all hospitals, and I must bear it. I did, armed with lavender water, with which I so besprinkled myself and premises, that I was soon known among my patients as "the nurse with the

1. "Contraband" was the peculiar Civil War term for a slave in the Confederate states who escaped from slave-holders and reached a Union camp; the "contraband" was thus claimed, on the basis of the slave-holders' own definition, as enemy "property" and immediately freed by the Union army.

bottle." Having been run over by three excited surgeons, bumped against by migratory coal-hods, water-pails, and small boys, nearly scalded by an avalanche of newly filled tea-pots, and hopelessly entangled in a knot of colored sisters coming to wash, I progressed by slow stages up stairs and down, till the main hall was reached, and I paused to take breath and a survey. There they were! "our brave boys," as the papers justly call them, for cowards could hardly have been so riddled with shot and shell, so torn and shattered, nor have borne suffering for which we have no name, with an uncomplaining fortitude, which made one glad to cherish each like a brother. In they came, some on stretchers, some in men's arms, some feebly staggering along propped on rude crutches, and one lay stark and still with covered face, as a comrade gave his name to be recorded before they carried him away to the dead house. All was hurry and confusion; the hall was full of these wrecks of humanity, for the most exhausted could not reach a bed till duly ticketed and registered; the walls were lined with rows of such as could sit, the floor covered with the more disabled, the steps and doorways filled with helpers and lookers on; the sound of many feet and voices made that usually quiet hour as noisy as noon; and, in the midst of it all, the matron's motherly face brought more comfort to many a poor soul, than the cordial draughts she administered, or the cheery words that welcomed all, making of the hospital a home.

The sight of several stretchers, each with its legless, armless, or desperately wounded occupant, entering my ward, admonished me that I was there to work, not to wonder or weep; so I corked up my feelings, and returned to the path of duty, which was rather "a hard road to travel" just then. The house had been a hotel before hospitals were needed, and many of the doors still bore their old names; some not so inappropriate as might be imagined, for that ward was in truth a *ball-room*, if gunshot wounds could christen it. Forty beds were prepared, many already tenanted by tired men who fell down anywhere, and drowsed till the smell of food roused them. Round the great stove was gathered the dreariest group I ever saw—ragged, gaunt and pale, mud to the knees, with bloody bandages untouched since put on days before; many bundled up in blankets, coats being lost or useless; and all wearing that disheartened look which proclaimed defeat, more plainly than any telegram of the Burnside blunder. I pitied them so much, I dared not speak to them, though, remembering all they had been through since the fight at Fredericksburg, I yearned to serve the dreariest of them all. Presently, Miss Blank tore me from my refuge behind piles of one-sleeved shirts, odd socks, bandages and lint; put basin, sponge, towels, and a block of brown soap into my hands, with these appalling directions:

"Come, my dear, begin to wash as fast as you can. Tell them to take off socks, coats and shirts, scrub them well, put on clean shirts, and the attendants will finish them off, and lay them in bed."

If she had requested me to shave them all, or dance a hornpipe on the stove funnel, I should have been less staggered; but to scrub some dozen lords of creation at a moment's notice, was really—really—. However, there was no time for nonsense, and, having resolved when I came to do everything I was bid, I drowned my scruples in my washbowl, clutched my soap manfully, and, assuming a businesslike air, made a dab at the first dirty specimen I saw, bent on performing my task *vi et armis*[2] if necessary. I chanced to light on a withered old Irishman, wounded in the head, which caused that portion of his frame to be tastefully laid out like a garden, the bandages being the walks, his hair the shrubbery. He was so overpowered by the honor of having a lady wash him, as he expressed it, that he did nothing but roll up his eyes, and bless me, in an irresistible style which was too much for my sense of the ludicrous; so we laughed together, and when I knelt down to take off his shoes, he "flopped" also, and wouldn't hear of my touching "them dirty craters. May your bed above be aisy darlin', for the day's work ye are doon!—Whoosh! there ye are, and bedad, it's hard tellin' which is the dirtiest, the fut or the shoe." It was; and if he hadn't been to the fore, I should have gone on pulling, under the impression that the "fut" was a boot, for trousers, socks, shoes and legs were a mass of mud. This comical tableau produced a general grin, at which propitious beginning I took heart and scrubbed away like any tidy parent on a Saturday night. Some of them took the performance like sleepy children, leaning their tired heads against me as I worked, others looked grimly scandalized, and several of the roughest colored like bashful girls. One wore a soiled little bag about his neck, and, as I moved it, to bathe his wounded breast, I said,

"Your talisman didn't save you, did it?"

---

2. (Latin) *vi et armis*: by force of arms.

"Well, I reckon it did, marm, for that shot would a gone a couple a inches deeper but for my old mammy's camphor bag," answered the cheerful philosopher.

Another, with a gunshot wound through the cheek, asked for a looking-glass, and when I brought one, regarded his swollen face with a dolorous expression, as he muttered—

"I vow to gosh, that's too bad! I warn't a bad looking chap before, and now I'm done for; won't there be a thunderin' scar? and what on earth will Josephine Skinner say?"

He looked up at me with his one eye so appealingly, that I controlled my risibles, and assured him that if Josephine was a girl of sense, she would admire the honorable scar, as a lasting proof that he had faced the enemy, for all women thought a wound the best decoration a brave soldier could wear. I hope Miss Skinner verified the good opinion I so rashly expressed of her, but I shall never know.

The next scrubbee was a nice-looking lad, with a curly brown mane, honest blue eyes, and a merry mouth. He lay on a bed, with one leg gone, and the right arm so shattered that it must evidently follow: yet the little sergeant was as merry as if his afflictions were not worth lamenting over; and when a drop or two of salt water mingled with my suds at the sight of this strong young body, so marred and maimed, the boy looked up, with a brave smile, though there was a little quiver of the lips, as he said,

"Now don't you fret yourself about me, miss; I'm first rate here, for it's nuts to lie still on this bed, after knocking about in those confounded ambulances, that shake what there is left of a fellow to jelly. I never was in one of these places before, and think this cleaning up a jolly thing for us, though I'm afraid it isn't for you ladies."

"Is this your first battle, Sergeant?"

"No, miss; I've been in six scrimmages, and never got a scratch till this last one; but it's done the business pretty thoroughly for me, I should say. Lord! what a scramble there'll be for arms and legs, when we old boys come out of our graves, on the Judgment Day: wonder if we shall get our own again? If we do, my leg will have to tramp from Fredericksburg, my arm from here, I suppose, and meet my body, wherever it may be."

The fancy seemed to tickle him mightily, for he laughed blithely, and so did I; which, no doubt, caused the new nurse to be regarded as a light-minded sinner by the Chaplain, who roamed vaguely about, with his hands in his pockets, preaching resignation to cold, hungry, wounded men, and evidently feeling himself, what he certainly was, the wrong man in the wrong place.

"I say, Mrs.!" called a voice behind me; and, turning, I saw a rough Michigander, with an arm blown off at the shoulder, and two or three bullets still in him—as he afterwards mentioned, as carelessly as if gentlemen were in the habit of carrying such trifles about with them. I went to him, and, while administering a dose of soap and water, he whispered, irefully:

"That red-headed devil, over yonder, is a reb, hang him! He's got shet of a foot, or he'd a cut like the rest of the lot. Don't you wash him, nor feed him, but jest let him holler till he's tired. It's a blasted shame to fetch them fellers in here, along side of us; and so I'll tell the chap that bosses this concern; cuss me if I don't."

I regret to say that I did not deliver a moral sermon upon the duty of forgiving our enemies, and the sin of profanity, then and there; but, being a red-hot Abolitionist, stared fixedly at the tall rebel, who was a copperhead, in every sense of the word, and privately resolved to put soap in his eyes, rub his nose the wrong way, and excoriate his cuticle generally, if I had the washing of him.

My amiable intentions, however, were frustrated; for, when I approached, with as Christian an expression as my principles would allow, and asked the question—"Shall I try to make you more comfortable, sir?" all I got for my pains was a gruff—

"No; I'll do it myself."

"Here's your Southern chivalry, with a witness," thought I, dumping the basin down before him, thereby quenching a strong desire to give him a summary baptism, in return for his ungraciousness; for my angry passions rose, at this rebuff, in a way that would have scandalized good Dr. Watts. He was a disappointment in all respects, (the rebel, not the blessed Doctor,) for he was neither fiendish, romantic, pathetic, or anything interesting; but a long, fat man, with a head like a burning bush, and a perfectly expressionless face: so I could dislike him without the slightest drawback, and ignored his existence from that day forth. One redeeming trait he certainly did possess, as the floor speedily testified; for his ablutions were so vigorously performed, that his bed soon stood like an isolated island, in a sea of soap-suds, and he resembled a dripping merman, suffering from the loss of a fin. If cleanliness is a near neighbor to godliness, then was the big rebel the godliest man in my ward that day.

Having done up our human wash, and laid it out to dry, the second syllable of our version of the word War-fare was enacted with much success. Great trays of bread, meat, soup and coffee appeared; and both nurses and attendants turned waiters, serving bountiful rations to all who could eat. I can call my pinafore to testify to my good will in the work, for in ten minutes it was reduced to a perambulating bill of fare, presenting samples of all the refreshments going or gone. It was a lively scene; the long room lined with rows of beds, each filled by an occupant, whom water, shears, and clean raiment had transformed from a dismal ragamuffin into a recumbent hero, with a cropped head. To and fro rushed matrons, maids, and convalescent "boys," skirmishing with knives and forks; retreating with empty plates; marching and counter-marching, with unvaried success, while the clash of busy spoons made most inspiring music for the charge of our Light Brigade:

"Beds to the front of them,
Beds to the right of them,
Beds to the left of them,
  Nobody blundered.
Beamed at by hungry souls,
Screamed at with brimming bowls,
Steamed at by army rolls,
  Buttered and sundered.
With coffee not cannon plied,
Each must be satisfied,
Whether they lived or died;
  All the men wondered."

Very welcome seemed the generous meal, after a week of suffering, exposure, and short commons; soon the brown faces began to smile, as food, warmth, and rest, did their pleasant work; and the grateful "Thankee's" were followed by more graphic accounts of the battle and retreat, than any paid reporter could have given us. Curious contrasts of the tragic and comic met one everywhere; and some touching as well as ludicrous episodes, might have been recorded that day. A six-foot New Hampshire man, with a leg broken and perforated by a piece of shell, so large that, had I not seen the wound, I should have regarded the story as a Munchausenism, beckoned me to come and help him, as he could not sit up, and both his bed and beard were getting plentifully anointed with soup.

As I fed my big nestling with corresponding mouthfuls, I asked him how he felt during the battle.

"Well, 'twas my fust, you see, so I ain't ashamed to say I was a trifle flustered in the beginnin', there was such an all-fired racket; for ef there's anything I do spleen agin, it's noise. But when my mate, Eph Sylvester, fell, with a bullet through his head, I got mad, and pitched in, licketty cut. Our part of the fight didn't last long; so a lot of us larked round Fredericksburg, and give some of them houses a pretty consid'able of a rummage, till we was ordered out of the mess. Some of our fellows cut like time; but I warn't a-goin to run for nobody; and, fust thing I knew, a shell bust, right in front of us, and I keeled over, feelin' as if I was blowed higher'n a kite. I sung out, and the boys come back for me, double quick; but the way they chucked me over them fences was a caution, I tell you. Next day I was most as black as that darkey yonder, lickin' plates on the sly. This is bully coffee, ain't it? Give us another pull at it, and I'll be obleeged to you."

I did; and, as the last gulp subsided, he said, with a rub of his old handkerchief over eyes as well as mouth:

"Look a here; I've got a pair a earbobs and a handkercher pin I'm a goin' to give you, if you'll have them; for you're the very moral o' Lizy Sylvester, poor Eph's wife: that's why I signalled you to come over here. They ain't much, I guess, but they'll do to memorize the rebs by."

Burrowing under his pillow, he produced a little bundle of what he called "truck," and gallantly presented me with a pair of earrings, each representing a cluster of corpulent grapes, and the pin a basket of astonishing fruit, the whole large and coppery enough for a small warming-pan. Feeling delicate about depriving him of such valuable relics, I accepted the earrings alone, and was obliged to depart, somewhat abruptly, when my friend stuck the warming-pan in the bosom of his night-gown, viewing it with much complacency, and, perhaps, some tender memory, in that rough heart of his, for the comrade he had lost.

Observing that the man next him had left his meal untouched, I offered the same service I had performed for his neighbor, but he shook his head.

"Thank you, ma'am; I don't think I'll ever eat again, for I'm shot in the stomach. But I'd like a drink of water, if you ain't too busy."

I rushed away, but the water-pails were gone to be refilled, and it was some time before they reappeared. I did not forget my patient patient, meanwhile, and, with the first mugful, hurried back to him. He seemed asleep; but something in the tired white face caused me to listen at his lips for a breath. None came. I touched his forehead; it was cold: and then I knew that, while he waited, a better nurse than I had given him a cooler draught, and healed him with a touch. I laid the sheet over the quiet sleeper, whom no noise could now disturb; and, half an hour later, the bed was empty. It seemed a poor requital for all he had sacrificed and suffered,—that hospital bed, lonely even in a crowd; for there was no familiar face for him to look his last upon; no friendly voice to say, Goodbye; no hand to lead him gently down into the Valley of the Shadow; and he vanished, like a drop in that red sea upon whose shores so many women stand lamenting. For a moment I felt bitterly indignant at this seeming carelessness of the value of life, the sanctity of death; then consoled myself with the thought that, when the great muster roll was called, these nameless men might be promoted above many whose tall monuments record the barren honors they have won.

All having eaten, drank, and rested, the surgeons began their rounds; and I took my first lesson in the art of dressing wounds. It wasn't a festive scene, by any means; for Dr. P., whose Aid I constituted myself, fell to work with a vigor which soon convinced me that I was a weaker vessel, though nothing would have induced me to confess it then. He had served in the Crimea, and seemed to regard a dilapidated body very much as I should have regarded a damaged garment; and, turning up his cuffs, whipped out a very unpleasant looking housewife, cutting, sawing, patching and piecing, with the enthusiasm of an accomplished surgical seamstress; explaining the process, in scientific terms, to the patient, meantime; which, of course, was immensely cheering and comfortable. There was an uncanny sort of fascination in watching him, as he peered and probed into the mechanism of those wonderful bodies, whose mysteries he understood so well. The more intricate the wound, the better he liked it. A poor private, with both legs off, and shot through the lungs, possessed more attractions for him than a dozen generals, slightly scratched in some "masterly retreat"; and had anyone appeared in small pieces, requesting to be put together again, he would have considered it a special dispensation.

The amputations were reserved till the morrow, and the merciful magic of ether was not thought necessary that day, so the poor souls had to bear their pains as best they might. It is all very well to talk of the patience of woman; and far be it from me to pluck that feather from her cap, for, heaven knows, she isn't allowed to wear many; but the patient endurance of these men, under trials of the flesh, was truly wonderful. Their fortitude seemed contagious, and scarcely a cry escaped them, though I often longed to groan for them, when pride kept their white lips shut, while great drops stood upon their foreheads, and the bed shook with the irrepressible tremor of their tortured bodies. One or two Irishmen anathematized the doctors with the frankness of their nation, and ordered the Virgin to stand by them, as if she had been the wedded Biddy to whom they could administer the poker, if she didn't; but, as a general thing, the work went on in silence, broken only by some quiet request for roller, instruments, or plaster, a sigh from the patient, or a sympathizing murmur from the nurse.

It was long past noon before these repairs were even partially made; and, having got the bodies of my boys into something like order, the next task was to minister to their minds, by writing letters to the anxious souls at home; answering questions, reading papers, taking possession of money and valuables; for the eighth commandment was reduced to a very fragmentary condition, both by the blacks and whites, who ornamented our hospital with their presence. Pocket books, purses, miniatures, and watches, were sealed up, labelled, and handed over to the matron, till such times as the owners thereof were ready to depart homeward or campward again. The letters dictated to me, and revised by me, that afternoon, would have made an excellent chapter for some future history of the war; for, like that which Thackeray's "Ensign Spooney" wrote his mother just before Waterloo, they were "full of affection, pluck, and bad spelling"; nearly all giving lively accounts of the battle, and ending with a somewhat sudden plunge from patriotism to provender, desiring "Marm," "Mary Ann," or "Aunt Peters," to send along some pies, pickles, sweet stuff, and apples, "to yourn in haste," Joe, Sam, or Ned, as the case might be.

My little Sergeant insisted on trying to scribble something with his left hand, and patiently accomplished some half dozen lines of hieroglyphics, which he gave me to fold and direct, with a boyish blush, that rendered a glimpse of "My Dearest Jane," unnecessary, to assure me that the heroic lad had been more successful in the service of Commander-in-Chief Cupid than that of Gen. Mars; and a charming little romance blossomed instanter in Nurse Periwinkle's romantic fancy, though no further confidences were made that day, for Sergeant fell asleep, and, judging from his tranquil face, visited his absent sweetheart in the pleasant land of dreams.

At five o'clock a great bell rang, and the attendants flew, not to arms, but to their trays, to bring up supper, when a second uproar announced that it was ready. The newcomers woke at the sound; and I presently discovered that it took a very bad wound to incapacitate the defenders of the faith for the consumption of their rations; the amount that some of them sequestered was amazing; but when I suggested the probability of a famine hereafter, to the matron, that motherly lady cried out: "Bless their hearts, why shouldn't they eat? It's their only amusement; so fill everyone, and, if there's not enough ready tonight, I'll lend my share to the Lord by giving it to the boys." And, whipping up her coffee-pot and plate of toast, she gladdened the eyes and stomachs of two or three dissatisfied heroes, by serving them with a liberal hand; and I haven't the slightest doubt that, having cast her bread upon the waters, it came back buttered, as another large-hearted old lady was wont to say.

Then came the doctor's evening visit; the administration of medicines; washing feverish faces; smoothing tumbled beds; wetting wounds; singing lullabies; and preparations for the night. By twelve, the last labor of love was done; the last "goodnight" spoken; and, if any needed a reward for that day's work, they surely received it, in the silent eloquence of those long lines of faces, showing pale and peaceful in the shaded rooms, as we quitted them, followed by grateful glances that lighted us to bed, where rest, the sweetest, made our pillows soft, while Night and Nature took our places, filling that great house of pain with the healing miracles of Sleep, and his diviner brother, Death.

SOURCE: Louisa May Alcott. *Hospital Sketches*. Boston: James Redpath, Publisher, 1863.

ABRAHAM LINCOLN

We conclude the anthology with the writings of the man who, more than any other person, represents the Civil War, the sixteenth President of the United States. "Lincoln's most memorable writings have been at the heart of whatever positive interpretation Americans have been able to put on the Civil War. In fact, it is by now hard to imagine how we could engage the question of what that terrible war was about without Lincoln's words," writes Douglas L. Wilson in his study of Lincoln's most effective weapon—his pen.[1] *The following are a sampling of Lincoln's personal notes and official letters, as well as a handful of the history-making speeches. Born in the backwoods of Kentucky in 1809 and largely self-educated, Lincoln's writing voice throughout his life was as distinct as that of any man of letters. The writings are almost invariably patient and farseeing, logical and to the point. (The inconsistent punctuation and spelling, however, have been more or less regularized, and paragraph breaks added.)*

First Debate with Senator Stephen A. Douglas
(Ottawa, Illinois, August 21, 1858)

The incumbent U.S. Senator from Illinois, Stephen A. Douglas, led off the first of the seven statewide debates as they campaigned for the senatorship and spoke for an hour. Lincoln's reply follows, in the course of which he quotes from his own 1854 Peoria, Illinois, speech on the Missouri Compromise. (Douglas was then allowed a half-hour to respond to Lincoln's reply.) These debates and the newspaper coverage and the book publication of them (as revised by the debaters) helped bring Lincoln to national prominence on the issue of slavery and led to his nomination for president.

1. Douglas L. Wilson. *Lincoln's Sword: The Presidency and the Power of Words*. New York: Alfred A. Knopf, 2006. 9.

My Fellow Citizens:

When a man hears himself somewhat misrepresented, it provokes him,—at least, I find it so with myself; but when misrepresentation becomes very gross and palpable, it is more apt to amuse him. The first thing I see fit to notice is the fact that Judge Douglas alleges, after running through the history of the old Democratic and the old Whig parties, that Judge Trumbull and myself made an arrangement in 1854, by which I was to have the place of General Shields in the United States Senate, and Judge Trumbull was to have the place of Judge Douglas. Now, all I have to say upon that subject is, that I think no man—not even Judge Douglas—can prove it, *because it is not true.* I have no doubt he is "*conscientious*" in saying it.

As to those resolutions that he took such a length of time to read, as being the platform of the Republican party in 1854, I say I never had anything to do with them, and I think Trumbull never had. Judge Douglas cannot show that either of us ever did have anything to do with them. I believe *this* is true about those resolutions: There was a call for a Convention to form a Republican party at Springfield, and I think that my friend, Mr. Lovejoy, who is here upon this stand, had a hand in it. I think this is true, and I think if he will remember accurately, he will be able to recollect that he tried to get me into it, and I would not go in. I believe it is also true that I went away from Springfield when the Convention was in session to attend court in Tazewell county. It is true they did place my name, though without authority, upon the committee, and afterward wrote me to attend the meeting of the committee; but I refused to do so, and I never had anything to do with that organization. This is the plain truth about all that matter of the resolutions.

Now, about this story that Judge Douglas tells of Trumbull bargaining to sell out the old Democratic party, and Lincoln agreeing to sell out the old Whig party, I have the means of *knowing* about that; Judge Douglas cannot have; and I know there is no substance to it whatever. Yet I have no doubt he is "*conscientious*" about it. I know that after Mr. Lovejoy got into the Legislature that winter, he complained of me that I had told all the old Whigs of his district that the old Whig party was good enough for them, and some of them voted against him because I told them so. Now, I have no means of totally disproving such charges as this which the Judge makes. A man cannot prove a negative; but he has a right to claim that when a man makes an affirmative charge, he must offer some proof to show the truth of what he says. I certainly cannot introduce testimony to show the negative about things, but I have a right to claim that if a man says he *knows* a thing, then he must show *how* he knows it. I always have a right to claim this, and it is not satisfactory to me that he may be "conscientious" on the subject.

Now, gentlemen, I hate to waste my time on such things; but in regard to that general Abolition tilt that Judge Douglas makes, when he says that I was engaged at that time in selling out and abolitionizing the old Whig party, I hope you will permit me to read a part of a printed speech that I made then at Peoria, which will show altogether a different view of the position I took in that contest of 1854.

VOICE: Put on your specs.

LINCOLN: Yes, sir, I am obliged to do so; I am no longer a young man:

[Reads] "This is the *repeal* of the Missouri Compromise. The foregoing history may not be precisely accurate in every particular, but I am sure it is sufficiently so for all the uses I shall attempt to make of it, and in it we have before us the chief materials enabling us to correctly judge whether the repeal of the Missouri Compromise is right or wrong.

"I think, and shall try to show, that it is wrong—wrong in its direct effect, letting slavery into Kansas and Nebraska, and wrong in its prospective principle, allowing it to spread to every other part of the wide world, where men can be found inclined to take it.

"This *declared* indifference, but, as I must think, covert *real* zeal for the spread of slavery, I cannot but hate. I hate it because of the monstrous injustice of slavery itself. I hate it because it deprives our republican example of its just influence in the world—enables the enemies of free institutions, with plausibility, to taunt us as hypocrites; causes the real friends of freedom to doubt our sincerity, and especially because it forces so many really good men amongst ourselves into an open war with the very fundamental principles of civil liberty—criticizing the Declaration of Independence, and insisting that there is no right principle of action but *self-interest*.

"Before proceeding, let me say I think I have no prejudice against the Southern people. They are just what we would be in their situation. If slavery did not now exist among them, they would not introduce it. If it did now exist amongst us, we should not instantly give it up. This I believe of the masses North and South. Doubtless there are individuals on both sides who would not hold slaves under any circumstances; and others who would gladly introduce slavery anew, if it were out of existence. We know that some Southern men do free their slaves, go North, and become tip-top Abolitionists; while some Northern ones go South, and become most cruel slave-masters.

"When Southern people tell us they are no more responsible for the origin of slavery than we, I acknowledge the fact. When it is said that the institution exists, and that it is very difficult to get rid of it, in any satisfactory way, I can understand and appreciate the saying. I surely will not blame them for not doing what I should not know how to do myself. If all earthly power were given me, I should not know what to do, as to the existing institution. My first impulse would be to free all the slaves, and send them to Liberia—to their own native land. But a moment's reflection would convince me that whatever of high hope (as I think there is) there may be in this, in the long run, its sudden execution is impossible. If they were all landed there in a day, they would all perish in the next ten days; and there are not surplus shipping and surplus money enough in the world to carry them there in many times ten days. What then? Free them all, and keep them among us as underlings? Is it quite certain that this betters their condition? I think I would not hold one in slavery, at any rate; yet the point is not clear enough to me to denounce people upon. What next? Free them, and make them politically and socially our equals? My own feelings will not admit of this; and if mine would, we well know that those of the great mass of white people will not. Whether this feeling accords with justice and sound judgment is not the sole question, if, indeed, it is any part of it. A universal feeling, whether well or ill-founded, cannot be safely disregarded. We cannot, then, make them equals. It does seem to me that systems of gradual emancipation might be adopted; but for their tardiness in this, I will not undertake to judge our brethren of the South.

"When they remind us of their Constitutional rights, I acknowledge them, not grudgingly, but fully and fairly; and I would give them any legislation for the reclaiming of their fugitives, which should not, in its stringency, be more likely to carry a free man into slavery than our ordinary criminal laws are to hang an innocent one.

"But all this, to my judgment, furnishes no more excuse for permitting slavery to go into our own free territory than it would for reviving the African slave-trade by law. The law which forbids the bringing of slaves *from* Africa, and that which has so long forbid the taking of them *to* Nebraska, can hardly be distinguished on any moral principle; and the repeal of the former could find quite as plausible excuses as that of the latter."

I have reason to know that Judge Douglas *knows* that I said this. I think he has the answer here to one of the questions he put to me. I do not mean to allow him to catechise me unless he pays back for it in kind. I will not answer questions one after another, unless he reciprocates; but as he has made this inquiry, and I have answered it before, he has got it without my getting anything in return. He has got my answer on the Fugitive Slave law.

Now, gentlemen, I don't want to read at any greater length; but this is the true complexion of all I have ever said in regard to the instruction of slavery and the black race. This is the whole of it; and anything that argues me into his idea of perfect social and political equality with the negro is but a specious and fantastic arrangement of words by which a man can prove a horsechestnut to be a chestnut horse.

I will say here, while upon this subject, that I have no purpose, directly or indirectly, to interfere with the institution of slavery in the States where it exists. I believe I have no lawful right to do so, and I have no inclination to do so. I have no purpose to introduce political and social equality between the white and the black races. There is a physical difference between the two which, in my judgment, will probably forever forbid their living together upon the footing of perfect equality; and inasmuch as it becomes a necessity that there must be a difference, I, as well as Judge Douglas, am in favor of the race to which I belong having the superior position. I have never said anything to the contrary, but I hold that, notwithstanding all this, there is no reason in the world why the negro is not entitled to all the natural rights enumerated in the Declaration of Independence—the right to life, liberty, and the pursuit of happiness. I hold that he is as much entitled to these as the white man. I agree with Judge Douglas he is not my equal in many respects—certainly not in color, perhaps not in moral or intellectual endowment. But in the right to eat the bread, without the leave of anybody else, which his own hand earns, *he is my equal, and the equal of Judge Douglas, and the equal of every living man.*

Now I pass on to consider one or two more of these little follies. The Judge is woefully at fault about his early friend Lincoln being a "grocery-keeper." I don't know as it would be a great sin, if I had been; but he is mistaken. Lincoln never kept a grocery anywhere in the world. It is true that Lincoln did work the latter part of one winter in a little still-house, up at the head of a hollow.

And so I think my friend the Judge is equally at fault when he charges me at the time when I was in Congress of having opposed our soldiers who were fighting in the Mexican War. The Judge did not make his charge very distinctly, but I can tell you what he can prove, by referring to the record. You remember I was an old Whig, and whenever the Democratic party tried to get me to vote that the war had been righteously begun by the President, I would not do it. But whenever they asked for any money, or land-warrants, or anything to pay the soldiers there, during all that time, I gave the same vote that Judge Douglas did. You can think as you please as to whether that was consistent. Such is the truth; and the Judge has the right to make all he can out of it. But when he, by a general charge, conveys the idea that I withheld supplies from the soldiers who were fighting in the Mexican War, or did anything else to hinder the soldiers, he is, to say the least, grossly and altogether mistaken, as a consultation of the records will prove to him.

As I have not used up so much of my time as I had supposed, I will dwell a little longer upon one or two of these minor topics upon which the Judge has spoken. He has read from my speech in Springfield, in which I say that "a house divided against itself cannot stand." Does the Judge say it *can* stand? I don't know whether he does or not. The Judge does not seem to be attending to me just now, but I would like to know if it is his opinion that a house divided against itself *can stand.* If he does, then there is a question of veracity, not between him and me, but between the Judge and an authority of a somewhat higher character.

Now, my friends, I ask your attention to this matter for the purpose of saying something seriously. I know that the Judge may readily enough agree with me that the maxim which was put forth by the Savior is true, but he may allege that I misapply it; and the Judge has a right to urge that, in my application, I do misapply it, and then I have a right to show that I do *not* misapply it. When he undertakes to say that because I think this nation, so far as the question of slavery is concerned, will all become one thing or all the other, I am in favor of bringing about a dead uniformity in the various States, in all their institutions, he argues erroneously. The great variety of the local institutions in the States, springing from differences in the soil, differences in the face of the country, and in the climate, are bonds of union. They do not make "a house divided against itself," but they make a house united. If they produce in one section of the country what is called for by the wants of another section, and this other section can supply the wants of the first, they are not matters of discord but bonds of union, true bonds of union.

But can this question of slavery be considered as among *these* varieties in the institutions of the country? I leave it to you to say whether, in the history of our Government, this institution of slavery has not always failed to be a bond of union, and, on the contrary, been an apple of discord and an element of division in the house. I ask you to consider whether, so long as the moral constitution of men's minds shall continue to be the same, after this generation and assemblage shall sink into the grave, and another race shall arise, with the same moral and intellectual development we have—whether, if that institution is standing in the same irritating position in which it now is, it will not continue an element of division? If so, then I have a right to say that, in regard to this question, the Union is a house divided against itself; and when the Judge reminds me that I have often said to him that the institution of slavery has existed for eighty years in some States, and yet it does not exist in some others, I agree to the fact, and I account for it by looking at the position in which our fathers originally placed it—restricting it from the new Territories where it had not gone, and legislating to cut off its source by the abrogation of the slave-trade, thus putting the seal of legislation *against its spread.*

The public mind *did* rest in the belief that it was in the course of ultimate extinction. But lately, I think—and in this I charge nothing on the Judge's motives—lately, I think, that he, and those acting with him, have placed that institution on a new basis, which looks to the *perpetuity and nationalization of slavery*. And while it is placed upon this new basis, I say, and I have said, that I believe we shall not have peace upon the question until the opponents of slavery arrest the further spread of it, and place it where the public mind shall rest in the belief that it is in the course of ultimate extinction; or, on the other hand, that its advocates will push it forward until it shall become alike lawful in all the States, old as well as new, North as well as South. Now, I believe if we could arrest the spread, and place it where Washington and Jefferson and Madison placed it, it *would be* in the course of ultimate extinction, and the public mind *would*, as for eighty years past, believe that it was in the course of ultimate extinction. The crisis would be past and the institution might be let alone for a hundred years, if it should live so long, in the States where it exists; yet it would be going out of existence in the way best for both the black and the white races.

A VOICE: Then do you repudiate popular sovereignty?

LINCOLN: Well, then, let us talk about popular sovereignty! What is popular sovereignty? Is it the right of the people to have slavery or not have it, as they see fit, in the Territories? I will state—and I have an able man to watch me—my understanding is that Popular Sovereignty, as now applied to the question of slavery, does allow the people of a Territory to have slavery if they want to, but does not allow them *not* to have it if they *do not* want it. I do not mean that if this vast concourse of people were in a Territory of the United States, any one of them would be obliged to have a slave if he did not want one; but I do say that, as I understand the Dred Scott decision, if any one man wants slaves, all the rest have no way of keeping that one man from holding them.

When I made my speech at Springfield, of which the Judge complains, and from which he quotes, I really was not thinking of the things which he ascribes to me at all. I had no thought in the world that I was doing anything to bring about a war between the Free and Slave States. I had no thought in the world that I was doing anything to bring about a political and social equality of the black and white races. It never occurred to me that I was doing anything or favoring anything to reduce to a dead uniformity all the local institutions of the various States. But I must say, in all fairness to him, if he thinks I am doing something which leads to these bad results, it is none the better that I did not mean it. It is just as fatal to the country, if I have any influence in producing it, whether I intend it or not. But can it be true that placing this institution upon the original basis—the basis upon which our fathers placed it—can have any tendency to set the Northern and the Southern States at war with one another, or that it can have any tendency to make the people of Vermont raise sugar-cane, because they raise it in Louisiana, or that it can compel the people of Illinois to cut pine logs on the Grand Prairie, where they will not grow, because they cut pine logs in Maine, where they do grow?

The Judge says this is a new principle started in regard to this question. Does the Judge claim that he is working on the plan of the founders of government? I think he says in some of his speeches—indeed, I have one here now—that he saw evidence of a policy to allow slavery to be south of a certain line, while north of it it should be excluded, and he saw an indisposition on the part of the country to stand upon that policy, and therefore he set about studying the subject upon *original principles,* and upon *original principles* he got up the Nebraska bill! I am fighting it upon these "original principles"—fighting it in the Jeffersonian, Washingtonian, and Madisonian fashion.

Now, my friends, I wish you to attend for a little while to one or two other things in that Springfield speech. My main object was to show, so far as my humble ability was capable of showing to the people of this country, what I believed was the truth—that there was a *tendency,* if not a conspiracy, among those who have engineered this slavery question for the last four of five years to make slavery perpetual and universal in this nation. Having made that speech principally for that object, after arranging the evidences that I thought tended to prove my proposition, I concluded with this bit of comment:

"We cannot absolutely know that these exact adaptations are the result of preconcert; but when we see a lot of framed timbers, different portions of which we know have been gotten out at different times and places, and by different workmen—Stephen, Franklin, Roger, and James, for instance—and when we see these timbers joined together, and see they exactly make the frame of a house or a mill, all the beams and mortises exactly fitting, and all the lengths and proportions of the different pieces exactly adapted to their respective places, and not a piece too many or too few—not omitting even the scaffolding—or if a single piece be lacking, we see the place in the frame exactly fitted and prepared yet to bring such piece in,—in such a case we feel it impossible not to believe that Stephen and Franklin, and Roger and James all understood one another from the beginning, and all worked upon a common plan or draft drawn before the first blow was struck."

When my friend Judge Douglas came to Chicago on the 9th of July, this speech having been delivered on the 16th of June, he made an harangue there, in which he took hold of this speech of mine, showing that he had carefully read it; and while he paid no attention to *this* matter at all, but complimented me as being a "kind, amiable, and intelligent gentleman," notwithstanding I had said this, he goes on and eliminates, or draws out, from my speech this tendency of mine to set the States at war with one another, to make all the institutions uniform, and set the negroes and white people to marrying together. Then, as the Judge had complimented me with these pleasant titles (I must confess to my weakness), I was a little "taken," for it came from a great man. I was not very much accustomed to flattery, and it came the sweeter to me. I was rather like the Hoosier, with the gingerbread, when he said he reckoned he loved it better than any other man, and got less of it. As the Judge had so flattered me, I could not make up my mind that he meant to deal unfairly with me; so I went to work to show him that he misunderstood the whole scope of my speech, and that I really never intended to set the people at war with one another.

As an illustration, the next time I met him, which was at Springfield, I used this expression, that I claimed no right under the Constitution, nor had I any inclination, to enter into the Slave States and interfere with the institutions of slavery. He says upon that: Lincoln will not enter into the Slave States, but will go to the banks of Ohio, on this side, and shoot over! He runs on, step by step, in the horse-chestnut style of argument, until in the Springfield speech he says: "Unless he shall be successful in firing his batteries, until he shall have extinguished slavery in all the States, the Union shall be dissolved." Now, I don't think that was exactly the way to treat "a kind, amiable, intelligent gentleman." I know if I had asked the Judge to show when or where it was I had said that, if I didn't succeed in firing into the Slave States until slavery should be extinguished, the Union should be dissolved, he could not have shown it. I understand what he would do. He would say, "I don't mean to quote from you, but this was the *result* of what you say." But I have the right to ask, and I do ask now, Did you not put it in such a form that an ordinary reader or listener would take it as an expression *from me?*

In a speech at Springfield, on the night of the 17th, I thought I might as well attend to my own business a little, and I recalled his attention as well as I could to this charge of conspiracy to nationalize slavery. I called his attention to the fact that he had acknowledged, in my hearing twice, that he had carefully read the speech, and, in the language of the lawyers, as he had twice read the speech, and still had put in no plea or answer, I took a default on him. I insisted that I had a right then to renew that charge of conspiracy. Ten days afterward I met the Judge at Clinton—that is to say, I was on the ground, but not in the discussion—and heard him make a speech. Then he comes in with his plea to this charge, for the first time, and his plea when put in, as well as I can recollect it, amounted to this: that he never had any talk with Judge Taney or the President of the United States with regard to the Dred Scott decision before it was made. I (Lincoln) ought to know that the man who makes a charge without knowing it to be true, falsifies as much as he who knowingly tells a falsehood; and, lastly, that he would pronounce the whole thing a falsehood; but he would make no personal application of the charge of falsehood, not because of any regard for the "kind, amiable, intelligent gentleman," but because of his own personal self-respect!

I have understood since then (but *[turning to Senator Douglas]* will not hold the Judge to it if he is not willing) that he has broken through the "self-respect," and has got to saying the thing *out.* The Judge nods to me that it is so. It is fortunate for me that I can keep as good-humored as I do, when the Judge acknowledges that he has been trying to make a question of veracity with me. I know the Judge is a great man, while I am only a small man, but *I feel that I have got him.* I demur to that plea. I waive all objections that it was not filed till after default was taken, and demur to it upon the merits. What if Judge Douglas never did talk with Chief Justice Taney and the President before the Dred Scott decision was made, does it follow that he could not have had as perfect an understanding without talking as with it? I am not disposed to stand upon my legal advantage. I am disposed to take his denial as being like an answer in chancery, that he neither had any knowledge, information, or belief in the existence of such a conspiracy. I am disposed to take his answer as being as broad as though he had put it in these words. And now, I ask, even if he had done so, have not I a right to *prove it on him,* and to offer the evidence of more than two witnesses, by whom to prove it; and if the evidence proves the existence of the conspiracy, does his broad answer denying all knowledge, information, or belief, disturb the fact? It can only show that he was *used* by conspirators, and was not a *leader* of them.

Now, in regard to his reminding me of the moral rule that persons who tell what they do not know to be true, falsify as much as those who knowingly tell falsehoods. I remember the rule, and it must be borne in mind that in what I have read to you, I do not say that I *know* such a conspiracy to exist. To that I reply, *I believe it.* If the Judge says that I do *not* believe it, then *he* says what *he* does not know, and falls within his own rule, that he who asserts a thing which he does not know to be true, falsifies as much as he who knowingly tells a falsehood.

I want to call your attention to a little discussion on that branch of the case, and the evidence which brought my mind to the conclusion which I expressed as my *belief*. If, in arraying that evidence, I had stated anything which was false or erroneous, it needed but that Judge Douglas should point it out, and I would have taken it back, with all the kindness in the world. I do not deal in that way. If I have brought forward anything not a fact, if he will point it out, it will not even ruffle me to take it back. But if he will not point out anything erroneous in the evidence, is it not rather for him to show, by a comparison of the evidence, that I have *reasoned* falsely, than to call the "kind, amiable, intelligent gentleman" a liar? If I have reasoned to a false conclusion, it is the vocation of an able debater to show by argument that I have wandered to an erroneous conclusion.

I want to ask your attention to a portion of the Nebraska bill, which Judge Douglas has quoted: "It being the true intent and meaning of this Act, not to legislate slavery into any Territory or State, nor to exclude it therefrom, but to leave the people thereof perfectly free to form and regulate their domestic institutions in their own way, subject only to the Constitution of the United States." Thereupon Judge Douglas and others began to argue in favor of "Popular Sovereignty"—the right of the people to have slaves if they wanted them, and to exclude slavery if they did not want them. "But," said, in substance, a Senator from Ohio (Mr. Chase, I believe), "we more than suspect that you do not mean to allow the people to exclude slavery if they wish to; and if you do mean it, accept an amendment which I propose expressly authorizing the people to exclude slavery."

I believe I have the amendment here before me, which was offered, and under which the people of the Territory, through their representatives, might, if they saw fit, prohibit the existence of slavery therein. And now I state it as a *fact,* to be taken back if there is any mistake about it, that Judge Douglas and those acting with him *voted that amendment down.* I now think that those men who voted it down had a *real reason* for doing so. They know what that reason was. It looks to us, since we have seen the Dred Scott decision pronounced, holding that, "under the Constitution," the people cannot exclude slavery—I say it looks to outsiders, poor, simple, "amiable, intelligent gentlemen," as though the niche was left as a place to put that Dred Scott decision in—a niche which would have been spoiled by adopting the amendment. And now, I say again, if *this* was not the reason, it will avail the Judge much more to calmly and good-humoredly point out to these people what that *other* reason was for voting the amendment down, than, swelling himself up, to vociferate that he may be provoked to call somebody a liar.

Again: There is in that same quotation from the Nebraska bill this clause: "It being the true intent and meaning of this bill not to legislate slavery into any Territory or *State.*" I have always been puzzled to know what business the word "State" had in that connection. Judge Douglas knows. *He put it there.* He knows what he put it there for. We outsiders cannot say what he put it there for. The law they were passing was not about States, and was not making provisions for States. What was it placed there for? After seeing the Dred Scott decision, which holds that the people cannot exclude slavery from a *Territory,* if another Dred Scott decision shall come, holding that they cannot exclude it from a *State,* we shall discover that when the word was originally put there, it was in view of something which was to come in due time, we shall see that it was the *other half* of something. I now say again, if there is any different reason for putting it there, Judge Douglas, in a good-humored way, without calling anybody a liar, *can tell what the reason was.*

When the Judge spoke at Clinton, he came very near making a charge of falsehood against me. He used, as I found it printed in a newspaper, which, I remember, was very nearly like the real speech, the following language:

"I did not answer the charge [of conspiracy] before, for the reason that I did not suppose there was a man in America with a heart so corrupt as to believe such a charge could be true. I have too much respect for Mr. Lincoln to suppose he is serious in making the charge."

I confess this is rather a curious view, that out of respect for me he should consider I was making what I deemed rather a grave charge in fun. I confess it strikes me rather strangely. But I let it pass. As the Judge did not for a moment believe that there was a man in America whose heart was so "corrupt" as to make such a charge, and as he places me among the "men in America" who have hearts base enough to make such a charge, I hope he will excuse me if I hunt out another charge very like this; and if it should turn out that in hunting I should find that other, and it should turn out to be Judge Douglas himself who made it, I hope he will reconsider this question of the deep corruption of heart he has thought fit to ascribe to me. In Judge Douglas's speech of March 22, 1858, which I hold in my hand, he says:

"In this connection there is another topic to which I desire to allude. I seldom refer to the course of newspapers, or notice the articles which they publish in regard to myself; but the course of the Washington *Union* has been so extraordinary, for the last two or three months, that I think it well enough to make some allusion to it. It has read me out of the Democratic party every other day, at least for two or three months, and keeps reading me out, and, as if it had not succeeded, still continues to read me out, using such terms as 'traitor,' 'renegade,' 'deserter,' and other kind and polite epithets of that nature. Sir, I have no vindication to make of my Democracy against the Washington *Union,* or any other newspapers. I am willing to allow my history and action for the last twenty years to speak for themselves as to my political principles and my fidelity to political obligations. The Washington *Union* has a personal grievance. When its editor was nominated for public printer I declined to vote for him, and stated that at some time I might give my reasons for doing so. Since I declined to give that vote, this scurrilous abuse, these vindictive and constant attacks have been repeated almost daily on me. Will my friend from Michigan read the article to which I allude?"

This is a part of the speech. You must excuse me from reading the entire article of the Washington *Union,* as Mr. Stuart read it for Mr. Douglas. The Judge goes on and sums up, as I think, correctly:

"Mr. President, you here find several distinct propositions advanced boldly by the Washington *Union* editorially, and apparently *authoritatively;* and any man who questions any of them is denounced as an Abolitionist, a Freesoiler, a fanatic. The propositions are, first, that the primary object of all government at its original institution is the protection of person and property; second, that the Constitution of the United States declares that the citizens of each State shall be entitled to all the privileges and immunities of citizens in the several States; and that, therefore, thirdly, all State laws, whether organic or otherwise, which prohibit the citizens of one State from settling in another with their slave property, and especially declaring it forfeited, are direct violations of the original intention of the Government and Constitution of the United States; and, fourth, that the emancipation of the slaves of the Northern States was a gross outrage on the rights of property, inasmuch as it was involuntarily done on the part of the owner.

"Remember that this article was published in the *Union* on the 17th of November, and on the 18th appeared the first article giving the adhesion of the *Union* to the Lecompton Constitution. It was in these words:

"'KANSAS AND HER CONSTITUTION.—The vexed question is settled. The problem is solved. The dead point of danger is passed. All serious trouble to Kansas affairs is over and gone.'

"And a column nearly of the same sort. Then, when you come to look into the Lecompton Constitution, you find the same doctrine incorporated in it which was put forth editorially in the *Union*. What is it?

"'ARTICLE 7, *Section* 1. The right of property is before and higher than any Constitutional sanction; and the right of the owner of a slave to such slave and its increase is the same and as inviolable as the right of the owner of any property whatever.'

"Then in the schedule is a provision that the Constitution may be amended after 1864 by a two-thirds vote.

"'But no alteration shall be made to affect the right of property in the ownership of slaves.'

"It will be seen by these clauses in the Lecompton Constitution, that they are identical in spirit with the *authoritative* article in the Washington *Union* of the day previous to its indorsement of this Constitution."

I pass over some portions of the speech, and I hope that any one who feels interested in this matter will read the entire section of the speech, and see whether I do the Judge justice. He proceeds:

"When I saw that article in the *Union* of the 17th of November, followed by the glorification of the Lecompton Constitution on the 18th of November, and this clause in the Constitution asserting the doctrine that a State has no right to prohibit slavery within its limits, I saw that there was a *fatal blow* being struck at the sovereignty of the States of this Union."

I stop the quotation there, again requesting that it may all be read. I have read all of the portion I desire to comment upon. What is this charge that the Judge thinks I must have a very corrupt heart to make? It was a purpose on the part of certain high functionaries to make it impossible for the people of one State to prohibit the people of any other State from entering it with their "property," so called, and making it a Slave State. In other words, it was a charge implying a design to make the institution of slavery national. And now I ask your attention to what Judge Douglas has himself done here. I know he made that part of the speech as a reason why he had refused to vote for a certain man for public printer; but when we get at it, the charge itself is the very one I made against him, that he thinks I am so corrupt for uttering. Now, whom does he make that charge against? Does he make it against that newspaper editor merely? No; he says it is identical in spirit with the Lecompton Constitution, and so the framers of that Constitution are brought in with the editor of the newspaper in that "fatal blow being struck." He did not call it a "conspiracy." In his language, it is a "fatal blow being struck." And if the words carry the meaning better when changed from a "conspiracy" into a "fatal blow being struck," I will change *my* expression, and call it a "fatal blow being struck." We see the charge made not merely against the editor of the *Union,* but all the framers of the Lecompton Constitution; and not only so, but the article was an *authoritative* article. By whose authority? Is there any question but he means it was by the authority of the President and his Cabinet—the Administration?

Is there any sort of question but he means to make that charge? Then there are the editors of the *Union,* the framers of the Lecompton Constitution, the President of the United States and his Cabinet, and all the supporters of the Lecompton Constitution, in Congress and out of Congress, who are all involved in this "fatal blow being struck." I commend to Judge Douglas's consideration the question of *how corrupt a man's heart must be to make such a charge!*

Now, my friends, I have but one branch of the subject, in the little time I have left, to which to call your attention, and as I shall come to a close at the end of that branch, it is probable that I shall not occupy quite all the time allotted to me. Although on these questions I would like to talk twice as long as I have, I could not enter upon another head and discuss it properly without running over my time. I ask the attention of the people here assembled and elsewhere, to the course that Judge Douglas is pursuing every day as bearing upon this question of making slavery national. Not going back to the records, but taking the speeches he makes, the speeches he made yesterday and day before, and makes constantly all over the country—I ask your attention to them. In the first place, what is necessary to make the institution national? Not war. There is no danger that the people of Kentucky will shoulder their muskets, and, with a young nigger stuck on every bayonet, march into Illinois and force them upon us. There is no danger of our going over there and making war upon them. Then what is necessary for the nationalization of slavery? It is simply the next Dred Scott decision. It is merely for the Supreme Court to decide that no *State* under the Constitution can exclude it, just as they have already decided that under the Constitution neither Congress nor the Territorial Legislature can do it. When that is decided and acquiesced in, the whole thing is done.

This being true, and this being the way, as I think, that slavery is to be made national, let us consider what Judge Douglas is doing every day to that end. In the first place, let us see what influence he is exerting on public sentiment. In this and like communities, public sentiment is everything. With public sentiment, nothing can fail; without it nothing can succeed. Consequently, he who molds public sentiment goes deeper than he who enacts statutes or pronounces decisions. He makes statutes and decisions possible or impossible to be executed. This must be borne in mind, as also the additional fact that Judge Douglas is a man of vast influence, so great that it is enough for many men to profess to believe anything, when they once find out that Judge Douglas professes to believe it. Consider also the attitude he occupies at the head of a large party—a party which he claims has a majority of all the voters in the country. This man sticks to a decision which forbids the people of a Territory from excluding slavery, and he does so not because he says it is right in itself—he does not give any opinion on that—but because it has been *decided by the court;* and being decided by the court, he is, and you are, bound to take it in your political action as *law,* not that he judges at all of its merits, but because a decision of the court is to him a "*Thus saith the Lord.*" He places it on that ground alone; and you will bear in mind that thus committing himself unreservedly to this decision *commits him to the next one* just as firmly as to this. He did not commit himself on account of the merit or demerit of the decision, but it is a

"*Thus saith the Lord.*" The next decision, as much as this, will be a "*Thus saith the Lord.*"

There is nothing that can divert or turn him away from this decision. It is nothing that I point out to him that his great prototype, General Jackson, did not believe in the binding force of decisions. It is nothing to him that Jefferson did not so believe. I have said that I have often heard him approve of Jackson's course in disregarding the decision of the Supreme Court pronouncing a National Bank constitutional. He says, I did not hear him say so. He denies the accuracy of my recollection. I say he ought to know better than I, but I will make no question about this thing, though it still seems to me that I heard him say it twenty times. I will tell him though, that he now claims to stand on the Cincinnati platform, which affirms that Congress *cannot* charter a National Bank, in the teeth of that old standing decision that Congress *can* charter a bank.

And I remind him of another piece of history, on the question of respect for judicial decisions, and it is a piece of Illinois history belonging to a time when the large party to which Judge Douglas belonged were displeased with a decision of the Supreme Court of Illinois, because they had decided that a Governor could not remove a Secretary of State. You will find the whole story in Ford's *History of Illinois*, and I know that Judge Douglas will not deny that he was then in favor of oversloughing that decision by the mode of adding five new Judges, so as to vote down the four old ones. Not only so, but it ended in *the Judge's sitting down on that very bench as one of the five new judges to break down the four old ones.* It was in this way precisely that he got his title of Judge. Now, when the Judge tells me that men appointed conditionally to sit as members of a court will have to be catechised beforehand upon some subject, I say, "You know, Judge; you have tried it." When he says a court of this kind will lose the confidence of all men, will be prostituted and disgraced by such a proceeding, I say, "You know best, Judge; you have been through the mill."

But I cannot shake Judge Douglas's teeth loose from the Dred Scott decision. Like some obstinate animal (I mean no disrespect) that will hang on when he has once got his teeth fixed; you may cut off a leg, or you may tear away an arm, still he will not relax his hold. And so I may point out to the Judge, and say that he is bespattered all over, from the beginning of his political life to the present time, with attacks upon judicial decision; I may cut off limb after limb of his public record, and strive to wrench him from a single dictum of the court, yet I cannot divert him from it. He hangs, to the last, to the Dred Scott decision. These things show there is a purpose *strong as death and eternity* for which he adheres to this decision, and for which he will adhere to *all other decisions* of the same court.

A HIBERNIAN: Give us something besides Dred Scott.

LINCOLN: Yes; no doubt you want to hear something that don't hurt. Now, having spoken of the Dred Scott decision, one more word and I am done. Henry Clay, my beau ideal of a statesman, the man for whom I fought all my humble life—Henry Clay once said of a class of men who would repress all tendencies to liberty and ultimate emancipation, that they must, if they would do this, go back to the era of our Independence, and muzzle the cannon which thunders its annual joyous return; they must blow out the moral lights around us; they must penetrate the human soul, and eradicate there the love of liberty; and then, and not till then, could they perpetuate slavery in this country! To my thinking, Judge Douglas is, by his example and vast influence, doing that very thing in this community, when he says that the negro has nothing in the Declaration of Independence. Henry Clay plainly understood the contrary.

Judge Douglas is going back to the era of our Revolution, and, to the extent of his ability, muzzling the cannon which thunders its annual joyous return. When he invites any people willing to have slavery to establish it, he is blowing out the moral lights around us. When he says he "cares not whether slavery is voted down or voted up"—that it is a sacred right of self-government—he is, in my judgment, penetrating the human soul and eradicating the light of reason and the love of liberty in this American people. And now I will only say that when, by all these means and appliances, Judge Douglas shall succeed in bringing public sentiment to an exact accordance with his own views; when these vast assemblages shall echo back all these sentiments; when they shall come to repeat his views and to avow his principles, and to say all that he says on these mighty questions—then it needs only the formality of the second Dred Scott decision, which he indorses in advance, to make slavery alike lawful in all the States—old as well as new, North as well as South.

My friends, that ends the chapter. The Judge can take his half-hour.

Letter: To Jesse W. Fell
(December 20, 1859)

Fell was an Illinois Republican who foresaw the possibility of Lincoln's entrance onto the national political scene as a presidential candidate. Fell would use Lincoln's "little sketch" as a source for newspaper articles.

MY DEAR SIR:

Herewith is a little sketch, as you requested. There is not much of it, for the reason, I suppose, that there is not much of me. If anything is made out of it, I wish it to be modest, and not to go beyond the materials. If it were thought necessary to incorporate anything from any of my speeches, I suppose there would be no objection. Of course it must not appear to have been written by myself.

Yours very truly,
A. Lincoln

[Enclosure:]

I was born Feb. 12, 1809, in Hardin County, Kentucky. My parents were both born in Virginia, of undistinguished families—second families, perhaps I should say. My mother, who died in my tenth year, was of a family of the name of Hanks, some of whom now reside in Adams, and others in Macon counties, Illinois. My paternal grandfather, Abraham Lincoln, emigrated from Rockingham County, Virginia, to Kentucky, about 1781 or '2, where, a year or two later, he was killed by Indians, not in battle, but by stealth, when he was laboring to open a farm in the forest. His ancestors, who were Quakers, went to Virginia from Berks County, Pennsylvania. An effort to identify them with the New England family of the same name ended in nothing more definite than a similarity of Christian names in both families, such as Enoch, Levi, Mordecai, Solomon, Abraham, and the like.

My father, at the death of his father, was but six years of age; and he grew up, literally without education. He removed from Kentucky to what is now Spencer County, Indiana, in my eighth year. We reached our new home about the time the State came into the Union. It was a wild region, with many bears and other wild animals still in the woods. There I grew up. There were some schools, so called; but no qualification was ever required of a teacher, beyond the "readin, writin, and cipherin" to the Rule of Three. If a straggler supposed to understand Latin happened to sojourn in the neighborhood, he was looked upon as a wizard. There was absolutely nothing to excite ambition for education. Of course when I came of age I did not know much. Still, somehow, I could read, write, and cipher to the Rule of Three, but that was all. I have not been to school since. The little advance I now have upon this store of education, I have picked up from time to time under the pressure of necessity.

I was raised to farm work, which I continued till I was twenty two. At twenty one I came to Illinois, and passed the first year in Macon County. Then I got to New Salem (at that time in Sangamon, now in Menard County), where I remained a year as a sort of clerk in a store. Then came the Black Hawk War; and I was elected a Captain of Volunteers—a success which gave me more pleasure than any I have had since. I went the campaign, was elated, ran for the Legislature the same year (1832) and was beaten—the only time I ever have been beaten by the people. The next, and three succeeding biennial elections, I was elected to the Legislature. I was not a candidate afterwards. During this Legislative period I had studied law, and removed to Springfield to practice it. In 1846 I was once elected to the lower House of Congress. Was not a candidate for reelection. From 1849 to 1854, both inclusive, practiced law more assiduously than ever before. Always a Whig in politics, and generally on the Whig electoral tickets, making active canvasses. I was losing interest in politics when the repeal of the Missouri Compromise aroused me again.What I have done since then is pretty well known.

If any personal description of me is thought desirable, it may be said, I am, in height, six feet, four inches, nearly; lean in flesh, weighing, on an average, one hundred and eighty pounds; dark complexion, with coarse black hair, and grey eyes—no other marks or brands recollected.

Yours truly,
A. Lincoln

Meditation on the Divine Will
(c. September 2, 1862)

This discarded note was discovered at the time and preserved by one of Lincoln's secretaries. Lincoln would announce his preliminary Emancipation Proclamation, upon which this meditation seems to bear, a few weeks later.

THE WILL OF God prevails. In great contests each party claims to act in accordance with the will of God. Both may be, and one must be, wrong. God cannot be for and against the same thing at the same time. In the present civil war it is quite possible that God's purpose is something different from the purpose of either party; and yet the human instrumentalities, working just as they do, are of the best adaptation to effect his purpose. I am almost ready to say that this is probably true; that God wills this contest, and wills that it shall not end yet. By his mere great power on the minds of the now contestants, he could have either saved or destroyed the Union without a human contest. Yet the contest began. And, having begun, he could give the final victory to either side any day. Yet the contest proceeds.

Letter: To James C. Conkling
(August 26, 1863)

The President insisted to his friend Conkling that he read this response "very slowly." While Lincoln could not return to speak in Springfield as he would have liked to do, he instead composed this succinct and persuasive argument about the war's development and the necessity of the Emancipation Proclamation.

MY DEAR SIR:

Your letter inviting me to attend a mass meeting of unconditional Union men, to be held at the Capitol of Illinois, on the 3rd day of September, has been received. It would be very agreeable to me to thus meet my old friends at my own home; but I can not, just now, be absent from here so long as a visit there would require.

The meeting is to be of all those who maintain unconditional devotion to the Union; and I am sure my old political friends will thank me for tendering, as I do, the nation's gratitude to those other noble men, whom no partisan malice or partisan hope can make false to the nation's life.

There are those who are dissatisfied with me. To such I would say: You desire peace; and you blame me that we do not have it. But how can we attain it? There are but three conceivable ways. First, to suppress the rebellion by force of arms. This I am trying to do. Are you for it? If you are, so far we are agreed. If you are not for it, a second way is to give up the Union. I am against this. Are you for it? If you are, you should say so plainly. If you are not for force, nor yet for dissolution, there only remains some imaginable compromise. I do not believe any compromise, embracing the maintenance of the Union, is now possible. All I learn leads to a directly opposite belief. The strength of the rebellion is its military—its army. That army dominates all the country and all the people within its range. Any offer of terms made by any man or men within that range, in opposition to that army, is simply nothing for the present; because such man or men have no power whatever to enforce their side of a compromise, if one were made with them.

To illustrate: Suppose refugees from the South and peace men of the North get together in convention and frame and proclaim a compromise embracing a restoration of the Union; in what way can that compromise be used to keep Lee's army out of Pennsylvania? Meade's army can keep Lee's army out of Pennsylvania; and, I think, can ultimately drive it out of existence. But no paper compromise, to which the controllers of Lee's army are not agreed can at all affect that army. In an effort at such compromise we should waste time, which the enemy would improve to our disadvantage; and that would be all. A compromise, to be effective, must be made either with those who control the rebel army, or with the people first liberated from the domination of that army, by the success of our own army. Now allow me to assure you that no word or intimation from that rebel army, or from any of the men controlling it, in relation to any peace compromise, has ever come to my knowledge or belief. All charges and insinuations to the contrary are deceptive and groundless. And I promise you that if any such proposition shall hereafter come, it shall not be rejected and kept a secret from you. I freely acknowledge myself the servant of the people, according to the bond of service—the United States Constitution—and that, as such, I am responsible to them.

But to be plain, you are dissatisfied with me about the negro. Quite likely there is a difference of opinion between you and myself upon that subject. I certainly wish that all men could be free, while I suppose you do not. Yet I have neither adopted, nor proposed any measure, which is not consistent with even your view, provided you are for the Union. I suggested compensated emancipation; to which you replied you wished not to be taxed to buy negroes. But I had not asked you to be taxed to buy negroes, except in such way as to save you from greater taxation to save the Union exclusively by other means.

You dislike the emancipation proclamation and, perhaps, would have it retracted. You say it is unconstitutional—I think differently. I think the constitution invests its Commander-in-Chief with the law of war in time of war. The most that can be said, if so much, is that slaves are property. Is there—has there ever been—any question that by the law of war, property, both of enemies and friends, may be taken when needed? And is it not needed whenever taking it helps us or hurts the enemy? Armies the world over destroy enemy's property when they can not use it; and even destroy their own to keep it from the enemy. Civilized belligerents do all in their power to help themselves or hurt the enemy, except a few things regarded as barbarous or cruel. Among the exceptions are the massacre of vanquished foes and noncombatants, male and female.

But the proclamation, as law, either is valid or is not valid. If it is not valid, it needs no retraction. If it is valid, it cannot be retracted, any more than the dead can be brought to life. Some of you profess to think its retraction would operate favorably for the Union. Why better after the retraction than before the issue? There was more than a year and a half of trial to suppress the rebellion before the proclamation issued, the last one hundred days of which passed under an explicit notice that it was coming, unless averted by those in revolt, returning to their allegiance. The war has certainly progressed as favorably for us since the issue of proclamation as before. I know, as fully as one can know the opinions of others, that some of the commanders of our armies in the field who have given us our most important successes believe the emancipation policy and the use of the colored troops constitute the heaviest blow yet dealt to the Rebellion, and that at least one of these important successes could not have been achieved when it was but for the aid of black soldiers. Among the commanders holding these views are some who have never had any affinity with what is called abolitionism or with the Republican party policies but who held them purely as military opinions. I submit these opinions as being entitled to some weight against the objections often urged that emancipation and arming the blacks are unwise as military measures and were not adopted as such in good faith.

You say you will not fight to free negroes. Some of them seem willing to fight for you; but no matter. Fight you, then, exclusively to save the Union. I issued the proclamation on purpose to aid you in saving the Union. Whenever you shall have conquered all resistance to the Union, if I shall urge you to continue fighting, it will be an apt time, then, for you to declare you will not fight to free negroes.

I thought that in your struggle for the Union, to whatever extent the negroes should cease helping the enemy, to that extent it weakened the enemy in his resistance to you. Do you think differently? I thought that whatever negroes can be got to do as soldiers leaves just so much less for white soldiers to do, in saving the Union. Does it appear otherwise to you? But negroes, like other people, act upon motives. Why should they do anything for us, if we will do nothing for them? If they stake their lives for us, they must be prompted by the strongest motive—even the promise of freedom. And the promise being made must be kept.

The signs look better. The Father of Waters again goes unvexed to the sea. Thanks to the great Northwest for it. Nor yet wholly to them. Three hundred miles up, they met New England, Empire, Keystone, and Jersey, hewing their way right and left. The Sunny South, too, in more colors than one, also lent a hand. On the spot, their part of the history was jotted down in black and white. The job was a great national one; and let none be banned who bore an honorable part in it. And while those who have cleared the great river may well be proud, even that is not all. It is hard to say that anything has been more bravely and well done than at Antietam, Murfreesboro, Gettysburg, and on many fields of lesser note. Nor must Uncle Sam's web-feet be forgotten. At all the watery margins they have been present. Not only on the deep sea, the broad bay, and the rapid river, but also up the narrow muddy bayou, and wherever the ground was a little damp, they have been, and made their tracks. Thanks to all. For the great republic—for the principle it lives by and keeps alive—for man's vast future—thanks to all.

Peace does not appear so distant as it did. I hope it will come soon, and come to stay; and so come as to be worth the keeping in all future time. It will then have been proved that among free men there can be no successful appeal from the ballot to the bullet; and that they who take such appeal are sure to lose their case and pay the cost. And then, there will be some black men who can remember that, with silent tongue and clenched teeth and steady eye and well-poised bayonet, they have helped mankind on to this great consummation; while I fear there will be some white ones unable to forget that with malignant heart and deceitful speech, they strove to hinder it.

Still, let us not be oversanguine of a speedy final triumph. Let us be quite sober. Let us diligently apply the means, never doubting that a just God, in his own good time, will give us the rightful result.

Yours very truly,
A. Lincoln

Gettysburg Address
(Gettysburg, Pennsylvania, November 19, 1863)

Lincoln delivered his most famous speech at the dedication of the National Cemetery on the site of one of the most important victories of the war.

FOURSCORE AND SEVEN years ago our fathers brought forth on this continent a new nation, conceived in liberty, and dedicated to the proposition that all men are created equal.

Now we are engaged in a great civil war, testing whether that nation, or any nation so conceived and so dedicated, can long endure. We are met on a great battlefield of that war. We have come to dedicate a portion of that field as a final resting place for those who here gave their lives that that nation might live. It is altogether fitting and proper that we should do this.

But, in a larger sense, we cannot dedicate—we cannot consecrate—we cannot hallow—this ground. The brave men, living and dead, who struggled here, have consecrated it far above our poor power to add or detract. The world will little note nor long remember what we say here, but it can never forget what they did here. It is for us, the living, rather, to be dedicated here to the unfinished work which they who fought here have thus far so nobly advanced. It is rather for us to be here dedicated to the great task remaining before us—that from these honored dead we take increased devotion to that cause for which they gave the last full measure of devotion; that we here highly resolve that these dead shall not have died in vain; that this nation, under God, shall have a new birth of freedom; and that government of the people, by the people, for the people, shall not perish from the earth.

Second Inaugural Address
(March 4, 1865)

About a week after delivering this address, the President wrote: "I expect it to wear as well as—perhaps better than—anything I have produced; but I believe it is not immediately popular. Men are not flattered by being shown that there has been a difference of purpose between the Almighty and them. To deny it, however, in this case, is to deny that there is a God governing the world. It is a truth, which I thought needed to be told; and as whatever of humiliation there is in it falls most directly on myself, I thought others might afford for me to tell it."

AT THIS SECOND appearing to take the oath of the presidential office, there is less occasion for an extended address than there was at the first. Then a statement, somewhat in detail, of a course to be pursued seemed fitting and proper. Now, at the expiration of four years, during which public declarations have been constantly called forth on every point and phase of the great contest which still absorbs the attention and engrosses the energies of the nation, little that is new could be presented. The progress of our arms, upon which all else chiefly depends, is as well known to the public as to myself, and it is, I trust, reasonably satisfactory and encouraging to all. With high hope for the future, no prediction in regard to it is ventured.

On the occasion corresponding to this four years ago all thoughts were anxiously directed to an impending civil war. All dreaded it, all sought to avert it. While the inaugural address was being delivered from this place, devoted altogether to *saving* the Union without war, insurgent agents were in the city seeking to *destroy* it without war—seeking to dissolve the Union and divide effects by negotiation. Both parties deprecated war, but one of them would *make* war rather than let the nation survive, and the other would *accept* war rather than let it perish. And the war came.

One-eighth of the whole population were colored slaves, not distributed generally over the Union, but localized in the southern part of it. These slaves constituted a peculiar and powerful interest.

All knew that this interest was somehow the cause of the war. To strengthen, perpetuate, and extend this interest was the object for which the insurgents would rend the Union even by war, while the government claimed no right to do more than to restrict the territorial enlargement of it. Neither party expected for the war the magnitude or the duration which it has already attained. Neither anticipated that the *cause* of the conflict might cease with or even before the conflict itself should cease. Each looked for an easier triumph, and a result less fundamental and astounding. Both read the same Bible and pray to the same God, and each invokes His aid against the other. It may seem strange that any men should dare to ask a just God's assistance in wringing their bread from the sweat of other men's faces, but let us judge not, that we be not judged. The prayers of both could not be answered. That of neither has been answered fully. The Almighty has His own purposes. "Woe unto the world because of offenses; for it must needs be that offenses come, but woe to that man by whom the offense cometh." If we shall suppose that American slavery is one of those offenses which, in the providence of God, must needs come, but which, having continued through His appointed time, He now wills to remove, and that He gives to both North and South this terrible war as the woe due to those by whom the offense came, shall we discern therein any departure from those divine attributes which the believers in a living God always ascribe to Him? Fondly do we hope, fervently do we pray, that this mighty scourge of war may speedily pass away. Yet, if God wills that it continue until all the wealth piled by the bondsman's two hundred and fifty years of unrequited toil shall be sunk, and until every drop of blood drawn with the lash shall be paid by another drawn with the sword, as was said three thousand years ago, so still it must be said "the judgments of the Lord are true and righteous altogether."

With malice toward none, with charity for all, with firmness in the right as God gives us to see the right, let us strive on to finish the work we are in, to bind up the nation's wounds, to care for him who shall have borne the battle and for his widow and his orphan, to do all which may achieve and cherish a just and lasting peace among ourselves and with all nations.

SOURCES: Various.

Index of Authors